"Sanderson's outstand[...]n-plete unto itself and f[...]rs something for everyon[...]al wrangling, religious co[...]g, and wonderful, robust [...] of Elantris, once the capit[...]er-ated into powerless, tortured souls, unable to die, after the city's magic inexplicably broke ten years earlier. When the same curse strikes Prince Raoden of Arelon and he's imprisoned in Elantris, he refuses to surrender to his grim fate and instead strives to create a society out of the fallen and to unlock the secret that will restore the city's glory. Meanwhile, Princess Sarene of Teod [in] Kae (Arelon's new capital), who was betrothed to Raoden sight unseen, believes her intended has died. Officially declared his widow, she must use her political savvy and wit to protect Kae from malevolent forces without and within the city, chiefly Hrathen, a leader of the creepy Shu-Dereth faith, who aims to either convert Kae or destroy it within three months. The intrigue and excitement grow steadily in this smoothly written, perfectly balanced narrative; by the end readers won't want to put it down. As the blurb from Orson Scott Card suggests, Sanderson is a writer to watch." —*Publishers Weekly* (starred review)

"Sanderson's fantasy debut offers a vibrant cast of characters and a story of faith and determination set against a vividly portrayed world where magic is based on channeling power through the depiction of runes. The author's skill at turning conventional fantasy on its head produces a tale filled with surprising twists and turns and a conclusion both satisfying and original." —*Library Journal* (starred review)

"*Elantris* is a new *Ben-Hur* for the fantasy genre, with a sweeping, epic story line and well-drawn and sympathetic characters." —Kevin J. Anderson, *New York Times* bestselling coauthor of *Dune: The Battle of Corrin*

"*Elantris,* Brandon Sanderson's excellent debut novel, is marked by vivid, strongly drawn characters (including a memorable female character) and ingenious plot twists that will keep the reader turning pages. Don't miss it!" —Katherine Kurtz

BY BRANDON SANDERSON®

ELANTRIS

BRANDON
SANDERSON

TOR®
fantasy

Tor Publishing Group
New York

This is a work of fiction. All of the characters, organizations, and events portrayed in this novel are either products of the author's imagination or are used fictitiously.

ELANTRIS

Spot illustrations throughout by Stephen de las Heras

Map by Jeffrey Creer

Edited by Moshe Feder

A Tor Book
Published by Tom Doherty Associates/Tor Publishing Group
120 Broadway
New York, NY 10271

www.torpublishinggroup.com

Tor® is a registered trademark of Macmillan Publishing Group, LLC.

ISBN 978-0-7653-5037-4

Our books may be purchased in bulk for promotional, educational, or business use. Please contact your local bookseller or the Macmillan Corporate and Premium Sales Department at 1-800-221-7945, ext. 5442, or by email at MacmillanSpecialMarkets@macmillan.com.

First Edition: May 2005
First Mass Market Edition: June 2006

Printed in the United States of America

28 27 26 25 24 23 22 21 20

Dedicated to my mother,

Who wanted a doctor,
    Ended up with a writer,
But loved him enough not to complain
    (Very much).

ACKNOWLEDGMENTS

FIRST and foremost, I would like to thank my agent, Joshua Bilmes, and my editor, Moshe Feder, for helping me squeeze the fullest potential out of this manuscript. Without their masterful editorial vision, you'd be holding a very different book right now.

Next, high praise and thanks must be offered to the members of my various writing groups. Alan Layton, Janette Layton, Kaylynn ZoBell, and Ethan Skarstedt. Daniel Wells, Benjamin R. Olsen, Nathan Goodrich, and Peter Ahlstrom. Ryan Dreher, Micah Demoux, Annie Gorringe, and Tom Conrad. (You guys were a writing group, even if you didn't know it!) Thank you all so much for your work and suggestions.

In addition, there are dozens of people who read this book and others during my years struggling to get published, and I am inexpressibly grateful for their enthusiasm, criticism, and praise. Kristina Kugler, Megan Kauffman, Izzy Whiting, Eric Ehlers, Greg Creer, Ethan Sproat, Robert ZoBell, Deborah Anderson, Laura Bellamy, Mr. M, Kraig Hausmann, Nate Hatfield, Steve Frandson, Robison E. Wells, and Krista Olsen. If I forgot anyone, I'll get you in the next book!

I'd also like to give special thanks to those teachers who have helped me in my university career. Professors Sally Taylor, Dennis Perry, and John Bennion (who worked on my master's thesis committee). Professor Jacqueline Thursby for her faith in me. Dave Wolverton, who sent me out into the world, and Professor Douglas Thayer, whom I'll someday convince to read a fantasy book. (He's getting a copy of this one, whether he wants it or not!)

Finally, I'd like to thank my family. My father for buying me books when I was a kid, my mother for turning me into a scholar, my sisters for their smiles, and Jordan for putting up with a domineering older brother. You can check out his programming skills—along with Jeff Creer's amazing artistic design—on my Web site, www.brandonsanderson.com.

Thank you so much, everyone, for believing in me.

to
Teod

Elantris   Kae

Aredel River

Kondeon

ARELON

FJORDEN

Kaltii

The
Chasm   JINDO

Lake
Alonoe   HaiKo

Kalomo
River

DULADEL   JAADOR
Fellavoo

PROLOGUE

ELANTRIS was beautiful, once. It was called the city of the gods: a place of power, radiance, and magic. Visitors say that the very stones glowed with an inner light, and that the city contained wondrous arcane marvels. At night, Elantris shone like a great silvery fire, visible even from a great distance.

Yet, as magnificent as Elantris was, its inhabitants were more so. Their hair a brilliant white, their skin an almost metallic silver, the Elantrians seemed to shine like the city itself. Legends claim that they were immortal, or at least nearly so. Their bodies healed quickly, and they were blessed with great strength, insight, and speed. They could perform magics with a bare wave of the hand; men visited Elantris from all across Opelon to receive Elantrian healings, food, or wisdom. They were divinities.

And anyone could become one.

The Shaod, it was called. The Transformation. It struck randomly—usually at night, during the mysterious hours when life slowed to rest. The Shaod could take beggar, craftsman, nobleman, or warrior. When it came, the fortunate person's life ended and began anew; he would discard his old, mundane existence, and move to Elantris. Elantris, where he could live in bliss, rule in wisdom, and be worshipped for eternity.

Eternity ended ten years ago.

PART ONE

THE
SHADOW
OF
ELANTRIS

CHAPTER 1

PRINCE Raoden of Arelon awoke early that morning, completely unaware that he had been damned for all eternity. Still drowsy, Raoden sat up, blinking in the soft morning light. Just outside his open balcony windows he could see the enormous city of Elantris in the distance, its stark walls casting a deep shadow over the smaller city of Kae, where Raoden lived. Elantris's walls were incredibly high, but Raoden could see the tops of black towers rising behind them, their broken spires a clue to the fallen majesty hidden within.

The abandoned city seemed darker than usual. Raoden stared at it for a moment, then glanced away. The huge Elantrian walls were impossible to ignore, but people of Kae tried very hard to do just that. It was painful to remember the city's beauty, to wonder how ten years ago the blessing of the Shaod had become a curse instead. . . .

Raoden shook his head, climbing out of bed. It was unusually warm for such an early hour; he didn't feel even a bit chilly as he threw on his robe, then pulled the servant's cord beside his bed, indicating that he wanted breakfast.

That was another odd thing. He was hungry—*very* hungry. Almost ravenous. He had never liked large breakfasts, but this morning he found himself waiting impatiently for his meal to arrive. Finally, he decided to send someone to see what was taking so long.

"Ien?" he called in the unlit chambers.

There was no response. Raoden frowned slightly at the Seon's absence. Where could Ien be?

Raoden stood, and as he did, his eyes fell on Elantris

again. Resting in the great city's shadow, Kae seemed like an insignificant village by comparison. Elantris. An enormous, ebony block—not really a city anymore, just the corpse of one. Raoden shivered slightly.

A knock came at his door.

"Finally," Raoden said, walking over to pull open the door. Old Elao stood outside with a tray of fruit and warm bread.

The tray dropped to the ground with a crash, slipping from the stunned maid's fingers even as Raoden reached out to accept it. Raoden froze, the tray's metallic ring echoing through the silent morning hallway.

"Merciful Domi!" Elao whispered, her eyes horrified and her hand trembling as she reached up to grab the Korathi pendant at her neck.

Raoden reached out, but the maid took a quivering step away, stumbling on a small melon in her haste to escape.

"What?" Raoden asked. Then he saw his hand. What had been hidden in the shadows of his darkened room was now illuminated by the hallway's flickering lantern.

Raoden turned, throwing furniture out of his way as he stumbled to the tall mirror at the side of his chambers. The dawn's light had grown just strong enough for him to see the reflection that stared back at him. A stranger's reflection.

His blue eyes were the same, though they were wide with terror. His hair, however, had changed from sandy brown to limp gray. The skin was the worst. The mirrored face was covered with sickly black patches, like dark bruises. The splotches could mean only one thing.

The Shaod had come upon him.

THE Elantris city gate boomed shut behind him with a shocking sound of finality. Raoden slumped against it, thoughts numbed by the day's events.

It was as if his memories belonged to another person. His father, King Iadon, hadn't met Raoden's gaze as he ordered the priests to prepare his son and throw him into Elantris. It had been done swiftly and quietly; Iadon couldn't afford to let it be known that the crown prince was an Elantrian. Ten years ago, the Shaod would have made Raoden a god. Now, instead of making people into silver-skinned deities, it changed them into sickly monstrosities.

Raoden shook his head in disbelief. The Shaod was a thing that happened to other people—distant people. People who deserved to be cursed. Not the crown prince of Arelon. Not Raoden.

The city of Elantris stretched out before him. Its high walls were lined with guardhouses and soldiers—men intended not to keep enemies out of the city, but to keep its inhabitants from escaping. Since the Reod, every person taken by the Shaod had been thrown into Elantris to rot; the fallen city had become an expansive tomb for those whose bodies had forgotten how to die.

Raoden could remember standing on those walls, looking down on Elantris's dread inhabitants, just as the guards now looked down on him. The city had seemed far away then, even though he had been standing just outside of it. He had wondered, philosophically, what it would be like to walk those blackened streets.

Now he was going to find out.

Raoden pushed against the gate for a moment, as if to force his body through, to cleanse his flesh of its taint. He lowered his head, releasing a quiet moan. He felt like curling into a ball on the grimy stones and waiting until he woke from this dream. Except, he knew he would never awaken. The priests said that this nightmare would never end.

But, somewhere, something within urged him forward. He knew he had to keep moving—for if he stopped, he feared he'd simply give up. The Shaod had taken his body. He couldn't let it take his mind as well.

So, using his pride like a shield against despair, dejection, and—most important—self-pity, Raoden raised his head to stare damnation in the eyes.

BEFORE, when Raoden had stood on the walls of Elantris to look down—both literally and figuratively—on its inhabitants, he had seen the filth that covered the city. Now he stood in it.

Every surface—from the walls of the buildings to the numerous cracks in the cobblestones—was coated with a patina of grime. The slick, oily substance had an equalizing effect on Elantris's colors, blending them all into a single, depressing hue—a color that mixed the pessimism of black with the polluted greens and browns of sewage.

Before, Raoden had been able to see a few of the city's inhabitants. Now he could hear them as well. A dozen or so Elantrians lay scattered across the courtyard's fetid cobblestones. Many sat uncaringly, or unknowingly, in pools of dark water, the remains of the night's rainstorm. And they were moaning. Most of them were quiet about it, mumbling to themselves or whimpering with some unseen pain. One woman at the far end of the courtyard, however, screamed with a sound of raw anguish. She fell silent after a moment, her breath or her strength giving out.

Most of them wore what looked like rags—dark, loose-fitting garments that were as soiled as the streets. Looking closely, however, Raoden recognized the clothing. He glanced down at his own white burial cloths. They were long and flowing, like ribbons sewn together into a loose robe. The linen on his arms and legs was already stained with grime from brushing up against the city gate and stone pillars. Raoden suspected they would soon be indistinguishable from the other Elantrians' garb.

This is what I will become, Raoden thought. *It has already begun. In a few weeks I will be nothing more than a dejected body, a corpse whimpering in the corner.*

A slight motion on the other side of the courtyard brought Raoden out of his self-pity. Some Elantrians were crouching in a shadowed doorway across from him. He couldn't make out much from their silhouetted forms, but they seemed to be waiting for something. He could feel their eyes on him.

Raoden raised an arm to shade his eyes, and only then did he remember the small thatch basket in his hands. It held the ritual Korathi sacrifice sent with the dead into the next life—or, in this case, into Elantris. The basket contained a loaf of bread, a few thin vegetables, a handful of grain, and a small flask of wine. Normal death sacrifices were far more extensive, but even a victim of the Shaod had to be given something.

Raoden glanced back at the figures in the doorway, his mind flashing to rumors he'd heard on the outside—stories of Elantrian brutality. The shadowed figures had yet to move, but their study of him was unnerving.

Taking a deep breath, Raoden took a step to the side, moving along the city wall toward the east side of the courtyard. The forms still seemed to be watching him, but they didn't follow. In a moment, he could no longer see through the doorway, and a second later he had safely passed into one of the side streets.

Raoden released his breath, feeling that he had escaped something, though he didn't know what. After a few moments, he was certain that no one followed, and he began to feel foolish for his alarm. So far, he had yet to see anything that corroborated the rumors about Elantris. Raoden shook his head and continued moving.

The stench was almost overwhelming. The omnipresent sludge had a musty, rotten scent, like that of dying fungus. Raoden was so bothered by the smell that he nearly stepped directly on the gnarled form of an old man huddled next to a building's wall. The man moaned piteously, reaching up with a thin arm. Raoden looked down, and felt a sudden chill. The "old man" was no more than sixteen years old. The creature's soot-covered skin was dark and spotted, but his face was that of a child, not a man. Raoden took an involuntary step backward.

The boy, as if realizing that his chance would soon pass, stretched his arm forward with the sudden strength of desperation. "Food?" he mumbled through a mouth only half full of teeth. "Please?"

Then the arm fell, its endurance expended, and the body slumped back against the cold stone wall. His eyes, however, continued to watch Raoden. Sorrowful, pained eyes. Raoden had seen beggars before in the Outer Cities, and he had probably been fooled by charlatans a number of times. This boy, however, was not faking.

Raoden reached up and pulled the loaf of bread from his

sacrificial offerings, then handed it to the boy. The look of disbelief that ran across the boy's face was somehow more disturbing than the despair it had replaced. This creature had given up hope long ago; he probably begged out of habit rather than expectation.

Raoden left the boy behind, turning to continue down the small street. He had hoped that the city would grow less gruesome as he left the main courtyard—thinking, perhaps, that the dirt was a result of the area's relatively frequent use. He had been wrong; the alley was covered with just as much filth as the courtyard, if not more.

A muffled thump sounded from behind. Raoden turned with surprise. A group of dark forms stood near the mouth of the side street, huddled around an object on the ground. The beggar. Raoden watched with a shiver as five men devoured his loaf of bread, fighting among themselves and ignoring the boy's despairing cries. Eventually, one of the newcomers—obviously annoyed—brought a makeshift club down on the boy's head with a crunch that resounded through the small alley.

The men finished the bread, then turned to regard Raoden. He took an apprehensive step backward; it appeared that he had been hasty in assuming he hadn't been followed. The five men slowly stalked forward, and Raoden spun, taking off at a run.

Sounds of pursuit came from behind. Raoden scrambled away in fear—something that, as a prince, he had never needed to do before. He ran madly, expecting his breath to run short and a pain to stab him in the side, as usually happened when he overextended himself. Neither occurred. Instead, he simply began to feel horribly tired, weak to the point that he knew he would soon collapse. It was a harrowing feeling, as if his life were slowly seeping away.

Desperate, Raoden tossed the sacrificial basket over his head. The awkward motion threw him off balance, and an unseen schism in the cobblestones sent him into a maladroit skip that didn't end until he collided with a rotting mass of wood. The wood—which might once have been a pile of crates—squished, breaking his fall.

Raoden sat up quickly, the motion tossing shreds of wood

pulp across the damp alleyway. His assailants, however, were no longer concerned with him. The five men crouched in the street's muck, picking scattered vegetables and grain off the cobblestones and out of the dark pools. Raoden felt his stomach churn as one of the men slid his finger down a crack, scraped up a dark handful that was more sludge than corn, then rammed the entire mass between eager lips. Brackish spittle dribbled down the man's chin, dropping from a mouth that resembled a mud-filled pot boiling on the stove.

One man saw Raoden watching. The creature growled, reaching down to grab the almost-forgotten cudgel at his side. Raoden searched frantically for a weapon, finding a length of wood that was slightly less rotten than the rest. He held the weapon in uncertain hands, trying to project an air of danger.

The thug paused. A second later, a cry of joy from behind drew his attention: one of the others had located the tiny skin of wine. The struggle that ensued apparently drove all thoughts of Raoden from the men's minds, and the five were soon gone—four chasing after the one who had been fortunate, or foolish, enough to escape with the precious liquor.

Raoden sat in the debris, overwhelmed. *This is what you will become. . . .*

"Looks like they forgot about you, sule," a voice observed.

Raoden jumped, looking toward the sound of the voice. A man, his smooth bald head reflecting the morning light, reclined lazily on a set of steps a short distance away. He was definitely an Elantrian, but before the transformation he must have been of a different race—not from Arelon, like Raoden. The man's skin bore the telltale black splotches of the Shaod, but the unaffected patches weren't pale, they were a deep brown instead.

Raoden tensed against possible danger, but this man showed no signs of the primal wildness or the decrepit weakness Raoden had seen in the others. Tall and firm-framed, the man had wide hands and keen eyes set in a dark-skinned face. He studied Raoden with a thoughtful attitude.

Raoden breathed a sigh of relief. "Whoever you are, I'm

glad to see you. I was beginning to think everyone in here was either dying or insane."

"We can't be dying," the man responded with a snort. "We're already dead. Kolo?"

"Kolo." The foreign word was vaguely familiar, as was the man's strong accent. "You're not from Arelon?"

The man shook his head. "I'm Galladon, from the sovereign realm of Duladel. I'm most recently from Elantris, land of sludge, insanity, and eternal perdition. Nice to meet you."

"Duladel?" Raoden said. "But the Shaod only affects people from Arelon." He picked himself up, brushing away pieces of wood in various stages of decomposition, grimacing at the pain in his stubbed toe. He was covered with slime, and the raw stench of Elantris now rose from him as well.

"Duladel is of mixed blood, sule. Arelish, Fjordell, Teoish—you'll find them all. I—"

Raoden cursed quietly, interrupting the man.

Galladon raised an eyebrow. "What is it, sule? Get a splinter in the wrong place? There aren't many *right* places for that, I suppose."

"It's my toe!" Raoden said, limping across the slippery cobblestones. "There's something wrong with it—I stubbed it when I fell, but the pain isn't going away."

Galladon shook his head ruefully. "Welcome to Elantris, sule. You're dead—your body won't repair itself like it should."

"What?" Raoden flopped to the ground next to Galladon's steps. His toe continued to hurt with a pain as sharp as the moment he stubbed it.

"Every pain, sule," Galladon whispered. "Every cut, every nick, every bruise, and every ache—they will stay with you until you go mad from the suffering. As I said, welcome to Elantris."

"How do you stand it?" Raoden asked, massaging his toe, an action that didn't help. It was such a silly little injury, but he had to fight to keep the pained tears from his eyes.

"We don't. We're either *very* careful, or we end up like those rulos you saw in the courtyard."

"In the courtyard. . . . Idos Domi!" Raoden pulled himself to his feet and hobbled toward the courtyard. He found the beggar boy in the same location, near the mouth of the alley. He was still alive . . . in a way.

The boy's eyes stared blankly into the air, the pupils quivering. His lips worked silently, no sound escaping. The boy's neck had been completely crushed, and there was a massive gash in its side, exposing the vertebrae and throat. The boy tried without success to breathe through the mess.

Suddenly Raoden's toe didn't seem so bad. "Idos Domi . . ." Raoden whispered, turning his head as his stomach lurched. He reached out and grabbed the side of a building to steady himself, his head bowed, as he tried to keep from adding to the sludge on the cobblestones.

"There isn't much left for this one," Galladon said with a matter-of-fact tone, crouching down next to the beggar.

"How . . . ?" Raoden began, then stopped as his stomach threatened him again. He sat down in the slime with a plop and, after a few deep breaths, continued. "How long will he live like that?"

"You still don't understand, sule," Galladon said, his accented voice sorrowful. "He isn't alive—none of us are. That's why we're here. Kolo? The boy will stay like this forever. That is, after all, the typical length of eternal damnation."

"Is there nothing we can do?"

Galladon shrugged. "We could try burning him, assuming we could make a fire. Elantrian bodies seem to burn better than those of regular people, and some think that's a fitting death for our kind."

"And . . ." Raoden said, still unable to look at the boy. "And if we do that, what happens to him—his soul?"

"He doesn't have a soul," Galladon said. "Or so the priests tell us. Korathi, Derethi, Jesker—they all say the same thing. We're damned."

"That doesn't answer my question. Will the pain stop if he is burned?"

Galladon looked down at the boy. Eventually, he just shrugged. "Some say that if you burn us, or cut off our head, or do anything that completely destroys the body, we'll just stop existing. Others, they say the pain goes on—that we *become* pain. They think we'd float thoughtlessly, unable to feel anything but agony. I don't like either option, so I just try to keep myself in one piece. Kolo?"

"Yes," Raoden whispered. "I kolo." He turned, finally getting the courage to look back at the wounded boy. The enormous gash stared back at him. Blood seeped slowly from the wound—as if the liquid were just sitting in the veins, like stagnant water in a pool.

With a sudden chill Raoden reached up and felt his chest. "I don't have a heartbeat," he realized for the first time.

Galladon looked at Raoden as if he had made an utterly idiotic statement. "Sule, you're *dead*. Kolo?"

THEY didn't burn the boy. Not only did they lack the proper implements to make fire, but Galladon forbade it. "We can't make a decision like that. What if he really has no soul? What if he stopped existing when we burned his body? To many, an existence of agony is better than no existence at all."

So, they left the boy where he had fallen—Galladon doing so without a second thought, Raoden following because he couldn't think of anything else to do, though he felt the pain of guilt more sharply than even the pain in his toe.

Galladon obviously didn't care whether Raoden followed him, went in another direction, or stood staring at an interesting spot of grime on the wall. The large, dark-skinned man walked back the way they had come, passing the occasional moaning body in a gutter, his back turned toward Raoden with a posture of complete indifference.

Watching the Dula go, Raoden tried to gather his thoughts. He had been trained for a life in politics; years of preparation had conditioned him to make quick decisions. He made one just then. He decided to trust Galladon.

There was something innately likable about the Dula, something Raoden found indefinably appealing, even if it was covered by a grime of pessimism as thick as the slime on the ground. It was more than Galladon's lucidity, more than just his leisurely attitude. Raoden had seen the man's eyes when he regarded the suffering child. Galladon claimed to accept the inevitable, but he felt sad that he had to do so.

The Dula found his former perch on the steps and settled back down. Taking a determined breath, Raoden walked over and stood expectantly in front of the man.

Galladon glanced up. "What?"

"I need your help, Galladon," Raoden said, squatting on the ground in front of the steps.

Galladon snorted. "This is Elantris, sule. There's no such thing as help. Pain, insanity, and a whole lot of slime are the only things you'll find here."

"You almost sound like you believe that."

"You are asking in the wrong place, sule."

"You're the only noncomatose person I've met in here who hasn't attacked me," Raoden said. "Your actions speak much more convincingly than your words."

"Perhaps I simply haven't tried to hurt you because I know you don't have anything to take."

"I don't believe that."

Galladon shrugged an "I don't care what you believe" shrug and turned away, leaning back against the side of the building and closing his eyes.

"Are you hungry, Galladon?" Raoden asked quietly.

The man's eyes snapped open.

"I used to wonder when King Iadon fed the Elantrians," Raoden mused. "I never heard of any supplies entering the city, but I always assumed that they were sent. *After all,* I thought, *the Elantrians stay alive.* I never understood. If the people of this city can exist without heartbeats, then they can probably exist without food. Of course, that doesn't mean the hunger goes away. I was ravenous when I awoke this morning, and I still am. From the looks in the eyes of those men who attacked me, I'd guess the hunger only gets worse."

Raoden reached under his grime-stained sacrificial robe, pulling out a thin object and holding it up for Galladon to see. A piece of dried meat. Galladon's eyes opened all the way, his face changing from bored to interested. There was a glint in his eyes—a bit of the same wildness that Raoden had seen in the savage men earlier. It was more controlled, but it was there. For the first time, Raoden realized just how much he was gambling on his first impression of the Dula.

"Where did that come from?" Galladon asked slowly.

"It fell out of my basket when the priests were leading me here, so I stuffed it under my sash. Do you want it or not?"

Galladon didn't answer for a moment. "What makes you think I won't simply attack you and take it?" The words were not hypothetical; Raoden could tell that a part of Galladon was actually considering such an action. How large a part was still indeterminable.

"You called me 'sule,' Galladon. How could you kill one you've dubbed a friend?"

Galladon sat, transfixed by the tiny piece of meat. A thin drop of spittle ran unnoticed from the side of his mouth. He looked up at Raoden, who was growing increasingly anxious. When their eyes met, something sparked in Galladon, and the tension snapped. The Dula suddenly bellowed a deep, resounding laugh. "You speak Duladen, sule?"

"Only a few words," Raoden said modestly.

"An educated man? Rich offerings for Elantris today! All right, you conniving rulo, what do you want?"

"Thirty days," Raoden said. "For thirty days you will show me around and tell me what you know."

"Thirty days? Sule, you're kayana."

"The way I see it," Raoden said, moving to tuck the meat back in his sash, "the only food that ever enters this place arrives with the newcomers. One must get pretty hungry with so few offerings and so many mouths to feed. One would think the hunger would be almost maddening."

"Twenty days," Galladon said, a hint of his former intensity showing again.

"Thirty, Galladon. If you won't help me, someone else will."

Galladon ground his teeth for a moment. "Rulo," he muttered, then held out his hand. "Thirty days. Fortunately, I wasn't planning any extended trips during the next month."

Raoden tossed him the meat with a laugh.

Galladon snatched the meat. Then, though his hand jerked reflexively toward his mouth, he stopped. With a careful motion he tucked the meat into a pocket and stood up. "So, what should I call you?"

Raoden paused. *Probably best if people don't know I'm royalty, for now.* "'Sule' works just fine for me."

Galladon chuckled. "The private type, I see. Well, let's go then. It's time for you to get the grand tour."

CHAPTER 2

SARENE stepped off of the ship to discover that she was a widow. It was shocking news, of course, but not as devastating as it could have been. After all, she had never met her husband. In fact, when Sarene had left her homeland, she and Raoden had only been engaged. She had assumed that the kingdom of Arelon would wait to hold the wedding until she actually arrived. Where she came from, at least, it was expected that both partners would be present when they were married.

"I never liked that clause in the wedding contract, my lady," said Sarene's companion—a melon-sized ball of light hovering at her side.

Sarene tapped her foot in annoyance as she watched the packmen load her luggage onto a carriage. The wedding contract had been a fifty-page beast of a document, and one of its many stipulations made her betrothal legally binding if either she or her fiancé died before the actual wedding ceremony.

"It's a fairly common clause, Ashe," she said. "That way, the treaty of a political marriage isn't voided if something happens to one of the participants. I've never seen it invoked."

"Until today," the ball of light replied, its voice deep and its words well enunciated.

"Until today," Sarene admitted. "How was I to know Prince Raoden wouldn't last the five days it took us to cross the Sea of Fjorden?" She paused, frowning in thought. "Quote the clause to me, Ashe. I need to know exactly what it says."

"'If it happens that one member of the aforementioned couple is called home to Merciful Domi before the pre-arranged wedding time,'" Ashe said, "'then the engagement will be considered equivalent to marriage in all legal and social respects.'"

"Not much room for argument, is there?"

"Afraid not, my lady."

Sarene frowned distractedly, folding her arms and tapping her cheek with her index finger, watching the packmen. A tall, gaunt man directed the work with bored eyes and a resigned expression. The man, an Arelish court attendant named Ketol, was the only reception King Iadon had seen fit to send her. Ketol had been the one to "regretfully inform her" that her fiancé had "died of an unexpected disease" during her journey. He had made the declaration with the same dull, uninterested tone that he used to command the packmen.

"So," Sarene clarified, "as far as the law is concerned, I'm now a princess of Arelon."

"That is correct, my lady."

"And the widowed bride of a man I never met."

"Again, correct."

Sarene shook her head. "Father is going to laugh himself sick when he hears about this. I'll never live it down."

Ashe pulsed slightly in annoyance. "My lady, the king would never take such a solemn event with levity. The death of Prince Raoden has undoubtedly brought great grief to the sovereign family of Arelon."

"Yes. So much grief, in fact, that they couldn't even spare the effort it would take to come meet their new daughter."

"Perhaps King Iadon would have come himself if he'd had more warning of our arrival. . . ."

Sarene frowned, but the Seon had a point. Her early arrival, several days ahead of the main wedding party, had been intended as a prewedding surprise for Prince Raoden.

She'd wanted a few days, at least, to spend time with him privately and in person. Her secrecy, however, had worked against her.

"Tell me, Ashe," she said. "How long do Arelish people customarily wait between a person's death and their burial?"

"I'm not sure, my lady," Ashe confessed. "I left Arelon long ago, and I lived here for such a short time that I can't remember many specifics. However, my studies tell me that Arelish customs are generally similar to those of your homeland."

Sarene nodded, then waved over King Iadon's attendant.

"Yes, my lady?" Ketol asked in a lazy tone.

"Is a funeral wake being held for the prince?" Sarene asked.

"Yes, my lady," the attendant replied. "Outside the Korathi chapel. The burial will happen this evening."

"I want to go see the casket."

Ketol paused. "Uh . . . His Majesty asked that you be brought to him immediately. . . ."

"Then I won't spend long at the funeral tent," Sarene said, walking toward her carriage.

SARENE surveyed the busy funeral tent with a critical eye, waiting as Ketol and a few of the packmen cleared a way for her to approach the casket. She had to admit, everything was irreproachable—the flowers, the offerings, the praying Korathi priests. The only oddity about the event was how crowded the tent was.

"There certainly are a lot of people here," she noted to Ashe.

"The prince was very well liked, my lady," the Seon replied, floating beside her. "According to our reports, he was the most popular public figure in the country."

Sarene nodded, walking down the passageway Ketol had made for her. Prince Raoden's casket sat at the very center of the tent, guarded by a ring of soldiers who let the masses approach only so far. As she walked, she sensed true grief in the faces of those in attendance.

So it is true, she thought. *The people did love him.*

The soldiers made way for her, and she approached the casket. It was carved with Aons—most of them symbols of hope and peace—after the Korathi way. The entire wooden casket was surrounded by a ring of lavish foods—an offering made on behalf of the deceased.

"Can I see him?" she asked, turning toward one of the Korathi priests—a small, kindly-looking man.

"I'm sorry, child," the priest said. "But the prince's disease was unpleasantly disfiguring. The king has asked that the prince be allowed dignity in death."

Sarene nodded, turning back to the casket. She wasn't sure what she had expected to feel, standing before the dead man she would have married. She was oddly . . . angry.

She pushed that emotion away for the moment, instead turning to look around the tent. It almost seemed *too* formal. Though the visiting people were obviously grieved, the tent, the offerings, and the decorations seemed sterile.

A man of Raoden's age and supposed vigor, she thought. *Dead of the coughing shivers. It could happen—but it certainly doesn't seem likely.*

"My . . . lady?" Ashe said quietly. "Is something wrong?"

Sarene waved to the Seon and walked back toward their carriage. "I don't know," she said quietly. "Something just doesn't feel right here, Ashe."

"You have a suspicious nature, my lady," Ashe pointed out.

"Why isn't Iadon having a vigil for his son? Ketol said he was holding court, as if his own son's death didn't even bother him." Sarene shook her head. "I spoke with Raoden just before I left Teod, and he seemed fine. Something is wrong, Ashe, and I want to know what it is."

"Oh, dear . . ." Ashe said. "You know, my lady, your father *did* ask me to try and keep you out of trouble."

Sarene smiled. "Now, there's an impossible task. Come on, we need to go meet my new father."

SARENE leaned against the carriage window, watching the city pass as she rode toward the palace. She sat in silence for the moment, a single thought crowding everything else out of her mind.

What am I doing here?

Her words to Ashe had been confident, but she had always been good at hiding her worries. True, she was curious about the prince's death, but Sarene knew herself very well. A large part of that curiosity was an attempt to take her mind off of her feelings of inferiority and awkwardness—anything to keep from acknowledging what she was: a lanky, brusque woman who was almost past her prime. She was twenty-five years old; she should have been married years ago. Raoden had been her last chance.

How dare you die on me, prince of Arelon! Sarene thought indignantly. Yet, the irony did not escape her. It was fitting that this man, one she had thought she might actually grow to like, would die before she even got to meet him. Now she was alone in an unfamiliar country, politically bound to a king she did not trust. It was a daunting, lonely feeling.

You've been lonely before, Sarene, she reminded herself. *You'll get through it. Just find something to occupy your mind. You have an entire new court to explore. Enjoy it.*

With a sigh, Sarene turned her attention back to the city. Despite considerable experience serving in her father's diplomatic corps, she had never visited Arelon. Ever since the fall of Elantris, Arelon had been unofficially quarantined by most other kingdoms. No one knew why the mystical city had been cursed, and everyone worried that the Elantrian disease might spread.

Sarene was surprised, however, by the lushness she saw in Kae. The city thoroughfares were wide and well maintained. The people on the street were well dressed, and she didn't see a single beggar. To one side, a group of blue-robed Korathi priests walked quietly through the crowd, leading an odd, white-robed person. She watched the procession, wondering what it could be, until the group disappeared around a corner.

From her vantage, Kae reflected none of the economic hardship Arelon was supposed to be suffering. The carriage passed dozens of fenced-in mansions, each one built in a different style of architecture. Some were expansive, with large wings and pointed roofs, following Duladen construction.

Others were more like castles, their stone walls looking as if they had been directly transported from the militaristic countryside of Fjorden. The mansions all shared one thing, however: wealth. The people of this country might be starving, but Kae—seat of Arelon's aristocracy—didn't appear to have noticed.

Of course, one disturbing shadow still hung over the city. The enormous wall of Elantris rose in the distance, and Sarene shivered as she glanced at its stark, imposing stones. She had heard stories about Elantris for most of her adult life, tales of the magics it had once produced and the monstrosities that now inhabited its dark streets. No matter how gaudy the houses, no matter how wealthy the streets, this one monument stood as a testament that all was not well in Arelon.

"Why do they even live here, I wonder?" Sarene asked.

"My lady?" Ashe asked.

"Why did King Iadon build his palace in Kae? Why choose a city that is so close to Elantris?"

"I suspect the reasons are primarily economic, my lady," Ashe said. "There are only a couple of viable ports on the northern Arelish coast, and this is the finest."

Sarene nodded. The bay formed by the merging of the Aredel River with the ocean made for an enviable harbor. But even still . . .

"Perhaps the reasons are political," Sarene mused. "Iadon took power during turbulent times—maybe he thinks that remaining close to the old capital will lend him authority."

"Perhaps, my lady," Ashe said.

It's not like it really matters that much, she thought. Apparently, proximity to Elantris—or Elantrians—didn't actually increase one's chances of being taken by the Shaod.

She turned away from the window, looking over at Ashe, who hovered above the seat beside her. She had yet to see a Seon in the streets of Kae, though the creatures—said to be the ancient creations of Elantris magic—were supposed to be even more common in Arelon than in her homeland. If she squinted, she could barely make out the glowing Aon at the center of Ashe's light.

"At least the treaty is safe," Sarene finally said.

"Assuming you remain in Arelon, my lady," Ashe said in his deep voice. "At least, that is what the wedding contract says. As long as you stay here, and 'remain faithful to your husband,' King Iadon must honor his alliance with Teod."

"Remain faithful to a dead man," Sarene mumbled with a sigh. "Well, that means I have to stay, husband or no husband."

"If you say so, my lady."

"We need this treaty, Ashe," Sarene said. "Fjorden is expanding its influence at an incredible rate. Five years ago I would have said we didn't need to worry, that Fjorden's priests would never be a power in Arelon. But now . . ." Sarene shook her head. The collapse of the Duladen Republic had changed so much.

"We shouldn't have kept ourselves so removed from Arelon these last ten years, Ashe," she said. "I probably wouldn't be in this predicament if we had forged strong ties with the new Arelish government ten years ago."

"Your father was afraid their political turmoil would infect Teod," Ashe said. "Not to mention the Reod—no one was certain that whatever struck the Elantrians wouldn't affect normal people as well."

The carriage slowed, and Sarene sighed, letting the topic drop. Her father knew that Fjorden was a danger, and he understood that old allegiances needed to be reforged; that was why she was in Arelon. Ahead of them, the palace gates swung open. Friendless or not, she had arrived, and Teod was depending on her. She had to prepare Arelon for the war that was coming—a war that had become inevitable the moment Elantris fell.

SARENE'S new father, King Iadon of Arelon, was a thin man with a shrewd face. He was conferring with several of his administrators when Sarene entered the throne room, and she stood unnoticed for nearly fifteen minutes before he even nodded to her. Personally, she didn't mind the wait—it gave her a chance to observe the man she was now sworn to obey—but her dignity couldn't help being a little offended by the treatment. Her station as a princess of Teod alone should have earned her a reception that was, if not grand, at least punctual.

As she waited, one thing struck her immediately. Iadon did not look like a man mourning the passing of his son and heir. There was no sign of grief in his eyes, none of the haggard fatigue that generally accompanied the passing of a loved one. In fact, the air of the court itself seemed remarkably free of mourning signs.

Is Iadon a heartless man, then? Sarene wondered curiously. *Or is he simply one who knows how to control his emotions?*

Years spent in her father's court had taught Sarene to be a connoisseur of noble character. Though she couldn't hear what Iadon was saying—she had been told to stay near the back of the room and wait for permission to approach—the king's actions and mannerisms gave her an idea of his character. Iadon spoke firmly, giving direct instruction, occasionally pausing to stab his table map with a thin finger. He was a man with a strong personality, she decided—one with a definite idea of how he wanted things done. It wasn't a bad sign. Tentatively, Sarene decided that this was a man with whom she might be able to work.

She was to revise that opinion shortly.

King Iadon waved her over. She carefully hid her annoyance at the wait, and approached him with the proper air of noble submission. He interrupted her halfway through her curtsy.

"No one told me you would be so tall," he declared.

"My lord?" she said, looking up.

"Well, I guess the only one who would have cared about that isn't around to see it. Eshen!" he snapped, causing an almost unseen woman near the far side of the room to jump in compliance.

"Take this one to her rooms and see that she has plenty of things to keep her occupied. Embroidery or whatever else it is that entertains you women." With that, the king turned to his next appointment—a group of merchants.

Sarene stood in midcurtsy, stunned at Iadon's complete lack of courtesy. Only years of courtly training kept her jaw from dropping. Quick but unassertive, the woman Iadon had ordered—*Queen* Eshen, the king's wife—scuttled over and took Sarene's arm. Eshen was short and slight of frame, her brownish blond Aonic hair only beginning to streak with gray.

"Come, child," Eshen said in a high-pitched voice. "We mustn't waste the king's time."

Sarene allowed herself to be pulled through one of the room's side doors. "Merciful Domi," she muttered to herself. "What have I gotten myself into?"

". . . AND you'll love it when the roses come in. I have the gardeners plant them so you can smell them without even leaning out the window. I wish they weren't so big, though."

Sarene frowned in confusion. "The roses?"

"No, dear," the queen continued, barely pausing, "the windows. You can't believe how bright the sun is when it shines through them in the morning. I asked them—the gardeners, that is—to find me some orange ones, because I *so* adore orange, but so far all they found were some ghastly yellow ones. 'If I wanted yellow,' I said to them, 'I would have had you plant aberteens.' You should have seen them apologize—I'm sure we'll have some orange ones by the end of next year. Don't you think that would be lovely, dear? Of course, the windows will still be too big. Maybe I can have a couple of them bricked off."

Sarene nodded, fascinated—not by the conversation, but by the queen. Sarene had assumed that the lecturers at her father's academy had been skilled at saying nothing with lots of words, but Eshen put them all to shame. The queen flitted from one topic to the next like a butterfly looking for a place to land, but never finding one suitable enough for an extended stay. Any one of the topics would have been potential fuel for an interesting conversation, but the queen never let Sarene grab hold of one long enough to do it justice.

Sarene took a calming breath, telling herself to be patient. She couldn't blame the queen for being the way she was; Domi taught that all people's personalities were gifts to be enjoyed. The queen was charming, in her own meandering way. Unfortunately, after meeting both king and queen,

Sarene was beginning to suspect that she would have trouble finding political allies in Arelon.

Something else bothered Sarene—something odd about the way Eshen acted. No one could *possibly* talk as much as the queen did; she never let a silent moment pass. It was almost like the woman was uncomfortable around Sarene. Then, in a moment of realization, Sarene understood what it was. Eshen spoke on every imaginable topic except for the one most important: the departed prince. Sarene narrowed her eyes with suspicion. She couldn't be certain—Eshen was, after all, a very flighty person—but it seemed that the queen was acting far too cheerful for a woman who had just lost her son.

"Here is your room, dear. We unpacked your things, and added some as well. You have clothing in every color, even yellow, though I can't imagine why you would want to wear it. Horrid color. Not that your hair is horrid, of course. Blond isn't the same as yellow, no. No more than a horse is a vegetable. We don't have a horse for you yet, but you are welcome to use any in the king's stables. We have lots of fine animals, you see, Duladel is beautiful this time of year."

"Of course," Sarene said, looking over the room. It was small, but suited her tastes. Too much space could be as daunting as too little could be cramped.

"Now, you'll be needing these, dear," Eshen said, pointing a small hand at a pile of clothing that wasn't hanging like the rest—as if it had been delivered more recently. All of the dresses in the pile shared a single attribute.

"Black?" Sarene asked.

"Of course. You're . . . you're in . . ." Eshen fumbled with the words.

"I'm in mourning," Sarene realized. She tapped her foot with dissatisfaction—black was *not* one of her favorite colors.

Eshen nodded. "You can wear one of those to the funeral this evening. It should be a nice service—I did the arrangements." She began talking about her favorite flowers again, and the monologue soon degenerated into a discourse on how much she hated Fjordell cooking. Gently but firmly, Sarene led the woman to the door, nodding pleasantly. As soon as they reached the hallway, Sarene pled fatigue from her travels, and plugged the queen's verbal torrent by closing the door.

"That's going to get old *very* quickly," Sarene said to herself.

"The queen does have a robust gift for conversation, my lady," a deep voice agreed.

"What did you find out?" Sarene asked, walking over to pick through the pile of dark clothing as Ashe floated in through the open window.

"I didn't find as many Seons as I had expected. I seem to recall that this city was once overflowing with us."

"I noticed that too," Sarene said, holding up a dress in front of the mirror, then discarding it with a shake of her head. "I guess things are different now."

"They are indeed. As per your instructions, I asked the other Seons what they knew of the prince's untimely death. Unfortunately, my lady, they were hesitant to discuss the event—they consider it extremely ill omened for the prince to die so soon before he was to be married."

"Especially for him," Sarene mumbled, pulling off her clothing to try on the dress. "Ashe, something strange is going on. I think maybe someone killed the prince."

"Killed, my lady?" Ashe's deep voice was disapproving, and he pulsed slightly at the comment. "Who would do such a thing?"

"I don't know, but . . . something feels odd. This doesn't seem like a court that is in mourning. Take the queen, for instance. She didn't appear distraught when she spoke to me—you'd think she would be at least a little bothered by the fact that her son died yesterday."

"There is a simple explanation for that, my lady. Queen Eshen is not Prince Raoden's mother. Raoden was born of Iadon's first wife, who died over twelve years ago."

"When did he remarry?"

"Right after the Reod," Ashe said. "Just a few months after he took the throne."

Sarene frowned. "I'm still suspicious," she decided, reaching around awkwardly to button the back of her dress. Then she regarded herself in the mirror, looking at the dress critically. "Well, at least it fits—even if it does make me look pale. I was half afraid it would cut off at my knees. These Arelish women are all so unnaturally short."

"If you say so, my lady," Ashe replied. He knew as well as she did that Arelish women weren't that short; even in Teod, Sarene had been a head taller than most of the other women. Her father had called her Leky Stick as a child—borrowing the name of the tall thin post that marked the goal line in his favorite sport. Even after filling out during adolescence, Sarene was still undeniably lanky.

"My lady," Ashe said, interrupting her contemplations.

"Yes, Ashe?"

"Your father is desperate to talk to you. I think you have some news he deserves to hear."

Sarene nodded, holding in a sigh, and Ashe began to pulse brightly. A moment later the ball of light that formed his essence melted into a bustlike glowing head. King Eventeo of Teod.

"'Ene?" her father asked, the glowing head's lips moving. He was a robust man, with a large oval face and a thick chin.

"Yes, Father. I'm here." Her father would be standing beside a similar Seon—probably Dio—who would have changed to resemble a glowing approximation of Sarene's head.

"Are you nervous for the wedding?" Eventeo asked anxiously.

"Well, about that wedding . . ." she said slowly. "You'll probably want to cancel your plans to come next week. There won't be much for you to see."

"What?"

Ashe had been right—her father didn't laugh when he heard that Raoden was dead. Instead, his voice turned to one of sharp concern, the glowing face worried. His worry increased when Sarene explained how the death was as binding as an actual wedding.

"Oh, 'Ene, I'm sorry," her father said. "I know how much you were expecting from this marriage."

"Nonsense, Father." Eventeo knew her far too well. "I hadn't even met the man—how could I have had any expectations?"

"You hadn't met him, but you had spoken with him through Seon, and you had written all those letters. I know you, 'Ene—you're a romantic. You would never have decided to go through with this if you hadn't thoroughly convinced yourself that you could love Raoden."

The words rang true, and suddenly Sarene's loneliness returned. She had spent the trip across the Sea of Fjorden in a state of disbelieving nervousness, both excited and apprehensive at the prospect of meeting the man who was to become her husband. More excited, however, than apprehensive.

She had been away from Teod many times, but she had always gone with others from her homeland. This time she had come by herself, traveling ahead of the rest of the wedding party to surprise Raoden. She had read and reread the prince's letters so many times that she had begun to feel that she knew him, and the person she'd constructed from those sheets of paper was a complex, compassionate man whom she had been very anxious to meet.

And now she never would. She felt more than alone, she felt rejected—again. Unwanted. She had waited all these years, suffered by a patient father who didn't know how the men of her homeland avoided her, how they were frightened by her forward, even arrogant, personality. Finally, she had found a man who was willing to have her, and Domi had snatched him away at the last moment.

Sarene finally began to let herself feel some of the emotions she had been keeping in a tight noose since stepping off the ship. She was glad the Seon transferred only her features, for she would have been mortified if her father had seen the tear rolling down her cheek.

"That's silly, Father," she said. "This was a simple political marriage, and we all knew it. Now our countries have more in common than just language—our royal lines are related."

"Oh, honey . . ." her father whispered. "My little Sarene. I had so hoped this would work out—you don't know how your mother and I prayed that you would find happiness there. Idos Domi! We shouldn't have gone through with this."

"I would have made you, Father," Sarene said. "We need the treaty with Arelon far too badly. Our armada won't keep Fjorden off our shores for much longer—the entire Svordish navy is under Wyrn's command."

"Little Sarene, all grown up now," her father said through the Seon link.

"All grown up and fully capable of marrying herself off to a corpse." Sarene laughed weakly. "It's probably for the best. I don't think Prince Raoden would have turned out as I had imagined—you should meet his father."

"I've heard stories. I hoped they weren't true."

"Oh, they are," Sarene said, letting her dissatisfaction with the Arelish monarch burn away her sorrow. "King Iadon has to be just about the most disagreeable man I have ever met. He barely even acknowledged me before sending me off to, as he put it, 'go knit, and whatever else you women do.' If Raoden was anything like his father, then I'm better off this way."

There was a momentary pause before her father responded. "Sarene, do you want to come home? I can void the contract if I want, no matter what the laws say."

The offer was tempting—more tempting than she would ever admit. She paused. "No, Father," she finally said with an unconscious shake of her head. "I have to stay. This was my idea, and Raoden's death doesn't change the fact that we need this alliance. Besides, returning home would break tradition—we both know that Iadon is my father now. It would be unseemly for you to take me back into your household."

"I will always be your father, 'Ene. Domi curse the customs—Teod will always be open for you."

"Thank you, Father," Sarene said quietly. "I needed to hear that. But I still think I should stay. For now, at least. Besides, it could be interesting. I have an entirely new court full of people to play with."

"'Ene . . ." her father said apprehensively. "I know that tone. What are you planning?"

"Nothing," she said. "There's just a few things I want to poke my nose into before I give up completely on this marriage."

There was a pause, and then her father chuckled. "Domi

protect them—they don't know what we've shipped over there. Go easy on them, Leky Stick. I don't want to get a note from Minister Naolen in a month telling me that King Iadon has run off to join a Korathi monastery and the Arelish people have named you monarch instead."

"All right," Sarene said with a wan smile. "I'll wait at least two months then."

Her father burst into another round of his characteristic laughter—a sound that did her more good than any of his consolations or counsels. "Wait for a minute, 'Ene," he said after his laughter subsided. "Let me get your mother—she'll want to speak with you." Then, after a moment, he chuckled, continuing, "She's going to faint dead away when I tell her you've already killed off poor Raoden."

"Father!" Sarene said—but he was already gone.

CHAPTER 3

NONE of Arelon's people greeted their savior when he arrived. It was an affront, of course, but not an unexpected one. The people of Arelon—especially those living near the infamous city of Elantris—were known for their godless, even heretical, ways. Hrathen had come to change that. He had three months to convert the entire kingdom of Arelon; otherwise Holy Jaddeth—lord of all creation—would destroy it. The time had finally come for Arelon to accept the truths of the Derethi religion.

Hrathen strode down the gangplank. Beyond the docks, with their continuous bustle of loading and unloading, stretched the city of Kae. A short distance beyond Kae, Hrathen could see a towering stone wall—the old city of Elantris.

On the other side of Kae, to Hrathen's left, the land sloped steeply, rising to a tall hill—a foothill of what would become the Dathreki Mountains. Behind him was the ocean.

Overall, Hrathen was not impressed. In ages past, four small cities had surrounded Elantris, but only Kae—the new capital of Arelon—was still inhabited. Kae was too unorganized, too spread out, to be defensible, and its only fortification appeared to be a small, five-foot-high wall of stones—more a border than anything else.

Retreat into Elantris would be difficult, and only marginally effective. Kae's buildings would provide wonderful cover for an invading force, and a few of Kae's more peripheral structures looked like they were built almost against Elantris's wall. This was not a nation accustomed to war. Yet, of all the kingdoms on the Syclan continent—the land named Opelon by the Arelish people—only Arelon itself had avoided domination by the Fjordell Empire. Of course, that too was something Hrathen would soon change.

Hrathen marched away from the ship, his presence causing quite a stir among the people. Workers halted their labors as he passed, staring at him with impressed amazement. Conversations died when eyes fell upon him. Hrathen didn't slow for anyone, but that didn't matter, for people moved quickly from his path. It could have been his eyes, but more likely it was his armor. Bloodred and glittering in the sunlight, the plate armor of a Derethi imperial high priest was an imposing sight even when one was accustomed to it.

He was beginning to think he would have to find his own way to the city's Derethi chapel when he made out a spot of red weaving its way through the crowd. The speck soon resolved into a stumpy, balding figure clad in red Derethi robes. "My lord Hrathen!" the man called.

Hrathen stopped, allowing Fjon—Kae's Derethi head arteth—to approach. Fjon puffed and wiped his brow with a silken handkerchief. "I'm terribly sorry, Your Grace. The register had you scheduled to come in on a different ship. I didn't find out you weren't on board until they were halfway done unloading. I'm afraid I had to leave the carriage behind; I couldn't get it through the crowd."

Hrathen narrowed his eyes with displeasure, but he said nothing. Fjon continued to blather for a moment before finally deciding to lead Hrathen to the Derethi chapel, apologizing again for the lack of transportation. Hrathen followed his pudgy guide with a measured stride, dissatisfied. Fjon trotted along with a smile on his lips, occasionally waving to passers on the streets, shouting pleasantries. The people responded in kind—at least, until they saw Hrathen, his blood cloak billowing behind him and his exaggerated armor cut with sharp angles and harsh lines. Then they fell silent, greetings withering, their eyes following Hrathen until he passed. Such was as it should be.

The chapel was a tall stone structure, complete with bright red tapestries and towering spires. Here, at least, Hrathen found some of the majesty he was accustomed to. Within, however, he was confronted by a disturbing sight—a crowd of people involved in some kind of social activity. People milled around, ignoring the holy structure in which they stood, laughing and joking. It was too much. Hrathen had heard, and believed, the reports. Now he had confirmation.

"Arteth Fjon, assemble your priests," Hrathen said—the first words he had spoken since his arrival on Arelish soil.

The arteth jumped, as if surprised to finally hear sounds coming from his distinguished guest. "Yes, my lord," he said, motioning for the gathering to end.

It took a frustratingly long time, but Hrathen endured the process with a flat expression. When the people had left, he approached the priests, his armored feet clicking against the chapel's stone floor. When he finally spoke, his words were directed at Fjon.

"Arteth," he said, using the man's Derethi title, "the ship that brought me here will leave for Fjorden in one hour. You are to be on board."

Fjon's jaw dropped in alarm. "Wha—"

"Speak Fjordell, man!" Hrathen snapped. "Surely ten years amongst the Arelish heathens hasn't corrupted you to the point that you have forgotten your native tongue?"

"No, no, Your Grace," Fjon replied, switching from Aonic to Fjordell. "But I—"

"Enough," Hrathen interrupted again. "I have orders from

Wyrn himself. You have spent far too long in the Arelish culture—you have forgotten your holy calling, and are unable to see to the progress of Jaddeth's empire. These people don't need a friend; they need a priest. A Derethi priest. One would think you were Korathi, watching you fraternize. We're not here to love the people; we are here to help them. You will go."

Fjon slumped back against one of the room's pillars, his eyes widening and his limbs losing their strength. "But who will be head arteth of the chapel in my absence, my lord? The other arteths are so inexperienced."

"These are pivotal times, Arteth," Hrathen said. "I'll be remaining in Arelon to personally direct the work here. May Jaddeth grant me success."

HE had hoped for an office with a better view, but the chapel, majestic as it was, held no second floor. Fortunately, the grounds were well kept, and his office—Fjon's old room—overlooked nicely trimmed hedges and carefully arranged flower beds.

Now that he had cleared the walls of paintings—agrarian nature scenes, for the most part—and thrown out Fjon's numerous personal effects, the chamber was approaching a level of dignified orderliness appropriate for a Derethi gyorn. All it needed was a few tapestries and maybe a shield or two.

Nodding to himself, Hrathen turned his attention back to the scroll on his desk. His orders. He barely dared hold them in his profane hands. He read the words over and over again in his mind, imprinting both their physical form and their theological meaning on his soul.

"My lord . . . Your Grace?" a quiet voice asked in Fjordell.

Hrathen looked up. Fjon entered the room, then crouched in a subservient huddle on the floor, his forehead rubbing the ground. Hrathen allowed himself to smile, knowing that the penitent arteth couldn't see his face. Perhaps there was hope for Fjon yet.

"Speak," Hrathen said.

"I have done wrong, my lord. I have acted contrary to the plans of our lord Jaddeth."

"Your sin was complacency, Arteth. Contentment has destroyed more nations than any army, and it has claimed the souls of more men than even Elantris's heresies."

"Yes, my lord."

"You still must leave, Arteth," Hrathen said.

The man's shoulders slumped slightly. "Is there no hope for me then, my lord?"

"That is Arelish foolishness speaking, Arteth, not Fjordell pride." Hrathen reached down, grasping the man's shoulder. "Rise, my brother!" he commanded.

Fjon looked up, hope returning to his eyes.

"Your mind may have become tainted with Arelish thoughts, but your soul is still Fjordell. You are of Jaddeth's chosen people—all of the Fjordell have a place of service in His empire. Return to our homeland, join a monastery to reacquaint yourself with those things you have forgotten, and you will be given another way to serve the empire."

"Yes, my lord."

Hrathen's grip grew hard. "Understand this before you leave, Arteth. My arrival is more of a blessing than you can possibly understand. All of Jaddeth's workings are not open to you; do not think to second-guess our God." He paused, debating his next move. After a moment he decided: This man still had worth. Hrathen had a unique chance to reverse much of Arelon's perversion of Fjon's soul in a single stroke. "Look there on the table, Arteth. Read that scroll."

Fjon looked toward the desk, eyes finding the scroll resting thereon. Hrathen released the man's shoulder, allowing him to walk around the desk and read.

"This is the official seal of Wyrn himself!" Fjon said, picking up the scroll.

"Not just the seal, Arteth," Hrathen said. "That is his signature as well. The document you hold was penned by His Holiness himself. That isn't just a letter—it is scripture."

Fjon's eyes opened wide, and his fingers began to quiver. "Wyrn himself?" Then, realizing in full what he was holding in his unworthy hand, he dropped the parchment to the desk with a quiet yelp. His eyes didn't turn away from the letter, however. They were transfixed—reading the words as voraciously as a starving man devoured a joint of beef. Few people actually had an opportunity to read words written by the hand of Jaddeth's prophet and Holy Emperor.

Hrathen gave the priest time to read the scroll, then reread it, and then read it again. When Fjon finally looked up, there was understanding—and gratitude—in his face. The man was intelligent enough. He knew what the orders would have required of him, had he remained in charge of Kae.

"Thank you," Fjon mumbled.

Hrathen nodded graciously. "Could you have done it? Could you have followed Wyrn's commands?"

Fjon shook his head, eyes darting back to the parchment. "No, Your Grace. I could not have . . . I couldn't have functioned—couldn't have even thought—with that on my conscience. I do not envy your place, my lord. Not anymore."

"Return to Fjorden with my blessing, brother," Hrathen said, taking a small envelope from a bag on the table. "Give this to the priests there. It is a letter from me telling them you accepted your reassignment with the grace befitting a servant of Jaddeth. They will see that you are assigned to a monastery. Perhaps someday you will be allowed to lead a chapel again—one well within Fjorden's borders."

"Yes, my lord. Thank you, my lord."

Fjon withdrew, closing the door behind him. Hrathen walked to his desk and slid another envelope—identical to the one he had given Fjon—from his letter bag. He held it for a few moments, then turned it to one of the desk's candles. The words it held—condemning Arteth Fjon as a traitor and an apostate—would never be read, and the poor, pleasant arteth would never know just how much danger he had been in.

"WITH your leave, my lord gyorn," said the bowing priest, a minor dorven who had served under Fjon for over a decade. Hrathen waved his hand, bidding the man to leave. The door shut silently as the priest backed from the room.

Fjon had done some serious damage to his underlings. Even a small weakness would build enormous flaws over two decades' time, and Fjon's problems were anything but small. The man had been lenient to the point of flagrancy. He had run a chapel without order, bowing before Arelish culture rather than bringing the people strength and discipline. Half of the priests serving in Kae were hopelessly corrupted—including men as new to the city as six months. Within the next few weeks, Hrathen would be sending a veritable fleet of priests back to Fjorden. He'd have to pick a new head arteth from those who remained, few though they would be.

A knock came at the door. "Come," Hrathen said. He had been seeing the priests one at a time, feeling out the extent of their contamination. So far, he had not often been impressed.

"Arteth Dilaf," the priest said, introducing himself as he entered.

Hrathen looked up. The name and words were Fjordell, but the accent was slightly off. It sounded almost . . . "You're Arelish?" Hrathen said with surprise.

The priest bowed with the proper amount of subservience; his eyes, however, were defiant.

"How did you become a priest of Derethi?" Hrathen asked.

"I wanted to serve the empire," the man replied, his voice quietly intense. "Jaddeth provided a way."

No, Hrathen realized. *It isn't defiance in this man's eyes—it's religious fervor.* One did not often find zealots in the Derethi religion; such people were more often drawn to the frenzied lawlessness of the Jeskeri Mysteries than to the militaristic organization of Shu-Dereth. This man's face, however, burned with fanatical passion. It was not a bad thing; while Hrathen himself spurned such lack of control, he had often found zealots to be useful tools.

"Jaddeth always provides a way, Arteth," Hrathen said carefully. "Be more specific."

"I met a Derethi arteth in Duladel twelve years ago. He preached to me, and I believed. He gave me copies of the *Do-Keseg* and the *Do-Dereth,* and I read them both in one night. The holy arteth sent me back to Arelon to help convert those in my home country, and I set up in Rain. I taught there for seven years, until the day I heard that a Derethi chapel had been built in Kae itself. I overcame my loathing for the Elantrians, knowing that Holy Jaddeth had struck them down with an eternal punishment, and came to join with my Fjordell brethren.

"I brought my converts with me—fully half of the believers in Kae came with me ·from Rain. Fjon was impressed with my diligence. He granted me the title of arteth and allowed me to continue teaching."

Hrathen rubbed his chin thoughtfully, regarding the Arelish priest. "You know what Arteth Fjon did was wrong."

"Yes, my lord. An arteth cannot appoint another to his own position. When I speak to the people, I never refer to myself as a priest of Derethi, only a teacher."

A very good teacher, Dilaf's tone implied. "What did you think of Arteth Fjon?" Hrathen asked.

"He was an undisciplined fool, my lord. His laxness kept Jaddeth's kingdom from growing in Arelon, and has made a mockery of our religion."

Hrathen smiled: Dilaf, though not of the chosen race, was obviously a man who understood the doctrine and culture of his religion. However, his ardor could be dangerous. The wild intensity in Dilaf's eyes was barely under control. Either he would have to be watched very closely, or he would have to be disposed of.

"It appears that Arteth Fjon did one thing right, even if he didn't have the proper authority," Hrathen said. Dilaf's eyes burned even more brightly at the declaration. "I make you a full arteth, Dilaf."

Dilaf bowed, touching his head to the ground. His mannerisms were perfectly Fjordell, and Hrathen had never heard a foreigner speak the Holy Tongue so well. This man could prove useful indeed; after all, one common complaint against Shu-Dereth was that it favored the Fjordell. An Arelish priest could help prove that all were welcome within Jaddeth's empire—even if the Fjordell were the most welcome.

Hrathen congratulated himself on creating such a useful tool, completely satisfied until the moment Dilaf looked up from his bow. The passion was still there in Dilaf's eyes—but there was something else as well. Ambition. Hrathen frowned slightly, wondering whether or not he had just been manipulated.

There was only one thing to do. "Arteth, are you sworn as any man's odiv?"

Surprise. Dilaf's eyes opened wide as he stared up at Hrathen, uncertainty flashing therein. "No, my lord."

"Good. Then I will make you mine."

"My lord . . . I am, of course, your humble servant."

"You will be more than that, Arteth," Hrathen said, "if you would be my odiv, I your hroden. You will be mine, heart and soul. If you follow Jaddeth, you follow Him *through me*. If you serve the empire, you do it under me. Whatever you think, act, or say will be by my direction. Am I understood?"

Fire burned in Dilaf's eyes. "Yes," he hissed. The man's fervor wouldn't let him reject such an offer. Though his lowly rank of arteth would remain unchanged, being odiv to a gyorn would enormously increase Dilaf's power and respectability. He *would* be Hrathen's slave, if that slavery would carry him higher. It was a very Fjordell thing to do— ambition was the one emotion Jaddeth would accept as readily as devotion.

"Good," Hrathen said. "Then your first order is to follow the priest Fjon. He should be getting on the ship to Fjordell right at this moment—I want you to make sure he does so. If Fjon gets off for any reason, kill him."

"Yes, my gyorn." Dilaf rushed from the room. He finally had an outlet for his enthusiasm. All Hrathen had to do now was keep that enthusiasm focused in the right direction.

Hrathen stood for a moment after the Arelish man had gone, then shook his head and turned back to his desk. The scroll still lay where it had fallen from Fjon's unworthy fingers; Hrathen picked it up with a smile, his touch reverent. He was not a man who delighted in possessions; he set his sights on much grander accomplishments than the simple accumulation of useless baubles. However, occasionally an object came along that was so unique, Hrathen reveled in simply knowing it belonged to him. One did not own such a thing for its usefulness, or for its ability to impress others, but because it was a privilege to possess. The scroll was such an object.

It had been scribed in front of Hrathen by Wyrn's own hand. It was revelation directly from Jaddeth; scripture intended for only one man. Few people ever got to meet Jaddeth's anointed, and even among the gyorns, private audiences were rare. To receive orders directly from Wyrn's hand . . . such was the most exquisite of experiences.

Hrathen ran his eyes over the sacred words again, even though he had long since memorized their every detail.

> *Behold the words of Jaddeth, through His servant Wyrn Wulfden the Fourth, Emperor and King.*
>
> *High Priest and Son, your request has been granted. Go to the heathen peoples of the West and declare to them my final warning, for while my Empire is eternal, my patience will soon end. Not much longer will I slumber within a tomb of rock. The Day of Empire is at hand, and my glory will soon shine forth, a second sun blazing forth from Fjorden.*
>
> *The pagan nations of Arelon and Teod have been blackened scars upon my land for long enough. Three hundred years have my priests served amongst those tainted by Elantris, and few have harkened to their call. Know this, High Priest: My faithful warriors are prepared and they wait only the word of my Wyrn. You have three months to prophesy to the people of Arelon. At the end of that time, the holy soldiers of Fjorden will descend on the nation like hunting predators, rending and tearing the unworthy life from those who heed not my words. Only three months will pass before the destruction of all who oppose my Empire.*
>
> *The time for my ascension nears, my son. Be stalwart, and be diligent.*
>
> *Words of Jaddeth, Lord of all Creation, through his servant Wyrn Wulfden the Fourth, Emperor of Fjorden, Prophet of Shu-Dereth, Ruler of Jaddeth's Holy Kingdom, and Regent of all Creation.*

The time had finally come. Only two nations resisted. Fjorden had regained its former glory, glory lost hundreds of years ago when the First Empire collapsed. Once again,

Arelon and Teod were the only two kingdoms who resisted Fjordell rule. This time, with the might of Jaddeth's holy calling behind it, Fjorden would prevail. Then, with all mankind united under Wyrn's rule, Jaddeth could rise from His throne beneath the earth and reign in glorious majesty.

And Hrathen would be the one responsible for it. The conversion of Arelon and Teod was his urgent duty. He had three months to change the religious temperament of an entire culture; it was a monumental task, but it was vital that he succeed. If he did not, Fjorden's armies would destroy every living being in Arelon, and Teod would soon follow; the two nations, though separated by water, were the same in race, religion, and obstinance.

The people might not yet know it, but Hrathen was the only thing standing between them and utter annihilation. They had resisted Jaddeth and His people in arrogant defiance for far too long. Hrathen was their last chance.

Someday they would call him their savior.

CHAPTER 4

THE woman screamed until she grew too tired, calling for help, for mercy, for Domi. She clawed at the broad gate, her fingernails leaving marks in the film of slime. Eventually, she slumped to the ground in a quiet heap, shaking from occasional sobs. Seeing her agony reminded Raoden of his own pain—the sharp twinge of his toe, the loss of his life outside.

"They won't wait much longer," Galladon whispered, his hand firmly on Raoden's arm, holding the prince back.

The woman finally stumbled to her feet, looking dazed, as

if she had forgotten where she was. She took a single, uncertain step to her left, her palm resting on the wall, as if it were a comfort—a connection to the outside world, rather than the barrier separating her from it.

"It's done," Galladon said.

"Just like that?" Raoden asked.

Galladon nodded. "She picked well—or, as well as one could. Watch."

Shadows stirred in an alleyway directly across the courtyard; Raoden and Galladon watched from inside a ramshackle stone building, one of many that lined Elantris's entry courtyard. The shadows resolved into a group of men, and they approached the woman with determined, controlled steps, surrounding her. One reached out and took her basket of offerings. The woman didn't have the strength left to resist; she simply collapsed again. Raoden felt Galladon's fingers dig into his shoulder as he involuntarily pulled forward, wanting to dash out to confront the thieves.

"Not a good idea. Kolo?" Galladon whispered. "Save your courage for yourself. If stubbing your toe nearly knocked you out, think how it would feel to have one of those cudgels cracking across your brave little head."

Raoden nodded, relaxing. The woman had been robbed, but it didn't look like she was in further danger. It hurt, however, to watch her. She wasn't a young maiden; she bore the stout figure of a woman accustomed to childbirth and the running of a household. A mother, not a damsel. The strong lines of the woman's face bespoke hard-won wisdom and courage, and somehow that made watching her more difficult. If such a woman could be defeated by Elantris, what hope was there for Raoden?

"I told you she chose well," Galladon continued. "She might be a few pounds of food lighter, but she doesn't have any wounds. Now, if she had turned right—like you did, sule—she would have been at the dubious mercy of Shaor's men. If she had gone forward, then Aanden would have had the right to her offerings. The left turn is definitely best— Karata's men take your food, but they rarely hurt you. Better to be hungry than spend the next few years with a broken arm."

"Next few years?" Raoden asked, turning away from the courtyard to regard his tall, dark-skinned companion. "I thought you said our wounds would last us an eternity."

"We only assume they will, sule. Show me an Elantrian who has managed to keep his wits until eternity ends, and maybe he'll be able to prove the theory."

"How long do people usually last in here?"

"A year, maybe two," Galladon said.

"What?"

"Thought we were immortal, did you? Just because we don't age, we'll last forever?"

"I don't know," Raoden said. "I thought you said we couldn't die."

"We can't," Galladon said. "But the cuts, the bruises, the stubbed toes . . . they pile up. One can only take so much."

"They kill themselves?" Raoden asked quietly.

"That's not an option. No, most of them lie around mumbling or screaming. Poor rulos."

"How long have you been here, then?"

"A few months."

The realization was another shock to pile on the already teetering stack. Raoden had assumed that Galladon had been an Elantrian for at least a few years. The Dula spoke of life in Elantris as if it had been his home for decades, and he was impressively adept at navigating the enormous city.

Raoden looked back at the courtyard, but the woman had already gone. She could have been a maid in his father's palace, a wealthy merchant's lady, or a simple housewife. The Shaod respected no classes; it took from all equally. She was gone now, having entered the gaping pit that was Elantris. He should have been able to help her.

"All that for a single loaf of bread and a few flaccid vegetables," Raoden muttered.

"It may not seem like much now, but just wait a few days. The only food that enters this place comes clutched in the arms of its new arrivals. You wait, sule. You will feel the desire as well. It takes a strong man to resist when the hunger calls."

"You do it," Raoden said.

"Not very well—and I've only been here a few months.

There's no telling what the hunger will drive me to do a year from now."

Raoden snorted. "Just wait until my thirty days are done before you become a primordial beast, if you please. I'd hate to feel that I hadn't got my beef's worth out of you."

Galladon paused for a moment, then laughed. "Does nothing frighten you, sule?"

"Actually, pretty much everything here does—I'm just good at ignoring the fact that I'm terrified. If I ever realize how scared I am, you'll probably find me trying to hide under those cobblestones over there. Now, tell me more about these gangs."

Galladon shrugged, walking away from the broken door and pulling a chair away from the wall. He turned a critical eye on its legs, then carefully settled down. He moved just quickly enough to stand again as the legs cracked. He tossed the chair away with disgust, and settled on the floor.

"There are three sections of Elantris, sule, and three gangs. The market section is ruled by Shaor; you met a few members of his court yesterday, though they were too busy licking the slime off your offerings to introduce themselves. In the palace section you'll find Karata—she's the one who so very politely relieved that woman of her food today. Last is Aanden. He spends most of his time in the university section."

"A learned man?"

"No, an opportunist. He was the first one who realized that many of the library's older texts were written on vellum. Yesterday's classics have become tomorrow's lunch. Kolo?"

"Idos Domi!" Raoden swore. "That's atrocious! The old scrolls of Elantris are supposed to hold countless original works. They're priceless!"

Galladon turned him a suffering eye. "Sule, do I need to repeat my speech about hunger? What good is literature when your stomach hurts so much your eyes water?"

"That's a terrible argument. Two-century-old lambskin scrolls can't possibly taste very good."

Galladon shrugged. "Better than slime. Anyway, Aanden supposedly ran out of scrolls a few months back. They tried boiling books, but that didn't work very well."

"I'm surprised they haven't tried boiling one another."

"Oh, it's been tried," Galladon said. "Fortunately, something happens to us during the Shaod—apparently the flesh of a dead man doesn't taste too good. Kolo? In fact, it's so violently bitter that no one can keep it down."

"It's nice to see that cannibalism has been so logically ruled out as an option," Raoden said dryly.

"I told you, sule. The hunger makes men do strange things."

"And that makes it all right?"

Wisely, Galladon didn't answer.

Raoden continued. "You talk about hunger and pain as if they are forces which can't be resisted. Anything is acceptable, as long as the hunger made you do it—remove our comforts, and we become animals."

Galladon shook his head. "I'm sorry, sule, but that's just the way things work."

"It doesn't have to be."

TEN years wasn't long enough. Even in Arelon's thick humidity, it should have taken longer for the city to deteriorate so much. Elantris looked as if it had been abandoned for centuries. Its wood was decaying, its plaster and bricks were disintegrating—even stone buildings were beginning to crumble. And coating everything was the omnipresent film of brown sludge.

Raoden was finally getting used to walking on the slippery, uneven cobblestones. He tried to keep himself clean of the slime, but the task proved impossible. Every wall he brushed and every ledge he grasped left its mark on him.

The two men walked slowly down a broad street; the thoroughfare was far larger than any of its kind back in Kae. Elantris had been built on a massive scale, and while the size had seemed daunting from without, Raoden was only now beginning to grasp just how enormous the city was. He and Galladon had been walking for hours, and Galladon said they were still a moderate distance from their destination.

The two did not rush, however. That was one of the first things Galladon had taught: In Elantris, one took one's time.

Everything the Dula did was performed with an air of utter precision, his movements relaxed and careful. The slightest scratch, no matter how negligible, added to an Elantrian's pain. The more careful one was, the longer one would stay sane. So, Raoden followed, trying to mimic Galladon's attentive gait. Every time Raoden began to feel that the caution was excessive, all he had to do was look at one of the numerous forms that lay huddled in gutters and on street corners, and his determination would return.

The Hoed, Galladon called them: those Elantrians who had succumbed to the pain. Their minds lost, their lives were filled with continual, unrelenting torture. They rarely moved, though some had enough feral instinct to remain crouched in the shadows. Most of them were quiet, though few were completely silent. As he passed, Raoden could hear their mumbles, sobs, and whines. Most seemed to be repeating words and phrases to themselves, a mantra to accompany their suffering.

"Domi, Domi, Domi . . ."

"So beautiful, once so very beautiful . . ."

"Stop, stop, stop. Make it stop. . . ."

Raoden forced himself to close his ears to the words. His chest was beginning to constrict, as if he were suffering with the poor, faceless wretches. If he paid too much attention, he would go mad long before the pain took him.

However, if he let his mind wander, it invariably turned to his outside life. Would his friends continue their clandestine meetings? Would Kiin and Roial be able to hold the group together? And what of his best friend, Lukel? Raoden had barely gotten to know Lukel's new wife; now he would never get to see their first child.

Even worse were the thoughts of his own marriage. He had never met the woman he was to have married, though he had spoken to her via Seon on many occasions. Was she really as witty and interesting as she had seemed? He would never know. Iadon had probably covered up Raoden's transformation, pretending that his son was dead. Sarene would never come to Arelon now; once she heard the news, she would stay in Teod and seek another husband.

If only I had been able to meet her, if just once. But, such thoughts were useless. He was an Elantrian now.

Instead, he focused on the city itself. It was difficult to believe that Elantris had once been the most beautiful city in Opelon, probably in the world. The slime was what he saw—the rot and the erosion. However, beneath the filth were the remnants of Elantris's former greatness. A spire, the remains of a delicately carved wall relief, grand chapels and vast mansions, pillars and arches. Ten years ago this city had shone with its own mystical brightness, a city of pure white and gold.

No one knew what had caused the Reod. There were those who theorized—most of them Derethi priests—that the fall of Elantris had been caused by God. The pre-Reod Elantrians had lived as gods, allowing other religions in Arelon, but suffering them the same way a master lets his dog lick fallen food off the floor. The beauty of Elantris, the powers its inhabitants wielded, had kept the general population from converting to Shu-Keseg. Why seek an unseen deity when you had gods living before you?

It had come with a tempest—that much even Raoden remembered. The earth itself had shattered, an enormous chasm appearing in the south, all of Arelon quaking. With the destruction, Elantris had lost its glory. The Elantrians had changed from brilliant white-haired beings to creatures with splotchy skin and bald scalps—like sufferers of some horrible disease in the advanced stages of decay. Elantris had stopped glowing, instead growing dark.

And it had happened only ten years ago. Ten years was not enough. Stone should not crumble after just a decade of neglect. The filth should not have piled up so quickly—not with so few inhabitants, most of whom were incapacitated. It was as if Elantris were intent on dying, a city committing suicide.

"THE market section of Elantris," Galladon said. "This place used to be one of the most magnificent marketplaces in the world—merchants came from across Opelon to sell their exotic goods to the Elantrians. A man could also come here to buy the more luxurious Elantrian magics. They didn't give *everything* away for free. Kolo?"

They stood atop a flat-roofed building; apparently, some Elantrians had preferred flat roofs as opposed to peaks or domes, for the flat sections allowed for rooftop gardens. Before them lay a section of city that looked pretty much the same as the rest of Elantris—dark and falling apart. Raoden could imagine that its streets had once been decorated with the colorful canvas awnings of street vendors, but the only remains of such was the occasional filth-covered rag.

"Can we get any closer?" Raoden asked, leaning over the ledge to look down on the market section.

"You can if you want, sule," Galladon said speculatively. "But I'm staying here. Shaor's men are fond of chasing people; it's probably one of the few pleasures they have left."

"Tell me about Shaor himself, then."

Galladon shrugged. "In a place like this, many look for leaders—someone to ward off a bit of the chaos. Like any society, those who are strongest often end up in command. Shaor is one who finds pleasure in controlling others, and for some reason the most wild and morally corrupt Elantrians find their way to him."

"And he gets to take the offerings of one-third of the newcomers?" Raoden asked.

"Well, Shaor himself rarely bothers with such things—but yes, his followers get first call on one-third of the offerings."

"Why the compromise?" Raoden asked. "If Shaor's men are as uncontrollable as you imply, then what convinced them to hold to such an arbitrary agreement?"

"The other gangs are just as big as Shaor's, sule," Galladon explained. "On the outside, people tend to be convinced of their own immortality. We are more realistic. One rarely wins a battle without at least a few wounds, and here even a couple of slight cuts can be more devastating, and more agonizing, than a swift decapitation. Shaor's men are wild, but they are not complete idiots. They won't fight unless they have incredible odds or a promising reward. You think it was your physique that kept that man from attacking you yesterday?"

"I wasn't sure," Raoden admitted.

"Even the slightest hint that you might fight back is enough to scare these men off, sule," Galladon said. "The pleasure of torturing you just isn't worth the gamble that you might get in a lucky blow."

Raoden shivered at the thought. "Show me where the other gangs live."

THE university and the palace bordered one another. According to Galladon, Karata and Aanden had a very uneasy truce, and guards were usually posted on both sides to keep watch. Once again, Raoden's companion led him to a flat-roofed building, an untrustworthy set of stairs leading to the top.

However, after climbing the stairs—and nearly falling when one of the steps cracked beneath him—Raoden had to admit that the view was worth the effort. Elantris's palace was large enough to be magnificent despite the inevitable decay. Five domes topped five wings, each with a majestic spire. Only one of the spires—the one in the middle—was still intact, but it rose high into the air, by far the tallest structure Raoden had ever seen.

"That's said to be the exact center of Elantris," Galladon said, nodding to the spire. "Once you could climb the steps winding around it and look out over the entire city. Nowadays, I wouldn't trust it. Kolo?"

The university was large, but less magnificent. It consisted of five or six long, flat buildings and a lot of open space—ground that had probably once held grass or gardens, both things that would have been eaten to their roots long ago by Elantris's starving inhabitants.

"Karata is both the harshest and most lenient of the gang leaders," Galladon said, gazing down on the university. There was something odd in his eyes, as if he were seeing things Raoden couldn't. His description continued in its characteristic rambling tone, as if his mouth wasn't aware that his mind was focused elsewhere.

"She doesn't often let new members into her gang, and she is extremely territorial. Shaor's men might chase you for a while if you wander onto his turf, but only if they feel like it. Karata suffers no intruders. However, if you leave Karata alone, she leaves you alone, and she rarely harms newcomers when she takes their food. You saw her earlier today—she always takes the food personally. Maybe she doesn't trust her underlings enough to handle it."

"Perhaps," Raoden said. "What else do you know about her?"

"Not much—leaders of violent thieving gangs don't tend to be the type to spend their afternoons chatting."

"Now who's taking things lightly?" Raoden said with a smile.

"You're a bad influence, sule. Dead people aren't supposed to be cheerful. Anyway, the only thing I can tell you about Karata is that she doesn't like being in Elantris very much."

Raoden frowned. "Who does?"

"We all hate it, sule, but few of us have the courage to try and escape. Karata has been caught in Kae three times now—always in the vicinity of the king's palace. One more time and the priests will have her burned."

"What does she want at the palace?"

"She hasn't been kind enough to explain it to me," Galladon replied. "Most people think she intends to assassinate King Iadon."

"The king?" Raoden said. "What would that accomplish?"

"Revenge, discord, bloodlust. All very good reasons when you're already damned. Kolo?"

Raoden frowned. Perhaps living with his father—who was absolutely paranoid about the prospect of getting killed by an assassin—had desensitized him, but murdering the king just didn't seem like a likely goal to him. "What about the other gang leader?"

"Aanden?" Galladon asked, looking back over the city. "He claims he was some kind of noble before he was thrown in here—a baron, I think. He's tried to establish himself as monarch of Elantris, and he is incredibly annoyed that Karata has control of the palace. He holds court, claims he will feed those who join him—though all they've gotten so far are a few boiled books—and makes plans for attacking Kae."

"What?" Raoden asked with surprise. "Attacking?"

"He isn't serious," Galladon said. "But he *is* good at propaganda. He claims to have a plan to free Elantris, and it's gained him a large following. However, he's also brutal. Karata only harms people who try to sneak into the palace—Aanden is notorious for dispensing judgments at a whim. Personally, sule, I don't think he's completely sane."

Raoden frowned. If this Aanden really had been a baron, then Raoden would have known him. However, he didn't recognize the name. Either Aanden had lied about his background, or he had chosen a new name after entering Elantris.

Raoden studied the area in between the university and the palace. A certain object had caught his attention. Something so mundane he wouldn't have given it a second look, had it not been the first of its kind he had seen in all of Elantris.

"Is that a well?" he asked uncertainly.

Galladon nodded. "The only one in the city."

"How is that possible?"

"Indoor plumbing, sule, courtesy of AonDor magic. Wells weren't necessary."

"Then why build that one?"

"I think it was used in religious ceremonies. Several Elantrian worship services required water that had been freshly gathered from a moving river."

"Then the Aredel river *does* run under the city," Raoden said.

"Of course. Where else would it go. Kolo?"

Raoden narrowed his eyes thoughtfully, but he didn't volunteer any information. As he stood, watching the city, he noticed a small ball of light floating through one of the streets below. The Seon meandered with an aimless air, occasionally floating in circles. It was far too distant for him to make out the Aon at its center.

Galladon noticed Raoden's scrutiny. "A Seon," the Dula noted. "Not uncommon in the city."

"It's true, then?" Raoden asked.

Galladon nodded. "When a Seon's master gets taken by the Shaod, the Seon itself is driven mad. There's a number of them floating through the city. They don't talk, they just hover about, mindless."

Raoden glanced away. Since being thrown into Elantris, he'd avoided thinking about his own Seon, Ien. Raoden had heard what happened to Seons when their masters became Elantrians.

Galladon glanced up at the sky. "It will rain soon."

Raoden raised an eyebrow at the cloudless sky. "If you say so."

"Trust me. We should get inside, unless you want to spend the next few days in damp clothing. Fires are hard to make in Elantris; the wood is all too wet or too rotten to burn."

"Where should we go?"

Galladon shrugged. "Pick a house, sule. Chances are it won't be inhabited."

They had spent the previous night sleeping in an abandoned house—but now, something occurred to Raoden. "Where do *you* live, Galladon?"

"In Duladel," Galladon immediately answered.

"I mean nowadays."

Galladon thought for a moment, eyeing Raoden uncertainly. Then, with a shrug, he waved Raoden to follow him down the unstable stairs. "Come."

"BOOKS!" Raoden said with excitement.

"Should never have brought you here," Galladon muttered. "Now I'll never get rid of you."

Galladon had led Raoden into what had seemed to be a deserted wine cellar, but had turned out to be something quite different indeed. The air was drier here—even though it was below ground—and much cooler as well. As if to revoke his earlier cautions about fire, Galladon had pulled a lantern from a hidden alcove and lit it with a bit of flint and steel. What the light had revealed was surprising indeed.

It looked like a learned man's study. There were Aons—the mystical ancient characters behind the Aonic language—painted all over the walls, and there were several shelves of books.

"How did you ever find this place?" Raoden asked eagerly.

"I stumbled upon it," Galladon said with a shrug.

"All these books," Raoden said, picking one up off its shelf. It was a bit moldy, but still legible. "Maybe these could teach us the secret behind the Aons, Galladon! Did you ever think of that?"

"The Aons?"

"The magic of Elantris," Raoden said. "They say that before the Reod, Elantrians could create powerful magics just by drawing Aons."

"Oh, you mean like this?" the large dark-skinned man asked, raising his hand. He traced a symbol in the air, Aon Deo, and his finger left a glowing white line behind it.

Raoden's eyes opened wide, and the book dropped from his stunned fingers. The Aons. Historically, only the Elantrians had been able to call upon the power locked within them. That power was supposed to be gone; it was said to have failed when Elantris fell.

Galladon smiled at him through the glowing symbol that hovered in the air between them.

CHAPTER 5

"MERCIFUL Domi," Sarene asked with surprise, "where did *he* come from?"

The gyorn strode into the king's throne room with the arrogance characteristic of his kind. He wore the shining bloodred armor of a Derethi high priest, an extravagant crimson cloak billowing out behind him, though he bore no weapon. It was a costume meant to impress—and, despite what Sarene thought of the gyorns themselves, she had to admit that their clothing was effective. Of course, it was mostly for show; even in Fjorden's martial society, few people could walk as easily as this gyorn while wearing full plate armor. The metal was probably so thin and light that it would be useless in battle.

The gyorn marched past her without a second glance, his eyes focused directly on the king. He was young for a gyorn, probably in his forties, and his short, well-styled black hair had only a trace of gray in it.

"You knew there was a Derethi presence in Elantris, my lady," Ashe said, floating beside her as usual, one of only two Seons in the room. "Why should you be surprised to see a Fjordell priest?"

"That is a full *gyorn*, Ashe. There are only twenty of them in the entire Fjordell Empire. There may be some Derethi believers in Kae, but not enough to warrant a visit from a high priest. Gyorns are extremely miserly with their time."

Sarene watched the Fjordell man stride through the room, cutting through groups of people like a bird tearing through a cloud of gnats. "Come on," she whispered to Ashe, making her way through the peripheral crowd toward the front of the room. She didn't want to miss what the gyorn said.

She needn't have worried. When the man spoke, his firm voice boomed through the throne room. "King Iadon," he said, with only the slightest nod of his head in place of a bow. "I, Gyorn Hrathen, bring you a message from Wyrn Wulfden the Fourth. He thinks that it is time our two nations shared more than a common border." He spoke with the thick, melodic accent of a native Fjordell.

Iadon looked up from his ledgers with a barely masked scowl. "What more does Wyrn want? We already have a trade treaty with Fjorden."

"His Holiness fears for the souls of your people, Your Majesty," Hrathen said.

"Well, then, let him convert them. I have always allowed your priests complete freedom to preach in Arelon."

"The people respond too slowly, Your Majesty. They require a push—a sign, if you will. Wyrn thinks it is time you yourself converted to Shu-Dereth."

This time Iadon didn't even bother masking the annoyance in his tone. "I already believe in Shu-Korath, priest. We serve the same God."

"Derethi is the only true form of Shu-Keseg," Hrathen said darkly.

Iadon waved a dismissive hand. "I care nothing for the squabbles between the two sects, priest. Go convert someone who doesn't believe—there are still plenty of Arelenes who hold to the old religion."

"You should not dismiss the offering of Wyrn so casually," the gyorn warned.

"Honestly, priest, do we need to go through this? Your threats hold no weight—Fjorden hasn't held any real influence for two centuries. Do you seriously think to intimidate me with how powerful you *used* to be?"

Hrathen's eyes grew dangerous. "Fjorden is more powerful now than it ever was before."

"Really?" Iadon asked. "Where is your vast empire? Where are your armies? How many countries have you conquered in the last century? Maybe someday you people will realize that your empire collapsed three hundred years ago."

Hrathen paused for a moment; then he repeated his introductory nod and spun around, his cloak billowing dramatically as he stalked toward the door. Sarene's prayers were not answered, however—he didn't step on it and trip himself. Just before Hrathen left, he turned to shoot one final, disappointed look at the throne room. His gaze however, found Sarene instead of the king. Their eyes locked for a moment, and she could see a slight hint of confusion as he studied her unusual height and blond Teoish hair. Then he was gone, and the room burst into a hundred prattling conversations.

King Iadon snorted and turned back to his ledgers.

"He doesn't see," Sarene whispered. "He doesn't understand."

"Understand what, my lady?" Ashe asked.

"How dangerous that gyorn is."

"His Majesty is a merchant, my lady, not a true politician. He doesn't see things the same way you do."

"Even so," Sarene said, speaking quietly enough that only

Ashe could hear. "King Iadon should be experienced enough to recognize that what Hrathen said—at least about Fjorden—was completely true. The Wyrns *are* more powerful now than they were centuries ago, even at the height of the Old Empire's power."

"It is hard to look past military might, especially when one is a relatively new monarch," Ashe said. "King Iadon cannot fathom how Fjorden's army of priests could be more influential than its warriors ever were."

Sarene tapped her cheek for a moment in thought. "Well, Ashe, at least now you don't have to worry about my causing too much unrest amongst Kae's nobility."

"I seriously doubt that, my lady. How else would you spend your time?"

"Oh, Ashe," she said sweetly. "Why would I bother with a bunch of incompetent would-be nobles when I can match wits with a full gyorn?" Then, more seriously, she continued. "Wyrn picks his high priests well. If Iadon doesn't watch that man—and it doesn't seem like he will—then Hrathen will convert this city out from under him. What good will my sacrificial marriage do for Teod if Arelon gives itself to our enemies?"

"You may be overreacting, my lady," Ashe said with a pulse. The words were familiar—it seemed that Ashe often felt a need to say them to her.

Sarene shook her head. "Not this time. Today was a test, Ashe. Now Hrathen will feel justified in taking action against the king—he has convinced himself that Arelon is indeed ruled by a blasphemer. He'll try to find a way to overthrow Iadon's throne, and Arelon's government will collapse for the second time in ten years. This time it won't be the merchant class that fills the void of leadership—it will be the Derethi priesthood."

"So you are going to help Iadon?" Ashe said with an amused tone.

"He is my sovereign king."

"Despite your opinion that he is insufferable?"

"*Anything* is better than Fjordell rule. Besides, maybe I was wrong about Iadon." Things hadn't gone *too* poorly between the two of them since that first embarrassing meeting.

Iadon had practically ignored her at Raoden's funeral, which had suited Sarene just fine; she'd been too busy watching for discrepancies in the ceremony. Unfortunately, the event had occurred with a disappointing level of orthodoxy, and no predominant noblemen had given themselves away by failing to show up or by looking too guilty during the proceedings.

"Yes . . ." she said. "Perhaps Iadon and I can get along by just ignoring each other."

"What in the name of Burning Domi are you doing back in my court, girl!" the king swore from behind her.

Sarene raised her eyes to the sky in a look of resignation, and Ashe pulsed a quiet laugh as she turned to face King Iadon.

"What?" she asked, trying her best to sound innocent.

"You!" Iadon barked, pointing at her. He was understandably in a bad mood—of course, from what she heard, Iadon was rarely in a good mood. "Don't you understand that women aren't to come to my court unless they're invited?"

Sarene blinked her eyes in confusion. "No one told me that, Your Majesty," she said, intentionally trying to sound as if she didn't have a wit in her head.

Iadon grumbled something about foolish women, shaking his head at her obvious lack of intelligence.

"I just wanted to see the paintings," Sarene said, putting a quaver in her voice, as if she were on the brink of crying.

Iadon held his hand palm-forward in the air to forestall any more of her drivel, turning back to his ledgers. Sarene barely kept herself from smiling as she wiped her eyes and pretended to study the painting behind her.

"That was unexpected," Ashe said quietly.

"I'll deal with Iadon later," Sarene mumbled. "I have someone more important to worry about now."

"I just never thought I'd see the day when you, of all women, gave into the feminine stereotype—even if it was just an act."

"What?" Sarene asked, fluttering her eyes. "Me, act?"

Ashe snorted.

"You know, I've never been able to figure out how you Seons manage sounds like that," Sarene said. "You don't have noses—how can you snort?"

"Years of practice, my lady," Ashe replied. "Am I truly going to have to suffer your whimpering every time you speak with the king?"

Sarene shrugged. "He expects women to be foolish, so I'll be foolish. It's much easier to manipulate people when they assume you can't gather enough wits to remember your own name."

"'Ene?" a sudden voice bellowed. "Is that you?" The deep, scratchy voice was oddly familiar. It was as if the speaker had a sore throat, though she had never heard someone with a sore throat yell so loudly.

Sarene turned hesitantly. An enormous man—taller, broader, pudgier, and more muscled than seemed possible—shoved his way through the crowd in her direction. He was dressed in a broad blue silken doublet—she shuddered to think of how many worms had toiled to make it—and wore the ruffle-cuffed trousers of an Arelish courtier.

"It is you!" the man exclaimed. "We thought you weren't coming for another week!"

"Ashe," Sarene mumbled, "who is this lunatic and what does he want with me?"

"He looks familiar, my lady. I'm sorry, my memory isn't what it used to be."

"Ha!" the enormous man said, scooping her up into a bear hug. It was an odd feeling—her bottom half squished into his oversized gut while her face was crushed by his hard, well-muscled chest. She resisted the urge to whimper, waiting and hoping the man would drop her before she passed out. Ashe would probably go for help if her face started to change colors.

Fortunately, the man let go long before she asphyxiated, instead holding her by her shoulders at arms length. "You've changed. When I last saw you, you were only knee high." Then he looked over her tall figure. "Well . . . I doubt you were ever *knee* high, but you were certainly no taller than a waist. Your mother always said you'd be a lanky one!"

Sarene shook her head. The voice was slightly familiar, but she couldn't place his features. She usually had such a good memory for faces. . . . Unless, ...

"Hunkey Kay?" she asked hesitantly. "Gracious Domi! What happened to your beard?"

"Arelish nobles don't wear beards, little one. I haven't had one in years."

It *was* him. The voice was different, the beardless face unfamiliar, but the eyes were the same. She remembered looking up at those wide brown eyes, always full of laughter. "Hunkey Kay," she mumbled distractedly. "Where's my present?"

Her uncle Kiin laughed, his odd scratchy voice making it sound more like a wheeze than a chortle. Those had always been the first words out of her mouth when he came to visit; her uncle brought the most exotic of gifts, delights that were extravagant enough to be unique even to the daughter of a king.

"I'm afraid I forgot the present this time, little one."

Sarene blushed. However, before she could squeak out an apology, Hunkey Kay wrapped a large arm around her shoulder and began towing her out of the throne room.

"Come, you have to meet my wife."

"Wife?" Sarene asked with a shocked voice. It had been over a decade since she had seen Kiin, but she remembered one fact quite clearly. Her uncle had been a sworn bachelor and a confirmed rascal. "Hunkey Kay is *married*?"

"You aren't the only one who has grown over the last ten years," Kiin rasped. "Oh, and as cute as it is to hear you call me 'Hunkey Kay,' you'll probably want to call me Uncle Kiin now."

Sarene blushed again. "Hunkey Kay" had been the creation of a child unable to pronounce her uncle's name.

"So, how's your father doing?" the large man asked. "Acting properly regal, I assume."

"He's doing fine, Uncle," she replied. "Though I'm sure he would be surprised to find you living in the court of Arelon."

"He knows."

"No, he thinks you left on one of your voyages and settled on one of the far islands."

"Sarene, if you're as quick-witted a woman as you were a

girl, then you should have learned by now to separate the truth from the stories."

The statement came like a bucketful of icy water. She vaguely remembered watching her uncle's ship sail away one day and asking her father when Hunkey Kay was going to return. Eventeo's face had been morose when he replied that this time Hunkey Kay would be taking a long, long voyage.

"But why?" she asked. "All this time you were living just a few days' trip from home, and you never came to visit?"

"Stories for another day, little one," Kiin said with a shake of his head. "Right now, you need to meet the monster of a woman who finally managed to capture your uncle."

KIIN'S wife was hardly a monster. In fact, she was one of the most beautiful mature women Sarene had ever seen. Daora had a strong face with sharp, statuesque features and a well-styled head of auburn hair. She was not what Sarene would ever have placed with her uncle—of course, her most recent memories of Kiin were over a decade old.

Kiin's large, castle-like mansion was not a surprise. She remembered that her uncle had been a merchant of some sort, and her memories were highlighted by expensive gifts and Kiin's exotic clothing. He had not only been the younger son of a king, but he had also been an extremely successful businessman. Something he still was, apparently. He'd been out of the city on business until that morning, which was why she hadn't seen him at the funeral.

The greatest shock was the children. Despite the fact that Sarene knew he was married, she just couldn't reconcile her recollections of the unruly Hunkey Kay with the concept of fatherhood. Her preconceptions were neatly shattered the moment Kiin and Daora opened the door to the mansion's dining hall.

"Father's home!" called the voice of a young girl.

"Yes, Father's home," Kiin said with a suffering voice. "And no, I didn't bring you anything. I've only been gone a few minutes."

"I don't care what you did or didn't bring me. I just want to *eat*." The speaker, a young girl about ten years old, had a very serious, adult-sounding voice. She wore a pink dress tied with white ribbon, and had a bob of stark blond hair on her head.

"When do you *not* want to eat, Kaise?" a little boy, who looked almost identical to the girl, asked with a sour look.

"Children, don't squabble," Daora said firmly. "We have a guest."

"Sarene," Kiin declared, "meet your cousins. Kaise and Daorn. The two biggest headaches in your poor uncle's life."

"Now, Father, you know you would have gone mad from boredom long ago without them," a man said from the far doorway. The newcomer was of average Arelish height, which meant he was an inch or two shorter than Sarene, with a lean build and a strikingly handsome, hawkish face. His hair had been parted down the center and flopped down on either side of his face. A woman with black hair stood at his side, her lips slightly pursed as she studied Sarene.

The man bowed slightly to Sarene. "Your Highness," he said with only a hint of a smile on his lips.

"My son Lukel," Kiin explained.

"Your son?" Sarene asked with surprise. Young children she could accept, but Lukel was a few years older than she was. That meant . . .

"No," Kiin said with a shake of his head. "Lukel is from Daora's previous marriage."

"Not that that makes me any less his son," Lukel said with a broad smile. "You can't escape responsibility for me that easily."

"Domi himself wouldn't dare take responsibility for you," Kiin said. "Anyway, that's Jalla next to him."

"Your daughter?" Sarene asked as Jalla curtsied.

"Daughter-in-law," the dark-haired woman explained, her speech thick with an accent.

"You're Fjordell?" Sarene asked. The hair had been a clue, but the name and accent were giveaways.

"Svordish," Jalla corrected—not that it was much different. The small kingdom of Svorden was all but a Fjordell province.

"Jalla and I studied together at the Svordish university," Lukel explained. "We were married last month."

"Congratulations," Sarene said. "It's nice to know I'm not the only newlywed in the room." Sarene meant the comment lightly, but was unable to keep the bitterness out of her voice. She felt Kiin's large hand grip her shoulder.

"I'm sorry, 'Ene," he said softly. "I wasn't going to bring it up, but . . . You deserved better than this; you were always such a happy child."

"No loss to me," Sarene said with an indifference she didn't feel. "It isn't like I knew him, Uncle."

"Even still," Daora said, "it must have been a shock."

"You could say that," Sarene agreed.

"If it helps," Kiin said, "Prince Raoden was a good man. One of the best I have ever known. If you knew a little more about Arelish politics, then you would understand that I don't use those words lightly when referring to a member of Iadon's court."

Sarene nodded slightly. Part of her was happy to hear she hadn't misjudged Raoden by his letters; the other half thought it would have been easier to continue thinking that he was like his father.

"Enough talk about dead princes!" a small but insistent voice decided from the table. "If we don't eat soon, Father will have to stop complaining about me because *I'll* be dead."

"Yes, Kiin," Daora agreed, "you should probably go to the kitchen and make sure your feast isn't burning."

Kiin snorted. "I have each dish cooking on a precise schedule. It would be impossible for one to . . ." The large man trailed off, sniffing the air. Then he swore and barreled out of the room.

"Uncle Kiin is cooking dinner?" Sarene asked with amazement.

"Your uncle is one of the best chefs in this town, dear," Daora said.

"Uncle Kiin?" Sarene repeated. *"Cook?"*

Daora nodded, as if it were an everyday occurrence. "Kiin has traveled more places in this world than anyone in Arelon, and he brought back recipes from each one. I believe tonight he's fixing something he learned in Jindo."

"Does this mean we're going to eat?" Kaise asked pointedly.

"I hate Jindoeese food," Daorn complained, his voice almost indistinguishable from that of his sister. "It's too spicy."

"You don't like anything unless it has a handful of sugar mixed in," Lukel teased, mussing his half brother's hair.

"Daorn, go run and get Adien."

"Another one?" Sarene asked.

Daora nodded. "The last. Lukel's full brother."

"He's probably sleeping," Kaise said. "Adien's always sleeping. I think it's because his mind is only half awake."

"Kaise, little girls who say such things about their brothers often end up in bed without supper," Daora informed. "Daorn, get moving."

"YOU don't look like a princess," Kaise said. The girl sat primly on her chair beside Sarene. The dining room had a homey, studylike feel, filled with dark wood paneling and relics from Kiin's traveling days.

"What do you mean?" Sarene asked, trying to figure out how to use the odd Jindoeese dining utensils. There were two of them, one with a sharp pointed end and the other with a flat shoveled end. Everyone else was eating with them as if it were second nature, and Sarene was determined not to say anything. She would figure them out on her own or she wouldn't get much to eat. The latter was looking much more likely.

"Well, for one thing you're way too tall," Kaise said.

"Kaise," her mother warned in a threatening tone.

"Well it's true. All of the books say princesses are petite. I'm not exactly sure what petite means, but I don't think she's it."

"I'm Teoish," Sarene said, successfully spearing something that looked like a marinated piece of shrimp. "We're all this tall."

"Father's Teoish too, Kaise," Daorn said. "And you know how tall he is."

"But father's fat," Kaise pointed out. "Why aren't you fat too, Sarene?"

Kiin, who had just appeared out of the kitchen doors, absently rapped his daughter on the head with the bottom of a serving tray as he passed. "Just as I thought," he mumbled, listening to the ringing sound created by the metal pan, "your head is completely hollow. I guess that explains a lot."

Kaise rubbed her head petulantly before turning back to her meal, muttering, "I still think princesses should be smaller. Besides, princesses are supposed to have good table manners; cousin Sarene's dropped about half of her meal on the floor. Who ever heard of a princess that didn't know how to use MaiPon sticks?"

Sarene blushed, looking down at the foreign utensils.

"Don't listen to her, 'Ene," Kiin laughed, setting another succulent-smelling dish on the table. "This is Jindoeese food—it's made with so much grease that if half of it *doesn't* end up on the floor, then something's wrong. You'll get the hang of those sticks eventually."

"You can use a spoon, if you want," Daorn said helpfully. "Adien always does."

Sarene's eyes were immediately drawn to the fourth child. Adien was a thin-faced boy in his late teens. He had a pale white complexion and a strange, discomforting cast to his face. He ate awkwardly, his motions stiff and uncontrolled. As he ate, he mumbled to himself—repeating numbers, as far as Sarene could tell. Sarene had met people like him before, children whose minds weren't completely whole.

"Father, the meal is delicious," Lukel said, drawing the attention away from his brother. "I don't believe you've ever fixed this shrimp dish before."

"It's called HaiKo," Kiin said in his raspy voice. "I learned it off a traveling merchant while you were studying in Svorden last year."

"Sixteen million four hundred thousand seven hundred and seventy-two," Adien mumbled. "That's how many steps it is to Svorden."

Sarene paused slightly at Adien's addition, but the rest of the family paid him no heed, so she did likewise. "It truly is wonderful, Uncle," Sarene said. "I would never have figured you for a chef."

"I've always enjoyed it," Kiin explained, sitting down in his chair. "I would have fixed you some things back when I visited Teod, but your mother's head cook had this inane idea that royalty didn't belong in the kitchen. I tried to explain to her that, in a way, I partially *owned* the kitchens, but she still would never let me set foot inside to prepare a meal."

"Well, she did us all a disservice," Sarene said. "You don't do all of the cooking, do you?"

Kiin shook his head. "Fortunately, no. Daora is quite the cook herself."

Sarene blinked in surprise. "You mean you don't have a cook to fix your meals for you?"

Kiin and Daora shook their heads in unison.

"Father *is* our cook," Kaise said.

"No servers or butlers either?" Sarene asked. She had assumed the lack of servants was due to an odd desire on Kiin's part to keep this particular meal personal.

"None at all," Kiin said.

"But why?"

Kiin looked at his wife, then back at Sarene. "Sarene, do you know what happened here ten years ago?"

"The Reod?" Sarene asked. "The Punishment?"

"Yes, but do you know what that means?"

Sarene thought for a moment, then shrugged slightly. "The end of the Elantrians."

Kiin nodded. "You probably never met an Elantrian—you were still young when the Reod hit. It is hard to explain how much this country changed when the disaster struck. Elantris used to be the most beautiful city in the world—trust me, I've been everywhere else. It was a monument of glowing stone and lustrous metal, and its inhabitants looked like they were chiseled from the same materials. Then . . . they fell."

"Yes, I've studied this before," Sarene said with a nod. "Their skin turned dark with black spots, and their hair began to fall from their skulls."

"You can say that with the knowledge of books," Kiin said, "but you weren't here when it happened. You can't know the horror that comes from seeing gods turn wretched and foul. Their fall destroyed the Arelish government, throwing the country into total chaos."

He paused for a moment, then continued. "It was the servants who started the revolution, Sarene. The very day their masters fell, the servants turned on them. Some—mostly the country's current nobility—say it was because the lower class in Elantris was treated too well, that their pampered natures inspired them to cast down their former rulers at the first sign of weakness. I think it was simply fear—ignorant fear that the Elantrians had a vile disease, mixed with the terror that comes from seeing someone you had worshipped stricken down before you.

"Either way, the servants are the ones who did the most damage. First in small groups, then in an incredibly destructive riot, killing any Elantrian they could find. The most powerful Elantrians went first, but the killings spread to the weaker ones as well.

"It didn't stop with the Elantrians either—the people attacked families, friends, and even those who had been appointed to positions by the Elantrians. Daora and I watched it all, horrified and thankful that there were no Elantrians in the family. Because of that night, we haven't ever been able to convince ourselves to hire servants."

"Not that we really need them," Daora said. "You'd be surprised at how much you can get done on your own."

"Especially when you have a couple of children to do the dirty jobs," Kiin said with a sly smile.

"Is that all we're good for, Father?" Lukel said with a laugh. "Scrubbing floors?"

"It's the only reason *I've* ever found for having kids," Kiin said. "Your mother and I only had Daorn because we decided we needed another couple of hands to wash chamber pots."

"Father, *please*," Kaise said. "I'm trying to eat."

"Merciful Domi help the man who interrupts Kaise's supper," Lukel said with a chuckle.

"*Princess* Kaise," the little girl corrected.

"Oh, so my little girl's a princess now?" Kiin asked with amusement.

"If Sarene can be one, then so can I. After all, you're her uncle, and that should make you a prince. Right, Father?"

"Technically yes," Kiin said. "Though I don't think I officially have a title anymore."

"They probably kicked you out because you spoke of chamber pots during supper," Kaise said. "Princes can't do that sort of thing, you know. It's horrible table manners."

"Of course," Kiin said with a fond smile. "I wonder why I never realized that before."

"So," Kaise continued. "If you are a prince, then your daughter is a princess."

"I'm afraid it doesn't work that way, Kaise," Lukel said. "Father's not king, so his kids would be barons or counts, not princes."

"Is that true?" Kaise asked with a disappointed tone.

"I'm afraid so," Kiin said. "However, trust me. Anyone who claims you're not a princess, Kaise, hasn't ever listened to you complain at bedtime."

The little girl thought for a moment and, apparently unsure how to take the comment, simply turned back to her dinner. Sarene wasn't paying much attention; her mind had frozen at the part where her uncle had said "I don't think I officially have a title anymore." It smelled of politics. Sarene thought she knew every important event that had happened in Teod's court during the last fifty years, and she knew nothing of Kiin being officially stripped of his title.

Before she could ponder any more on the incongruity, Ashe floated in through a window. In the excitement of the dinner, Sarene had almost forgotten that she'd sent him to follow the Gyorn Hrathen.

The ball of light stopped hesitantly in the air near the window. "My lady, am I interrupting?"

"No, Ashe, come in and meet my family."

"You have a Seon!" Daorn exclaimed with amazement. For once his sister seemed too stunned to speak.

"This is Ashe," Sarene explained. "He's been serving my house for over two centuries, and he's the wisest Seon I've ever known."

"My lady, you exaggerate," Ashe said modestly, yet at the same time she noticed he was glowing a bit brighter.

"A Seon . . ." Kaise said with quiet wonder, her dinner forgotten.

"They've always been rare," Kiin said, "now more than ever."

"Where did you get him?" Kaise asked.

"From my mother," Sarene said. "She Passed Ashe to me when I was born." The Passing of a Seon—it was one of the finest gifts a person could receive. Someday, Sarene would have to Pass Ashe, selecting a new ward for him to watch over and care for. She had planned it to be one of her children, or perhaps grandchildren. The possibility of either ever existing, however, was looking increasingly unlikely. . . .

"A Seon," Kaise said with wonder. She turned to Sarene, eyes alight with excitement. "Can I play with him after supper?"

"*Play* with me?" Ashe asked uncertainly.

"Can I please, Cousin Sarene?" Kaise begged.

"I don't know," Sarene said with a smile. "I seem to recall a few comments about my height."

The little girl's look of disappointed chagrin was a source of great amusement to all. It was at that moment, among their laughter, that Sarene began to feel her tension ease for the first time since leaving her homeland a week before.

CHAPTER 6

"THERE is no hope for the king, I'm afraid." Hrathen folded his arms across his breastplate thoughtfully as he looked back at the throne room.

"Your Grace?" Dilaf asked.

"King Iadon," Hrathen explained. "I had hoped to save him—though I never really expected the nobility to follow me without a fight. They're too entrenched in their ways. Perhaps if we had gotten to them right after the Reod. Of course, we weren't sure that whatever disease had taken the Elantrians wouldn't affect us as well."

"Jaddeth struck down the Elantrians," Dilaf said fervently.

"Yes," Hrathen said, not bothering to look down at the shorter man. "But ofttimes Jaddeth uses natural processes to bring about His will. A plague will kill Fjordell as well as Arelene."

"Jaddeth would protect his chosen."

"Of course," Hrathen said distractedly, shooting one more dissatisfied glance down the hallway toward the throne room. He had made the offer out of duty, knowing that the easiest way to save Arelon would be to convert its ruler, but he hadn't expected Iadon to respond favorably. If only the king knew how much suffering he could forestall with a simple profession of faith.

It was too late now; Iadon had formally rejected Jaddeth. He would have to become an example. However, Hrathen would have to be careful. Memories of the Duladen revolution were still stark in Hrathen's mind—the death, blood, and chaos. Such a cataclysm had to be avoided. Hrathen was a stern man, and a determined one, but he was no lover of carnage.

Of course, with only three months' time, he might not have a choice. If he was going to succeed, he might have to incite a revolt. More death and more chaos—horrible things to throw upon a nation that still hadn't recovered from its last violent revolution. However, Jaddeth's empire would not sit still and wait because a few ignorant nobles refused to accept the truth.

"I suppose I expected too much of them," Hrathen mumbled. "They are, after all, only Arelenes."

Dilaf made no response to the comment.

"I noticed someone odd in the throne room, Arteth," Hrathen said as they turned and walked out of the palace, passing both sculpture and servant without so much as a glance. "Perhaps you can help me identify her. She was Aonic, but she was taller than most Arelenes, and her hair was much lighter than the average Arelish brown. She looked out of place."

"What was she wearing, Your Holiness?" Dilaf asked.

"Black. All black with a yellow sash."

"The new princess, Your Grace," Dilaf hissed, his voice suddenly hateful.

"New princess?"

"She arrived yesterday, the same as yourself. She was to be married to Iadon's son Raoden."

Hrathen nodded. He hadn't attended the prince's funeral, but he had heard of the event. He hadn't known, however, of the impending marriage. The betrothal must have occurred recently. "She's still here," he asked, "even though the prince died?"

Dilaf nodded. "Unfortunately for her, the royal engagement contract made her his wife the moment he died."

"Ah," Hrathen said. "Where is she from?"

"Teod, Your Grace," Dilaf said.

Hrathen nodded, understanding the hatred in Dilaf's voice. Arelon, despite the blasphemous city of Elantris, at least showed some possibility for redemption. Teod, however, was the homeland of Shu-Korath—a degenerate sect of Shu-Keseg, the parent religion of Shu-Dereth. The day

Teod fell beneath Fjorden's glory would be a joyous day indeed.

"A Teoish princess could be a problem," Hrathen mused.

"Nothing can hinder Jaddeth's empire."

"If nothing could hinder it, Arteth, then it would already encompass the entire planet. Jaddeth takes pleasure in allowing His servants to serve Him, and grants us glory in bending the foolish before our will. And of all the fools in the world, Teoish fools are the most dangerous."

"How could one woman be a danger to you, Your Holiness?"

"Well, for one thing, her marriage means that Teod and Arelon have a formal blood bond. If we aren't careful, we'll have to fight them both at once. A man is more likely to think himself a hero when he has an ally to support him."

"I understand, Your Grace."

Hrathen nodded, sweeping out into the sunlight. "Pay attention, Arteth, and I will teach you a very important lesson—one that few people know, and even fewer can properly use."

"What lesson is that?" Dilaf asked, following close behind.

Hrathen smiled slightly. "I will show you the way to destroy a nation—the means by which the man of Jaddeth can topple kingdoms and seize control of the people's souls."

"I am . . . eager to learn, Your Grace."

"Good," Hrathen said, looking across Kae at the enormous wall of Elantris. It rose above the city like a mountain. "Take me up there. I wish to view the fallen lords of Arelon."

WHEN Hrathen had first arrived at the Outer City of Kae, he had noted how indefensible it was. Now, standing atop the wall of Elantris, Hrathen could see that he had actually underestimated how pathetic Kae's fortifications were. Beautiful, terraced steps ran up the outside of Elantris's wall, providing outside access to the top. They were firm, stone constructions; it would be impossible to destroy them in an emergency. If Kae's inhabitants retreated into Elantris, they would be trapped, not protected.

There were no archers. The Elantris City Guard members carried large, unwieldy spears that looked like they were far too heavy to be thrown. They held themselves with a proud air, wearing unarmored yellow-and-brown uniforms, and they obviously considered themselves far above the regular city militia. From what Hrathen had heard, however, the Guard wasn't even really necessary to keep the Elantrians in. The creatures rarely tried to escape, and the city wall was far too large for the Guard to patrol extensively. The force was more of a public-relations operation than a true military; the people of Kae felt much more comfortable living beside Elantris when they knew a troop of soldiers watched the city. However, Hrathen suspected that in a war, the Guard members would be hard-pressed to defend themselves, let alone protect Kae's population.

Arelon was a ripe jewel waiting to be pillaged. Hrathen had heard of the days of chaos directly following Elantris's fall, and of the incalculable treasures that had been plundered from the magnificent city. Those valuables were now concentrated in Kae, where the new nobility lived practically unguarded. He had also heard that, despite the thievery, a large percentage of Elantris's wealth—pieces of art too large to move easily, or smaller items that hadn't been plundered before Iadon began enforcing the city's isolation—remained locked within Elantris's forbidden walls.

Only superstition and inaccessibility kept Elantris and Kae from being raped by invaders. The smaller thieving bands were still too frightened of Elantris's reputation. The larger bands were either under Fjordell control—and therefore wouldn't attack unless instructed to do so—or had been bribed to stay away by Kae's nobles. Both situations were extremely temporary in nature.

And that was the basic reason Hrathen felt justified in taking extreme action to bring Arelon under Fjorden control—and protection. The nation was an egg balanced on the peak of a mountain, just waiting for the first breeze to plunge it to the hard ground below. If Fjorden didn't conquer Arelon soon, then the kingdom would certainly collapse beneath the weight of a dozen different problems. Beyond inept leadership, Arelon suffered from an overtaxed working class, religious uncertainty, and dwindling resources. All of these factors competed to deliver the final blow.

His thoughts were interrupted by the sound of harsh breathing behind him. Dilaf stood on the other side of the wall walk, looking out over Elantris. His eyes were wide, like those of a man who had been punched in the stomach, and his teeth were clenched. Hrathen half expected him to start frothing at the mouth.

"I hate them," Dilaf whispered in a harsh, almost unintelligible voice.

Hrathen crossed the wall walk to stand beside Dilaf. Since the wall had not been constructed for military purposes, there were no battlements, but both sides had raised parapets for safety. Hrathen rested against one of these, looking out to study Elantris.

There wasn't much to see; he'd been in slums more promising than Elantris. The buildings were so decayed that it was a miracle any of them still had roofs, and the stench was revolting. At first he doubted anything could possibly be alive inside the city, but then he saw some forms running furtively along the side of a building. They were crouched with their hands outstretched, as if prepared to fall on all fours. One paused, looking up, and Hrathen saw his first Elantrian.

It was bald, and at first Hrathen thought its skin was dark, like that of a member of the Jindo noble caste. However, he could see splotches of light gray on the creature's skin as well—great uneven pale masses, like lichen on a stone. He squinted, leaning forward against the parapet. He couldn't make out the Elantrian's eyes, but somehow Hrathen knew they would be wild and feral, darting around like those of an anxious animal.

The creature took off with its companions—its pack. *So this is what the Reod did,* Hrathen mused to himself. *It made beasts out of gods.* Jaddeth had simply taken what was in their hearts and showed it for the world to see. According to Derethi philosophy, the only thing that separated men from the animals was religion. Men could serve Jaddeth's empire; beasts could serve only their lusts. The Elantrians represented the ultimate flaw of human arrogance: they had set themselves up as gods. Their hubris had earned their fate. In another situation, Hrathen would have been content in leaving them to their punishment.

However, he happened to need them.

Hrathen turned to Dilaf. "The first step in taking control of a nation, Arteth, is the simplest. You find someone to hate."

"TELL me of them, Arteth," Hrathen requested, entering his room inside the chapel. "I want to know everything you know."

"They are foul, loathsome creatures," Dilaf hissed, entering behind Hrathen. "Thinking of them makes my heart grow sick and my mind feel tainted. I pray every day for their destruction."

Hrathen closed the door to his chambers, dissatisfied. It was possible for a man to be *too* passionate. "Arteth, I understand you have strong feelings," Hrathen said sternly, "but if you are to be my odiv you will need to see through your prejudices. Jaddeth has placed these Elantrians before us with a purpose in mind, and I cannot discover that purpose if you refuse to tell me anything useful."

Dilaf blinked, taken aback. Then, for the first time since their visit to Elantris, a level of sanity returned to his eyes. "Yes, Your Grace."

Hrathen nodded. "Did you see Elantris before its fall?"

"Yes."

"Was it as beautiful as people say?"

Dilaf nodded sullenly. "Pristine, kept white by the hands of slaves."

"Slaves?"

"All of Arelon's people were slaves to the Elantrians, Your Grace. They were false gods, giving promises of salvation in exchange for sweat and labor."

"And their legendary powers?"

"Lies, like their supposed divinity. A carefully crafted hoax to earn them respect and fear."

"Following the Reod, there was chaos, correct?"

"Chaos, killing, riots, and panic, Your Grace. Then the merchants seized power."

"And the Elantrians?" Hrathen asked, walking over to take a seat at his desk.

"There were few left," Dilaf said. "Most had been killed in the riots. Those remaining were confined to Elantris, as were all men that the Shaod took from that day forward. They looked much as you just saw them, wretched and sub-human. Their skin was patched with black scars, like some-one had pulled away the flesh and revealed the darkness underneath."

"And the transformations? Did they abate at all after the Reod?" Hrathen asked.

"They continue, Your Grace. They happen all across Arelon."

"Why do you hate them so, Arteth?"

The question came suddenly, and Dilaf paused. "Because they are unholy."

"And?"

"They lied to us, Your Grace. They made promises of eter-nity, but they couldn't even maintain their own divinity. We listened to them for centuries, and were rewarded with a group of impotent, vile cripples."

"You hate them because they disappointed you," Hrathen said.

"Not me, my people. I was a follower of Derethi years be-fore the Reod."

Hrathen frowned. "Then you are convinced that there is nothing supernatural about the Elantrians other than the fact that Jaddeth has cursed them?"

"Yes, Your Grace. As I said, the Elantrians created many falsehoods to reinforce their divinity."

Hrathen shook his head, then stood and began to remove his armor. Dilaf moved to help, but Hrathen waved the arteth away. "How, then, do you explain the sudden transformation of ordinary people into Elantrians, Arteth?"

Dilaf didn't have a response.

"Hate has weakened your ability to see, Arteth," Hrathen said, hanging his breastplate on the wall beside his desk and smiling. He had just experienced a flash of brilliance; a por-tion of his plan suddenly fit into place. "You assume because Jaddeth did not give them powers, they did not have any."

Dilaf's face grew pale. "What you say is—"

"Not blasphemy, Arteth. Doctrine. There is another supernatural force besides our God."

"The Svrakiss," Dilaf said quietly.

"Yes." Svrakiss. The souls of the dead men who hated Jaddeth, the opponents to all that was holy. According to Shu-Dereth, there was nothing more bitter than a soul who had had its chance and thrown it away.

"You think the Elantrians are Svrakiss?" Dilaf asked.

"It is accepted doctrine that the Svrakiss can control the bodies of the evil," Hrathen said, unbuckling his greaves. "Is it so hard to believe that all this time they have been controlling bodies of the Elantrians, making them appear as gods to fool the simpleminded and unspiritual?"

There was a light in Dilaf's eyes; the concept was not new to the arteth, Hrathen realized. Suddenly his flash of inspiration didn't seem quite so brilliant.

Dilaf regarded Hrathen for a moment, then spoke. "You don't really believe it, do you?" he asked, his voice uncomfortably accusatory for one speaking to his hroden.

Hrathen was careful not to let discomfort show. "It doesn't matter, Arteth. The connection is logical; people will follow it. Right now all they see are the abject remnants of what were once aristocrats—men do not loathe such, they pity them. Demons, however, are something everyone can hate. If we denounce the Elantrians as devils, then we will have success. You already hate the Elantrians; that is fine. To make others join you, however, you'll have to give them more of a reason than 'they disappointed us.'"

"Yes, Your Grace."

"We are religious men, Arteth, and we must have religious enemies. The Elantrians are our Svrakiss, no matter if they possess the souls of evil men long dead or evil men now living."

"Of course, Your Holiness. We will destroy them then?" There was eagerness in Dilaf's face.

"Eventually. Right now, we will use them. You will find that hate can unify people more quickly and more fervently than devotion ever could."

CHAPTER 7

RAODEN stabbed the air with his finger. The air bled light. His fingertip left a glowing white trail behind it as he moved his arm, as if he were writing with paint on a wall—except without the paint, and without the wall.

He moved cautiously, careful not to let his finger waver. He drew a line about a handspan long from left to right, then pulled his finger down at a slight slant, drawing a curved line downward at the corner. Next he lifted his finger from the unseen canvas and replaced it to draw a dot in the center. Those three marks—two lines and a dot—were the starting point of every Aon.

He continued, drawing the same three-line pattern at different angles, then added several diagonal lines. The finished drawing looked something like an hourglass, or perhaps two boxes placed on top of each other, pulling in just slightly near the middles. This was Aon Ashe, the ancient symbol for light. The character brightened momentarily, seeming to pulse with life; then it flashed weakly like a man heaving his last breath. The Aon disappeared, its light fading from brightness, to dimness, to nothing.

"You're much better at that than I am, sule," Galladon said. "I usually make one line a little too big, or slant it a bit too much, and the whole thing fades away before I'm done."

"It's not supposed to be like this," Raoden complained. It had been a day since Galladon had shown him how to draw Aons, and he had spent nearly every moment since then practicing. Every Aon he had finished properly had acted the same way, disappearing without producing any visible effect.

His first acquaintance with the legendary magic of the Elantrians had been decidedly anticlimactic.

The most surprising thing was how easy it was. In ignorance he had assumed that AonDor, the magic of the Aons, would require some sort of incantation or ritual. A decade without AonDor had spawned hordes of rumors; some people, mostly Derethi priests, claimed the magic had been a hoax, while others, also mostly Derethi priests, had denounced the art as blasphemous rites involving the power of evil. The truth was that no one, not even the Derethi priests, knew just what AonDor had been. Every one of its practitioners had fallen to the Reod.

Yet Galladon claimed AonDor required nothing more than a steady hand and an intimate knowledge of the Aons. Since only Elantrians could draw the characters in light, only they could practice AonDor, and no one outside Elantris had been allowed to know just how simple it was. No incantations, no sacrifices, no special potions or ingredients; anyone who was taken by the Shaod could perform AonDor, assuming, of course, they knew the characters.

Except, it didn't work. The Aons were supposed to do something—at least, something more than flash weakly and disappear. Raoden could remember images of Elantris as a child—visions of men flying through the air, incredible feats of power, and merciful healings. He had broken his leg once, and although his father had objected, his mother had taken him to Elantris for healing. A bright-haired figure had reknit Raoden's bones with barely a wave of her hand. She had drawn an Aon, just as he was doing, but the rune had released a powerful burst of arcane magic.

"They're supposed to do something," Raoden said again, this time out loud.

"They did once, sule, but not since the Reod. Whatever took the life from Elantris also stole AonDor's power. Now all we can do is paint pretty characters in the air."

Raoden nodded, drawing his own Aon, Aon Rao. Four circles with one large square in the center, all five connected by lines. The Aon reacted as all of the others had, building as if for some release of power, then dying with a whimper.

"Disappointing. Kolo?"

"Very," Raoden admitted, pulling over a chair and sitting down. They were still in Galladon's small underground study. "I'll be honest with you, Galladon. When I saw that first Aon hovering in the air in front of you, I forgot about everything—the filth, the depression, even my toe."

Galladon smiled. "If AonDor worked, the Elantrians would still rule in Arelon—Reod or no Reod."

"I know. I just wonder what happened. What changed?"

"The world wonders with you, sule," Galladon said with a shrug.

"They must be related," Raoden mused. "The change in Elantris, the way the Shaod started making people demons rather than gods, the ineffectiveness of AonDor. . . ."

"You aren't the first person to notice that. Not by far. However, no one is likely to find the answer—the powerful in Arelon are much too comfortable with Elantris the way it is."

"Trust me, I know," Raoden said. "If the secret is to be found, it will have to come from us." Raoden looked over the small laboratory. Remarkably clean and free from the grime that coated the rest of Elantris, the room had an almost homey feeling—like the den or study in a large mansion.

"Maybe the answer is in here, Galladon," Raoden said. "In those books, somewhere."

"Perhaps," Galladon said noncommittally.

"Why were you so reluctant to bring me here?"

"Because it's special, sule—surely you can see that? Let the secret out, and I won't be able to leave for fear it will be pillaged while I am gone."

Raoden stood, nodding as he walked around the room. "Then why bring me?"

Galladon shrugged, as if not completely sure himself. Eventually he answered, "You aren't the first to think the answer might be in those books. Two men can read more quickly than one."

"Twice as quickly, I'd guess," Raoden agreed with a smile. "Why do you keep it so dark in here?"

"We are in *Elantris,* sule. We can't just go to the lamp-lighter's store every time we run out of oil."

"I know, but surely there's enough. Elantris must have had stores of oil before the Reod."

"Ah, *sule*," Galladon said with a shake of his head. "You still don't understand, do you? This is Elantris, city of the gods. What need have gods of such mundane things as lamps and oil? Look at the wall beside you."

Raoden turned. There was a metal plate hanging on the wall beside him. Though it was tarnished with time, Raoden could still make out the shape etched into its surface—Aon Ashe, the character he had drawn just a few moments ago.

"Those plates used to glow more brightly and steadily than any lamp, *sule*," Galladon explained. "The Elantrians could shut them off with a bare brush of their fingers. Elantris didn't need oil—it had a far more reliable source of light. For the same reason, you won't find coal—or even furnaces—in Elantris, nor are there many wells, for water flowed from pipes like rivers trapped within the walls. Without AonDor, this city is barely fit to be inhabited."

Raoden rubbed his finger against the plate, feeling the lines of Aon Ashe. Something catastrophic must have happened—an event lost in just ten brief years' time. Something so terrible it caused the land to shatter and gods to stumble. However, without an understanding of how AonDor had worked, he couldn't even begin to imagine what had caused it to fail. He turned from the plate and considered the two squat bookcases. It was unlikely that any of the books contained direct explanations of AonDor. However, if they had been written by Elantrians, then maybe they would have references to the magic. References that could lead the careful reader to an understanding of how AonDor worked. Maybe.

His thoughts were interrupted by a pain from his stomach. It wasn't like hunger he had experienced on the outside. His stomach didn't rumble. Yet, the pain was there—somehow even more demanding. He had gone three days now without food, and the hunger was beginning to grow insistent. He was only just beginning to see why it, and the other pains, were enough to reduce men to the beasts that had attacked him on his first day.

"Come," he said to Galladon. "There is something we need to do."

THE square was much as it had been the day before: grime, moaning unfortunates, tall unforgiving gates. The sun was almost three-quarters finished with its trek through the sky. It was time for new inductees to be cast into Elantris.

Raoden studied the square, watching from atop a building beside Galladon. As he looked, he realized that something was different. There was a small crowd gathered on top of the wall.

"Who's that?" Raoden asked with interest, pointing to a tall figure standing high on the wall above Elantris's gates. The man's arms were outstretched, and his bloodred cloak was flapping in the wind. His words were hardly audible from such a distance, but it was obvious that he was yelling.

Galladon grunted in surprise. "A Derethi gyorn. I didn't know there was one here in Arelon."

"A gyorn? As in high priest?" Raoden squinted, trying to make out the details of the figure far above them.

"I'm surprised one would come this far east," Galladon said. "They hated Arelon even before the Reod."

"Because of the Elantrians?"

Galladon nodded. "Though not so much because of Elantrian worship, no matter what they claim. The Derethi have a particular loathing for your country because their armies never figured a way to get through those mountains to attack you."

"What do you suppose he's doing up there?" Raoden asked.

"Preaching. What else would a priest do? He's probably decided to denounce Elantris as some sort of judgment from his god. I'm surprised it took them so long."

"People have been whispering it for years," Raoden said, "but no one had the courage to actually teach such things. They're secretly afraid that the Elantrians are just testing them—that they will return to their former glory someday and punish all the unbelievers."

"Still?" Galladon asked. "I would have thought such beliefs would be gone after ten years."

Raoden shook his head. "Even yet there are many who pray for, or fear, the Elantrians' return. The city was strong, Galladon. You can't know how beautiful it once was."

"I know, sule," Galladon said. "I didn't spend all of my life in Duladel."

The priest's voice rose to a crescendo, and he delivered one final wave of screams before spinning around and disappearing from view. Even from a distance, Raoden could hear the hate and anger in the gyorn's voice. Galladon was right: This man's words had been no blessing.

Raoden shook his head, looking from the wall to the gates. "Galladon," he asked, "what are the chances of someone being thrown in here today?"

Galladon shrugged. "Hard to say, sule. Sometimes weeks go without a new Elantrian, but I have seen as many as five cast in at once. You came two days ago, that woman yesterday—who knows, maybe Elantris will have new flesh for the third day in a row. Kolo?"

Raoden nodded, watching the gate expectantly.

"Sule, what do you intend to do?" Galladon asked uncomfortably.

"I intend to wait."

THE newcomer was an older man, perhaps in his late forties, with a gaunt face and nervous eyes. As the gate slammed shut, Raoden climbed down from the rooftop, pausing just inside the courtyard. Galladon followed, a worried look on his face. He obviously thought Raoden might do something foolish.

He was right.

The unfortunate newcomer just stared morosely at the gate. Raoden waited for him to take a step, to make the unwitting decision that would determine who got the privilege of robbing him. The man stood where he was, watching the courtyard with nervous eyes, his thin frame pulled up inside his robes like he was trying to hide within them. After a few minutes of waiting, he finally took his first hesitant step—to the right, the same way Raoden had chosen.

"Come on," Raoden declared, striding out of the alleyway. Galladon groaned, mumbling something in Duladen.

"Teoren?" Raoden called, choosing a common Aonic name.

The spindly newcomer looked up with surprise, then glanced over his shoulder with confusion.

"Teoren, it *is* you!" Raoden said, wrapping his hand around the man's shoulder. Then, in a lower voice, he continued. "Right now you have two choices, friend. Either you do what I tell you, or you let those men in the shadows over there chase you down and beat you senseless."

The man turned around to search the shadows with apprehensive eyes. Fortunately, at that moment, Shaor's men decided to move, their shadowed forms emerging into the light, their carnal eyes staring at the new man with hunger. It was all the encouragement the newcomer needed.

"What do I do?" the man asked with a quavering voice.

"Run!" Raoden ordered, then took off toward one of the alleys at a dash.

The man didn't need to be told twice; he bolted so quickly that Raoden was afraid he would go careering down a side alley and get lost. There was a muffled yell of surprise from behind as Galladon realized what Raoden was doing. The large Duladen man obviously wouldn't have any problems keeping up; even considering his time in Elantris, Galladon was in much better shape than Raoden.

"What in the name of Doloken do you think you are doing, you idiot?" Galladon swore.

"I'll tell you in a moment," Raoden said, conserving strength as he ran. Again, he noticed that he didn't get out of breath, though his body did begin to grow tired. A dull feeling of fatigue began to grow within him, and of the three of them, Raoden was soon proven the slowest runner. However, he was the only one who knew where they were going.

"Right!" he yelled to Galladon and the new man, then took off down a side alley. The two men followed, as did the group of thugs, who were gaining quickly. Fortunately, Raoden's destination wasn't far away.

"Rulo," Galladon cursed, realizing where they were going. It was one of the houses he had shown Raoden the day before, the one with the unstable staircase. Raoden sprinted through the door and up the stairs, nearly falling twice as steps gave out beneath him. Once on the roof, he used the last of his strength to push over a stack of bricks—the remnants of what had once been a planter—toppling the entire pile of crumbling clay into the stairwell just as Galladon and the newcomer reached the top. The weakened steps didn't even begin to hold the weight, collapsing to the ground with a furious crash.

Galladon walked over and looked through the hole with a critical eye. Shaor's men gathered around the fallen steps below, their feral intensity dulled a bit by realization.

Galladon raised an eyebrow. "Now what, genius?"

Raoden walked over to the newcomer, who had collapsed after stumbling up the stairs. Raoden carefully removed each of the man's food offerings and, after tucking a certain one into his belt, he dumped the rest to the houndlike men waiting below. The sounds of battle came from below as they fought over the food.

Raoden stepped back from the hole. "Let's just hope they realize that they're not going to get anything more out of us, and decide to leave."

"And if they don't?" Galladon asked pointedly.

Raoden shrugged. "We can live forever without food or water, right?"

"Yes, but I'd rather not spend the rest of eternity on the top of this building." Then, shooting a look at the new man, Galladon pulled Raoden to the side and demanded in a low voice, "Sule, what was the point of that? You could have just thrown them the food back in the courtyard. In fact, why 'save' him? For all we know, Shaor's men might not have even hurt him."

"We don't know that. Besides, this way he thinks he owes me his life."

Galladon snorted. "So now you have another follower—at the cheap price of the hatred of an entire third of Elantris's criminal element."

"And this is only the beginning," Raoden said with a smile. However, despite the brave words, he wasn't quite so certain of himself. He was still amazed at how much his toe hurt, and he had scraped his hands while pushing the bricks. While not as painful as the toe, the scrapes also continued to hurt, threatening to draw his attention away from his plans.

I have to keep moving, Raoden repeated to himself. *Keep working. Don't let the pain take control.*

"I'M a jeweler," the man explained. "Mareshe is my name."

"A jeweler," Raoden said with dissatisfaction, his arms folded as he regarded Mareshe. "That won't be of much use. What else can you do?"

Mareshe looked at him indignantly, as if having forgotten that he had, just a few moments ago, been cowering in fear. "Jewelry making is an extremely useful skill, sir."

"Not in Elantris, sule," Galladon said, peeking through the hole to see if the thugs had decided to leave. Apparently they hadn't, for he gave Raoden a withering look.

Pointedly ignoring the Dula, Raoden turned back to Mareshe. "What else can you do?"

"Anything."

"That's quite broad, friend," Raoden said. "Could you be a bit more specific?"

Mareshe brought his hand up beside his head with a dramatic gesture. "I . . . am a craftsman. An artisan. I can make anything, for Domi himself has granted me the soul of an artist."

Galladon snorted from his seat beside the stairwell.

"How about shoes?" Raoden asked.

"Shoes?" Mareshe replied with a slightly offended tone.

"Yes, shoes."

"I suppose I could," Mareshe said, "though such hardly demands the skill of a man who is a full artisan."

"And a full id—" Galladon began before Raoden hushed him.

"Artisan Mareshe," Raoden continued in his most diplomatic of tones. "Elantrians are cast into the city wearing only an Arelish burial shroud. A man who could make shoes would be very valuable indeed."

"What kind of shoes?" Mareshe asked.

"Leather ones," Raoden said. "It won't be an easy calling, Mareshe. You see, Elantrians don't have the luxury of trial and error—if the first pair of shoes do not fit, then they will cause blisters. Blisters that will never leave."

"What do you mean, never leave?" Mareshe asked uncomfortably.

"We are Elantrians now, Mareshe," Raoden explained. "Our wounds no longer heal."

"No longer heal . . . ?"

"Would you care for an example, artisan?" Galladon asked helpfully. "I can arrange one quite easily. Kolo?"

Mareshe's face turned pale, and he looked back at Raoden. "He doesn't seem to like me very much," he said quietly.

"Nonsense," Raoden said, putting his arm around Mareshe's shoulder and turning him away from Galladon's grinning face. "That's how he shows affection."

"If you say so, Master . . ."

Raoden paused. "Just call me Spirit," he decided, using the translation of Aon Rao.

"Master Spirit." Then Mareshe's eyes narrowed. "You look familiar for some reason."

"You've never seen me before in your life. Now, about those shoes . . ."

"They have to fit perfectly, without a bit of scraping or rubbing?" Mareshe asked.

"I know it sounds difficult. If it's beyond your ability . . ."

"Nothing is beyond *my* ability," Mareshe said. "I'll do it, Master Spirit."

"Excellent."

"They're not leaving," Galladon said from behind them.

Raoden turned to regard the large Dula. "What does it matter? It's not like we have anything pressing to do. It's actually quite pleasant up here—you should just sit back and enjoy it."

An ominous crash came from the clouds above them, and Raoden felt a wet drop splat against his head.

"Fantastic," Galladon grumbled. "I'm enjoying myself already."

CHAPTER 8

ARENE decided not to accept her uncle's offer to stay
with him. As tempting as it was to move in with his family, she was afraid of losing her foothold in the palace.
The court was a lifeline of information, and the Arelish nobility were a fountain of gossip and intrigue. If she was going to do battle with Hrathen, she would need to stay up to
date.

So it was that the day after her meeting with Kiin, Sarene
procured herself an easel and paints, and set them up directly in the middle of Iadon's throne room.

"What in the name of Domi are you doing, girl!" the king
exclaimed as he entered the room that morning, a group of
apprehensive attendants at his side.

Sarene looked up from her canvas with imitation surprise.
"I'm painting, Father," she said, helpfully holding up her
brush—an action that sprayed droplets of red paint across
the chancellor of defense's face.

Iadon sighed. "I can see that you're painting. I meant why
are you doing it *here*?"

"Oh," Sarene said innocently. "I'm painting your paintings, Father. I do like them so."

"You're painting my . . . ?" Iadon asked with a dumbfounded expression. "But . . ."

Sarene turned her canvas with a proud smile, showing the
king a painting that only remotely resembled a picture of
some flowers.

"Oh for Domi's sake!" Iadon bellowed. "Paint if you
must, girl. Just don't do it in the *middle* of my *throne room*!"

Sarene opened her eyes wide, blinked a few times, then pulled her easel and chair over to the side of the room near one of the pillars, sat down, and continued to paint.

Iadon groaned. "I meant . . . Bah, Domi curse it! You're not worth the effort." With that, the king turned and stalked over to his throne and ordered his secretary to announce the first item of business—a squabble between two minor nobles over some possessions.

Ashe hovered down next to Sarene's canvas, speaking to her softly. "I thought he was going to expel you for good, my lady."

Sarene shook her head, a self-congratulatory smile on her lips. "Iadon has a quick temper, and grows frustrated with ease. The more I convince him of my brainlessness, the fewer orders he's going to give me. He knows I'll just misunderstand him, and he'll just end up aggravated."

"I am beginning to wonder how one such as he obtained the throne in the first place," Ashe noted.

"A good point," Sarene admitted, tapping her cheek in thought. "Though, perhaps we aren't giving him enough credit. He might not make a very good king, but he was apparently a very good businessman. To him, I'm an expended resource—he has his treaty. I'm just of no further concern."

"I'm not convinced, my lady," Ashe noted. "He seems too shortsighted to remain king for long."

"Which is why he's probably going to lose his throne," Sarene said. "I suspect that is why the gyorn is here."

"A good point, my lady," Ashe noted in his deep voice. He floated in front of her painting for a moment, studying its irregular blotches and semistraight lines. "You're getting better, my lady."

"Don't patronize me."

"No, really, Your Highness. When you started painting five years ago, I could never tell what it was you were trying to depict."

"And this is a painting of . . ."

Ashe paused. "A bowl of fruit?" he asked hopefully.

Sarene sighed in frustration. She was usually good at everything she tried, but the secrets of painting completely eluded her. At first, she had been astounded at her lack of talent, and she had pressed on with a determination to prove herself. Artistic technique, however, had totally refused to bow beneath her royal will. She was a master of politics, an unquestionable leader, and could grasp even Jindoeese mathematics with ease. She was also a horrible painter. Not that she let it stop her—she was also undeniably stubborn.

"One of these days, Ashe, something will click, and I'll figure out how to make the images in my head appear on canvas."

"Of course, my lady."

Sarene smiled. "Until then, let's just pretend I was trained by someone from some Svordish school of extreme abstractionism."

"Ah yes. The school of creative misdirection. Very good, my lady."

Two men entered the throne room to present their case to the king. There was little to distinguish them; both wore fashionable vests over colorful frilled shirts and loose, wide-cuffed trousers. Much more interesting to Sarene was a third man, one who was brought into the room by a palace guard. He was a nondescript, light-haired man of Aonic blood dressed in a simple brown smock. It was obvious that he was horribly underfed, and there was a look of despairing hopelessness in his eyes that Sarene found haunting.

The dispute regarded the peasant. Apparently, he had escaped from one of the noblemen about three years ago, but had been captured by the second. Instead of returning the man, the second noble had kept him and put him to work. The argument wasn't over the peasant himself, however, but his children. He had married about two years ago, and had fathered two children during his stay with the second noble. Both nobles claimed ownership of the babies.

"I thought slavery was illegal in Arelon," Sarene said quietly.

"It is, my lady," Ashe said with a confused voice. "I don't understand."

"They speak of figurative ownership, Cousin," a voice

said from in front of her. Sarene peeked around the side of her canvas with surprise. Lukel, Kiin's oldest son, stood smiling beside her easel.

"Lukel! What are you doing here?"

"I'm one of the most successful merchants in the city, Cousin," he explained, walking around the canvas to regard the painting with a raised eyebrow. "I have an open invitation to the court. I'm surprised you didn't see me when you came in."

"You were there?"

Lukel nodded. "I was near the back, reacquainting myself with some old contacts. I've been out of town for some time."

"Why didn't you say anything?"

"I was too interested in what you were doing," he said with a smile. "I don't think anyone has ever decided to requisition the middle of Iadon's throne room to use as an art studio."

Sarene felt herself blushing. "It worked, didn't it?"

"Beautifully—which is more than I can say for the painting." He paused for a moment. "It's a horse, right?"

Sarene scowled.

"A house?" he asked.

"It is not a bowl of fruit either, my lord," Ashe said. "I already tried that."

"Well, she said it was one of the paintings in this room," Lukel said. "All we have to do is keep guessing until we find the right one."

"Brilliant deduction, Master Lukel," Ashe said.

"That's enough, you two," Sarene growled. "It's the one across from us. The one I was facing while I painted."

"That one?" Lukel asked. "But that's a picture of flowers."

"And?"

"What's that dark spot in the middle of your painting?"

"Flowers," Sarene said defensively.

"Oh." Lukel looked once more at Sarene's painting, then looked up at her model again. "Whatever you say, Cousin."

"Maybe you could explain Iadon's legal case before I turn violent, Cousin," Sarene said with threatening sweetness.

"Right. What do you want to know?"

"Our studies tell us slavery is illegal in Arelon, but those men keep referring to the peasant as their possession."

Lukel frowned, turning eyes on the two contesting nobles. "Slavery is illegal, but it probably won't be for long. Ten years ago there weren't any nobles or peasants in Arelon— just Elantrians and everyone else. Over the past decade, commoners have changed from families that owned their own land, to peasants beneath feudal lords, to indentured servants, to something more resembling ancient Fjordell serfs. It won't be much longer before they're nothing more than property."

Sarene frowned. The mere fact that the king would hear a case such as this—that he would even consider taking a man's children away from him to save some nobleman's honor—was atrocious. Society was supposed to have progressed beyond that point. The peasant watched the proceedings with dull eyes, eyes that had systematically and deliberately had the light beaten out of them.

"This is worse than I had feared," Sarene said.

Lukel nodded at her side. "The first thing Iadon did when he took the throne was eliminate individual landholding rights. Arelon had no army to speak of, but Iadon could afford to hire mercenaries, forcing the people into compliance. He declared that all land belonged to the Crown, and then he rewarded those merchants who had supported his ascension with titles and holdings. Only a few men, such as my father, had enough land and money that Iadon didn't dare try to take their property."

Sarene felt her disgust for her new father rise. Once Arelon had boasted the happiest, most advanced society in the world. Iadon had crushed that society, transforming it into a system not even Fjordell used anymore.

Sarene glanced at Iadon, then turned to Lukel. "Come," she said, pulling her cousin to the side of the room, where they could speak a little more openly. They were close enough to keep an eye on Iadon, but far enough away from other groups of people that a quiet conversation wouldn't be overheard.

"Ashe and I were discussing this earlier," she said. "How did that man ever manage to get the throne?"

Lukel shrugged. "Iadon is . . . a complex man, Cousin. He's remarkably shortsighted in some areas, but he can be extremely crafty when dealing with people—that's part of what makes him a good merchant. He was head of the local merchants' guild before the Reod—which probably made him the most powerful man in the area who wasn't directly connected to the Elantrians.

"The merchants' guild was an autonomous organization—and many of its members didn't get along too well with the Elantrians. You see, Elantris provided free food for everyone in the area, something that made for a happy populace, but was terrible for the merchants."

"Why didn't they just import other things?" Sarene asked. "Something besides food?"

"The Elantrians could make almost anything, Cousin," Lukel said. "And while they didn't give it all away for free, they could provide many materials at far cheaper prices than the merchants could—especially if you consider shipping costs. Eventually, the merchants' guild struck a deal with Elantris, getting the Elantrians to promise that they would only provide 'basic' items to the populace for free. That left the merchants' guild to import the more expensive luxury items, catering to the more wealthy crowd in the area—which, ironically, tended to be other members of the merchants' guild."

"And then the Reod struck," Sarene said, beginning to understand.

Lukel nodded. "Elantris fell, and the merchants' guild—of which Iadon was chairman—was the largest, most powerful organization in the four Outer Cities. Its members were wealthy, and they were intimately familiar with the other wealthy people in the area. The fact that the guild had a history of disagreement with Elantris only strengthened its reputation in the eyes of the people. Iadon was a natural fit for king. That doesn't mean that he's a particularly good monarch, though."

Sarene nodded. Sitting on his throne, Iadon finally made his decision regarding the case. He declared with a loud voice that the runaway peasant did indeed belong to the first noble, but his children would remain with the second. "For,"

Iadon pointed out, "the children have been fed all this time by their current master."

The peasant didn't cry out at the decision, he simply looked down at his feet, and Sarene felt a stab of sorrow. When the man looked up, however, there was something in his eyes—something beneath the enforced subservience. Hate. There was still enough spirit left in him for that ever-powerful emotion.

"This won't go on much longer," she said quietly. "The people won't stand for it."

"The working class lived for centuries under the Fjordell feudal system," Lukel pointed out. "And they were treated worse than farm animals."

"Yes, but they were raised to it," Sarene said. "People in ancient Fjorden didn't know better—to them, the feudal system was the only system. These people are different. Ten years really isn't all that long—the Arelish peasantry can remember a time when the men they now call masters were simple shopkeepers and tradesmen. They know that there is a better life. More importantly, they know a government can collapse, making those who were once servants into masters. Iadon has put too much on them too quickly."

Lukel smiled. "You sound like Prince Raoden."

Sarene paused. "Did you know him well?"

"He was my best friend," Lukel said with a sorrowful nod. "The greatest man I have ever known."

"Tell me about him, Lukel," she requested, her voice soft.

Lukel thought for a moment, then spoke with a reminiscent voice. "Raoden made people happy. Your day could have been as sour as winter, and the prince and his optimism would arrive, and with a few gentle words he would make you realize just how silly you were being. He was brilliant as well; he knew every Aon, and could draw them with perfection, and he was always coming up with some weird new philosophy that no one but Father could understand. Even with my training at the university in Svorden, I still couldn't follow half of his theories."

"He sounds like he was flawless."

Lukel smiled. "In everything but cards. He always lost when we played tooledoo, even if he did talk me into paying for dinner afterward. He would have made a horrible merchant—he didn't really care about money. He would lose a game of tooledoo just because he knew I got a thrill from the victory. I never saw him sad, or angry—except when he was at one of the outer plantations, visiting the people. He did that often; then he would come back to the court and speak his thoughts on the matter quite directly."

"I'll bet the king didn't think much of that," Sarene said with a slight smile.

"He hated it," Lukel said. "Iadon tried everything short of banishing Raoden to keep him quiet, but nothing worked. The prince would find a way to work his opinion into any and every royal ruling. He was the crown prince, and so court laws—written by Iadon himself—gave Raoden a chance to speak his mind in every matter brought before the king. And let me tell you, Princess, you don't know what a scolding is until you've had one from Raoden. The man could be so stern at times that even the stone walls would shrivel beneath his tongue."

Sarene sat back, enjoying the image of Iadon being denounced by his own son before the entire court.

"I miss him," Lukel said quietly. "This country needed Raoden. He was beginning to make some real differences; he had gathered quite a following amongst the nobles. Now the group is fragmenting without his leadership. Father and I are trying to hold them together, but I've been gone so long that I'm out of touch. And, of course, few of them trust Father."

"What? Why not?"

"He has something of a reputation for being a scoundrel. Besides, he doesn't have a title. He's refused every one the king tried to give him."

Sarene's brow furled. "Wait a moment—I thought Uncle Kiin opposed the king. Why would Iadon try to give him a title?"

Lukel smiled. "Iadon can't help it. The king's entire government is built on the idea that monetary success is justification for rule. Father is extremely successful, and the law says that money equals nobility. You see, the king was foolish enough to think that everyone rich would think the same way he does, and so he wouldn't have any opposition as long as he gave titles to everyone affluent. Father's refusal to accept a title is really a way of undermining Iadon's sovereignty, and the king knows it. As long as there's even one rich man who isn't technically a nobleman, the Arelish aristocratic system is flawed. Old Iadon nearly has a fit every time Father appears in court."

"He should come by more often then," Sarene said wickedly.

"Father finds plenty of opportunities to show his face. He and Raoden met nearly every afternoon here in the court to play a game of ShinDa. It was an unending source of discomfort to Iadon that they chose to do this in his own throne room, but again, his own laws proclaimed that the court was open to everyone his son invited, so he couldn't throw them out."

"It sounds like the prince had a talent for using the king's own laws against him."

"It was one of his more endearing traits," Lukel said with a smile. "Somehow Raoden would twist every one of Iadon's new decrees until they turned around and slapped the king in the face. Iadon spent nearly every moment of the last five years trying to find a way to disinherit Raoden. It turns out Domi solved that problem for him in the end."

Either Domi, Sarene thought with growing suspicion, *or one of Iadon's own assassins. . . .* "Who inherits now?" she asked.

"That's not exactly certain," Lukel said. "Iadon probably plans to have another son—Eshen is young enough. One of the more powerful dukes would probably be next in line. Lord Telrii or Lord Roial."

"Are they here?" Sarene asked, scanning the crowd.

"Roial isn't," Lukel said, "but that's Duke Telrii over there." Lukel nodded toward a pompous-looking man standing near the far wall. Lean and strong-postured, he might have been handsome had he not displayed signs of gross indulgence. His clothing sparkled with sewn-in gemstones, and his fingers glittered gold and silver. As he turned, Sarene could see that the left side of his face was marred by a massive, purplish birthmark.

"Let us hope the throne never falls to him," Lukel said. "Iadon is disagreeable, but at least he's fiscally responsible.

Iadon is a miser. Telrii, however, is a spender. He likes money, and he likes those who give it to him. He'd probably be the richest man in Arelon if he weren't so lavish—as it is, he's a poor third, behind the king and Duke Roial."

Sarene frowned. "The king would have disinherited Raoden, leaving the country with no visible heir? Doesn't he know anything about succession wars?"

Lukel shrugged. "Apparently, he'd rather have no heir than risk leaving Raoden in charge."

"He couldn't have things like freedom and compassion ruining his perfect little monarchy," Sarene said.

"Exactly."

"These nobles who followed Raoden. Do they ever meet?"

"No," Lukel said with a frown. "They're too afraid to continue without the prince's protection. We've convinced a few of the more dedicated ones to gather one last time tomorrow, but I doubt anything will come of it."

"I want to be there," Sarene said.

"These men don't like newcomers, Cousin," Lukel warned. "They've grown very jumpy—they know their meetings could be considered treasonous."

"It's the last time they plan to meet anyway. What are they going to do if I show up? Refuse to come anymore?"

Lukel paused, then smiled. "All right, I'll tell Father, and he'll find a way to get you in."

"We can both tell him over lunch," Sarene said, taking one last dissatisfied look at her canvas, then walking over to pack up her paints.

"So you're coming to lunch after all?"

"Well, Uncle Kiin did promise he'd fix Fjordell revertiss. Besides, after what I've learned today, I don't think I can sit here and listen to Iadon's judgments much longer. I'm liable to start throwing paints if he makes me much more angry."

Lukel laughed. "That probably wouldn't be a good idea, princess or not. Come on, Kaise is going to be ecstatic that you're coming. Father always fixes better food when we have company."

LUKEL was right.

"She's *here!*" Kaise declared with an enthusiastic squeal as she saw Sarene walk in. "Father, you have to fix lunch!"

Jalla appeared from a nearby doorway to meet her husband with a hug and a brief kiss. The Svordish woman whispered something to Lukel in Fjordell, and he smiled, rubbing her shoulder affectionately. Sarene watched with envy, then steeled herself with gritted teeth. She was a royal Teoish princess; it wasn't her place to complain about the necessities of state marriages. If Domi had taken her husband before she even met him, then He obviously wanted to leave her mind clear for other concerns.

Uncle Kiin emerged from the kitchen, stuffed a book in his apron, then gave Sarene one of his crushing hugs. "So you couldn't stay away after all. The lure of Kiin's magical kitchen was too much for you, eh?"

"No, Papa, she's just *hungry,*" Kaise announced.

"Oh, is that all. Well, sit down, Sarene, I'll have lunch out in a few moments."

The meal proceeded in much the same way as dinner had the night before, Kaise complaining about the slowness, Daorn trying to act more mature than his sister, and Lukel teasing them both mercilessly—as was the solemn duty of any elder brother. Adien made his appearance late, looking distracted as he mumbled some numbers softly to himself. Kiin brought out several steaming platters of food, apologizing for his wife's absence because of a prior engagement.

The meal was delightful—the food good, the conversation enjoyable. Until, that was, Lukel took it upon himself to inform the family of Sarene's painting talents.

"She was engaged in some sort of new-abstractionism," her cousin proclaimed with a completely serious voice.

"Is that so?" Kiin asked.

"Yes," Lukel said. "Though I can't quite say what kind of statement she was trying to make by representing a flower patch with a brown smudge that only vaguely resembles a horse."

Sarene blushed as the table laughed. However, it wasn't over—Ashe chose that moment to betray her as well.

"She calls it the school of creative misdirection," the Seon explained solemnly in his deep, stately voice. "I believe the princess feels empowered by crafting art that completely baffles one's ability to distinguish what the subject could be."

This was too much for Kiin, who nearly collapsed from laughter. Sarene's torment was soon over, however, as the topic of conversation met with a slight change—the source of which was of some interest to the princess.

"There's no such thing as a school of creative misdirection," Kaise informed them.

"There isn't?" her father asked.

"No. There's the impressionist school, the neorepresentational school, the abstract derivational school, and the revivationist school. That's it."

"Oh, is that so?" Lukel asked with amusement.

"Yes," Kaise pronounced. "There was the realist movement, but that's the same as the neorepresentational school. They just changed names to sound more important."

"Stop trying to show off for the princess," Daorn mumbled.

"I'm not showing off," Kaise huffed. "I'm being *educated.*"

"You are too showing off," Daorn said. "Besides, the realist school is *not* the same as the neorepresentational school."

"Daorn, stop grumbling at your sister," Kiin ordered. "Kaise, stop showing off."

Kaise scowled, then sat back with a sullen look on her face and began mumbling incoherently.

"What's she doing?" Sarene asked with confusion.

"Oh, she's cursing at us in Jindoeese," Daorn said offhandedly. "She always does that when she loses an argument."

"She thinks she can save face by speaking in other languages," Lukel said. "As if that proves that she's actually more intelligent than the rest of the world."

With that, the torrent of words from the small blond girl's mouth changed directions. With a start, Sarene realized Kaise was now muttering in Fjordell. Kaise wasn't done, however; she topped of the tirade with a brief, but biting, accusation in what sounded like Duladen.

"How many languages does she speak?" Sarene asked in amazement.

"Oh, four or five, unless she's learned a new one while I wasn't looking," Lukel said. "Though she's going to have to stop soon. Svordish scientists claim that the human mind can only maintain six languages before it starts to jumble them."

"It's one of little Kaise's life quests to prove them wrong," Kiin explained in his deep, scratchy voice. "That, and to eat every morsel of food to be found in all of Arelon."

Kaise stuck out her chin at her father with a dismissive sniff, then turned back to her meal.

"They're both so . . . well informed," Sarene said with surprise.

"Don't be too impressed," Lukel said. "Their tutors have been covering art history lately, and the two of them have been working hard to prove they can outdo one another."

"Even so," Sarene said.

Kaise, still displeased at her loss, mumbled something over her meal.

"What was that?" Kiin asked with a firm tone.

"I said, 'If the prince were here, *he* would have listened to me.' He always took my side."

"He just *sounded* like he was agreeing with you," Daorn said. "That is called sarcasm, Kaise."

Kaise stuck out her tongue at her brother. "He thought I was beautiful, and he loved me. He was waiting for me to grow up so he could marry me. Then I would be queen, and I'd throw you all in the dungeon until you admitted that I was right."

"He wouldn't have married you, stupid," Daorn said with a scowl. "He married Sarene."

Kiin must have noticed the way Sarene's face fell when the prince's name came up, for he quickly hushed the two children with hard looks. However, the damage had been done. The more she learned of him, the more Sarene remembered the prince's soft, encouraging voice traveling hundreds of miles through the Seon to speak with her. She thought of the rambling way his letters told her of life in Arelon, explaining how he was preparing a place for her. She had been so excited to meet him that she had decided to leave Teod a week early. Not early enough, apparently.

Perhaps she should have listened to her father. He had been hesitant to agree to the marriage, even though he knew Teod needed a solid alliance with the new Arelish government. Though the two countries were descendants of the same racial and cultural heritage, there had been little contact between Teod and Arelon during the last decade. The uprisings after the Reod threatened anyone associated with the Elantrians—and that certainly included the Teoish royalty. But with Fjorden pushing the boundaries of its influence again—this time instigating the collapse of the Duladen Republic—it became obvious that Teod needed to either reacquaint itself with its ancient ally, or face Wyrn's hordes alone.

And so Sarene had suggested the marriage. Her father had objected at first, but then had bowed beneath its utter practicality. There was no stronger bond than that of blood, especially when the marriage involved a crown prince. Never mind that a royal marriage contract forbade Sarene to ever marry again; Raoden was young and strong. They all assumed he would live for decades.

Kiin was talking to her. "What was that, Uncle?" she asked.

"I just wanted to know if there was anything you wanted to see in Kae. You've been here a couple of days; it's probably time someone gave you a tour. I'm sure Lukel would be happy to show you the sights."

The thin man raised his hands. "Sorry, Father. I'd love to show our beautiful cousin around the town, but Jalla and I have to go discuss the purchase of some silk for shipment to Teod."

"Both of you?" Sarene asked with surprise.

"Of course," Lukel said, dropping his napkin to the table and rising. "Jalla's a fierce bargainer."

"That be the only reason he married me," the Svorden woman confessed with her thick accent and a slight smile. "Lukel is a merchant. Profit in everything, even marriage."

"That's right," Lukel said with a laugh, taking his wife's hand as she rose. "The fact that she's brilliant and beautiful didn't even enter into it. Thanks for the meal, Father. It was delicious. Good day, all."

With that the couple left, staring into each other's eyes as they walked. Their exit was followed by a series of gagging sounds from Daorn. "Ugh. Father, you should speak to them. They're so dopey-eyed they make it hard to eat."

"Our dear brother's mind has turned to mush," Kaise agreed.

"Be patient, children," Kiin said. "Lukel has only been married for a month now. Give him a while longer, and he'll turn back to normal."

"I hope so," Kaise said. "He's making me sick." Of course, she didn't *look* very sick to Sarene; she was still packing down the food with a vengeance.

Beside Sarene, Adien continued to mumble in his way. He didn't seem to say much, except to quote numbers—that, and the occasional word that sounded a lot like "Elantris."

"I would like to see the town, Uncle," Sarene said, the boy's comments reminding her of something. "Especially Elantris—I want to know what all of the furor is about."

Kiin rubbed his chin. "Well," he said, "I suppose the twins can show you. They know how to get to Elantris, and it will keep them out of my hair for a little while."

"Twins?"

Kiin smiled. "It's Lukel's nickname for them."

"One we hate," Daorn said. "We aren't twins—we don't even look alike."

Sarene studied the two children, with their similar bobs of blond hair and their identical determined expressions, and smiled. "Not at all," she agreed.

THE wall of Elantris stood over Kae like a disapproving sentry. Walking at its base, Sarene finally realized how truly formidable it was. She had once visited Fjordell, and had been impressed by many of that nation's fortified cities—but even they couldn't compete with Elantris. The wall was so high, its sides so smooth, that it obviously hadn't been crafted by normal human hands. There were enormous, intricate Aons carved into its sides—many of which Sarene didn't recognize, and she liked to consider herself well educated.

The children led her to a massive set of stone stairs that ran up the side of the outer wall. Magnificently carved, with archways and frequent viewing platforms, the stairs themselves were sculpted with a certain regality. There was also a sense of . . . arrogance about the tiered stairway. It was obviously part of the original Elantris city design, and proved that the massive walls had been constructed not as a means of defense, but as a means of separation. Only people supremely confident in themselves would craft such an amazing fortification, then place a wide set of stairs on the outside, leading up to the top.

That confidence had been proven unjustified, for Elantris had fallen. Yet, Sarene reminded herself, it hadn't been invaders who had claimed the city, but something else. Something not yet understood. The Reod.

Sarene paused along a stone railing about halfway up to the top of the wall, looking out over the city of Kae. The smaller city stood like a little brother to the grand Elantris—it tried so hard to prove its significance, but next to the massive city it couldn't help but seem inferior. Its buildings might have been impressive somewhere else, but they seemed tiny—petty, even—when compared with the majesty of Elantris.

Petty or not, Sarene told herself, *Kae will have to be my focus. Elantris's day has passed.*

Several little bubbles of light floated along the outside of the wall—some of the first Seons Sarene had seen in the area. She was excited at first, but then remembered the stories. Once, Seons had been unaffected by the Shaod—but that had changed with the fall of Elantris. When a person was taken by the Shaod now, their Seon—if they had one—gained a kind of madness. The Seons by the wall floated aimlessly, like lost children. She knew without asking that the city was where such maddened Seons gathered, once their masters had fallen.

She looked away from the Seons, nodded to the children, and continued her trek up the enormous set of stairs. Kae would be her focus, true, but she still wanted to see Elantris. There was something about it—its size, its Aons, its reputation—that she had to experience for herself.

As she walked, she was able to reach out and rub her hand across the groove of a carved Aon sculpted into the side of the city wall. The line was as wide as her hand. There were no gaps where stone met stone. It was as she had read: the entire wall was one seamless piece of rock.

Except, it was no longer flawless. Pieces of the enormous monolith were crumbling and cracking, especially near the top. As they neared the end of their climb there were places where great chunks of the wall had torn away, leaving jagged wounds in the stone reminiscent of bite marks. Still, the wall was impressive, especially when one was standing on top of it, looking down at the ground below.

"Oh my," Sarene said, feeling herself grow dizzy.

Daorn pulled against the back of her dress urgently. "Don't get too close, Sarene."

"I'm all right," she said with a dazed voice. She did, however, let him pull her back.

Ashe hovered next to her, glowing with concern. "Perhaps this wasn't a good idea, my lady. You know how you are with heights."

"Nonsense," Sarene said, recovering. Then she noticed for the first time the large gathering on the wall's top a short distance away. There was a piercing voice rising over the group—one she couldn't quite make out. "What's that?"

The twins exchanged mutual shrugs of confusion. "I don't know," Daorn said.

"This place is usually empty, except for the guards," Kaise added.

"Let's have a look," Sarene said. She wasn't sure, but she thought she recognized the voice's accent. As they approached the back of the crowd, Sarene confirmed her suspicion.

"It's the gyorn!" Kaise said excitedly. "I wanted to see him." And she was gone, shooting in to the crowd. Sarene could hear muffled cries of surprise and annoyance as the little girl pushed her way to the front of the group. Daorn shot his sister a longing look and took a step forward, but then looked back at Sarene and instead decided to remain beside her like a dutiful guide.

Daorn needn't have worried about seeing the gyorn, however. Sarene was a bit more reserved than her young cousin, but she was just as determined to get close enough to hear Hrathen. So, her small guard at her side, Sarene politely—but resolutely—made her way through the crowd until she was standing at the front.

Hrathen stood on a small overlook built into the Elantris wall. His back was to the crowd, but he was angled in such a way as to let his words reach them. His speech was obviously intended for their ears, and not those down below. Sarene spared barely a glance for Elantris itself—she would study it later.

"Look at them!" Hrathen commanded, gesturing toward Elantris. "They have lost their right to be men. They are animals, having no will or desire to serve Lord Jaddeth. They know no God, and can follow only after their lusts."

Sarene frowned. Shu-Dereth taught that the only difference between men and animals was mankind's ability to worship God, or "Jaddeth" in Fjordell. The doctrine was not new to Sarene; her father had made sure to include an extensive knowledge of Shu-Dereth in her education. What she couldn't figure out was why a full gyorn would waste his time with the Elantrians. What could he possibly gain from denouncing a group that had already been beaten down so soundly?

One thing was clear, however. If the gyorn saw reason to preach against Elantris, then it was her duty to defend it. It was possible to block her enemy's schemes before she fully understood them.

". . . as all know, animals are far beneath men in the eyes of Lord Jaddeth," Hrathen was saying, his speech rising toward its conclusion.

Sarene saw her chance and took it. She opened her eyes wide, assumed a dull look of confusion, and—with her most high-pitched innocent voice—asked a single word.

"Why?"

Hrathen stopped. She had timed the question so it fell directly in the awkward space between two of his sentences. The gyorn stumbled at the piercing inquiry, obviously trying to regain his momentum. However, Sarene's placement had been too skillful, and the moment was gone. He turned around with harsh eyes to search out the one who had so foolishly interrupted him. All he found was a demure, perplexed Sarene.

"Why what?" Hrathen demanded.

"Why are animals beneath humans in Mr. Jaddeth's eyes?" she asked.

The gyorn gritted his teeth at her use of the term "Mr. Jaddeth." "Because, unlike men, they can do nothing but follow their own lusts."

The standard follow-up question to such a statement would have been "But men follow their lusts as well," which would have given Hrathen an opportunity to explain the difference between a man of God and a carnal, sinful man. Sarene didn't oblige.

"But I heard that Mr. Jaddeth rewarded arrogance," Sarene said with confusion.

The gyorn's eyes grew suspicious. The question was just a bit too well placed to have come from one as simple as Sarene was pretending to be. He knew, or at least suspected, that she was toying with him. However, he still had to answer the question—if not for her, then for the rest of the crowd.

"*Lord* Jaddeth rewards ambition, not arrogance," he said carefully.

"I don't understand," Sarene said. "Isn't ambition serving our own lusts? Why does Mr. Jaddeth reward that?"

Hrathen was losing his audience, and he knew it. Sarene's question was a century-old theological argument against Shu-Dereth, but the crowd knew nothing of ancient disputes or scholarly refutations. All they knew was that someone was asking questions Hrathen couldn't answer quickly enough, or interestingly enough, to hold their attention.

"Arrogance is different from carnality," Hrathen declared in a snappish voice, making use of his commanding position to take control of the conversation. "People's service in

Jaddeth's empire is quickly rewarded both here and in the afterlife."

It was a masterful attempt: he managed not only to switch the topic, but to draw the crowd's attention to another idea. Everyone found rewards fascinating. Unfortunately for him, Sarene wasn't done yet.

"So if we serve Jaddeth, our lusts are fulfilled?"

"No one serves Jaddeth but Wyrn," Hrathen said offhandedly as he considered how to best answer her objections.

Sarene smiled; she had been hoping he would make that mistake. It was a basic tenet of Shu-Dereth that only one man could serve Jaddeth directly; the religion was very regimented, and its structure was reminiscent of the feudal government that had once ruled in Fjorden. One served those above him, who served those above him, and so on until it reached Wyrn, who served Jaddeth directly. Everyone served Jaddeth's empire, but only one man was holy enough to serve God directly. There was much confusion about the distinction, and it was common for the Derethi priesthood to correct it as Hrathen just had.

Unfortunately, he had also just given Sarene another opportunity.

"No one can serve Jaddeth?" she asked with confusion. "Not even you?"

It was a silly argument—a misinterpretation of Hrathen's point, not a true attack on Shu-Dereth. In a debate of pure religious merit, Sarene would never have been able to stand against a fully-trained gyorn. However, Sarene wasn't looking to disprove Hrathen's teachings, just ruin his speech.

Hrathen looked up at her comment, immediately realizing his mistake. All of his former thinking and planning was now useless—and the crowd was wondering at this new question.

Nobly, the gyorn tried to cover for his mistake, attempting to bring the conversation back to more familiar grounds, but Sarene had the crowd now, and she held on to them with the viselike grip only a woman on the verge of hysterics could manage.

"What will we do?" she asked with a shake of her head. "I fear these things of priests are beyond common people such as myself."

And it was over. The people began talking among themselves and wandering away. Most of them were laughing at the eccentricities of priests, and the abstruseness of theological reasonings. Sarene noticed that most of them were nobles; it must have taken a great deal of effort for the gyorn to lead them all up to Elantris's wall. She found herself smiling wickedly at all of his wasted planning and coaxing.

Hrathen watched his carefully arranged gathering dribble away. He didn't try speaking again; he probably knew that if he yelled or fumed, he would only do more damage than good.

Surprisingly, the gyorn turned away from the scattering people and nodded appreciatively at Sarene. It wasn't a bow, but it was the most respectful gesture she had ever received from a Derethi priest. It was an acknowledgment of a battle well won, a concession given to a worthy opponent.

"You play a dangerous game, Princess," he said softly in his slightly accented voice.

"You'll find I am very good at games, Gyorn," she replied.

"Until the next round, then," he said, waving for a shorter, light-haired priest to follow him as he climbed down from the wall. In this other man's eyes there was no hint of respect or even tolerance. They burned with hatred, and Sarene shivered as he focused them on her. The man's teeth were clenched tightly, and Sarene got the feeling that there wasn't much holding the man back from grabbing her by the neck and hurling her off the side of the wall. She grew dizzy just thinking about it.

"That one worries me," Ashe observed by her side. "I have seen such men before, and my experience has not been favorable. A dam so poorly constructed must eventually collapse."

Sarene nodded. "He was Aonic—not a Fjordell. He looks like a page or attendant of Hrathen's."

"Well, let us hope that the gyorn can keep his pet under control, my lady."

She nodded, but her response was cut off by a sudden peal of laughter from beside her. She looked down to find Kaise rolling on the ground with mirth; apparently, she had managed to hold her outburst until the gyorn was out of sight.

"Sarene," she said between gasps of breath, "that was *wonderful*! You were so stupid! And his face . . . he got even redder than Papa after he finds out I've eaten all of his sweets. His face almost matched his armor!"

"I didn't like him at all," Daorn said solemnly from beside Sarene. He stood near an open part of the parapet, looking down toward Hrathen as the man descended the enormous flight of stairs to the city. "He was too . . . hard. Didn't he know you were only *acting* stupid?"

"Probably," Sarene said, motioning for Kaise to stand up and then brushing off the girl's pink dress. "But there was no way for him to prove it, so he had to pretend that I was serious."

"Father says the gyorn is here to convert us all to Shu-Dereth," Daorn said.

"Does he now?" Sarene asked.

Daorn nodded. "He also says he's afraid Hrathen will be successful. He says the crops didn't do well last year, and a lot of the people are without food. If the planting this month doesn't go well, next winter will be even harder, and hard times make people willing to accept a man who preaches change."

"Your father is a wise man, Daorn," Sarene said. Her confrontation with Hrathen had been little more than sport; people's minds were fickle, and they would quickly forget this day's debate. Whatever Hrathen had been doing was only part of something much larger—something to do with Elantris—and Sarene needed to discover what his intentions were. Finally remembering her original reason for visiting the wall, Sarene took her first good look at the city below.

It had once been beautiful. The feel of the city, how the buildings worked together, the way the roads crossed—the entire mass was . . . intentional. Art on a grand scale. Most of the arches had collapsed, many of the domed roofs had fallen, and even some of the walls looked as if they had little time left. Still, she could tell one thing. Elantris had been beautiful, once.

"They're so sad," Kaise said next to her, on her tiptoes so she could see over the side of the stone safety wall.

"Who?"

"Them," Kaise said, pointing to the streets below.

There were people down there—huddled forms that barely moved. They were camouflaged against the dark streets. Sarene couldn't hear their groans, but she could feel them.

"No one takes care of them," Kaise said.

"How do they eat?" Sarene asked. "Someone must feed them." She couldn't make out many details about the people below—only that they were human. Or, at least, they had the forms of humans; she had read many confusing things about the Elantrians.

"No one," Daorn said from her other side. "No one feeds them. They should all be dead—there's nothing for them to eat."

"They must get it somewhere," Sarene argued.

Kaise shook her head. "They're dead, Sarene. They don't need to eat."

"They may not move much," Sarene said dismissively, "but they obviously aren't dead. Look, those ones over there are standing."

"No, Sarene. They're dead too. They don't need to eat, they don't need to sleep, and they don't age. They're all dead." Kaise's voice was uncharacteristically solemn.

"How do you know so much about it?" Sarene said, trying to dismiss the words as productions of a child's imagination. Unfortunately, these children had proven themselves remarkably well informed.

"I just do," Kaise said. "Trust me. They're dead."

Sarene felt the hair on her arms rising, and she sternly told herself not to give in to the mysticism. The Elantrians were odd, true, but they were not dead. There had to be another explanation.

She scanned the city once more, trying to put Kaise's disturbing comments out of her mind. As she did, her eyes fell on a particular pair of figures—ones who didn't appear to be as pitiful as the rest. She squinted at the figures. They were Elantrian, but one seemed to have darker skin than the other. They crouched on the top of a building, and they looked mobile, unlike most of the other Elantrians she had seen. There was something . . . different about these two.

"My lady?" Ashe's concerned voice sounded in her ear, and she realized that she had begun to lean out over the stone parapet.

With a start, she looked down, realizing just how high up they were. Her eyes unfocused, and she began to lose her balance, transfixed by the undulating ground below. . . .

"My lady!" Ashe's voice came again, shocking her out of her stupor.

Sarene stumbled back from the wall, squatting down and wrapping her arms around her knees. She breathed deeply for a moment. "I'll be all right, Ashe."

"We're leaving this place as soon as you regain your balance," the Seon ordered, his voice firm.

Sarene nodded distractedly.

Kaise snorted. "You know, considering how tall she is, you'd think she'd get used to heights."

CHAPTER 9

IF Dilaf had been a dog, he would have been growling. Probably frothing at the mouth as well, Hrathen decided. The arteth was even worse than he usually was after visiting Elantris's wall.

Hrathen turned to look back at the city. They had nearly reached their chapel, but the enormous wall surrounding Elantris was still visible behind them. Atop it somewhere was the infuriating young woman who had somehow gotten the best of him this day.

"She was magnificent," Hrathen said in spite of himself. Like any of his kind, he had an unquestioned prejudice when it came to the Teoish people. Teod had banished Derethi ministers from the country fifty years ago following a small misunderstanding, and had never consented to let them back in. The Teoish king had come quite near to banishing the Fjordell ambassadors as well. There wasn't a single known Teoish member of Shu-Dereth, and the Teoish royal house was infamous for its biting denunciations of all things Derethi.

Still, it was invigorating to meet a person who could so easily foil one of his sermons. Hrathen had preached Shu-Dereth so long, had made such an art of manipulating the public mind, that he hardly found challenge in it any longer. His success in Duladel a half year ago had proven that one could even cause nations to crumble, if one were capable enough.

Unfortunately, in Duladel there had been little opposition. The Dulas themselves were too open, too accepting, to present a true challenge. In the end, with the shambles of a government dead at his feet, Hrathen had found himself disappointed. It had been almost too easy.

"Yes, she is impressive," he said.

"She is accursed above all others," Dilaf hissed. "A member of the only race hated by Lord Jaddeth."

So that was what was bothering him. Many Fjordells assumed that there was no hope for the Teos. It was foolishness, of course—a simple justification that infused Fjorden's historical enemies with theological hatred. Still, many people believed it—and apparently Dilaf was among them.

"Jaddeth hates no one but those who hate Him," Hrathen said.

"They do hate Him."

"Most of them have never even heard His name preached, Arteth," Hrathen said. "Their king, yes; he is most likely cursed for his injunction against Derethi priests. However, the people haven't even been given a chance. Once Arelon falls to Lord Jaddeth, then we can worry about penetrating Teod. The country won't last long with the rest of the civilized world pitted against it."

"It will be destroyed," Dilaf prophesied with angry eyes. "Jaddeth will not wait while our arteths preach His name against the unyielding walls of Teoish hearts."

"Lord Jaddeth can only come when all men are united beneath Fjordell rule, Arteth," Hrathen said, turning away from his contemplation of Elantris and moving to enter the chapel. "That includes the ones in Teod."

Dilaf's response was softly spoken, but every word sounded powerfully in Hrathen's ears. "Perhaps," the Arelish priest whispered. "But there is another way. Lord Jaddeth will rise when every *living* soul is united—the Teoish will be no obstacle if we destroy them. When the final Teo heaves his last sigh, when the Elantrians have been burned from the face of Sycla, then all men will follow Wyrn. Then Jaddeth will come."

The words were disturbing. Hrathen had come to save Arelon, not to burn it. It might be necessary to undermine the monarchy, and perhaps he would have to spill some noble blood, but the end result would be the redemption of an entire nation. To Hrathen, uniting all mankind meant converting them to Derethi, not murdering those who didn't believe.

Except, perhaps his way was wrong. Wyrn's patience seemed only slightly greater than Dilaf's—the three-month time limit proved that much. Suddenly Hrathen felt an extreme sense of urgency. Wyrn meant his words: Unless Hrathen converted Arelon, the country would be destroyed.

"Great Jaddeth Below . . ." Hrathen whispered, invoking his deity's name—an action he reserved for only the most sacred of times. Right or wrong, he didn't want the blood of an entire kingdom—even a heretical one—on his hands. He *must* succeed.

FORTUNATELY, his loss to the Teoish girl hadn't been as complete as she probably assumed. When Hrathen arrived at the meeting place—a large suite in one of Kae's finest inns—many of the nobles he had invited were waiting for him. The speech on Elantris's wall had been only one part of his plan to convert these men.

"Greetings, Lords," Hrathen said with a nod of his head.

"Don't pretend everything is fine between us, priest," said Idan, one of the younger, more vocal nobles. "You promised your words would bring power. It appears powerful confusion was the only thing they produced."

Hrathen waved his hand dismissively. "My speech baffled one simpleminded girl. It is said the fair princess has trouble remembering which is her right hand and which is her left. I wouldn't have expected her to understand my speech—don't tell me that you, Lord Idan, were similarly lost."

Idan blushed. "Of course not, my lord. It's just that . . . I failed to see how conversion could grant us power."

"The power, my lord, comes in the perception of your enemy." Hrathen strolled through the room, the ever-present Dilaf at his side, and chose a seat. Some gyorns preferred to use a standing posture as a form of intimidation, but Hrathen found it more useful to sit. More often than not, sitting made his listeners—especially those who were standing—uncomfortable. One appeared more in control when one could captivate an audience without towering over them.

Sure enough, Idan and the others soon found their seats as well. Hrathen rested his elbows on the armrests, then clasped his hands and regarded his audience in silence. His brow furled slightly as his eyes fell on one face near the back of the room. The man was older, perhaps in his late forties, and wore rich clothing. The most telling part of the man's appearance was the large purplish birthmark on the left side of his neck and face.

Hrathen hadn't invited Duke Telrii to the meeting. The duke was one of the most powerful men in Arelon, and Hrathen had kept his invitations to the younger nobles. He had assumed that he had little chance in convincing powerful men to follow him; young men impatient to move up the aristocratic ladder were usually easier to manipulate. Hrathen would have to speak carefully this night—a powerful alliance could be his reward.

"Well?" Idan finally asked, fidgeting beneath Hrathen's stare. "Who are they then? Who do *you* perceive as our enemy?"

"The Elantrians," Hrathen said simply. He could feel Dilaf tense by his side as he mentioned the word.

Idan's discomfort left as he chuckled, shooting looks at several of his companions. "The Elantrians have been dead for a decade, Fjordell. They are hardly a threat."

"No, my young lord," Hrathen said. "They live on."

"If you can call it that."

"I don't mean those pitiful mongrels inside the city," Hrathen said. "I mean the Elantrians that live in the people's minds. Tell me, Idan. Have you ever met a man who thought the Elantrians would return someday?"

Idan's chuckles faded away as he considered the question.

"Iadon's rule is far from absolute," Hrathen said. "He is more of a regent than a king. The people don't really expect him to be monarch for long—they're waiting for their blessed Elantrians to return. Many call the Reod false, a kind of 'test' to see who will remain true to the old pagan religion. You have all heard how people speak of Elantris in whispers."

Hrathen's words held weight. He had been in Kae for only a few days, but he had listened and researched well during that time. He was exaggerating the opinion, but he knew it existed.

"Iadon doesn't see the danger," Hrathen continued softly. "He doesn't see that his leadership is suffered, rather than accepted. As long as the people have a physical reminder of Elantris's might, they will fear—and as long as they fear something more than they fear their king, none of *you* will have power. Your titles came from the king; your power is connected to him. If he is impotent, then you are as well."

They were listening now. At the heart of every nobleman was an incurable insecurity. Hrathen hadn't met an aristocrat yet who wasn't at least in part convinced that the peasants laughed at him behind his back.

"Shu-Korath doesn't recognize the danger," Hrathen continued. "The Korathi do nothing to denounce the Elantrians, and therefore perpetuate the public's hope. Irrational though it may be, the people *want* to believe Elantris will be restored. They imagine how grand it used to be, their memories enhanced by a decade of stories—it is human nature to believe that other places and other times are better than the here and now. If you ever want to hold true domination over Arelon, my dear noble friends, then you must abolish your people's foolish hopes. You must find a way to free them from Elantris's grip."

Young Idan nodded enthusiastically. Hrathen pursed his lips with dissatisfaction: The boy noble had been too easily swayed. As was often the case, the most outspoken man was the least discerning. Ignoring Idan, Hrathen judged the expressions of the others. They were thoughtful, but not convinced. The more mature Telrii sat quietly at the back, rubbing the large ruby on one of his rings, watching Hrathen with a musing expression.

Their uncertainty was good. Men as fickle-minded as Idan were of no use to him; those so easily won would be lost just as quickly. "Tell me, men of Arelon," Hrathen said, changing his argument subtly, "have you traveled the countries of the East?"

There were several nods. During the last few years, the East had seen a flood of visitors from Arelon touring through the old Fjordell Empire. Hrathen strongly suspected that the new aristocracy of Arelon, even more insecure than most nobles, felt a desire to prove its level of cultured refinement by associating with kingdoms such as Svorden, the cultural epicenter of the East.

"If you have visited the powerful countries of the East, my friends, then you know of the influence available to those who align themselves with the Derethi priesthood." "Influence" was, perhaps, an understatement. No king ruled east of the Dathreki Mountains unless he professed allegiance to Shu-Dereth, and the most desirable and lucrative governmental positions always fell to those who were diligent in their worship of Jaddeth.

There was a promise implicit in Hrathen's words and—no matter what else they might discuss this night, no matter what other arguments Hrathen put forth—this was what would win their support. It was no secret that Derethi priests took a keen interest in politics; and most people knew that gaining the endorsement of the church was usually enough to insure political victory. This was the promise the noblemen had come expecting to hear, and this was why the Teoish girl's complaints hadn't affected them. Theological disputes were far from these men's minds; Shu-Dereth or Shu-Korath, it mattered little to them. All they needed was an assurance that a sudden outpouring of piety on their parts would in turn be rewarded with temporal blessings—very tangible and spendable ones.

"Enough wordplay, priest," said Ramear, one of the younger nobles. He was a hawk-faced second son of an unimportant baron, a man with a sharp Aonic nose and a reputation for straightforwardness—a reputation he apparently deserved. "I want promises. Are you saying that if we convert to Derethi, you will grant us greater holdings?"

"Jaddeth rewards his followers," Hrathen said noncommittally.

"And how will he reward us?" Ramear demanded. "Shu-Dereth holds no power in *this* kingdom, priest."

"Lord Jaddeth holds power everywhere, friend," Hrathen said. Then, to forestall further demands, he continued. "It is true that as of yet He has few followers in Arelon. The world, however, is dynamic, and few things can stand against Jaddeth's empire. Remember Duladel, my friends. Arelon has remained untouched for so long because we haven't bothered to spare the effort it would take to convert her." A lie, but only a modest one. "The first problem is Elantris. Remove it from the people's minds, and they will gravitate toward Shu-Dereth—Shu-Korath is too tranquil, too indolent. Jaddeth will grow in the people's awareness, and as He does, they will look for role models within the ranks of the aristocracy—men who hold to the same ideals as themselves."

"And then we will be rewarded?" Ramear asked pointedly.

"The people will never suffer rulers who don't believe as they do. As recent history has shown, my friends, kings and monarchies are hardly eternal."

Ramear sat back to contemplate the priest's words. Hrathen had to be careful yet; it was quite possible that only a few of these men would end up supporting him, and he didn't want to give the others evidence against him. Lenient as he may be with regards to religion, King Iadon wouldn't suffer Hrathen's preaching long if he found it treasonous.

Later, after Hrathen sensed firm conviction in his fledgling nobles, he would give them more concrete promises. And, no matter what his opponents might say, Hrathen's promises were trustworthy: as little as he liked working with men whose allegiance could be bought, it was a firm tenet of Shu-Dereth that ambition should be rewarded. Besides, it was beneficial to have a reputation for honesty, if only so that one could lie at crucial moments.

"It will take time to unseat an entire religion and set up a new one in its place," mused Waren, a thin man with a head of nearly white blond hair. Waren was known for his strict piety; Hrathen had been rather surprised when he accompanied his cousin Idan to the meeting. It appeared that Waren's renowned faith was less a matter of religious fervor than it was one of political advantage. Winning him, and his reputation, would be a great help to Hrathen's cause.

"You would be surprised, young Lord Waren," Hrathen said. "Until very recently, Duladel was the seat of one of the world's oldest religions. Now, as far as Fjordell recorders can tell, that religion has been completely wiped out—at least in its pure form."

"Yes," Waren said, "but the collapse of the Jesker religion and the Duladen Republic are events that had been building for years, perhaps even centuries."

"But you cannot deny that when that change in power occurred, it came swiftly," Hrathen said.

Waren paused. "True."

"The fall of the Elantrians was likewise swift," Hrathen said. "Change can come with blinding speed, Lord Waren—but those who are prepared can profit quite substantially from it. You say that the fall of Jesker was building for years . . . well, I suggest to you that the Korathi religion has been in decline for a similar amount of time. It used to hold much sway in the East. Now, its influence has been relegated to only Teod and Arelon."

Waren paused thoughtfully. He appeared to be a man of intelligence and shrewdness, and seemed swayed by Hrathen's logic. It was possible that Hrathen had misjudged the Arelish nobility. Most of them were as hopeless as their king, but a surprising number showed promise. Perhaps they realized just how precarious their positions were—their people starving, their aristocracy inexperienced, and the full attention of the Fjordell Empire turned upon them. When the storm hit, most of Arelon would be surprised like rodents stunned by a bright light. These few lords, however, might just be worth saving.

"My lords, I hope you will review my offers with more wisdom than your king," Hrathen said. "These are difficult times, and those who don't have the Church's support will find life harsh in the coming months. Remember who and what I represent."

"Remember Elantris," a voice, Dilaf's, hissed from beside Hrathen. "Do not forget the well of desecration that pollutes our land. They sleep, and they wait, clever as always. They wait to capture you—all of you—and drag you into their embrace. You must cleanse the world of them before they cleanse it of *you*."

There was an uncomfortable moment of silence. Finally—the arteth's sudden exclamation having spoiled his rhythm—Hrathen leaned back in his chair, crossing his fingers before him to show that the meeting was at an end. The nobles left, their troubled faces showing that they understood the difficult decision Hrathen had placed before them. Hrathen studied them, deciding which ones it would be safe to contact again. Idan was his, and with him would inevitably come several of his followers. Hrathen probably had Ramear as well, assuming he met privately with the man and offered him a solid promise of backing. There were a couple of others like Ramear, and then there was Waren, whose eyes were tinged with what looked like respect. Yes, he could do grand things with that one.

They were a politically weak, relatively unimportant lot, but they were a beginning. As Shu-Dereth gained followers, increasingly important nobles would throw their weight behind Hrathen. Then, when the country finally collapsed beneath the weight of political unrest, economic uncertainty, and martial threats, Hrathen would reward his followers with positions in the new government.

The key to reaching that success was still sitting at the back of the meeting, watching quietly. Duke Telrii's air was stately, his face calm, but his reputation for extravagance spoke of great potential.

"My lord Telrii, a moment please," Hrathen requested, rising. "I have a special proposal that might be of interest to you."

CHAPTER 10

S ULE, I don't think this is a good idea." Galladon's whisper was unenthusiastic as he crouched next to Raoden.

"Hush," Raoden ordered, peeking around the corner toward the courtyard. The gangs had heard about Raoden's recruitment of Mareshe, and were convinced that he intended to start his own rival gang. When Raoden and Galladon had arrived the day before to look for newcomers, they had found a group of Aanden's men waiting for them. The reception hadn't been pleasant. Fortunately, they had escaped without any broken bones or stubbed toes, but this time Raoden intended to be a little more subtle.

"What if they're waiting for us again?" Galladon asked.

"They probably are," Raoden said. "Which is why you should keep your voice down. Come on."

Raoden slipped around the corner and into an alleyway. His toe pained him as he walked, as did his scraped hands and a bruise he had picked up on his arm. In addition, the hunger called to him, a phantom passion from within.

Galladon sighed. "I'm not so bored with death that I want to abandon it in favor of an existence of pure pain. Kolo?"

Raoden turned back with tolerant eyes. "Galladon, someday you're going to get over this determined pessimism of yours, and all of Elantris will collapse from the shock."

"Pessimism?" Galladon demanded as Raoden crept down the alleyway. "Pessimism? Me? Dulas are the most lighthearted, easygoing people in Opelon! We look at each day with— Sule? Don't you dare leave when I'm defending myself!"

Raoden ignored the large Dula. He also tried to ignore his pains, sharp though they were. His new leather shoes helped immensely; despite Galladon's reservations, Mareshe had created a product to match his considerable ego. The shoes were sturdy, with a strong, protective sole, but the soft leather—from the covers of Galladon's books—fit perfectly and didn't rub.

Peeking carefully around the corner, Raoden studied the courtyard. Shaor's men weren't visible, but they were probably hiding nearby. Raoden perked up as he saw the city gate swinging open. The day had brought a new arrival. However, he was shocked when the Elantris City Guard pushed not one, but three separate white-clothed forms through the gate.

"Three?" Raoden said.

"The Shaod is unpredictable, sule," Galladon said, creeping up behind him.

"This changes everything," Raoden said with annoyance.

"Good. Let's go—the others can have today's offering. Kolo?"

"What? And miss such a grand opportunity? Galladon, I'm disappointed in you."

The Dula grumbled something Raoden couldn't catch, and Raoden reached back to clap the big man reassuringly on the shoulder. "Don't worry—I have a plan."

"Already?"

"We have to move quickly—any minute now one of those three is going to take a step, and then our opening will be gone."

"Doloken," Galladon muttered. "What are you going to do?"

"Nothing. You, however, are going to have a nice stroll out there in the courtyard."

"What?" Galladon asked. "Sule, you've gone kayana again. If I go out there, the gangs are going to see me!"

"Exactly," Raoden said with a smile. "Just make sure you run very quickly, my friend. We wouldn't want them to catch you."

"You're serious," Galladon said with growing apprehension.

"Unfortunately. Now get moving—lead them off to the left, and I'll do the rest. We'll meet back where we left Mareshe."

Galladon huffed something about "not being worth all the dried meat in the world," but he let Raoden push him into the courtyard. A moment later a series of startled growls came from the building where Shaor's men usually hid. The feral men burst out, forgetting the three newcomers in their hatred of the man who had wronged them just a few days earlier.

Galladon shot one final withering look in Raoden's direction, then took off at a dash, choosing a street at random and leading Shaor's men away. Raoden gave him a moment, then ran out into the middle of the courtyard, making a great show of breathing deeply, as if from exhaustion.

"Which way did he go?" he demanded sharply of the three confused newcomers.

"Who?" one of them finally ventured.

"The large Dula! Quickly, man, which way did he go? He has the cure!"

"The cure?" the man asked with surprise.

"Of course. It's very rare, but there should be enough for all of us, if you tell me which way he went. Don't you want to get out of here?"

The newcomer raised a wavering hand and pointed at the path Galladon had taken.

"Come on!" Raoden urged. "Unless we move quickly we'll lose him forever!" With that, he started running.

The three newcomers stood for a moment; then, Raoden's sense of urgency too much for them, they followed. All three of their first steps, therefore, were to the north—the direction that would have made them the property of Shaor's men. The other two gangs could only watch with frustration as all three dashed away.

"WHAT can you do?" Raoden asked.

The woman shrugged. "Maare is my name, my lord. I was a simple housewife. I have no special skills to speak of."

Raoden snorted. "If you're like any other housewife, then you're probably more skilled than anyone here. Can you weave?"

"Of course, my lord."

Raoden nodded thoughtfully. "And you?" he asked of the next man.

"Riil, a workman, my lord. I spent most of my time building on my master's plantation."

"Hauling bricks?"

"At first, my lord," the man said. He had the wide hands and ingenuous face of a worker, but his eyes were keen and intelligent. "I spent years learning with the journeymen. I hoped that my master would send me to apprentice."

"You're very old to be an apprentice," Raoden noted.

"I know, my lord, but it was a hope. Not many of the peasantry have room for hopes anymore, even ones so simple."

Raoden nodded again. The man didn't speak like a peasant, but few people in Arelon did. Ten years ago, Arelon had been a land of opportunity, and most of its people had been at least slightly educated. Many of the men in his father's court complained that learning had ruined the peasantry for good work, selectively forgetting that they themselves had been members of the same "peasantry" a decade earlier.

"All right, how about you?" Raoden asked the next man.

The third newcomer, a well-muscled man with a nose that appeared to have been broken at least a dozen times, regarded Raoden with hesitant eyes. "Before I answer, I want to know just why I should listen to you."

"Because I just saved your life," Raoden said.

"I don't understand. What happened to that other man?"

"He should show up in a few minutes."

"But—"

"We weren't really chasing him," Raoden said. "We were getting you three out of danger. Mareshe, please explain."

The artisan jumped at the chance. With wild gestures he explained his narrow escape two days earlier, making it appear that he had been on the verge of death before Raoden appeared and helped him to safety. Raoden smiled; Mareshe had a melodramatic soul. The artist's voice rose and fell like a well-written symphony. Listening to the man's narrative, even Raoden nearly believed he had done something incredibly noble.

Mareshe finished with a proclamation that Raoden was

trustworthy, and encouraged them all to listen to him. At the end, even the burly, hook-nosed man was attentive.

"My name is Saolin, Lord Spirit," the man said, "and I was a soldier in Count Eondel's personal legion."

"I know Eondel," Raoden said with a nod. "He's a good man—a soldier himself before he was granted a title. You were probably trained well."

"We are the best soldiers in the country, sir," Saolin said proudly.

Raoden smiled. "It isn't hard to best most of the soldiers in our poor country, Saolin. However, I'd match Eondel's legion against soldiers from any nation—I always found them to be men of honor, discipline, and skill. Much like their leader. Giving Eondel a title is one of the few intelligent things Iadon has done recently."

"As I understand it, my lord, the king didn't have much choice," Saolin said with a smile, showing a mouth that was missing a couple of teeth. "Eondel has amassed quite a large fortune by hiring out his personal forces to the Crown."

"That's the truth," Raoden said with a laugh. "Well, Saolin, I am glad to have you. A professional soldier of your skill will certainly make us all feel a lot safer around here."

"Whatever Your Lordship needs," Saolin said, his face growing serious. "I pledge you my sword. I know little about religion besides saying my prayers, and I don't really understand what's going on here, but a man who speaks well of Lord Eondel is a good man in my estimation."

Raoden clasped Saolin on the shoulder, ignoring the fact that the grizzled soldier didn't have a sword to pledge anymore. "I appreciate and accept your protection, friend. But I warn you, this is no easy burden you take upon yourself. I'm quickly amassing enemies in here, and it is going to require a great deal of vigilance to make sure we aren't surprised by an attack."

"I understand, my lord," Saolin said fervently. "But, by Domi, I won't let you down!"

"And what of us, my lord?" asked Riil the builder.

"I have a grand project in store for you two as well," Raoden said. "Look up and tell me what you see."

Riil raised his eyes to the sky, his eyes confused. "I see nothing, my lord. Should I?"

Raoden laughed. "Not a thing, Riil. That's the problem—the roof to this building must have fallen in years ago. Despite that, it's one of the largest and least-degenerate buildings I've found. I don't suppose your training included some experience in roof building?"

Riil smiled. "It certainly did, my lord. You have materials?"

"That's going to be the tricky part, Riil. All of the wood in Elantris is either broken or rotted."

"That is a problem," Riil acknowledged. "Perhaps if we dried out the wood, then mixed it with clay. . . ."

"It isn't an easy task, Riil, Maare," Raoden said.

"We'll give it our best try, my lord," Maare assured him.

"Good," Raoden said with an approving nod. His bearing, coupled with their insecurity, made them quick to listen. It wasn't loyalty, not yet. Hopefully, time would gain him their trust as well as their words.

"Now, Mareshe," Raoden continued, "please explain to our new friends about what it means to be an Elantrian. I don't want Riil falling off the top of a building before he realizes breaking his neck won't necessarily mean an end to the pain."

"Yes, my lord," Mareshe said, eyeing the newcomers' food, which was sitting on a relatively clean section of the floor. The hunger was affecting him already.

Raoden carefully chose a few items from the offerings, then nodded to the rest. "Divide this up amongst yourselves and eat it. Saving it won't do any good—the hunger is going to start immediately, and you might as well get this down before it has time to make you greedy."

The four nodded, and Mareshe began to explain the limitations of life in Elantris as he divided the food. Raoden watched for a moment, then turned away to think.

"Sule, my hama would love you. She always complained that I don't get enough exercise." Raoden looked up as Galladon strode into the room.

"Welcome back, my friend," Raoden said with a smile. "I was beginning to worry."

Galladon snorted. "I didn't see you worrying when you shoved me out into that courtyard. Seen worms on hooks treated more kindly. Kolo?"

"Ah, but you made such fantastic bait," Raoden said. "Besides, it worked. We got the newcomers, and you appear remarkably bruise-free."

"A state of being that is most likely a source of grand displeasure to Shaor's dogs."

"How did you escape them?" Raoden asked, handing Galladon the loaf of bread he had grabbed for the Dula. Galladon regarded it, then ripped it in half and offered one part to Raoden, who held up his hand forestallingly.

Galladon shrugged an "okay, starve if it suits you" shrug, and began to gnaw on the loaf. "Ran into a building with a collapsed set of stairs, then went out the back door," he explained between mouthfuls. "I threw some rocks up onto the roof when Shaor's men entered. After what you did to them the other day, they just assumed I was up there. They're probably still sitting there waiting for me."

"Smooth," Raoden said.

"Somebody didn't leave me much choice."

Galladon continued to eat in quiet, listening to the newcomers discuss their various "important duties." "You going to tell all of them that?" he asked in a quiet voice.

"What's that?"

"The newcomers, sule. You made them all think they are of vital importance, just like Mareshe. Shoes are nice, but not a matter of life and death."

Raoden shrugged. "People do a better job when they assume they're important."

Galladon was quiet for another short moment before speaking again. "They're right."

"Who?"

"The other gangs. You are starting your own gang."

Raoden shook his head. "Galladon, that is just a tiny part of it. No one accomplishes anything in Elantris—they're all either too busy squabbling over food or contemplating their misery. The city needs a sense of purpose."

"We're dead, sule," Galladon said. "What purpose can we have besides suffering?"

"That's exactly the problem. Everyone's convinced that their lives are over just because their hearts stopped beating."

"That's usually a pretty good indication, sule," Galladon said dryly.

"Not in our case, my friend. We need to convince ourselves that we can go on. The Shaod isn't causing all the pain here—I've seen people on the outside lose hope too, and their souls end up just as emaciated as those poor wretches in the square. If we can restore even a tiny bit of hope to these people, then their lives will improve drastically." He emphasized the word "lives," looking Galladon right in the eyes.

"The other gangs aren't just going to sit around and watch you steal all their offerings, sule," Galladon said. "They're going to get tired of you very quickly."

"Then I'll just have to be ready for them." Raoden nodded toward the large building around them. "This will make a rather good base of operations, wouldn't you say? It has this open room in the middle, with all of those smaller ones at the back."

Galladon squinted upward. "You could have picked a building with a roof."

"Yes, I know," Raoden replied. "But this one suits my purpose. I wonder what it used to be."

"A church," Galladon said. "Korathi."

"How do you know?" Raoden asked with surprise.

"Has the feel, sule."

"Why would there be a Korathi church in Elantris?" Raoden argued. "The Elantrians were their own gods."

"But they were very lenient gods. There was supposed to be a grand Korathi chapel here in Elantris, the most beautiful of its kind. It was built as an offering of friendship to the people of Teod."

"That seems so odd," Raoden said with a shake of his head. "Gods of one religion building a monument to Domi."

"Like I said. The Elantrians were very lax gods. They didn't really care if the people worshipped them—they were secure in their divinity. Until the Reod came along. Kolo?"

"You seem to know quite a bit, Galladon," Raoden noted.

"And since when has that been a sin?" Galladon said with a huff. "You've lived in Kae all your life, sule. Maybe instead of asking why I know these things, you should wonder why you *don't*."

"Point taken," Raoden said, glancing to the side. Mareshe was still deeply involved in his explanation of an Elantrian's danger-fraught life. "He's not going to be done anytime soon. Come on, there's something I want to do."

"Does it involve running?" Galladon asked in a pained voice.

"Only if they spot us."

RAODEN recognized Aanden. It was difficult to see—the Shaod brought profound changes—but Raoden had a knack for faces. The so-called Baron of Elantris was a short man with a sizable paunch and a long drooping mustache that was obviously fake. Aanden did not look noble—of course, few noblemen Raoden knew looked very aristocratic.

Regardless, Aanden was no baron. The man before Raoden, seated on a throne of gold and presiding over a court of sickly-looking Elantrians, had been called Taan. He had been one of Kae's finest sculptors before the Shaod took him, but he had not been of noble blood. Of course, Raoden's own father had been nothing more than a simple trader until chance had made him king. In Elantris, Taan had apparently taken advantage of a similar opportunity.

The years in Elantris had not been kind to Taan. The man was blubbering incoherently to his court of rejects.

"He's mad?" Raoden asked, crouched outside the window they were using to spy on Aanden's court.

"We each have our own way of dealing with death, sule," Galladon whispered. "The rumors say Aanden's insanity was a conscious decision. They say that after being thrown into Elantris he looked around and said, 'There's no way I can face this sane.' After that, he declared himself Baron Aanden of Elantris and began giving orders."

"And people follow him?"

"Some do," Galladon whispered with a shrug. "He may be mad, but so is the rest of the world—at least, to the eyes of one who's been thrown in here. Kolo? Aanden is a source of authority. Besides, maybe he was a baron on the outside."

"He wasn't. He was a sculptor."

"You knew him?"

"I met him once," Raoden said with a nod. Then he looked back at Galladon with inquisitive eyes. "Where did you hear the rumors about him?"

"Can we move back first, sule?" Galladon requested. "I'd rather not end up a participant in one of Aanden's mock trials and executions."

"Mock?"

"Everything's mock but the axe."

"Ah. Good idea—I've seen all I needed to."

The two men moved back, and as soon as they were a few streets away from the university, Galladon answered Raoden's question. "I talk to people, sule; that's where I get my information. Granted, the great majority of the city's people are Hoed, but there're enough conscious ones around to talk with. Of course, my mouth is what got me in trouble with you. Maybe if I'd kept it shut I'd still be sitting on those steps enjoying myself, rather than spying on one of the most dangerous men in the city."

"Perhaps," Raoden said. "But you wouldn't be having half as much fun. You'd be chained to your boredom."

"I'm so glad you liberated me, sule."

"Anytime."

Raoden thought as they walked, trying to decide on a plan of action should Aanden ever come looking for him. It hadn't taken Raoden long to adjust to walking on Elantris's uneven, slime-covered streets; his still painful toe was a wonderful motivator. He was actually beginning to regard the dun-colored walls and grime as normal, which bothered him much more than the city's dirtiness ever had.

"Sule," Galladon eventually asked. "Why did you want to see Aanden? You couldn't have known you'd recognize him."

Raoden shook his head. "If Aanden had been a baron from the outside, I would have known him almost immediately."

"You're certain?"

Raoden nodded absently.

Galladon was silent for a few more streets, then spoke with sudden understanding. "Now, sule, I'm not very good with these Aons you Arelenes hold in such esteem, but unless I'm completely wrong, the Aon for 'spirit' is Rao."

"Yes," Raoden said hesitantly.

"And doesn't the king of Arelon have a son named Raoden?"

"He did."

"And here you are, sule, claiming to know all the barons in Arelon. You're obviously a man with a good education, and you give commands easily."

"You could say that," Raoden said.

"Then, to top it all off, you call yourself 'Spirit.' Pretty suspicious. Kolo?"

Raoden sighed. "I should have picked a different name, eh?"

"By Doloken, boy! You're telling me you're the crown prince of Arelon?"

"I *was* the crown prince of Arelon, Galladon," Raoden corrected. "I lost the title when I died."

"No wonder you're so frustrating. I've spent my entire life trying to avoid royalty, and here I end up with you. Burning Doloken!"

"Oh quiet down," Raoden said. "It's not like I'm really royalty—it's been in the family for less than a generation."

"That's long enough, sule," Galladon said sullenly.

"If it helps, my father didn't think I was fit to rule. He tried everything to keep me from the throne."

Galladon snorted. "I'd be scared to see the man Iadon found fit to rule. Your father's an idiot—no offense intended."

"None taken," Raoden replied. "And I trust you'll keep my identity secret."

Galladon sighed. "If you wish."

"I do. If I'm going to do any good in Elantris, I need to win followers because they like what I'm doing, not because they feel a patriotic obligation."

Galladon nodded. "You could have at least told me, sule."

"You said we shouldn't talk about our pasts."

"True."

Raoden paused. "Of course, you know what this means."

Galladon eyed him suspiciously. "What?"

"Now that you know who I was, you have to tell me who you were. It's only fair."

Galladon's response was long in coming. They had almost arrived at the church before he spoke. Raoden slowed his walk, not wanting to break off his friend's narration by arriving at their destination. He needn't have worried—Galladon's declaration was brief and pointed.

"I was a farmer," he said curtly.

"A farmer?" Raoden had been expecting something more.

"And an orchard-keeper. I sold my fields and bought an apple farm because I figured it would be easier—you don't have to replant trees every year."

"Was it?" Raoden asked. "Easier, I mean?"

Galladon shrugged. "I thought it was, though I know a couple of wheat farmers that would argue with me until the sun set. Kolo?" The larger man looked at Raoden with an insightful eye. "You don't think I'm telling the truth about my past, do you?"

Raoden smiled, spreading his hands before him. "I'm sorry, Galladon, but you just don't seem like a farmer to me. You have the build for it, but you seem too . . ."

"Intelligent?" Galladon asked. "Sule, I've seen some farmers with minds so sharp you could have used their heads to scythe grain."

"I don't doubt that you have," Raoden said. "But, intelligent or not, those types still tend to be uneducated. You are a learned man, Galladon."

"Books, sule, are a wonderful thing. A wise farmer has time to study, assuming he lives in a country such as Duladen, where men are free."

Raoden raised an eyebrow. "So, you're going to hold to this farmer story?"

"It's the truth, sule," Galladon said. "Before I became an Elantrian, I was a farmer."

Raoden shrugged. Perhaps. Galladon had been able to predict the rain, as well as do a number of other eminently practical things. Still, it seemed like there was something more, something he wasn't ready to share yet.

"All right," Raoden said appreciatively. "I believe you."

Galladon nodded curtly, his expression saying he was very glad the matter was settled. Whatever he was hiding, it wouldn't come out this day. So, instead, Raoden took the opportunity to ask a question that had been bothering him since the first day he came into Elantris.

"Galladon," he asked, "where are the children?"

"Children, sule?"

"Yes, if the Shaod strikes randomly, then it should strike children as well as adults."

Galladon nodded. "It does. I've seen babes barely old enough to walk get thrown in those gates."

"Then where are they? I only see adults."

"Elantris is a harsh place, sule," Galladon said quietly as they strode through the doors to Raoden's broken-down church. "Children don't last very long here."

"Yes, but—" Raoden cut himself off as he saw something flicker in the corner of his eye. He turned with surprise.

"A Seon," Galladon said, noticing the glowing ball.

"Yes," Raoden said, watching the Seon float slowly through the open ceiling and spin in a lazy circle around the two men. "It's so sad how they just drift around the city like this. I . . ." he trailed off, squinting slightly, trying to make out which Aon glowed at the center of the strange, silent Seon.

"Sule?" Galladon asked.

"Idos Domi," Raoden whispered. "It's Ien."

"The Seon? You recognize it?"

Raoden nodded, holding out his hand with the palm up. The Seon floated over and alighted on his proffered palm for a moment; then it began to float away, flitting around the room like a careless butterfly.

"Ien was my Seon," Raoden said. "Before I was thrown in here." He could see the Aon at Ien's center now. The character looked . . . weak, somehow. It glowed unevenly, sections of the character very dim, like . . .

Like the blotches on an Elantrian's skin, Raoden realized, watching Ien float away. The Seon headed for the wall of the church, continuing on until he bounced against it. The small ball of light hovered for a moment, contemplating the wall, then spun away to float in a different direction. There was an awkwardness to the Seon's motion—as if Ien could barely keep himself upright in the air. He jerked occasionally, and constantly moved in slow, dizzy loops.

Raoden's stomach turned as he regarded what was left of his friend. He'd avoided thinking about Ien too much during his days in Elantris; he knew what happened to Seons when their masters were taken by the Shaod. He'd assumed—perhaps hoped—that Ien had been destroyed by the Shaod, as sometimes happened.

Raoden shook his head. "Ien used to be so wise. I never knew a creature, Seon or man, more thoughtful than he."

"I'm . . . sorry, sule," Galladon said solemnly.

Raoden held out his hand again, and the Seon approached dutifully, as it had once done for the young boy Raoden—a boy who hadn't yet learned that Seons were more valuable as friends than as servants.

Does he recognize me? Raoden wondered, watching the Seon lurch slightly in the air before him. *Or is it just the familiar gesture that he recognizes?*

Raoden would probably never know. After hovering above the palm for a second, the Seon lost interest and floated away again.

"Oh, my dear friend," Raoden whispered. "And I thought the Shaod had been harsh to *me*."

CHAPTER 11

ONLY five men responded to Kiin's request. Lukel scowled at the meager turnout. "Raoden had as many as thirty men at his meetings before he died," the handsome merchant explained. "I didn't expect them all to come running, but *five*? That's barely even worth our time."

"It's enough, son," Kiin said thoughtfully, peeking through the kitchen door. "They may be few in number, but we got the best of the lot. Those are five of the most powerful men in the nation, not to mention five of the most intelligent. Raoden had a way of attracting clever men to his side."

"Kiin, you old bear," one of the men called from the dining room. He was a stately man with graying lines of silver hair who wore a sharp martial uniform. "Are you going to feed us or not? Domi knows I only came because I heard you were going to fix some of your roast ketathum."

"The pig is turning as we speak, Eondel," Kiin called back. "And I made sure to prepare a double portion for you. Keep your stomach in check for a little while longer."

The man laughed heartily, patting his belly—which, as far as Sarene could tell, was as flat and hard as that of a man many years younger. "Who is he?" she asked.

"The Count of Eon Plantation," Kiin said. "Lukel, go check on the pork while your cousin and I gossip about our guests."

"Yes, Father," Lukel said, accepting the poker and moving to the firepit room at the back of the kitchen.

"Eondel is the only man besides Raoden that I've ever seen openly oppose the king and get away with it," Kiin explained. "He's a military genius, and owns a small personal army. There are only a couple hundred men in it, but they're extremely well trained."

Next Kiin pointed through the slightly open door toward a man with dark brown skin and delicate features. "That man beside Eondel is Baron Shuden."

"Jindoeese?" Sarene asked.

Her uncle nodded. "His family took up residence in Arelon about a century ago, and they've amassed a fortune directing the Jindoeese trade routes through the country. When Iadon came to power, he offered them a barony to keep their caravans running. Shuden's father passed away about five years ago, and the son is much more traditional than the father ever was. He thinks Iadon's method of rule contradicts the heart of Shu-Keseg, which is why he's willing to meet with us."

Sarene tapped her cheek in thought, studying Shuden. "If his heart is as Jindoeese as his skin, Uncle, then he could be a powerful ally indeed."

"That's what your husband thought," Kiin said.

Sarene pursed her lips. "Why do you keep referring to Raoden as 'your husband'? I know I'm married. No need to keep pointing it out."

"You know it," Kiin said in his deep-throated rasp, "but you don't believe it yet."

Either Kiin didn't see the question in her face, or he simply ignored it, for he continued with his explanations as if he hadn't just made an infuriatingly unfair judgment.

"Beside Shuden is the Duke Roial of Ial Plantation," Kiin said, nodding to the oldest man in the room. "His holdings include the port of Iald—a city that is second only to Kae in wealth. He's the most powerful man in the room, and probably the wisest as well. He's been loath to take action against the king, however. Roial and Iadon have been friends since before the Reod."

Sarene raised an eyebrow. "Why does he come, then?"

"Roial is a good man," Kiin explained. "Friendship or not, he knows that Iadon's rule has been horrible for this nation. That, and I suspect he also comes because of boredom."

"He engages in traitorous conferences simply because he's bored?" Sarene asked incredulously.

Her uncle shrugged. "When you've been around as long as Roial, you have trouble finding things to keep you interested. Politics is so ingrained in the duke that he probably can't sleep at night unless he's involved in at least five different wild schemes—he was governor of Iald before the Reod, and was the only Elantris-appointed official to remain in power after the uprising. He's fabulously wealthy—the only way Iadon keeps ahead is by including national tax revenues in his own earnings."

Sarene studied the duke as the group of men laughed at one of Roial's comments. He seemed different from other elderly statesmen she had met: Roial was boisterous instead of reserved, almost more mischievous than distinguished. Despite the duke's diminutive frame, he dominated the conversation, his thin locks of powder-white hair bouncing as he laughed. One man, however, didn't seem captivated by the duke's company.

"Who is that sitting next to Duke Roial?"

"The portly man?"

"Portly?" Sarene said with a raised eyebrow. The man was so overweight his stomach bulged over the sides of his chair.

"That's how we fat men describe one another," Kiin said with a smile.

"But Uncle," Sarene said with a sweet grin. "You're not fat. You're . . . robust."

Kiin laughed a scratchy-throated chuckle. "All right, then. The 'robust' gentleman next to Roial is Count Ahan. You wouldn't know it by watching them, but he and the duke are very good friends. Either that or they're very old enemies. I can never remember which it is."

"There's a bit of a distinction there, Uncle," Sarene pointed out.

"Not really. The two of them have been squabbling and sparring for so long that neither one would know what to do without the other. You should have seen their faces when they realized they were both on the same side of this particular argument—Raoden laughed for days after that first meeting. Apparently, he'd gone to them each separately and gained their support, and they both came to that first meeting with the belief they were outdoing the other."

"So why do they keep coming?"

"Well, they both seem to agree with our point of view—not to mention the fact that they really do enjoy one another's company. That or they just want to keep an eye on each other." Kiin shrugged. "Either way they help us, so we don't complain."

"And the last man?" Sarene asked, studying the table's final occupant. He was lean, with a balding head and a pair of very fidgety eyes. The others didn't let nervousness show; they laughed and spoke together as if they were meeting to discuss bird-watching rather than treason. This last man, however, wiggled in his seat uncomfortably, his eyes in constant motion—as if he were trying to determine the easiest way to escape.

"Edan," Kiin said, his lips turning downward. "Baron of Tii Plantation to the south. I've never liked him, but he's probably one of our strongest supporters."

"Why is he so nervous?"

"Iadon's system of government lends itself well to greed—the better a noble does financially, the more likely he is to be granted a better title. So, the minor nobles squabble like children, each one trying to find new ways to milk their subjects and increase their holdings.

"The system also encourages financial gambling. Edan's fortune was never very impressive—his holdings border the Chasm, and the lands nearby just aren't very fertile. In an attempt to gain a bit more status, Edan made some risky investments—but lost them. Now he doesn't have the wealth to back his nobility."

"He might lose his title?"

"Not 'might'—he's going to lose it as soon as the next tax period comes around and Iadon realizes just how poor the baron's become. Edan has about three months to either discover a gold mine in his backyard or overthrow Iadon's system of allocating noble titles." Kiin scratched his face, as if looking for whiskers to pull in thought. Sarene smiled—ten years might have passed since the burly man's face had held a beard, but old habits were more difficult to shave away.

"Edan is desperate," Kiin continued, "and desperate people do things completely out of character. I don't trust him, but of all the men in that room, he's probably the most anxious for us to succeed."

"Which would mean?" Sarene asked. "What exactly do these men expect to accomplish?"

Kiin shrugged. "They'll do about anything to get rid of this silly system that requires them to prove their wealth. Noblemen will be nobleman, 'Ene—they're worried about maintaining their place in society."

Further discussion was halted as a voice called from the dining room. "Kiin," Duke Roial noted pointedly, "we could have raised our own hogs and had them slaughtered in the time this is taking you."

"Good meals take time, Roial," Kiin huffed, sticking his head out the kitchen door. "If you think you can do better, you're welcome to come cook your own."

The duke assured him that wouldn't be necessary. Fortunately, he didn't have to wait much longer. Kiin soon proclaimed the pig cooked to perfection, and ordered Lukel to begin cutting it. The rest of the meal quickly followed—a feast so large it would even have satisfied Kaise, if her father hadn't ordered her and the other children to visit their aunt's house for the evening.

"You're still determined to join us?" Kiin asked Sarene as he reentered the kitchen to grab the final dish.

"Yes," Sarene said firmly.

"This isn't Teod, Sarene," Kiin said. "The men here are a lot more . . . traditional. They don't feel it's proper for a woman to be involved in politics."

"This from a man who's doing the evening's cooking?" Sarene asked.

Kiin smiled. "Good point," he noted in his scratchy voice. Someday, she would have to find out what had happened to his throat.

"I can handle myself, Uncle," Sarene said. "Roial isn't the only one who likes a good challenge."

"All right, then," Kiin said, picking up a large steaming bean dish. "Let's go." Kiin led the way through the kitchen doors and then, after setting down the plate, gestured to Sarene. "Everyone, I'm sure you've all met my niece, Sarene, princess of our realm."

Sarene curtsied to Duke Roial, then nodded to the others, before taking her seat.

"I was wondering who that extra seat was for," mumbled the aged Roial. "Niece, Kiin? You have connections to the Teoish throne?"

"Oh come now!" The overweight Ahan laughed merrily. "Don't tell me you don't know Kiin is old Eventeo's brother? My spies told me that years ago."

"I was being polite, Ahan," Roial said. "It's bad form to spoil a man's surprise just because your spies are efficient."

"Well, it's also bad form to bring an outsider to a meeting of this nature," Ahan pointed out. His voice was still happy, but his eyes were quite serious.

All faces turned toward Kiin, but it was Sarene who answered. "One would think that after such a drastic reduction in your numbers, my lord, you would appreciate additional support—no matter how unfamiliar, or how feminine, it may be."

The table went silent at her words, ten eyes studying her through the steam rising from Kiin's several masterpieces. Sarene felt herself grow tense beneath their unaccepting gaze. These men knew just how quickly a single error could bring destruction upon their houses. One did not dabble lightly with treason in a country where civil upheaval was a fresh memory.

Finally, Duke Roial laughed, the chuckle echoing lightly from his slight frame. "I knew it!" he proclaimed. "My dear, no person could possibly be as stupid as you made yourself out to be—not even the queen herself is that empty-headed."

Sarene pasted a smile over her nervousness. "I believe you're wrong about Queen Eshen, Your Grace. She's simply . . . energetic."

Ahan snorted. "If that's what you want to call it." Then, as it appeared no one else was going to begin, he shrugged and began helping himself to the food. Roial, however, did not follow his rival's lead; mirth had not erased his concerns. He folded his hands in front of himself and regarded Sarene with a very practiced gaze.

"You may be a fine actress, my dear," the duke said as Ahan reached in front of him to grab a basket of rolls, "but I see no reason why you should attend this dinner. Through no fault of your own, you are young and inexperienced. The things we say tonight will be very dangerous to hear and even more dangerous to remember. An unnecessary set of ears—no matter how pretty the head to which they are attached—will not help."

Sarene narrowed her eyes, trying to decide whether the duke was attempting to provoke her or not. Roial was as hard a man to read as any she had ever met. "You'll find that I am hardly inexperienced, my lord. In Teod we don't shelter our women behind a curtain of weaving and embroidering. I have spent years serving as a diplomat."

"True," Roial said, "but you are hardly familiar with the delicate political situations here in Arelon."

Sarene raised an eyebrow. "I have often found, my lord, that a fresh, unbiased opinion is an invaluable tool in any discussion."

"Don't be silly, girl," spat the still nervous Edan as he filled his plate. "I'm not going to risk my safety simply because you want to assert your liberated nature."

A dozen snide retorts snapped to Sarene's lips. However, even as she was deciding which was the most witty, a new voice entered the debate.

"I beseech you, my lords," said the young Jindo, Shuden. His words were very soft, but still distinct. "Answer me a question. Is 'girl' the proper title for one who, had things turned out a bit differently, might have been our queen?"

Forks stopped on the way to mouths, and once again Sarene found herself the focus of the room's attention. This time, however, the looks were slightly more appreciative. Kiin nodded, and Lukel shot her an encouraging smile.

"I warn you, my lords," Shuden continued, "forbid her or accept her as you will, but do not treat her with disrespect. Her Arelish title is no stronger and no more flimsy than our own. Where we ignore one, we must ignore all others."

Sarene blushed furiously on the inside, chastising herself. She had overlooked her most valuable asset—her marriage to Raoden. She had been a Teoish princess all her life; the position formed the cornerstone of who she was. Unfortunately, that self-concept was outdated. She was no longer just Sarene, daughter of Teod; she was also Sarene, wife to the crown prince of Arelon.

"I applaud your caution, my lords," she said. "You have good reason to be careful—you have lost your patron, the only man who could have given you a measure of protection. Remember, however, that I am his wife. I am no substitute for the prince, but I am still a connection to the throne. Not just this throne, but others as well."

"That's well and good, Sarene," Roial said, "but 'connections' and promises will do us little good in the face of the king's wrath."

"Little good is not the same as no good, my lord," Sarene replied. Then, in a softer, less argumentative tone, she continued. "My lord duke, I will never know the man that I now call my husband. You all respected and, if I am to believe my uncle, loved Raoden—but I, who should have come to love him best, can never even meet him. This work in which you are involved was his passion. I want to be a part of it. If I cannot know Raoden, at least let me share his dreams."

Roial watched her for a second, and she knew that he was measuring her sincerity. The duke was not a man to be fooled by mock sentimentality. Eventually, he nodded and began cutting himself a piece of pork. "I have no problem with her staying."

"Neither do I," Shuden said.

Sarene looked at the others. Lukel was smiling openly at her speech, and the stately mercenary Lord Eondel was nearly in tears. "I give my assent to the lady."

"Well, if Roial wants her here, then I have to object out of principle," Ahan said with a laugh. "But, happily, it looks as if I'm outvoted." He winked at her with a broad smile. "I get tired of looking at the same crusty old faces anyway."

"Then she stays?" Edan asked with surprise.

"She stays," Kiin said. Her uncle still hadn't touched his meal. He wasn't the only one—neither Shuden nor Eondel had begun to eat either. As soon as the debate ended, Shuden bowed his head in a short prayer, then turned to eating. Eondel, however, waited until Kiin had taken his first bite—a fact Sarene noticed with interest. Despite Roial's higher rank, the meeting was at Kiin's home. According to the older traditions, it should have been his privilege to eat first. Only Eondel, however, had waited. The others were probably so accustomed to being the most important person at their respective tables that they gave no thought to when they should eat.

After the intensity of the debate surrounding Sarene's place, or lack thereof, the lords were quick to turn their minds to a topic less controversial.

"Kiin," Roial declared, "this is by far the best meal I have eaten in decades."

"You humble me, Roial," Kiin said. He apparently avoided calling the others by their titles—but, oddly, none of them seemed to mind.

"I agree with Lord Roial, Kiin," Eondel said. "No chef in this country can outdo you."

"Arelon is a large place, Eondel," Kiin said. "Be careful not to encourage me too much, lest you find someone better and disappoint me."

"Nonsense," Eondel said.

"I can't believe that you make all of it by yourself," Ahan said with a shake of his large round head. "I'm absolutely certain that you have a fleet of Jaadorian chefs hiding underneath one of those counters back there."

Roial snorted. "Just because it keeps an army of men to keep you fed, Ahan, doesn't mean that a single cook isn't satisfactory for the rest of us." Then, to Kiin, he continued. "Still, Kiin, it is very odd of you to insist on doing this all yourself. Couldn't you at least hire an assistant?"

"I enjoy it, Roial. Why would I let someone else steal my pleasure?"

"Besides, my lord," Lukel added, "it gives the king chest pains every time he hears that a man as wealthy as my father does something as mundane as cook."

"Quite clever," Ahan agreed. "Dissidence through subservience."

Kiin held up his hands innocently. "All I know, my lords, is that a man can take care of himself and his family quite easily without any assistance, no matter how wealthy he supposedly is."

"Supposedly, my friend?" Eondel laughed. "The little bit

you let us see is enough to earn you a barony at least. Who knows, maybe if you told everyone how much you're really worth we wouldn't have to worry about Iadon—you'd be king."

"Your assumptions are a bit inflated, Eondel," Kiin said. "I'm just a simple man who likes to cook."

Roial smiled. "A simple man who likes to cook—and whose brother is king of Teod, whose niece is now the daughter of *two* kings, and whose wife is a ranked noblewoman in our own court."

"I can't help that I'm related to important people," Kiin said. "Merciful Domi gives us each different trials."

"Speaking of trials," Eondel said, turning eyes on Sarene. "Has Your Ladyship decided what to do for her Trial yet?"

Sarene furled her brow in confusion. "Trial, my lord?"

"Yes, uh, your . . ." The dignified man looked to the side, a bit embarrassed.

"He's talking about your Widow's Trial," Roial explained.

Kiin shook his head. "Don't tell me you expect her to perform one of those, Roial? She never even met Raoden—it's preposterous to expect her to go through mourning, let alone a Trial."

Sarene felt herself grow annoyed. No matter how much she claimed she enjoyed surprises, she didn't like the way this conversation was going. "Would one of you please explain exactly what this Trial is?" she requested in a firm voice.

"When an Arelish noblewoman is widowed, my lady," Shuden explained, "she is expected to perform a Trial."

"So what am I supposed to do?" Sarene asked, frowning. She did *not* like unfulfilled duties hanging over her.

"Oh, hand out some food or blankets to the poor," Ahan said with a dismissive wave of his hand. "No one expects you to take any real interest in the process, it's just one of the traditions that Iadon decided to hold over from the old days—the Elantrians used to do something similar whenever one of their kind died. I never liked the custom myself. It seems to me we shouldn't encourage the people to look forward to our deaths; it doesn't bode well for an aristocrat's popularity to be at its greatest just after he dies."

"I think it's a fine tradition, Lord Ahan," Eondel said.

Ahan chuckled. "You would, Eondel. You're so conservative that even your socks are more traditional than the rest of us."

"I can't believe no one's told me about it," Sarene said, still annoyed.

"Well," Ahan said, "perhaps somebody would have mentioned it to you if you didn't spend all of your time holed up in the palace or in Kiin's house."

"What else am I supposed to do?"

"Arelon has a fine court, Princess," Eondel said. "I believe there have been two balls since you arrived, and there is another happening as we speak."

"Well, why didn't anyone invite me?" she asked.

"Because you're in mourning," Roial explained. "Besides, the invitations only go out to men, who in turn bring their sisters and wives."

Sarene frowned. "You people are so backward."

"Not backward, Your Highness," Ahan said. "Just traditional. If you like, we could arrange to have some men invite you."

"Wouldn't that look bad?" Sarene asked. "Me, not even a week widowed, accompanying some young bachelor to a party?"

"She has a point," Kiin noted.

"Why don't you all take me?" Sarene asked.

"Us?" Roial asked.

"Yes, you," Sarene said. "Your Lordships are old enough that people won't talk too much—you'll just be introducing a young friend to the joys of court life."

"Many of these men are married, Your Highness," Shuden said.

Sarene smiled. "What a coincidence. So am I."

"Don't worry about our honor, Shuden," Roial said. "I'll make the princess's intentions known, and as long as she doesn't go with any one of us too often, no one will infer much from it."

"Then it's settled," Sarene decided with a smile. "I'll be expecting to hear from each of you, my lords. It's essential that I get to these parties—if I am ever going to fit into Arelon, then I'll need to get to know the aristocracy."

There was general agreement, and the conversation turned to other topics, such as the upcoming lunar eclipse. As they spoke, Sarene realized that her question about the mysterious "Trial" hadn't yielded much information. She would have to corner Kiin later.

Only one man wasn't enjoying the conversation or, apparently, the meal. Lord Edan had filled his plate, but had barely taken a few bites. Instead, he poked at his food with dissatisfaction, mixing the different dishes into an adulterated mush only vaguely resembling the delicacies Kiin had prepared.

"I thought we had decided not to meet anymore," Edan finally blurted out, the comment forcing its way into the conversation like an elk wandering into the middle of a pack of wolves. The others paused, turning toward Edan.

"We had decided not to meet for a while, Lord Edan," Eondel said. "We never intended to stop meeting completely."

"You should be happy, Edan," Ahan said, waving a fork topped with a chunk of pork. "You, of all people, should be eager to keep these meetings going. How long is it before the next taxing period arrives?"

"I believe it is on the first day of Eostek, Lord Ahan," Eondel said helpfully. "Which would put it just under three months away."

Ahan smiled. "Thank you, Eondel—you're such a useful man to have around. Always knowing things that are proper and such. Anyway . . . three months, Edan. How are the coffers doing? You know how picky the king's auditors are. . . ."

Edan squirmed even more beneath the count's brutal mockery. It appeared that he was quite aware of his time constraints—yet, at the same time, he seemed to be trying to forget his troubles in the hope that they would disappear. The conflict was visible in his face, and Ahan seemed to take great pleasure in watching.

"Gentlemen," Kiin said, "we are not here to squabble. Remember that we all have much to gain from reform—including stability for our country and freedom for our people."

"The good baron does bring up a valid concern, however," Duke Roial said, sitting back in his chair. "Despite this young lady's promise of aid, we are completely exposed without Raoden. The people loved the prince—even if Iadon had discovered our meetings, he could never have taken action against Raoden."

Ahan nodded. "We don't have the power to oppose the king anymore. We were gaining strength before—it probably wouldn't have been long before we had enough of the nobility to go public. Now, however, we have nothing."

"You still have a dream, my lord," Sarene said quietly. "That is hardly nothing."

"A dream?" Ahan said with a laugh. "The dream was Raoden's, my lady. We were just along to see where he took us."

"I can't believe that, Lord Ahan," Sarene said with a frown.

"Perhaps Her Highness would tell us what that dream is?" Shuden requested, his voice inquisitive but not argumentative.

"You are intelligent men, dear lords," Sarene replied. "You have the brains and the experience to know that a country cannot withstand the stress that Iadon is placing on it. Arelon is not a business to be run with a grip of steel—it is much more than its production minus its costs. The dream, my lords, is an Arelon whose people work with her king, instead of against him."

"A fine observation, Princess," Roial said. His tone, however, was dismissive. He turned to the others, and they continued talking—every one of them politely ignoring Sarene. They had allowed her into the meeting, but they obviously didn't intend to let her join the discussion. She sat back with annoyance.

". . . having a goal is not the same thing as having the means to accomplish it," Roial was saying. "I believe that we should wait—to let my old friend run himself into a corner before we move in to help."

"But Iadon will destroy Arelon in the process, Your Grace," Lukel objected. "The more time we give him, the harder it will be to recover."

"I do not see another option," Roial said with raised hands. "We cannot continue to move against the king in the way we were."

Edan jumped slightly at the proclamation, sweat forming

on his brow. He was finally beginning to realize that, dangerous or not, continuing to meet was a much better choice than
waiting for Iadon to strip him of rank.

"You have a point, Roial," Ahan grudgingly admitted.
"The prince's original plan will never work now. We won't
be able to pressure the king unless we have at least half of
the nobility—and their fortunes—on our side."

"There is another way, my lords," Eondel said with a hesitant voice.

"What is that, Eondel?" the duke asked.

"It would take me less than two weeks to gather the legion
from their watchpoints along the nation's highways. Monetary might isn't the only kind of power."

"Your mercenaries could never stand against Arelon's
armies," Ahan scoffed. "Iadon's military might be small
compared to those of some kingdoms, but it's far larger than
your few hundred men—especially if the king calls in the
Elantris City Guard."

"Yes, Lord Ahan, you are correct," Eondel agreed. "However, if we strike quickly—while Iadon is still ignorant of
our intentions—we could get my legion into the palace and
take the king hostage."

"Your men would have to fight their way into the king's
quarters," Shuden said. "Your new government would be
born out of the blood of the old, as Iadon's rule was birthed
from the death of Elantris. You would set the cycle again for
another fall, Lord Eondel. As soon as one revolution
achieves its goal, another will begin to scheme. Blood,
death, and coups will only lead to further chaos. There must
be a way to persuade Iadon without resorting to anarchy."

"There is," Sarene said. Annoyed eyes turned her direction. They still assumed she was simply there to listen. They
should have known better.

"I agree," Roial said, turning away from Sarene, "and that
way is to wait."

"No, my lord," Sarene countered. "I am sorry, but that is
not the answer. I have seen the people of Arelon, and while
there is still hope in their eyes, it is growing weak. Give
Iadon time, and he will create the despondent peasants he
desires."

Roial's mouth turned downward. He had probably intended to be in control, now that Raoden was gone. Sarene hid her smile of satisfaction: Roial had been the first to allow her in, and therefore he would have to let her speak. Refusing to listen now would show that he had been wrong to grant her his support.

"Speak, Princess," the old man said with reservation.

"My lords," Sarene said in a frank voice, "you have been trying to find a way to overthrow Iadon's system of rule, a system that equates wealth with ability to lead. You claim it is unwieldy and unfair—that its foolishness is a torture to the Arelish people."

"Yes," Roial said curtly. "And?"

"Well, if Iadon's system is so bad, why worry about overthrowing it? Why not let the system overthrow itself?"

"What do you mean, Lady Sarene?" Eondel asked with interest.

"Turn Iadon's own creation against him, and force him to acknowledge its faults. Then, hopefully, you can work out one that is more stable and satisfactory."

"Interesting, but impossible," Ahan said with a shake of his many-jowled face. "Perhaps Raoden could have done it, but we are too few."

"No, you're perfect," Sarene said, rising from her chair and strolling around the table. "What we want to do, my lords, is make the other aristocrats jealous. That won't work if we have too many on our side."

"Speak on," Eondel said.

"What is the biggest problem with Iadon's system?" Sarene asked.

"It encourages the lords to treat their people brutally," Eondel said. "King Iadon threatens the noblemen, taking away the titles of those who do not produce. So, in turn, the lords grow desperate, and they beat extra effort out of their people."

"It is an unconscionable arrangement," Shuden agreed, "one based on greed and fear rather than loyalty."

Sarene continued to stroll around the table. "Have any of you looked at Arelon's production charts over the last ten years?"

"Is there such a thing?" Ahan asked.

Sarene nodded. "We keep them in Teod. Would you be surprised to find, my lords, that Arelon's level of production has plummeted since Iadon took control?"

"Not at all," Ahan said. "We've had quite the decade of misfortune."

"Kings make their own misfortune, Lord Ahan," Sarene said with a cutting motion of her hand. "The saddest thing about Iadon's system is not what it does to the people, nor is it the fact that it destroys the morality of the country. No, most pitiful is the fact that it does both of these things without making the noblemen any richer.

"We have no slaves in Teod, my lords, and we get along just fine. In fact, not even Fjorden uses a serf-based system anymore. They found something better—they discovered that a man will work much more productively when he works for himself."

Sarene let the words hang in the air for a moment. The lords sat thoughtfully. "Continue," Roial finally said.

"The planting season is upon us, my lords," Sarene said. "I want you to divide your land amongst your peasants. Give them each a section of field, and tell them they can keep ten percent of whatever that land produces. Tell them that you will even let them buy their homes and the land they occupy."

"That would be a very difficult thing to do, young princess," Roial said.

"I'm not done yet," Sarene said. "I want you to feed your people well, my lords. Give them clothing and supplies."

"We are not beasts, Sarene," Ahan warned. "Some lords treat their peasants poorly, but we would never accept such into our fellowship. The people on our lands have food to eat and clothing to keep them warm."

"That may be true, my lord," Sarene continued, "but the people must feel that you love them. Do not trade them to other nobles or squabble over them. Let the peasants know that you care, and they will give you their hearts and their sweat. Prosperity need not be limited to a small percentage of the population."

Sarene reached her seat and stood behind it. The lords were thinking—that was good—but they were scared as well.

"It will be risky," Shuden ventured.

"As risky as attacking Iadon with Lord Eondel's army?" Sarene asked. "If this doesn't work, you lose a bit of money and some pride. If the honorable general's plan doesn't work, you lose your heads."

"She has a point," Ahan agreed.

"A good one," Eondel said. There was relief in his eyes: soldier or not, he didn't want to attack his countrymen. "I will do it."

"That's easy for you to say, Eondel," Edan said, wiggling in his seat. "You can always just order your legion to work on the farms when the peasants turn lazy."

"My men are policing our country's highways, Lord Edan," Eondel huffed. "Their service there is invaluable."

"And you are handsomely rewarded for it," Edan spat. "I have no income but that of my farms—and while my lands *look* big, I've got that blasted crack running right through the center of them. I don't have any room for laziness. If my potatoes don't get planted, weeded, and harvested, then I will lose my title."

"You'll probably lose it anyway," Ahan said with a helpful smile.

"Enough, Ahan," Roial ordered. "Edan has a point. How can we be certain the peasants will produce more if we give them so much liberty?"

Edan nodded. "I have found the Arelish peasantry to be a lazy, unproductive lot. The only way I can get enough work out of them is by force."

"They aren't lazy, my lord," Sarene said. "They are angry. Ten years is not so long a time, and these people can remember what it is to be their own masters. Give them the promise of autonomy, and they will work hard to achieve it. You will be surprised how much more profitable an independent man is than a slave who thinks of nothing more than his next meal. After all, which situation would make *you* more likely to be productive?"

The nobles mused over her words.

"Much of what you say makes sense," Shuden noted.

"But, Lady Sarene's evidence is vague," Roial said. "Times were different before the Reod. The Elantrians provided food, and the land could survive without a peasant class. We no longer have that luxury."

"Then help me *find* evidence, my lord," Sarene said. "Give me a few months and we will create our own proof."

"We will . . . consider your words," Roial said.

"No, Lord Roial, you will make a decision," Sarene said. "Beneath everything else, I believe that you are a patriot. You know what is right, and this is it. Don't tell me you've never felt any guilt for what you have done to this country."

Sarene regarded Roial anxiously. The elderly duke had impressed her, but there was no way for her to be sure he felt ashamed for Arelon. She had to depend on her impression that his heart was good, and that in his long life he had seen and understood how far his country had fallen. The collapse of Elantris had been a catalyst, but the greed of the nobility had been the true destroyer of this once grand nation.

"We have all been blinded at one time or another by Iadon's promises of wealth," Shuden said with his soft, wise voice. "I will do as Her Highness asks." Then the brown-skinned man turned his eyes on Roial and nodded. His acceptance had given the duke an opportunity to agree without losing too much face.

"All right," the elderly duke said with a sigh. "You are a wise man, Lord Shuden. If you find merit in this plan, then I will follow it as well."

"I suppose we have no choice," Edan said.

"It's better than waiting, Lord Edan," Eondel noted.

"True. I agree as well."

"That leaves me," Ahan said with a sudden realization. "Oh, my. What shall I do?"

"Lord Roial agreed only grudgingly, my lord," Sarene said. "Don't tell me you are going to do the same?"

Ahan bellowed a laugh, his entire frame shaking. "What a delightful girl you are! Well, then, I guess I have to accept wholeheartedly, with the admonition that I knew she was right all along. Now, Kiin, please tell me you haven't forgotten dessert. I've heard such lovely things about your confections."

"Forget dessert?" her uncle rasped. "Ahan, you wound me." He smiled as he rose from his chair and moved toward the kitchen.

"SHE is good at this, Kiin—perhaps better than I am." It was Duke Roial's voice. Sarene froze; she had gone looking for the washroom after bidding everyone farewell, and had expected them to be gone by now.

"She is a very special young woman," Kiin agreed. Their voices were coming from the kitchen. Silently, Sarene slipped forward and listened outside the door.

"She neatly slipped control away from me, and I still don't know where I went wrong. You should have warned me."

"And let you escape, Roial?" Kiin said with a laugh. "It's been a long time since anyone, including Ahan, got the better of you. It does a man good to realize he can still be taken by surprise once in a while."

"She nearly lost it near the end there, though," Roial said. "I don't like being backed into corners, Kiin."

"It was a calculated risk, my lord," Sarene said, pushing open the door and strolling in.

Her appearance didn't give the duke even a moment's pause. "You all but threatened me, Sarene. That is no way to make an ally—especially of a crotchety old man such as myself." The duke and Kiin were sharing a bottle of Fjordell wine at the kitchen table, and their manner was even more relaxed than the dinner had been. "A few days wouldn't have hurt our position, and I certainly would have given you my support. I've found that thoughtful, well-considered commitment is much more productive than spurious professions."

Sarene nodded, slipping a glass from one of Kiin's shelves and pouring herself some wine before sitting. "I understand, Roial." If he could drop formalities, then so could she. "But the others look to you. They trust your judgment. I needed more than your support—which, by the way, I know you would have given—I needed your *open* support. The others had to see you accept the plan before they would agree. It wouldn't have had the same impact a few days later."

"Perhaps," Roial said. "One thing is certain, Sarene—you give us hope again. Raoden was our unity before; now you will take his place. Kiin or I couldn't do it. Kiin has refused nobility for too long—no matter what they say, the people still want a leader with a title. And me . . . they all know that I helped Iadon start this monstrosity that has slowly killed our country."

"That was long ago, Roial," Kiin said clasping the elderly duke on the shoulder.

"No," Roial said with a shake of his head. "As the fair princess said, ten years isn't long in the life span of nations. I am guilty of a grave mistake."

"We will make it right, Roial," Kiin said. "This plan is a good one—perhaps even better than Raoden's."

Roial smiled. "She would have made him a fine wife, Kiin."

Kiin nodded. "Fine indeed—and an even better queen. Domi moves in ways that are sometimes strange to our mortal minds."

"I'm not convinced it was Domi's will that took him from us, Uncle," Sarene said over her wine. "Have either of you ever wondered if, perhaps, someone might have been behind the prince's death?"

"The answer to that question borders on treason, Sarene," Kiin warned.

"Any more than the other things we have said tonight?"

"We were only accusing the king of greed, Sarene," Roial said. "The murder of his own son is another matter entirely."

"Think about it, though," Sarene said, waving her hand in a wide gesture, and nearly spilling her wine. "The prince took a contrary stance on everything his father did—he ridiculed Iadon in court, he planned behind the king's back, and he had the love of the people. Most importantly, everything he said about Iadon was true. Is that the kind of person a monarch can afford to have running free?"

"Yes, but his own son?" Roial said with a disbelieving shake of his head.

"It wouldn't be the first time such a thing has happened," Kiin said.

"True," Roial said. "But, I don't know if the prince was as much of a problem to Iadon as you assume. Raoden wasn't so much rebellious as he was critical. He never said that Iadon shouldn't be king, he simply claimed that Arelon's government was in trouble—which it is."

"Weren't either of you even a little suspicious when you heard the prince was dead?" Sarene asked, contemplatively sipping her wine. "It came at such a convenient time. Iadon has the benefit of an alliance with Teod, but now he doesn't have to worry about Raoden producing any heirs."

Roial looked at Kiin, who shrugged. "I think we have to at least consider the possibility, Roial."

Roial nodded regretfully. "So what do we do? Try and find proof that Iadon executed his son?"

"Knowledge will bring strength," Sarene said simply.

"Agreed," Kiin said. "You, however, are the only one of us with free access to the palace."

"I'll poke around and see what I can uncover."

"Is it possible he isn't dead?" Roial asked. "It would have been easy enough to find a look-alike for the casket—the coughing shivers is a very disfiguring disease."

"It's possible," Sarene said doubtfully.

"But you don't believe it."

Sarene shook her head. "When a monarch decides to destroy a rival, he usually makes sure to do so in a permanent way. There are too many stories about lost heirs that reappear after twenty years in the wilderness to claim their rightful throne."

"Still, perhaps Iadon isn't as brutal as you assume," Roial said. "He was a better man, once—never what I would call a good man, but not a bad one either. Just greedy. Something's happened to him over the last few years, something that has . . . changed him. Still, I think there remains enough compassion in Iadon to keep him from murdering his own son."

"All right," Sarene said. "I'll send Ashe to search through

the royal dungeons. He's so meticulous he'll know the name of every rat in the place before he's satisfied."

"Your Seon?" Roial realized. "Where is he?"

"I sent him to Elantris."

"Elantris?" Kiin asked.

"That Fjordell gyorn is interested in Elantris for some reason," Sarene explained. "And I make it my business never to ignore what a gyorn finds interesting."

"You seem to be rather preoccupied with a single priest, 'Ene," Kiin said.

"Not a priest, Uncle," Sarene corrected. "A full gyorn."

"Still only one man. How much damage can he do?"

"Ask the Duladen Republic," Sarene said. "I think this is the same gyorn who was involved in that disaster."

"There's no sure evidence that Fjorden was behind the collapse," Roial noted.

"There is in Teod, but no one else would believe it. Just believe me when I tell you that this single gyorn could be more dangerous than Iadon."

The comment struck a lull in the conversation. Time passed silently, the three nobles drinking their wine in thought until Lukel entered, having traveled to retrieve his mother and siblings. He nodded to Sarene and bowed to the duke before pouring himself a cup of wine.

"Look at you," Lukel said to Sarene as he took a seat. "A confident member of the boys' club."

"Leader of it, more truthfully," Roial noted.

"Your mother?" Kiin asked.

"Is on her way," Lukel said. "They weren't finished, and you know how Mother is. Everything must be done in its proper order; no rushing allowed."

Kiin nodded, downing the last of his wine. "Then you and I should get to cleaning before she returns. We wouldn't want her to see what a mess our collected noble friends have made of the dining room."

Lukel sighed, giving Sarene a look that suggested he sometimes wished he lived in a traditional household—one with servants, or at least women, to do such things. Kiin was already moving, however, and his son had no choice but to follow.

"Interesting family," Roial said, watching them go.

"Yes. A little odd even by Teoish standards."

"Kiin had a long life on his own," the duke observed. "It accustomed him to doing things by himself. He once hired a cook, I hear, but grew frustrated with the woman's methods. I seem to recall that she quit before he had the heart to fire her—she claimed she couldn't work in such a demanding environment."

Sarene laughed. "That sounds appropriate."

Roial smiled, but continued in a more serious tone. "Sarene, we are indeed fortunate. You might very well be our last chance for saving Arelon."

"Thank you, Your Grace," Sarene said, flushing despite herself.

"This country will not last much longer. A few months, maybe, a half a year if we are lucky."

Sarene's brow furled. "But, I thought you wanted to wait. At least, that's what you told the others."

Roial made a dismissive gesture. "I'd convinced myself that little could be gained by their aid—Edan and Ahan are too contrary, and Shuden and Eondel are both too inexperienced. I wanted to mollify them while Kiin and I decided what to do. I fear our plans may have centered around more . . . dangerous methods.

"Now, however, there is another chance. If your plan works—though I'm still not convinced that it will—we might be able to forestall collapse for a little longer. I'm not sure; ten years of Iadon's rule has built momentum. It will be difficult to change it in only a few months' time."

"I think we can do it, Roial," Sarene said.

"Just make sure you don't get ahead of yourself, young lady," Roial said, eyeing her. "Do not dash if you only have the strength to walk, and do not waste your time pushing on walls that will not give. More importantly, don't shove where a pat would be sufficient. You backed me into a corner today. I'm still a prideful old man. If Shuden hadn't saved me, I honestly can't say if I would have been humble enough to acknowledge fault in front of all those men."

"I'm sorry," Sarene said, now blushing for another reason. There was something about this powerful, yet grandfatherly, old duke that made her suddenly desperate to have his respect.

"Just be careful," Roial said. "If this gyorn is as dangerous as you claim, then there are some very powerful forces moving through Kae. Do not let Arelon get crushed between them."

Sarene nodded, and the duke leaned back, pouring the last of the wine into his cup.

CHAPTER 12

ARLY in his career, Hrathen had found it difficult to accept other languages. Fjordell was Jaddeth's own chosen tongue—it was holy, while other languages were profane. How, then, did one convert those who didn't speak Fjordell? Did one speak to them in their own language, or did one force all true supplicants to study Fjordell first? It seemed foolish to require an entire nation to learn a new language before allowing them to hear of Jaddeth's empire.

So, when forced to make the decision between profanity and infinite delay, Hrathen chose profanity. He had learned to speak Aonic and Duladen, and had even picked up a little Jindoeese. When he taught, he taught the people in their own tongue—though, admittedly, it still bothered him to do so. What if they never learned? What if his actions made people think that they didn't need Fjordell, since they could learn of Jaddeth in their mother language?

These thoughts, and many like them, passed through Hrathen's mind as he preached to the people of Kae. It wasn't that he lacked focus or dedication; he had simply given the same speeches so many times that they had become rote. He spoke almost unconsciously, raising and lowering his voice to the rhythm of the sermon, performing the ancient art that was a hybrid offspring of prayer and theater.

When he urged, they responded with cheers. When he condemned, they looked at one another with shame. When he raised his voice, they focused their attention, and when he lowered it to a bare whisper, they were even more captivated. It was as if he controlled the ocean waves themselves, emotion surging through the crowd like froth-covered tides.

He finished with a stunning admonition to serve in Jaddeth's kingdom, to swear themselves as odiv or krondet to one of the priests in Kae, thereby becoming part of the chain that linked them directly to Lord Jaddeth. The common people served the arteths and dorven, the arteths and dorven served the gradors, the gradors served the ragnats, the ragnats served the gyorns, the gyorns served Wyrn, and Wyrn served Jaddeth. Only the gragdets—leaders of the monasteries—weren't directly in the line. It was a superbly organized system. Everyone knew whom he or she had to serve; most didn't need to worry about the commands of Jaddeth, which were often above their understanding. All they had to do was follow their arteth, serve him as best they could, and Jaddeth would be pleased with them.

Hrathen stepped down from the podium, satisfied. He had only been preaching in Kae for a few days, but the chapel was already so packed that people had to line up at the back once the seats were full. Only a few of the newcomers were actually interested in converting; most came because Hrathen himself was a novelty. However, they would return. They could tell themselves that they were only curious—that their interest had nothing to do with religion—but they *would* return.

As Shu-Dereth grew more popular in Kae, the people at these first meetings would find themselves important by association. They would brag that they had discovered Shu-Dereth long before their neighbors, and as a consequence they would have to continue attending. Their pride, mixed with Hrathen's powerful sermons, would override doubts, and soon they would find themselves swearing servitude to one of the arteths.

Hrathen would have to call a new head arteth soon. He'd put off the decision for a time, waiting to see how the priests remaining in the chapel dealt with their tasks. Time was growing slim, however, and soon the local membership would be too great for Hrathen to track and organize by himself, especially considering all of the planning and preaching he had to do.

The people at the back were beginning to file out of the chapel. However, a sudden sound stopped them. Hrathen looked up at the podium with surprise. The meeting was to have ended after his sermon, but someone thought differently. Dilaf had decided to speak.

The short Arelish man screamed his words with fiery energy. In barely a few seconds, the crowd grew hushed, most of the people sliding back into their seats. They had seen Dilaf following Hrathen, and most of them probably knew he was an arteth, but Dilaf had never addressed them before. Now, however, he made himself impossible to ignore.

He disobeyed all of the rules of public speaking. He didn't vary the loudness of his voice, nor did he look members of the audience in the eyes. He didn't maintain a stately, upright posture to appear in control; instead he hopped across the podium energetically, gesturing wildly. His face was covered with sweat; his eyes were wide and haunting.

And they listened.

They listened more acutely than they had to Hrathen. They followed Dilaf's insane jumps with their eyes, transfixed by his every unorthodox motion. Dilaf's speech had a single theme: hatred of Elantris. Hrathen could feel the audience's zeal growing. Dilaf's passion worked like a catalyst, like a mold that spread uncontrollably once it found a dank place to grow. Soon the entire audience shared in his loathing, and they screamed along with his denunciations.

Hrathen watched with concern and, admittedly, jealousy. Unlike Hrathen, Dilaf hadn't been trained in the greatest schools of the East. However, the short priest had something Hrathen lacked. Passion.

Hrathen had always been a calculating man. He was organized, careful, and attentive to detail. Similar things in Shu-Dereth—its standardized, orderly method of governing along with its logical philosophy—were what had first attracted him to the priesthood. He had never doubted the church. Something so perfectly organized couldn't help but be right.

Despite that loyalty, Hrathen had never felt what Dilaf now expressed. Hrathen had no hatreds so severe that he wept, no loves so profound that he would risk everything in their name. He had always believed that he was the perfect follower of Jaddeth; that his Lord needed levelheadedness more than He needed unbridled ardor. Now, however, he wondered.

Dilaf had more power over this audience than Hrathen ever had. Dilaf's hatred of Elantris wasn't logical—it was irrational and feral—but they didn't care. Hrathen could spend years explaining to them the benefits of Shu-Dereth and never get the reaction they now expressed. Part of him scoffed, trying to convince himself that the power of Dilaf's words wouldn't last, that the passion of the moment would be lost in the mundanity of life—but another, more truthful part of him was simply envious. What was wrong with Hrathen that, in thirty years of serving Jaddeth's kingdom, he had never once felt as Dilaf seemed to at every moment?

Eventually, the arteth fell silent. The room remained completely quiet for a long moment after Dilaf's speech. Then they burst into discussion, excited, speaking as they began to trail from the chapel. Dilaf stumbled off the podium and collapsed onto one of the pews near the front of the room.

"That was well done," a voice noted from beside Hrathen. Duke Telrii watched the sermons from a private booth at the side of the chapel. "Having the short man speak after yourself was a wonderful move, Hrathen. I was worried when I saw people growing bored. The young priest refocused everyone's attention."

Hrathen hid his annoyance at Telrii's use of his name rather than his title; there would be time to change such disrespect at a later date. He also restrained himself from making a comment about the audience's supposed boredom during his sermon.

"Dilaf is a rare young man," Hrathen said instead. "There are two sides to every argument, Lord Telrii: the logical and the passionate. We have to make our attack from both directions if we are to be victorious."

Telrii nodded.

"So, my lord, have you considered my proposal?"

Telrii hesitated for a moment, then nodded again. "It is tempting, Hrathen. Very tempting. I don't think there is any man in Arelon who could refuse it, let alone myself."

"Good. I will contact Fjorden. We should be able to begin within the week."

Telrii nodded, the birthmark on his neck looking like a large bruise in the shadows. Then, gesturing to his numerous attendants, the duke made his way out the side door to the chapel, disappearing into the twilight. Hrathen watched the door shut, then walked over to Dilaf, who was still sprawled on the pew.

"That was unexpected, Arteth," he said. "You should have spoken with me first."

"It was not planned, my lord," Dilaf explained. "I suddenly felt the need to speak. It was only done in your service, my hroden."

"Of course," Hrathen said, dissatisfied. Telrii was right: Dilaf's addition had been valuable. As much as Hrathen wanted to reproach the arteth, he could not. He would be negligent in his service to Wyrn if he didn't use every tool at his command to convert the people of Arelon, and Dilaf had proven himself a very useful tool. Hrathen would need the arteth to speak at later meetings. Once again, Dilaf had left him without many choices.

"Well, it is done," Hrathen said with calculated dismissiveness. "And they appear to have liked it. Perhaps I will have you speak again sometime. However, you must remember your place, Arteth. You are my odiv; you do not act unless I specifically tell you. Is that understood?"

"Perfectly, my lord Hrathen."

HRATHEN quietly shut the door to his personal chambers. Dilaf was not there; Hrathen would never let him see what was about to take place. In this Hrathen could still feel superior to the young Arelish priest. Dilaf would never rise to the highest ranks of the priesthood, for he could never do what Hrathen was about to do—something known only to the gyorns and Wyrn.

Hrathen sat in his chair quietly, preparing himself. Only after a half hour of meditation did he feel controlled enough to act. Taking a measured breath, Hrathen rose from his seat and moved to the large trunk in the corner of his room. It was topped with a stack of folded tapestries, carefully draped to obscure. Hrathen moved the tapestries reverently, then reached beneath his shirt to pull forth the gold chain that encircled his neck. At the end of the chain was a small key. With this he opened the trunk, revealing the contents— a small metal box.

The box was about the size of four stacked books, and its weight rested heavily in Hrathen's hands as he lifted it from the trunk. Its sides had been constructed of the best steel, and on its front was a small dial and several delicate levers. The mechanism had been designed by Svorden's finest locksmiths. Only Hrathen and Wyrn knew the proper method of turning and twisting that would open the box.

Hrathen spun the dial and turned the levers in a pattern he had memorized soon after being appointed to the position of gyorn. The combination had never been written down. It would be a source of extreme embarrassment to Shu-Dereth if anyone outside the inner priesthood discovered what was inside this box.

The lock clicked, and Hrathen pulled the top open with a firm hand. A small glowing ball sat patiently inside.

"You need me, my lord?" the Seon asked in a soft, feminine voice.

"Be quiet!" Hrathen ordered. "You know you are not to speak."

The ball of light bobbed submissively. It had been months since Hrathen had last opened the box, but the Seon showed no signs of rebelliousness. The creatures—or whatever they were—seemed to be unfailingly obedient.

The Seons had been Hrathen's greatest shock upon his appointment to the rank of gyorn. Not that he had been surprised to find that the creatures were real—though many in the East dismissed Seons as Aonic myths, Hrathen had, by that time, been taught that there were . . . things in the world that were not understood by normal people. The memories of his early years in Dakhor still caused him to shiver in fear.

No, Hrathen's surprise had come in discovering that Wyrn would consent to using heathen magics to further Jaddeth's empire. Wyrn himself had explained the necessity of using Seons, but it had taken years for Hrathen to accept the idea. In the end, logic had swayed him. Just as it was sometimes necessary to speak in heathen languages to preach Jaddeth's empire, there were instances where the enemy's arts proved valuable.

Of course, only those with the most self-control and holiness could use the Seons without being tainted. Gyorns used them to contact Wyrn when in a far country, and they did so infrequently. Instantaneous communication across such distances was a resource worth the price.

"Get me Wyrn," Hrathen ordered. The Seon complied, hovering up a bit, questing with its abilities to seek out Wyrn's own hidden Seon—one attended at all times by a mute servant, whose only sacred duty was to watch over the creature.

Hrathen eyed the Seon as he waited. The Seon hovered patiently. It always *appeared* obedient; indeed, the other gyorns didn't even seem to question the loyalty of the creatures. They claimed it was part of the Seons' magic to be faithful to their masters, even if those masters detested them.

Hrathen wasn't quite as certain. Seons could contact others of their kind, and they apparently didn't need half as much sleep as men. What did the Seons do, while their masters slept? What secrets did they discuss? At one point, most of the nobility in Duladel, Arelon, Teod, and even Jindo had kept Seons. During those days, how many state secrets had been witnessed, and perhaps gossiped about, by the unobtrusive floating balls?

He shook his head. It was a good thing those days were past. Out of favor because of their association with fallen Elantris, prevented from any further reproduction by the loss of Elantrian magics, the Seons were growing more and more rare. Once Fjorden conquered the West, Hrathen doubted one would ever see Seons floating around freely again.

His Seon began to drip like water, and then it formed into Wyrn's proud face. Noble, squareish features regarded Hrathen.

"I am here, my son." Wyrn's voice floated through the Seon.

"O great lord and master, Jaddeth's anointed, and emperor in the light of His favor," Hrathen said, bowing his head.

"Speak on, my odiv."

"I have a proposal involving one of the lords of Arelon, great one. . . ."

CHAPTER 13

"THIS is it!" Raoden exclaimed. "Galladon, get over here!" The large Dula set down his own book with raised eyebrows, then stood with his characteristic relaxed style and wandered over to Raoden. "What have you found, sule?"

Raoden pointed to the coverless book in front of him. He sat in the former Korathi church that had become their center of operations. Galladon, still determined to keep his small book-filled study a secret, had insisted that they lug the necessary volumes up to the chapel rather than let anyone else into his sanctuary.

"Sule, I can't read that," Galladon protested, looking down at the book. "It's written completely in Aons."

"That's what made me suspicious," Raoden said.

"Can *you* read it?" Galladon asked.

"No," Raoden said with a smile. "But I do have this." He

reached down and pulled out a similar coverless volume, its cover pages stained with Elantris grime. "A dictionary of the Aons."

Galladon studied the first book with a critical eye. "Sule, I don't even recognize a tenth of the Aons on this page. Do you have any idea how long it's going to take you to translate it?"

Raoden shrugged. "It's better than searching for clues in those other books. Galladon, if I have to read one more word about the landscape of Fjorden, I am going to be sick."

Galladon grunted his agreement. Whoever had owned the books before the Reod must have been a geography scholar, for at least half of the volumes dealt with the topic.

"You're sure this is the one we want?" Galladon asked.

"I've had a little training in reading pure Aon texts, my friend," Raoden said, pointing at an Aon on a page near the beginning of the book. "This says AonDor."

Galladon nodded. "All right, sule. I don't envy you the task, however. Life would be much simpler if it hadn't taken your people so long to invent an alphabet. Kolo?"

"The Aons were an alphabet," Raoden said. "Just an incredibly complex one. This won't take as long as you think—my schooling should start to come back to me after a little while."

"Sule, sometimes you're so optimistic it's sickening. I suppose then we should cart these other books back to where we got them?" There was a measure of anxiety in Galladon's voice. The books were precious to him; it had taken Raoden a good hour of arguing to convince the Dula to let him take off their covers, and he could see how much it bothered the larger man to have the books exposed to the slime and dirt of Elantris.

"That should be all right," Raoden said. None of the other books were about AonDor, and while some of them were journals or other records that could hold clues, Raoden suspected that none of them would be as useful as the one in front of him. Assuming he could translate it successfully.

Galladon nodded and began gathering up the books; then he looked upward apprehensively as he heard a scraping sound from the roof. Galladon was convinced that sooner or later the entire assemblage would collapse and, inevitably, fall on his shiny dark head.

"Don't worry so much, Galladon," Raoden said. "Maare and Riil know what they're doing."

Galladon frowned. "No they don't, sule. I seem to recall that neither of them had any idea what to do before you pressed them into it."

"I meant that they're competent." Raoden looked up with satisfaction. Six days of working had completed a large portion of the roof. Mareshe had devised a claylike combination of wood scraps, soil, and the ever-prevalent Elantris sludge. This mixture, when added to the fallen support beams and some less-rotted sections of cloth, had provided materials to make a ceiling that was, if not superior, at least adequate.

Raoden smiled. The pain and hunger were always there, but things were going so well that he could almost forget the pain of his half-dozen bumps and cuts. Through the window to his right he could see the newest member of his band, Loren. The man worked in the large area beside the church that had probably once been a garden. According to Raoden's orders, and equipped with a newly fashioned pair of leather gloves, Loren moved rocks and cleared away refuse, revealing the soft dirt underneath.

"What good is that going to do?" Galladon asked, following Raoden's gaze out the window.

"You'll see," Raoden said with a secretive smile.

Galladon huffed as he picked up an armload of books and left the chapel. The Dula had been right about one thing: They could not count on new Elantrians being thrown into the city as fast as Raoden had first anticipated. Before Loren's arrival the day before, five solid days had passed without even a quiver from the city gates. Raoden had been very fortunate to find Mareshe and the others in such a short period of time.

"Lord Spirit?" a hesitant voice asked.

Raoden looked up at the chapel's doorway to find an unfamiliar man waiting to be acknowledged. He was thin, with a stooped-over form and an air of practiced subservience. Raoden couldn't tell his age for certain; the Shaod tended to make everyone look much older than they really were.

However, he had the feeling that this man's age was no illusion. If his head had held any hair, then it would have been white, and his skin had been long wrinkled before the Shaod took him.

"Yes?" Raoden asked with interest. "What can I do for you?"

"My lord . . ." the man began.

"Go on," Raoden prodded.

"Well, Your Lordship, I've just heard some things, and I was wondering if I could join with you."

Raoden smiled, rising and walking over to the man. "Certainly, you may join us. What have you heard?"

"Well . . ." The aged Elantrian fidgeted nervously. "Some people on the streets say that those who follow you aren't as hungry. They say you have a secret that makes the pain go away. I've been in Elantris for nearly a year now, my lord, and my injuries are almost too much. I figured I could either give you a chance, or go find myself a gutter and join the Hoed."

Raoden nodded, clasping the man on the shoulder. He could still feel his toe burning—he was growing used to the pain, but it was still there. It was accompanied by a gnawing from his stomach. "I'm glad you came. What is your name?"

"Kahar, my lord."

"All right then, Kahar, what did you do before the Shaod took you?"

Kahar's eyes grew unfocused, as if his mind were traveling back to a time long ago. "I was a cleaner of some sort, my lord. I think I washed streets."

"Perfect! I've been waiting for one of your particular skill. Mareshe, are you back there?"

"Yes, my lord," the spindly artisan called from one of the rooms in the back. His head poked out a moment later.

"By chance, did those traps you set up catch any of last night's rainfall?"

"Of course, my lord," Mareshe said indignantly.

"Good. Show Kahar here where the water is."

"Certainly." Mareshe motioned for Kahar to follow.

"What am I to do with water, my lord?" Kahar asked.

"It is time that we stopped living in filth, Kahar," Raoden

said. "This slime that covers Elantris can be cleaned off; I've seen a place where it was done. Take your time and don't strain yourself, but clean this building inside and out. Scrape away every bit of slime and wash off every hint of dirt."

"Then you will show me the secret?" Kahar asked hopefully.

"Trust me."

Kahar nodded, following Mareshe from the room. Raoden's smile faded as the man left. He was finding that the most difficult part of leadership here in Elantris was maintaining the attitude of optimism that Galladon teased him about. These people, even the newcomers, were dangerously close to losing hope. They thought that they were damned, and assumed that nothing could save their souls from rotting away like Elantris itself. Raoden had to overcome years of conditioning teamed with the ever-present forces of pain and hunger.

He had never considered himself an overly cheerful person. Here in Elantris, however, Raoden found himself reacting to the air of despair with defiant optimism. The worse things got, the more determined he was to take it on without complaint. But the forced cheerfulness took its toll. He could feel the others, even Galladon, relying on him. Of all the people in Elantris, only Raoden couldn't let his pain show. The hunger gnawed at his chest like a horde of insects trying to escape from within, and the pain of several injuries beat at his resolve with merciless determination.

He wasn't sure how long he would last. After barely a week and a half in Elantris, he was already in so much pain it was sometimes difficult to focus. How long would it be before he couldn't function at all? Or, how long before he was reduced to the subhuman level of Shaor's men? One question was more frightening than them all. When he fell, how many people would fall with him?

And yet, he had to bear the weight. If he didn't accept the responsibility, no one else would—and these people would become slaves either to their own agony or to the bullies on the streets. Elantris needed him. If it used him up, then so be it.

"Lord Spirit!" called a frantic voice.

Raoden looked as a worried Saolin rushed into the room. The hook-nosed mercenary had fashioned a spear from a piece of only half-rotten wood and a sharp stone, and had taken to patrolling the area around the chapel. The man's scarred Elantrian face was wrinkled with concern.

"What is it, Saolin?" Raoden asked, alarmed. The man was an experienced warrior, and was not easily unsettled.

"A group of armed men coming this way, my lord. I counted twelve of them, and they are carrying steel weapons."

"Steel?" Raoden said. "In Elantris? I wasn't aware that there was any to be found."

"They're coming quickly, my lord," Saolin said. "What do we do—they're almost here."

"They *are* here," Raoden said as a group of men forced their way through the chapel's open doorway. Saolin was right: several carried steel weapons, though the blades were chipped and rusted. The group was a dark-eyed, unpleasant lot, and at their lead was a familiar figure—or, at least, familiar from a distance.

"Karata," Raoden said. Loren should have been hers the other day, but Raoden had stolen him. Apparently, she had come to make a complaint. It had only been a matter of time.

Raoden glanced toward Saolin, who was inching forward as if anxious to try his makeshift spear. "Stand your ground, Saolin," Raoden commanded.

Karata was completely bald, a gift from the Shaod, and she had been in the city long enough that her skin was beginning to wrinkle. However, she held herself with a proud face and determined eyes—the eyes of a person who hadn't given in to the pain, and who wasn't going to do so any time soon. She wore a dark outfit composed of torn leather—for Elantris, it was well made.

Karata turned her head around the chapel, studying the new ceiling, then the members of Raoden's band, who had gathered outside the window to watch with apprehension. Mareshe and Kahar stood immobile at the back of the room. Finally, Karata turned her gaze on Raoden.

There was a tense pause. Eventually, Karata turned to one

of her men. "Destroy the building, chase them out, and break some bones." She turned to leave.

"I can get you into Iadon's palace," Raoden said quietly.

Karata froze.

"That is what you want, isn't it?" Raoden asked. "The Elantris City Guards caught you in Kae. They won't suffer you forever—they burn Elantrians who escape too often. If you really want to get into the palace, I can take you there."

"We'll never get out of the city," Karata said, turning skeptical eyes back on him. "They've doubled the guard recently; something to do with looking good for a royal wedding. I haven't even been able to get out in a month."

"I can get you out of the city too," Raoden promised.

Karata's eyes narrowed with suspicion. There was no talk of price. They both knew that Raoden could demand only one thing: to be left alone. "You're desperate," she finally concluded.

"True. But I'm also an opportunist."

Karata nodded slowly. "I will return at nightfall. You will deliver as promised, or my men will break the limbs of every person here and leave them to rot in their agony."

"Understood."

"SULE, I—"

"Don't think this is a good idea," Raoden finished with a slight smile. "Yes, Galladon, I know."

"Elantris is a big city," Galladon said. "There are plenty of places to hide that not even Karata could find us. She can't spread herself too thin, otherwise Shaor and Aanden will attack her. Kolo?"

"Yes, but what then?" Raoden asked, trying the strength of a rope Mareshe had fashioned from some rags. It seemed like it would hold his weight. "Karata wouldn't be able to find us, but neither would anyone else. People are finally beginning to realize we're here. If we move now, we'll never grow."

Galladon looked pained. "Sule, do we have to grow? Do you have to start another gang? Aren't three warlords enough?"

Raoden stopped, looking up at the large Dula with concern. "Galladon, is that really what you think I am doing?"

"I don't know, sule."

"I have no wish for power, Galladon," Raoden said flatly. "I am worried about life. Not just survival, Galladon, *life*. These people are dead because they have given up, not because their hearts no longer beat. I am going to change that."

"Sule, it's impossible."

"So is getting Karata into Iadon's palace," Raoden said, pulling the rope into a coil around his arm. "I'll see you when I get back."

"WHAT is this?" Karata asked suspiciously.

"It's the city well," Raoden explained, peering over the side of the stone lip. The well went deep, but he could hear water moving in the darkness below.

"You expect us to swim out?"

"No," Raoden said, tying Mareshe's rope to a rusted iron rod jutting from the well's side. "We'll just let the current take us along. More like floating than swimming."

"That's insane—that river runs underground. We'll drown."

"We can't drown," Raoden said. "As my friend Galladon is fond of saying, 'Already dead. Kolo?'"

Karata didn't look convinced.

"The Aredel River runs directly underneath Elantris, then continues on to Kae," Raoden explained. "It runs around the city and past the palace. All we have to do is let it drag us. I've already tried holding my breath; I went an entire half hour, and my lungs didn't even burn. Our blood doesn't flow anymore, so the only reason we need air is to talk."

"This could destroy us both," Karata warned.

Raoden shrugged. "The hunger would just take us in a few months anyway."

Karata smiled slightly. "All right, Spirit. You go first."

"Gladly," Raoden said, not feeling glad about that particular fact at all. Still, it was his idea. With a rueful shake of his head, Raoden swung over the side of the lip and began to lower himself. The rope ran out before he touched water and so, taking a deep but ineffectual breath, he let go.

He splashed into a shockingly cold river. The current threatened to pull him away, but he quickly grabbed hold of a rock and held himself steady, waiting for Karata. Her voice soon sounded in the darkness above.

"Spirit?"

"I'm here. You're about ten feet above the river—you'll have to drop the rest of the way."

"And then?"

"Then the river continues underground—I can feel it sucking me down right now. We'll just have to hope it's wide enough the entire distance, otherwise we'll end up as eternal subterranean plugs."

"You could have mentioned that before I got down here," Karata said nervously. However, a splash soon sounded, followed by a quiet groan that ended in a gurgle as something large was sucked past Raoden in the current.

Muttering a prayer to Merciful Domi, Raoden released the rock and let the river drag him beneath its unseen surface.

RAODEN did indeed have to swim. The trick was to keep himself in the middle of the river, lest he be slammed against the rock tunnel's walls. He did his best as he moved in the blackness, using outspread arms to position himself. Fortunately, time had smoothed the rocks to the point that they bruised rather than sliced.

An eternity passed in that silent underworld. It was as if he floated through darkness itself, unable to speak, completely alone. Perhaps this was what death would bring, his soul set adrift in an endless, lightless void.

The current changed, pulling him upward. He moved his arms to brace himself against the stone roof, but they met no resistance. A short moment later his head broke into open air, his wet face cold in the passing wind. He blinked uncertainly as the world focused, starlight and the occasional street lantern granting only dim illumination. It was enough to restore his orientation—and, perhaps, his sanity.

He floated lethargically; the river grew wide after rising to the surface, and the current slowed considerably. He felt a form approach in the water, and he tried to speak, but his lungs were full. He only succeeded in vocalizing a loud, un-controllable fit of coughing.

A hand clamped around his mouth, cutting off his cough with a gurgle.

"Quiet, fool!" Karata hissed.

Raoden nodded, struggling to control his fit. Perhaps he should have concentrated less on the theological metaphors of the trip, and more on keeping his mouth closed.

Karata released his mouth, but continued to hold on to his shoulder, keeping them together as they drifted past the city of Kae. Its shops were closed for the night, but an occasional guard patrolled the streets. The two continued to float in silence until they reached the northern edge of the city, where Iadon's castle-like palace rose in the night. Then, still not speaking, they swam to the shore beside the palace.

The palace was a dark, sullen edifice—a manifestation of Iadon's one insecurity. Raoden's father was not often afraid; in fact, he was often belligerent when he should have been intelligently apprehensive. The trait had earned him wealth as a businessman trading with the Fjordell, but it had brought him failure as a king. In one thing only was Iadon paranoid: sleeping. The king was terrified that assassins would somehow sneak in and murder him as he slumbered. Raoden remembered well his father's irrational muttering on the subject each night before retiring. The worries of kingship had only made Iadon worse, causing him to outfit his already fortresslike house with a battalion of guards. The soldiers lived near Iadon's own quarters to facilitate quick response.

"All right," Karata whispered, watching uncertainly as guards crossed on the battlements, "you got us out. Now get us in."

Raoden nodded, trying to drain his sodden lungs as silently as possible—an act not accomplished without a fair bit of muffled retching.

"Try not to cough so much," Karata advised. "You'll irritate your throat and make your chest sore, and then you'll spend eternity feeling like you have a cold."

Raoden groaned, pushing himself to his feet. "We need to get to the west side," he said, his voice a croak.

Karata nodded. She walked silently and quickly—much

more so than Raoden could manage—like a person well acquainted with danger. Several times she put back her hand in warning, halting their progress just before a squad of guards appeared out of the darkness. Her aptitude gained them the western side of Iadon's palace without mishap, despite Raoden's lack of skill.

"Now what?" she asked quietly.

Raoden paused. A question now confronted him. Why did Karata want access to the palace? From what Raoden had heard of her, she didn't seem like the type to exact revenge. She was brutal, but not vindictive. But, what if he were wrong? What if she did want Iadon's blood?

"Well?" Karata asked.

I won't let her kill my father, he decided. *No matter how poor a king he is, I won't let her do that.* "You have to answer something for me first."

"Now?" she asked with annoyance.

Raoden nodded. "I need to know why you want into the palace."

She frowned in the darkness. "You aren't in any position to make demands."

"Nor are you in any position to refuse them," Raoden said. "All I have to do is raise an alarm, and we'll both be taken by the guards."

Karata waited quietly in the darkness, obviously debating whether or not he would do it.

"Look," Raoden said. "Just tell me one thing. Do you intend to harm the king?"

Karata met his eyes, then shook her head. "My quibble is not with him."

Do I believe her, or not? Raoden thought. *Do I have a choice?*

He reached over, pulling back a patch of bushes that abutted the wall; then he threw his weight against one of the stones. The stone sank into the wall with a quiet grinding noise, and a section of ground fell away before them.

Karata raised her eyebrows. "A secret passage? How quaint."

"Iadon is a paranoid sleeper," Raoden explained, crawling through the small space between ground and wall. "He had this passage installed to give him one last means of escape should someone attack his palace."

Karata snorted as she followed him through the hole. "I thought things like this only existed in children's tales."

"Iadon likes those tales quite a bit," Raoden said.

The passage widened after a dozen feet, and Raoden felt along the wall until he found a lantern, complete with flint and steel. He kept the shield mostly closed, releasing only a sliver of light, but it was enough to reveal the narrow, dust-filled passage.

"You seem to have quite an extensive knowledge of the palace," Karata observed.

Raoden didn't answer, unable to think of a response that wasn't too revealing. His father had shown the passage to Raoden when he had barely been into his teenage years, and Raoden and his friends had found it an instant and irresistible attraction. Ignoring cautions that the passage was only for emergencies, Raoden and Lukel had spent hours playing inside of it.

The passage seemed smaller now, of course. There was barely enough room for Raoden and Karata to maneuver. "Come," he said, holding the lantern aloft and inching sideways through the passageway. The trip to Iadon's rooms took less time than he remembered; it really wasn't much of a passage, despite what his imagination had claimed. It slanted upward to the second floor at a steep angle, heading straight to Iadon's room.

"This is it," Raoden said as they reached the end. "Iadon should be in bed by now, and—despite his paranoia—he is a deep sleeper. Perhaps the one causes the other." He slid open the door, which was hidden behind a tapestry in the royal sleeping chamber. Iadon's massive bed was dark and quiet, though the open window provided enough starlight to see that the king was, in fact, present.

Raoden grew tense, eyeing Karata. The woman, however, held to her word: she barely gave the slumbering king a passing glance as she moved through the room and into the outer hallway. Raoden sighed in quiet relief, following her with a less practiced gait of stealth.

The darkened outer hallway connected Iadon's rooms with those of his guards. The right path led toward the guard barracks; the left led to a guard post, then the rest of the palace. Karata turned away from this option, continuing down the right hallway to the barrack annex, her bare feet making no sound on the stone floor.

Raoden followed her into the barracks, his nervousness returning. She had decided not to kill his father, but now she was sneaking into the most dangerous part of the palace. A single misplaced sound would wake dozens of soldiers.

Fortunately, sneaking down a stone hallway didn't require much skill. Karata quietly opened any doors in their path, leaving them open enough that Raoden didn't even have to move them to slip through.

The dark hallway joined with another, this one lined with doors—the quarters of the lesser officers, as well as those guards allowed room to raise a family. Karata picked a door. Inside was the single room allotted to a married guard's family; starlight illuminated a bed by one wall and a dresser beside the other.

Raoden fidgeted anxiously, wondering if all this had been so Karata could procure herself a sleeping guard's weapons. If so, she was insane. Of course, sneaking into a paranoid king's palace wasn't exactly a sign of mental stability.

As Karata moved into the room, Raoden realized that she couldn't have come to steal the guard's accouterments—he wasn't there. The bed was empty, its sheets wrinkled with a slept-in look. Karata stooped beside something that Raoden hadn't noticed at first: a mattress on the floor, occupied by a small lump that could only have been a sleeping child, its features and sex lost to Raoden in the darkness. Karata knelt beside the child for a quiet moment.

Then she was done, motioning Raoden out of the room and closing the door behind her. Raoden raised his eyebrows questioningly, and Karata nodded. They were ready to go.

The escape was accomplished in the reverse order of the incursion. Raoden went first, sliding through the still open doors, and Karata followed, pulling them closed behind her.

In all, Raoden was relieved at how easily the night was going—or, at least, he was relieved right up to the moment
when he slipped through the door to that final hallway outside Iadon's chamber.

A man stood on the other side of the door, his hand frozen
in the act of reaching for the doorknob. He regarded them
with a startled expression.

Karata pushed past Raoden. She wrapped her arm around
the man's neck, clamping his mouth closed in a smooth motion, then grabbed his wrist as he reached for the sword at
his side. The man, however, was larger and stronger than
Karata's weakened Elantrian form, and he broke her grip,
blocking her leg with his own as she tried to trip him.

"Stop!" Raoden snapped quietly, his hand held before him
menacingly.

Both of their eyes flickered at him in annoyance, but then
they stopped struggling as they saw what he was doing.

Raoden's finger moved through the air, an illuminated
line appearing behind it. Raoden continued to write, curving
and tracing until he had finished a single character. Aon
Sheo, the symbol for death.

"If you move," Raoden said quietly, "you will die."

The guard's eyes widened in horror. The Aon sat glowing
above his chest, casting harsh light on the otherwise caligi-
nous room, throwing shadows across the walls. The character flashed as they always did, then disappeared. However,
the light had been enough to illuminate Raoden's black-
spotted Elantrian face.

"You know what we are."

"Merciful Domi . . ." the man whispered.

"That Aon will remain for the next hour," Raoden lied. "It
will hang where I drew it, unseen, waiting for you to so
much as quiver. If you do, it will destroy you. Do you understand?"

The man didn't move, sweat beading on his terrified face.

Raoden reached down and undid the man's sword belt,
then tied the weapon around his own waist.

"Come," Raoden said to Karata.

The woman still squatted next to the wall where the guard

had pushed her, regarding Raoden with an indecipherable look.

"Come," Raoden repeated, a bit more urgently.

Karata nodded, regaining her composure. She pulled open the king's door, and the two of them vanished the way they had come.

"HE didn't recognize me," Karata said to herself, her voice amused yet sorrowful.

"Who?" Raoden asked. The two of them squatted in the doorway of a shop near the middle of Kae, resting for a moment before continuing their trek back to Elantris.

"That guard. He was my husband, during another life."

"Your *husband*?"

Karata nodded. "We lived together for twelve years, and now he's forgotten me."

Raoden did some quick connecting of events. "That means the room we entered . . ."

"That was my daughter," Karata said. "I doubt anyone ever told her what happened to me. I just . . . wanted her to know."

"You left her a note?"

"A note and a keepsake," Karata explained with a sad voice, though no tears could fall from her Elantrian eyes. "My necklace. I managed to sneak it past the priests a year ago. I wanted her to have it—I always intended to give it to her. They took me so quickly. . . . I never said goodbye."

"I know," Raoden said putting his arm around the woman comfortingly. "I know."

"It takes them all from us. It takes everything, and leaves us with nothing." Her voice was laced with vehemence.

"As Domi wills."

"How can you say that?" she demanded harshly. "How can you invoke His name after all that He has done to us?"

"I don't know," Raoden confessed, feeling inadequate. "I just know we need to keep going, as everyone does. At least you got to see her again."

"Yes," Karata said. "Thank you. You have done me a great service this night, my prince."

Raoden froze.

"Yes, I know you. I lived in the palace for years, with my husband, protecting your father and your family. I watched you from your childhood, Prince Raoden."

"You knew all this time?"

"Not the entire time," Karata said. "But for enough of it. Once I figured it out, I couldn't decide whether to hate you for being related to Iadon, or to be satisfied that justice took you as well."

"And your decision?"

"Doesn't matter," Karata said, wiping her dry eyes by reflex. "You fulfilled your bargain admirably. My people will leave you alone."

"That's not enough, Karata," Raoden said, standing up.

"You would demand more beyond our bargain?"

"I demand nothing, Karata," Raoden said, offering his hand to help her to her feet. "But you know who I am, and you can guess what I am trying to do."

"You're like Aanden," Karata said. "You think to lord over Elantris as your father rules the rest of this cursed land."

"People certainly are quick to judge me today," Raoden said with a wry smile. "No, Karata, I don't want to 'lord over' Elantris. But I do want to help it. I see a city full of people feeling sorry for themselves, a people resigned to seeing themselves as the rest of the world sees them. Elantris doesn't have to be the pit that it is."

"How can you change that?" Karata demanded. "As long as food is scarce, the people will fight and destroy to sate their hunger."

"Then we'll just have to fill them," Raoden said.

Karata snorted.

Raoden reached inside a pocket he had formed in his ragged clothing. "Do you recognize this, Karata?" he asked, showing her a small cloth pouch. It was empty, but he kept it as a reminder of his purpose.

Karata's eyes blazed with desire. "It held food."

"What kind?"

"It's one of the pouches of corn that is part of the sacrifice that comes with a new Elantrian," Karata said.

"Not just corn, Karata," Raoden said holding up a finger.

"*Seed corn.* Part of the ceremony requires that a grain offering be plantable."

"Seed corn?" Karata whispered.

"I've been collecting it from the newcomers," Raoden explained. "The rest of the offerings don't interest me—only the corn. We can plant it, Karata. There aren't that many people in Elantris; it wouldn't be hard to feed them all. Goodness knows we have enough free time to work a garden or two."

Karata's eyes were wide with shock. "No one's ever tried that before," she said, dumbfounded.

"I figured as much. It requires foresight, and the people of Elantris are too focused on their immediate hunger to worry about tomorrow. I intend to change that."

Karata looked up from the small pouch to Raoden's face. "Amazing," she mumbled.

"Come on," Raoden said, tucking the pouch away, then hiding the stolen sword beneath his rags. "We're almost to the gate."

"How do you intend to get us back in?"

"Just watch."

As they walked, Karata paused beside a dark home.

"What?" Raoden asked.

Karata pointed. On the window, inside the glass, sat a loaf of bread.

Suddenly, Raoden felt his own hunger stab sharply at his insides. He couldn't blame her—even in the palace, he'd been watching for something to swipe.

"We can't take that chance, Karata," Raoden said.

Karata sighed. "I know. It's just that . . . we're so close."

"All the shops are closed, all the houses locked," Raoden said. "We'll never find any."

Karata nodded, lethargically moving again. They turned a corner and approached the broad gate to Elantris. A squat building sat beside it, light pouring from the windows. Several guards lounged inside, their brown-and-yellow Elantris City Guard uniforms bright in the lamplight. Raoden approached the building and tapped on a window with the back of his fist.

"Excuse me," he said politely, "but would you mind opening the gates please?"

The guards, who had been playing a game of cards, threw back their chairs in alarm, shouting and cursing as they recognized his Elantrian features.

"Be quick about it," Raoden said airily. "I'm getting tired."

"What are you doing out?" one of the guards—an officer by appearances—demanded as his men piled out of the building. Several of them pointed their wicked spears at Raoden's chest.

"Trying to get back in," Raoden said impatiently.

One of the guards raised his spear.

"I wouldn't do that, if I were you," Raoden said. "Not unless you want to explain how you managed to kill an Elantrian *outside* of the gates. You are supposed to keep us in—it would be quite an embarrassment if the people found out that we were escaping beneath your noses."

"How did you escape?" the officer asked.

"I'll tell you later," Raoden said. "Right now, you should probably put us back in the city before we wake the entire neighborhood and start a panic. Oh, and I wouldn't get too close to me. The Shaod is, after all, highly contagious."

The guards backed away at his words. Watching Elantris was one thing; being confronted by a talking corpse was another. The officer, uncertain what else to do, ordered the gates opened.

"Thank you, my good man," Raoden said with a smile. "You're doing a wonderful job. We'll have to see if we can get you a raise." With that, Raoden held out his arm to Karata and strolled through the gates to Elantris as if the soldiers were his personal butlers, rather than prison guards.

Karata couldn't help snickering as the gate closed behind them. "You made it sound as if we *wanted* to be in here. Like it was a privilege."

"And that is exactly the way we should feel. After all, if we're going to be confined to Elantris, we might as well act as if it were the grandest place in the entire world."

Karata smiled. "You have a measure of defiance in you, my prince. I like that."

"Nobility is in one's bearing as much as it is in one's breeding. If we *act* like living here is a blessing, then maybe we'll start to forget how pathetic we think we are. Now, Karata, I want you to do some things for me."

She raised an eyebrow.

"Don't tell anyone who I am. I want loyalty in Elantris based on respect, not based on my title."

"All right."

"Second, don't tell anyone about the passage into town through the river."

"Why not?"

"It's too dangerous," Raoden said. "I know my father. If the guards start finding too many Elantrians in the city, he'll come and destroy us. The only way Elantris is going to progress is if it becomes self-sufficient. We can't risk sneaking into the city to support ourselves."

Karata listened, then nodded in the affirmative. "All right." Then she paused in thought for a moment. "Prince Raoden, there's something I want to show you."

THE children were happy. Though most slept, a few were awake, and they giggled and played with one another. They were all bald, of course, and they bore the marks of the Shaod. They didn't seem to mind.

"So *this* is where they all go," Raoden said with interest.

Karata led him farther into the room, which was buried deep within the palace of Elantris. Once, this building had housed the leaders elected by the Elantrian elders. Now it hid a playroom for babes.

Several men stood watchful guard over the children, eyeing Raoden with suspicion. Karata turned toward him. "When I first came to Elantris, I saw the children huddled in the shadows, frightened of everything that passed, and I thought of my own little Opais. Something within my heart healed when I began to help them—I gathered them, showed them a little bit of love, and they clung to me. Every one of the men and women you see here left a little child back on the outside."

Karata paused, affectionately rubbing a small Elantrian child on the head. "The children unite us, keep us from giving in to the pain. The food we gather is for them. Somehow, we can endure the hunger a little better if we know it has come, in part, because we gave what we had to the children."

"I wouldn't have thought . . ." Raoden began quietly, watching a pair of young girls playing a clapping game together.

"That they would be happy?" Karata finished. She motioned for Raoden to follow her and they moved back, out of the children's hearing range. "We don't understand it either, my prince. They seem better at dealing with the hunger than the rest of us."

"A child's mind is a surprisingly resilient thing," Raoden said.

"They seem to be able to endure a certain amount of pain as well," Karata continued, "bumps and bruises and the like. However, they eventually snap, just like everyone else. One moment a child is happy and playful. Then he falls down or cuts himself one too many times, and his mind gives up. I have another room, kept far away from these little ones, filled with dozens of children who do nothing but whimper all day."

Raoden nodded. Then, after a moment, he asked, "Why are you showing me this?"

Karata paused. "Because I want to join with you. I once served your father, despite what I thought of him. Now I will serve his son *because* of what I think of him. Will you accept my loyalty?"

"With honor, Karata."

She nodded, turning back to the children with a sigh. "I don't have much left in me, Lord Raoden," she whispered. "I've worried what would happen to my children when I am lost. This dream you have, this crazy idea of an Elantris where we grow food and we ignore our pain . . . I want to see you try to create it. I don't think you can, but I think you will make something better of us in the process."

"Thank you," Raoden said, realizing that he had just accepted a monumental responsibility. Karata had lived for over a year under the burden he was just beginning to feel. She was tired; he could see it in her eyes. Now, if the time came, she could rest. She had passed her weight on to him.

"Thank you," Karata said, looking at the children.

"Tell me, Karata," Raoden said after a moment of thought. "Would you really have broken my people's limbs?"

Karata didn't respond at first. "You tell me, my prince. What would you have done if I'd tried to kill your father to-night?"

"Questions both better left unanswered."

Karata nodded, her tired eyes bearing a calm wisdom.

RAODEN smiled as he recognized the large figure standing outside of the chapel, waiting for him to return. Galladon's concerned face was illuminated by the tiny flame of his lantern.

"A light to guide me home, my friend?" Raoden asked from the darkness as he approached.

"Sule!" Galladon cried. "By Doloken, you're not dead?"

"Of course I am," Raoden said with a laugh, clapping his friend on the shoulder. "We all are—at least, that's what you seem to be fond of telling me."

Galladon grinned. "Where's the woman?"

"I walked her home, as any gentleman would," Raoden said, entering the chapel. Inside, Mareshe and the others were rousing.

"Lord Spirit has returned!" Saolin said with enthusiasm.

"Here, Saolin, a gift," Raoden said, pulling the sword out from under his rags and tossing it to the soldier.

"What is this, my lord?" Saolin asked.

"That spear is amazing considering what you had to work with," Raoden said, "but I think you ought to have something a little more sturdy if you intend to do any real fighting."

Saolin pulled the blade free of its scabbard. The sword, nothing special on the outside, was a wondrous work of beauty within the confines of Elantris. "Not a spot of rust on her," Saolin said with amazement. "And it is engraved with the symbol of Iadon's own personal guard!"

"Then the king is dead?" Mareshe asked eagerly.

"Nothing of the sort," Raoden said dismissively. "Our mission was of a personal nature, Mareshe, and it did not involve killing—though the guard who owned that sword is probably fairly angry."

"I'll bet," Galladon said with a snort. "Then we don't have to worry about Karata anymore?"

"No," Raoden said with a smile. "As a matter of fact, her gang will be joining with us."

There were a few mutters of surprise at the announcement, and Raoden paused before continuing. "Tomorrow we're going to visit the palace sector. Karata has something there I want you all to see—something everyone in Elantris should see."

"What is that, sule?" Galladon asked.

"Proof that the hunger can be defeated."

CHAPTER 14

SARENE had about as much talent for needlepoint as she did for painting. Not that she let it stop her from trying— no matter how much she worked to become a part of what were traditionally considered masculine activities, Sarene felt an intense need to prove that she could be as feminine and ladylike as anyone else. It wasn't her fault that she just wasn't any good at it.

She held up her embroidering hoop. It was supposed to depict a crimson sisterling sitting on a branch, its beak open in song. Unfortunately, she had drawn the pattern herself— which meant it hadn't been all that good in the first place. That, coupled with her startling inability to follow the lines, had produced something that resembled a squashed tomato more than it did a bird.

"Very nice, dear," Eshen said. Only the incurably bubbly queen could deliver such a compliment without sarcasm.

Sarene sighed, dropping her hoop to her lap and grabbing some brown thread for the branch.

"Don't worry, Sarene," Daora said. "Domi gives everyone different levels of talent, but he always rewards diligence. Continue to practice and you will improve."

You say that with such ease, Sarene thought with a mental scowl. Daora's own hoop was filled with a detailed masterpiece of embroidered perfection. She had entire flocks of birds, each one tiny yet intricate, hovering and spinning through the branches of a statuesque oak. Kiin's wife was the embodiment of aristocratic virtue.

Daora didn't walk, she glided, and her every action was smooth and graceful. Her makeup was striking—her lips bright red and her eyes mysterious—but it had been applied with masterful subtlety. She was old enough to be stately, yet young enough to be known for her remarkable beauty. In short, she was the type of woman Sarene would normally hate—if she weren't also the kindest, most intelligent woman in the court.

After a few moments of quiet, Eshen began to talk, as usual. The queen seemed frightened of silence, and was constantly speaking or prompting others to do so. The other women in the group were content to let her lead—not that anyone would have wanted to try wrestling control of a conversation from Eshen.

The queen's embroidery group consisted of about ten women. At first, Sarene had avoided their meetings, instead focusing her attention on the political court. However, she had soon realized that the women were as important as any civil matter; gossip and idle chatting spread news that couldn't be discussed in a formal setting. Sarene couldn't afford to be out of the chain, she just wished she didn't have to reveal her ineptitude to take part.

"I heard that Lord Waren, son of the Baron of Kie Plantation, has had quite the religious experience," Eshen said. "I knew his mother—she was a very decent woman. Quite proficient at knitting. Next year, when sweaters come back in,

I'm going to force Iadon to wear one—it isn't seemly for a king to appear unconscious of fashion. His hair is quite too long."

Daora pulled a stitch tight. "I have heard the rumors about young Waren. It seems odd to me that now, after years of being a devout Korathi, he would suddenly convert to Shu-Dereth."

"They're all but the same religion anyway," Atara said offhandedly. Duke Telrii's wife was a small woman—even for an Arelene—with shoulder-length auburn curls. Her clothing and jewelry was by far the richest in the room, a compliment to her husband's extravagance, and her stitching patterns were always conservative and unimaginative.

"Don't say such things around the priests," warned Seaden, Count Ahan's wife. The largest woman in the room, her girth nearly matched that of her husband. "They act as if your soul depends on whether you call God Domi or Jaddeth."

"The two do have some very striking differences," Sarene said, trying to shield her mangled embroidering from the eyes of her companions.

"Maybe if you're a priest," Atara said with a quiet twitter of a laugh. "But those things hardly make any difference to *us*."

"Of course," Sarene said. "We are, after all, only women." She looked up from her needlepoint discreetly, smiling at the reaction her statement sparked. Perhaps the women of Arelon weren't quiet as subservient as their men assumed.

The quiet continued for only a few moments before Eshen spoke again. "Sarene, what do women do in Teod to pass the time?"

Sarene raised an eyebrow in surprise; she had never heard the queen ask such a straightforward question. "What do you mean, Your Majesty?"

"What do they do?" Eshen repeated. "I've heard things, you understand—as I have about Fjorden, where they say it gets so cold in the winter that trees sometimes freeze and explode. An easy way to make wood chips, I suppose. I wonder if they can make it happen on command."

Sarene smiled. "We find things to do, Your Majesty. Some women like to embroider, though others of us find different pursuits."

"Like what?" asked Torena, the unmarried daughter of Lord Ahan—though Sarene still found it hard to believe that a person so slight of frame could have come from a pair as bulbous as Ahan and Seaden. Torena was normally quiet during these gatherings, her wide brown eyes watching the proceedings with a spark that hinted at a buried intelligence.

"Well, the king's courts are open to all, for one thing," Sarene said nonchalantly. Her heart sang, however: this was the kind of opportunity she had been anticipating with excitement.

"You would go listen to the cases?" Torena asked, her quiet, high-pitched voice growing increasingly interested.

"Often," Sarene said. "Then I would talk about them with my friends."

"Did you fight one another with swords?" asked the overweight Seaden, her face eager.

Sarene paused, a little taken aback. She looked up to find nearly every head in the room staring at her. "What makes you ask that?"

"That's what they say about women from Teod, dear," Daora said calmly, the only woman who was still working on her needlepoint.

"Yes," Seaden said. "We've always heard it—they say that women in Teod kill one another for the sport of the men."

Sarene raised an eyebrow. "We call it fencing, Lady Seaden. We do it for our own amusement, not that of our men—and we definitely do *not* kill one another. We use swords, but the tips have little knobs on them, and we wear thick clothing. I've never heard of anyone suffering an injury greater than a twisted ankle."

"Then it's true?" little Torena breathed with amazement. "You *do* use swords."

"Some of us," Sarene said. "I rather enjoyed it, actually. Fencing was my favorite sport." The women's eyes shone with an appalling level of bloodlust—like the eyes of hounds that had been locked in a very small room for far too long. Sarene had hoped to instill a measure of political interest in these women, to encourage them to take an active role in the management of the country, but apparently that was too subtle an approach. They needed something more direct.

"I could teach you, if you wanted," Sarene offered.

"To fight?" Atara asked, astounded.

"Of course," Sarene said. "It's not that difficult. And please, Lady Atara, we call it fencing. Even the most understanding of men gets a bit uncomfortable when he thinks of women 'fighting.'"

"We couldn't . . ." Eshen began.

"Why not?" Sarene asked.

"Swordplay is frowned upon by the king, dear," Daora explained. "You've probably noticed that none of the noblemen here carry swords."

Sarene frowned. "I was going to ask about that."

"Iadon considers it too commonplace," Eshen said. "He calls fighting peasant's work. He's studied them rather a lot—he's a fine leader, you know, and a fine leader has to know a lot about a lot of things. Why, he can tell you what the weather is like in Svorden at any time of the year. His ships are the most sturdy, and fastest in the business."

"So none of the men can fight?" Sarene asked with amazement.

"None except for Lord Eondel and perhaps Lord Shuden," Torena said, her face taking on a dreamy look as she mentioned Shuden's name. The young, dark-skinned nobleman was a favorite among the women of court, his delicate features and impeccable manners capturing even the most steady of hearts.

"Don't forget Prince Raoden," Atara added. "I think he had Eondel teach him to fight just to spite his father. He was always doing things like that."

"Well, all the better," Sarene said. "If none of the men fight, then King Iadon can't very well object to our learning."

"What do you mean?" Torena asked.

"Well, he says it's beneath him," Sarene explained. "If that's true, then it should be perfect for us. After all, we *are* only women."

Sarene smiled mischievously, an expression that spread across most of the faces in the room.

"ASHE, where did I put my sword?" Sarene said, on her knees beside her bed, fumbling around beneath it.

"Your sword, my lady?" Ashe asked.

"Never mind, I'll find it later. What did you discover?"

Ashe pulsed quietly, as if wondering just what sort of trouble she was getting into, before speaking. "I'm afraid I don't have much to report, my lady. Elantris is a very delicate subject, and I have been able to learn very little."

"Anything will help," Sarene said, turning to her wardrobe. She had a ball to attend this night.

"Well, my lady, most of the people in Kae don't want to speak of the city. Kae's Seons didn't know very much, and the mad Seons inside of Elantris seem incapable of enough thought to respond to my questions. I even tried approaching the Elantrians themselves, but many appeared scared of me, and the others only begged me for food—as if I could carry it to them. Eventually, I found the best source of information to be the soldiers that guard the city walls."

"I've heard of them," Sarene said, looking over her clothing. "They're supposed to be the most elite fighting group in Arelon."

"And they are very quick to tell you so, my lady," Ashe said. "I doubt many of them would know what to do in a battle, though they seem quite proficient at cards and drinking. They tend to keep their uniforms well pressed, however."

"Typical of a ceremonial guard," Sarene said, picking through the row of black garments, her skin quivering at the thought of donning yet another flat, colorless monstrosity of a dress. As much as she respected the memory of Raoden, she couldn't possibly wear black again.

Ashe bobbed in the air at her comment. "I am afraid, my lady, that Arelon's most 'elite' military group hardly does the country any credit. Yet, they are the city's most informed experts regarding Elantris."

"And what did they have to say?"

Ashe drifted over to the closet, watching as she rifled through her choices. "Not much. People in Arelon don't talk to Seons as quickly as they once did. There was a time, I barely recall, when the population loved us. Now they are . . . reserved, almost frightened."

"They associate you with Elantris," Sarene said, glancing longingly toward the dresses she had brought with her from Teod.

"I know, my lady," Ashe said. "But we had nothing to do with the fall of the city. There is nothing to fear from a Seon. I wish . . . But, well, that is irrelevant. Despite their reticence, I did get some information. It appears that Elantrians lose more than their human appearance when the Shaod takes them. The guards seem to think that the individual completely forgets who he or she used to be, becoming something more like an animal than a human. This certainly seems the case for the Elantrian Seons I spoke to."

Sarene shivered. "But, Elantrians can talk—some asked you for food."

"They did," Ashe said. "The poor souls hardly even seemed animal; most of them were crying or mumbling in some way. I'm inclined to think they had lost their minds."

"So the Shaod is mental as well as physical," Sarene said speculatively.

"Apparently, my lady. The guards also spoke of several despotic lords that rule the city. Food is so valuable that the Elantrians vigorously attack anyone bearing it."

Sarene frowned. "How are the Elantrians fed?"

"They aren't, as far as I can tell."

"Then how do they live?" Sarene asked.

"I do not know, my lady. It is possible that the city exists in a feral state, with the mighty living upon the weak."

"No society could survive like that."

"I don't believe they *have* a society, my lady," Ashe said. "They are a group of miserable, cursed individuals that your God appears to have forgotten—and the rest of the country is trying very hard to follow His example."

Sarene nodded thoughtfully. Then, determined, she pulled off her black dress and rifled through the clothing at the back of her closet. She presented herself for Ashe's appraisal a few minutes later.

"What do you think?" she asked, twirling. The dress was crafted of a thick, golden material that was almost metallic in its shine. It was overlaid with black lace, and had a high, open collar, like a man's. The collar was constructed from a stiff material, which was matched in the cuffs. The sleeves were very wide, as was the body of the dress, which billowed outward and continued all the way to the floor, hiding her feet. It was the kind of dress that made one feel regal. Even a princess needed reminders once in a while.

"It isn't black, my lady," Ashe pointed out.

"This part is," Sarene objected, pointing to the long cape at the back. The cape was actually part of the dress, woven into the neck and shoulders so carefully that it seemed to grow from the lace.

"I don't think that the cape is enough to make it a widow's dress, my lady."

"It will have to do," Sarene said, studying herself in the mirror. "If I wear one more of those dresses Eshen gave me, then you'll have to throw *me* into Elantris for going insane."

"Are you certain the front is . . . appropriate?"

"What?" Sarene said.

"It's rather low-cut, my lady,"

"I've seen much worse, even here in Arelon."

"Yes, my lady, but those were all unmarried women."

Sarene smiled. Ashe was always so sensitive—especially in regards to her. "I have to at least wear it once—I've never had the chance. I got it in from Duladel the week before I left Teod."

"If you say so, my lady," Ashe said, pulsing slightly. "Is there anything else you would like me to try and find out?"

"Did you visit the dungeons?"

"I did," Ashe said. "I'm sorry, my lady—I found no secret alcoves hiding half-starved princes. If Iadon locked his son away, then he wasn't foolish enough to do it in his own palace."

"Well, it was worth a look," Sarene said with a sigh. "I didn't think you would find anything—we should probably be searching for the assassin who wielded the knife instead."

"True," Ashe said. "Perhaps you might try prompting the queen for information? If the prince really was killed by an intruder, she might know something."

"I've tried, but Eshen is . . . well, it's not hard to get information out of her. Getting her to stay on topic, however . . .

Honestly, how a woman like that ended up married to Iadon is beyond me."

"I suspect, my lady," Ashe said, "that the arrangement was more financial than it was social. Much of Iadon's original governmental funds came from Eshen's father."

"That makes sense," Sarene said, smiling slightly and wondering what Iadon thought of the bargain now. He'd gotten his money, true, but he'd also ended up spending several decades listening to Eshen's prattle. Perhaps that was why he seemed so frustrated by women in general.

"Regardless," Sarene said, "I don't think the queen knows anything about Raoden—but I'll keep trying."

Ashe bobbed. "And, what shall I do?"

Sarene paused. "Well, I've been thinking about Uncle Kiin lately. Father never mentions him anymore. I was wondering—do you know if Kiin was ever officially disinherited?"

"I don't know, my lady," Ashe said. "Dio might know; he works much more closely with your father."

"See if you can dig anything up—there might be some rumors here in Arelon about what happened. Kiin is, after all, one of the most influential people in Kae."

"Yes, my lady. Anything else?"

"Yes," Sarene decided with a wrinkle of her nose. "Find someone to take those black dresses away—I've decided I won't be needing them anymore."

"Of course, my lady," Ashe said with a suffering tone.

SARENE glanced out the carriage window as it approached Duke Telrii's mansion. Reports said that Telrii had been very free with ball invitations, and the number of carriages on the road this evening seemed to confirm the information. Torches lined the pathway, and the mansion grounds were brilliantly lit with a combination of lanterns, torches, and strange colorful flames.

"The duke has spared no expense," Shuden noted.

"What are they, Lord Shuden?" Sarene asked, nodding toward one of the bright flames, which burned atop a tall metal pole.

"Special rocks imported from the south."

"Rocks that burn? Like coal?"

"They burn much more quickly than coal," the young Jindoeese lord explained. "And they are extremely expensive. It must have cost Telrii a fortune to light this pathway." Shuden frowned. "This seems extravagant, even for him."

"Lukel mentioned that the duke is somewhat wasteful," Sarene said, remembering her conversation in Iadon's throne room.

Shuden nodded. "But he's far more clever than most will credit. The duke is easy with his money, but there is usually a purpose behind his frivolity." Sarene could see the young baron's mind working as the coach pulled to a stop, as if trying to discern the exact nature of the aforementioned "purpose."

The mansion itself was bursting with people. Women in bright dresses accompanied men in the straight-coated suits that were the current masculine fashion. The guests only slightly outnumbered the white-clothed servants who bustled through the crowd, carrying food and drink or changing lanterns. Shuden helped Sarene from the carriage, then led her into the main ballroom with a gait that was practiced at navigating crowds.

"You have no idea how happy I am you offered to come with me," Shuden confided as they entered the room. A large band played at one end of the hallway, and couples either spun through the center of the room in dance or stood around the wide periphery in conversation. The room was bright with colored lights, the rocks they had seen outside burning intensely from placements atop banisters or poles. There were even chains of tiny candles wrapped around several of the pillars—contraptions that probably had to be refilled every half hour.

"Why is that, my lord?" Sarene asked, gazing at the colorful scene. Even living as a princess, she had never seen such beauty and opulence. Light, sound, and color mixed intoxicatingly.

Shuden followed her gaze, not really hearing her question. "One would never know this country is dancing on the lip of destruction," he muttered.

The statement struck like a solemn death knell. There was a reason Sarene had never seen such lavishness—wondrous as it was, it was also incredibly wasteful. Her father was a prudent ruler; he would never allow such profligacy.

"That is always how it is, though, isn't it?" Shuden asked. "Those who can least afford extravagance seem to be the ones most determined to spend what they have left."

"You are a wise man, Lord Shuden," Sarene said.

"No, just a man who tries to see to the heart of things," he said, leading her to a side gallery where they could find drinks.

"What was that you were saying before?"

"What?" Shuden asked. "Oh, I was explaining how you are going to save me quite a bit of distress this evening."

"Why is that?" she asked as he handed her a cup of wine.

Shuden smiled slightly, taking a sip of his own drink. "There are some who, for one reason or another, consider me quite . . . eligible. Many of them won't realize who you are, and will stay away, trying to judge their new competitor. I might actually have some time to enjoy myself tonight."

Sarene raised an eyebrow. "Is it really that bad?"

"I usually have to beat them away with a stick," Shuden replied, holding out his arm to her.

"One would almost think you never intended to marry, my lord," Sarene said with a smile, accepting his proffered arm.

Shuden laughed. "No, it is nothing like that, my lady. Let me assure you, I am quite interested in the concept—or, at least, the theory behind it. However, finding a woman in this court whose twittering foolishness doesn't cause my stomach to turn, that is another thing entirely. Come, if I am right, then we should be able to find a place much more interesting than the main ballroom."

Shuden led her through the masses of ballgoers. Despite his earlier comments, he was very civil—even pleasant—to the women who appeared from the crowd to welcome him. Shuden knew every one by name—a feat of diplomacy, or good breeding, in itself.

Sarene's respect for Shuden grew as she watched the reactions of those he met. No faces turned dark as he approached, and few gave him the haughty looks that were common in so-called genteel societies. Shuden was well liked, though he was far from the most lively of men. She

sensed that his popularity came not from his ability to enter-
tain, but from his refreshing honesty. When Shuden spoke,
he was always polite and considerate, but completely frank.
His exotic origin gave him the license to say things that others could not.

Eventually they arrived at a small room at the top of a
flight of stairs. "Here we are," Shuden said with satisfaction,
leading her through the doorway. Inside they found a
smaller, but more skilled, band playing stringed instruments.
The decorations in this room were more subdued, but the
servants were holding plates of food that seemed even more
exotic than those down below. Sarene recognized many of
the faces from court, including the one most important.

"The king," she said, noticing Iadon standing near the far
corner. Eshen was at his side in a slim green dress.

Shuden nodded. "Iadon wouldn't miss a party like this,
even if it is being held by Lord Telrii."

"They don't get along?"

"They get along fine. They're just in the same business.
Iadon runs a merchant fleet—his ships travel the sea of Fjorden, as do those of Telrii. That makes them rivals."

"I think it's odd that he's here either way," Sarene said.
"My father never goes to these kinds of things."

"That is because he has grown up, Lady Sarene. Iadon is
still infatuated with his power, and takes every opportunity
to enjoy it." Shuden looked around with keen eyes. "Take
this room, for example."

"This room?"

Shuden nodded. "Whenever Iadon comes to a party, he
chooses a room aside from the main one and lets the important people gravitate toward him. The nobles are used to it.
The man throwing the ball usually hires a second band, and
knows to start a second, more exclusive party apart from the
main ball. Iadon has made it known that he doesn't want to
associate with people who are too far beneath him—this
gathering is only for dukes and well-placed counts."

"But *you* are a baron," Sarene pointed out as the two of
them drifted into the room.

Shuden smiled, sipping his wine. "I am a special case. My
family forced Iadon to give us our title, where most of the

others gained their ranks through wealth and begging. I can take certain liberties that no other baron would assume, for Iadon and I both know I once got the better of him. I can usually only spend a short time here in the inner room—an hour at most. Otherwise I stretch the king's patience. Of course, that is all beside the point tonight."

"Why is that?"

"Because I have you," Shuden said. "Do not forget, Lady Sarene. You outrank everyone in this room except for the royal couple themselves."

Sarene nodded. While she was quite accustomed to the idea of being important—she was, after all, the daughter of a king—she wasn't used to the Arelish penchant for pulling rank.

"Iadon's presence changes things," she said quietly as the king noticed her. His eyes passed over her dress, obviously noting its less than black state, and his face grew dark.

Maybe the dress wasn't such a good idea, Sarene admitted to herself. However, something else quickly drew her attention. "What is *he* doing here?" she whispered as she noticed a bright form standing like a red scar in the midst of the ball-goers.

Shuden followed her eyes. "The gyorn? He's been coming to the court balls since the day he got here. He showed up at the first one without an invitation, and held himself with such an air of self-importance that no one has dared neglect inviting him since."

Hrathen spoke with a small group of men, his brilliant red breastplate and cape stark against the nobles' lighter colors. The gyorn stood at least a head taller than anyone in the room, and his shoulder plates extended a foot on either side. All in all, he was very hard to miss.

Shuden smiled. "No matter what I think of the man, I am impressed with his confidence. He simply walked into the king's private party that first night and began talking to one of the dukes—he barely even nodded to the king. Apparently, Hrathen considers the title of gyorn equal to anything in this room."

"Kings bow to gyorns in the East," Sarene said. "They practically grovel when Wyrn visits."

"And it all came from one elderly Jindo," Shuden noted, pausing to replace their cups with wine from a passing servant. It was a much better vintage. "It always interests me to see what you people have done with Keseg's teachings."

"'You people'?" Sarene asked. "I'm Korathi—don't lump me together with the gyorn."

Shuden held up a hand. "I apologize. I didn't mean to be offensive."

Sarene paused. Shuden spoke Aonic as a native and lived in Arelon, so she had assumed him to be Korathi. She had misjudged. Shuden was still Jindoeese—his family would have believed in Shu-Keseg, the parent religion of both Korath and Dereth. "But," she said, thinking out loud, "Jindo is Derethi now."

Shuden's face darkened slightly, eyeing the gyorn. "I wonder what the great master thought when his two students, Korath and Dereth, left to preach to the lands northward. Keseg taught of unity. But what did he mean? Unity of mind, as my people assume? Unity of love, as your priests claim? Or is it the unity of obedience, as the Derethi believe? In the end, I am left to ponder how mankind managed to complicate such a simple concept."

He paused, then shook his head. "Anyway, yes, my lady, Jindo is Derethi now. My people allow Wyrn to assume that the Jindo have been converted because it is better than fighting. Many are now questioning that decision, however. The arteths are growing increasingly demanding."

Sarene nodded. "I agree. Shu-Dereth must be stopped—it is a perversion of the truth."

Shuden paused. "I didn't say that, Lady Sarene. The soul of Shu-Keseg is acceptance. There is room for all teachings. The Derethi think they are doing what is right." Shuden stopped, looking over at Hrathen, before continuing. "That one, however, is dangerous."

"Why him and not others?"

"I visited one of Hrathen's sermons," Shuden said. "He doesn't preach from his heart, Lady Sarene, he preaches from his mind. He looks for numbers in his conversions, paying no attention to the faith of his followers. This is dangerous."

Shuden scanned Hrathen's companions. "That one bothers me as well," he said, pointing to a man whose hair was so blond it was almost white.

"Who is he?" Sarene asked with interest.

"Waren, first son of Baron Diolen," Shuden said. "He shouldn't be here in this room, but he is apparently using his close association with the gyorn as an invitation. Waren used to be a notably pious Korathi, but he claims to have seen a vision of Jaddeth commanding that he convert to Shu-Dereth."

"The ladies were talking about this earlier," Sarene said, eyeing Waren. "You don't believe him?"

"I have always suspected Waren's religiousness to be an exhibition. He is an opportunist, and his extreme piety gained him notoriety."

Sarene studied the white-haired man, worried. He was very young, but he carried himself as a man of accomplishment and control. His conversion was a dangerous sign. The more such people Hrathen gathered, the more difficult he would be to stop.

"I shouldn't have waited so long," she said.

"For what?"

"To come to these balls. Hrathen has a week's edge on me."

"You act as if it were a personal struggle between you two," Shuden noted with a smile.

Sarene didn't take the comment lightly. "A personal struggle with the fates of nations at stake."

"Shuden!" a voice said. "I see that you are lacking your customary circle of admirers."

"Good evening, Lord Roial," Shuden said, bowing slightly as the old man approached. "Yes, thanks to my companionship, I have been able to avoid most of that tonight."

"Ah, the lovely Princess Sarene," Roial said, kissing her hand. "Apparently, your penchant for black has waned."

"It was never that strong to begin with, my lord," she said with a curtsy.

"I can imagine," Roial said with a smile. Then he turned

back to Shuden. "I had hoped that you wouldn't realize your good fortune, Shuden. I might have stolen the princess and kept off a few of the leeches myself."

Sarene regarded the elderly man with surprise.

Shuden chuckled. "Lord Roial is, perhaps, the only bachelor in Arelon whose affection is more sought-after than my own. Not that I am jealous. His Lordship diverts some of the attention from me."

"You?" Sarene asked, looking at the spindly old man. "Women want to marry *you*?" Then, remembering her manners, she added a belated "my lord," blushing furiously at the impropriety of her words.

Roial laughed. "Don't worry about offending me, young Sarene. No man my age is much to look at. My dear Eoldess has been dead for twenty years, and I have no son. My fortune has to pass to someone, and every unmarried girl in the realm realizes that fact. She would only have to indulge me for a few years, bury me, then find a lusty young lover to help spend my money."

"My lord is too cynical," Shuden noted.

"My lord is too realistic," Roial said with a snort. "Though I'll admit, the idea of forcing one of those young puffs into my bed is tempting. I know they all think I'm too old to make them perform their duties as a wife, but they assume wrong. If I were going to let them steal my fortune, I'd at least make them work for it."

Shuden blushed at the comment, but Sarene only laughed. "I knew it. You really are nothing but a dirty old man."

"Self-professedly so," Roial agreed with a smile. Then, looking over at Hrathen, he continued. "How's our overly armored friend doing?"

"Bothering me by his mere noxious presence, my lord," Sarene replied.

"Watch him, Sarene," Roial said. "I hear that our dear lord Telrii's sudden good fortune isn't a matter of pure luck."

Shuden's eyes grew suspicious. "Duke Telrii has declared no allegiance to Derethi."

"Not openly, no," Roial agreed. "But my sources say that there is something between those two. One thing is certain:

There has rarely been a party like this in Kae, and the duke is throwing it for no obvious reason. One begins to wonder just what Telrii is advertising, and why he wants us to know how wealthy he is."

"An interesting thought, my lord," Sarene said.

"Sarene?" Eshen's voice called from the other side of the room. "Dear, would you come over here?"

"Oh no," Sarene said, looking over at the queen, who was waving her to approach. "What do you suppose this is about?"

"I'm intrigued to find out," Roial said with a sparkle in his eyes.

Sarene acknowledged the queen's gesture, approaching the royal couple and curtsying politely. Shuden and Roial followed more discreetly, placing themselves within earshot.

Eshen smiled as Sarene approached. "Dear, I was just explaining to my husband about the idea we came up with this morning. You know, the one about exercising?" Eshen nodded her head toward the king enthusiastically.

"What is this nonsense, Sarene?" the king demanded. "Women playing with swords?"

"His Majesty wouldn't want us to get fat, would he?" Sarene asked innocently.

"No, of course not," the king said. "But you could just eat less."

"But, I do so like to exercise, Your Majesty."

Iadon took a deep, suffering breath. "But surely there is some *other* form of exercise you women could do?"

Sarene blinked, trying to hint that she might be close to tears. "But, Your Majesty, I've done this ever since I was a child. Surely the king can have nothing against a foolish womanly pastime."

The king stopped, eyeing her. She might have overdone it that last time. Sarene assumed her best look of hopeless idiocy and smiled.

Finally, he just shook his head. "Bah, do whatever you want, woman. I don't want you spoiling my evening."

"The king is very wise," Sarene said, curtsying and backing away.

"I had forgotten about that," Shuden whispered to her as

she rejoined him. "The act must be quite the burden to maintain."

"It is useful sometimes," Sarene said. They were about to withdraw when Sarene noticed a courier approaching the king. She placed her hand on Shuden's arm, indicating that she wanted to wait a moment where she could still hear Iadon.

The messenger whispered something in Iadon's ear, and the king's eyes grew wide with frustration. "What!"

The man moved to whisper again, and the king pushed him back. "Just say it, man. I can't stand all that whispering."

"It happened just this week, Your Majesty," the man explained.

Sarene edged closer.

"How odd." A slightly accented voice suddenly drifted in their direction. Hrathen stood a short distance away. He wasn't watching them, but somehow he was directing his voice at the king—as if he were intentionally allowing his words to be overheard. "I wouldn't have thought the king would discuss important matters where the dull-minded can hear. Such people tend to be so confused by events that it is a disservice to allow them the opportunity."

Most of the people around her didn't even appear to have heard the gyorn's comment. The king, however, had. Iadon regarded Sarene for a moment, then grabbed his messenger by the arm and strode quickly from the room, leaving a startled Eshen behind. As Sarene watched the king leave, Hrathen's eyes caught her own, and he smiled slightly before turning back to his companions.

"Can you believe that?" Sarene said, fuming. "He did that on purpose!"

Shuden nodded. "Often, my lady, our deceptions turn on us."

"The gyorn is good," Roial said. "It's always a masterful stroke when you can turn someone's guise to your advantage."

"I have often found that no matter what the circumstance, it is most useful to be oneself," Shuden said. "The more faces we try to wear, the more confused they become."

Roial nodded slightly, smiling. "True. Boring, perhaps, but true."

Sarene was barely listening. She had assumed that she was the one doing the manipulating; she had never realized the disadvantage it gave her. "The façade is troubling," she admitted. Then she sighed, turning back to Shuden. "But I am stuck with it, at least with the king. Honestly though, I doubt he would have regarded me any other way, no matter how I acted."

"You're probably right," Shuden said. "The king is rather shortsighted when it comes to women."

The king returned a few moments later, his face dark, his humor obviously ruined by whatever news he had received. The courier escaped with a look of relief, and as he left, Sarene caught sight of a new figure entering the room. Duke Telrii was customarily pompous in bright reds and golds, his fingers speckled with rings. Sarene watched him closely, but he didn't join—or even acknowledge—the gyorn Hrathen. In fact, he seemed to doggedly ignore the priest, instead making the proper hostly overtures, visiting with each group of guests in turn.

"You're right, Lord Roial," Sarene finally said.

Roial looked up from his conversation with Shuden. "Hum?"

"Duke Telrii," Sarene said, nodding to the man. "There's something between him and the gyorn."

"Telrii is a troublesome one," Roial said. "I've never quite been able to figure out his motivations. At times, it seems he wants nothing more than coin to pad his coffers. At others . . ."

Roial trailed off as Telrii, as if noticing their study of him, turned toward Sarene's group. He smiled and drifted in their direction, Atara at his side. "Lord Roial," he said with a smooth, almost uncaring, voice. "Welcome. And, Your Highness. I don't believe we've been properly introduced."

Roial did the honors. Sarene curtsied as Telrii sipped at his wine and exchanged pleasantries with Roial. There was a startling level of . . . nonchalance about him. While few noblemen actually cared about the topics they discussed, most had the decency to at least sound interested. Telrii made no such concession. His tone was flippant, though not quite to the level of being insulting, and his manner uninterested. Beyond the initial address, he completely ignored Sarene, obviously satisfied that she was of no discernible significance.

Eventually, the duke sauntered away, and Sarene watched him go with annoyance. If there was one thing she loathed, it was being ignored. Finally, she sighed and turned to her companion. "All right, Lord Shuden, I want to mingle. Hrathen has a week's lead, but Domi be cursed if I'm going to let him stay ahead of me."

IT was late. Shuden had wanted to leave hours ago, but Sarene had been determined to forge on, plowing through hundreds of people, making contacts like a madwoman. She made Shuden introduce her to everyone he knew, and the faces and names had quickly become a blur. However, repetition would bring familiarity.

Eventually, she let Shuden bring her back to the palace, satisfied with the day's events. Shuden let her off and wearily bid her goodnight, claiming he was glad that Ahan was next in line to take her to a ball. "Your company was delightful," he explained, "but I just can't keep up with you!"

Sarene found it hard to keep up with *herself* sometimes. She practically stumbled her way into the palace, so drowsy with fatigue and wine that she could barely keep her eyes open.

Shouts echoed through the hallway.

Sarene frowned, turning a corner to find the king's guard scrambling around, yelling at one another and generally making a rather large nuisance of themselves.

"What is going on?" she asked, holding her head.

"Someone broke into the palace tonight," a guard explained. "Snuck right through the king's bedchambers."

"Is anyone hurt?" Sarene asked, suddenly coming alert. Iadon and Eshen had left the party hours before her and Shuden.

"Thank Domi, no," the guard said. Then, he turned to two soldiers. "Take the princess to her room and stand guard at the door," he ordered. "Goodnight, Your Highness. Don't worry—they're gone now."

Sarene sighed, noting the yelling and bustle of the guards, their armor and weapons clanking as they periodically ran through the hallways. She doubted that she would be able to have a good night with so much ruckus, no matter how tired she was.

CHAPTER 15

AT night, when all melted into a uniform blackness, Hrathen could almost see Elantris's grandeur. Silhouetted against the star-filled sky, the fallen buildings cast off their mantle of despair and became memories; memories of a city crafted with skill and care, a city where every stone was a piece of functional art; memories of towers that stretched to the sky—fingers tickling the stars—and of domes that spread like venerable hills.

And it had all been an illusion. Beneath the greatness had been wreckage, a filthy sore now exposed. How easy it was to look past heresies gilded with gold. How simple it had been to assume that outward strength bespoke inward righteousness.

"Dream on, Elantris," Hrathen whispered, turning to stroll along the top of the great wall that enclosed the city. "Remember what you used to be and try to hide your sins beneath the blanket of darkness. Tomorrow the sun will rise, and all will be revealed once again."

"My lord? Did you say something?"

Hrathen turned. He had barely noticed the guard passing

him on the wall, the man's heavy spear resting over his shoulder and his wan torch nearly dead.

"No. I was only whispering to myself."

The guard nodded, continuing his rounds. They were growing accustomed to Hrathen, who had visited Elantris nearly every night this week, pacing its walls in thought. Though he had an additional purpose behind his visit this particular time, most nights he simply came to be alone and think. He wasn't sure what drew him to the city. Part of it was curiosity. He had never beheld Elantris in its power, and couldn't understand how anything—even a city so grand— had repeatedly withstood the might of Fjorden, first militarily, then theologically.

He also felt a responsibility toward the people—or whatever they were—that lived in Elantris. He was using them, holding them up as an enemy to unite his followers. He felt guilty; the Elantrians he had seen were not devils, but wretches afflicted as if by a terrible disease. They deserved pity, not condemnation. Still, his devils they would become, for he knew that it was the easiest, and most harmless, way to unify Arelon. If he turned the people against their government, as he had done in Duladel, there would be death. This way would lead to bloodshed as well, but he hoped much less.

Oh, what burdens we must accept in the service of Your empire, Lord Jaddeth, Hrathen thought to himself. It didn't matter that he had acted in the name of the Church, or that he had saved thousands upon thousands of souls. The destruction Hrathen had caused in Duladel ground against his soul like a millstone. People who had trusted him were dead, and an entire society had been cast into chaos.

But, Jaddeth required sacrifices. What was one man's conscience when compared with the glory of His rule? What was a little guilt when a nation was now unified beneath Jaddeth's careful eye? Hrathen would ever bear the scars of what he had done, but it was better that one man suffer than an entire nation continue in heresy.

Hrathen turned away from Elantris, looking instead toward the twinkling lights of Kae. Jaddeth had given him another opportunity. This time he would do things differently.

There would be no dangerous revolution, no bloodbath caused by one class turning against another. Hrathen would apply pressure carefully until Iadon folded, and another, more agreeable man took his place. The nobility of Arelon would convert easily, then. The only ones who would truly suffer, the scapegoats in his strategy, were the Elantrians.

It was a good plan. He was certain he could crush this Arelish monarchy without much effort; it was already cracked and weak. The people of Arelon were so oppressed that he could institute a new government swiftly, before they even received word of Iadon's fall. No revolution. Everything would be clean.

Unless he made a mistake. He had visited the farms and cities around Kae; he knew that the people were stressed beyond their ability to bend. If he gave them too much of a chance, they would rise up and slaughter the entire noble class. The possibility made him nervous—mostly because he knew that if it happened, he would make use of it. The logical gyorn within him would ride the destruction as if it were a fine stallion, using it to make Derethi followers out of an entire nation.

Hrathen sighed, turning and continuing his stroll. The wall walk here was kept clean by the guard, but if he strayed too far, he would reach a place covered with a dark, oily grime. He wasn't certain what had caused it, but it seemed to completely coat the wall, once one got away from the central gate area.

Before he reached the grime, however, he spotted the group of men standing along the wall walk. They were dressed in cloaks, though the night wasn't cold enough to require it. Perhaps they thought the garments made them more nondescript. However, if that was the intention, then perhaps Duke Telrii should have chosen to wear something other than a rich lavender cloak set with silver embroidery.

Hrathen shook his head at the materialism. *The men we must work with to accomplish Jaddeth's goals. . . .*

Duke Telrii did not lower his hood, nor did he bow properly, as Hrathen approached—though, of course, Hrathen hadn't really expected him to do either. The duke did, however, nod to his guards, who withdrew to allow them privacy.

Hrathen strolled over to stand beside Duke Telrii, resting against the wall's parapet and staring out over the city of Kae. Lights twinkled; so many people in the city were rich that lamp oil and candles were plentiful. Hrathen had visited some large cities that grew as dark as Elantris when night fell.

"Aren't you going to ask why I wanted to meet with you?" Telrii asked.

"You're having second thoughts about our plan," Hrathen said simply.

Telrii paused, apparently surprised that Hrathen understood him so readily. "Yes, well. If you know that already, then perhaps you are having second thoughts as well."

"Not at all," Hrathen said. "Your mannerism—the furtive way you wanted to meet—was what gave you away."

Telrii frowned. This was a man accustomed to being dominant in any conversation. Was that why he was wavering? Had Hrathen offended him? No, studying Telrii's eyes, Hrathen could tell that wasn't it. Telrii had been eager, at first, to enter into the bargain with Fjorden, and he had certainly seemed to enjoy throwing his party this evening. What had changed?

I can't afford to let this opportunity pass, Hrathen thought. If only he had more time. Fewer than eighty days remained of his three-month deadline. If he had been given even a year, he could have worked with more delicacy and precision. Unfortunately, he had no such luxury, and a blunt attack using Telrii was his best bet for a smooth change in leadership.

"Why don't you tell me what is bothering you?" Hrathen said.

"Yes, well," Telrii said carefully. "I'm just not sure that I want to work with Fjorden."

Hrathen raised an eyebrow. "You didn't have that uncertainty before."

Telrii eyed Hrathen from beneath his hood. In the dark moonlight, it looked like his birthmark was simply a continuation of the shadows, and it gave his features an ominous cast—or, at least, it would have, had his extravagant costume not ruined the effect.

Telrii simply frowned. "I heard some interesting things at the party tonight, Gyorn. Are you really the one who was assigned to Duladel before its collapse?"

Ah, so that's it, Hrathen thought. "I was there."

"And now you're here," Telrii said. "You wonder why a nobleman is made uncomfortable by that news? The entire Republican class—the rulers of Duladel—were slaughtered in that revolution! And my sources claim that *you* had a great deal to do with that."

Perhaps the man wasn't as foolish as Hrathen thought. Telrii's concern was a valid one; Hrathen would have to speak with delicacy. He nodded toward Telrii's guards, who stood a short distance down the wall walk. "Where did you get those soldiers, my lord?"

Telrii paused. "What does that have to do with anything?"

"Humor me," Hrathen said.

Telrii turned, glancing at the soldiers. "I recruited them away from the Elantris City Guard. I hired them to be my bodyguards."

Hrathen nodded. "And, how many such guards do you employ?"

"Fifteen," Telrii said.

"How would you judge their skill?"

Telrii shrugged. "Good enough, I suppose. I've never actually seen them fight."

"That's probably because they never *have* fought," Hrathen said. "None of the soldiers here in Arelon have ever seen combat."

"What is your point, Gyorn?" Telrii asked testily.

Hrathen turned, nodding toward the Elantris City Guard post, lit in the distance by torches at the base of the wall. "The Guard is what, five hundred strong? Perhaps seven hundred? If you include local policing forces and personal guards, such as your own, there are perhaps a thousand soldiers in the city of Kae. Added to Lord Eondel's legion, you still have well below fifteen hundred professional soldiers in the vicinity."

"And?" Telrii asked.

Hrathen turned. "Do you really think that Wyrn needs a revolution to take control of Arelon?"

"Wyrn doesn't have an army," Telrii said. "Fjorden only has a basic defense force."

"I didn't speak of Fjorden," Hrathen said. "I spoke of Wyrn, Regent of all Creation, leader of Shu-Dereth. Come now, Lord Telrii. Let us be frank. How many soldiers are there in Hrovell? In Jaador? In Svorden? In the other nations of the East? These are people who have sworn themselves Derethi. You don't think they would rise up at Wyrn's command?"

Telrii paused.

Hrathen nodded as he saw understanding growing in the duke's eyes. The man didn't understand the half of it. The truth was, Wyrn didn't even need an army of foreigners to conquer Arelon. Few outside the high priesthood understood the second, more powerful force Wyrn had at his call: the monasteries. For centuries, the Derethi priesthood had been training its monks in war, assassination, and . . . other arts. Arelon's defenses were so weak that a single monastery's personnel could probably conquer the country.

Hrathen shivered at the thought of the . . . monks trained inside of Dakhor Monastery gaining access to defenseless Arelon. He glanced down at his arm, the place where—beneath his plate armor—he bore the marks of his time there. These were not things that could be explained to Telrii, however.

"My lord," Hrathen said frankly, "I am here in Arelon because Wyrn wants to give the people a chance for peaceful conversion. If he wanted to crush the country, he could. Instead, he sent me. My only intention is to find a way to convert the people of Arelon."

Telrii nodded slowly.

"The first step in converting this country," Hrathen said, "is making certain that the government is favorable to the Derethi cause. This would require a change in leadership—it would require putting a new king on the throne."

"I have your word, then?" Telrii said.

"You will have the throne," Hrathen said.

Telrii nodded—this was obviously what he had been waiting for. Hrathen's promises before had been vague, but he could no longer afford to be uncommitted. His promises gave Telrii verbal proof that Hrathen was trying to undermine the throne—a calculated risk, but Hrathen was very good at such calculations.

"There will be those who oppose you," Telrii warned.

"Such as?"

"The woman, Sarene," Telrii said. "Her supposed idiocy is an obvious act. My informants say that she's taken an unhealthy interest in your activities, and she was asking about you at my party this evening."

Telrii's astuteness surprised Hrathen. The man seemed so pretentious, so flagrant—yet there was obviously a measure of competence to him. That could be an advantage or a disadvantage.

"Do not worry about the girl," Hrathen said. "Just take the money we have provided and wait. Your opportunity will come soon. You heard of the news the king received tonight?"

Telrii paused, then nodded.

"Things are moving along as promised," Hrathen said. "Now we just have to be patient."

"Very well," Telrii said. He still had his reservations, but Hrathen's logic—mixed with the outright promise of the throne—had obviously been enough to sway him. The duke nodded with uncustomary respect to Hrathen. Then he waved to his guards, moving to walk away.

"Duke Telrii," Hrathen said, a thought occurring to him.

Telrii paused, turning back.

"Do your soldiers still have friends in the Elantris City Guard?" Hrathen asked.

Telrii shrugged. "I assume so."

"Double your men's pay," Hrathen said, too quietly for Telrii's bodyguards to hear. "Speak well of the Elantris City Guard to them, and give them time off to spend with their former comrades. It might be . . . beneficial to your future to have it known amongst the Guard that you are a man who rewards those that give him allegiance."

"You'll provide the funds to pay my men extra?" Telrii asked carefully.

Hrathen rolled his eyes. "Very well."

Telrii nodded, then walked off to join his guards.

Hrathen turned, leaning against the wall, looking back out over Kae. He would have to wait for a short period before returning to the steps and descending. Telrii was still worried about proclaiming Derethi allegiance, and hadn't wanted to be seen openly meeting with Hrathen. The man was overly worried, but perhaps it was better for him to appear religiously conservative for the moment.

It disturbed Hrathen that Telrii had mentioned Sarene. For some reason, the pert Teoish princess had decided to oppose Hrathen, though he had given her no overt reason to do so. It was ironic, in a way; she didn't know it, but Hrathen was her greatest ally, not her dire enemy. Her people would convert one way or another. Either they would respond to Hrathen's humane urgings, or they would be crushed by the Fjordell armies.

Hrathen doubted he would ever be able to convince her of that truth. He saw the mistrust in her eyes—she would immediately assume that whatever he said was a lie. She loathed him with the irrational hatred of one who subconsciously knew that her own faith was inferior. Korathi teachings had withered in every major nation to the East, just as they would in Arelon and Teod. Shu-Korath was too weak; it lacked virility. Shu-Dereth was strong and powerful. Like two plants competing for the same ground, Shu-Dereth would strangle Shu-Korath.

Hrathen shook his head, waited for a safe period of time, then finally turned to walk back along the wall toward the steps that ran down into Kae. As he arrived, he heard an echoing thump from below, and he paused in surprise. It sounded like the city gates had just been closed.

"What was that?" Hrathen asked, approaching several guards who stood in a ring of glittering torchlight.

The guards shrugged, though one pointed at two forms walking through the darkened courtyard below. "They must have caught someone trying to escape."

Hrathen wrinkled his brow. "Does that happen often?"

The guard shook his head. "Most of them are too mindless to try escaping. Every once in a while, one tries to scurry away, but we always catch 'em."

"Thank you," Hrathen said, leaving the guards behind as

he began the long descent to the city below. At the foot of the stairs he found the main guardhouse. The captain was inside, his eyes drowsy as if he had just awakened.

"Trouble, Captain?" Hrathen asked.

The captain turned with surprise. "Oh, it's you, Gyorn. No, no trouble. Just one of my lieutenants doing something he shouldn't have."

"Letting some Elantrians back into the city?" Hrathen asked.

The captain frowned, but nodded. Hrathen had met the man several times, and at each encounter he had fostered the captain's greed with a few coins. This man was nearly his.

"Next time, Captain," Hrathen said, reaching onto his belt and pulling out a pouch, "I can offer you a different option."

The captain's eyes shone as Hrathen began to pull gold wyrnings—stamped with Wyrn Wulfden's head—out of the pouch.

"I have been wanting to study one of these Elantrians up close, for theological reasons," Hrathen explained, setting a pile of coins on the table. "I would be appreciative if the next captured Elantrian found his way to my chapel before being thrown back into the city."

"That can probably be arranged, my lord," the captain said, slipping the coins off the table with an eager hand.

"No one would have to know about it, of course," Hrathen said.

"Of course, my lord."

CHAPTER 16

RAODEN had once tried to set Ien free. He had been a young boy then, simple of mind but pure of intention. He had been learning about slavery from one of his tutors, and had somehow gotten it into his mind that the Seons were being held against their will. He had gone to Ien tearfully that day, demanding that the Seon accept his freedom.

"But I *am* free, young master," Ien had replied to the crying boy.

"No you're not!" Raoden had argued. "You're a slave—you do whatever people tell you."

"I do it because I want to, Raoden."

"Why? Don't you want to be free?"

"I want to serve, young master," Ien explained, pulsing reassuringly. "My freedom is to be here, with you."

"I don't understand."

"You look at things as a human, young master," Ien said with his wise, indulgent voice. "You see rank and distinction; you try to order the world so that everything has a place either above you or beneath you. To a Seon, there is no above or beneath, there are only those we love. And we serve those we love."

"But you don't even get paid!" had been Raoden's indignant response.

"But I do, young master. My payment is that of a father's pride and a mother's love. My wages come from the satisfaction of seeing you grow."

It had been many years before Raoden understood those words, but they had always remained in his mind. As he had grown and learned, listening to countless Korathi sermons on the unifying power of love, Raoden had come to see Seons in a new way. Not as servants, or even as friends, but as something much more deep and more powerful. It was as if the Seons were an expression of Domi himself, reflections of God's love for his people. Through their service, they were much closer to heaven than their supposed masters could ever really understand.

"You're finally free, my friend," Raoden said with a wan smile as he watched Ien float and bob. He still hadn't been able to get even a flicker of recognition from the Seon, though Ien did seem to stay in Raoden's general vicinity. Whatever the Shaod had done to Ien, it had taken away more than just his voice. It had broken his mind.

"I think I know what's wrong with him," Raoden said to Galladon, who sat in the shade a short distance away. They were on a rooftop a few buildings down from the chapel, ejected from their habitual place of study by an apologetic Kahar. The old man had been cleaning furiously in the days since his arrival, and the time had finally come for the final polishing. Early in the morning he had contritely, but insistently, thrown them all out so he could finish.

Galladon looked up from his book. "Who? The Seon?"

Raoden nodded, lying on his stomach near the edge of what was once a garden wall, still watching Ien. "His Aon isn't complete."

"Ien," Galladon said thoughtfully. "That's healing. Kolo?"

"That's right. Except his Aon isn't complete anymore—there are tiny breaks in its lines, and patches of weakness in its color."

Galladon grunted, but didn't offer anything more; he wasn't as interested in Aons or Seons as Raoden was. Raoden watched Ien for a few more moments before turning back to his study of the AonDor book. He didn't get far, however, before Galladon brought up a topic of his own.

"What do you miss most, sule?" the Dula asked contemplatively.

"Miss most? About the outside?"

"Kolo," Galladon said. "What one thing would you bring here to Elantris if you could?"

"I don't know," Raoden said. "I'd have to think about it. What about you?"

"My house," Galladon said with a reminiscent tone. "I built it myself, sule. Felled every tree, worked every board, and pounded every nail. It was beautiful—no mansion or palace can compete with the work of one's own hands."

Raoden nodded, imagining the cabin in his mind. What had he owned that he missed the most strongly? He had been the son of a king, and had therefore had many possessions. The answer he came up with, however, surprised him.

"Letters," he said. "I'd bring a stack of letters."

"Letters, sule?" It obviously hadn't been the response he had been expecting. "From whom?"

"A girl."

Galladon laughed. "A woman, sule? I never figured you for the romantic type."

"Just because I don't mope around dramatically like a character from one of your Duladen romances doesn't mean I don't think about such things."

Galladon held up his hands defensively. "Don't get DeluseDoo on me, sule. I'm just surprised. Who was this girl?"

"I was going to marry her," Raoden explained.

"Must have been some woman."

"Must have been," Raoden agreed. "I wish I could have met her."

"You never met her?"

Raoden shook his head. "Hence the letters, my friend. She lived in Teod—she was the king's daughter, as a matter of fact. She started sending me letters about a year ago. She was a beautiful writer, her words were laced with such wit that I couldn't help but respond. We continued to write for the better part of five months; then she proposed."

"*She* proposed to *you*?" Galladon asked.

"Unabashedly," Raoden said with a smile. "It was, of course, politically motivated. Sarene wanted a firm union between Teod and Arelon."

"And you accepted?"

"It was a good opportunity," Raoden explained. "Ever since the Reod, Teod has kept its distance from Arelon.

Besides, those letters were intoxicating. This last year has been . . . difficult. My father seems determined to run Arelon to its ruin, and he is not a man who suffers dissent with patience. But, whenever it seemed that my burdens were too great, I would get a letter from Sarene. She had a Seon too, and after the engagement was formalized we began to speak regularly. She would call in the evenings, her voice drifting from Ien to captivate me. We left the link open for hours sometimes."

"What was that you said about not moping around like a character from a romance?" Galladon said with a smile.

Raoden snorted, turning back to his book. "So, there you have it. If I could have anything, I'd want those letters. I was actually excited about the marriage, even if the union was just a reaction to the Derethi invasion of Duladel."

There was silence.

"What was that you just said, Raoden?" Galladon finally asked in a quiet voice.

"What? Oh, about the letters?"

"No. About Duladel."

Raoden paused. Galladon had claimed to have entered Elantris a "few months" ago, but Dulas were known for understatement. The Duladen Republic had fallen just over six months previously. . . .

"I assumed you knew," Raoden said.

"What, sule?" Galladon demanded. "Assumed I knew what?"

"I'm sorry, Galladon," Raoden said with compassion, turning around and sitting up. "The Duladen Republic collapsed."

"No," Galladon breathed, his eyes wide.

Raoden nodded. "There was a revolution, like the one in Arelon ten years ago, but even more violent. The republican class was completely destroyed, and a monarchy was instituted."

"Impossible. . . . The republic was *strong*—we all believed in it so much."

"Things change, my friend," Raoden said, standing and walking over to place a hand on Galladon's shoulder.

"Not the republic, sule," Galladon said, his eyes unfocused. "We all got to *choose* who ruled, sule. Why rise up against that?"

Raoden shook his head. "I don't know—not much information escaped. It was a chaotic time in Duladel, which is why the Fjordell priests were able to step in and seize power."

Galladon looked up. "That means Arelon is in trouble. We were always there to keep the Derethi away from your borders."

"I realize that."

"What happened to Jesker?" he asked. "My religion, what happened to it?"

Raoden simply shook his head.

"You have to know something!"

"Shu-Dereth is the state religion in Duladel now," Raoden said quietly. "I'm sorry."

Galladon's eyes fell. "It's gone then."

"There are still the Mysteries," Raoden offered weakly.

Galladon frowned, his eyes hard. "The Mysteries are *not* the same thing as Jesker, sule. They are a mockery of things sacred. A perversion. Only outsiders—those without any sort of true understanding of the Dor—practice the Mysteries."

Raoden left his hand on the grieving man's shoulder, unsure how to comfort him. "I thought you knew," he said again, feeling helpless.

Galladon simply groaned, staring absently with morose eyes.

RAODEN left Galladon on the rooftop; the large Dula wanted to be alone with his grief. Unsure what else to do, Raoden returned to the chapel, distracted by his thoughts. He didn't remain distracted for long.

"Kahar, it's beautiful!" Raoden exclaimed, looking around with wonder.

The old man looked up from the corner he had been cleaning. There was a deep look of pride on his face. The chapel was empty of sludge; all that remained was clean, whitish gray marble. Sunlight flooded through the western windows, reflecting off the shiny floor and illuminating the entire chapel with an almost divine brilliance. Shallow reliefs covered nearly every surface. Only half an inch deep, the detailed sculptures had been lost in the sludge. Raoden ran his fingers across one of the tiny masterpieces, the expressions on the people's faces so detailed as to be lifelike.

"They're amazing," he whispered.

"I didn't even know they were there, my lord," Kahar said, hobbling over to stand next to Raoden. "I didn't see them until I started cleaning, and then they were lost in the shadows until I finished the floor. The marble is so smooth it could be a mirror, and the windows are placed just right to catch the light."

"And the reliefs run all around the room?"

"Yes, my lord. Actually, this isn't the only building that has them. You'll occasionally run across a wall or a piece of furniture with carvings on it. They were probably common in Elantris before the Reod."

Raoden nodded. "It was the city of the gods, Kahar."

The old man smiled. His hands were black with grime, and a half-dozen ragged cleaning cloths hung from his sash. But he was happy.

"What next, my lord?" he asked eagerly.

Raoden paused, thinking quickly. Kahar had attacked the chapel's grime with the same holy indignation a priest used to destroy sin. For the first time in months, perhaps years, Kahar had been needed.

"Our people have started living in the nearby buildings, Kahar," Raoden said. "What good will all your cleaning here do if they track slime in every time we meet?"

Kahar nodded thoughtfully. "The cobblestones are a problem," he mumbled. "This is a big project, my lord." His eyes, however, were not daunted.

"I know." Raoden agreed. "But it is a desperate one. A people who live in filth will feel like filth—if we are ever going to rise above our opinions of ourselves, we are going to need to be clean. Can you do it?"

"Yes, my lord."

"Good. I'll assign you some workers to speed the process." Raoden's band had grown enormously over the last few days as the people of Elantris had heard of Karata's merger with him. Many of the random, ghostlike Elantrians who wandered the streets alone had begun to make their way to Raoden's band, seeking fellowship as a final, desperate attempt to avoid madness.

Kahar turned to go, his wrinkled face turning around the chapel one last time, admiring it with satisfaction.

"Kahar," Raoden called.

"Yes, my lord?"

"Do you know what it is? The secret, I mean?"

Kahar smiled. "I haven't been hungry in days, my lord. It is the most amazing feeling in the world—I don't even notice the pain anymore."

Raoden nodded, and Kahar left. The man had come looking for a magical solution to his woes, but he had found an answer much more simple. Pain lost its power when other things became more important. Kahar didn't need a potion or an Aon to save him—he just needed something to do.

Raoden strolled through the glowing room, admiring the different sculptures. He paused, however, when he reached the end of a particular relief. The stone was blank for a short section, its white surface polished by Kahar's careful hand. It was so clean, in fact, that Raoden could see his reflection.

He was stunned. The face that stared out of the marble was unknown to him. He had wondered why so few people recognized him; he had been prince of Arelon, his face known even in many of the outer plantations. He had assumed that the Elantrians simply didn't expect to find a prince in Elantris, so they didn't think to associate "Spirit" with Raoden. However, now that he saw the changes in his face, he realized that there was another reason people didn't recognize him.

There were hints in his features, clues to what had been. The changes, however, were drastic. Only two weeks had passed, but his hair had already fallen out. He had the usual Elantris blotches on his skin, but even the parts that had been flesh-toned a few weeks ago had turned a flat gray. His skin was wrinkling slightly, especially around the lips, and his eyes were beginning to take on a sunken look.

Once, before his own transformation, he had envisioned the Elantrians as living corpses, their flesh rotting and torn. That wasn't the case; Elantrians retained their flesh and most of their figure, though their skin wrinkled and darkened. They were more withering husks than they were decaying corpses. Yet, even though the transformation wasn't as drastic as he had once assumed, it was still a shock to see it in himself.

"We are a sorry people, are we not?" Galladon asked from the doorway.

Raoden looked up, smiling encouragingly. "Not as bad as we could be, my friend. I can get used to the changes."

Galladon grunted, stepping into the chapel. "Your cleaning man does good work, sule. This place looks almost free from the Reod."

"The most beautiful thing, my friend, is the way it freed its cleanser in the process."

Galladon nodded, joining Raoden beside the wall, looking out at the large crew of people who were clearing the chapel's garden area. "They've been coming in droves, haven't they, sule?"

"They hear that we offer something more than life in an alley. We don't even have to watch the gates anymore—Karata brings us everyone she can rescue."

"How do you intend to keep them all busy?" Galladon asked. "That garden is big, and it's nearly completely cleared."

"Elantris is a very large city, my friend. We'll find things to keep them occupied."

Galladon watched the people work, his eyes unreadable. He appeared to have overcome his grief, for the moment.

"Speaking of jobs," Raoden began. "I have something I need you to do."

"Something to keep *my* mind off the pain, sule?"

"You could think that. However, this project is a little more important than cleaning sludge." Raoden waved Galladon to follow as he walked to the back corner of the room and pried a loose stone from the wall. He reached inside and pulled out a dozen small bags of corn. "As a farmer, how would you judge the grade of this seed?"

Galladon picked up a kernel with interest, turning it over in his hand a few times, testing its color and its hardness. "Not bad," he said. "Not the best I've seen, but not bad."

"The planting season is almost here, isn't it?"

"Considering how warm it's been lately, I'd say that it's here already."

"Good," Raoden said. "This corn won't last long in this hole, and I don't trust leaving it out in the open."

Galladon shook his head. "It won't work, sule. Farming takes time before it brings rewards—those people will pull up and eat the first little sprouts they see."

"I don't think so," Raoden said, pushing a few kernels of corn around in his palm. "Their minds are changing, Galladon. They can see that they don't have to live as animals anymore."

"There isn't enough room for a decent crop," Galladon argued. "It will be little more than a garden."

"There's enough space to plant this little amount. Next year we'll have more corn, and then we can worry about room. I hear the palace gardens were rather large—we could probably use those."

Galladon shook his head. "The problem in that statement, sule, is the part about 'next year.' There won't be a 'next year.' Kolo? People in Elantris don't last that long."

"Elantris will change," Raoden said. "If not, then those who come here after us will plant the next season."

"I still doubt it will work."

"You'd doubt the sun's rising if you weren't proven wrong each day," Raoden said with a smile. "Just give it a try."

"All right, sule," Galladon said with a sigh. "I suppose your thirty days aren't up yet."

Raoden smiled, passing the corn to his friend and placing his hand on the Dula's shoulder. "Remember, the past need not become our future as well."

Galladon nodded, putting the corn back in its hiding place. "We won't need this for another few days—I'm going to have to figure out a way to plow that garden."

"Lord Spirit!" Saolin's voice called faintly from above, where he had constructed himself a makeshift watchtower. "Someone is coming."

Raoden stood, and Galladon hurriedly replaced the stone. A moment later one of Karata's men burst into the room.

"My lord," the man said, "Lady Karata begs your presence immediately!"

"YOU are a fool, Dashe!" Karata snapped.

Dashe—the extremely large, well-muscled man who was her second-in-command—simply continued to strap on his weapons.

Raoden and Galladon stood confused at the doorway to the palace. At least ten of the men in the entryway—a full two-thirds of Karata's followers—looked as if they were preparing for battle.

"You can continue to dream with your new friend, Karata," Dashe replied gruffly, "but I will wait no longer— especially not as long as that man threatens the children."

Raoden edged closer to the conversation, pausing beside a thin-limbed, anxious man named Horen. Horen was the type who avoided conflict, and Raoden guessed that he was neutral in this argument.

"What's happening?" Raoden asked quietly.

"One of Dashe's scouts overheard Aanden planning to attack our palace tonight," Horen whispered, carefully watching his leaders argue. "Dashe has wanted to strike at Aanden for months now, and this is just the excuse he needed."

"You're leading these men into something far worse than death, Dashe," Karata warned. "Aanden has more people than you do."

"He doesn't have weapons," Dashe replied, sliding a rusted sword into its sheath with a click. "All that university held was books, and he already ate those."

"Think about what you are doing," Karata said.

Dashe turned, his boardlike face completely frank. "I have, Karata. Aanden is a madman; we cannot rest while he shares our border. If we strike unexpectedly, then we can stop him permanently. Only then will the children be safe."

With that, Dashe turned to his grim band of would-be soldiers and nodded. The group moved out the door with purposeful strides.

Karata turned to Raoden, her face a mixture of frustration and pained betrayal. "This is worse than suicide, Spirit."

"I know," Raoden said. "We're so few we can't afford to lose a single man—not even those who follow Aanden. We have to stop this."

"He's already gone," Karata said, leaning back against the wall. "I know Dashe well. There's no stopping him now."

"I refuse to accept that, Karata."

"SULE, if you don't mind my asking, what in Doloken are you planning?"

Raoden loped along beside Galladon and Karata, barely keeping up with the two. "I have no idea," he confessed. "I'm still working on that part."

"I figured as much," Galladon muttered.

"Karata," Raoden asked, "what route will Dashe take?"

"There's a building that runs up against the university," she replied. "Its far wall collapsed a while ago, and some of the stones knocked a hole in the university wall it abuts. I'm sure Dashe will try to get in there—he assumes Aanden doesn't know about the breach."

"Take us there," Raoden said. "But take a different route. I don't want to run into Dashe."

Karata nodded, leading them down a side street. The building she'd mentioned was a low, single-story structure. One of the walls had been built so close to the university that Raoden was at a loss to guess what the architect had been thinking. The building had not fared well over the years; although it still had its roof—which was sagging horribly— the entire structure seemed on the edge of collapse.

They approached apprehensively, poking their heads through a doorway. The building was open on the inside. They stood near the center of the rectangular structure, the collapsed wall a short distance to their left, another doorway a short distance to their right.

Galladon cursed quietly. "I don't trust this."

"Neither do I," Raoden said.

"No, it's more than that. Look, sule." Galladon pointed to the building's inner support beams. Looking closely, Raoden recognized the marks of fresh cuts in the already weakened wood. "This entire place is rigged to fall."

Raoden nodded. "It appears as if Aanden is better informed than Dashe assumed. Maybe Dashe will notice the danger and use a different entrance."

Karata shook her head immediately. "Dashe is a good man, but very single-minded. He'll march right through this building without bothering to look up."

Raoden cursed, kneeling beside the doorframe to think. He soon ran out of time, however, as he heard voices approaching. A moment later Dashe appeared in the doorway on the far side, to Raoden's right.

Raoden—halfway between Dashe and the fallen wall— took a deep breath and called out. "Dashe, stop! This is a trap—the building is rigged to collapse!"

Dashe halted, half of his men already in the building. There was a cry of alarm from the university side of the room, and a group of men appeared behind the rubble. One, bearing Aanden's familiar mustached face, held a worn fire axe in his hands. Aanden jumped into the room with a cry of defiance, axe raised toward the support pillar.

"Taan, stop!" Raoden yelled.

Aanden stopped his axe in midswing, shocked at the sound of his real name. One half of his fake mustache drooped limply, threatening to fall off.

"Don't try to reason with him!" Dashe warned, pulling his men from the room. "He's insane."

"No, I don't think he is," Raoden said, studying Aanden's eyes. "This man is not insane—just confused."

Aanden blinked a few times, his hands growing tense on the axe handle. Raoden searched desperately for a solution, and his eyes fell on the remnants of a large stone table near the center of the room. Gritting his teeth and muttering a silent prayer to Domi, Raoden stood and walked into the building.

Karata gasped behind him, and Galladon cursed. The roof moaned ominously.

Raoden looked at Aanden, who stood with the axe prepared to swing. His eyes followed Raoden into the center of the room.

"I'm right, am I not? You aren't mad. I heard you babbling insanely at your court, but anyone can babble. An insane man doesn't think to boil parchment for food, and a madman doesn't have the foresight to plan a trap."

"I am not Taan," Aanden finally said. "I am Aanden, Baron of Elantris!"

"If you wish," Raoden said, taking the remnants of his sleeve and wiping it against the top of the fallen table. "Though I can't imagine why you would rather be Aanden than Taan. This is, after all, Elantris."

"I know that!" Aanden snapped. No matter what Raoden had said, this man wasn't completely stable. The axe could fall at any moment.

"Do you?" Raoden asked. "Do you really understand what it means to live in Elantris, the city of the gods?" He turned toward the table, still wiping, his back to Aanden. "Elantris, city of beauty, city of art . . . and city of sculpture." He stepped back, revealing the now clean tabletop. It was covered with intricate carvings, just like the walls of the chapel.

Aanden's eyes opened wide, the axe drooping in his hand.

"This city is a stonecarver's dream, Taan," Raoden said. "How many artists did you hear on the outside complain about the lost beauty of Elantris? These buildings are amazing monuments to the art of sculpture. I want to know who, when faced with such opportunity, would choose to be Aanden the baron instead of Taan the sculptor."

The axe clanged to the ground. Aanden's face was stunned.

"Look at the wall next to you, Taan," Raoden said quietly.

The man turned, his fingers brushing against a relief hidden in slime. His sleeve came up, his arm quivering as he buffed away the slime. "Merciful Domi," he whispered. "It's beautiful."

"Think of the opportunity, Taan," Raoden said. "Only you, out of all the sculptors in the world, can see Elantris. Only you can experience its beauty and learn from its masters. You are the luckiest man in Opelon."

A trembling hand ripped the mustache away. "And I would have destroyed it," he mumbled. "I would have knocked it down. . . ."

With that, Aanden bowed his head and collapsed in a crying heap. Raoden exhaled thankfully—then noticed that the danger wasn't over. Aanden's squad of men was armed with stones and steel rods. Dashe and his people entered the room again, convinced that it wasn't going to collapse on them any time soon.

Raoden stood directly between the two groups. "Stop!" he commanded, raising an arm at each one. They halted, but warily.

"What are you people doing?" Raoden demanded. "Hasn't Taan's realization taught you anything?"

"Step aside, Spirit," Dashe warned, hefting his sword.

"I will not!" Raoden said. "I asked you a question—did you learn nothing from what just happened?"

"We aren't sculptors," Dashe said.

"That doesn't matter," Raoden replied. "Don't you understand the opportunity you have living in Elantris? We have a chance here that no one outside can ever achieve—we are free."

"Free?" scoffed someone from Aanden's group.

"Yes, free," Raoden said. "For eternity man has struggled just to fill his mouth. Food is life's one desperate pursuit, the first and the last thought of carnal minds. Before a person can dream, he must eat, and before he can love, he must fill his stomach. But we are different. At the price of a little hunger, we can be loosed from the bonds that have held every living thing since time began."

Weapons lowered slightly, though Raoden couldn't be certain if they were considering his words, or just confused by them.

"Why fight?" Raoden asked. "Why worry about killing? Outside they fight for wealth—wealth that is ultimately used to buy food. They fight for land—land to raise food. Eating is the source of all struggle. But, we have no needs. Our bodies are cold—we barely need clothing or shelter to warm us—and they continue on even when we don't eat. It's amazing!"

The groups still eyed each other warily. Philosophic debate wasn't a match for the sight of their enemies.

"Those weapons in your hands," Raoden said. "Those be-

long to the outside world. They have no purpose in Elantris.
Titles and class, those are ideas for another place.

"Listen to me! There are so few of us that we can't afford
to lose a single one of you. Is it really worth it? An eternity
of pain in exchange for a few moments of released hatred?"

Raoden's words echoed through the silent room. Finally, a
voice broke the tension.

"I will join you," Taan said, rising to his feet. His voice
wavered slightly, but his face was resolute. "I thought I had
to be mad to live in Elantris, but madness was what kept me
from seeing the beauty. Put down your weapons, men."

They balked at the order.

"I said put them down." Taan's voice grew firm, his short,
large-bellied form suddenly commanding. "I still lead here."

"Baron Aanden ruled us," one of the men said.

"Aanden was a fool," Taan said with a sigh, "and so was
anyone who followed him. Listen to this man—there is more
royalty in his argument than there ever was in my pretend
court."

"Give up your anger," Raoden pled. "And let me give you
hope instead."

A clank sounded behind him—Dashe's sword falling to
the stones. "I cannot kill today," he decided, turning to leave.
His men regarded Aanden's group for a moment, then joined
their leader. The sword sat abandoned in the center of the
room.

Aanden—Taan—smiled at Raoden. "Whoever you are,
thank you."

"Come with me, Taan," Raoden said. "There is a building
you should see."

CHAPTER 17

SARENE strode into the palace dance hall, a long black bag on her shoulder. There were several gasps from the women inside.

"What?" she asked.

"It's your clothing, dear," Daora finally answered. "These women aren't accustomed to such things."

"It looks like men's clothing!" Seaden exclaimed, her double chin jiggling indignantly.

Sarene looked down at her gray jumpsuit with surprise, then back at the collected women. "Well, you didn't really expect us to fight in dresses, did you?" However, after studying the women's faces, she realized that that was exactly what they had expected.

"You have a long way to go here, Cousin," Lukel warned quietly, entering behind her and taking a seat on the far side of the room.

"Lukel?" Sarene asked. "What are you doing here?"

"I fully expect this to be the most entertaining experience of the week," he said, reclining in his chair and putting his hands behind his head. "I wouldn't miss it for all the gold in Wyrn's coffers."

"Me too," Kaise's voice declared. The small girl pushed her way past Sarene and scuttled toward the chairs. Daorn, however, darted in from the side and hopped into Kaise's chosen seat. Kaise stamped her foot with pique, then, realizing that every chair along the wall was exactly the same, chose another.

"I'm sorry," Lukel said with an embarrassed shrug. "I was stuck with them."

"Be nice to your siblings, dear," Daora chided.

"Yes, Mother," Lukel responded immediately.

Slightly put off by the sudden audience, Sarene turned to her prospective students. Every woman from the embroidery circle had come—even the stately Daora and the equally scatterbrained Queen Eshen. Sarene's clothing and actions might have mortified them, but their hunger for independence was greater than their indignation.

Sarene allowed the bag to slide off her shoulder and into her hands. One side opened with some snaps, and she reached inside to whip out one of her practice swords. The long, thin blade made a slight metallic scrape as she pulled it free, and the collected women shied away.

"This is a syre," Sarene said, making a few slices in the air. "It's also called a kmeer or a jedaver, depending on which country you're in. The swords were first crafted in Jaador as light weapons for scouts, but they fell into disuse after only a few decades. Then, however, the swords were adopted by Jaadorian nobility, who favored them for their grace and delicacy. Duels are common in Jaador, and the quick, neat style of syre fencing requires a great deal of skill."

She punctuated her sentences with a few thrusts and swipes—mostly moves she would never use in a real fight, but ones that looked good nonetheless. The women were captivated.

"The Dulas were the first ones to turn fencing into a sport, rather than a means of killing the man who had decided to woo the same woman as yourself," Sarene continued. "They placed this little knob on the tip and dulled the blade's edge. The sport soon became quite popular amongst the republicans—Dula neutrality usually kept the country out of war, and so a form of fighting that didn't have martial applications appealed to them. Along with the dulled edge and tip, they added rules that forbid the striking of certain body parts.

"Fencing skipped Arelon, where the Elantrians frowned upon anything resembling combat, but was very well received in Teod—with one notable change. It became a woman's sport. The Teoish men prefer more physical contests, such as jousting or broadsword fencing. For a woman, however, the syre is perfect. The light blade allows us to make full use of our dexterity and," she added, eyeing Lukel with a smile, "allows us to capitalize on our superior intelligence."

With that, Sarene whipped out her second blade and tossed it to the young Torena, who stood at the front of the group. The reddish-gold-haired girl caught the sword with a confused look.

"Defend yourself," Sarene warned, raising her blade and falling into an attack stance.

Torena brought up the syre clumsily, trying to imitate Sarene's posture. As soon as Sarene attacked, Torena abandoned the stance with a yelp of surprise, swinging her syre in wild two-handed sweeps. Sarene easily batted the girl's sword away and placed a thrust directly between her breasts.

"You're dead," Sarene informed her. "Fencing does not depend on strength; it requires skill and precision. Only use one hand—you'll have better control and reach that way. Turn your body a little to the side. It allows for a greater lunging distance and makes you more difficult to hit."

As she spoke, Sarene brought out a bundle of thin sticks she'd had made earlier. They were, of course, poor substitutes for a real sword, but they would do until the armorer finished the practice syres. After each woman received a weapon, Sarene began to teach them how to lunge.

It was difficult work—much more difficult than Sarene had expected. She considered herself a decent fencer, but it had never occurred to her that having knowledge was entirely different from explaining that knowledge to others. The women seemed to find ways to hold their weapons that Sarene would have thought physically impossible. They thrust wildly, were frightened of oncoming blades, and tripped over their dresses.

Eventually Sarene left them to practice their thrusts—she wouldn't trust them to spar with one another until they had proper face masks and clothing—and seated herself beside Lukel with a sigh.

"Exhausting work, Cousin?" he asked, obviously enjoying the sight of his mother trying to wield a sword in a dress.

"You have no idea," Sarene said, wiping her brow. "Are you sure you don't want to give it a try?"

Lukel raised his hands. "I may be flamboyant at times, Cousin, but I'm not stupid. King Iadon would blacklist any man who took part in such a supposedly demeaning activity. Being on the king's bad side is fine if you happen to be Eondel, but I'm just a simple merchant. I can't afford royal displeasure."

"I'm sure," Sarene said, watching the women trying to master their lunges. "I don't think I taught them very well."

"Better than I could have done," Lukel said with a shrug.

"*I* could have done better," Kaise informed from her seat. The little girl was obviously growing bored with the repetitious fighting.

"Oh really?" Lukel asked dryly.

"Of course. She didn't teach them about riposting or Proper Form, and she didn't even bother with tournament rules."

Sarene raised an eyebrow. "You know about fencing?"

"I read a book on it," Kaise said airily. Then she reached over to slap away Daorn's hand, which was poking her with a stick he had taken from Sarene's pile.

"The sad thing is she probably did," Lukel said with a sigh. "Just so she could try and impress you."

"I think Kaise must be the most intelligent little girl I've ever met," Sarene confessed.

Lukel shrugged. "She's smart, but don't let her impress you too much—she's still only a child. She may comprehend like a woman, but she still reacts like a little girl."

"I still think she's astounding," Sarene said, watching as the two children played.

"Oh, she's that," Lukel agreed. "It only takes Kaise a few hours to devour a book, and her language-learning ability is unreal. I feel sorry for Daorn sometimes. He tries his best, but I think he just feels inadequate—Kaise can be domineering, if you haven't noticed. But, smart or not, they're still children, and they're still a pain to take care of."

Sarene watched the children playing. Kaise, having stolen the stick from her brother, was proceeding to chase him around the room, cutting and thrusting in parodies of the methods Sarene had taught. As Sarene watched, her eyes fell on the doorway. It was open, and two figures watched the women practice.

The ladies fell still as Lords Eondel and Shuden, realizing they had been noticed, slipped into the room. The two men, though very different in age, were reportedly becoming good friends. Both were something of outsiders in Arelon—Shuden, a foreigner with dark skin, and Eondel, a former soldier whose very presence seemed to offend.

If Eondel's presence was distasteful to the women, however, Shuden's more than made up for it. A serious wave of blushing ran through the fencers as they realized that the handsome Jindoeese lord had been watching them. Several of the younger girls clutched friends' arms for support, whispering excitedly. Shuden himself flushed at the attention.

Eondel, however, ignored the women's reactions. He walked among the would-be fencers, his eyes contemplative. Finally, he picked up a spare length of wood, and stepped into a fencing posture and began a series of swipes and thrusts. After testing the weapon, he nodded to himself, set it aside, then moved toward one of the women.

"Hold the wood like so," he instructed, positioning her fingers. "You were gripping it so tightly you lost flexibility. Now, place your thumb along the top of the hilt to keep it pointed in the right direction, step back, and thrust."

The woman, Atara, complied—flustered that Eondel had dared touch her wrist. Her thrust, amazingly, was straight and well aimed—a fact that surprised no one more than Atara herself.

Eondel moved through the group, carefully correcting posture, grip, and stance. He took each woman in turn, giving advice to their several individual problems. After just a few brief minutes of instruction, the women's attacks were more focused and accurate than Sarene would have thought possible.

Eondel backed away from the women with a satisfied eye. "I hope you aren't offended by my intrusion, Your Highness."

"Not at all, my lord," Sarene assured him—even though

she did feel a stab of jealousy. She had to be woman enough to recognize superior skill when she saw it, she told herself.

"You are obviously talented," the older man said. "But you seem to have had little experience in training others."

Sarene nodded. Eondel was a military commander—he had probably spent decades instructing novices in the basics of fighting. "You know quite a bit about fencing, my lord."

"It interests me," Eondel said, "and I have visited Duladel on numerous occasions. The Dulas refuse to recognize a man's fighting ability unless he can fence, no matter how many battles he has won."

Sarene stood, reaching over and pulling out her practice syres. "Care to spar then, my lord?" she asked offhandedly, testing one of the blades in her hand.

Eondel looked surprised. "I . . . I have never sparred with a woman before, Your Highness. I don't think it would be proper."

"Nonsense," she said, tossing him a sword. "Defend yourself."

Then, without giving him another chance to object, she attacked. Eondel stumbled at first, taken aback by her sudden offense. However, his warrior training soon took control, and he began to parry Sarene's attack, with amazing skill. From what he'd said, Sarene had assumed that his knowledge of fencing would be cursory. She was mistaken.

Eondel threw himself into the bout with determination. His blade whipped through the air so quickly it was impossible to follow, and only years of training and drills told Sarene where to parry. The room rang with the sound of metal against metal, and the women paused to gawk as their two instructors moved across the floor, engaged in intense battle.

Sarene wasn't used to sparring with someone as good as Eondel. Not only was he as tall as she was—negating any advantage she had in reach—he had the reflexes and training of a man who had spent his entire life fighting. The two of them pushed through the crowd, using women, chairs, and other random objects as foils for the other's attack. Their swords cracked and whipped, lunging out and then snapping back to block.

Eondel was too good for her. She could hold him, but was so busy with defense that she had no time to attack. With sweat streaming down her face, Sarene became acutely aware that everyone in the room was watching her.

At that moment, something changed in Eondel. His stance weakened slightly, and Sarene struck reflexively. Her round tipped blade slipped past his defenses came up against his neck. Eondel smiled slightly.

"I have no choice but to yield, my lady," Eondel said.

Suddenly, Sarene felt very ashamed for putting Eondel in a situation where he had obviously let her win, lest he make her look bad in front of the others. Eondel bowed, and Sarene was left feeling silly.

They walked back to the side of the room, accepting cups from Lukel, who complimented them on the performance. As Sarene drank, something struck her. She had been treating her time here in Arelon like a contest, as she did with most political endeavors—a complex, yet enjoyable, game.

Arelon was different. Eondel had let her win because he wanted to protect her image. To him, it was no game. Arelon was his nation, his people, and he would make any sacrifice in order to protect them.

This time is different, Sarene. If you fail, you won't lose a trade contract or building rights. You'll lose lives. The lives of real people. The thought was sobering.

Eondel regarded his cup, eyebrows raised skeptically. "It's only water?" he asked, turning to Sarene.

"Water is good for you, my lord."

"I'm not so sure about that," Eondel said. "Where did you get it?"

"I had it boiled and then poured between two buckets to restore its flavor," Sarene said. "I wasn't going to have the women falling over each other in drunken stupors while they tried to practice."

"Arelish wine isn't that strong, Cousin," Lukel pointed out.

"It's strong enough," Sarene replied. "Drink up, Lord Eondel. We wouldn't want you to get dehydrated."

Eondel complied, though he maintained his look of dissatisfaction.

Sarene turned back toward her students, intending to order them to their practicing—however, their attention had been captured by something else. Lord Shuden stood near the back of the room. His eyes were closed as he moved slowly through a delicate set of motions. His taut muscles rippled as his hands spun in controlled loops, his body flowing in response. Even though his motions were slow and precise, there was sweat glistening on his skin.

It was like a dance. Shuden took long steps, legs rising high in the air, toes pointed, before placing them on the floor. His arms were always moving, his muscles stretched tightly, as if he were struggling against some unseen force. Slowly, Shuden accelerated. As if building in tension, Shuden swept faster and faster, his steps becoming leaps, his arms whipping.

The women watched in silence, their eyes wide, more than one jaw gaping open. The only sounds came from the wind of Shuden's moves and the thumping of his feet.

He stopped suddenly, landing in a final jump, feet pounding to the ground in unison, arms outspread, hands flat. He folded his arms inward like two heavy gates swinging shut. Then he bowed his head and exhaled deeply.

Sarene let the moment hang before mumbling, "Merciful Domi. Now I'll *never* get them to focus."

Eondel chuckled quietly. "Shuden's an interesting lad. He complains repeatedly about the way women chase him, but he can't resist the urge to show off. Despite it all, he's still a man, and he's still rather young."

Sarene nodded as Shuden completed his ritual, then turned sheepishly as he realized how much attention he had drawn. He quickly wove his way through the women with downcast eyes, joining Sarene and Eondel.

"That was . . . unexpected," Sarene said as Shuden accepted a cup of water from Lukel.

"I apologize, Lady Sarene," he replied between gulps. "Your sparring made me want to exercise. I thought everyone would be so busy practicing that they wouldn't notice me."

"Women always notice you, my friend," Eondel said with a shake of his gray-streaked head. "Next time you complain

about being mauled by adoring women, I'll point out this little fiasco."

Shuden bowed his head in acquiescence, blushing again.

"What was that exercise?" Sarene asked curiously. "I've
never seen anything like it."

"We call it ChayShan," Shuden explained. "It's a kind of
warm-up—a way to focus your mind and body when preparing for a battle."

"It's impressive," Lukel said.

"I'm just an amateur," Shuden said with a modestly
bowed head. "I lack speed and focus—there are men in
Jindo who can move so quickly you grow dizzy watching
them."

"All right, ladies," Sarene declared, turning to the women,
most of whom were still staring at Shuden. "Thank Lord
Shuden for his exhibition later. Right now, you have some
lunges to practice—don't think I'm going to let you leave
after just a few minutes of work!"

There were several groans of complaint as Sarene took up
her syre and began the practice session anew.

"THEY'LL all be devilishly sore tomorrow," Sarene said
with a smile.

"You say that with such passion, my lady, that one is inclined to think you're enjoying the prospect." Ashe throbbed
slightly as he spoke.

"It will be good for them," Sarene said. "Most of those
women are so pampered that they've never felt anything
more serious than the prick of a stitching needle."

"I'm sorry I missed the practice," Ashe said. "I haven't
watched a ChayShan in decades."

"You've seen one before?"

"I've seen many things, my lady," Ashe replied. "A Seon's
life is very long."

Sarene nodded. They walked down a street in Kae, the
enormous wall of Elantris looming in the background.
Dozens of street vendors offered their wares eagerly as she
passed, recognizing from her dress that she was a member of
the court. Kae existed to support the Arelish nobility, and it

catered to very pompous tastes. Gold-plated cups, exotic spices, and extravagant clothes all vied for her attention—though most of it just made her feel sick to her stomach.

From what she understood, these merchants were the only real middle class left in Arelon. In Kae they competed for King Iadon's favor, and hopefully a title—usually at the expense of their competitors, a few peasants, and their dignity. Arelon was quickly becoming a nation of fervent, even terrified, commercialism. Success no longer brought just wealth, and failure no longer just poverty—income determined just how close one was to being sold into virtual slavery.

Sarene waved off the merchants, though her efforts did little to discourage them. She was relieved to finally turn a corner and see the Korathi chapel. She resisted the urge to sprint the rest of the way, keeping her pace steady until she reached the doors to the broad building and slipped in.

She dropped a few coins—nearly the last of the money she had brought with her from Teod—into the donations box, then went looking for the priest. The chapel felt comfortable to Sarene. Unlike Derethi chapels—which were austere and formal, hung with shields, spears, and the occasional tapestry—Korathi chapels were more relaxed. A few quilts hung on the walls—probably donations from elderly patrons—and flowers and plants sat lined up beneath them, their buds peeking out in the spring weather. The ceiling was low and unvaulted, but the windows were broad and wide enough to keep the building from feeling cramped.

"Hello, child," a voice said from the side of the room. Omin, the priest, was standing next to one of the far windows, looking out at the city.

"Hello, Father Omin," Sarene said with a curtsey. "Am I bothering you?"

"Of course not, child," Omin said, waving her over. "Come, how have you been? I missed you at the sermon last night."

"I'm sorry, Father Omin," Sarene said with a slight flush. "There was a ball I had to attend."

"Ah. Do not feel guilty, child. Socializing is not to be underestimated, especially when one is new in town."

Sarene smiled, walking between a set of pews to join the

short priest next to the window. His small stature wasn't usually so noticeable; Omin had constructed a podium at the front of the chapel to fit his size, and while he gave sermons it was hard to distinguish his height. Standing next to the man, however, Sarene couldn't help feeling that she was towering over him. He was terribly short even for an Arelene, the top of his head barely reaching her chest.

"You are troubled by something, child?" Omin asked. He was mostly bald, and wore a loose-fitting robe tied at the waist with a white sash. Other than his strikingly blue eyes, the only color on his body was a jade Korathi pendant at his neck, carved in the shape of Aon Omi.

He was a good man—something Sarene couldn't say about everyone, even priests. There were several back in Teod who absolutely infuriated her. Omin, however, was thoughtful and fatherly—even if he did have an annoying habit of letting his thoughts drift. He sometimes got so distracted that minutes would pass without his realizing someone was waiting for him to speak.

"I wasn't sure who else to ask, Father," Sarene said. "I need to do a Widow's Trial, but no one will explain what it is."

"Ah," Omin said with a nod of his shiny hairless head. "That would be confusing for a newcomer."

"Why won't anyone explain it to me?"

"It is a semireligious ceremony left over from days when the Elantrians ruled," Omin explained. "Anything involving the city is a taboo topic in Arelon, especially for the Faithful."

"Well, then how am I going to learn what is expected of me?" Sarene asked with exasperation.

"Do not get frustrated, child," Omin said soothingly. "It is taboo, but only by custom, not by doctrine. I don't think Domi would have any objection to my assuaging your curiosity."

"Thank you, Father," Sarene said with a sigh of relief.

"Since your husband died," Omin explained, "you are expected to show your grief openly, otherwise the people won't think you loved him."

"But I didn't love him—not really. I didn't even know him."

"Nonetheless, it would be proper for you to do a Trial.

The severity of a Widow's Trial is an expression of how important she thought her union, and how much she respected her husband. To go without one, even for an outsider, could be a bad sign."

"But wasn't it a pagan ritual?"

"Not really," Omin said with a shake of his head. "The Elantrians started it, but it had nothing to do with their religion. It was simply an act of kindness that developed into a benevolent and worthy tradition."

Sarene raised her eyebrows. "Honestly, I am surprised to hear you speak that way about the Elantrians, Father."

Omin's eyes sparkled. "Just because the Derethi arteths hated the Elantrians doesn't mean that Domi did, child. I do not believe they were gods, and many of them had inflated opinions of their own majesty, but I had a number of friends in their ranks. The Shaod took men both good and bad, selfish and selfless. Some of the most noble men I ever knew lived in that city—I was very sorry to see what happened to them."

Sarene paused. "Was it Domi, Father? Did he curse them as they say?"

"Everything happens according to Domi's will, child," Omin answered. "However, I do not think that 'curse' is the right word. At times, Domi sees fit to send disasters upon the world; other times he will give the most innocent of children a deadly disease. These are no more curses than what happened to Elantris—they are simply the workings of the world. All things must progress, and progression is not always a steady incline. Sometimes we must fall, sometimes we will rise—some must be hurt while others have fortune, for that is the only way we can learn to rely on one another. As one is blessed, it is his privilege to help those whose lives are not as easy. Unity comes from strife, child."

Sarene paused. "So you don't think the Elantrians—what's left of them—are devils?"

"Svrakiss, as the Fjordells call them?" Omin asked with amusement. "No, though I hear that is what this new gyorn teaches. I fear his pronouncements will only bring hatred."

Sarene tapped her cheek in thought. "That may be what he wants."

"What purpose could that accomplish?"

"I don't know," Sarene admitted.

Omin shook his head again. "I cannot believe any follower of God, even a gyorn, would do such a thing." He took on an abstracted look as he considered the prospect, a slight frown on his face.

"Father?" Sarene asked. "Father?"

At the second prod Omin shook his head, as if startled to realize she was still there. "I'm sorry, child. What were we discussing?"

"You never finished telling me what a Widow's Trial was," she reminded. Tangents were all too frequent when one was speaking with the diminutive priest.

"Ah, yes. The Widow's Trial. Put simply, child, you are expected to do some favor for the country—the more you loved your husband, and the more lofty your station, the more extravagant your Trial is supposed to be. Most women give food or clothing to the peasantry. The more personal your involvement, the better the impression you give. The Trial is a method of service—a means of bringing humility to the exalted."

"But where will I get the money?" She hadn't decided just how to go about asking her new father for a stipend.

"Money?" Omin asked with surprise. "Why, you're one of the richest people in Arelon. Didn't you know that?"

"What?"

"You inherited Prince Raoden's estate, child," Omin explained. "He was a very wealthy man—his father made sure of that. Under King Iadon's government, it would not be good for the crown prince to be any less rich than a duke. By the same token, it would be a source of extreme embarrassment to him if his daughter-in-law weren't fabulously wealthy. All you need to do is speak to the royal treasurer, and I'm certain he will take care of you."

"Thank you, Father," Sarene said, giving the little man a fond hug. "I have work to do."

"Your visit was welcome, child," Omin said, looking back at the city with contemplative eyes. "That is what I am here for." However, she could tell that soon after making the comment, he had already forgotten her presence, traveling, once again, the long roads within his mind.

ASHE waited for her outside, hovering beside the door with characteristic patience.

"I don't see why you're so worried," Sarene said to him. "Omin *liked* Elantris; he wouldn't have anything against your entering his chapel."

Ashe pulsed slightly. He hadn't entered a Korathi chapel since the day many years ago when Seinalan, the patriarch of Shu-Korath, had thrown him out of one.

"It is all right, my lady," Ashe said. "I have a feeling that no matter what the priests may say, both of us will be happier if we stay out of one another's sight."

"I disagree," Sarene said, "but I don't want to argue it. Did you hear anything of our conversation?"

"Seons have very good ears, my lady."

"You don't have ears at all," she pointed out. "What did you think?"

"It sounds like a good way for my lady to gain some notoriety in the city."

"My thought exactly."

"One other thing, my lady. You two spoke of the Derethi gyorn and Elantris. The other night, when I was inspecting the city, I noticed the Gyorn Hrathen walking the city wall of Elantris. I have gone back several nights now, and have found him there on a couple of occasions. He appears quite friendly with the captain of the Elantris City Guard."

"What is he trying to do with that city?" Sarene said, frustrated.

"It baffles me as well, my lady."

Sarene frowned, trying to piece together what she knew of the gyorn's actions and Elantris. She could make no connections. However, as she thought, something else occurred to her. Perhaps she could solve one of her other problems and inconvenience the gyorn at the same time.

"Maybe I don't need to know what he is doing to block him," she said.

"It would certainly help, my lady."

"I don't have that luxury. But, we do know this: If the gyorn wants the people to hate the Elantrians, then it is my job to see the opposite happen."

Ashe paused. "What are you planning, my lady?"

"You'll see," she said with a smile. "First, let's get back to my rooms. I've wanted to speak with Father for some time now."

"'ENE? I'm glad you called. I've been worried about you." Eventeo's glowing head hovered before her.

"You could have sent for me at any time, Father," Sarene said.

"I didn't want to intrude, honey. I know how you value your independence."

"Independence is second to duty right now, Father," Sarene said. "Nations are falling—we don't have time to worry about one another's feelings."

"I stand corrected," her father said with a chuckle.

"What is happening in Teod, Father?"

"It isn't good," Eventeo warned, his voice growing uncharacteristically somber. "These are dangerous times. I just had to put down another Jeskeri Mystery cult. They always seem to spring up when an eclipse is near."

Sarene shivered. The Mystery cultists were an odd bunch, one her father didn't like to deal with. There was reservation in his voice, however—something else was bothering him. "There's more, isn't there?"

"I'm afraid there is, 'Ene," her father admitted. "Something worse."

"What?"

"You know Ashgress, the Fjordell ambassador?"

"Yes," Sarene said with a frown. "What has he done? Denounced you in public?"

"No, something worse." Her father's face looked troubled. "He left."

"*Left?* The country? After all the trouble Fjorden went through to get representatives back in?"

"That's right, 'Ene," Eventeo said. "He took his entire entourage, made a last speech on the docks, and left us behind. There was a disturbing air of finality about the event."

"This isn't good," Sarene agreed. Fjorden had been dogmatic about keeping a presence in Teod. If Ashgress had left, he had gone in response to a personal command from Wyrn. It smelled of their having given up on Teod for good.

"I'm scared, 'Ene." The words chilled her like nothing else—her father was the strongest man she knew.

"You shouldn't say things like that."

"Only to you, 'Ene," Eventeo said. "I want you to understand how serious the situation is."

"I know," Sarene said. "I understand. There's a gyorn here in Kae."

Her father muttered a few curses she had never heard him speak before.

"I think I can handle him, Father," Sarene said quickly. "We're keeping our eyes on one another."

"Which one is it?"

"His name is Hrathen."

Her father cursed again, this time even more vehemently. "Idos Domi, Sarene! Do you know who that is? Hrathen was the gyorn assigned to Duladen the six months before it collapsed."

"I guessed that was who he was."

"I want you out of there, Sarene," Eventeo said. "That man is dangerous—do you know how many people died in the Duladen revolution? There were tens of thousands of casualties."

"I know, Father."

"I'm sending a ship for you—we'll make our stand back here, where no gyorn is welcome."

"I'm not leaving, Father," Sarene said resolutely.

"Sarene, be logical." Eventeo's voice took on the quiet, prodding tone it did every time he wanted her to do something. He usually got his way; he was one of the few who knew how to sway her. "Everyone knows the Arelish government is a mess. If this gyorn toppled Duladen, then he'll have no trouble doing the same to Arelon. You can't hope to stop him when the entire country is against you."

"I have to stay, Father, regardless of the situation."

"What loyalty do you owe them, Sarene?" Eventeo pled. "A husband you never knew? A people who are not your own?"

"I am the daughter of their king."

"You are the daughter of a king here as well. What is the difference? Here the people know and respect you."

"They know me, Father, but respect . . ." Sarene sat back, beginning to feel sick. The old feelings were returning—the feelings that had made her willing to leave her homeland in the first place, abandoning all she knew in favor of a foreign land.

"I don't understand, 'Ene." Her father's voice was pained.

Sarene sighed, closing her eyes. "Oh, Father, you could never see it. To you I was a delight—your beautiful, intelligent daughter. No one would dare tell you what they really thought of me."

"What are you talking about?" he demanded, now speaking with the voice of a king.

"Father," Sarene said, "I am twenty-five years old, and I am blunt, conniving, and ofttimes offensive. You must have noticed that no man ever sought my hand."

Her father didn't respond for a moment. "I thought about it," he finally admitted.

"I was the king's spinster daughter, a shrew no one wanted to touch," Sarene said, trying—and failing—to keep the bitterness out of her voice. "Men laughed at me behind my back. No one would dare approach me with romantic intentions, for it was well known that whoever did would be mocked by his peers."

"I just thought you were independent—that you didn't consider any of them worthy of your time."

Sarene laughed wryly. "You love me, Father—no parent wants to admit that his daughter is unattractive. The truth of the matter is, no man wants an intelligent wife."

"That isn't true," her father objected immediately. "Your mother is brilliant."

"You are an exception, Father, which is why you can't see it. A strong woman is not an asset in this world—not even in Teod, which I always claim is so much more advanced than the continent. It really isn't all that different, Father. They say they give their women more freedom, but there's still the impression that the freedom was theirs to 'give' in the first place.

"In Teod I am an unmarried daughter. Here in Arelon, I am a widowed wife. That is an enormous distinction. As much as I love Teod, I would have to live with the constant knowledge that no one wants me. Here, at least, I can try to convince myself that someone was willing to have me— even if it was for political reasons."

"We can find you someone else."

"I don't think so, Father," Sarene said with a shake of her head, sitting back in her chair. "Now that Teorn has children, no husband of mine would end up on the throne—which is the only reason anyone in Teod would consider marrying me. No one under Derethi control will consider marriage with a Teo. That only leaves Arelon, where my betrothal contract forbids me from marrying again. No, there is no one for me now, Father. The best I can do is make use of my situation here. At least I can command a measure of respect in Arelon without having to worry about how my actions will affect my future marriageability."

"I see," her father said. She could hear the displeasure in his voice.

"Father, do I need to remind you not to worry about me?" she asked. "We have much larger problems to deal with."

"I can't help worrying about you, Leky Stick. You're my only daughter."

Sarene shook her head, determined to change the topic before she started crying. Suddenly very ashamed for destroying his idyllic vision of her, Sarene searched for anything she could say that would divert the conversation. "Uncle Kiin is here in Kae."

That did it. She heard an intake of breath from the other side of the Seon bond. "Do not mention his name to me, 'Ene."

"But—"

"No."

Sarene sighed. "All right, then, tell me about Fjorden instead. What do you think Wyrn is planning?"

"This time I really have no idea," Eventeo said, allowing

himself to be diverted. "It must be something massive. Borders are closing to Teoish merchants north and south, and our ambassadors are beginning to disappear. I am very close to calling them home."

"And your spies?"

"Are vanishing almost as quickly," her father said. "I haven't been able to get anyone into the Velding in over a month, and Domi only knows what Wyrn and the gyorns are scheming in there. Sending spies to Fjorden these days is almost the same as sending them to die."

"But you do it anyway," Sarene said quietly, understanding the source of the pain in her father's voice.

"I have to. What we find could end up saving thousands, though that doesn't make it any easier. I just wish I could get someone into Dakhor."

"The monastery?"

"Yes," Eventeo said. "We know what the other monasteries do—Rathbore trains assassins, Fjeldor spies, and most of the others simple warriors. Dakhor, however, worries me. I've heard some horrible stories about that monastery—and I can't fathom why anyone, even the Derethi, would do such things."

"Does it look like Fjorden's massing for war?"

"I can't tell—it doesn't appear so, but who knows. Wyrn could send a multination army in our direction at almost a moment's notice. One small consolation is I don't think he knows we understand that fact. Unfortunately, the knowledge does put me in a difficult position."

"What do you mean?"

Her father's voice was hesitant. "If Wyrn declares holy war on us, then it will mean the end of Teod. We can't stand against the united might of the Eastern countries, 'Ene. I will not sit back and watch my people be slaughtered."

"You would consider surrendering?" Sarene asked with outrage.

"A king's duty is to protect his people. When faced with the choice of conversion or letting my people be destroyed, I think I would have to choose conversion."

"You would be as spineless as the Jindoeese," Sarene said.

"The Jindoeese are a wise people, Sarene," her father

said, his voice growing firm. "They did what they needed to survive."

"But that would mean giving up!"

"It would mean doing what we have to do," her father said. "I won't do anything yet. As long as there are two nations left, we have hope. However, if Arelon falls, I will be forced to surrender. We cannot fight the entire world, 'Ene, no more than one grain of sand can fight an entire ocean."

"But . . ." Sarene's voice trailed off. She could see her father's predicament. Fighting Fjorden on the battlefield would be an exercise in complete futility. Convert or die—both options were sickening, but conversion was obviously the more logical choice. However, a quiet voice inside her argued that it was worth dying, if death would prove that truth was more powerful than physical strength.

She had to make sure her father was never given that choice. If she could stop Hrathen, then she might be able to stop Wyrn. For a time, at least.

"I'm definitely staying, Father," she declared.

"I know, 'Ene. It will be dangerous."

"I understand. However, if Arelon does fall, then I would probably rather be dead than watch what happens in Teod."

"Be careful, and keep an eye on that gyorn. Oh, by the way—if you find out why Wyrn is sinking Iadon's ships, tell me."

"What?" Sarene asked with shock.

"You didn't know?"

"Know what?" Sarene demanded.

"King Iadon has lost nearly his entire merchant fleet. The official reports claim that the sinkings are the work of pirates, some remnant of Dreok Crushthroat's navy. However, my sources link the sinkings with Fjorden."

"So *that*'s what it was!" Sarene said.

"What?"

"Four days ago I was at a party," Sarene explained. "A servant delivered a message to the king, and whatever it was unsettled the king a great deal."

"That would be about the right time frame," her father said. "I found out two days ago myself."

"Why would Wyrn sink innocent merchant vessels?"

Sarene wondered. "Unless . . . *Idos Domi*! If the king loses his income, then he would be in danger of losing his throne!"

"Is all that nonsense about rank being tied to money true?"

"Insanely true," Sarene said. "Iadon takes away a family's title if they can't maintain their income. If he lost his own source of wealth, it would destroy the foundation of his rule. Hrathen could replace him with someone else—a man more willing to accept Shu-Dereth—without even bothering to start a revolution."

"It sounds feasible. Iadon asked for such a situation by concocting such an unstable basis for rule."

"It's probably Telrii," Sarene said. "That's why he spent so much money on that ball—the duke wants to show that he is financially sound. I would be very surprised if there wasn't a mountain of Fjordell gold behind his expenditures."

"What are you going to do?"

"Stop him," Sarene said. "Even though it hurts. I really don't like Iadon, Father."

"Unfortunately, it looks like Hrathen has chosen our allies for us."

Sarene nodded. "He has placed me with Elantris and Iadon—not a very enviable position."

"We all do the best with what Domi has given us."

"You sound like a priest."

"I have found reason to become very religious lately."

Sarene thought for a moment before replying, tapping her cheek as she considered his words. "A wise choice, Father. If Domi were ever going to help us, it would be now. The end of Teod means the end of Shu-Korath."

"For a time, perhaps," her father said. "Truth can never be defeated, Sarene. Even if people do forget about it occasionally."

SARENE was in bed, the lights down. Ashe hovered on the far side of the room, his light dimmed so much that he was barely an outline of Aon Ashe against the wall.

The conversation with her father had ended an hour ago,

but its implications would likely plague her mind for months. She had never considered surrender an option, but now it looked almost inevitable. The prospect worried her. She knew that it was unlikely that Wyrn would let her father continue to rule, even if he did convert. She also knew that Eventeo would willingly give his life if it would spare his people.

She also thought about her own life, and her mixed memories of Teod. The kingdom contained the things she loved most—her father, brother, and mother. The forests around the port city of Teoin, the capital, were another very fond memory. She remembered the way the snow settled on the landscape. One morning she had awoken to find everything outside coated in a beautiful film of ice; the trees had looked like jewels sparkling in the winter daylight.

Yet, Teod also reminded her of pain and loneliness. It represented her exclusion from society and her humiliation before men. She had established early in life that she had a quick wit and an even quicker tongue. Both things had set her apart from the other women—not that some of them weren't intelligent; they just had the wisdom to hide it until they were married.

Not all men wanted a stupid wife—but there also weren't a lot of men who felt comfortable around a woman they assumed was their intellectual superior. By the time Sarene had realized what she was doing to herself, she had found that the few men who might have accepted her were already married. Desperate, she had ferreted out the masculine opinion of her in court, and had been mortified to learn just how much they mocked her. After that, it had only grown worse—and she had only grown older. In a land where nearly every woman was at least engaged by the age of eighteen, she was an old maid by twenty-five. A very tall, gangly, argumentative old maid.

Her self-recrimination was interrupted by a noise. It didn't come from the hallway or window, however, but from inside her room. She sat up with a start, breath catching in her throat as she prepared to jump away. Only then did she realize it wasn't actually coming from her room, but from the wall beside her room. She frowned in confusion. There weren't any rooms on the other side; she was at the very edge of the palace. She had a window looking out over the city.

The noise was not repeated, and, determined to get some sleep despite her anxieties, Sarene told herself it had simply been the building settling.

CHAPTER 18

DILAF walked in the door, looking a bit distracted. Then he saw the Elantrian sitting in the chair in front of Hrathen's desk.

The shock nearly killed him.

Hrathen smiled, watching as Dilaf's breath audibly caught in his throat, his eyes grew wide as shields, and his face turned a shade not unlike the color of Hrathen's armor. "Hruggath Ja!" Dilaf yelped in surprise, the Fjordell curse rising quickly to his lips.

Hrathen raised his eyebrows at the expletive—not so much because it offended him, but because he was surprised that it should come so easily to Dilaf. The arteth had submerged himself in Fjorden's culture deeply indeed.

"Say hello to Diren, Arteth," Hrathen said, gesturing to the black-and-gray-faced Elantrian. "And kindly refrain from using Lord Jaddeth's name as a curse. That is one Fjordell habit I would rather you hadn't assumed."

"An Elantrian!"

"Yes," Hrathen said. "Very good, Arteth. And no, you may not set fire to him."

Hrathen leaned back slightly in his seat, smiling as Dilaf glared at the Elantrian. Hrathen had summoned Dilaf to the room knowing full well the kind of reaction he would get, and he felt a little petty at the move. That, however, didn't stop him from enjoying the moment.

Finally, Dilaf shot Hrathen a hateful look—though he quickly masked it with one of barely controlled submissiveness. "What is he doing here, my hroden?"

"I thought it would be good to know the face of our enemy, Arteth," Hrathen said, rising and walking over to the frightened Elantrian. The two priests were, of course, conversing in Fjordell. There was confusion in the Elantrian's eyes, along with a feral sort of fear.

Hrathen squatted down beside the man, studying his demon. "Are they all bald, Dilaf?" he asked with interest.

"Not at first," the arteth answered sullenly. "They usually have a full head when the Korathi dogs prepare them for the city. Their skin is paler as well."

Hrathen reached out, feeling the man's cheek. The skin was tough and leathery. The Elantrian watched him with frightened eyes. "These black spots—these are what distinguish an Elantrian?"

"It is the first sign, my hroden," Dilaf said, subdued. Either he was getting used to the Elantrian, or he had simply gotten over his initial burst of hatred and had moved on to a more patient, smoldering form of disgust. "It usually happens overnight. When the accursed one wakes up, he or she will have dark blotches all over their body. The rest of their skin turns grayish brown, like this one, over time."

"Like the skin of an embalmed corpse," Hrathen noted. He had visited the university in Svorden on occasion, and knew of the bodies they kept there for study.

"Very similar," Dilaf agreed quietly. "The skin isn't the only sign, my hroden. Their insides are rotten as well."

"How can you tell?"

"Their hearts do not beat," Dilaf said. "And their minds do not work. There are stories from the early days ten years ago, before they were all locked away in that city. Within a few months they turn comatose, barely able to move, except to bemoan their pain."

"Pain?"

"The pain of their soul being burned by Lord Jaddeth's

fire," Dilaf explained. "It builds within them until it con-
sumes their consciousness. It is their punishment."

Hrathen nodded, turning away from the Elantrian.

"You shouldn't have touched him, my hroden," Dilaf said.

"I thought you said that Lord Jaddeth would protect his
faithful," Hrathen said. "What need have I to fear?"

"You invited evil into the chapel, my hroden."

Hrathen snorted. "There is nothing sacred about this
building, Dilaf, as you know. No holy ground can be dedicated in a country that hasn't allied itself with Shu-Dereth."

"Of course," Dilaf said. His eyes were growing eager for
some reason.

The look in Dilaf's eyes made Hrathen uncomfortable.
Perhaps it would be best to minimize the time the arteth
spent in the same room as the Elantrian.

"I summoned you because I'm going to need you to make
the preparations for the evening sermon," Hrathen said. "I
can't do them myself—I want to spend a bit of time interro-
gating this Elantrian."

"As you command, my hroden," Dilaf said, still eyeing the
Elantrian.

"You are dismissed, Arteth," Hrathen said firmly.

Dilaf growled quietly, then scuttled from the room, off to
do Hrathen's bidding.

Hrathen turned back to the Elantrian. The creature didn't
seem "mindless," as Dilaf had put it. The Guard captain
who'd brought the Elantrian had even mentioned the creature's name; that implied that it could speak.

"Can you understand me, Elantrian?" Hrathen asked in
Aonic.

Diren paused, then nodded his head.

"Interesting," Hrathen said musingly.

"What do you want with me?" the Elantrian asked.

"Just to ask you some questions," Hrathen said, stepping
back to his desk and sitting down. He continued to study the
creature with curiosity. Never in all of his varied travels had
he seen a disease such as this.

"Do you . . . have any food?" the Elantrian asked. There
was a slight edge of wildness to his eyes as he mentioned the
word "food."

"If you answer my questions, I promise to send you back to Elantris with a full basket of bread and cheese."

This got the creature's attention. He nodded vigorously.

So hungry, Hrathen thought with curiosity. *And, what was it that Dilaf said? No heartbeat? Perhaps the disease does something to the metabolism—makes the heart beat so quickly that it's hard to detect, increases the appetite somehow?*

"What were you before you were thrown into the city, Diren?" Hrathen asked.

"A peasant, my lord. I worked the fields of Aor Plantation."

"And, how long have you been an Elantrian?"

"I was thrown in during the fall," Diren said. "Seven months? Eight? I lose track. . . ."

So Dilaf's other assertion, that Elantrians fell "comatose" within a few months, was incorrect. Hrathen sat thoughtfully, trying to decide what kind of information this creature might have that could be of use to him.

"What is it like in Elantris?" Hrathen asked.

"It's . . . terrible, my lord," Diren said, looking down. "There's the gangs. If you go the wrong place, they'll chase you, or hurt you. No one tells the newcomers about things, so if you aren't careful, you'll walk into the market. . . . That's not good. And, there's a new gang now—so say a few of the Elantrians I know on the streets. A fourth gang, more powerful than the others."

Gangs. That implied a basic level of society, at least. Hrathen frowned to himself. If the gangs were as harsh as Diren implied, then perhaps he could use them as an example of Svrakiss for his followers. However, speaking with the complacent Diren, Hrathen was beginning to think that perhaps he should continue making his condemnations from a distance. If any percentage of the Elantrians were as harmless as this man, then the people of Kae would probably be disappointed in the Elantrians as "demons."

As the interrogation proceeded, Hrathen realized that Diren didn't know much more that was of use. The Elantrian couldn't explain what the Shaod was like—it had happened to him while he was sleeping. He claimed that he was "dead," whatever that meant, and that his wounds no longer healed. He even showed Hrathen a cut in his skin. The wound wasn't bleeding, however, so Hrathen just suspected that the pieces of skin hadn't sealed properly as they healed.

Diren knew nothing of the Elantrian "magic." He claimed that he'd seen others doing magical drawings in the air, but Diren himself didn't know how to do likewise. He did know that he was hungry—very hungry. He reiterated this idea several times, as well as mentioning twice more that he was frightened of the gangs.

Satisfied that he knew what he'd wanted to find out—that Elantris was a brutal place, but disappointingly human in its methods of brutality—Hrathen sent for the Guard captain who had brought Diren.

The captain of the Elantris City Guard entered obsequiously. He wore thick gloves, and he prodded the Elantrian out of its chair with a long stick. The captain eagerly accepted a bag of coins from Hrathen, then nodded as Hrathen made him promise to purchase Diren a basket of food. As the captain forced his prisoner out of the room, Dilaf appeared at Hrathen's door. The arteth watched his prey leave with a look of disappointment.

"Everything ready?" Hrathen asked.

"Yes, my hroden," Dilaf said. "People are already beginning to arrive for the services."

"Good," Hrathen said, leaning back in his chair, lacing his fingers thoughtfully.

"Does something concern you, my hroden?"

Hrathen shook his head. "I was just planning for the evening speech. I believe it is time for us to move on to the next step in our plans."

"The next step, my hroden?"

Hrathen nodded. "I think we have successfully established our stance against Elantris. The masses are always quick to find devils around them, as long as you give them proper motivation."

"Yes, my hroden."

"Do not forget, Arteth," Hrathen said, "that there is a point to our hatred."

"It unifies our followers—it gives them a common enemy."

"Correct," Hrathen said, resting his arms on his desk. "There is another purpose, however. One just as important. Now that we have given the people someone to hate, we need to create an association between Elantris and our rivals."

"Shu-Korath," Dilaf said with a sinister smile.

"Again correct. The Korathi priests are the ones who prepare new Elantrians—they are the motivation behind the mercy this country shows its fallen gods. If we imply that Korathi tolerance makes its priests sympathizers, the people's loathing of Elantris will shift to Shu-Korath instead. Their priests will be faced with two options: Either they accept our incrimination, or they side with us against Elantris. If they choose the former, then the people will turn against them. If they choose the latter, then it puts them under our theological control. After that, a few simple embarrassments will make them appear impotent and irrelevant."

"It is perfect," Dilaf said. "But will it happen quickly enough? There is so little time."

Hrathen started, looking over at the still smiling arteth. How had the man known about his deadline? He couldn't—he must be guessing.

"It will work," Hrathen said. "With their monarchy unstable and their religion wavering, the people will look for a new source of leadership. Shu-Dereth will be like a rock amidst shifting sands."

"A fine analogy, my hroden."

Hrathen could never tell if Dilaf mocked him with such statements or not. "I have a task for you, Arteth. I want you to make the connection in your sermon tonight—turn the people against Shu-Korath."

"Will my hroden not do it himself?"

"I will speak second, and my speech will offer logic. You, however, are more passionate—and their disgust for Shu-Korath must first come from their hearts."

Dilaf nodded, bowing his head to show that he acceded to the command. Hrathen waved his hand, indicating the conversation was over, and the arteth backed away, closing the door behind him.

DILAF spoke with characteristic zeal. He stood outside the chapel, on a podium Hrathen had commissioned once the crowds became too large to fit in the building. The warm spring nights were conducive to such meetings, and the half-light of sunset, combined with torches, gave the proper mixture of visibility and shadow.

The people watched Dilaf with rapture, even though most of what he said was repetitious. Hrathen spent hours preparing his sermons, careful to combine both duplication for reinforcement and originality to provide excitement. Dilaf just spoke. It didn't matter if he spouted the same denunciations of Elantris and the same redundant praises to Jaddeth's empire; the people listened anyway. After a week of hearing the arteth speak, Hrathen had learned to ignore his own envy—to an extent, at least. He replaced it with pride.

As he listened, Hrathen congratulated himself on the arteth's effectiveness. Dilaf did as Hrathen had ordered, beginning with his normal ravings about Elantris, then moving boldly into a full accusation of Shu-Korath. The crowd moved with him, allowing their emotions to be redirected. It was as Hrathen had planned; there was no reason for him to be jealous of Dilaf. The man's rage was like a river Hrathen himself had diverted toward the crowd. Dilaf might have the raw talent, but Hrathen was the master behind it.

He told himself that right up to the moment Dilaf surprised him. The sermon progressed well, Dilaf's fury investing the crowd with a loathing of everything Korathi. But then the tide shifted as Dilaf turned his attention back to Elantris. Hrathen thought nothing of it at first—Dilaf had an incorrigible tendency to wander during his sermons.

"And now, behold!" Dilaf suddenly commanded. "Behold the Svrakiss! Look into its eyes, and find form for your hate! Feed the outrage of Jaddeth that burns within you all!"

Hrathen felt himself grow cold. Dilaf gestured to the side of the stage, where a pair of torches suddenly burst into flame. Diren the Elantrian stood tied to a post, his head bowed. There were cuts on his face that had not been there before.

"Behold the enemy!" Dilaf screamed. "Look, see! He does not bleed! No blood runs through his veins, and no heart beats in his chest. Did not the philosopher Grondkest say that you can judge the equality of all men by their common unity of blood? But what of one who has no blood? What shall we call him?"

"Demon!" a member of the crowd yelled.

"Devil!"

"Svrakiss!" Dilaf screamed.

The crowd raged, each member yelling his own accusations at the wretched target. The Elantrian himself screamed with wild, feral passion. Something had changed within this man. When Hrathen had spoken with him, the Elantrian's answers had been unenthusiastic, but lucid. Now there was nothing of sanity in his eyes—only pain. The sound of the creature's voice reached Hrathen even over the congregation's fury.

"Destroy me!" the Elantrian pled. "End the pain! *Destroy me!*"

The voice shocked Hrathen out of his stupor. He realized one thing immediately: that Dilaf couldn't be allowed to murder this Elantrian in public. Visions of Dilaf's crowd becoming a mob flashed through Hrathen's mind, of them burning the Elantrian in a fit of collective passion. It would destroy everything; Iadon would never suffer something as violent as a public execution, even if the victim was an Elantrian. It smelled too much of chaos a decade old, chaos that had overthrown a government.

Hrathen stood at the side of the podium dais, amid a group of priests. There was a pressing crowd bunched up against the front of the dais, and Dilaf stood in front of the podium itself, hands outstretched as he spoke.

"They must be *destroyed*!" Dilaf screamed. "All of them! Cleansed by holy fire!"

Hrathen leaped up onto the dais. "And so they shall be!" he yelled, cutting the arteth off.

Dilaf paused only briefly. He turned to the side, nodding toward a lesser priest holding a lit torch. Dilaf probably assumed that there was nothing Hrathen could do to stop the execution—at least, nothing he could do that wouldn't undermine his own credibility with the crowd.

Not this time, Arteth, Hrathen thought. *I won't let you do whatever you wish.* He couldn't contradict Dilaf, not without making it seem like there was a division in the Derethi ranks.

He could, however, twist what Dilaf had said. That particular vocal feat was one of Hrathen's specialties.

"But, what good would that do?" Hrathen yelled, struggling to speak over the screaming crowd. They were surging forward in anticipation of the execution, calling out curses at the Elantrian.

Hrathen gritted his teeth, pushing past Dilaf and grabbing the torch from the passing priest's hand. Hrathen heard Dilaf hissing in annoyance, but he ignored the arteth. If he didn't gain control of the crowd, they would simply push forward and attack the Elantrian on their own.

Hrathen held aloft the torch, thrusting it upward repeatedly, causing the crowd to yell with pleasure, building a kind of chanting rhythm.

And in between pulses of rhythm, there was silence.

"I ask you again, people!" Hrathen bellowed as the crowd fell silent, preparing for another yell.

They paused.

"What good would killing this creature do?" Hrathen asked.

"It's a demon!" one of the men in the crowd yelled.

"Yes!" Hrathen said. "But it is *already* tormented. Jaddeth himself gave this demon its curse. Listen to it pleading for death! Is that what we want to do? Give the creature what it wants?"

Hrathen waited tensely. While some of the crowd's members screamed "Yes!" out of habit, others paused. Confusion showed, and a bit of the tension deflated.

"The Svrakiss are our enemies," Hrathen said, speaking with more control now, his voice firm rather than passionate. His words calmed the people further. "However, they are not ours to punish. That is Jaddeth's pleasure! We have another task.

"This creature, this demon, this is the thing that the Korathi priests would have you pity! You wonder why Arelon is poor compared to the nations of the East? It is because you suffer the Korathi foolishness. *That* is why you lack the riches and blessings found in nations like Jindo and Svorden. The Korathi are too lenient. It may not be our task to destroy these creatures, but neither is it our task to care for them! We certainly shouldn't pity them or suffer them to live in such a grand, rich city as Elantris."

Hrathen extinguished the torch, then waved for a priest to go and do the same for the lights illuminating the poor Elantrian. As those torches winked out, the Elantrian disappeared from view, and the crowd began to settle down.

"Remember," Hrathen said. "The Korathi are the ones who care for the Elantrians. Even now, they still hedge when asked if the Elantrians are demons. The Korathi are afraid that the city will return to its glory, but we know better. We know that Jaddeth has pronounced His curse. There is no mercy for the damned!

"Shu-Korath is the cause of your pains. *It* is the thing that supports and protects Elantris. You will never be rid of the Elantrian curse as long as the Korathi priests hold sway in Arelon. So, I say to you, go! Tell your friends what you have learned, and urge them to shun Korathi heresies!"

There was silence. Then people began to call out in agreement, their dissatisfaction successfully transferred. Hrathen watched them carefully as they yelled approval, then finally began to disperse. Their vengeful hatred had mostly dissipated. Hrathen sighed with relief—there would be no midnight attacks on Korathi priests or temples. Dilaf's speech had been too fleeting, too quick, to have done lasting damage. The disaster had been averted.

Hrathen turned, eyeing Dilaf. The arteth had left the stage after Hrathen had seized control, and now he stood watching his crowd disappear with petulant anger.

He would turn them all into zealous replicas of himself, Hrathen thought. Except, their passion would burn out quickly once the moment passed. They needed more. They needed knowledge, not just hysteria.

"Arteth," Hrathen said sternly, catching Dilaf's attention. "We need to speak."

The arteth contained a glare, then nodded. The Elantrian

was still screaming for death. Hrathen turned to another pair of arteths, waving toward the Elantrian. "Collect the creature and meet me in the gardens."

Hrathen turned to Dilaf, nodding curtly toward the gate at the back of the Derethi chapel. Dilaf did as ordered, moving toward the gardens. Hrathen followed him, on the way passing the confused Elantris City Guard captain.

"My lord?" the man asked. "The young priest caught me before I got back to the city. He said you wanted the creature back. Did I do wrong?"

"You are fine," Hrathen said curtly. "Go back to your post; we'll deal with the Elantrian."

THE Elantrian seemed to welcome the flames, despite the terrible pain they must have caused.

Dilaf huddled to the side, watching eagerly, though it had been Hrathen's hand—not Dilaf's—that had dropped the torch onto the oil-soaked Elantrian. Hrathen watched the poor creature as it burned, its cries of pain finally silenced by the roaring fire. The creature's body seemed to burn easily—too easily—within the licking flames.

Hrathen felt a stab of guilt for betraying Diren, though that emotion was foolish; the Elantrian might not have been a true devil, but he was certainly a creature that Jaddeth had cursed. Hrathen owed the Elantrian nothing.

Still, he regretted having to burn the creature. Unfortunately, Dilaf's cuts had obviously maddened the Elantrian, and there was no sending him back to the city in his current state. The flames had been the only option.

Hrathen watched the pitiful man's eyes until the flames consumed him completely.

"And the burning fire of Jaddeth's displeasure shall cleanse them," Dilaf whispered, quoting the *Do-Dereth*.

"Judgment belongs to Jaddeth alone, and it is executed by his only servant Wyrn," Hrathen quoted, using a different passage from the same book. "You should not have forced me to kill this creature."

"It was inevitable," Dilaf said. "Eventually all things must bow before Jaddeth's will—and it is his will that all of Elantris burn. I was simply following fate."

"You nearly lost control of that crowd with your ravings, Arteth," Hrathen snapped. "A riot must be very carefully planned and executed, otherwise it will just as likely turn against its creators as their enemies."

"I . . . got carried away," Dilaf said. "But, killing one Elantrian would not have made them riot."

"You don't know that. Besides, what of Iadon?"

"How could he object?" Dilaf said. "It is his own order that escaping Elantrians can be burned. He would never take a stand in favor of Elantris."

"But he could take a stand against us!" Hrathen said. "You were wrong to bring this creature to the meeting."

"The people deserved to see what they are to hate."

"The people are not ready for that yet," Hrathen said harshly. "We want to keep their hatred formless. If they start to tear up the city, Iadon will put an end to our preaching."

Dilaf's eyes narrowed. "You sound as if you are trying to avoid the inevitable, my hroden. You fostered this hatred—are you unwilling to accept responsibility for the deaths it will cause? Hate and loathing cannot remain 'formless' for long—they will find an outlet."

"But that outlet will come when *I* decide it," Hrathen said coldly. "I am aware of my responsibility, Arteth, though I question your understanding of it. You just told me that killing this Elantrian was fated by Jaddeth—that you were simply following Jaddeth's fate by forcing my hand. Which is it to be? Would the deaths I cause in riot be my doing, or simply the will of God? How can you be an innocent servant while I must accept full accountability for this city's people?"

Dilaf exhaled sharply. He knew, however, when he had been defeated. He bowed curtly, then turned and entered the chapel.

Hrathen watched the arteth go, fuming quietly. Dilaf's action this night had been foolish and impulsive. Was he trying to undermine Hrathen's authority, or was he simply acting on his zealous passions? If it was the second, the near riot was Hrathen's own fault. He had, after all, been so proud of himself for using Dilaf as an effective tool.

Hrathen shook his head, releasing a tense breath. He had defeated Dilaf this evening, but the tension was growing between them. They couldn't afford to get into visible arguments. Rumors of dissension in the Derethi ranks would erode their credibility.

I will have to do something about the arteth, Hrathen decided with resignation. Dilaf was becoming too much of a liability.

His decision made, Hrathen turned to leave. As he did, however, his eyes fell again on the Elantrian's charred remains, and he shuddered despite himself. The man's willful acceptance of immolation brought memories to Hrathen's mind—memories he had long tried to banish. Images of pain, of sacrifice, and of death.

Memories of Dakhor.

He turned his back on the charred bones, walking toward the chapel. He still had one other task to complete this evening.

THE Seon floated free from its box, responding to Hrathen's command. Mentally, Hrathen chided himself—this was the second time in one week he had used the creature. Reliance on the Seon was something to be avoided. However, Hrathen could think of no other way to accomplish his goal. Dilaf was right: Time was very scarce. Fourteen days had already passed since his arrival in Arelon, and he had spent a week traveling before that. Only seventy days remained of his original allotment, and, despite the size of the night's congregation, Hrathen had converted only a tiny fraction of Arelon.

Only one fact gave him hope: Arelon's nobility was concentrated in Kae. To be away from Iadon's court was political suicide; the king granted and took away titles willfully, and a high profile was necessary to assure a firm place in the aristocracy. Wyrn didn't care if Hrathen converted the masses or not; as long as the nobility bowed, the country was considered Derethi.

So, Hrathen had a chance, but he still had much work to do. An important piece of it lay in the man Hrathen was about to call. His contact was not a gyorn, which made Hrathen's use of the Seon a little unorthodox. However, Wyrn had never directly commanded him *not* to call other people with his Seon, so Hrathen was able to rationalize the use.

The Seon responded promptly, and soon Forton's large-eared, mouselike face appeared in its light.

"Who is it?" he asked in the harsh Fjordell dialect spoken in the country of Hrovell.

"It is I, Forton."

"My lord Hrathen?" Forton asked with surprise. "My lord, it has been a long time."

"I know, Forton. I trust you are well."

The man laughed happily, though the laugh quickly turned to a wheeze. Forton had a chronic cough—a condition caused, Hrathen was certain, by the various substances the man was fond of smoking.

"Of course, my lord," Forton said through his coughing. "When am I not well?" Forton was a man utterly contented with his life—a condition that was also caused by the various substances he was fond of smoking. "What can I do for you?"

"I have need of one of your elixirs, Forton," Hrathen said.

"Of course, of course. What must it do?"

Hrathen smiled. Forton was an unparalleled genius, which was why Hrathen suffered his eccentricities. The man not only kept a Seon, but was a devout follower of the Mysteries—a degenerate form of the Jesker religion common in rural areas. Though Hrovell was officially a Derethi nation, most of it was a primitive, sparsely populated countryside which was difficult to supervise. Many of the peasants attended their Derethi services with devotion, then took part in their midnight Mystery ceremonies with equal devotion. Forton himself was considered something of a mystic in his town, though he always put on a show of Derethi orthodoxy when he spoke with Hrathen.

Hrathen explained what he wanted, and Forton repeated it back. Though Forton was often drugged, he was very accomplished at the mixing of potions, poisons, and elixirs.

Hrathen had met no man in Sycla who could match Forton's skill. One of the eccentric man's concoctions had restored Hrathen to health after he had been poisoned by a political enemy. The slow-acting substance was said to have no antidote.

"This will be no problem, my lord," Forton promised Hrathen in his thick dialect. Even after years of dealing with the Hroven, Hrathen had trouble understanding them. He was certain that most of them didn't even know there was a pure, correct form of their language back in Fjorden.

"Good," Hrathen said.

"Yes, all I'll need to do is combine two formulas I already have," Forton said. "How much do you want?"

"At least two doses. I will pay you the standard price."

"My true payment is the knowledge I have served Lord Jaddeth," the man said piously.

Hrathen resisted the urge to laugh. He knew how much of a hold the Mysteries had on Hrovell's people. It was a distasteful form of worship, a syncretic combination of a dozen different faiths, with some aberrations—such as ritual sacrifice and fertility rites—added in to make it more alluring. Hrovell, however, was a task for another day. The people did what Wyrn commanded, and they were too politically insignificant to cause Fjorden distress. Of course, their souls were in serious danger; Jaddeth was not known for his leniency toward the ignorant.

Another day, Hrathen told himself. *Another day.*

"When will my lord be needing this potion?" the man asked.

"That is the thing, Forton. I need it immediately."

"Where are you?"

"In Arelon," Hrathen said.

"Ah, good," Forton said. "My lord has finally decided to convert those heathens."

"Yes," Hrathen said with a slight smile. "We Derethi have been patient with the Arelenes long enough."

"Well, Your Lordship couldn't have picked a place farther away," Forton said. "Even if I finish the potion tonight and send it in the morning, it will take at least two weeks to arrive."

Hrathen chafed at the delay, but there was no other option. "Then do so, Forton. I will compensate you for working on such short notice."

"A true follower of Jaddeth will do anything to bring about His Empire, my lord."

Well, at least he knows his Derethi doctrine, Hrathen thought with a mental shrug.

"Is there anything else, my lord?" Forton asked, coughing slightly.

"No. Get to work, and send the potions as quickly as possible."

"Yes, my lord. I'll get started immediately. Feel free to pray to me any time you need to."

Hrathen frowned—he had forgotten about that little inaccuracy. Perhaps Forton's mastery of Derethi doctrine wasn't all that sound after all. Forton didn't know Hrathen had a Seon; he simply assumed that a gyorn could pray to Jaddeth and that God would direct his words through the Seons. As if Lord Jaddeth were a member of the post.

"Goodnight, Forton," Hrathen said, keeping the displeasure from his voice. Forton was a drug addict, a heretic, and a hypocrite—but he was still an invaluable resource. Hrathen had long ago decided that if Jaddeth would suffer his gyorns to communicate using Seons, then He would certainly let Hrathen use men such as Forton.

After all, Jaddeth had created all men—even the heretics.

CHAPTER 19

THE city of Elantris glowed brilliantly. The very stones shone, as if each one held a fire within. The shattered domes had been restored, their smooth, egglike surfaces blossoming across the landscape. Thin spires stabbed the air like streaks of light. The wall was no longer a barrier, for its gates were left permanently open—it existed not to protect, but for cohesion. The wall was part of the city somehow, an essential element of the whole, without which Elantris would not be complete.

And amid the beauty and the glory were the Elantrians. Their bodies seemed to shine with the same inner light as the city, their skin a luminous pale silver. Not metallic, just . . . pure. Their hair was white, but not the worn-out dull gray or yellow of the aged. It was the blazing white of steel heated to an extreme temperature—a color free of impurities, a powerful, focused white.

Their bearings were equally striking. The Elantrians moved through their city with an air of complete control. The men were handsome and tall—even the short ones— and the women were undeniably beautiful—even the homely ones. They were unhurried; they strolled rather than walked, and they were quick to greet those they met. There was a power in them, however. It radiated from their eyes and underlay their motions. It was easy to understand why these beings were worshipped as gods.

Equally unmistakable were the Aons. The ancient glyphs covered the city; they were etched into walls, painted on doors, and written on signs. Most of them were inert—simple markings, rather than runes with an arcane purpose. Others, however, obviously held energy. Throughout the city stood large metal plates carved with Aon Tia, and occasionally an Elantrian would approach and place his or her hand in the center of the character. The Elantrian's body would flash, and then disappear in a circular burst of light, his body instantly transported to another section of the city.

Amid the glory was a small family of Kae townspeople. Their clothing was rich and fine, their words were educated, but their skin did not glow. There were other regular people in the city—not as many as the Elantrians, but a fair number nonetheless. This comforted the boy, giving him a familiar reference.

The father carried his young son tightly, looking around with distrust. Not everyone adored the Elantrians; some were suspicious. The boy's mother gripped her husband's arm with tense fingers. She had never been inside Elantris, though she had lived in Kae for over a decade. Unlike the boy's father, she was more nervous than distrustful. She was worried about her son's wound, anxious as any mother whose child was near death.

Suddenly, the boy felt the pain in his leg. It was blinding and intense, stemming from the festering wound and shattered bone in his thigh. He had fallen from someplace high, and his leg had snapped so soundly the shattered bone had torn through the skin to jut into the air.

His father had hired the best surgeons and doctors, but they had been unable to stop the infection. The bone had been set as well as possible, considering that it had fractured in at least a dozen places. Even without the infection, the boy would walk with a limp the rest of his days. With the infection . . . amputation seemed the only recourse. Secretly, the doctors feared it was too late for even that solution; the wound had occurred high on the leg, and the infection had probably spread to the torso. The father had demanded the truth. He knew his son was dying. And so he had come to Elantris, despite his lifelong distrust of its gods.

They took the boy to a domed building. He nearly forgot his pain as the door opened on its own, sliding inward without a sound. His father stopped abruptly before the door, as if reconsidering his actions, but his mother tugged insistently on the man's arm. His father nodded, bowing his head and entering the building.

Light shone from glowing Aons on the walls. A woman approached, her white hair long and full, her silvery face smiling encouragingly. She ignored his father's distrust, her eyes sympathetic as she took the boy from hesitant arms. She laid him carefully on a soft mat, then brought her hand into the air above him, her long, thin index finger pointing at nothing.

The Elantrian moved her hand slowly, and the air began to glow. A trail of light followed her finger. It was like a rupture in the air, a line that radiated with deep intensity. It was as if a river of light were trying to force its way through the small crack. The boy could feel the power, he could sense it raging to be free, but only this little was allowed to escape. Even that little was so bright that he could barely see for the light.

The woman traced carefully, completing Aon Ien—but it wasn't just Aon Ien, it was more complex. The core was the familiar Aon of healing, but there were dozens of lines and curves at the sides. The boy's brow wrinkled—he had been taught the Aons by his tutors, and it seemed odd that the woman should change this one so drastically.

The beautiful Elantrian made one final mark at the side of her complex construction, and the Aon began to glow even more intensely. The boy felt a burning in his leg, then a burning up through his torso. He began to yell, but the light suddenly vanished. The boy opened his eyes with surprise; the afterimage of Aon Ien still burned into his vision. He blinked, looking down. The wound was gone. Not even a scar remained.

But he could still feel the pain. It burned him, cut him, caused his soul to tremble. It should have been gone, but it was not.

"Rest now, little one," the Elantrian said in a warm voice, pushing him back.

His mother was weeping with joy, and even his father looked satisfied. The boy wanted to yell at them, to scream that something was wrong. His leg hadn't been healed. The pain still remained.

No! Something is wrong! He tried to say, but he couldn't. He couldn't speak. . . .

"*NO!*" Raoden yelled, sitting upright with a sudden motion. He blinked a few times, disoriented in the darkness. Finally, he took a few deep breaths, putting his hand to his head. The pain did remain; it was growing so strong that it even corrupted his dreams. He had dozens of tiny wounds and bruises now, even though he had been in Elantris for only three weeks. He could feel each one distinctly, and together they formed a unified frontal assault on sanity.

Raoden groaned, leaning forward and grabbing his legs as he fought the pain. His body could no longer sweat, but he could feel it trembling. He clamped his teeth shut, gritting them against the surge of agony. Slowly, laboriously, he reasserted control. He rebuffed the pain, soothing his tortured body until, finally, he released his legs and stood.

It was growing worse. He knew it shouldn't be so bad yet; he hadn't even been in Elantris for a month. He also knew that the pain was supposed to be steady, or so everyone said, but for him it seemed to come in waves. It was always there—always ready to pounce on him in a moment of weakness.

Sighing, Raoden pushed open the door to his chambers. He still found it odd that Elantrians should sleep. Their hearts no longer beat, they no longer needed breath. Why did they need sleep? The others, however, could give him no answers. The only true experts had died ten years previously.

So, Raoden slept, and with that sleep came dreams. He had been eight when he broke his leg. His father had been loath to bring him into the city; even before the Reod, Iadon had been suspicious of Elantris. Raoden's mother, dead some twelve years now, had insisted.

The child Raoden hadn't understood how close he'd come to death. He had felt the pain, however, and the beautiful peace of its removal. He remembered the beauty of both the city and its occupants. Iadon had spoken harshly of Elantris as they left, and Raoden had contradicted the words with vehemence. It was the first time Raoden could remember taking a position against his father. After that, there had been many others.

As Raoden entered the main chapel, Saolin left his attendant position beside Raoden's chamber, falling into place beside him. Over the last week, the soldier had gathered a group of willing men and formed them into a squad of guards.

"You know I am flattered by your attentiveness, Saolin," Raoden said. "But is it really necessary?"

"A lord requires an honor guard, Lord Spirit," Saolin explained. "It wouldn't be proper for you to go about alone."

"I'm not a lord, Saolin," Raoden said. "I'm just a leader—there is to be no nobility in Elantris."

"I understand, my lord," Saolin said with a nod, obviously not seeing the paradox within his own words. "However, the city is still a dangerous place."

"As you wish, Saolin," Raoden said. "How goes the planting?"

"Galladon has finished his plowing," Saolin said. "He has already organized the planting teams."

"I shouldn't have slept so long," Raoden said, looking out the chapel window to notice how high the sun had risen. He left the building, Saolin close behind, and walked around a neat cobblestone path to the gardens. Kahar and his crew had cleaned off the stones, and then Dahad—one of Taan's followers—had used his skills with stoneworking to reset them.

The planting was already well under way. Galladon oversaw the work with a careful eye, his gruff tongue quick to point out any errors. However, there was a peace about the Dula. Some men were farmers because they had no other choice, but Galladon seemed to find true enjoyment in the activity.

Raoden remembered clearly that first day, when he had tempted Galladon with the bit of dried meat. His friend's pain had barely been under control back then—Raoden had been scared of the Dula several times during those first days. Now none of that remained. Raoden could see it in Galladon's eyes and in his bearing: He had found the "secret," as Kahar had put it. Galladon was in control again. Now the only one Raoden had to fear was himself.

His theories were working better than even he had expected—but only on everyone else. He had brought peace and purpose to the dozens who followed him, but he couldn't do the same for himself. The pain still burned him. It threatened him every morning when he awoke and stayed with him every moment he was conscious. He was more purposeful than any of the others, and was the most determined to see Elantris succeed. He filled his days, leaving no empty moments to contemplate his suffering. Nothing worked. The pain continued to build.

"My lord, watch out!" Saolin yelled.

Raoden jumped, turning as a growling, bare-chested Elantrian charged from a darkened hallway, running toward Raoden. Raoden barely had time to step backward as the wildman lifted a rusted iron bar and swung it directly at Raoden's face.

Bare steel flashed out of nowhere, and Saolin's blade parried the blow. The bestial newcomer halted, reorienting himself to a new foe. He moved too slowly. Saolin's practiced hand delivered a thrust directly through the madman's abdomen. Then, knowing that such a blow wouldn't stop an Elantrian, Saolin swung a mighty backhand, separating the madman's head from his body. There was no blood.

The corpse tumbled to the ground, and Saolin saluted Raoden with his blade, shooting him a gap-toothed smile of reassurance. Then he spun around to face a group of wildmen charging down a nearby street toward them.

Stunned, Raoden stumbled backward. "Saolin, no! There are too many of them!"

Fortunately, Saolin's men had heard the commotion. Within seconds, there were five of them—Saolin, Dashe, and three other soldiers—standing against the attack. They fought in an efficient line, blocking their enemy's path to the rest of the gardens, working with the coordination of trained soldiers.

Shaor's men were more numerous, but their rage was no match for martial efficiency. They attacked solitarily, and their fervor made them stupid. In moments the battle was over, the few remaining attackers dashing away in retreat.

Saolin cleaned his blade efficiently, then turned with the others. They saluted Raoden in coordination.

The entire battle had happened almost more quickly than Raoden could follow. "Good work," he finally managed to say.

A grunt came from his side, where Galladon knelt beside the decapitated body of the first attacker. "They must have heard we had corn in here," the Dula mumbled. "Poor rulos."

Raoden nodded solemnly, regarding the fallen madmen. Four of them lay on the ground, clutching various wounds—all of which would have been fatal had they not been Elantrians. As it was, they could only moan in torment. Raoden felt a stab of familiarity. He knew what that pain felt like.

"This cannot continue," he said quietly.

"I don't see how you can stop it, sule," Galladon replied at his side. "These are Shaor's men; not even he has much control over them."

Raoden shook his head. "I will *not* save the people of Elantris and leave them to fight all the days of their lives. I will not build a society on death. Shaor's followers might have forgotten that they are men, but I have not."

Galladon frowned. "Karata and Aanden, they were possibilities—if distant ones. Shaor is another story, sule. There isn't a smear of humanity left in these men—you can't reason with them."

"Then I'll have to give them their reason back," Raoden said.

"And how, sule, do you intend to do that?"

"I will find a way."

Raoden knelt by the fallen madman. A tickle in the back of his mind warned him that he recognized this man from recent experience. Raoden couldn't be certain, but he thought that the man had been one of Taan's followers, one of the men Raoden had confronted during Dashe's attempted raid.

So, it's true, Raoden thought with a crimp in his stomach. Many of Taan's followers had come to join Raoden, but the larger part had not. It was whispered that many of these had found their way to the merchant sector of Elantris, joining with Shaor's wildmen. It wasn't all that unlikely, Raoden supposed—the men had been willing to follow the obviously unbalanced Aanden, after all. Shaor's band was only a short step away from that.

"Lord Spirit?" Saolin asked hesitantly. "What should we do with them?"

Raoden turned pitying eyes on the fallen. "They are of no danger to us now, Saolin. Let's put them with the others."

SOON after his success with Aanden's gang, and the subsequent swell in his band's numbers, Raoden had done something he'd wanted to from the beginning. He started gathering the fallen of Elantris.

He took them off the streets and out of the gutters, searched through buildings both destroyed and standing, trying to find every man, woman, and child in Elantris who had given in to their pain. The city was large, and Raoden's manpower was limited, but so far they had collected hundreds of people. He ordered them placed in the second building Kahar had cleaned, a large open structure he had originally intended to use as a meeting place. The Hoed would still suffer, but at least they could do it with a little decency.

And they wouldn't have to do it alone. Raoden had asked the people in his band to visit the Hoed. There were usually a couple of Elantrians walking among them, talking soothingly and trying to make them as comfortable as possible considering the circumstances. It wasn't much—and no one could stomach much time among the Hoed—but Raoden had convinced himself that it helped. He followed his own counsel, visiting the Hall of the Fallen at least once a day, and it seemed to him that they were improving. The Hoed still groaned, mumbled, or stared blankly, but the more vocal ones seemed quieter. Where the Hall had once been a place of fearful screams and echoes, it was now a subdued realm of quiet mumblings and despair.

Raoden moved among them gravely, helping carry one of the fallen wildmen. There were only four to deposit; he had ordered the fifth man, the one Saolin had beheaded, buried. As far as anyone could tell, an Elantrian died when he was completely beheaded—at least, their eyes didn't move, nor did their lips try to speak, if the head was completely separated from the body.

As he walked through the Hoed, Raoden listened to their quiet murmurings.

"Beautiful, once so very beautiful. . . ."

"Life, life, life, life, life. . . ."

"Oh Domi, where are you? When will it end? Oh Domi. . . ."

He usually had to block the words out after a time, lest they drive him insane—or worse, reawaken the pain within his own body. Ien was there, floating around sightless heads and weaving between fallen bodies. The Seon spent a lot of time in the room. It was strangely fitting.

They left the Hall a solemn group, quiet and content to keep to their own thoughts. Raoden only spoke when he noticed the tear in Saolin's robes.

"You're wounded!" Raoden said with surprise.

"It is nothing, my lord," Saolin said indifferently.

"That kind of modesty is fine on the outside, Saolin, but not here. You must accept my apology."

"My lord," Saolin said seriously. "Being an Elantrian only makes me *more* proud to wear this wound. I received it protecting our people."

Raoden turned a tormented look back at the Hall. "It only brings you one step closer . . ."

"No, my lord, I don't think it does. Those people gave in to their pain because they couldn't find purpose—their torture was meaningless, and when you can't find reason in life, you tend to give up on it. This wound will hurt, but each stab of pain will remind me that I earned it with honor. That is not such a bad thing, I think."

Raoden regarded the old soldier with a look of respect. On the outside he probably would have been close to retirement. In Elantris, with the Shaod as an equalizer, he looked about the same as anyone else. One couldn't tell age by looks, but perhaps one could tell it through wisdom.

"You speak discerningly, my friend," Raoden said. "I accept your sacrifice with humility."

The conversation was interrupted by the slap of feet against cobblestones. A moment later Karata dashed into view, her feet coated with fresh sludge from outside the chapel area. Kahar would be furious: she had forgotten to wipe down her feet, and now she was tracking slime over his clean cobblestones.

Karata obviously didn't care about slime at the moment. She surveyed the group quickly, making sure no one was missing. "I heard Shaor attacked. Were there any casualties?"

"Five. All on their side," Raoden said.

"I should have been here," she said with a curse. During the last few days, the determined woman had been overseeing the relocation of her people to the chapel area; she agreed that a central, unified group would be more effective, and the chapel area was cleaner. Oddly enough, the idea of cleaning the palace had never occurred to her. To most Elantrians, the sludge was accepted as an irrevocable part of life.

"You have important things to do," Raoden said. "You couldn't have anticipated Shaor would attack."

Karata didn't like the answer, but she fell into line beside him without further complaint.

"Look at him, sule," Galladon said, smiling slightly beside him. "I would never have thought it possible."

Raoden looked up, following the Dula's gaze. Taan knelt beside the road, inspecting the carvings on a short wall with childlike wonder. The squat-bodied former baron had spent the entire week cataloguing each carving, sculpture, or relief in the chapel area. He had already discovered, in his words, "at least a dozen new techniques." The changes in Taan were remarkable, as was his sudden lack of interest in leadership. Karata still maintained a measure of influence in the group, accepting Raoden as the ultimate voice but retaining most of her authority. Taan, however, didn't bother to give orders; he was too busy with his studies.

His people—the ones who had decided to join with Raoden—didn't seem to mind. Taan now estimated that about thirty percent of his "court" had found its way to Raoden's band, trickling in as small groups. Raoden hoped that most of the others had chosen solitude instead; he found the idea of seventy percent of Taan's large band joining with Shaor very disturbing. Raoden had all of Karata's people, but her gang had always been the smallest—if most efficient—of the three. Shaor's had always been the largest; its members had just lacked the cohesion and the motivation to attack the other gangs. The occasional newcomers Shaor's men had been given had sated their bloodlust.

No longer. Raoden would accept no quarter with the madmen, would not allow them to torment innocent newcomers. Karata and Saolin now retrieved everyone thrown into the city, bringing them safely to Raoden's band. So far, the reaction from Shaor's men had not been good—and Raoden feared that it would only grow worse.

I'll have to do something about them, he thought. That, however, was a problem for another day. He had studies he needed to get to for the moment.

Once they reached the chapel, Galladon went back to his planting, Saolin's men dispersed to their patrols, and Karata decided—despite her earlier protests—that she should return to the palace. Soon only Raoden and Saolin were left.

After the battle and sleeping so late, over half the day's light had already been wasted, and Raoden attacked his studies with determination. While Galladon planted and Karata evacuated the palace, it was Raoden's self-appointed duty to decipher as much as he could about AonDor. He was becoming increasingly convinced that the ancient magic of the characters held the secret of Elantris's fall.

He reached through one of the chapel windows and pulled out the thick AonDor tome sitting on a table inside. So far, it hadn't been as helpful as he had hoped. It was not an instruction manual, but a series of case studies explaining odd or interesting events surrounding AonDor. Unfortunately, it was extremely advanced. Most of the book gave examples of what *wasn't* supposed to happen, and so Raoden needed to use reverse reasoning to decipher the logic of AonDor.

So far he had been able to determine very little. It was becoming obvious that the Aons were only starting points— the most basic figures one could draw to produce an effect. Just like the expanded healing Aon from his dream, advanced AonDor consisted of drawing a base Aon in the center, then proceeding to draw other figures—sometimes just dots and lines—around it. The dots and lines were stipulations, narrowing or broadening the power's focus. With careful drawing, for instance, a healer could specify which limb was to be healed, what exactly was to be done to it, and how an infection was to be cleansed.

The more Raoden read, the less he was beginning to see Aons as mystical symbols. They seemed more like mathematical computations. While most any Elantrian could draw the Aons—all it required was a steady hand and a basic knowledge of how to write the characters—the masters of AonDor were the ones who could swiftly and accurately delineate dozens of smaller modifications around the central Aon. Unfortunately, the book assumed that its reader had a comprehensive knowledge of AonDor, and passed over most of the basic principles. The few illustrations included were so incredibly complex that Raoden usually couldn't even tell which character was the base Aon without referring to the text.

"If only he would explain what it means to 'channel the Dor'!" Raoden exclaimed, rereading a particularly annoying passage that kept using the phrase.

"Dor, sule?" Galladon asked, turning away from his planting. "That sounds like a Duladen term."

Raoden sat upright. The character used in the book to represent "Dor" was an uncommon one—not really an Aon at all, but simply a phonetic representation. As if the word had been transliterated from a different language.

"Galladon, you're right!" Raoden said. "It isn't Aonic at all."

"Of course not—it can't be an Aon, it only has one vowel in it."

"That's a simplistic way of putting it, my friend."

"But it's true. Kolo?"

"Yes, I suppose it is," Raoden said. "That doesn't matter right now—what matters is Dor. Do you know what it means?"

"Well, if it's the same word, then it refers to something in Jesker."

"What do the Mysteries have to do with this?" Raoden asked suspiciously.

"Doloken, sule!" Galladon swore. "I've told you, Jesker and the Mysteries are not the same thing! What Opelon calls the 'Jeskeri Mysteries' is no more related to Duladel's religion than it is to Shu-Keseg."

"Point taken," Raoden said, raising his hands. "Now, tell me about Dor."

"It's hard to explain, sule," Galladon said, leaning on a makeshift hoe he had crafted out of a pole and some rocks. "Dor is the unseen power—it is in everything, but cannot be touched. It affects nothing, yet it controls everything. Why do rivers flow?"

"Because the water is pulled downwards, just like everything else. The ice melts in the mountains, and it has to have a place to go."

"Correct," Galladon said. "Now, a different question. What makes the water *want* to flow?"

"I wasn't aware that it needed to."

"It does, and the Dor is its motivation," Galladon said. "Jesker teaches that only humans have the ability—or the curse—of being oblivious to the Dor. Did you know that if you take a bird away from its parents and raise it in your house, it will still learn to fly?"

Raoden shrugged.

"How did it learn, sule? Who taught it to fly?"

"The Dor?" Raoden asked hesitantly.

"That is correct."

Raoden smiled; the explanation sounded too religiously mysterious to be useful. But then he thought of his dream, his memories of what had happened so long ago. When the Elantrian healer had drawn her Aon, it appeared as if a tear were appearing in the air behind her finger. Raoden could still feel the chaotic power raging behind that tear, the massive force trying to press its way through the Aon to get at him. It sought to overwhelm him, to break him down until he became part of it. However, the healer's carefully constructed Aon had funneled the power into a usable form, and it had healed Raoden's leg instead of destroying him.

That force, whatever it had been, was real. It was there behind the Aons he drew, weak though they were. "That must be it. . . . Galladon, that's why we are still alive!"

"What are you babbling about, sule?" Galladon said, looking up from his work with tolerance.

"That is why we live on, even though our bodies don't work anymore!" Raoden said with excitement. "Don't you see? We don't eat, yet we get the energy to keep moving. There must be some link between Elantrians and the Dor—it feeds our bodies, providing the energy we need to survive."

"Then why doesn't it give us enough to keep our hearts moving and our skin from turning gray?" Galladon asked, unconvinced.

"Because it's barely enough," Raoden explained. "Aon-Dor no longer works—the power that once fueled the city has been reduced to a bare trickle. The important thing is, *it's not gone*. We can still draw Aons, even if they are weak and don't do anything, and our minds continue to live, even if our bodies have given up. We just need to find a way to restore it to full power."

"Oh, is that all?" Galladon asked. "You mean we need to fix what is broken?"

"I guess so," Raoden said. "The important thing is realizing there's a link between ourselves and the Dor, Galladon. Not only that—but there must be some sort of link between this land and the Dor."

Galladon frowned. "Why do you say that?"

"Because AonDor was developed in Arelon and nowhere else," Raoden said. "The text says that the farther one traveled from Elantris, the weaker the AonDor powers became. Besides—only people from Arelon are taken by the Shaod. It can take Teoish people, but only if they're living in Arelon at the time. Oh, and it takes the occasional Dula as well."

"I hadn't noticed."

"There's some link between this land, the Arelish people, and the Dor, Galladon," Raoden said. "I've never heard of a Fjordell getting taken by the Shaod, no matter how long he lives in Arelon. Dulas are a mixed people—half Jindo, half Aonic. Where was your farm in Duladen?"

Galladon frowned. "In the north, sule."

"The part that borders Arelon," Raoden said triumphantly. "It has something to do with the land, and with our Aonic bloodlines."

Galladon shrugged. "It sounds like it makes sense, sule, but I'm just a simple farmer—what know I of such things?"

Raoden snorted, not bothering to respond to the comment. "But why? What's the connection? Maybe the Fjordell are right—maybe Arelon is cursed."

"Hypothesize away, sule," Galladon said, turning back to his work. "I don't see much empirical good to it, though."

"All right. Well, I'll stop theorizing as soon as you tell me where a *simple farmer* learned the word 'empirical.'"

Galladon didn't respond, but Raoden thought he could hear the Dula chuckling softly.

CHAPTER 20

"LET me see if I understand you, Princess dear," Ahan said, holding aloft a chubby finger. "You want us to *help* Iadon? How foolish I am—I thought we didn't like the fellow."

"We don't," Sarene agreed. "Helping the king financially doesn't have anything to do with our personal feelings."

"I'm afraid I have to agree with Ahan, Princess," Roial said with outspread hands. "Why the sudden change? What good will it do to aid the king now?"

Sarene gritted her teeth in annoyance. Then, however, she caught a twinkle in the elderly duke's eye. He knew. The duke reportedly had a spy network as extensive as most kings'—he had figured out what Hrathen was trying to do. He had asked the question not to provoke her, but to give her an opportunity to explain. Sarene exhaled slowly, grateful for the duke's tact.

"Someone is sinking the king's ships," Sarene said. "Common sense confirms what my father's spies say. Dreok Crushthroat's fleets couldn't be sinking the boats—most of

Dreok's ships were destroyed fifteen years ago when he tried to take the throne of Teod, and any remnants have long since disappeared. Wyrn must be behind the sinkings."

"All right, we accept that much," Ahan said.

"Fjorden is also giving financial support to Duke Telrii," Sarene continued.

"You don't have any proof of that, Your Highness," Eondel pointed out.

"No, I don't," Sarene admitted, pacing between the men's chairs, the ground soft with new spring grass. They had eventually decided to hold this meeting in the gardens of Kae's Korathi chapel, and so there was no table for her to circle. Sarene had managed to remain seated during the first part of the meeting, but had eventually stood. She found it easier to address others when she was on her feet—something of a nervous habit, she realized, but she also knew that her height lent her an air of authority.

"I do, however, have logical conjecture," she said. Eondel would respond well to anything following the word "logical." "We all attended Telrii's party a week ago. He must have spent more on that ball than most men make in a year."

"Extravagance isn't always a sign of wealth," Shuden pointed out. "I've seen men poor as a peasant put on dazzling shows to maintain an illusion of security in the face of collapse." Shuden's words rang true—a man at their own meeting, Baron Edan, was doing just what Shuden described.

Sarene frowned. "I've done some checking around—I had a lot of free time this last week, since none of you managed to get this meeting together, despite its urgency." None of the noblemen would meet her eyes after that comment. She'd finally gotten them together. But, unfortunately, Kiin and Lukel hadn't been able to attend because of a prior engagement. "Anyway, rumors say that Telrii's accounts have swelled drastically during the last two weeks, and his shipments to Fjorden turn fantastic profits no matter what he chooses to send, whether it be fine spices or cow dung."

"The fact remains that the duke has not aligned himself with Shu-Dereth," Eondel pointed out. "He still attends his Korathi meetings piously."

Sarene folded her arms, tapping her cheek in thought. "If

Telrii openly aligned himself with Fjorden, his earnings would be suspicious. Hrathen is far too crafty to be so transparent. It would be much smarter for Fjorden to remain separate from the duke, allowing Telrii to appear a pious conservative. Despite Hrathen's recent advances, it would be much easier for a traditional Korathi to usurp the throne than it would be for a Derethi."

"He'll take the throne, *then* make good on his pact with Wyrn," Roial agreed.

"Which is why we have to make sure Iadon starts earning money again very soon," Sarene said. "The nation is running dry—it is very possible that Telrii will earn more in this next accounting period than Iadon, even including taxes. I doubt the king would abdicate. However, if Telrii were to stage a coup, the other nobles might go along with him."

"How do you like that, Edan?" Ahan asked, directing a hearty laugh at the anxious baron. "You might not be the only one who loses his title in a few months—old Iadon himself might join you."

"If you please, Count Ahan," Sarene said. "It's our duty to make sure that doesn't happen."

"What do you want us to do?" Edan asked nervously. "Send gifts to the king? I don't have any money to spare."

"None of us do, Edan," Ahan responded, hands resting on his ample belly. "If it were 'spare' it wouldn't be valuable now, would it?"

"You know what he means, Ahan," Roial chided. "And I doubt gifts are what the princess had in mind."

"Actually, I'm open for suggestions, gentlemen," Sarene said, spreading out her hands. "I'm a politician, not a merchant. I'm a confessed amateur at making money."

"Gifts wouldn't work," Shuden said, hands laced before his chin contemplatively. "The king is a proud man who has earned his fortune through sweat, work, and scheming. He would never take handouts, even to save his throne. Besides, merchants are notoriously suspicious of gifts."

"We could go to him with the truth," Sarene suggested. "Maybe then he'd accept our help."

"He wouldn't believe us," Roial said with a shake of his aged head. "The king is a very literal man, Sarene—even more so than our dear Lord Eondel. Generals have to think abstractly to outguess their opponents, but Iadon—I seriously doubt he's had an abstract thought in his life. The king accepts things as they appear to be, especially if they are the way he thinks they should be."

"Which is why Lady Sarene fooled His Majesty with her apparent lack of wits," Shuden agreed. "He expected her to be foolish, and when she appeared to fit his expectations he dismissed her—even if her act was terribly overdone."

Sarene chose not to rebut that remark.

"Pirates are something Iadon understands," Roial said. "They make sense in the world of shipping—in a way, every merchant considers himself a pirate. However, governments are different. In the king's eyes, it wouldn't make sense for a kingdom to sink ships filled with valuable merchandise. The king would never attack merchants, no matter how tense the war. And as far as he knows, Arelon and Fjorden are good friends. He was the first one to let Derethi priests into Kae, and he has given that gyorn Hrathen every liberty of a visiting nobleman. I seriously doubt we could convince him that Wyrn is trying to depose him."

"We could try framing Fjorden," Eondel suggested. "Making it obvious that the sinkings are Wyrn's work."

"It would take too long, Eondel," Ahan said, shaking his jowls. "Besides, Iadon doesn't have many ships left—I doubt he'll risk them in those same waters again."

Sarene nodded. "It would also be very difficult for us to establish a connection to Wyrn. He's probably using Svordish warships for the task—Fjorden itself doesn't have much of a navy."

"Was Dreok Crushthroat Svordish?" Eondel asked with a frown.

"I heard he was Fjordell," Ahan said.

"No," Roial said. "I think he was supposed to be Aonic, wasn't he?"

"Anyway," Sarene said impatiently, trying to keep the meeting on track as she paced across the loamy garden floor. "Lord Ahan said he wouldn't risk his ships in those waters again, but the king obviously has to keep them shipping somewhere."

Ahan nodded in agreement. "He can't afford to stop now—spring is one of the best buying seasons. People have been cooped up all winter with drab colors and drabber relatives. As soon as the snows melt, they're ready to splurge a little. This is the time when expensive colored silks go for a premium, and that is one of Iadon's best products.

"These sinkings are a disaster. Not only did Iadon lose the ships themselves, he lost the profit he would have made off all those silks, not to mention the other cargo. Many merchants nearly bankrupt themselves this time of year by stockpiling goods that they know they can eventually sell."

"His Majesty got greedy," Shuden said. "He bought more and more ships, and filled them with as much silk as he could afford."

"We're all greedy, Shuden," Ahan said. "Don't forget, your family earned its fortune by organizing the spice route from Jindo. You didn't even ship anything—you just built the roads and charged the merchants to use them."

"Let me rephrase, Lord Ahan," Shuden said. "The king let his greed make him foolish. Disasters are something every good merchant should plan for. Never ship what you can't afford to lose."

"Well put," Ahan agreed.

"Anyway," Sarene said, "if the king only has a couple of ships left, then they have to deliver a solid profit."

"'Solid' isn't the right word, my dear," Ahan said. "Try 'extraordinary.' It is going to take a miracle for Iadon to recoup from this little catastrophe—especially before Telrii humiliates him irreparably."

"What if he had an agreement with Teod?" Sarene asked. "An extremely lucrative contract for silks?"

"Maybe," Ahan said with a shrug. "It's clever."

"But impossible," Duke Roial said.

"Why?" Sarene demanded. "Teod can afford it."

"Because," the duke explained, "Iadon would never accept such a contract. He's too experienced a merchant to make a deal that appears too fabulous to be realistic."

"Agreed," Shuden said with a nod. "The king wouldn't be against making a horrible profit off of Teod, but only if he thought he was cheating you."

The others nodded at Shuden's statement. Although the Jindoeese man was the youngest in the group, Shuden was quickly proving himself to be as shrewd as Roial—perhaps more so. That capability, mixed with his deserved reputation for honesty, earned him respect beyond his years. It was a powerful man indeed who could mix integrity with savvy.

"We'll have to think on this some more," Roial said. "But not too long. We must solve the problem by the accounting day, otherwise we'll be dealing with Telrii instead of Iadon. As bad as my old friend is, I know we'd have less luck with Telrii—especially if Fjorden is backing him."

"Is everyone doing as I asked with their planting?" Sarene asked as the nobles prepared to leave.

"It wasn't easy," Ahan admitted. "My overseers and minor nobles all objected to the idea."

"But you did it."

"I did," Ahan said.

"As did I," Roial said.

"I had no choice," Edan muttered.

Shuden and Eondel each gave her quiet nods.

"We started planting last week," Edan said. "How long before we see results?"

"Hopefully within the next three months, for your sake, my lord," Sarene said.

"That is usually long enough to get an estimate of how good a crop will do," Shuden said.

"I still don't see how it matters whether the people think they're free or not," Ahan said. "The same seeds get planted, and so the same crop should come up."

"You'll be surprised, my lord," Sarene promised.

"May we go now?" Edan asked pointedly. He still chafed at the idea of Sarene running these meetings.

"One more question, my lords. I've been considering my Widow's Trial, and would like to hear what you think."

The men began to shift uncomfortably at the statement, looking at each other uneasily.

"Oh, come now," Sarene said with a displeased frown, "you're grown men. Get over your childish fear of Elantris."

"It is a very delicate topic in Arelon, Sarene," Shuden said.

"Well, it appears that Hrathen isn't worried about that," she said. "You all know what he's begun to do."

"He's drawing a parallel between Shu-Korath and Elantris," Roial said with a nod. "He's trying to turn the people against the Korathi priests."

"And he's going to be successful if we don't stop him," Sarene said, "which requires you all to get over your squeamishness and stop pretending that Elantris doesn't exist. The city is a major part of the gyorn's plans."

The men shot each other knowing looks in the dense Korathi garden. The men thought she paid undue attention to the gyorn; they saw Iadon's government as a major problem, but religion didn't seem a tangible threat. They didn't understand that in Fjorden, at least, religion and war were almost the same thing.

"You're just going to have to trust me, my lords," Sarene said. "Hrathen's schemes are important. You said the king sees things concretely—well, this Hrathen is the opposite. He views everything by its potential, and his goal is to make Arelon another Fjordell protectorate. If he is using Elantris against us, we must respond."

"Just have that short Korathi priest agree with him," Ahan suggested. "Put them on the same side, then no one can use the city against anyone else."

"Omin won't do that, my lord," Sarene said with a shake of her head. "He bears the Elantrians no ill will, and he would never consent to labeling them devils."

"Couldn't he just . . ." Ahan said.

"Merciful Domi, Ahan," Roial said. "Don't you ever attend his sermons? The man would never do that."

"I go," Ahan said indignantly. "I just thought he might be willing to serve his kingdom. We could compensate him."

"No, my lord," Sarene said insistently. "Omin is a man of the Church—a good and sincere one, at that. To him, truth is not subject to debate—or sale. I'm afraid we have no choice. We have to side with Elantris."

Several faces, including Eondel and Edan's, blanched at that statement.

"That might not be an easy proposition to carry out,

Sarene," Roial warned. "You may think us childish, but these four are among the most intelligent and open-minded men in Arelon. If you find them nervous about Elantris, then you will find the rest of Arelon more so."

"We have to change that sentiment, my lord," Sarene said. "And my Widow's Trial is our opportunity. I am going to take food to the Elantrians."

This time she succeeded in getting a reaction even from Shuden and Roial.

"Did I hear your correctly, my dear?" Ahan asked with a shaky voice. "You're going to go into Elantris?"

"Yes," Sarene said.

"I need something to drink," Ahan decided, unstoppering his wine flask.

"The king will never allow it," Edan said. "He doesn't even let the Elantris City Guards go inside."

"He's right," Shuden agreed. "You will never get through those gates, Your Highness."

"Let me deal with the king," Sarene said.

"Your subterfuge won't work this time, Sarene," Roial warned. "No amount of stupidity will convince the king to let you into the city."

"I'll think of something," Sarene said, trying to sound more certain than she was. "It's not your concern, my lord. I just want your word that you will help me."

"Help you?" Ahan asked hesitantly.

"Help me distribute food in Elantris," Sarene said.

Ahan's eyes bugged out. "Help you?" he repeated. "In there?"

"My goal is to demystify the city," Sarene explained. "To do that, I'll need to convince the nobility to go inside and see for themselves that there's nothing horrifying about the Elantrians."

"I'm sorry to sound objectionable," Eondel began. "But, Lady Sarene, what if there is? What if everything they say about Elantris is true?"

Sarene paused. "I don't think they're dangerous, Lord Eondel. I've looked in on the city and its people. There is nothing frightening about Elantris—well, nothing besides the way its people are treated. I don't believe the tales about monsters or Elantrian cannibalism. I just see a collection of men and women who have been mistreated and misjudged."

Eondel didn't look convinced, and neither did the others.

"Look, I'll go in first and test it," Sarene said. "I want you lords to join me after the first few days."

"Why us?" Edan said with a groan.

"Because I need to start somewhere," Sarene explained. "If you lords brave the city, then others will feel foolish if they object. Aristocrats have a group mentality; if I can build some momentum, then I can probably get most of them to come in with me at least once. Then they'll see that there is nothing horrible about Elantris—that its people are just poor wretches who want to eat. We can defeat Hrathen with simple truth. It is hard to demonize a man after you have seen tears in his eyes as he thanks you for feeding him."

"This is all pointless anyway," Edan said, his hand twitching at the thought of entering Elantris. "The king will never let her in."

"And if he does?" Sarene asked quickly. "Then will you go, Edan?"

The baron blinked in surprise, realizing he had been caught. She waited for him to respond, but he stubbornly refused to answer the question.

"I will," Shuden declared.

Sarene smiled at the Jindo. This was the second time he had been the first to offer her support.

"If Shuden's going to do it, then I doubt the rest of us will have the humility to say no," Roial said. "Get your permission, Sarene, then we will discuss this further."

"MAYBE I was a little too optimistic," Sarene admitted, standing outside the doors to Iadon's study. A pair of guards stood a short distance away, watching her suspiciously.

"Do you know what you are going to do, my lady?" Ashe asked. The Seon had spent the meeting floating just outside the chapel walls—well within his range of hearing—making certain that no one else was eavesdropping on their meeting.

Sarene shook her head. She had displayed bravado when

confronted by Ahan and the others, but now she realized
how misplaced that sentiment had been. She had no idea
how she was going to get Iadon to let her into Elantris—let
alone get him to accept their help.

"Did you speak with Father?" she asked.

"I did, my lady," Ashe replied. "He said he would give you
whatever financial help you required."

"All right," Sarene said. "Let's go." She took a deep
breath and strode toward the soldiers. "I would speak with
my father," she announced.

The guards glanced at each other. "Um, we were told not
to . . ."

"That doesn't apply to family, soldier," Sarene said insistently. "If the queen came to speak with her husband would
you turn her away?"

The guards frowned in confusion; Eshen probably didn't
come to visit. Sarene had noticed that the bubbly queen
tended to keep her distance from Iadon. Even silly women
resent being described that way to their faces.

"Just open the door, soldier," Sarene said. "If the king
doesn't want to talk to me, he'll throw me out, and next time
you will know not to let me in."

The guards hesitated, and Sarene simply pushed her way
between them and opened the door herself. The guards, obviously unused to dealing with forceful women—especially
in the royal family—simply let her pass.

Iadon looked up from his desk, a pair of spectacles she
had never seen him wear before balanced on the end of his
nose. He quickly pulled them off and stood, slamming his
hands against the desktop in annoyance, disturbing several
invoice stacks in the process.

"You aren't content to annoy me in public, so you have to
follow me to my study as well?" he demanded. "If I'd known
what a foolish, spindly girl you were, I would never have
signed that treaty. Be gone, woman, and leave me to work!"

"I tell you what, Father," Sarene said with frankness. "I'll
pretend to be an intelligent human being capable of a semi-
lucid conversation, and you pretend the same thing."

Iadon's eyes grew wide at the comment, and his face
turned a bright red. "Rag Domi!" he swore, using a curse so

vile Sarene had only heard it twice. "You tricked me, woman. I could have you beheaded for making me look the fool."

"Start decapitating your children, Father, and people will begin to ask questions." She watched his reaction carefully, hoping to glean something about Raoden's disappearance, but she was disappointed. Iadon brushed off the comment with only passing attention.

"I should ship you back to Eventeo right now," he said.

"Fine, I'd be happy to go," she lied. "However, realize that if I go, you lose your trade treaty with Teod. That could be a problem, considering the luck you've had peddling your silks in Fjorden lately."

Iadon gritted his teeth at the comment.

"Careful, my lady," Ashe whispered. "Do not unsettle him too much. Men often place pride before reason."

Sarene nodded. "I can give you a way out, Father. I have come to offer you a deal."

"What reason do I have to accept any offers from you, woman?" he snapped. "You have been here nearly a month, and now I find that you have been deceiving me the whole time."

"You will trust me, Father, because you have lost seventy-five percent of your fleet to pirates. In a few short months you could lose your throne unless you listen to me."

Iadon betrayed surprise at her knowledge. "How do you know these things?"

"Everyone knows, Father," Sarene said lightly. "It's all over the court—they expect you to fall at the next taxing period."

"I knew it!" Iadon said, his eyes widening with rage. He began to sweat and curse at the courtiers, railing at their determination to see him off the throne.

Sarene blinked in surprise. She had made the comment passingly to keep Iadon off balance, but hadn't expected such a strong reaction. *He's paranoid!* she realized. *Why hasn't anyone noticed this before?* However, the speed with which Iadon recovered gave her a clue—he was paranoid, but he kept it well hidden. The way she was jerking his emotions must have weakened his control.

"You propose a deal?" the king demanded.

"I do," Sarene said. "Silk is going for a premium in Teod

right now, Father. One could make quite a profit selling it to the king. And, considering certain familial relationships, you might be able to talk Eventeo into giving you sole mercantile rights in his country."

Iadon grew suspicious, his rage cooling as he sensed a bargain. However, the merchant in him immediately began to sniff for problems. Sarene gritted her teeth in frustration: It was as the others had told her. Iadon would never accept her offer; it stank too much of deceit.

"An interesting proposal," he admitted. "But I'm afraid that I—"

"I would, of course, require something in return," Sarene interrupted, thinking quickly. "Call it a fee for setting up the deal between Eventeo and yourself."

Iadon paused. "What kind of fee are we talking about?" he asked warily. An exchange was different from a gift—it could be weighed, measured, and, to an extent, trusted.

"I want to go inside Elantris," Sarene declared.

"What?"

"I have to perform a Widow's Trial," Sarene said. "So, I am going to bring food to the Elantrians."

"What possible motivation could you have for doing that, woman?"

"Religious reasons, Father," Sarene explained. "Shu-Korath teaches us to help those most lowly, and I challenge you to find anyone more lowly than the Elantrians."

"It's out of the question," Iadon said. "Entry into Elantris is forbidden by law."

"A law you made, Father," Sarene said pointedly. "And, therefore, you can make exceptions. Think carefully—your fortune, and your throne, could balance on your answer."

Iadon ground his teeth audibly as he considered the trade. "You want to enter Elantris with food? For how long?"

"Until I am convinced my duty as Prince Raoden's wife has been fulfilled," Sarene said.

"You would go alone?"

"I would take any who were willing to accompany me."

Iadon snorted. "You'll have trouble finding anyone to fill that requirement."

"My problem, not yours."

"First that Fjordell devil starts whipping my people into mobs, now you would do the same," the king mumbled.

"No, Father," Sarene corrected. "I want quite the opposite—chaos would only benefit Wyrn. Believe as you wish, but it is my sole concern to see stability in Arelon."

Iadon continued to think for a moment. "No more than ten at a time, excluding guards," he finally said. "I don't want mass pilgrimages going into Elantris. You will enter an hour before noon and you will be gone by an hour after noon. No exceptions."

"Done," Sarene agreed. "You may use my Seon to call King Eventeo to work out the details of the deal."

"I must admit, my lady, that was rather clever." Ashe bobbed along beside her in the hallway on the way to her room.

Sarene had stayed as Iadon spoke with Eventeo, mediating as the two worked out the deal. Her father's voice had contained a hearty measure of "I hope you know what you're doing, 'Ene" in it. Eventeo was a kind and good king, but he was an absolutely horrible businessman; he kept a fleet of accountants to manage the royal finances. Once Iadon had sensed her father's inability, he struck with the enthusiasm of a raging predator, and only Sarene's presence had kept Iadon from leaking away Teod's entire tax revenue in a rampage of trading fervor. As it was, Iadon had managed to talk them into buying his silks for four times as much as they were worth. The king had been beaming so widely as Sarene left that he almost appeared to have forgiven her for her charade.

"Clever?" Sarene asked innocently in response to Ashe's comment. "Me?"

The Seon bobbed, chuckling softly. "Is there anyone you can't manipulate, my lady?"

"Father," Sarene said. "You know he gets the better of me three times out of five."

"He says the same thing about you, my lady," Ashe noted.

Sarene smiled, pushing open the door to her room to prepare for bed. "It really wasn't that clever, Ashe. We should have realized that our problems were really solutions to one another—one an offer with no catch, the other a request with no sweetener."

Ashe made noises of displeasure as he floated around the room, "tisking," offended at its messy state.

"What?" Sarene asked, unwrapping the black ribbon tied around her upper arm—the only remaining sign of her mourning.

"The room has not been cleaned again, my lady," Ashe explained.

"Well, it's not like I left it that messy in the first place," Sarene said with a huff.

"No, Your Highness is a very tidy woman," Ashe agreed. "However, the palace maids have been lax in their duties. A princess deserves proper esteem—if you allow them to neglect their work, it won't be long before they stop respecting you."

"I think you're reading too much into it, Ashe," Sarene said with a shake of her head, pulling off her dress and preparing her nightgown. "I'm supposed to be the suspicious one, remember?"

"This is a matter of servants, not lords, my lady," Ashe said. "You are a brilliant woman and a fine politician, but you betray a common weakness of your class—you ignore the opinions of servants."

"Ashe!" Sarene objected. "I always treated my father's servants with respect and kindness."

"Perhaps I should rephrase, my lady," Ashe said. "Yes, you lack unkind prejudices. However, you don't pay attention to what the servants think of you—not in the same way you are always aware of what the aristocracy thinks."

Sarene pulled her nightgown over her head, refusing to show even a hint of petulance. "I've always tried to be fair."

"Yes, my lady, but you are a child of nobility, raised to ignore those who work around you. I only suggest you remember that if the maids disrespect you, it could be as detrimental as if the lords did so."

"All right," Sarene said with a sigh. "Point taken. Fetch Meala for me; I'll ask her if she knows what happened."

"Yes, my lady."

Ashe floated toward the window. However, before he left, Sarene made one last comment.

"Ashe?" she asked. "The people loved Raoden, didn't they?"

"By all accounts, my lady. He was known for paying very personal heed to their opinions and needs."

"He was a better prince than I am a princess, wasn't he?" she asked, her voice falling.

"I wouldn't say that, my lady," Ashe said. "You are a very kindhearted woman, and you always treat your maids well. Do not compare yourself to Raoden—it is important to remember that you weren't preparing to run a country, and your popularity with the people wasn't an issue. Prince Raoden was the heir to the throne, and it was vital that he understand his subjects' feelings."

"They say he gave the people hope," Sarene said musingly. "That the peasants endured Iadon's outrageous burdens because they knew Raoden would eventually take the throne. The country would have collapsed years ago if the prince hadn't gone amongst them, encouraging them and reviving their spirits."

"And now he's gone," Ashe said quietly.

"Yes, he's gone," Sarene agreed, her voice detached. "We have to hurry, Ashe. I keep feeling that I'm not doing any good—that the country is heading for disaster no matter what I do. It's like I'm at the bottom of a hill watching an enormous boulder crash down toward me, and I'm throwing pebbles up to try and deflect it."

"Be strong, my lady," Ashe said in his deep, stately voice. "Your God will not sit and watch as Arelon and Teod crumble beneath Wyrn's heel."

"I hope the prince is watching as well," Sarene said. "Would he be proud of me, Ashe?"

"Very proud my lady."

"I just want them to accept me," she explained, realizing how silly she must sound. She had spent nearly three decades loving a country without ever feeling it loved her back. Teod had respected her, but she was tired of respect. She wanted something different from Arelon.

"They will, Sarene," Ashe promised. "Give them time. They will."

"Thank you Ashe," Sarene said with a quiet sigh. "Thank you for enduring the lamentations of a silly girl."

"We can be strong in the face of kings and priests, my lady," Ashe replied, "but to live is to have worries and uncertainties. Keep them inside, and they will destroy you for certain—leaving behind a person so callused that emotion can find no root in his heart."

With that the Seon passed out the window, in search of the maid Meala.

BY the time Meala arrived, Sarene had composed herself. There had been no tears, just time spent in thought. Sometimes it was too much for her, and her insecurity simply had to boil out. Ashe and her father had always been there to support her during those times.

"Oh dear," Meala said, regarding the state of the room. She was thin and rather young—definitely not what Sarene expected when she had first moved into the palace. Meala more resembled one of her father's accountants than she did a head maid.

"I'm sorry, my lady," Meala apologized, offering Sarene a wan smile. "I didn't even think of this. We lost another girl this afternoon, and it didn't occur to me that your room was on her list of duties."

"'Lost,' Meala?" Sarene asked with concern.

"A runaway, my lady," Meala explained. "They aren't supposed to leave—we're indentured like the rest of the peasants. For some reason we have trouble keeping maids in the palace, however. Domi knows why it is—no servant in the country is treated better than those here."

"How many have you lost?" Sarene asked with curiosity.

"She was the fourth this year," Meala said. "I'll send someone up immediately."

"No, don't bother tonight. Just make sure it doesn't happen again."

"Of course, my lady," Meala said with a curtsy.

"Thank you."

"THERE it is again!" Sarene said with excitement, jumping out of her bed.

Ashe instantly burst back to full illumination, hovering uncertainly by the wall. "My lady?"

"Quiet," Sarene ordered, pressing her ear against the stone wall beneath her window, listening to the scraping sound. "What do you think?"

"I am thinking that whatever my lady had for supper, it isn't agreeing with her," Ashe informed her curtly.

"There was definitely a noise there," Sarene said, ignoring the gibe. Though Ashe was always awake in the mornings when she got up, he didn't like being disturbed after he had fallen asleep.

She reached over to her nightstand and picked up a scrap of parchment. On it she made a mark with a thin piece of charcoal, not wanting to bother with pen and ink.

"Look," she declared, holding up the paper for Ashe to see. "The sounds always come on the same days of the week: MaeDal and OpeDal."

Ashe floated over and looked at the paper, his glowing Aon the room's only illumination besides starlight. "You've heard it twice on MaeDal and twice on OpeDal, four times in total," he said skeptically. "That is hardly grounds for a decision that they 'always come on the same days,' my lady."

"Oh, you think I'm hearing things anyway," Sarene said, dropping the parchment back onto her table. "I thought Seons were supposed to have excellent auditory senses."

"Not when we're sleeping, my lady," Ashe said, implying that that was exactly what he should have been doing at the moment.

"There must be a passage here," Sarene decided, ineffectually tapping the stone wall.

"If you say so, my lady."

"I do," she said, rising and studying her window. "Look how thick the stone is around this window, Ashe." She leaned against the wall and stuck her arm out the window. The tips of her fingers could barely curl around the outside ledge. "Does the wall really need to be so wide?"

"It offers much protection, my lady."

"It also offers room for a passage."

"A very thin one," Ashe replied.

"True," Sarene mused, kneeling down to view the bottom edge of the window at eye level. "It slopes upwards. The passage was constructed to angle up, passing between the bottoms of the windows on this level and the first story."

"But the only thing in that direction is . . ."

"The king's rooms," Sarene finished. "Where else would a passage lead?"

"Are you suggesting that the king takes secret excursions twice a week in the middle of the night, my lady?"

"At precisely eleven o'clock," Sarene said, eyeing the large grandfather clock in the corner of her room. "It's always at the same time."

"What possible reason could he have for such a thing?"

"I don't know," Sarene said, tapping her cheek in contemplation.

"Oh dear," Ashe mumbled. "My lady is concocting something, isn't she?"

"Always," Sarene said sweetly, climbing back into bed. "Turn down your light—some of us want to get some sleep."

CHAPTER 21

HRATHEN sat down in his chair, wearing a red Derethi robe instead of his armor, as he often did when he was in his chambers.

The knock that came at his door was expected. "Come in," he said.

Arteth Thered entered. A man of good Fjordell stock, Thered had a strong, tall frame, dark hair, and squareish features. He was still well muscled from his days training in the monastery.

"Your Grace," the man said, bowing and falling to his knees with a proper sign of respect.

"Arteth," Hrathen said, lacing his fingers in front of himself. "During my time here, I've been watching the local priests. I have been impressed with your service in Jaddeth's kingdom, and I have decided to offer you the position of head arteth of this chapel."

Thered looked up with surprise. "Your Grace?"

"I had thought that I would have to wait to appoint a new head arteth until a new batch of priests arrived from Fjorden," Hrathen said. "But, as I said, you have impressed me. I decided to offer you the position."

And, of course, he added in his mind, *I don't have time to wait. I need someone to administrate the chapel now so that I can focus on other tasks.*

"My lord . . ." the arteth said, obviously overwhelmed. "I cannot accept this position."

Hrathen froze. *"What?"* No Derethi priest would refuse a position of such power.

"I'm sorry, my lord," the man repeated, looking down.

"What reason have you for this decision, Arteth?" Hrathen demanded.

"I can give none, Your Grace. I just . . . It just wouldn't be right for me to take the position. May I withdraw?"

Hrathen waved his hand, disturbed. Ambition was such a cardinal Fjordell attribute; how had a man such as Thered lost his pride so quickly? Had Fjon really weakened the priests in Kae so soundly?

Or . . . was something else behind this man's refusal? A nagging voice inside of Hrathen whispered that the banished Fjon was not to blame. Dilaf—Dilaf had something to do with Thered's refusal.

The thought was probably just paranoia, but it spurred Hrathen forward with his next item of business. Dilaf had to be dealt with; despite his stunt with the Elantrian, the arteth was growing increasingly influential with the other priests. Hrathen reached into a desk drawer, pulling out a small envelope. He had made a mistake with Dilaf. While it was possible to channel a zealot's ardor, Hrathen currently had neither the time nor the energy to do so. The future of an entire kingdom depended on Hrathen's ability to focus, and he hadn't realized how much attention Dilaf would require.

It could not continue. Hrathen's world was one of control and predictability, his religion a logical exercise. Dilaf was like a boiling pot of water poured on Hrathen's ice. In the end, they would both just end up weakened and dissipated, like puffs of steam in the wind. And after they were gone, Arelon would die.

Hrathen put on his armor and left his room, entering the chapel. Several supplicants knelt in prayerful silence, and priests moved about busily. The chapel's vaulted ceilings and spirited architecture were familiar—this was where he should be most comfortable. Too often, however, Hrathen found himself fleeing up to the walls of Elantris. Though he told himself that he simply went to the walls because their height gave him a vantage over Kae, he knew that there was another reason. He went, in part, because he knew that Elantris was a place that Dilaf would never voluntarily go.

Dilaf's chamber was a small alcove much like the one Hrathen himself had occupied as an arteth many years ago. Dilaf looked up from his desk as Hrathen pushed open the room's simple wooden door.

"My hroden?" the arteth said, standing with surprise. Hrathen rarely visited his chambers.

"I have an important task for you, Arteth," Hrathen said. "One I cannot trust to anyone else."

"Of course, my hroden," Dilaf said submissively, bowing his head. However, his eyes narrowed with suspicion. "I serve with devotion, knowing I am part of the chain linked to Lord Jaddeth himself."

"Yes," Hrathen said dismissively. "Arteth, I need you to deliver a letter."

"A letter?" Dilaf looked up with confusion.

"Yes," Hrathen said flatly. "It is vital Wyrn know of our progress here. I have written him a report, but the matters discussed therein are very delicate. If it should be lost, irreparable damage could be done. I have chosen you, my odiv, to deliver it in person."

"That will take weeks, my hroden!"

"I know. I will have to go without your service for a time, but I will be comforted by the knowledge that you are engaged in a vital mission."

Dilaf lowered his eyes, his hands falling to rest lightly on the top of his table. "I go as my hroden commands."

Hrathen paused, frowning slightly. It was impossible for Dilaf to escape; the hroden-odiv relationship was irrevocably binding. When one's master commanded, one obeyed. Even so, Hrathen had expected more from Dilaf. A ploy of some kind. An attempt to wiggle out of the assignment.

Dilaf accepted the letter with apparent subservience. *Maybe this was what he wanted all along,* Hrathen realized. *A way into Fjorden.* His position as odiv to a gyorn would give him power and respect in the East. Perhaps Dilaf's only purpose in antagonizing Hrathen had been to get out of Arelon.

Hrathen turned and walked back out into the chapel's hollow sermon hall. The event had been even more painless than he had hoped. He held back a sigh of relief, stepping with a bit more confidence as he walked toward his chambers.

A voice sounded from behind. Dilaf's voice. Speaking softly—yet with enough projection to be heard. "Send out messengers," the arteth ordered to one of the dorvens. "We leave for Fjorden in the morning."

Hrathen nearly kept walking. He almost didn't care what Dilaf was planning or what he did, as long as he left. However, Hrathen had spent too long in positions of leadership—too long as a political being—to let such a statement pass. Especially from Dilaf.

Hrathen spun. "We? I ordered only you, Arteth."

"Yes, my lord," Dilaf said. "However, surely you don't expect me to leave my odivs behind."

"Odivs?" Hrathen asked. As an official member of the Derethi priesthood, Dilaf was able to swear odivs just as Hrathen had, continuing the chain that linked all men to Jaddeth. Hrathen hadn't even considered, however, that the man might call odivs of his own. When had he found the time?

"Who, Dilaf?" Hrathen asked sharply. "Whom did you make your odiv?"

"Several people, my hroden," Dilaf responded evasively.

"Names, Arteth."

And he began to name them. Most priests called one or two odivs, several of the gyorns had as many as ten. Dilaf had over thirty. Hrathen grew increasingly stunned as he listened. Stunned, and angry. Somehow, Dilaf made odivs out of all Hrathen's most useful supporters—including Waren and many of the other aristocrats.

Dilaf finished his list, turning traitorously humble eyes toward the floor.

"An interesting list," Hrathen said slowly. "And who do you intend to take with you, Arteth?"

"Why, all of them, my lord," Dilaf said innocently. "If this letter is as important as my lord implies, then I must give it proper protection."

Hrathen closed his eyes. If Dilaf took all of the people he had mentioned, then it would leave Hrathen stripped of supporters—assuming, that was, they would go. The calling of odiv was very demanding; most normal Derethi believers, even many priests, were sworn to the less restrictive position of krondet. A krondet listened to the counsel of his hroden, but was not morally bound to do what he was told.

It was well within Dilaf's power to make his odivs accompany him to Fjorden. Hrathen could have no control over what the arteth did with his sworn followers; it would be a grave breach of protocol to order Dilaf to leave them behind. However, if Dilaf did try to take them, it would undoubtedly be a disaster. These men were new to Shu-Dereth; they didn't know how much power they had given Dilaf. If the arteth tried to drag them to Fjorden, it was unlikely they would follow.

And if that happened, Hrathen would be forced to excommunicate every single one of them. Shu-Dereth would be ruined in Arelon.

Dilaf continued his preparations as if he hadn't noticed Hrathen's internal battle. Not that it was much of a conflict—Hrathen knew what he had to do. Dilaf was unstable.

It was possible that he was bluffing, but equally likely that he would destroy Hrathen's efforts in spiteful retribution.

Hrathen gritted his teeth until his jaw throbbed. Hrathen might have stopped Dilaf's attempt to burn the Elantrian, but the arteth had obviously realized what Hrathen's next move would be. No, Dilaf didn't want to go to Fjorden. He might have been unstable, but he was also much better prepared than Hrathen had assumed.

"Wait," Hrathen ordered as Dilaf's messenger turned to leave. If that man left the chapel, all would be ruined. "Arteth, I have changed my mind."

"My hroden?" Dilaf asked, poking his head out of his chamber.

"You will not go to Fjorden, Dilaf."

"But my lord . . ."

"No, I cannot do without you." The lie made Hrathen's stomach clinch tightly. "Find someone else to deliver the message."

With that, Hrathen spun and stalked toward his chambers.

"I am, as always, my hroden's humble servant," Dilaf whispered, the room's acoustics carrying the words directly to Hrathen's ears.

HRATHEN fled again.

He needed to think, to clear his mind. He had spent several hours stewing in his office, angry at both Dilaf and himself. Finally, he could stand it no longer, and so he absconded to the night streets of Kae.

As usual, he directed his path toward Elantris's wall. He sought height, as if rising above the dwellings of man could give him a better perspective on life.

"Spare some coins, sir?" pled a voice.

Hrathen stopped in surprise; he had been so distracted that he hadn't noticed the rag-clothed beggar at his feet. The man was old and obviously had poor sight, for he was squinting up at Hrathen in the darkness. Hrathen frowned, realizing for the first time that he had never seen a beggar in Kae.

A youth, dressed in clothing no better than that of the old man, hobbled around the corner. The boy froze, blanching pale white. "Not him, you old fool!" he hissed. Then, to Hrathen, he quickly said, "I'm sorry, my lord. My father loses his wits sometimes and thinks he is a beggar. Please forgive us." He moved to grab the old man's arm.

Hrathen held up his hand commandingly, and the youth stopped, growing another shade paler. Hrathen knelt down beside the elderly man, who was smiling with a half-senile daze. "Tell me, old man," Hrathen asked, "why do I see so few beggars in the city?"

"The king forbids begging in his city, good sir," the man croaked. "It is a poor sign of prosperity to have us on his streets. If he finds us, he sends us back to the farms."

"You say too much," the youth warned, his frightened face indicating that he was very close to abandoning the old man and bolting away.

The elderly beggar wasn't finished. "Yes, good sir, we mustn't let him catch us. Hide outside the city, we do."

"Outside the city?" Hrathen pressed.

"Kae isn't the only town here, you know. There used to be four of them, all surrounding Elantris, but the others dried up. Not enough food for so many people in such a small area, they said. We hide in the ruins."

"Are there many of you?" Hrathen asked.

"No, not many. Only those who've the nerve to run away from the farms." The old man's eyes took on a dreamy look. "I wasn't always a beggar, good sir. Used to work in Elantris—I was a carpenter, one of the best. I didn't make a very good farmer, though. The king was wrong there, good sir—he sent me to the fields, but I was too old to work in them, so I ran away. Came here. The merchants in the town, they give us money sometimes. But we can only beg after night comes, and never from the high nobles. No, sir, they would tell the king."

The old man squinted up at Hrathen—as if realizing for the first time why the boy was so apprehensive. "You don't look much like a merchant, good sir," he said hesitantly.

"I'm not," Hrathen responded, dropping a bag of coins in the man's hand. "That is for you." Then he dropped a second bag beside the first. "That is for the others. Good night, old man."

"Thank you, good sir!" the man cried.

"Thank Jaddeth," Hrathen said.

"Who is Jaddeth, good sir?"

Hrathen bowed his head. "You'll know soon enough, old man. One way or another, you'll know."

THE breeze was gusty and strong atop the wall of Elantris, and it whipped at Hrathen's cape with glee. It was a cool ocean wind, bearing the briny scent of saltwater and sea life. Hrathen stood between two burning torches, leaning against the low parapet and looking out over Kae.

The city wasn't very large, not when compared with the sheer mass of Elantris, but it could have been far better fortified. He felt his old dissatisfaction returning. He hated being in a place that couldn't protect itself. Perhaps that was part of the stress he was feeling with this assignment.

Lights sparked throughout Kae, most of them streetlamps, including a series that ran along the short wall that marked the formal border of the city. The wall ran in a perfect circle—so perfect, in fact, that Hrathen would have remarked upon it had he been in any other city. Here it was just another remnant of fallen Elantris's glory. Kae had spilled out beyond that inner wall, but the old border remained—a ring of flame running around the center of the city.

"It was so much nicer, once," a voice said behind him.

Hrathen turned with surprise. He had heard the footsteps approaching, but he had simply assumed it was one of the guards making his rounds. Instead he found a short, bald Arelene in a simple gray robe. Omin, head of the Korathi religion in Kae.

Omin approached the edge, pausing beside Hrathen and studying the city. "Of course, that was back then, when the Elantrians still ruled. The city's fall was probably good for our souls. Still, I can't help recalling those days with awe. Do you realize that no one in all of Arelon went without food? The Elantrians could turn stone into corn and dirt into steak. Confronted by those memories, I am left wondering. Could devils do that much good in this world? Would they even want to?"

Hrathen didn't respond. He simply stood, leaning with his arms crossed on top of the parapet, the wind churning his hair. Omin fell silent.

"How did you find me?" Hrathen finally asked.

"It is well known that you spend your nights up here," the squat priest explained. He could barely rest his arms on the parapet. Hrathen considered Dilaf short, but this man made the arteth look like a giant. "Your supporters say you come here and plan how to defeat the vile Elantrians," Omin continued, "and your opponents say you come because you feel guilty for condemning a people who have already been cursed."

Hrathen turned, looking down into the little man's eyes. "And what do you say?"

"I say nothing," Omin said. "It doesn't matter to me why you climb these stairs, Hrathen. I do, however, wonder why you preach hatred of the Elantrians when you yourself simply pity them."

Hrathen didn't respond immediately, tapping his gauntleted finger against the stone parapet with a repetitious click. "It's not so hard, once you accustom yourself to it," he finally said. "A man can force himself to hate if he wishes, especially if he convinces himself that it is for a higher good."

"The oppression of the few brings salvation to the many?" Omin asked, a slight smile on his face, as if he found the concept ridiculous.

"You'd best not mock, Arelene," Hrathen warned. "You have few options, and we both know the least painful one will require you to do as I do."

"To profess hatred where I have none? I will never do that, Hrathen."

"Then you will become irrelevant," Hrathen said simply.

"Is that the way it must be, then?"

"Shu-Korath is docile and unassuming, priest," Hrathen said. "Shu-Dereth is vibrant and dynamic. It will sweep you away like a roaring flood rushing through a stagnant pool."

Omin smiled again. "You act as if truth were something to be influenced by persistence, Hrathen."

"I'm not speaking of truth or falsehood; I am simply

referring to physical inevitability. You cannot stand against Fjorden—and where Fjorden rules, Shu-Dereth teaches."

"One cannot separate truth from actions, Hrathen," Omin said with a shake of his bald head. "Physically inevitable or not, truth stands above all things. It is independent of who has the best army, who can deliver the longest sermons, or even who has the most priests. It can be pushed down, but it will always surface. Truth is the one thing you can never intimidate."

"And if Shu-Dereth is the truth?" Hrathen demanded.

"Then it will prevail," Omin said. "But I didn't come to argue with you."

"Oh?" Hrathen said with raised eyebrows.

"No," Omin said. "I came to ask you a question."

"Then ask, priest, and leave me to my thoughts."

"I want to know what happened," Omin began speculatively. "What happened, Hrathen? What happened to your faith?"

"My faith?" Hrathen asked with shock.

"Yes," Omin said, his words soft, almost meandering. "You must have believed at one point, otherwise you wouldn't have pursued the priesthood long enough to become a gyorn. You lost it somewhere, though. I have listened to your sermons. I hear logic and complete understanding—not to mention determination. I just don't hear any faith, and I wonder what happened to it."

Hrathen hissed inward slowly, drawing a deep breath between his teeth. "Go," he finally ordered, not bothering to look down at the priest.

Omin didn't answer, and Hrathen turned. The Arelish man was already gone, strolling down the wall with a casual step, as if he had forgotten Hrathen were there.

Hrathen stood on the wall for a long time that night.

CHAPTER 22

RAODEN inched forward, slowly peeking around the corner. He should have been sweating—in fact, he kept reaching up to wipe his brow, though the motion did nothing but spread black Elantris grime across his forehead. His knees trembled slightly as he huddled against the decaying wooden fence, anxiously searching the cross street for danger.

"Sule, behind you!"

Raoden turned with surprise at Galladon's warning, sliding on the slimy cobblestones and slipping to the ground. The fall saved him. As he grappled for purchase, Raoden felt something whoosh through the air above him. The leaping madman howled in frustration as he missed and smashed through the fence, rotten wood chips spraying through the air.

Raoden stumbled to his feet. The madman moved far more quickly. Bald and nearly naked, the man howled as he ripped his way through the rest of the fence, growling and tearing at the wood like a mad hound.

Galladon's board smacked the man directly in the face. Then, while the man was stunned, Galladon grabbed a cobblestone and smashed it against the side of the man's head. The madman collapsed and did not rise.

Galladon straightened. "They're getting stronger somehow, sule," he said, dropping his cobblestone. "They seem almost oblivious to pain. Kolo?"

Raoden nodded, calming his nerves. "They haven't been able to capture a newcomer in weeks. They're getting desperate, falling more and more into their bestial state. I've heard of warriors who grow so enraged during combat that they ignore even mortal wounds." Raoden paused as Galladon poked at the attacker's body with a stick to make sure he wasn't feigning.

"Maybe they've found the final secret to stopping the pain," Raoden said quietly.

"All they have to do is surrender their humanity," Galladon said, shaking his head as they continued to sneak through what had been the Elantris market. They passed piles of rusted metal and crushed ceramics etched with Aons. Once these scraps had produced wondrous effects, their powerful magics demanding unparalleled prices. Now they were little more than obstacles for Raoden to avoid, lest they crunch noisily beneath his feet.

"We should have brought Saolin," Galladon said quietly.

Raoden shook his head. "Saolin is a wonderful soldier and a good man, but he's completely lacking in stealth. Even I can hear him approaching. Besides, he would have insisted on bringing a group of his guards. He refuses to believe I can protect myself."

Galladon glanced at the fallen madman, then back at Raoden with sardonic eyes. "Whatever you say, sule."

Raoden smiled slightly. "All right," he admitted, "he might have been useful. However, his men would have insisted on pampering me. Honestly, I thought I'd left that sort of thing behind in my father's palace."

"Men protect things they find important," Galladon said with a shrug. "If you object, you shouldn't have made yourself so irreplaceable. Kolo?"

"Point taken," Raoden said with a sigh. "Come on."

They fell quiet as they continued their infiltration. Galladon had protested for hours when Raoden had explained his plan to sneak in and confront Shaor. The Dula had called it foolhardy, pointless, dangerous, and just plain stupid. He hadn't, however, been willing to let Raoden go alone.

Raoden knew the plan probably was foolhardy, pointless, and all the other things Galladon said. Shaor's men would rip them apart without a second thought—probably without even a first thought, considering their mental state. However, during the last week, Shaor's men had tried to capture the garden three more times. Saolin's guards were collecting more and more wounds while Shaor's men seemed to be getting even more feral and wild.

Raoden shook his head. While his troop was growing, most of his followers were physically weak. Shaor's men, however, were frighteningly strong—and every one of them was a warrior. Their rage gave them strength, and Raoden's followers couldn't stand against them for much longer.

Raoden had to find Shaor. If only he could speak with the man, he was sure they could find a compromise. It was said that Shaor himself never went on the raids. Everyone referred to the band as "Shaor's men," but no one could ever remember seeing Shaor himself. It was entirely possible that he was just another maniac, indistinguishable from the rest. It was also possible that the man Shaor had joined the Hoed long ago, and the group continued without leadership.

Still, something told him that Shaor was alive. Or, perhaps Raoden simply wanted to believe so. He needed an adversary he could face; the madmen were too scattered to be efficiently defeated, and they outnumbered Raoden's soldiers by a significant number. Unless Shaor existed, unless Shaor could be swayed, and unless Shaor could control his men, Raoden's band was in serious trouble.

"We're close now," Galladon whispered as they approached one final street. There was movement to one side, and they waited apprehensively until it appeared to have passed on.

"The bank," Galladon said, nodding to a large structure across the street. It was large and boxy, its walls dark beyond even what the slime normally produced. "The Elantrians maintained the place for the local merchants to keep their wealth. A bank inside Elantris was seen as far more secure than one in Kae."

Raoden nodded. Some merchants, like his father, hadn't trusted the Elantrians. Their insistence on storing their fortunes outside of the city had eventually proven wise. "You think Shaor's in there?" he asked.

Galladon shrugged. "If I were going to choose a base, this would be it. Large, defensible, imposing. Perfect for a warlord."

Raoden nodded. "Let's go, then."

The bank was definitely occupied. The slime around the front door was scuffed by the frequent passing of feet, and they could hear voices coming from the back of the structure. Galladon looked at Raoden inquiringly, and Raoden nodded. They went in.

The inside was as drab as the outside—dull and stale, even for fallen Elantris. The vault door—a large circle etched with a thick Aon Edo—was open, and the voices came from inside. Raoden took a deep breath, ready to confront the last of the gang leaders.

"Bring me food!" wailed a high-pitched voice.

Raoden froze. He craned his neck to the side, peeking into the vault, then recoiled with surprise. At the back of the chamber, sitting on a pile of what appeared to be gold bars, was a young girl in a pristine, unsoiled pink dress. She had long Aonic blond hair, but her skin was black and gray like that of any other Elantrian. Eight men in ragged clothing knelt before her, their arms spread out in adoration.

"Bring me food!" the girl repeated in a demanding voice.

"Well, behead me and see me in Doloken," Galladon swore behind him. "What is that?"

"Shaor," Raoden said with amazement. Then his eyes refocused, and he realized that the girl was staring at him.

"Kill them!" Shaor screamed.

"Idos Domi!" Raoden yelped, spinning around and dashing toward the door.

"IF you weren't dead already, sule, I'd kill you," Galladon said.

Raoden nodded, leaning tiredly against a wall. He was getting weaker. Galladon had warned him it would happen—an Elantrian's muscles atrophied the most near the end of his first month. Exercise couldn't stop it. Even though the mind still worked and the flesh did not decay, the body was convinced that it was dead.

The old tricks worked the best—they had eventually lost Shaor's men by climbing up the side of a broken wall and hiding on a rooftop. The madmen might act like hounds, but they certainly hadn't acquired a dog's sense of smell. They had passed by Raoden and Galladon's hiding place a half-dozen times, and never thought to look up. The men were passionate, but they weren't very intelligent.

"Shaor is a little girl," Raoden said, still shocked.

Galladon shrugged. "I don't understand either, sule."

"Oh, I understand it—I just can't believe it. Didn't you see them kneeling before her? That girl, Shaor, is their god—a living idol. They've regressed to a more primitive way of life, and have adopted a primitive religion as well."

"Be careful, sule," Galladon warned, "many people called Jesker a 'primitive' religion."

"All right," Raoden said, gesturing that they should begin moving again. "Perhaps I should have said 'simplistic.' They found something extraordinary—a child with long golden hair—and decided that it should be worshipped. They placed it on an altar, and it makes demands of them. The girl wants food, so they get it for her. Then, ostensibly, she blesses them."

"What about that hair?"

"It's a wig," Raoden said. "I recognized her. She was the daughter of one of the most wealthy dukes in Arelon. She never grew hair, so her father had a wig made for her. I guess the priests didn't think to take it off before throwing her in here."

"When was she taken by the Shaod?"

"Over two years ago," Raoden said. "Her father, Duke Telrii, tried to keep the matter quiet. He always claimed she had died of dionia, but there were a lot of rumors."

"Apparently all true."

"Apparently," Raoden said with a shake of his head. "I only met her a few times. I can't even recall her name—it was based on Aon Soi, Soine or something like that—I only remember that she was the most spoiled, insufferable child I'd ever met."

"Probably makes a perfect goddess then," Galladon said with a sarcastic grimace.

"Well, you were right about one thing," Raoden said. "Speaking with Shaor isn't going to work. She was unreasonable on the outside; she's probably ten times worse now. All she knows is that she's very hungry, and those men bring her food."

"Good evening, my lord," a sentry said as they rounded a corner and approached their section of Elantris—or New Elantris, as the people were starting to call it. The sentry, a stout younger man named Dion, stood up tall as Raoden approached, a makeshift spear held firmly at his side. "Captain Saolin was quite disturbed by your disappearance."

Raoden nodded. "I'll be sure to apologize, Dion."

Raoden and Galladon pulled off their shoes and placed them along the wall next to several other dirty pairs, then put on the clean ones they had left behind. Also present was a bucket of water, which they used to wash off as much of the slime as they could manage. Their clothing was still dirty, but there was nothing else they could do; cloth was rare, despite the numerous scavenging parties Raoden had organized.

It was amazing how much they found. True, most of it was rusted or rotting, but Elantris was enormous. With a little organization—and some motivation—they had discovered a great number of useful items, from metal spearheads to furniture that could still hold weight.

With Saolin's help, Raoden had sectioned off a marginally defensible section of town to be New Elantris. Only eleven streets led into the area, and there was even a small wall—the original purpose of which baffled them—running along about half of the perimeter. Raoden had placed sentries at the tip of every road to watch for approaching marauders.

The system kept them from being overwhelmed. Fortunately, Shaor's men tended to attack in small bands. As long as Raoden's guards could get enough warning, they could gather and defeat any one group. If Shaor ever organized a larger, multidirectional assault, however, the result would be disastrous. Raoden's band of women, children, and weakened men just couldn't stand against the feral creatures. Saolin had begun teaching simple combat techniques to those capable, but he could use only the safest and most elementary training methods, lest the combatants' sparring wounds prove more dangerous than Shaor's attacks.

The people, however, never expected the fighting to go that far. Raoden heard what they said about him. They assumed that "Lord Spirit" would somehow find a way to bring Shaor to their side, just as he had with Aanden and Karata.

Raoden began to feel sick as they walked toward the chapel, the mounting pains of his several dozen bruises and scrapes suddenly pressing against him with suffocating pressure. It was as if his body were encased in a blazing fire—his flesh, bones, and soul being consumed in the heat.

"I've failed them," he said quietly.

Galladon shook his head. "We can't always get what we want on the first try. Kolo? You'll find a way—I would never have thought you'd get this far."

I was lucky. A lucky fool, Raoden thought as the pain pounded against him.

"Sule?" Galladon asked, suddenly looking at Raoden with concern. "Are you all right?"

Must be strong. They need me to be strong. With an inner groan of defiance, Raoden pushed through the haze of agony and managed a weak smile. "I'm fine."

"I've never seen you look like this, sule."

Raoden shook his head, leaning up against the stone wall of a nearby building. "I'll be all right—I was just wondering what we're going to do about Shaor. We can't reason with her, and we can't defeat her men by force. . . ."

"You'll think of something," Galladon said, his normal pessimism overridden by an obvious desire to encourage his friend.

Or we'll all die, Raoden thought, hands growing tense as they gripped the stone corner of the wall. *For good this time.*

With a sigh, Raoden pushed away from the wall, the stone crumbling beneath his fingers. He turned around and looked at the wall with surprise. Kahar had recently cleaned it, and its white marble glistened in the sun—except where Raoden's fingers had crushed it.

"Stronger than you thought?" Galladon asked with a smirk.

Raoden raised his eyebrows, brushing at the broken stone. It crumbled away. "This stone is as soft as pumice!"

"Elantris," Galladon said. "Things decay quickly here."

"Yes, but marble?"

"Everything. People too."

Raoden smacked the broken spot of stone with another rock; small flecks and chips cascaded to the ground at the impact. "It's all connected somehow, Galladon. The Dor is linked to Elantris, just as it's linked to Arelon itself."

"But why would the Dor do this, sule?" Galladon asked with a shake of his head. "Why destroy the city?"

"Maybe it's not the Dor," Raoden said. "Maybe it's the sudden *absence* of the Dor. The magic—the Dor—was a part of this city. Every stone burned with its own light. When that power was removed, the city was left hollow. Like the discarded shell of a small rivercrawler that has grown too big for its skin. The stones are empty."

"How can a stone be empty?" Galladon said skeptically.

Raoden cracked off another piece of marble, crumbling it between his fingers. "Like this, my friend. The rock spent so long infused by the Dor that it was weakened irreparably by the Reod. This city really is a corpse—its spirit has fled."

The discussion was interrupted by the approach of an exhausted Mareshe. "My lord Spirit!" he said urgently as he approached.

"What is it?" Raoden asked apprehensively. "Another attack?"

Mareshe shook his head, confusion in his eyes. "No. Something different, my lord. We don't know what to make of it. We're being invaded."

"By whom?"

Mareshe half smiled, then shrugged. "We think she's a princess."

RAODEN crouched on the rooftop, Galladon at his side. The building had been transformed into an observation area to watch the gates for newcomers. From its vantage, he could get a very good look at what was happening in the courtyard.

A crowd had gathered atop the Elantris city wall. The gate stood open. That fact was amazing enough; normally, after newcomers were cast in, the gate was immediately pulled shut, as if the guards were frightened to let it rest open for even a moment.

However, in front of the open gate sat a sight even more dumbfounding. A large horse-drawn cart rested in the middle of the courtyard, a cluster of well-dressed men huddled at its side. Only one person looked unafraid of what she saw before her—a tall woman with long blond hair. She wore a smooth, full-bodied brown dress with a black scarf tied around her right arm, and she stood with her arm raised to one of the horses' necks, patting the nervous beast. Her sharp face held a set of capable eyes, and she studied the dirty, slime-splattered courtyard with a calculating expression.

Raoden exhaled. "I only saw her through Seon," he mumbled. "I didn't realize she was so beautiful."

"You recognize her, sule?" Galladon asked in surprise.

"I . . . think I'm married to her. That could only be Sarene, the daughter of King Eventeo of Teod."

"What is she doing here?" Galladon asked.

"More importantly," Raoden said, "what is she doing here with a dozen of Arelon's most influential nobles? The older man near the back is Duke Roial—some say he's the second-most-powerful man in the kingdom."

Galladon nodded. "And I assume the young Jindo is Shuden, the Baron of Kaa Plantation?"

Raoden smiled. "I thought you were a simple farmer."

"Shuden's caravan route runs directly through the center of Duladel, sule. There isn't a Dula alive who doesn't know his name."

"Ah," Raoden said. "Counts Ahan and Eondel are there as well. What in Domi's name is that woman planning?"

As if in response to Raoden's question, Princess Sarene finished her contemplation of Elantris. She turned and walked to the back of the cart, shooing away apprehensive nobles with an intolerant hand. Then she reached up and whipped the cloth off the back of the cart, revealing its contents.

The cart was piled with food.

"Idos Domi!" Raoden cursed. "Galladon, we're in trouble."

Galladon regarded him with a frown. There was hunger in his eyes. "What in Doloken are you blabbering about, sule? That's food, and my intuition tells me she's going to give it to us. What could be wrong with that?"

"She must be doing her Widow's Trial," Raoden said. "Only a foreigner would think to come into Elantris."

"Sule," Galladon said instantly, "tell me what you're thinking."

"The timing is wrong, Galladon," Raoden explained. "Our people are just starting to get a sense of independence; they're beginning to focus on the future and forget their pain. If someone hands them food now, they'll forget everything else. For a short time they'll be fed, but Widow's Trials only last a few weeks. After that, it will be back to the pain, the hunger, and the self-pity. My princess out there could destroy everything we've been working for."

"You're right," Galladon realized. "I'd almost forgotten how hungry I was until I saw that food."

Raoden groaned.

"What?"

"What happens when Shaor hears about this? Her men will attack that cart like a pack of wolves. There's no telling what kind of damage it would do if one of them killed a count or a baron. My father only suffers Elantris because he doesn't have to think about it. If an Elantrian kills one of his nobles, however, he could very well decide to exterminate the lot of us."

People were appearing in the alleys around the courtyard. None appeared to be Shaor's men; they were the tired, wretched forms of those Elantrians who still lived on their own, wandering through the city like shades. More and more of them had been joining with Raoden—but now, with free food available, he would never get the rest of them. They would continue without thought or purpose, lost in their pain and damnation.

"Oh, my lovely princess," Raoden whispered. "You probably mean well, but handing these people food is the worst thing you could do to them."

MARESHE waited at the bottom of the stairs. "Did you see her?" he asked anxiously.

"We did," Raoden said.

"What does she want?"

Before Raoden could reply, a firm, feminine voice called out of the courtyard. "I would speak with the tyrants of this city—the ones who call themselves Aanden, Karata, and Shaor. Present yourselves to me."

"Where . . . ?" Raoden asked with surprise.

"Remarkably well informed, isn't she," Mareshe noted.

"A little outdated, though," Galladon added.

Raoden ground his teeth, thinking quickly. "Mareshe, send a runner for Karata. Tell her to meet us at the university."

"Yes, my lord," the man said, waving over a messenger boy.

"Oh," Raoden said, "and have Saolin bring half of his soldiers and meet us there. He's going to need to keep an eye on Shaor's men."

"I could go fetch them myself, if my lord wishes," offered Mareshe, ever watchful for a chance to impress.

"No," Raoden said. "You have to practice being Aanden."

CHAPTER 23

EONDEL and Shuden both insisted on going with her. Eondel kept one hand on his sword—he usually wore the weapon no matter what Arelish propriety said about them—and he watched both their guide and their complement of Elantris City Guards with equal amounts of suspicion. For their parts, the guards did a fair job of looking nonchalant, as if coming into Elantris were an everyday occurrence. Sarene could sense their anxiety, however.

Everyone had objected at first. It was unthinkable that she let herself be lured into the bowels of Elantris to meet with despots. Sarene, however, was determined to prove that the city was harmless. She couldn't very well balk at a short trip inside if she wanted to persuade the other nobles to enter the gates.

"We're nearly there," the guide said. He was a taller man, about the same height as Sarene in heels. The gray parts of his skin were a little lighter than those on the other Elantrians she had seen, though she didn't know if that meant he had been pale-skinned before, or if he had simply been in Elantris a shorter time than the rest. He had an oval face that might have been handsome before the Shaod destroyed it. He wasn't a servant; he walked with too proud a gait. Sarene guessed that even though he was acting as a simple messenger, he was one of the trusted minions of an Elantris gang leader.

"What is your name?" she asked, careful to keep her tone neutral. He belonged to one of three groups who, according to Ashe's sources, ruled the city like warlords and enslaved those who were newly cast inside.

The man didn't respond immediately. "They call me Spirit," he eventually said.

A fitting name, Sarene thought, *for this man who is so much a ghost of what he once must have been.*

They approached a large building that the man, Spirit, informed her used to be Elantris's university. Sarene regarded the building with a critical eye. It was covered with the same odd, brownish green sludge that coated the rest of the city, and while the structure might have once been great, now it was just another ruin. Sarene hesitated as their guide walked into the building. In Sarene's estimation, the upper floor was seriously considering a collapse.

She shot Eondel a look. The older man was apprehensive, rubbing his chin in thought. Then he shrugged, giving Sarene a nod. *We've come this far . . .* he seemed to be saying.

So, trying not to think about the sagging ceiling, Sarene

led her band of friends and soldiers into the structure. Fortunately, they didn't have to go far. A group of Elantrians stood near the back of the first room, their dark-skinned faces barely visible in the dim light. Two stood on what appeared to be the rubble of a fallen table, raising their heads a few feet above the others.

"Aanden?" Sarene asked.

"And Karata," replied the second form—apparently a woman, though her bald head and wrinkled face were virtually indistinguishable from those of a man. "What do you want of us?"

"I was led to believe you two were enemies," Sarene said suspiciously.

"We recently realized the benefits of an alliance," Aanden said. He was a short man with cautious eyes, his small face shriveled like that of a rodent. His pompous self-important attitude was about what Sarene had expected.

"And the man known as Shaor?" Sarene asked.

Karata smiled. "One of the aforementioned benefits."

"Dead?"

Aanden nodded. "We rule Elantris now, Princess. What do you want?"

Sarene didn't answer immediately. She had been planning to play the three different gang leaders against each other. She would have to present herself differently to a unified enemy. "I want to bribe you," she said straightforwardly.

The woman raised an eyebrow with interest, but the small man huffed. "What need have we of your bribes, woman?"

Sarene had played this game far too often; Aanden used the uninterested front of a man unaccustomed to serious politics. She had met men like him dozens of times while serving in her father's diplomatic corps—and she was very tired of them.

"Look," Sarene said, "let's be frank—you're obviously not very good at this, and so extended negotiations would be a waste of time. I want to bring food to the people of Elantris, and you're going to resist me because you think it will weaken your hold on them. Right now you're probably trying to figure out how to control who benefits from my offerings and who doesn't."

The man squirmed uncomfortably, and Sarene smiled.

"That is why I am going to bribe you. What will it take for you to let the people come and get food freely?"

Aanden balked, obviously uncertain how to proceed. The woman, however, spoke firmly. "You have a scribe to write down our demands?"

"I do," Sarene said, gesturing for Shuden to pull out his paper and charcoal-pen.

The list was extensive—even larger than Sarene had expected—and it included many odd items. She had assumed they would request weapons, perhaps even gold. Karata's demands, however, began with cloth, moved through various grains, some worked-metal sheets, lengths of wood, straw, and ended with oil. The message was clear: Rule of Elantris depended not on force or wealth, but on controlling basic necessities.

Sarene agreed to the demands curtly. If she had been dealing with Aanden only, she would have argued for less, but this Karata was a straightforward, unwavering woman—the type who didn't have much patience for haggling.

"Is that everything?" Sarene asked as Shuden scribbled down the final request.

"That will do for the first few days," Karata said.

Sarene narrowed her eyes. "Fine. But I have one rule you have to follow. You can't forbid anyone from coming to the courtyard. Rule as despots if you wish, but at least let the people suffer with full stomachs."

"You have my word," Karata said. "I will keep no one back."

Sarene nodded, motioning that the meeting was finished. Karata assigned a guide to lead them back to the gate—not Spirit, this time. He stayed behind, approaching the city's two tyrants as Sarene left the building.

"WAS that good enough, my lord?" Mareshe asked eagerly.

"Mareshe, that was perfect," Raoden replied, watching the retreating princess with satisfaction.

Mareshe smiled modestly. "Well, my lord, I do my best. I haven't much experience with acting, but I do think I played a properly decisive and intimidating leader."

Raoden caught Karata's eye. The gruff woman was trying very hard not to laugh. The pompous artisan had been perfect—neither decisive or intimidating. People outside Elantris saw the city as a lawless realm lorded over by harsh, thieving despots. Together Mareshe and Karata had portrayed exactly what the princess and her companions had expected to see.

"She suspected something, sule," Galladon noted, walking out of the shadows at the side of the room.

"Yes, but she doesn't know what," Raoden said. "Let her suspect that 'Aanden' and Karata are playing tricks on her; it will do no harm."

Galladon shook his head slightly, his bald head shining in the dim light. "What's the point? Why not bring her to the chapel; let her see what we really are?"

"I'd like to, Galladon," Raoden said. "But we can't afford to let out our secret. The people of Arelon tolerate Elantris because the Elantrians are so pitiful. If they discover we're establishing a civilized society, their fears will surface. A mass of moaning wretches is one thing, a legion of unkillable monstrosities is another."

Karata nodded, saying nothing. Galladon, the eternal skeptic, simply shook his head—as if unsure what to think. "Well, she certainly is determined. Kolo?" he finally asked, referring to Sarene.

"Determined indeed," Raoden agreed. Then, with amusement, he continued, "And I don't think she likes me very much."

"She thinks you're the lackey of a tyrant," Karata pointed out. "Is she supposed to like you?"

"True," Raoden said. "However, I think we should add a clause to our agreement that says I can attend all of her distributions. I want to keep an eye on our benevolent princess—she doesn't strike me as the type to do anything without several motives, and I wonder just what made her decide to do her Trial here in Elantris."

"THAT went well," Eondel said, watching their guide disappear back into Elantris.

"You got away easily," Shuden agreed. "The things they demanded can be obtained without much expenditure."

Sarene nodded slightly, rubbing her fingers along the cart's wooden side. "I just hate to deal with people like that."

"Perhaps you judge them too harshly," Shuden said. "They seemed less like tyrants and more like people trying to make the best of a very difficult life."

Sarene shook her head. "You should hear some of the stories Ashe told me, Shuden. The Guards say that when new Elantrians are thrown into the city, the gangs descend on them like sharks. What few resources enter this city go to the gang leaders, and they keep the rest of the people in a state of near starvation."

Shuden raised an eyebrow, looking over at the Elantris City Guards, the source of Sarene's information. The group leaned lazily on their spears, watching with uninterested eyes as the noblemen began unloading the cart.

"All right," Sarene admitted, climbing into the cart and handing Shuden a box of vegetables. "Perhaps they aren't the most reliable source, but we have proof in front of us." She swept her arm toward the emaciated forms that clustered in side streets. "Look at their hollow eyes and apprehensive steps. These are a people who live in fear, Shuden. I've seen it before in Fjorden, Hrovell, and a half-dozen other places. I know what an oppressed people looks like."

"True," Shuden admitted, accepting the box from Sarene, "but the 'leaders' didn't look much better to me. Perhaps they aren't oppressive, just equally oppressed."

"Perhaps," Sarene said.

"My lady," Eondel protested as Sarene lifted another box and handed it to Shuden, "I wish you would step back and let us move those. It just isn't proper."

"I'll be fine, Eondel," Sarene said, handing him a box. "There's a reason I didn't bring any servants—I want us all to take part. That includes you, my lord," Sarene added, nodding to Ahan, who had found a shaded spot near the gate to rest.

Ahan sighed, rising and waddling out into the sunlight. The day had turned remarkably hot for one so early in the spring, and the sun was blazing overhead—though even its heat hadn't been able to dry out the omnipresent Elantris muck.

"I hope you appreciate my sacrifice, Sarene," the over-weight Ahan exclaimed. "This slime is absolutely ruining my cloak."

"Serves you right," Sarene said, handing the count a box of boiled potatoes. "I told you to wear something inexpensive."

"I don't *have* anything inexpensive, my dear," Ahan said, accepting the box with a sullen look.

"You mean to tell me you actually paid money for that robe you wore to Neoden's wedding?" Roial asked, approaching with a laugh. "I wasn't even aware that shade of orange existed, Ahan."

The count scowled, lugging his box to the front of the cart. Sarene didn't hand Roial a box, nor did he move to receive one. It had been big news in the court a few days before when someone had noticed the duke walking with a limp. Rumors claimed he had fallen one morning while climbing out of bed. Roial's spry attitude sometimes made it difficult to remember that he was, in fact, a very old man.

Sarene got into a rhythm, giving out boxes as hands appeared to take them—which is why she didn't notice at first that a new figure had joined the others. Nearing the final few boxes, she happened to look up at the man accepting the load. She nearly dropped the box in shock as she recognized his face.

"You!" she said with amazement.

The Elantrian known as Spirit smiled, taking the box out of her stunned fingers. "I was wondering how long it would take you to realize I was here."

"How long . . ."

"Oh, about ten minutes now," he replied. "I arrived just after you began unloading."

Spirit took the box away, stacking it with the others. Sarene stood in muted stupefaction on the back of the cart—she must have mistaken his dark hands for Shuden's brown ones.

A throat cleared in front of her, and Sarene realized with a start that Eondel was waiting for a box. She rushed to comply.

"Why is *he* here?" she wondered as she dropped the box into Eondel's arms.

"He claims that his master ordered him to watch the

distribution. Apparently, Aanden trusts you about as much as you trust him."

Sarene delivered the last two boxes, then hopped down from the back of the cart. She hit the cobblestones at the wrong angle, however, and slipped in the muck. She tipped backward, waving her hands and yelping.

Fortunately, a pair of hands caught her and pulled her upright. "Be careful," Spirit warned. "Walking in Elantris takes a little getting used to."

Sarene pulled her arms out of his helpful grasp. "Thank you," she muttered in a very unprincesslike voice.

Spirit raised an eyebrow, then moved to stand next to the Arelish lords. Sarene sighed, rubbing her elbow where Spirit had caught her. Something about his touch seemed oddly tender. She shook her head to dispel such imaginings. More important things demanded her attention. The Elantrians were not approaching.

There were more of them now, perhaps fifty, clustered hesitantly and birdlike in the shadows. Some were obviously children, but most were of the same indeterminable age; their wrinkled Elantrian skin made them all look as old as Roial. None approached the food.

"Why aren't they coming?" Sarene asked with confusion.

"They're scared," Spirit said. "And disbelieving. This much food must seem like an illusion—a devilish trick their minds have surely played on them hundreds of times." He spoke softly, even compassionately. His words were not those of a despotic warlord.

Spirit reached down and selected a turnip from one of the carts. He held it lightly, staring at it as if he himself were unsure of its reality. There was a ravenousness in his eyes—the hunger of a man who hadn't seen a good meal in weeks. With a start, Sarene realized that this man was as famished as the rest of them, despite his favored rank. And he had patiently helped unload dozens of boxes filled with food.

Spirit finally lifted the turnip and took a bite. The vegetable crunched in his mouth, and Sarene could imagine how it must taste: raw and bitter. Yet, reflected in his eyes it seemed a feast.

Spirit's acceptance of the food seemed to give approval to

the others, for the mass of people surged forward. The Elantris City Guards finally perked up, and they quickly surrounded Sarene and the others, their long spears held out threateningly.

"Leave a space, here before the boxes," Sarene ordered.

The Guards parted, allowing Elantrians to approach a few at a time. Sarene and the lords stood behind the boxes, distributing food to the weary supplicants. Even Ahan stopped griping as he got into the work, doling out food in solemn silence. Sarene saw him give a bag to what must have been a little girl, though her head was bald and her lips creased with wrinkles. The girl smiled with an incongruous innocence, then scampered away. Ahan paused for a moment before continuing his labor.

It's working, Sarene thought with relief. If she could touch Ahan, then she might be able to do the same for the rest of the court.

As she worked, Sarene noticed the man Spirit standing near the back of the crowd. His hand was raised thoughtfully to his chin as he studied her. He seemed . . . worried. But why? What had he to be worried about? It was then, staring into his eyes, that Sarene knew the truth. This was no lackey. He was the leader, and for some reason he felt he needed to hide that fact from her.

So, Sarene did what she always did when she learned that someone was keeping things from her. She tried to find out what they were.

"THERE'S something about him, Ashe," Sarene said, standing outside the palace and watching the empty food cart pull away. It was hard to believe that for all the afternoon's work, they had distributed only three meals. It would all be gone by noon tomorrow—if it wasn't gone already.

"Who, my lady?" Ashe asked. He had watched the food distribution from the top of the wall, near where Iadon had been standing. He had wanted to accompany her, of course, but she had forbidden it. The Seon was her main source of information about Elantris and its leaders, and she didn't want to make an obvious connection between the two of them.

"The guide," Sarene explained as she turned and strolled through the broad tapestry-lined entryway of the king's palace. Iadon liked tapestries far too much for her taste.

"The man called Spirit?"

Sarene nodded. "He pretended to be following the others' orders, but he was no servant. Aanden kept shooting glances at him during our negotiations, as if looking for reassurance. Do you think perhaps we got the names of the leaders wrong?"

"It's possible, my lady," Ashe admitted. "However, the Elantrians I spoke with seemed very certain. Karata, Aanden, and Shaor were the names I heard at least a dozen times. No one mentioned a man named Spirit."

"Have you spoken with these people recently?" Sarene asked.

"Actually, I have been focusing my efforts on the Guards," Ashe said, bobbing to the side as a courier rushed past him. People had a tendency to ignore Seons with a level of indifference that would have been offensive to any human attendant. Ashe took it all without complaint, not even breaking his dialogue.

"The Elantrians were hesitant to give anything more than names, my lady—the Guards, however, were very free with their opinions. They have little to do all day besides watch the city. I put their observations together with the names I gathered, and produced what I told you."

Sarene paused for a moment, leaning against a marble pillar. "He's hiding something."

"Oh dear," Ashe mumbled. "My lady, don't you think you might be overextending yourself? You've decided to confront the gyorn, liberate the court women from masculine oppression, save Arelon's economy, and feed Elantris. Perhaps you should just let this man's subterfuge go unexplored."

"You're right," Sarene said, "I am too busy to deal with Spirit. That's why *you* are going to find out what he's up to."

Ashe sighed.

"Go back to the city," Sarene said. "You shouldn't have to go very far inside—a lot of Elantrians loiter near the gate.

Ask them about Spirit and see if you can discover anything about the treaty between Karata and Aanden."

"Yes, my lady."

"I wonder if maybe we misjudged Elantris," Sarene said.

"I don't know, my lady," Ashe said. "It is a very barbarous place. I witnessed several atrocious acts myself, and saw the aftermath of many others. Everyone in that city bears wounds of some sort—and from the sounds of their moans, I would guess that many of the injuries are severe. Fighting must be common."

Sarene nodded absently. However, she couldn't help thinking of Spirit, and how strikingly unbarbaric he had been. He'd put the lords at ease, conversing with them affably, as if he weren't damned and they the ones who had locked him away. She had found herself almost liking him by the end of the afternoon, though she worried that he was toying with her.

So she had remained indifferent, even cold, toward Spirit—reminding herself that many a murderer and tyrant could appear very friendly if he wanted to. Her heart, however, told her that this man was genuine. He was hiding things, as all men did, but he honestly wanted to help Elantris. For some reason, he seemed particularly concerned with Sarene's opinion of him.

And, walking out of the entryway toward her own rooms, Sarene had to try very hard before she convinced herself that she didn't care what *he* thought of *her*.

CHAPTER 24

HRATHEN was hot within his bloodred armor, exposed as he was to the bright sunlight. He was consoled by how imposing he must look, standing atop the wall with his armor shining in the light. Of course, no one was looking at him—they were all watching the tall Teoish princess distribute her food.

Her decision to enter Elantris had shocked the town, and the king's subsequent bestowal of permission had done so again. The walls of Elantris had filled early, nobles and merchants packing themselves along the open, wall-top walkway. They had come with faces like men watching a Svordish shark fight, leaning over the wall to get the best view of what many projected would be a thrilling disaster. It was commonly thought that the savages of Elantris would rip the princess apart within the first few minutes of her entrance, then proceed to devour her.

Hrathen watched with resignation as Elantris's monsters came placidly, refusing to ingest even a single guard—let alone the princess. His demons refused to perform, and he could see the disappointment in the crowd's faces. The princess's move had been masterful, castrating Hrathen's devils with a sweep of the brutal scythe known as truth. Now that Sarene's personal aristocrats had proven their courage by entering Elantris, pride would force the others to do so as well. Hatred of Elantris would evaporate, for people couldn't fear that which they pitied.

As soon as it became obvious that no princesses would be devoured this day, the people lost interest, returning down the wall's long flight of steps in a steady, dissatisfied trickle. Hrathen joined them, climbing down the steps, then turning toward the center of Kae and the Derethi chapel. As he walked, however, a carriage pulled up alongside him. Hrathen recognized the Aon on its side: Aon Rii.

The carriage pulled to a stop and the door opened. Hrathen paused for just a moment, then climbed in, seating himself opposite Duke Telrii.

The duke was obviously not pleased. "I warned you about that woman. The people will never hate Elantris now—and, if they don't hate Elantris, they won't hate Shu-Korath either."

Hrathen waved his hand. "The girl's efforts are irrelevant."

"I don't see how that is the case."

"How long can she keep this up?" Hrathen asked. "A few weeks, a month at the most? Right now, her excursions are a novelty, but that will wear off soon. I doubt many of the nobility will be willing to accompany her in the future, even if she does try and keep these feedings going."

"The damage is done," Telrii said insistently.

"Hardly," Hrathen said. "Lord Telrii, it has barely been a few weeks since I arrived in Arelon. Yes, the woman has dealt us a setback, but it will prove a minor inconvenience. You know, as I know, that the nobility are a fickle group. How long do you think it will take for them to forget their visits into Elantris?"

Telrii didn't look convinced.

"Besides," Hrathen said, trying another tactic, "my work with Elantris was only a small part of our plan. The instability of Iadon's throne—the embarrassment he will sustain at the next taxing period—is what we should be focusing on."

"The king recently found some new contracts in Teod," Telrii said.

"They won't be enough to recoup his losses," Hrathen said dismissively. "His finances are crippled. The nobility will never stand for a king who insists that they maintain their level of wealth, but who doesn't apply the same standard to himself.

"Soon, we can begin spreading rumors as to the king's reduced circumstances. Most of the high-ranking nobility are merchants themselves—they have means of discovering how their competitors are doing. They'll find out just how much Iadon is hurting, and they'll begin to complain."

"Complaints won't put me on the throne," Telrii said.

"You'd be surprised," Hrathen said. "Besides, at that same time we'll begin implying that if you were to take the throne, you would bring Arelon a lucrative trade treaty with the East. I can provide you with the proper documents. There will be money enough for all—and that is something that Iadon hasn't been able to provide. Your people know that this country is on the verge of financial ruin. Fjorden can bring you out of it."

Telrii nodded slowly.

Yes, Telrii, Hrathen thought with an inward sigh, *that's something you can understand, isn't it? If we can't convert the nobility, we can always just buy them.*

The tactic wasn't as certain as Hrathen implied, but the explanation would do for Telrii while Hrathen devised other plans. Once it was known that the king was bankrupt and Telrii was rich, certain other . . . pressures placed on the government would make for an easy—if abrupt—transfer in power.

The princess had countered the wrong scheme. Iadon's throne would collapse even as she handed out food to the Elantrians, thinking herself clever for having foiled Hrathen's plot.

"I warn you, Hrathen," Telrii said suddenly, "do not assume me a Derethi pawn. I go along with your plans because you were able to produce the wealth that you promised me. I won't just sit back and be pushed in any direction you wish, however."

"I wouldn't dream of it, Your Lordship," Hrathen said smoothly.

Telrii nodded, calling for the coachman to stop. They weren't even halfway to the Derethi chapel.

"My mansion is that direction," Telrii said airily, pointing down a side street. "You can walk the rest of the way to your chapel."

Hrathen clenched his jaw. Someday this man would have to learn proper respect for Derethi officials. For now, however, Hrathen simply climbed out of the carriage.

Considering the company, he preferred walking anyway.

"I'VE never seen this kind of response in Arelon," one priest noted.

"Agreed," said his companion. "I've been serving the empire in Kae for over a decade, and we've never had more than a few conversions a year."

Hrathen passed the priests as he entered the Derethi chapel. They were minor underpriests, of little concern to him; he noticed them only because of Dilaf.

"It has been a long while," Dilaf agreed. "Though I remember a time, just after the pirate Dreok Crushthroat assaulted Teod, when there was a wave of conversions in Arelon."

Hrathen frowned. Something about Dilaf's comment bothered him. He forced himself to continue walking, but he shot a glance back at the arteth. Dreok Crushthroat had attacked Teod fifteen years before. It was possible that Dilaf would remember such a thing from his childhood, but how would he have known about Arelon conversion rates?

The arteth had to be older than Hrathen had assumed. Much older. Hrathen's eyes widened as he studied Dilaf's face in his mind. He had placed Dilaf as no older than twenty-five, but he could now detect hints of age in the arteth's face. Only hints, however—he was probably one of those rare individuals who seemed many years younger than they really were. The "young" Arelish priest feigned lack of experience, but his planning and scheming revealed an otherwise hidden degree of maturity. Dilaf was far more seasoned than he led people to assume.

But, what did that mean? Hrathen shook his head, pushing the door open and walking into his rooms. Dilaf's power over the chapel was growing as Hrathen struggled to find an appropriate, and willing, new head arteth. Three more men had refused the position. That was more than just suspi-

cious—Hrathen was certain that Dilaf had something to do
with the matter.

He's older than you assumed, Hrathen thought. *He's also
had influence over Kae's priests for a very long time.*

Dilaf claimed that many of the original Derethi followers
in Kae had originally come from his personal chapel in
southern Arelon. How long had it been since he'd come to
Kae? Fjon had been head arteth when Dilaf arrived, but
Fjon's leadership in the city had lasted a long time.

Dilaf had probably been in the city for years. He had
probably been associating with the other priests—learning
to influence them, gaining authority over them—that entire
time. And, given Dilaf's ardor for Shu-Dereth, he had undoubtedly chosen the most conservative and effective of
Kae's arteths to be his associates.

And those were exactly the men Hrathen had let remain in
the city when he'd first arrived. He'd sent away the less devoted men, and they would have been the ones that would
have been insulted or disturbed by Dilaf's extreme ardor.
Unwittingly, Hrathen had culled the chapel's numbers in Dilaf's favor.

Hrathen sat down at his desk, this new revelation disturbing him. No wonder he was having trouble finding a new
head arteth. Those who remained knew Dilaf well; they
were probably either afraid to take a position above him, or
they had been bribed by him to step aside.

He can't have that kind of influence over them all, Hrathen thought firmly. *I'll just have to keep looking. Eventually, one of the priests will take the position.*

Still, he was worried about Dilaf's startling effectiveness.
The arteth held two firm grips over Hrathen. First, Dilaf still
had power over many of Hrathen's strongest converts
through his odiv oaths. Second, the arteth's unofficial leadership of the chapel was growing more and more secure.
Without a head arteth, and with Hrathen spending much of
his time giving sermons or meeting with nobility, Dilaf had
slowly been siphoning away power over the day-to-day
workings of the Derethi church in Arelon.

And, over it all, there was an even more disturbing problem—something Hrathen didn't want to confront, some-

thing even more disarming than Sarene's Trial or Dilaf's maneuverings. Hrathen could face external forces such as theirs, and he could be victorious.

His internal wavering, however, was something entirely different.

He reached into his desk, seeking out a small book. He remembered unpacking it into the drawer, as he had during countless other moves. He hadn't looked at it in years, but he had very few possessions, and so he had never found himself overburdened enough to discard the book.

Eventually, he located it. He flipped through the aging pages, selecting the one he was looking for.

I have found purpose, the book read. *Before, I lived, but I didn't know why. I have direction now. It gives glory to all that I do. I serve in Lord Jaddeth's empire, and my service is linked directly to Him. I am important.*

Priests in the Derethi faith were trained to record spiritual experiences, but Hrathen had never been diligent in this particular area. His personal record contained only a few entries—including this one, which he had written a few weeks after his decision to join the priesthood many years before. Just before he entered Dakhor monastery.

What happened to your faith, Hrathen?

Omin's questions plagued Hrathen's thoughts. He heard the Korathi priest whispering in his mind, demanding to know what had happened to Hrathen's beliefs, demanding to know the purpose behind his preaching. Had Hrathen become cynical, performing his duties simply because they were familiar? Had his preaching become a logical challenge and not a spiritual quest?

He knew, in part, that it had. He enjoyed the planning, the confrontation, and the thinking it took to convert an entire nation of heretics. Even with Dilaf distracting him, Hrathen found the challenge of Arelon invigorating.

But what of the boy Hrathen? What of the faith, the almost unthinking passion he had once felt? He could barely remember it. That part of his life had passed quickly, his faith transforming from a burning flame into a comfortable warmth.

Why did Hrathen want to succeed in Arelon? Was it for

the notoriety? The man who converted Arelon would be long remembered in the annals of the Derethi church. Was it a desire to be obedient? He did, after all, have a direct order from Wyrn. Was it because he seriously thought conversion would help the people? He had determined to succeed in Arelon without a slaughter such as he had instigated in Duladel. But, again, was it really because he wanted to save lives? Or was it because he knew that a smooth conquest was more difficult, and therefore more of a challenge?

His heart was as unclear to him as a room filled with smoke.

Dilaf was slowly seizing control. That in itself wasn't as frightening as Hrathen's own sense of foreboding. What if Dilaf was right to try and oust Hrathen? What if Arelon would be better off with Dilaf in control? Dilaf wouldn't have worried about the death caused by a bloody revolution; he would have known that the people would eventually be better off with Shu-Dereth, even if their initial conversion required a massacre.

Dilaf had faith. Dilaf believed in what he was doing. What did Hrathen have?

He wasn't certain anymore.

CHAPTER 25

"I think, perhaps, that she needs this food as much as we do," Raoden said, regarding the slight-framed Torena with a skeptical eye. Ahan's daughter had pulled her reddish gold hair up under a protective scarf, and she wore a simple blue dress—something she'd probably had to borrow from one of her maids, considering the average Arelish noblewoman's extravagant wardrobe.

"Be nice to her," Sarene ordered, handing Raoden a box from the cart. "She's the only woman brave enough to come—though she only agreed because I had Shuden ask her. If you scare that girl away, none of the others will ever come."

"Yes, Your Highness," Raoden said, bowing slightly. It seemed that a week's worth of distributing food together had softened her hatred of him somewhat, but she was still cold. She would respond to his comments, even converse with him, but she would not let herself be his friend.

The week had been surrealy unnerving for Raoden. He'd spent his time in Elantris accustoming himself to the strange and the new. This week, however, he had been forced to reacquaint himself with the familiar. It was worse, in a way. He could accept Elantris as a source of pain. It was entirely different to see his friends the same way.

Even now, Shuden stood next to the girl Torena, his hand on her elbow as he encouraged her to approach the line of food. Shuden had been one of Raoden's best friends; the solemn Jindo and he had spent hours at a time discussing their views on Arelon's civic problems. Now Shuden barely noticed him. It had been the same with Eondel, Kiin, Roial, and even Lukel. They had been companions to the handsome Prince Raoden, but never to the accursed creature known as Spirit.

Yet, Raoden found it hard to be bitter. He couldn't blame them for not recognizing him; he barely recognized himself anymore, with his wrinkled skin and spindly body. Even his voice was different. In a way, his own subterfuge hurt even more than his friends' ignorance. He couldn't tell them who he was, for news of his survival could destroy Arelon. Raoden knew very well that his own popularity exceeded that of his father—there would be some who would follow him, Elantrian or not. Civil war would serve no one, and at the end of it, Raoden would probably find himself beheaded.

No, he definitely had to remain hidden. Knowledge of his fate would only give his friends pain and confusion. However, concealing his identity required vigilance. His face and voice had changed, but his mannerisms had not. He made a point of staying away from anyone who had known him too well, trying to be cheerful and friendly, but not open.

Which was one reason why he found himself gravitating toward Sarene. She hadn't known him before, and so he could discard his act around her. In a way, it was kind of a test. He was curious to see how they would have gotten along as husband and wife, without their separate political necessities getting in the way.

His initial feelings seemed to have been correct. He liked her. Where the letters had hinted, Sarene fulfilled. She wasn't like the women he had grown accustomed to in the Arelish court. She was strong and determined. She didn't avert her eyes downward whenever a man addressed her, no matter how noble his rank. She gave orders easily and naturally, and never feigned weakness in order to draw a man's attentiveness.

Yet, the lords followed her. Eondel, Shuden, even Duke Roial—they deferred to her in judgment and responded to her commands as if she were king. There was never a look of bitterness in their eyes, either. She gave her orders courteously, and they responded naturally. Raoden could only smile in amazement. It had taken him years to earn these men's trust. Sarene had done it in a matter of weeks.

She was impressive in every attribute—intelligent, beautiful, and strong. Now, if only he could convince her not to hate him.

Raoden sighed and turned back to the work. Except for Shuden, all of the day's nobles were new to the process. Most were minor noblemen of little import, but there were a couple of important additions. Duke Telrii, for instance, stood to one side, watching the unloading process with lazy eyes. He didn't participate himself, but had brought a manservant to fill his place. Telrii obviously preferred to avoid any actual exertion.

Raoden shook his head. He had never cared much for the duke. He had once approached the man, hoping that Telrii might be persuaded to join in Raoden's opposition to the king. Telrii had simply yawned and asked how much Raoden was willing to pay for his support, then had laughed as Raoden stalked away. Raoden had never been able to decide whether Telrii had asked the question out of actual greed, or if he had simply known how Raoden would react to the demand.

Raoden turned to the other noblemen. As usual, the newcomers stood in a small, apprehensive cluster around the cart they had unloaded. Now it was Raoden's turn. He approached with a smile, introducing himself and shaking hands—mostly against the owners' wills. However, their tension began to wane after just a few minutes of mingling. They could see that there was at least one Elantrian who wasn't going to eat them, and none of the other food distributors had fallen to the Shaod, so they could dismiss their fears of infection.

The clot of people relaxed, falling to Raoden's affable proddings. Acclimatizing the nobles was a task he had taken upon himself. It had been obvious on the second day that Sarene had nowhere near as much influence with most aristocrats as she did with Shuden and the others of Raoden's former circle. If Raoden hadn't stepped in, that second group would probably still be standing frozen around the cart. Sarene hadn't thanked him for his efforts, but she had nodded in slight appreciation. Afterward, it had been assumed that Raoden would help each new batch of nobles as he had that second one.

It was odd to him, participating in the event that was singularly destroying everything he had worked to build in Elantris. However, beyond creating an enormous incident, there was little he could do to stop Sarene. In addition, Mareshe and Karata were receiving vital goods for their "cooperation." Raoden would have to do a great deal of rebuilding after Sarene's Trial finished, but the setbacks would be worth the effort. Assuming, of course, he survived long enough.

The casual thought brought a sudden awareness of his pains. They were with him as always, burning his flesh and eating at his resolve. He no longer counted them, though each one had its own feeling—an unformed name, a sense of individual agony. As far as he could tell, his pain was accelerating much more quickly than anyone else's. A scrape on his arm felt like a gash running from shoulder to fingers, and his once-stubbed toe blazed with a fire that ran all the way to his knee. It was as if he had been in Elantris a year, and not a single lonely month.

Or, maybe his pain wasn't stronger. Maybe he was just weaker than the others. Either way, he wouldn't be able to endure much longer. A day would soon come, in a month or maybe two, when he would not awaken from his pain, and they would have to lay him in the Hall of the Fallen. There, he could finally give full devotion to his jealous agony.

He pushed such thoughts away, forcing himself to start handing out food. He tried to let the work distract him, and it helped a little. However, the pain still lurked within, like a beast hiding in the shadows, its red eyes watching with intense hunger.

Each Elantrian received a small sack filled with a variety of ready-to-eat items. This day's portions were much like every other—though, surprisingly, Sarene had found some Jindoeese sourmelons. The fist-sized red fruits glistened in the crate beside Raoden, challenging the fact that they were supposed to be out of season. He dropped one fruit in every bag, followed by some steamed corn, various vegetables, and a small loaf of bread. The Elantrians accepted the offerings thankfully but greedily. Most of them scurried away from the cart as soon as they received their meal, off to eat it in solitude. They still couldn't believe that no one was going to take it away from them.

As Raoden worked, a familiar face appeared before him. Galladon wore his Elantris rags, as well as a tattered cloak they had made from dirty Elantris scavangings. The Dula held out his sack, and Raoden carefully switched it for one filled with five times the regular allotment; it was so full it was hard to lift with one weakened Elantrian hand. Galladon received the sack with an extended arm, the side of his cloak obscuring it from casual eyes. Then he was gone, disappearing through the crowd.

Saolin, Mareshe, and Karata would come as well, and each would receive a bag like Galladon's. They would store what items they could, then give the rest to the Hoed. Some of the fallen were able to recognize food, and Raoden hoped that regular eating would help restore their minds.

So far, it wasn't working.

THE gate thumped as it shut, the sound reminding Raoden of his first day in Elantris. His pain then had only been emotional, and comparatively weak at that. If he had truly understood what he was getting into, he probably would have curled up and joined the Hoed right then and there.

He turned, putting his back to the gate. Mareshe and Galladon stood in the center of the courtyard, looking down at several boxes Sarene had left behind—fulfillment of Karata's most recent demands.

"Please tell me you've figured out a way to transport those," Raoden said, joining his friends. The last few times, they had ended up carrying the boxes back to New Elantris one at a time, their weakened Elantrian muscles straining at the effort.

"Of course, I have," Mareshe said with a sniff. "At least, it *should* work."

The small man retrieved a slim metal sheet from behind a pile of rubble. All four sides curved up slightly, and there were three ropes connected to the front.

"A sled?" Galladon asked.

"Coated with grease on the bottom," Mareshe explained. "I couldn't find any wheels in Elantris that weren't rusted or rotted, but this should work—the slime on these streets will provide lubrication to keep it moving."

Galladon grunted, obviously biting off some sarcastic comment. No matter how poorly Mareshe's sled worked, it couldn't be any worse than walking back and forth between the gate and the chapel a dozen times.

In fact, the sled functioned fairly well. Eventually, the grease rubbed away and the streets grew too narrow to avoid the patches of torn-up cobblestones—and, of course, dragging it along the slime-free streets of New Elantris was even more difficult. On the whole, however, even Galladon had to admit that the sled saved them quite a bit of time.

"He finally did something useful," the Dula grunted after they had pulled up in front of the chapel.

Mareshe snorted indifferently, but Raoden could see the pleasure in his eyes. Galladon stubbornly refused to acknowledge the little man's ingenuity; the Dula complained that he didn't want to further inflate Mareshe's ego, something Raoden figured was just about impossible.

"Let's see what the princess decided to send us this time," Raoden said, prying open the first box.

"Watch out for snakes," Galladon warned.

Raoden chuckled, dropping the lid to the cobblestones. The box contained several bales of cloth—all of which were a sickeningly bright orange.

Galladon scowled. "Sule, that has to be the most vile color I have ever seen in my life."

"Agreed," Raoden said with a smile.

"You don't seem very disappointed."

"Oh, I'm thoroughly revolted," Raoden said. "I just enjoy seeing the ways she finds to spite us."

Galladon grunted, moving to the second box as Raoden held up an edge of the cloth, studying it with a speculative eye. Galladon was right; it was a particularly garish color. The exchange of demands and goods between Sarene and the "gang leaders" had become something of a game: Mareshe and Karata spent hours deciding how to word their demands, but Sarene always seemed to find a way to turn the orders against them.

"Oh, you're going to love this," Galladon said, peering into the second box with a shake of his head.

"What?"

"It's our steel," the Dula explained. Last time they had asked for twenty sheets of steel, and Sarene had promptly delivered twenty plates of the metal pounded so thin they almost floated when dropped. This time they had asked for their steel by weight.

Galladon reached into the box and pulled out a handful of nails. Bent nails. "There must be thousands of them in here."

Raoden laughed. "Well, I'm sure we can find something to do with them." Fortunately, Eonic the blacksmith had been one of the few Elantrians to remain true to Raoden.

Galladon dropped the nails back into their box with a skeptical shrug. The rest of the supplies weren't quite as bad. The food was stale, but Karata had stipulated that it had to be edible. The oil gave off a pungent smell when it was burned—Raoden had no idea where the princess had found that particular item—and the knives were sharp, but they had no handles.

"At least she hasn't figured out why we demand wooden boxes," Raoden said, inspecting the vessels themselves. The grain was good and strong. They would be able to pry the boxes apart and use the wood for a multitude of purposes.

"I wouldn't be surprised if she left them unsanded just to give us splinters," Galladon said, sorting through a pile of rope, looking for an end to begin unraveling the mess. "If that woman was your fate, sule, then your Domi blessed you by sending you to this place."

"She's not that bad," Raoden said, standing as Mareshe began to catalogue the acquisitions.

"I think it's odd, my lord," Mareshe said. "Why is she going to such lengths to aggravate us? Isn't she afraid of spoiling our deal?"

"I think she suspects how powerless we really are, Mareshe," Raoden said with a shake of his head. "She fulfills our demands because she doesn't want to back out of her promise, but she doesn't feel the need to keep us happy. She knows we can't stop the people from accepting her food."

Mareshe nodded, turning back to his list.

"Come on, Galladon," Raoden said, picking up the bags of food for the Hoed. "Let's find Karata."

NEW Elantris seemed hollow now. Once, right before Sarene's arrival, they had collected over a hundred people. Now barely twenty remained, not counting children and Hoed. Most of those who had stayed were newcomers to Elantris, people like Saolin and Mareshe that Raoden had "rescued." They didn't know any other life beyond New Elantris, and were hesitant to leave it behind. The others—those who had wandered into New Elantris on their own—

had felt only faint loyalty to Raoden's cause. They had left as soon as Sarene offered them something "better"; most now lined the streets surrounding the gate, waiting for their next handout.

"Sad. Kolo?" Galladon regarded the now clean, but empty, houses.

"Yes," Raoden said. "It had potential, if only for a week."

"We'll get there again, sule," Galladon said.

"We worked so hard to help them become human again, and now they've abandoned what they learned. They wait with open mouths—I wonder if Sarene realizes that her three-meal bags usually last only a few minutes. The princess is trying to stop hunger, but the people devour her food so fast that they end up feeling sick for a few hours, then starve for the rest of the day. An Elantrian's body doesn't work the same way as a regular person's."

"You were the one who said it, sule," Galladon said. "The hunger is psychological. Our bodies don't need food; the Dor sustains us."

Raoden nodded. "Well, at least it doesn't make them explode." He had worried that eating too much would cause the Elantrians' stomachs to burst. Fortunately, once an Elantrian's belly was filled, the digestive system started to work. Like Elantrian muscles, it still responded to stimulus.

They continued to walk, eventually passing Kahar scrubbing complacently at a wall with a brush they had gotten him in the last shipment. His face was peaceful and unperturbed; he hardly seemed to have noticed that his assistants had left. He did, however, look up at Raoden and Galladon with critical eyes.

"Why hasn't my lord changed?" he asked pointedly.

Raoden looked down at his Elantris rags. "I haven't had time yet, Kahar."

"After all the work Mistress Maare went to sew you a proper outfit, my lord?" Kahar asked critically.

"All right," Raoden said, smiling. "Have you seen Karata?"

"She's in the Hall of the Fallen, my lord, with the Hoed."

FOLLOWING the elderly cleaner's direction, Raoden and Galladon changed before continuing on to find Karata. Raoden was instantly glad that they had done so. He had nearly forgotten what it was like to put on fresh, clean clothing—cloth that didn't smell of muck and refuse, and that wasn't coated in a layer of brown slime. Of course, the colors left something to be desired—Sarene was rather clever with her selections.

Raoden regarded himself in a small piece of polished steel. His shirt was yellow dyed with blue stripes, his trousers were bright red, and his vest a sickly green. Over all, he looked like some kind of confused tropical bird. His only consolation was that as silly he looked, Galladon was much worse.

The large, dark-skinned Dula looked down at his pink and light green clothing with a resigned expression.

"Don't look so sour, Galladon," Raoden said with a laugh. "Aren't you Dulas supposed to be fond of garish clothing?"

"That's the aristocracy—the citizens and republicans. I'm a farmer; pink isn't exactly what I consider a flattering color. Kolo?" Then he looked up at Raoden with narrow eyes. "If you make even one comment about my resembling a kathari fruit, I will take off this tunic and hang you with it."

Raoden chuckled. "Someday I'm going to find that scholar who told me all Dulas were even-tempered, then force him to spend a week locked in a room with you, my friend."

Galladon grunted, declining to respond.

"Come on," Raoden said, leading the way out of the chapel's back room. They found Karata sitting outside of the Hall of the Fallen, a length of string and a needle held in her hand. Saolin sat in front of her, his sleeve pulled back, exposing a long, deep gash running along his entire arm. There was no flowing blood, but the flesh was dark and slick. Karata was efficiently sewing the gash back together.

"Saolin!" Raoden exclaimed. "What happened?"

The soldier looked down with embarrassment. He didn't seem pained, though the cut was so deep a normal man would have fainted long before from pain and blood loss. "I slipped, my lord, and one of them got to me."

Raoden regarded the wound with dissatisfaction. Saolin's soldiers had not thinned as badly as the rest of Elantris; they were a stern group, not so quick to abandon newfound responsibility. However, their numbers had never been that great, and they barely had enough men to watch the streets leading from Shaor's territory to the courtyard. Each day while the rest of Elantris glutted themselves on Sarene's offerings, Saolin and his men fought a bitter struggle to keep Shaor's beasts from overrunning the courtyard. Sometimes, howling could be heard in the distance.

"I am sorry, Saolin," Raoden said as Karata stitched.

"No mind, my lord," the soldier said bravely. However, this wound was different from previous ones. It was on his sword arm.

"My lord . . ." he began, looking away from Raoden's eyes.

"What is it?"

"We lost another man today. We barely kept them back. Now, without me . . . well, we'll have a very difficult time of it, my lord. My lads are good fighters, and they are well equipped, but we won't be able to hold out for much longer."

Raoden nodded. "I'll think of something." The man nodded hopefully, and Raoden, feeling guilty, spoke on. "Saolin, how did you get a cut like that? I've never seen Shaor's men wield anything other than sticks and rocks."

"They've changed, my lord," Saolin said. "Some of them have swords now, and whenever one of my men falls they drag his weapons away from him."

Raoden raised his eyebrows in surprise. "Really?"

"Yes, my lord. Is that important?"

"Very. It means that Shaor's men aren't quite as bestial as they would have us believe. There's room enough in their minds to adapt. Some of their wildness, at least, is an act."

"Doloken of an act," Galladon said with a snort.

"Well, perhaps not an act," Raoden said. "They behave like they do because it's easier than dealing with the pain. However, if we can give them another option, they might take it."

"We could just let them though to the courtyard, my lord," Saolin suggested hesitantly, grunting slightly as Karata finished her stitching. The woman was proficient; she had met her husband while serving as a nurse for a small mercenary group.

"No," Raoden said. "Even if they didn't kill some of the nobles, the Elantris City Guards would slaughter them."

"Isn't that what we want, sule?" Galladon asked with an evil twinkle in his eyes.

"Definitely not," Raoden said. "I think Princess Sarene has a secondary purpose behind this Trial of hers. She brings different nobles with her every day, as if she wanted to acclimatize them to Elantris."

"What good would that do?" Karata asked, speaking for the first time as she put away her sewing utensils.

"I don't know," Raoden said. "But it is important to her. If Shaor's men attacked the nobility, it would destroy whatever the princess is trying to accomplish. I've tried to warn her that not all Elantrians are as docile as the ones she's seen, but I don't think she believes me. We'll just have to keep Shaor's men away until Sarene is done."

"Which will be?" Galladon asked.

"Domi only knows," Raoden replied with a shake of his head. "She won't tell me—she gets suspicious every time I try to probe her for information."

"Well, sule," Galladon said, regarding Saolin's wounded arm, "you'd better find a way to make her stop soon—either that, or prepare her to deal with several dozen ravenous maniacs. Kolo?"

Raoden nodded.

A dot in the center, a line running a few inches above it, and another line running along its right side—Aon Aon, the starting point of every other Aon. Raoden continued to draw, his fingers moving delicately and quickly, leaving luminescent trails behind them. He completed the box around the center dot, then drew two larger circles around it. Aon Tia, the symbol for travel.

Raoden didn't stop here either. He drew two long lines extending from the corners of the box—a proscription that the Aon was to affect only him—then four smaller Aons down the side to delineate the exact distance it was to send him. A series of lines crossing the top instructed the Aon to wait to take effect until he tapped its center, indicating that he was ready.

He made each line or dot precisely; length and size was very important to the calculations. It was still a relatively simple Aon, nothing like the incredibly complex healing Aons that the book described. Still, Raoden was proud of his increasing ability. It had taken him days to perfect the four-Aon series that instructed Tia to transport him precisely ten body lengths away.

He watched the glowing pattern with a smile of satisfaction until it flashed and disappeared, completely ineffective.

"You're getting better, sule," Galladon said, leaning on the windowsill, peering into the chapel.

Raoden shook his head. "I have a long way to go, Galladon."

The Dula shrugged. Galladon had stopped trying to convince Raoden that practicing AonDor was pointless. No matter what else happened, Raoden always spent a few hours each day drawing his Aons. It comforted him—he felt the pain less when he was drawing Aons, and he felt more at peace during those few short hours than he had in a long time.

"How are the crops?" Raoden asked.

Galladon turned around, looking back at the garden. The cornstalks were still short, barely more than sprouts. Raoden could see their stems beginning to wilt. The last week had seen the disappearance of most of Galladon's workers, and now only the Dula remained to labor on the diminutive farm. Every day he made several treks to the well to bring water to his plants, but he couldn't carry much, and the bucket Sarene had given them leaked.

"They'll live," Galladon said. "Remember to have Karata send for some fertilizer in the next order."

Raoden shook his head. "We can't do that, my friend. The king mustn't find out that we're raising our own food."

Galladon scowled. "Well, I suppose you could order some dung instead."

"Too obvious."

"Well, ask for some fish then," he said. "Claim you've gotten a sudden craving for trike."

Raoden sighed, nodding. He should have thought a little more before he put the garden behind his own home; the scent of rotting fish was not something he looked forward to.

"You learned that Aon from the book?" Galladon asked, leaning through the window with a leisurely posture. "What was it supposed to do?"

"Aon Tia?" Raoden asked. "It's a transportation Aon. Before the Reod, that Aon could move a person from Elantris to the other side of the world. The book mentions it because it was one of the most dangerous Aons."

"Dangerous?"

"You have to be very precise about the distance it is to send you. If you tell it to transport you exactly ten feet, it will do so—no matter what happens to be ten feet away. You could easily materialize in the middle of a stone wall."

"You're learning much from the book, then?"

Raoden shrugged. "Some things. Hints, mostly." He flipped back in the book to a page he had marked. "Like this case. About ten years before the Reod, a man brought his wife to Elantris to receive treatment for her palsy. However, the Elantrian healer drew Aon Ien slightly wrong—and instead of just vanishing, the character flashed and bathed the poor woman in a reddish light. She was left with black splotches on her skin and limp hair that soon fell out. Sound familiar?"

Galladon raised an eyebrow in interest.

"She died a short time later," Raoden said. "She threw herself off a building, screaming that the pain was too much."

Galladon frowned. "What did the healer do wrong?"

"It wasn't an error so much as an omission," Raoden said. "He left out one of the three basic lines. A foolish error, but it shouldn't have had such a drastic effect." Raoden paused, studying the page thoughtfully. "It's almost like . . ."

"Like what, sule?"

"Well, the Aon wasn't completed, right?"

"Kolo."

"So, maybe the healing began, but couldn't finish because

its instructions weren't complete," Raoden said. "What if the mistake still created a viable Aon—one that could access the Dor, but couldn't provide enough energy to finish what it started?"

"What are you implying, sule?"

Raoden's eyes opened wide. "That we aren't dead, my friend."

"No heartbeat. No breathing. No blood. I couldn't agree with you more."

"No, really," Raoden said, growing excited. "Don't you see—our bodies are trapped in some kind of half transformation. The process began, but something blocked it—just like in that woman's healing. The Dor is still within us, waiting for the direction and the energy to finish what it started."

"I don't know that I follow you, sule," Galladon said hesitantly.

Raoden wasn't listening. "That's why our bodies never heal—it's like they're trapped in the same moment in time. Frozen, like a fish in a block of ice. The pain doesn't go away because our bodies think time isn't passing. They're stuck, waiting for the end of their transformation. Our hair falls away and nothing new grows to replace it. Our skin turns black in the spots where the Shaod began, then halted as it ran out of strength."

"It seems like a leap to me, sule," Galladon said.

"It is," Raoden agreed. "But I'm sure it's true. Something *is* blocking the Dor—I can sense it through my Aons. The energy is trying to get through, but there's something in the way—as if the Aon patterns are mismatched."

Raoden looked up at his friend. "We're not dead, Galladon, and we're not damned. We're just unfinished."

"Great, sule," Galladon said. "Now you just have to find out why."

Raoden nodded. They understood a little more, but the true mystery—the reason behind Elantris's fall—remained.

"But," the Dula continued, turning to tend to his plants again, "I'm glad the book was of help."

Raoden cocked his head to the side as Galladon walked away. "Wait a minute, Galladon."

The Dula turned with a quizzical look.

"You don't really care about my studies, do you?" Raoden asked. "You just wanted to know if your book was useful."

"Why would I care about that?" Galladon scoffed.

"I don't know," Raoden said. "But you've always been so protective of your study. You haven't shown it to anyone, and you never even go there yourself. What is so sacred about that place and its books?"

"Nothing," the Dula said with a shrug. "I just don't want to see them ruined."

"How did you find that place anyway?" Raoden asked, walking over to the window and leaning against the sill. "You say you've only been in Elantris a few months, but you seem to know your way through every road and alley. You led me straight to Shaor's bank, and the market's not exactly the kind of place you'd have casually explored."

The Dula grew increasingly uncomfortable as Raoden spoke. Finally he muttered, "Can a man keep nothing to himself, Raoden? Must you drag everything out of me?"

Raoden leaned back, surprised by his friend's sudden intensity. "I'm sorry," he stammered, realizing how accusatory his words had sounded. Galladon had given him nothing but support since his arrival. Embarrassed, Raoden turned to leave the Dula alone.

"My father was an Elantrian," Galladon said quietly.

Raoden paused. To the side, he could see his friend. The large Dula had taken a seat on the freshly watered soil and was staring at a small cornstalk in front of him.

"I lived with him until I was old enough to move away," Galladon said. "I always thought it was wrong for a Dula to live in Arelon, away from his people and his family. I guess that's why the Dor decided to give me the same curse.

"They always said that Elantris was the most blessed of cities, but my father was never happy here. I guess even in paradise there are those who don't fit in. He became a scholar—the study I showed you was his. However, Duladel never left his mind—he studied farming and agriculture, though both were useless in Elantris. Why farm when you can turn garbage into food?"

Galladon sighed, reaching out to pinch a piece of dirt

between his fingers. He rubbed them together for a moment, letting the soil fall back to the ground.

"He wished he had studied healing when he found my mother dying beside him in bed one morning. Some diseases strike so quickly even Elantris can't stop them. My father became the only depressed Elantrian I ever knew. That's when I finally understood that they weren't gods, for a god could never feel such agony. He couldn't return home—the Elantrians of old were as exiled as we are today, no matter how beautiful they might have been. People don't want to live with something so superior to themselves—they can't stand such a visible sign of their own inferiority.

"He was happy when I returned to Duladen. He told me to be a farmer. I left him a poor, lonely god in a divine city, wishing for nothing so much as the freedom to be a simple man again. He died about a year after I left. Did you know that Elantrians could die of simple things, such as heart-death? They lived much longer than regular people, but they could still die. Especially if they wanted to. My father knew the signs of heart-death; he could have gone in to be healed, but he chose to stay in his study and disappear. Just like those Aons you spend so much time drawing."

"So you hate Elantris?" Raoden asked, slipping quietly through the open window to approach his friend. He sat as well, looking across the small plant at Galladon.

"Hate?" Galladon asked. "No, I don't hate—that isn't the Dula way. Of course, growing up in Elantris with a bitter father made me a poor Dula. You've realized that—I can't take things as lightly as my people would. I see a taint on everything. Like the sludge of Elantris. My people avoided me because of my demeanor, and I was almost glad when the Shaod took me—I didn't fit Duladel, no matter how much I enjoyed my farming. I deserve this city, and it deserves me. Kolo?"

Raoden wasn't certain how to respond. "I suppose an optimistic comment wouldn't do much good right now."

Galladon smiled slightly. "Definitely not—you optimists just can't understand that a depressed person doesn't want you to try and cheer them up. It makes us sick."

"Then just let me say something true, my friend," Raoden

said. "I appreciate you. I don't know if you fit in here; I doubt any of us do. But I value your help. If New Elantris succeeds, then it will be because you were there to keep me from throwing myself off a building."

Galladon took a deep breath. His face was hardly joyful—yet, his gratitude was plain. He nodded slightly, then stood and offered Raoden a hand to help him up.

RAODEN turned fitfully. He didn't have much of a bed, just a collection of blankets in the chapel's back room. However, discomfort wasn't what kept him up. There was another problem—a worry in the back of his mind. He was missing something important. He had been close to it earlier, and his subconscious harried him, demanding that he make the connection.

But, what was it? What clue, barely registered, haunted him? After his discussion with Galladon, Raoden had returned to his Aon practice. Then he had gone for a short look around the city. All had been quiet—Shaor's men had stopped attacking New Elantris, instead focusing on the more promising potential presented by Sarene's visits.

It had to be related to his discussions with Galladon, he decided. Something to do with the Aons, or perhaps Galladon's father. What would it have been like to be an Elantrian back then? Could a man really have been depressed within these amazing walls? Who, capable of marvelous wonders, would be willing to trade them for the simple life of a farmer? It must have been beautiful back then, so beautiful. . . .

"Merciful Domi!" Raoden yelled, snapping upright in his blankets.

A few seconds later, Saolin and Mareshe—who made their beds in the main room of the chapel—burst through the door. Galladon and Karata weren't far behind. They found Raoden sitting in amazed stupefaction.

"Sule?" Galladon asked carefully.

Raoden stood and strode out of the room. A perplexed entourage followed. Raoden barely paused to light a lantern, and the pungent odor of Sarene's oil didn't even faze him.

He marched into the night, heading straight for the Hall of the Fallen.

The man was there, still mumbling to himself as many of the Hoed did even at night. He was small and wrinkled, his skin folded in so many places he appeared a thousand years old. His voice whispered a quiet mantra.

"Beautiful," he rasped. "Once so very beautiful. . . ."

The hint hadn't come during his discussions with Galladon at all. It had come during his short visit delivering food to the Hoed. Raoden had heard the man's mumbling a dozen times, and never made the connection.

Raoden placed a hand on each of the man's shoulders. "What was so beautiful?"

"Beautiful . . ." the man mumbled.

"Old man," Raoden pled. "If there is a soul left in that body of yours, even the slightest bit of rational thought, please tell me. What are you talking about?"

"Once so very beautiful . . ." the man continued, his eyes staring into the air.

Raoden raised a hand and began to draw in front of the man's face. He had barely completed Aon Rao before the man reached out, gasping as he put his hand through the center of the character.

"We were so beautiful, once," the man whispered. "My hair so bright, my skin full of light. Aons fluttered from my fingers. They were so beautiful. . . ."

Raoden heard several muttered exclamations of surprise from behind. "You mean," Karata asked, approaching, "all this time . . . ?"

"Ten years," Raoden said, still supporting the old man's slight body. "This man was an Elantrian before the Reod."

"Impossible," Mareshe said. "It's been too long."

"Where else would they go?" Raoden asked. "We know some of the Elantrians survived the fall of city and government. They were locked in Elantris. Some might have burned themselves, a few others might have escaped, but the rest would still be here. They would have become Hoed, losing their minds and their strength after a few years . . . forgotten in the streets."

"Ten years," Galladon whispered. "Ten years of suffering."

Raoden looked into the old man's eyes. They were lined with cracks and wrinkles, and seemed dazed, as if by some great blow. The secrets of AonDor hid somewhere in this man's mind.

The man's grip on Raoden's arm tightened almost imperceptibly, his entire body quivering with effort. Three straining words hissed from his lips as his agony-laden eyes focused on Raoden's face.

"Take. Me. Out."

"Where?" Raoden asked with confusion. "Out of the city?"

"The. Lake."

"I don't know what you mean, old one," Raoden whispered.

The man's eyes moved slightly, looking at the door.

"Karata, grab that light," Raoden ordered, picking up the old man. "Galladon, come with us. Mareshe and Saolin, stay here. I don't want any of the others to wake up and find us all gone."

"But . . ." Saolin began, but his words fell off. He recognized a direct order.

It was a bright night, moon hanging full in the sky, and the lantern almost wasn't necessary. Raoden carried the old Elantrian carefully. It was obvious that the man no longer had the strength to lift his arm and point, so Raoden had to pause at every intersection, searching the old man's eyes for some sign that they should turn.

It was a slow process, and it was nearly morning before they arrived at a fallen building at the very edge of Elantris. The structure looked much like any other, though its roof was mostly intact.

"Any idea what this was?" Raoden asked.

Galladon thought for a moment, digging through his memory. "Actually, I think I do, sule. It was some sort of meetinghouse for the Elantrians. My father came here occasionally, though I was never allowed to accompany him."

Karata gave Galladon a startled look at the explanation, but she held her questions for another time. Raoden carried

the old Elantrian into the hollow building. It was empty and
nondescript. Raoden studied the man's face. He was looking
at the floor.

Galladon knelt and brushed away debris as he searched
the floor. "There's an Aon here."

"Which one?"

"Rao, I think."

Raoden furled his brow. The meaning of Aon Rao was
simple: It meant "spirit" or "spiritual energy." However, the
AonDor book had mentioned it infrequently, and had never
explained what magical effect the Aon was meant to produce.

"Push on it," Raoden suggested.

"I'm trying, sule," Galladon said with a grunt. "I don't
think it's doing any—" The Dula cut off as the section of
floor began to fall away. He yelped and scrambled back as
the large stone block sank with a grinding noise. Karata
cleared her throat, pointing at an Aon she had pushed on the
wall. Aon Tae—the ancient symbol that meant "open."

"There are some steps here, sule," Galladon said, sticking
his head into the hole. He climbed down, and Karata followed with the lamp. After passing down the old Hoed, Raoden joined them.

"Clever mechanism," Galladon noted, studying the series
of gears that had lowered the enormous stone block.
"Mareshe would be going wild about now. Kolo?"

"I'm more interested in these walls," Raoden said, staring
at the beautiful murals. The room was rectangular and squat,
barely eight feet tall, but it was brilliantly decorated with
painted walls and a double row of sculpted columns. "Hold
the lantern up."

White-haired figures with silver skin coated the walls,
their two-dimensional forms engaged in various activities.
Some knelt before enormous Aons; others walked in rows,
heads bowed. There was a sense of formality about the figures.

"This place is holy," Raoden said. "A shrine of some
sort."

"Religion amongst the Elantrians?" Karata asked.

"They must have had something," Raoden said. "Perhaps

they weren't as convinced of their own divinity as the rest of Arelon." He shot an inquiring look at Galladon.

"My father never spoke of religion," the Dula said. "But his people kept many secrets, even from their families."

"Over there," Karata said, pointing at the far end of the rectangular room, where the wall held only a single mural. It depicted a large mirrorlike blue oval. An Elantrian stood facing the oval, his arms outstretched and his eyes closed. He appeared to be flying toward the blue disk. The rest of the wall was black, though there was a large white sphere on the other side of the oval.

"Lake." The old Elantrian's voice was quiet but insistent.

"It's painted sideways," Karata realized. "See, he's falling into a lake."

Raoden nodded. The Elantrian in the picture wasn't flying, he was falling. The oval was the surface of a lake, lines on its sides depicting a shore.

"It's like the water was considered a gate of some sort," Galladon said, head cocked to the side.

"And he wants us to throw him in," Raoden realized. "Galladon, did you ever see an Elantrian funeral?"

"Never," the Dula said with a shake of his head.

"Come on," Raoden said, looking down at the old man's eyes. They pointed insistently at a side passage.

Beyond the doorway was a room even more amazing than the first. Karata held up her lantern with a wavering hand.

"Books," Raoden whispered with excitement. Their light shone on rows and rows of bookshelves, extending into the darkness. The three wandered into the enormous room, feeling an incredible sense of age. Dust coated the shelves, and their footsteps left tracks.

"Have you noticed something odd about this place, sule?" Galladon asked softly.

"No slime," Karata realized.

"No slime," Galladon agreed.

"You're right," Raoden said with amazement. He had grown so used to New Elantris's clean streets that he'd almost forgotten how much work it took to make them that way.

"I haven't found a single place in this town that wasn't

covered with that slime, sule," Galladon said. "Even my father's study was coated with it before I cleaned it."

"There's something else," Raoden said, looking back at the room's stone wall. "Look up there."

"A lantern," Galladon said with surprise.

"They line the walls."

"But why not use Aons?" the Dula asked. "They did everywhere else."

"I don't know," Raoden said. "I wondered the same thing about the entrance. If they could make Aons that transported them instantly around the city, then they certainly could have made one that lowered a rock."

"You're right," Galladon said.

"AonDor must have been forbidden here for some reason," Karata guessed as they reached the far side of the library.

"No Aons, no slime. Coincidence?" Galladon asked.

"Perhaps," Raoden said, checking the old man's eyes. He pointed insistently at a small door in the wall. It was carved with a scene similar to the mural in the first room.

Galladon pulled open the door, revealing a long, seemingly endless passage cut into the stone. "Where in Doloken does this lead?"

"Out," Raoden said. "The man asked us to take him out of Elantris."

Karata walked into the passage, running her fingers along its smoothly carved walls. Raoden and Galladon followed. The path quickly grew steep, and they were forced to take frequent breaks to rest their weak Elantrian bodies. They took turns carrying the old man as the slope turned to steps. It took over an hour to reach the path's end—a simple wooden door, uncarved and unadorned.

Galladon pushed it open, and stepped out into the weak light of dawn. "We're on the mountain," he exclaimed with surprise.

Raoden stepped out beside his friend, walking onto a short platform cut into the mountainside. The slope beyond the platform was steep, but Raoden could make out the hints of switchbacks leading down. Abutting the slope was the city of Kae, and beyond that stood the enormous monolith that was Elantris.

He had never really realized just how big Elantris was. It made Kae look like a village. Surrounding Elantris were the ghostly remains of the three other Outer Cities—towns that, like Kae, had once squatted in the shadow of the great city. All were now abandoned. Without Elantris's magics, there was no way for Arelon to support such a concentration of people. The cities' inhabitants had been forcibly removed, becoming Iadon's workmen and farmers.

"Sule, I think our friend is getting impatient."

Raoden looked down at the Elantrian. The man's eyes twitched back and forth insistently, pointing at a wide path leading up from the platform. "More climbing," Raoden said with a sigh.

"Not much," Karata said from the top of the path. "It ends just up here."

Raoden nodded and hiked the short distance, joining Karata on the ridge above the platform.

"Lake," the man whispered in exhausted satisfaction.

Raoden frowned. The "lake" was barely ten feet deep— more like a pool. Its water was a crystalline blue, and Raoden could see no inlets or outlets.

"What now?" Galladon asked.

"We put him in," Raoden guessed, kneeling to lower the Elantrian into the pool. The man floated for a moment in the deep sapphire water, then released a blissful sigh. The sound opened a longing within Raoden, an intense desire to be free of his pains both physical and mental. The old Elantrian's face seemed to smooth slightly, his eyes alive again.

Those eyes held Raoden's for a moment, thanks shining therein. Then the man dissolved.

"Doloken!" Galladon cursed as the old Elantrian melted away like sugar in a cup of adolis tea. In barely a second, the man was gone, no sign remaining of flesh, bone, or blood.

"I'd be careful if I were you, my prince," Karata suggested.

Raoden looked down, realizing how close he was to the

pool's edge. The pain screamed; his body shook, as if it knew how close it was to relief. All he had to do was fall. . . .

Raoden stood, stumbling slightly as he backed away from the beckoning pool. He wasn't ready. He wouldn't be ready until the pain ruled him—as long as he had will left, he would struggle.

He placed a hand on Galladon's shoulder. "When I am Hoed, bring me here. Don't make me live in pain."

"You're young to Elantris yet, sule," Galladon said scoffingly. "You'll last for years."

The pain raged in Raoden, making his knees tremble. "Just promise, my friend. Swear to me you will bring me here."

"I swear, Raoden," Galladon said solemnly, his eyes worried.

Raoden nodded. "Come, we have a long trek back to the city."

CHAPTER 26

THE gate slammed shut as Sarene's cart rolled back into Kae. "You're certain he's the one in charge?" she asked.

Ashe bobbed slightly. "You were correct, my lady—my information about the gang leaders was outdated. They call this newcomer Lord Spirit. His rise was a recent event—most hadn't heard of him more than a month ago, though one man claims that Lord Spirit and Shaor are the same person. The reports agree that he defeated both Karata and Aanden. Apparently, the second confrontation involved an enormous battle of some sort."

"Then the people I'm meeting with are impostors," Sarene said, tapping her cheek as she rode in the back of the cart. It was hardly fitting transportation for a princess, but none of the day's nobles had offered her a ride in their coaches. She had intended to ask Shuden, but he had disappeared—the young Torena had beat Sarene to him.

"Apparently they are, my lady. Are you angered?" Ashe asked the question carefully. He had made it quite clear he still thought her preoccupation with Spirit was an unnecessary distraction.

"No, not really. You have to expect a measure of subterfuge in any political engagement." Or, so she said. Political necessity or not, she wanted Spirit to be honest with her. She was actually beginning to trust him, and that worried her.

He chose to confide in her for some reason. Around the others he was bright and cheerful, but no man could be that one-sidedly optimistic. When he spoke only to Sarene, he was more honest. She could see pain in his eyes, unexplained sorrows and worries. This man, warlord or not, cared about Elantris.

Like all Elantrians, he was more corpse than man: his skin wan and dry, his scalp and eyebrows completely hairless. Her revulsion was decreasing every day, however, as she grew accustomed to the city. She wasn't to the point where she could see beauty in the Elantrians, but at least she wasn't physically sickened by them any longer.

Still, she forced herself to remain aloof from Spirit's overtures of friendship. She had spent too long in politics to let herself become emotionally open with an opponent. And he was definitely an opponent—no matter how affable. He played with her, presenting false gang leaders to distract, while he himself supervised her distributions. She couldn't even be certain that he was honoring their agreements. For all she knew, the only ones allowed to receive food were Spirit's followers. Perhaps he seemed so optimistic because she was inadvertently helping him reign supreme over the city.

The cart hit an especially large bump, and Sarene

thumped against its wooden floor. A couple of empty boxes toppled off the pile, nearly falling on top of her.

"Next time we see Shuden," she mumbled sullenly, rubbing her posterior, "remind me to kick him."

"Yes, my lady," Ashe said complacently.

SHE didn't have to wait long. Unfortunately, she also didn't have a chance to do much kicking. She could probably have impaled Shuden if she had wished, but that wouldn't have made her very popular with the court women. This happened to be one of the days the women had chosen to practice their fencing, and Shuden attended the meeting, as usual—though he rarely participated. Thankfully, he also refrained from doing his ChayShan exercise. The women moped over him enough as it was.

"They're actually improving," Eondel said appreciatively, watching the women spar. Each had a steel practice sword, as well as a kind of uniform—a jumpsuit much like the on Sarene wore, but with a short ring of cloth hanging down from the waist, as if to imitate a skirt. The cloth loop was thin and useless, but it made the women comfortable, so Sarene didn't say anything—no matter how silly she thought it looked.

"You sound surprised, Eondel," Sarene said. "Were you that unimpressed with my ability to teach?"

The stately warrior stiffened. "No, Your Highness, never—"

"She's teasing you, my lord," Lukel said, rapping Sarene on the head with a rolled-up piece of paper as he approached. "You shouldn't let her get away with things like that. It only encourages her."

"What's this?" Sarene said, snatching the paper from Lukel.

"Our dear king's income figures," Lukel explained as he removed a bright red sourmelon from his pocket and took a bite. He still hadn't revealed how he'd managed to get a shipment of the fruit an entire month before the season began, a fact that was making the rest of the mercantile community rabid with jealousy.

Sarene looked over the figures. "Is he going to make it?"

"Barely," Lukel said with a smile. "But his earnings in Teod, coupled with his tax income, should be respectable enough to keep him from embarrassment. Congratulations, Cousin, you've saved the monarchy."

Sarene rerolled the paper. "Well, that's one less thing we have to worry about."

"Two," Lukel corrected, a bit of pink juice rolling down his cheek. "Our dear friend Edan has fled the country."

"What?" Sarene asked.

"It's true, my lady," Eondel said. "I heard the news just this morning. Baron Edan's lands border the Chasm down in southern Arelon, and recent rains caused some mudslides involving his fields. Edan decided to cut his losses, and was last seen heading for Duladel."

"Where he'll soon discover that the new monarchy is rather unimpressed with Arelish titles," Lukel added. "I think Edan will make a nice farmer, don't you?"

"Wipe your mouth," Sarene said with a reproving look. "It's not kind to make light of another's misfortune."

"Misfortune comes as Domi wills," Lukel said.

"You never liked Edan in the first place," Sarene said.

"He was spineless, arrogant, and would have betrayed us if he'd ever found the nerve. What wasn't there to like?" Lukel continued to munch on his fruit with a self-satisfied smirk.

"Well, someone is certainly proud of himself this afternoon," Sarene noted.

"He is always like that after he makes a good business deal, Your Highness," Eondel said. "He'll be insufferable for another week at least."

"Ah, just wait for the Arelene Market," Lukel said. "I'll make a killing. Anyway, Iadon is busy looking for someone rich enough to buy Edan's barony, so you shouldn't have to worry about him bothering you for a little while."

"I wish I could say the same for you," Sarene replied, turning her attention back to her still battling students. Eondel was right: They were improving. Even the older ones seemed to be bursting with energy. Sarene held up her hand, drawing their attention, and the sparring fell off.

"You're doing very well," Sarene said as the room fell silent. "I am impressed—some of you are already better than many of the women I knew back in Teod."

There was a general air of satisfaction about the women as they listened to Sarene's praise.

"However, there is one thing that bothers me," Sarene said, beginning to pace. "I thought you women intended to prove your strength, to show that you were good for more than making the occasional embroidered pillowcase. However, so far only one of you has truly shown me that she wants to change things in Arelon. Torena, tell them what you did today."

The thin girl yelped slightly as Sarene said her name, then looked sheepishly at her companions. "I went to Elantris with you?"

"Indeed," Sarene said. "I have invited each woman in this room several times, but only Torena has had the courage to accompany me into Elantris."

Sarene stopped her pacing to regard the uncomfortable women. None of them would look at her—not even Torena, who appeared to be feeling guilty by association.

"Tomorrow I will go into Elantris again, and this time, no men will accompany me beyond the regular guards. If you really want to show this town that you are as strong as your husbands, you will accompany me."

Sarene stood in her place, looking over the women. Heads raised hesitantly, eyes focusing on her. They would come. They were frightened near to death, but they would come. Sarene smiled.

The smile, however, was only half genuine. Standing as she was, before them like a general before his troops, she realized something. It was happening again.

It was just like Teod. She could see respect in their eyes; even the queen herself looked to Sarene for advice now. However, respect her as they did, they would never accept her. When Sarene entered a room, it fell silent; when she left, conversations began again. It was as if they thought her above their simple discussions. By serving as a model for what they wanted to become, Sarene had alienated herself from them.

Sarene turned, leaving the women to their practicing. The men were the same. Shuden and Eondel respected her—even considered her a friend—but they would never think about her romantically. Despite his professed annoyance with courtly games of matrimony, Shuden was reacting favorably to Torena's advances—but he had never once looked at Sarene. Eondel was far older than she, but Sarene could sense his feelings toward her. Respect, admiration, and a willingness to serve. It was as if he didn't even realize she was a woman.

Sarene knew that she was married now, and shouldn't be thinking about such things, but it was hard to regard herself as wedded. There had been no ceremony, and she had known no husband. She craved something—a sign that at least some of the men found her attractive, though she never would have responded to any such advances. The point was irrelevant; the men of Arelon feared her as much as they respected her.

She had grown up without affection outside of her family, and it appeared she would continue that way. At least she had Kiin and his family. Still, if she had come to Arelon searching for acceptance, then she had failed. She would have to be content with respect.

A deep, scratchy voice sounded behind her, and Sarene turned to find that Kiin had joined Lukel and Eondel.

"Uncle?" she asked. "What are you doing here?"

"I got home and found the house empty," Kiin said. "There's only one person who would dare steal a man's entire family."

"She didn't steal us, Father," Lukel joked. "We just heard that you were going to make Hraggish weed soup again."

Kiin regarded his jovial son for a moment, rubbing his chin where his beard once grew. "He got a good sale, then?"

"A very lucrative one," Eondel said.

"Domi protect us," Kiin grumbled, settling his stout body into a nearby chair. Sarene took a seat next to him.

"You heard about the king's projected earnings, 'Ene?" Kiin asked.

"Yes, Uncle."

Kiin nodded. "I never thought I'd see the day when I was

encouraged by Iadon's success. Your plan to save him worked, and from what I hear, Eondel and the rest are expected to bring forth exemplary crops."

"Then why do you look so worried?" Sarene asked.

"I'm getting old, 'Ene, and old men tend to worry. Most recently I've been concerned about your excursions into Elantris. Your father would never forgive me if something happened to you in there."

"Not that he's going to forgive you anytime soon anyway," Sarene said offhandedly.

Kiin grunted. "That's the truth." Then he stopped, turning suspicious eyes her direction. "What do you know of that?"

"Nothing," Sarene admitted. "But I'm hoping you will rectify my ignorance."

Kiin shook his head. "Some things are better left unrectified. Your father and I were both a whole lot more foolish when we were younger. Eventeo might be a great king, but he's a pathetic brother. Of course, I won't soon win any awards for my fraternal affection either."

"But what happened?"

"We had a . . . disagreement."

"What kind of disagreement?"

Kiin laughed his bellowing, raspy laugh. "No, 'Ene, I'm not as easy to manipulate as your larks over there. You just keep on wondering about this one. And don't pout."

"I never pout," Sarene said, fighting hard to keep her voice from sounding childish. When it became apparent that her uncle wasn't going to offer any more information, Sarene finally changed the subject. "Uncle Kiin, are there any secret passages in Iadon's palace?"

"I'd be surprised as the Three Virgins if there aren't," he replied. "Iadon is just about the most paranoid man I've ever known. He must have at least a dozen escape routes in that fortress he calls home."

Sarene resisted the urge to point out that Kiin's home was as much a fortress as the king's. As their conversation lulled, Kiin turned to ask Eondel about Lukel's sourmelon deal. Eventually, Sarene stood and retrieved her syre, then walked out onto the practice floor. She fell into form and began moving through a solo pattern.

Her blade whipped and snapped, the well-practiced motions now routine, and her mind soon began to wander. Was Ashe right? Was she allowing herself to become distracted by Elantris and its enigmatic ruler? She couldn't lose track of her greater tasks—Hrathen was planning something, and Telrii couldn't possibly be as indifferent as he made himself out to be. She had a lot of things she needed to watch, and she had enough experience with politics to realize how easy it was to overextend oneself.

However, she was increasingly interested in Spirit. It was rare to find someone politically skilled enough to hold her attention, but in Arelon she had found two. In a way, Spirit was even more fascinating than the gyorn. While Hrathen and she were very frank about their enmity, Spirit somehow manipulated and foiled her while at the same time acting like an old friend. Most alarmingly, she almost didn't care.

Instead of being outraged when she filled his demands with useless items, he had seemed impressed. He had even complimented her on her frugality, noting that the cloth she sent must have been bought at a discount, considering its color. In all things he remained friendly, indifferent to her sarcasm.

And she felt herself responding. There, in the center of the cursed city, was finally a person who seemed willing to accept her. She wished she could laugh at his clever remarks, agree with his observations, and share his concerns. The more confrontational she tried to be, the less threatened he was. He actually seemed to appreciate her defiance.

"Sarene, dear?" Daora's quiet voice broke through her contemplations. Sarene made one final sweep of her sword, then stood up, dazed. Sweat streamed down her face, running along the inside of her collar. She hadn't realized how vigorous her training had become.

She relaxed, resting the tip of her syre on the floor. Daora's hair was pulled into a neat bun, and her uniform was unstained by sweat. As usual, the woman did all things with grace—even exercise.

"Do you want to talk about it, dear?" Daora asked with a coaxing tone. They stood to the side of room, the thumping of feet and slapping of blades masking the conversation from prying ears.

"About what?" Sarene asked with confusion.

"I've seen that look before, child," Daora said comfortingly. "He's not for you. But, of course, you've realized that, haven't you?"

Sarene paled. How could she know? Could the woman read thoughts? Then, however, Sarene followed her aunt's gaze. Daora was looking at Shuden and Torena, who were laughing together as the young girl showed Shuden a few basic thrusts.

"I know it must be hard, Sarene," Daora said, "being locked into a marriage with no chance for affection . . . never knowing your husband, or feeling the comfort of his love. Perhaps in a few years, after your place here in Arelon is more secure, you could allow yourself a relationship that is . . . covert. It is much too soon for that now, however."

Daora's eyes softened as she watched Shuden clumsily drop the sword. The normally reserved Jindo was laughing uncontrollably at his mistake. "Besides, child," Daora continued, "this one is meant for another."

"You think . . . ?" Sarene began.

Daora placed a hand on Sarene's arm, squeezing it lightly and smiling. "I've seen the look in your eyes these last few days, and I've also seen the frustration. The two emotions go together more often than youthful hearts expect."

Sarene shook her head and laughed slightly. "I assure you, Aunt," she said affectionately, yet firmly, "I have no interest in Lord Shuden."

"Of course, dear," Daora said, patting her arm, then retreating.

Sarene shook her head, walking over to get a drink. What were these "signs" Daora had claimed to see in her? The woman was usually so observant; what had made her misjudge so grievously in this instance? Sarene liked Shuden, of course, but not romantically. He was too quiet and, like Eondel, a bit too rigid for her taste. Sarene was well aware that she would need a man who would know when to give her space, but who also wouldn't let her bend him in any way she chose.

With a shrug, Sarene put Daora's misguided assumptions from her mind, then sat down to contemplate just how she was going to throw awry Spirit's latest, and most detailed, list of demands.

CHAPTER 27

HRATHEN stared at the paper for a long, long period of time. It was an accounting of King Iadon's finances, as calculated by Derethi spies.

Somehow, Iadon had recovered from his lost ships and cargo. Telrii would not be king.

Hrathen sat at his desk, still in the armor he'd been wearing when he entered to find the note. The paper sat immobile in his stunned fingers. Perhaps if he hadn't been faced by other worries, the news wouldn't have shocked him so much—he had dealt with plenty of upset plans in his life. Beneath the paper, however, sat his list of local arteths. He had offered every single one of them the position of head arteth, and they had all refused. Only one man remained who could take the position.

Iadon's recovery was only one more fallen brick in the collapsing wall of Hrathen's sense of control. Dilaf all but ruled in the chapel; he didn't even inform Hrathen of half the meetings and sermons he organized. There was a vengefulness to the way Dilaf was wresting control away from Hrathen. Perhaps the arteth was still angered over the incident with the Elantrian prisoner, or perhaps Dilaf was just transferring his anger and frustration over Sarene's humanization of the Elantrians against Hrathen instead.

Regardless, Dilaf was slowly seizing power. It was subtle,

but it seemed inevitable. The crafty arteth claimed that menial organizational items were "beneath the time of my lord hroden"—a claim that was, to an extent, well founded. Gyorns rarely had much to do with day-to-day chapel practices, and Hrathen couldn't do everything himself. Dilaf stepped in to fill the gaps. Even if Hrathen didn't break down and make the obvious move—appointing Dilaf head arteth—the eventual result would be the same.

Hrathen was losing his grip on Arelon. Nobles went to Dilaf now instead of him, and while Derethi membership was still growing, it wasn't increasing quickly enough. Sarene had somehow foiled the plot to put Telrii on the throne—and after visiting the city, the people of Kae would no longer regard Elantrians as demons. Hrathen was setting a poor precedent for his activities in Arelon.

On top of it all stood Hrathen's wavering faith. This was not the time to call his beliefs into question. Hrathen understood this. However, understanding—as opposed to feeling—was the root of his problem. Now that the seed of uncertainty had been given purchase in his heart, he couldn't easily uproot it.

It was too much. Suddenly, it seemed as if his room were falling in on him. The walls and ceiling shrunk closer and closer, as if to crush him beneath their weight. Hrathen stumbled, trying to escape, and fell to the marble floor. Nothing worked, nothing could help him.

He groaned, feeling the pain as his armor bit into his skin at odd angles. He rolled to his knees, and began to pray.

As a priest of Shu-Dereth, Hrathen spent hours in prayer each week. However, those prayers were different—more a form of meditation than a communication, a means of organizing his thoughts. This time he begged.

For the first time in years he found himself pleading for aid. Hrathen reached out to that God that he had served so long he had almost forgotten Him. The God he had shuffled away in a flurry of logic and understanding, a God he had rendered impotent in his life, though he sought to further His influence.

For once, Hrathen felt unfit to perform on his own. For once he admitted a need for help.

He didn't know how long he knelt, praying fervently for aid, compassion, and mercy. Eventually, he was startled from his trancelike pleading by a knock at his door.

"Come," he said distractedly.

"I apologize for disturbing my lord," said a minor underpriest, cracking open the door. "But this just arrived for you." The priest pushed a small crate into the room, then closed the door.

Hrathen rose on unstable feet. It was dark outside, though he had begun his prayers before noon. Had he really spent that long in supplication? A little dazed, Hrathen picked up the box and placed it on his desk, prying loose the lid with a dagger. Inside, packed with hay, was a rack containing four vials.

My Lord Hrathen, the note read. *Here is the poison you requested. All of the effects are exactly as you specified. The liquid must be ingested, and the victim won't display any symptoms until about eight hours afterwards.*

In all things, praise to Lord Jaddeth.

Forton, apothecary and loyal subject of Wyrn.

Hrathen picked up a vial, regarding its dark contents with wonder. He had almost forgotten his late-night call to Forton. He vaguely remembered assuming he would administer the poison to Dilaf. That plan wouldn't work anymore. He needed something more spectacular.

Hrathen swished the poison around in its vial for a moment, then pulled off the stopper and drank it down in a single gulp.

PART TWO

THE
CALL
OF
ELANTRIS

CHAPTER 28

T HE most difficult part was deciding where to begin reading. The bookshelves extended out of sight, their information stretching as if to eternity. Raoden was certain that the
clues he needed were contained somewhere within the vast
sea of pages, but finding them seemed a daunting task indeed.

Karata was the one who made the discovery. She located a
low bookshelf near the side of the room opposite the entrance. A set of about thirty volumes squatted on the shelf,
waiting in their dust. They dictated a cataloguing system,
with numbers relating to the various columns and rows of
the library. From it, Raoden easily located the books on
AonDor. He selected the least complicated volume he could
find, and set to work.

Raoden restricted knowledge of the library to himself,
Galladon, and Karata. Not only did he fear a repeat of Aanden's book boiling, but he sensed a sacredness to the structure. It was not a place to be invaded by visitors,
misunderstanding fingers that would disorganize books and
shatter the calm.

They kept the pool a secret as well, giving Mareshe and
Saolin a simplified explanation. Raoden's own longings
warned him how dangerous the pool was. There was a part
of him that wanted to seek out its deadly embrace, the re-
freshment of destruction. If the people knew that there was
an easy, painless way to escape the suffering, many would
take it without deliberation. The city would be depopulated
in a matter of months.

Letting them do so was an option, of course. What right

had he to keep the others from their peace? Still, Raoden felt that it was too soon to give up on Elantris. In the weeks before Sarene began giving out food, he had seen that Elantris could forget its pains and its hungers. The Elantrians could move beyond their urges—there was an escape for them besides destruction.

But not for him. The pain swelled with each passing day. It drew strength from the Dor, bringing him a little closer to submission with its every assault. Fortunately, he had the books to distract him. He studied them with hypnotic fascination, finally discovering the simple explanations he had sought for so long.

He read how the complex Aon equations worked together. Drawing a line slightly longer in proportion to the rest of an Aon could have drastic effects. Two Aon equations could start the same, but—like two rocks rolled down a mountain on slightly different paths—they could end up doing completely different things. All by changing the length of a few lines.

He began to grasp the theory of AonDor. The Dor was as Galladon had described it: a powerful reservoir just beyond the normal senses. Its only desire was to escape. The books explained that the Dor existed in a place that was full of pressure, and so the energy pushed its way through any viable exit, moving from an area of high concentration to one of low.

However, because of the Dor's nature, it could enter the physical world only through gates of the proper size and shape. Elantrians could create rifts with their drawings, providing a means for the Dor to escape, and those drawings would determine what form the energy took when it appeared. However, if even one line was of the wrong proportion, the Dor would be unable to enter—like a square trying to force its way through a round hole. Some theorists described the process using unfamiliar words like "frequency" and "pulse length." Raoden was only beginning to understand how much scientific genius was held in the library's musty pages.

Still, for all of his studies, he was disappointingly unable to find out what had made AonDor stop working. He could only guess that the Dor had changed somehow. Perhaps now, instead of a square, the Dor was a triangle—and, no matter how many square-shaped Aons Raoden drew, the energy couldn't get through. What could have led to the Dor's sudden shift was beyond him.

"How did that get in here?" Galladon asked, interrupting Raoden's thoughts. The Dula pointed toward the Seon Ien, who floated along the top of a bookshelf, his light casting shadows on the books.

"I don't know," Raoden said, watching Ien loop a few times.

"I have to admit, sule. Your Seon is creepy."

Raoden shrugged. "All of the mad Seons are that way."

"Yes, but the others generally stay away from people." Galladon eyed Ien, shivering slightly. The Seon, as usual, didn't pay any apparent attention to Galladon—though Ien did seem to like staying near Raoden.

"Well, anyway," Galladon said, "Saolin's asking for you."

Raoden nodded, closing his book and rising from the small desk—one of many at the back of the library. He joined Galladon at the doorway. The Dula shot one last, uncomfortable look at Ien before closing the door, locking the Seon in darkness.

"I don't know, Saolin," Raoden said hesitantly.

"My lord, we have little choice," the soldier said. "My men have too many injuries. It would be pointless to stand against Shaor today—the wildmen would barely pause to laugh as they pushed us out of the way."

Raoden nodded with a sigh. The soldier was right: They couldn't keep holding Shaor's men away from Sarene. Though Saolin had grown quite proficient at fighting with his left hand, there just weren't enough warriors left to protect the courtyard. In addition, it seemed that Shaor's men were growing more and more dangerous in their ferocity. They could obviously sense that there was food in the courtyard, and the inability to reach it had driven them to an even deeper level of insanity.

Raoden had tried leaving food out for them, but the distraction only worked for a short time. They stuffed their faces, then rushed on, even more furious than before. They were driven by a single-minded, obsessive goal: to reach the carts of food in the courtyard.

If only we had more soldiers! Raoden thought with frustration. He'd lost many of his people to Sarene's handouts, while Shaor's numbers were apparently remaining strong. Raoden and Galladon had both offered to join Saolin's fighters, but the grizzled captain would hear nothing of it.

"Leaders don't fight," the broken-nosed man had said simply. "You're too valuable."

Raoden knew the man was right. Raoden and Galladon were not soldiers; they wouldn't do much besides disorder Saolin's carefully trained troops. They had few choices left, and it appeared Saolin's plan was the best of several bad options.

"All right," Raoden said. "Do it."

"Very good, my lord," Saolin said with a slight bow. "I will begin the preparations—we only have a few minutes until the princess arrives."

Raoden dismissed Saolin with a nod. The soldier's plan was a desperate last-ditch attempt at a trap. Shaor's men tended to take that same path each day before splitting up to try and work their way into the courtyard, and Saolin planned to ambush them as they approached. It was risky, but it was probably their only chance. The soldiers could not continue fighting as they were.

"I suppose we should go, then," Raoden said.

Galladon nodded. As they turned to walk toward the courtyard, Raoden couldn't help feeling uncomfortable with the decision he'd made. If Saolin lost, then the wildmen would break through. If Saolin won, it would mean the death or incapacitation of dozens of Elantrians—men, on both sides, that Raoden should have been able to protect.

Either way, I'm a failure, Raoden thought.

SARENE could tell something was wrong, but she wasn't sure what it could be. Spirit was nervous, his friendly banter subdued. It wasn't her—it was something else. Perhaps some burden of leadership.

She wanted to ask him what it was. She moved through the now familiar routine of food distribution, Spirit's worry making her nervous. Each time he approached to accept an item from the cart, she looked into his eyes and saw his tension. She couldn't force herself to ask about the problem. She had gone too long feigning coldness, too long rebuffing his attempts at friendship. Just as in Teod, she had locked herself into a role. And, just as before, she cursed herself, not quite knowing how to escape her self-imposed indifference.

Fortunately, Spirit didn't share her same inhibitions. As the noblemen gathered to begin the handouts, Spirit pulled Sarene aside, walking just a short distance from the main group.

She eyed him curiously. "What?"

Spirit glanced back at the collection of noblemen, and even a few noblewomen, who were waiting for the Elantrians to approach and receive their food. Finally, he turned to Sarene. "Something might happen today," he said.

"What?" she asked, frowning.

"Do you remember how I told you that not all Elantrians were as docile as the ones here?"

"Yes," Sarene said slowly. *What's your trick, Spirit? What game are you playing?* He seemed so honest, so earnest. Yet, she couldn't help worrying that he was just toying with her.

"Well, just . . ." Spirit said. "Just be ready. Keep your guards close."

Sarene frowned. She sensed a new emotion in his eyes—something she hadn't seen in him before. Guilt.

As he turned back toward the food line, leaving his foreboding words ringing in her mind, a part of Sarene was suddenly grateful that she had remained aloof. He was hiding something from her—something big. Her political senses warned her to be wary.

Whatever he had been expecting, however, it didn't come. By the time they had begun handing out food, Spirit had relaxed somewhat, speaking cheerfully. Sarene began to think that he had made a big show out of nothing.

Then the yelling began.

RAODEN cursed, dropping his bag of food as he heard the howl. It was close—far too close. A moment later he saw Saolin's beleaguered form appear at the mouth of an alley. The soldier was swinging his sword wildly at four separate opponents. One of the wildmen smashed a cudgel against Saolin's legs, and the soldier fell.

Then Shaor's men were upon them.

They spilled out of every alleyway—nearly two dozen howling madmen. The Elantris City Guards jumped up in surprise, startled from their leisurely idling near the gate, but they were too slow. Shaor's men leapt toward the group of aristocrats and Elantrians, their mouths open savagely.

Then Eondel appeared. By some fortune of chance, he had chosen to accompany Sarene on the day's trip and, as always, he had worn his sword—defying convention in favor of safety. In this instance, his caution was well placed.

Shaor's men weren't expecting resistance, and they stumbled over themselves before the general's swinging blade. Despite his accumulating years, Eondel fought with spry dexterity, beheading two wildmen in one breath. Eondel's weapon, powered by healthy muscles, easily cut through the Elantrian flesh. His attack slowed the wildmen long enough for the Guards to join the battle, and they formed a line beside him.

Finally realizing that they were in danger, the nobles began to scream. Fortunately, they were only a few steps away from the gate, and they easily fled the chaos. Soon only Raoden and Sarene remained, looking at each other through the battle.

One of Shaor's followers fell at their feet, knocking over a carton of grain mush. The creature's belly was sliced waist to neck, and his arms flailed awkwardly, mixing the white mush paste with the slime of the cobblestones. His lips trembled as he stared upward.

"Food. We only wanted a little food. Food . . ." the madman said, beginning the mantra of a Hoed.

Sarene looked down at the creature, then took a step back.

When she looked back up at Raoden, her eyes shone with the icy rage of betrayal.

"You held food back from them, didn't you?" she demanded.

Raoden nodded slowly, making no excuse. "I did."

"You tyrant!" she hissed. "You heartless despot!"

Raoden turned to look at Shaor's desperate men. In a way, she was right. "Yes. I am."

Sarene took another step backward. However, she stumbled against something. Raoden reached out to steady her, but then stopped as he realized what had tripped her. It was a sack of food, one of the overstuffed bags Raoden had prepared for the Hoed. Sarene looked down as well, realization dawning.

"I almost started trusting you," Sarene said bitterly. Then she was gone, dashing toward the gate as the soldiers fell back. Shaor's men did not follow, instead falling on the bounty that the nobles had abandoned.

Raoden stepped back from the food. Shaor's men didn't even seem to notice him as they tore into the scattered supplies, stuffing their faces with dirty hands. Raoden watched them with tired eyes. It was over. The nobles would not enter Elantris again. At least none of them had been killed.

Then he remembered Saolin. Raoden dashed across the courtyard to kneel beside his friend. The old soldier stared sightlessly into the sky, his head rocking back and forth as he mumbled, "Failed my lord. Failed my lord Spirit. Failed, failed, failed. . . ."

Raoden moaned, bowing his head in despair. *What have I done?* he wondered, helplessly cradling the newly made Hoed.

Raoden stayed there, lost in sorrow until long after Shaor's men had taken the last of the food and run off. Eventually, an incongruous sound brought him out of his grief.

The gates of Elantris were opening again.

CHAPTER 29

M Y lady, are you injured?" Ashe's deep voice was wrought with concern.

Sarene tried to wipe her eyes, but the tears kept coming. "No," she said through her quiet sobs. "I'm fine."

Obviously unconvinced, the Seon floated around her in a slow semicircle, searching for any outward signs of injury. Houses and shops passed quickly beyond the carriage window as the vehicle sped them back to the palace. Eondel, the carriage's owner, had stayed behind at the gate.

"My lady," Ashe said, his tone frank. "What is wrong?"

"I was right, Ashe," she said, trying to laugh at her stupidity through the tears. "I should be happy; I was right about him all along."

"Spirit?"

Sarene nodded, then rested her head against the back of the seat, staring up at the carriage's ceiling. "He was withholding food from the people. You should have seen them, Ashe—their starvation had driven them mad. Spirit's warriors kept them away from the courtyard, but they must have finally gotten hungry enough to fight back. I can't imagine how they did it—they didn't have armor or swords, just their hunger. He didn't even try to deny it. He just stood there, watching his schemes fall apart, a stash of hoarded food at his feet."

Sarene raised her hands to her face, holding her head in frustration. "Why am I *so stupid?*"

Ashe pulsed with concern.

"I knew what he was doing. Why does it bother me to find

out I was right?" Sarene took a deep breath, but it caught in her throat. Ashe had been right: She had allowed herself to get too caught up in Spirit and Elantris. She had become too emotionally involved to act on her suspicions.

The result was a disaster. The nobility had responded to Elantrian pain and wretchedness. Long-held prejudices had weakened, the Korathi teachings of temperate understanding proving their influence. Now, however, the nobility would only remember that they had been attacked. Sarene could only thank Domi that none of them had been hurt.

Sarene's thinking was interrupted by the sounds of armor clinking outside of her window. Recouping her composure the best she could, Sarene poked her head out the window to see what was causing the ruckus. A double line of men in chain and leather marched past her carriage, their livery black and red. It was Iadon's personal guard, and they were heading for Elantris.

Sarene felt a chill as she watched the grim-faced warriors. "Idos Domi," she whispered. There was hardness in these men's eyes—they were prepared to kill. To slaughter.

AT first, the coachman resisted Sarene's commands that he drive more quickly, but few men found it easy to resist a determined Teoish princess. They arrived at the palace shortly, and Sarene hopped from the carriage without waiting for the coachman to pull down the steps.

Her reputation with the palace staff was growing, and most knew to get out of her way as she stalked through the hallways. The guards at Iadon's study were also growing used to her, and they simply sighed resignedly as they pushed open the doors for her.

The king's face fell visibly as she entered. "Whatever it is, it will wait. We have a crisis—"

Sarene slammed her open palms down on Iadon's desk, shaking the wood and knocking over the penstand. "What in the blessed name of Domi do you think you're doing?"

Iadon reddened with frustrated anger, standing. "There has been an attack on members of my court! It is my duty to respond."

"Don't preach to me about duty, Iadon," Sarene countered. "You've been looking for an excuse to destroy Elantris for ten years now—only the people's superstitions kept you back."

"Your point?" he asked coldly.

"I am not going to be the one who gives you that excuse!" she said. "Withdraw your men."

Iadon snorted. "You of all people should appreciate the quickness of my response, Princess. It was your honor that was slighted by that attack."

"I'm perfectly capable of protecting my own honor, *Iadon*. Those troops move in direct opposition to everything I've accomplished these last few weeks."

"It was a fool's project, anyway," Iadon declared, dropping a collection of papers to the table. The top sheet ruffled from the motion, and Sarene could read its scribbled commands. The words "Elantris's" and "extermination" stood out, stark and foreboding.

"Go back to your room, Sarene," the king said. "This will all be over in a matter of hours."

For the first time Sarene realized how she must look, her face red and mussed from the tears, her simple monochrome dress stained with sweat and Elantris grime, and her disheveled hair pulled back into an unraveling braid.

The moment of insecurity disappeared as she looked back at the king and saw the satisfaction in his eyes. He would massacre the entire group of starving, helpless people in Elantris. He would kill Spirit. All because of her.

"You listen to me, Iadon," Sarene said, her voice sharp and cold. She held the king's eyes, drawing upon her nearly six-foot height to tower over the shorter man. "You *will* withdraw your soldiers from Elantris. You *will* leave those people alone. Otherwise, I will begin to tell people what I know about you."

Iadon snorted.

"Defiance, Iadon?" she asked. "I think you'll feel differently when everyone knows the truth. You know they already think you a fool. They pretend to obey you, but you know— you know in that whispering part of your heart that they mock you with their obedience. You think they didn't hear

about your lost ships? You think they weren't laughing to
themselves at how their king would soon be as poor as a
baron? Oh, they knew. How will you face them, Iadon, when
they learn how you *really* survived? When I show them how
I rescued your income, how I gave you the contracts in Teod,
how *I* saved your crown."

As she spoke, she punctuated each remark by stabbing her
finger at his chest. Beads of sweat appeared on his brow as
he began to crack beneath her unyielding gaze.

"You are a fool, Iadon," she hissed. "I know it, your nobles
know it, and the world knows it. You have taken a great nation
and squashed it in your greedy hands. You have enslaved the
people and you have defiled Arelon's honor. And, despite it
all, your country grows poorer. Even you, the king, are so des-
titute that only a gift from Teod lets you keep your crown."

Iadon shied away unnerved. The king seemed to shrink,
his arrogant act withering before her anger.

"How will it look, Iadon?" she whispered. "How will it
feel to have the entire court know you are indebted to a
woman? A foolish girl at that? You would be revealed.
Everyone would know what you are. Nothing more than an
insecure, trivial, incapable invalid."

Iadon plopped down into his seat. Sarene handed him a pen.

"Repeal it," she demanded.

His fingers shook as he scribbled a countermand at the
bottom of the page, then stamped it with his personal seal.

Sarene snatched up the paper, then stalked from the room.
"Ashe, stop those soldiers! Tell them new orders are coming."

"Yes, my lady," the Seon replied, shooting down the corridor toward a window, moving more quickly than even a gal-
loping horse.

"You!" Sarene ordered, slapping the rolled-up sheet of
paper against a guard's breastplate. "Take this to Elantris."

The man accepted the paper uncertainly.

"Run!" Sarene ordered.

He did.

Sarene folded her arms, watching the man dash down the
hallway. Then she turned to regard the second guard. He began to twitch nervously beneath her gaze.

"Um, I'll make sure he gets there," the man stuttered, then took off behind his companion.

Sarene stood for a moment, then turned back to the king's study, pulling the doors closed. She was left with the sight of Iadon, slumped in his chair, elbows on the desktop and head cradled in his hands. The king was sobbing quietly to himself.

BY the time Sarene reached Elantris, the new orders had long since arrived. Iadon's guard stood uncertainly before the gates. She told them to go home, but their captain refused, claiming that he had received orders not to attack, but he didn't have any orders to return. A short time later a courier arrived, delivering commands to do just that. The captain shot her an irritable look, then ordered his men back to the palace.

Sarene stayed a little longer, making the strenuous climb to the top of the wall to gaze down at the courtyard. Her food cart stood abandoned in the center of the square, overturned with broken boxes running in a jagged line before it. There were bodies, too—fallen members of the attacking party, their corpses rotting in the muck.

Sarene froze, her muscles stiffening. One of the corpses was still moving. She leaned over the stone railing, staring down at the fallen man. The distance was great, but she could still see the distinct lines of the man's legs—lying a dozen feet from his chest. Some powerful blow had separated him at the waist. There was no way he could have survived such a wound. Yet, insanely, his arms waved in the air with hopeless randomness.

"Merciful Domi," Sarene whispered, her hand rising to her breast, her fingers seeking out her small Korathi pendant. She scanned the courtyard with disbelieving eyes. Some of the other bodies were moving as well, despite horrible wounds.

They say that the Elantrians are dead, she realized. *That they are the deceased whose minds refuse to rest.* Her eyes open for the first time, Sarene realized how the Elantrians survived without food. *They didn't need to eat.*

But, why then did they?

Sarene shook her head, trying to clear her mind of both confusion and the struggling corpses below. As she did so, her eyes fell on another figure. It knelt in the shadow of Elantris's wall, its posture somehow bespeaking incredible sorrow. Sarene felt herself drawn along the walkway in the direction of the form, her hand dragging along the stone railing. She stopped when she stood above him.

Somehow she knew the figure belonged to Spirit. He was clutching a body in his arms, rocking back and forth with his head bowed. The message was clear: Even a tyrant could love those who followed him.

I saved you, Sarene thought. *The king would have destroyed you, but I saved your life. It wasn't for you, Spirit. It was for all those poor people that you rule over.*

Spirit didn't notice her.

She tried to remain angry at him. However, looking down and sensing his agony, she couldn't lie—even to herself. The day's events disturbed her for several reasons. She was angry at having her plans disrupted. She regretted that she would no longer be able to feed the struggling Elantrians. She was unhappy with the way the aristocracy would see Elantris.

But she was also saddened that she would never be able to see him again. Tyrant or not, he had seemed like a good man. Perhaps . . . perhaps only a tyrant could lead in a place like Elantris. Perhaps he was the best that the people had.

Regardless, she would probably never see him again. She would never again look into those eyes that, despite the emaciated form of his body, seemed so vibrant and alive. There was a complexity in them that she would never be able to unravel.

It was over.

SHE sought refuge in the only place in Kae she felt safe. Kiin let her in, then held her as she fell into his arms. It was a perfectly humiliating end to a very emotional day. However, the hug was worth it. She had decided as a child that her uncle was very good at hugging, his broad arms and enormous chest sufficient to envelope even a tall and gangly girl.

Sarene finally released him, wiping her eyes, disappointed in herself for crying again. Kiin simply placed a large hand on her shoulder and led her into the dining room, where the rest of the family sat around the table, even Adien.

Lukel had been talking animatedly, but he cut off as he saw Sarene. "Speak the name of the lion," he said, quoting a Jindoeese proverb, "and he will come to feast."

Adien's haunted, slightly unfocused eyes found her face. "Six hundred and seventy-two steps from here to Elantris," he whispered.

There was silence for a moment. Then Kaise jumped up onto her chair. "Sarene! Did they really try and eat you?"

"No, Kaise," Sarene replied, finding a seat. "They just wanted some of our food."

"Kaise, leave your cousin alone," Daora ordered firmly. "She has had a full day."

"And I missed it," Kaise said sullenly, plopping down in her seat. Then she turned angry eyes on her brother. "Why did *you* have to get sick?"

"It wasn't my fault," Daorn protested, still a little wan. He didn't seem very disappointed to have missed the battle.

"Hush, children," Daora repeated.

"It's all right," Sarene said. "I can talk about it."

"Well, then," Lukel said, "is it true?"

"Yes," Sarene said. "Some Elantrians attacked us, but no one got hurt—at least, not on our side."

"No," Lukel said. "Not that—I meant about the king. Is it true that you yelled him into submission?"

Sarene grew sick. "That got out?"

Lukel laughed. "They say your voice carried all the way to the main hall. Iadon still hasn't left his study."

"I might have gotten a little carried away," Sarene said.

"You did the right thing, dear," Daora assured her. "Iadon is far too accustomed to having the court jump when he so much as sneezes. He probably didn't know what to do when someone actually stood up to him."

"It wasn't that hard," Sarene said with a shake of her head. "Beneath all the bluster he's very insecure."

"Most men are, dear," Daora said.

Lukel chuckled. "Cousin, what did we ever do without you? Life was so boring before you decided to sail over and mess it all up for us."

"I would rather it stayed a little less messed up," Sarene mumbled. "Iadon isn't going to react too well when he recovers."

"If he gets out of line, you can always just yell at him again," Lukel said.

"No," Kiin said, his gruff voice solemn. "She's right. Monarchs can't afford to be reprimanded in public. We might have a much harder time of things when this is all through."

"Either that or he'll just give up and abdicate in favor of Sarene," Lukel said with a laugh.

"Just as your father feared," Ashe's deep voice noted as he floated in the window. "He always worried that Arelon wouldn't be able to deal with you, my lady."

Sarene smiled feebly. "Did they go back?"

"They did," the Seon said. She had sent him to follow Iadon's guards, in case they decided to ignore their orders. "The captain immediately went to see the king. He left when His Majesty refused to open his doors."

"It wouldn't do for a soldier to see his king bawling like a child," Lukel noted.

"Anyway," the Seon continued, "I—"

He was interrupted by an insistent knock at the door. Kiin disappeared, then returned with an eager Lord Shuden.

"My lady," he said bowing slightly to Sarene. Then he turned to Lukel. "I just heard some very interesting news."

"It's all true," Lukel said. "We asked Sarene."

Shuden shook his head. "It isn't about that."

Sarene looked up with concern. "What *else* could possibly happen today?"

Shuden's eyes twinkled. "You'll never guess who the Shaod took last night."

CHAPTER 30

HRATHEN didn't try to hide his transformation. He walked solemnly from his chambers, exposing his damnation to the entire chapel. Dilaf was in the middle of morning services. It was worth the loss of hair and skin color to see the short Arelish priest stumble backward in horrified shock.

The Korathi priests came for Hrathen a short time later. They gave him a large, enveloping white robe to hide his disfiguration, then led him from the now empty chapel. Hrathen smiled to himself as he saw the confused Dilaf watching from his alcove, his eyes openly hating Hrathen for the first time.

The Korathi priests took him to their chapel, stripped him, and washed his now black-spotted body with water from the Aredel river. Then they wrapped him in a white robe constructed of thick, raglike strips of cloth. After washing and clothing him, the priests stepped back and allowed Omin to approach. The short, balding leader of Arelish Korathi blessed Hrathen quietly, tracing the symbol of Aon Omi on his chest. The Arelish man's eyes betrayed just a hint of satisfaction.

After that, they led Hrathen through the city streets, chanting. However, at the city itself they found a large squadron of troops wearing Iadon's colors blocking their path. The soldiers stood with hands on weapons, speaking in hushed tones. Hrathen regarded them with surprise; he recognized men preparing for battle. Omin argued with the captain of the Elantris City Guard for a time while the other priests pulled Hrathen into a squat building beside the guardhouse—a holding place, carved with Aon Omi.

Hrathen watched through the room's small window as two winded guards galloped up and presented Iadon's soldiers with a rolled-up sheet of paper. The captain read it, frowning, then turned to argue with the messenger. After this Omin returned, explaining that they would have to wait.

And wait they did—the better part of two hours.

Hrathen had heard that the priests would only throw people into Elantris during a certain time of day, but apparently it was a window of time, and not a specific moment. Eventually, the priests stuffed a small basket of food in Hrathen's arms, offered one final prayer to their pitiful god, and pushed him through the gates.

He stood in the city, his head bald, his skin tainted with large black splotches. An Elantrian. The city was much the same at eye level as it had been from the wall—filthy, rotting, and unholy. It held nothing for him. He spun around, tossing aside the meager basket of food and dropping to his knees.

"Oh, Jaddeth, Lord of all Creation," he began, his voice loud and firm. "Hear now the petition of a servant in your empire. Lift this taint from my blood. Restore me to life. I implore you with all the power of my position as a holy gyorn."

There was no response. So, he repeated the prayer. Again, and again, and again. . . .

CHAPTER 31

$$SAOLIN$$ didn't open his eyes as he sank into the pool, but he did stop mumbling. He bobbed for a moment, then took a sharp breath, reaching his hands toward the heavens. After that, he melted into the blue liquid.

Raoden watched the process solemnly. They had waited for three days, hoping against all that the grizzled soldier would regain his wits. He had not. They had brought him to the pool partially because his wound was so terrible, and partially because Raoden knew that he could never enter the Hall of the Fallen with Saolin inside. The mantra "I have failed my lord Spirit" would have been too much.

"Come, sule," Galladon said. "He's gone."

"Yes, he is," Raoden said. *And it's my fault.* For once, the burdens and agonies of his body seemed insignificant compared with those of his soul.

THEY returned to him. First as a trickle, then as a flood. It took days for them to realize, and believe, that Sarene wasn't going to return. No more handouts—no more eating, waiting, and eating again. Then they came back, as if suddenly awakened from a stupor, remembering that once—not so long ago—there had been purpose in their lives.

Raoden turned them back to their old jobs—cleaning, farming, and building. With proper tools and materials, the work became less an exercise in intentional time wasting and more a productive means of rebuilding New Elantris. Piecemeal roofs were replaced with more durable, functional creations. Additional seed corn provided a chance for a second planting, one much larger and ambitious than the first. The short wall around New Elantris was reinforced and expanded—though, for the moment, Shaor's men remained quiet. Raoden knew, however, that the food they had gathered from Sarene's cart wouldn't last long. The wildmen would return.

The numbers that came to him after Sarene were much greater than those that had followed him before. Raoden was forced to acknowledge that despite the temporary setbacks they caused, Sarene's excursions into Elantris had ultimately been beneficial. She had proven to the people that no matter how much their hunger hurt, simply feeding their bellies wasn't enough. Joy was more than just an absence of discomfort.

So, when they came back to him, they no longer worked for food. They worked because they feared what they would become if they did not.

"HE shouldn't be here, Galladon," Raoden said as he studied the Fjordell priest from atop their garden-roof observation point.

"You're certain that's the gyorn?" Galladon asked.

"He says so in that prayer of his. Besides, he's definitely Fjordell. That frame of his is too large to be Aonic."

"Fjordells don't get taken by the Shaod," Galladon said stubbornly. "Only people from Arelon, Teod, and occasionally Duladel."

"I know," Raoden said, sitting back in frustration. "Perhaps it's just percentages. There aren't many Fjordells in Arelon—perhaps that's why they never get taken."

Galladon shook his head. "Then why don't Jindos ever get taken? There's plenty of them living along the spice route."

"I don't know," Raoden said.

"Listen to him pray, sule," Galladon said scoffingly. "As if the rest of us hadn't tried that already."

"I wonder how long he'll wait."

"Three days already," Galladon said. "Must be starting to get hungry. Kolo?"

Raoden nodded. Even after three days of almost continual prayer, the gyorn's voice was firm. Everything else considered, Raoden had to respect the man's determination.

"Well, when he finally realizes he's not getting anywhere, we'll invite him to join us," Raoden said.

"Trouble, sule," Galladon warned. Raoden followed the Dula's gesture, picking out a few huddled shapes in the shadows to the gyorn's left.

Raoden cursed, watching Shaor's men slink from the alleyway. Apparently, their food had run out even more quickly than Raoden had assumed. They had probably returned to the courtyard to look for scraps, but they found something much more promising: the still full basket of food at the gyorn's feet.

"Come on," Raoden urged, turning to climb down from the roof. There was a time when Shaor's men might have gone directly for the food. However, recent events had changed the wild men. They had begun wounding indiscriminately—as if they had realized that the fewer mouths opposed them, the more likely they were to get food.

"Doloken burn me for helping a gyorn," Galladon muttered, following. Unfortunately, he and Raoden moved too slowly. They were too late . . . to save Shaor's men.

Raoden rounded the side of the building as the first wildman jumped at the gyorn's back. The Fjordell leapt to his feet, spinning with near-inhuman speed and catching Shaor's man by the head. There was a snap as the gyorn cracked his opponent's neck, then threw him against the wooden gate. The other two attacked in unison. One met with a powerful spinning kick that tossed him across the courtyard like a pile of rags. The other received three successive punches to the face, then a kick to the midsection. The madman's howl of rage cut off with a whine as the gyorn placed another kick at the side of the man's head.

Raoden stumbled to a halt, mouth half open.

Galladon snorted. "Should have realized. Derethi priests can take care of themselves. Kolo?"

Raoden nodded slowly, watching the priest return smoothly to his knees and resume his prayers. Raoden had heard that all Derethi priests were trained in the infamous monasteries of Fjorden, where they were required to undergo vigorous physical training. However, he hadn't realized that a middle-aged gyorn would maintain his skills.

The two wildmen who could still move crawled away, while the other one lay where the gyorn had tossed him, whimpering pitifully with his broken neck.

"It's a waste," Raoden whispered. "We could have used those men back in New Elantris."

"I don't see what we can do about it," Galladon said with a shake of his head.

Raoden stood, turning toward the market section of Elantris. "I do," he said with determination.

THEY penetrated Shaor's territory so quickly and directly that they got nearly to the bank before they were noticed. Raoden didn't respond when Shaor's men began to howl—he continued to walk, resolute, focused on his goal. Galladon, Karata, and Dashe—Karata's former second was one of the few experienced fighting men left in Raoden's camp—accompanied him. Each nervously carried a medium-sized sack in his arms.

Shaor's men followed them, cutting off their escape. After the losses they had received over the last few weeks, there could only be a couple of dozen men left in Shaor's band, but those few seemed to multiply and shift in the shadows.

Galladon shot Raoden an apprehensive look. Raoden could tell what he was thinking. *You'd better be sure as Doloken you know what you're doing, sule. . . .*

Raoden set his jaw firmly. He had only a single hope—his belief in the rational nature of the human soul.

Shaor was much the same as before. Though her men must have delivered some of their spoils to her, one would never have known it from her screaming. "Bring me food!" she wailed, her voice audible long before they entered the bank. "I want food!"

Raoden led his small group into the bank. Shaor's remaining followers filed in behind, approaching slowly, waiting for their goddess's inevitable command to kill the intruders.

Raoden moved first. He nodded to the others, and each dropped their sacks. Corn spilled across the uneven floor of the bank, mixing with the slime and falling into cracks and crevices. Howls sounded behind them, and Raoden waved his people to the side as Shaor's men descended upon the corn.

"Kill them!" Shaor yelled belatedly, but her followers were too busy stuffing their mouths.

Raoden and the others left as simply as they had come.

THE first one approached New Elantris barely a few hours later. Raoden stood beside the large fire they had kindled atop one of the taller buildings. The blaze required many of their precious wood scraps, and Galladon had been against it from the start. Raoden ignored the objections. Shaor's men needed to see the fire to make the connection—the leap that would bring them back to sensibility.

The first wild man appeared out of the evening's darkness. He moved furtively, his stance nervous and bestial. He cradled a ripped sack, a couple of handfuls of grain clutched within.

Raoden motioned for his warriors to move back. "What do you want?" he asked the madman.

The man stared back dumbly.

"I know you understand me," Raoden said. "You can't have been in here long—six months at the most. That's not enough to forget language, even if you want to convince yourself that it is."

The man held up the sack, his hands glistening with slime.

"What?" Raoden insisted.

"Cook," the man finally said.

The grain they'd dropped had been seed corn, hardened over the winter to be planted in spring. Though they had most certainly tried, Shaor's men wouldn't have been able to chew or swallow it without great pain.

And so, Raoden had hoped that somewhere in the back of their abandoned minds, these men would remember that they had once been human. Hoped that they would recall civilization, and the ability to cook. Hoped they would confront their humanity.

"I won't cook your food for you," Raoden said. "But I will let you do it yourself."

CHAPTER 32

"SO, you've returned to wearing black, have you, my dear?" Duke Roial asked as he helped her into the carriage.

Sarene looked down at her dress. It wasn't one that Eshen had sent her, but something she'd asked Shuden to bring up on one of his caravans through Duladel. Less full than most current trends in Arelish fashion, it hugged tightly to her form. The soft velvet was embroidered with tiny silver patterns, and rather than a cape it had a short mantle that covered her shoulders and upper arms.

"It's actually blue, Your Grace," she said. "I never wear black."

"Ah." The older man was dressed in a white suit with a deep maroon undercoat. The outfit worked well with his carefully styled head of white hair.

The coachman closed the door and climbed into his place. A short moment later they were on their way to the ball.

Sarene stared out at the dark streets of Kae, her mood tolerant, but unhappy. She couldn't, of course, refuse to attend the ball—Roial had agreed to throw it at her suggestion. However, she had made those plans a week ago, before events in Elantris. The last three days had been devoted to reflection; she had spent them trying to work through her feelings and reorganize her plans. She didn't want to bother with a night of frivolities, even if there was a point behind it.

"You look at ill-ease, Your Highness," Roial said.

"I haven't quite recovered from what happened the other day, Your Grace," she said, leaning back in her seat.

"The day was rather overwhelming," he agreed. Then, leaning his head out the carriage's window, he checked the sky. "It is a beautiful night for our purposes."

Sarene nodded absently. It no longer mattered to her whether the eclipse would be visible or not. Ever since her tirade before Iadon, the entire court had begun to step lightly around her. Instead of growing angry as Kiin had predicted, Iadon simply avoided her. Whenever Sarene entered a room, heads turned away and eyes looked down. It was as if she were a monster—a vengeful Svrakiss sent to torment them.

The servants were no better. Where they had once been subservient, now they cringed. Her dinner had come late, and though the cook insisted it was because one of her serving women had suddenly run off, Sarene was certain it was simply because no one wanted to face the fearful princess's wrath. The entire situation was putting Sarene on edge. *Why, in the blessed name of Domi,* she wondered, *does everyone in this country feel so threatened by an assertive woman?*

Of course, this time she had to admit that woman or not, what she had done to the king had been too forward. Sarene was just paying the price for her loss of temper.

"All right, Sarene," Roial declared. "That is enough."

Sarene started, looking up at the elderly duke's stern face. "Excuse me, Your Grace?"

"I said it's enough. By all reports, you've spent the last three days moping in your room. I don't care how emotionally disturbing that attack in Elantris was, you need to get over it—and quickly. We're almost to my mansion."

"Excuse me?" she said again, taken aback.

"Sarene," Roial continued, his voice softening, "we didn't ask for your leadership. You wiggled your way in and seized control. Now that you've done so, you can't just leave us because of injured feelings. When you accept authority, you must be willing to take responsibility for it at all times— even when you don't particularly feel like it."

Suddenly abashed by the duke's wisdom, Sarene lowered her eyes in shame. "I'm sorry."

"Ah, Princess," Roial said, "we've come to rely on you so much in these last few weeks. You crept into our hearts and did what no one else, even myself, could have done—you unified us. Shuden and Eondel all but worship you, Lukel and Kiin stand by your side like two unmoving stones, I can barely unravel your delicate schemes, and even Ahan describes you as the most delightful young woman he's ever met. Don't leave us now—we need you."

Flushing slightly, Sarene shook her head as the carriage pulled up Roial's drive. "But what is left, Your Grace? Through no cleverness of my own, the Derethi gyorn has been neutralized, and it appears that Iadon has been quelled. It seems to me that the time of danger has passed."

Roial raised a bushy white eyebrow. "Perhaps. But Iadon is more clever than we usually credit. The king has some overwhelming blind spots, but he was capable enough to seize control ten years ago, and he has kept the aristocracy at one another's throats all this time. And as for the gyorn . . ."

Roial looked out the carriage window, toward a vehicle pulling up next to them. Inside was a short man dressed completely in red; Sarene recognized the young Aonic priest who had served as Hrathen's assistant.

Roial frowned. "I think we may have traded Hrathen for a foe of equal danger."

"Him?" Sarene asked with surprise. She'd seen the young man with Hrathen, of course—even remarked on his apparent fervor. However, he could hardly be as dangerous as the calculating gyorn, could he?

"I've been watching that one," the duke said. "His name is Dilaf—he's Arelish, which means he was probably raised Korathi. I've noticed that those who turn away from a faith are often more hateful toward it than any outsider could be."

"You might be right, Your Grace," Sarene admitted. "We'll have to change our plans. We can't deal with this one the same way we did Hrathen."

Roial smiled, a slight twinkle in his eyes. "That's the girl I remember. Come; it wouldn't do for me to be late to my own party."

Roial had decided to have the eclipse-observation party on the grounds behind his house—an action necessitated by the relative modesty of his home. For the third-richest man in Arelon, the duke was remarkably frugal.

"I've only been a duke for ten years, Sarene," Roial had explained when she first visited his home, "but I've been a businessman all my life. You don't make money by being wasteful. The house suits me—I fear I'd get lost in anything larger."

The grounds surrounding the home, however, were extensive—a luxury Roial admitted was a bit extravagant. The duke was a lover of gardens, and he spent more time outside wandering his grounds than he did in his house.

Fortunately, the weather had decided to comply with the duke's plans, providing a warm breeze from the south and a completely cloudless sky. Stars splattered the sky like specks of paint on a black canvas, and Sarene found her eyes tracing the constellations of the major Aons. Rao shone directly overhead, a large square with four circles at its sides and a dot in the center. Her own Aon, Ene, crouched barely visible on the horizon. The full moon rose ponderously toward its zenith. In just a few hours it would vanish completely—or, at least, that was what the astronomers claimed.

"So," Roial said, walking at her side, their arms linked, "are you going to tell me what this is all about?"

"What what's all about?"

"The ball," Roial said. "You can't claim that you had me organize it on a whim. You were much too specific about the date and location. What are you planning?"

Sarene smiled, rekindling the night's schemes. She had nearly forgotten about the party, but the more she considered it, the more excited she became. Before this night was over, she hoped to find the answer to a problem that had been bothering her almost since she'd arrived in Arelon.

"Let's just say I wanted to view the eclipse with company," she said with a sly smile.

"Ah, Sarene, ever dramatic. You've missed your calling in life, my dear—you should have been an actress."

"As a matter of fact, I considered it once," Sarene said reminiscently. "Of course, I was eleven years old at the time. A troop of players came through Teoin. After watching them, I informed my parents that I had decided not to grow up to be a princess, but an actress instead."

Roial laughed. "I would like to have seen old Eventeo's face when his prize daughter told him she wanted to become a traveling performer."

"You know my father?"

"Really, Sarene," Roial said with indignation, "I haven't been old and senile all my life. There was a time when I traveled, and every good merchant has a few contacts in Teod. I've had two audiences with your father, and both times he mocked my wardrobe."

Sarene chuckled. "He's merciless with visiting merchants."

Roial's grounds centered around a large courtyardlike patch of grass overlaid by a wooden dancing pavilion. Hedge-walled pathways led away from the pavilion, toward newly blooming flower beds, bridge-covered ponds, and sculpture displays. Torches lined the pavilion, providing full illumination. These would, of course, be doused prior to the eclipse. However, if things went as Sarene planned, she wouldn't be there to see it.

"The king!" Sarene exclaimed. "Is he here?"

"Of course," Roial said, pointing toward an enclosed sculpture garden to one side of the pavilion. Sarene could barely make out the form of Iadon inside, Eshen at his side.

Sarene relaxed. Iadon was the whole point of the night's activities. Of course, the king's pride wouldn't let him miss a ball thrown by one of his dukes. If he had attended Telrii's party, he would certainly make it to Roial's.

"What could the king have to do with little Sarene's schemes?" Roial mused to himself. "Maybe she sent someone to peruse his chambers while he's away. Her Seon, perhaps?"

However, at that moment Ashe floated into view a short distance away. Sarene shot Roial a sly look.

"All right, perhaps it wasn't the Seon," Roial said. "That would be too obvious anyway."

"My lady," Ashe said, bobbing in greeting as he approached.

"What did you find out?" Sarene asked.

"The cook did indeed lose a serving woman this afternoon, my lady. They claim she ran off to be with her brother, who was recently moved to one of the king's provincial mansions. The man, however, swears he hasn't seen anything of her."

Sarene frowned. Perhaps she had been too quick in judging the cook and her minions. "All right. Good work."

"What was that about?" Roial asked suspiciously.

"Nothing," Sarene said, this time completely honest.

Roial, however, nodded knowingly.

The problem with being clever, Sarene thought with a sigh, *is that everyone assumes you're always planning something.*

"Ashe, I want you to keep an eye on the king," Sarene said, aware of Roial's curious smile. "He'll probably spend most of his time in his exclusive portion of the party. If he decides to move, tell me immediately."

"Yes, my lady," Ashe said, hovering away to take an unobtrusive place next to one of the torches, where the flame's light masked his own.

Roial nodded again. He was obviously having a delightful time trying to decipher Sarene's plans.

"So, do you feel like joining the king's private gathering?" Sarene asked, trying to divert the duke's attention.

Roial shook his head. "No. As much good as it would do me to watch Iadon squirm in your presence, I've never approved of the way he holds himself aloof. I'm the host, thanks to you, and a host should mingle. Besides, being around Iadon tonight will be intolerable—he's looking for someone to replace Baron Edan, and every minor noble at the party will make a play for the title."

"As you wish," Sarene said, allowing Roial to lead her toward the open-walled pavilion where a group of musicians was playing and some couples were dancing, though most stood talking at the perimeter.

Roial chuckled, and Sarene followed his gaze. Shuden and Torena spun near the center of the dance floor, completely captivated by one another.

"What are you laughing about?" Sarene asked, watching the fire-haired girl and the young Jindo.

"It is one of the great joys of my old age to see young men proven hypocrites," Roial said with an evil smile. "After all those years swearing that he would never let himself be caught—after endless balls spent complaining when women fawned over him—his heart, and his mind, have turned to mush as surely as any other man's."

"You're a mean old man, Your Grace."

"And that is the way it should be," Roial informed. "Mean young men are trivial, and kindly old men boring. Here, let me get us something to drink."

The duke wandered away, and Sarene was left watching the young couple dance. The look in Shuden's eyes was so sickeningly dreamy that she had to turn away. Perhaps Daora's words had been more accurate than Sarene had been willing to admit. Sarene was jealous, though not because she had assumed any romantic possibilities with Shuden. However, ever since her arrival in Arelon, Shuden had been one of her most fervent supporters. It was hard to watch him giving his attention to another woman, even for a completely different purpose.

There was another reason as well—a deeper, more honest reason. She was jealous of that look in Shuden's eyes. She was envious of his opportunity to court, to fall in love, and to be swept up in the stupefying joy of romance.

They were ideals Sarene had dreamed about since early adolescence. As she grew older, Sarene realized such things would never be hers. She had rebelled at first, cursing her offensive personality. She knew she intimidated the court's men, and so, for a short while, she had forced herself to adopt a more subservient, docile temperament. Her engagement, and near marriage, to a young count named Graeo had been the result.

She still remembered the man—more a boy—with pity. Only Graeo had been willing to take a chance on the new, even-tempered Sarene—risking the mockery of his peers. The union had not been one of love, but she had liked Graeo despite his weak will. There had been a kind of childish hesitancy about him; an overdone compulsion to do what was right, to succeed in a world where most people understood things much better than he.

In the end, she had broken off the engagement—not because she knew living with the dull-minded Graeo would have driven her mad, but because she had realized that she was being unfair. She had taken advantage of Graeo's simple ingenuousness, knowing full well he was getting himself into something far over his head. It was better he bear the scorn of being refused at the last moment than live the rest of his life with a woman who would stifle him.

The decision had sealed her fate as an unmarried spinster. Rumors spread that she had led Graeo on simply to make a fool out of him, and the embarrassed young man had left the court, living the next three years holed up on his lands like a hermit. After that, no man had dared court the king's daughter.

She'd fled Teod at that point, immersing herself in her father's diplomatic corps. She served as an envoy in all the major cities of Opelon, from Fjorden itself to the Svordish capital of Seraven. The prospect of going to Arelon had intrigued her, of course, but her father had remained adamant about his prohibition. He barely allowed spies into the country, let alone his only daughter.

Still, Sarene thought with a sigh, she had made it eventually. It was worth it, she decided; her engagement to Raoden had been a good idea, no matter how horribly it had turned out. For a while, when they had been exchanging letters, she had allowed herself to hope again. The promise had eventually been crushed, but she still had the memory of that hope. It was more than she had ever expected to obtain.

"You look as if your best friend just died," Roial noted, returning to hand her a cup of blue Jaadorian wine.

"No, just my husband," Sarene said with a sigh.

"Ah," Roial said with an understanding nod. "Perhaps we should move somewhere else—a place where we won't have such a clear view of our young baron's rapture."

"A wonderful suggestion, Your Grace," Sarene said.

They moved along the pavilion's outer border, Roial nodding to those who complimented him on the fine party. Sarene strolled along at the elderly man's side, growing increasingly confused at the dark looks she occasionally got from noblewomen they passed. It was a few minutes before she realized the reason behind the hostility; she had completely forgotten Roial's status as the most marriageable man in Arelon. Many of the women had come this night expecting the duke to be unaccompanied. They had probably planned long and hard on how to corner the old man, intent on currying his favor. Sarene had ruined any chance of that.

Roial chuckled, studying her face. "You've figured it out then, haven't you?"

"This is why you never throw parties, isn't it?"

The duke nodded. "As difficult as it is to deal with them at another man's ball, it is nearly impossible to be a good host with those vixens nipping at my hide."

"Be careful, Your Grace," Sarene said. "Shuden complained about exactly the same sort of thing the first time he took me to a ball, and look where *he* ended up."

"Shuden went about it the wrong way," Roial said. "He just ran away—and everyone knows that no matter how hard you run, there's always going to be someone faster. I, on the other hand, don't run. I find far too much enjoyment in playing with their greedy little minds."

Sarene's chastising reply was cut off by the approach of a familiar couple. Lukel wore his customarily fashionable outfit, a blue, gold-embroidered vest and tan trousers, while Jalla, his dark-haired wife, was in a simple lavender dress—Jindoeese, by the look of its high-necked cut.

"Now, there's a mismatched couple if I've ever seen one," Lukel said with an open smile as he bowed to the duke.

"What?" Roial asked. "A crusty old duke and his lovely young companion?"

"I was referring more to the height difference, Your Grace," Lukel said with a laugh.

Roial glanced up with a raised eyebrow; Sarene stood a full head taller than him. "At my age, you take what you can get."

"I think that's true no matter what your age, Your Grace," Lukel said, looking down at his pretty, black-eyed wife. "We just have to accept whatever the women decide to allot us, and count ourselves blessed for the offering."

Sarene felt sick—first Shuden, now Lukel. She was definitely *not* in the mood to deal with happy couples this night.

Sensing her disposition, the duke bid Lukel farewell, pleading the need to check on the food in other parts of the garden. Lukel and Jalla turned back to their dancing as Roial led Sarene out of the lighted pavilion and back under the darkened sky and flickering torchlight.

"You're going to need to get over that, Sarene," the duke said. "You can't go running every time you meet someone with a stable relationship."

Sarene decided not to point out that young love was hardly stable. "I don't always get this way, Your Grace. I've just had a difficult week. Give me a few more days, and I'll be back to my regular, stone-hearted self."

Sensing her bitterness, Roial wisely decided not to respond to that particular remark. Instead, he glanced to the side, following the sound of a familiar voice's laughter.

Duke Telrii had apparently decided not to join the king's private section of the party. Quite the opposite, in fact. He stood entertaining a large group of noblemen in a small hedged courtyard opposite the pavilion of Iadon's private gathering. It was almost as if he were starting his own exclusive subparty.

"Not a good sign," Roial said quietly, voicing Sarene's own thoughts.

"Agreed," Sarene said. She did a quick count of Telrii's fawners, trying to distinguish rank, then glanced back toward Iadon's section of the party. Their numbers were about equal, but Iadon seemed to command more important nobility—for the moment.

"That's another unforeseen effect of your tirade before the king," Roial said. "The more unstable Iadon becomes, the more tempting other options appear."

Sarene frowned as Telrii laughed again, his voice melodious and unconcerned. He did not at all sound like a man whose most important supporter—Gyorn Hrathen—had just fallen.

"What is he planning?" Sarene wondered. "How could he take the throne now?"

Roial just shook his head. After a moment more of contemplation, he looked up and addressed open air. "Yes?"

Sarene turned as Ashe approached. Then, with astonishment, she realized it *wasn't* Ashe. It was a different Seon.

"The gardeners report that one of your guests has fallen

into the pond, my lord," the Seon said, bobbing almost to the ground as he approached. His voice was crisp and unemotional.

"Who?" Roial asked with a chuckle.

"Lord Redeem, Your Grace," the Seon explained. "It appears the wine proved too much for him."

Sarene squinted, searching deep into the ball of light and trying to make out the glowing Aon. She thought it was Opa.

Roial sighed. "He probably scared the fish right out of the pond. Thank you, Opa. Make sure that Redeem is given some towels and a ride home, if he needs it. Next time maybe he won't mix ponds with alcohol."

The Seon bobbed formally once more, then floated away to do his master's bidding.

"You never told me you had a Seon, my lord," Sarene said.

"Many of the nobles do, Princess," Roial said, "but it is no longer fashionable to bring them along with us wherever we go. Seons are reminders of Elantris."

"So he just stays here at your house?"

Roial nodded. "Opa oversees the gardeners of my estate. I think it fitting—after all, his name does mean 'flower.'"

Sarene tapped her cheek, wondering about the stern formality in Opa's voice. The Seons she knew back in Teod were much warmer with their masters, no matter what their personality. Perhaps it was because here, in the presumed land of their creation, Seons were now regarded with suspicion and dislike.

"Come," Roial said, taking her arm. "I was serious when I said I wanted to check on the serving tables."

Sarene allowed herself to be led away.

"Roial, you old prune," a blustery voice called out as they approached the serving tables, "I'm astounded. You actually know how to throw a party! I was afraid you'd try and cram us all into that box you call a house."

"Ahan," Roial said, "I should have realized I would find you next to the food."

The large count was draped in a yellow robe and clutched a plateful of crackers and shellfish. His wife's plate, however, held only a few slices of fruit. During the weeks Seaden had been attending Sarene's fencing lessons she had lost considerable weight.

"Of course—best part of a party!" the count said with a laugh. Then, nodding to Sarene, he continued, "Your Highness. I'd warn you not to let this old scoundrel corrupt you, but I'm just as worried about you doing the same to him."

"Me?" Sarene said with mock indignation. "What danger could I be?"

Ahan snorted. "Ask the king," he said, shoving a wafer into his mouth. "Actually, you can ask me—just look what you're doing to my poor wife. She refuses to eat!"

"I'm enjoying my fruit, Ahan," Seaden said. "I think you should try some of it."

"Maybe I'll try a plate of it after I'm done here," Ahan huffed. "You see what you're doing, Sarene? I would never have agreed to this 'fencing' thing if I had known how it would ruin my wife's figure."

"Ruin?" Sarene asked with surprise.

"I'm from southern Arelon, Princess," Ahan said, reaching for some more clams. "To us, round is beautiful. Not everyone wants their women to look like starving schoolboys." Then, realizing that he might have said too much, Ahan paused. "No offense intended, of course."

Sarene frowned. Ahan really was a delightful man, but he often spoke—and acted—without thought. Unsure how to properly respond, Sarene hesitated.

The wonderful Duke Roial came to her rescue. "Well, Ahan, we have to keep moving—I have a lot of guests to greet. Oh, by the way—you might want to tell your caravan to hurry."

Ahan looked up as Roial began to lead Sarene off. "Caravan?" he asked, suddenly very serious. "What caravan?"

"Why, the one you have carrying sourmelons from Duladel to Svorden, of course," the duke said offhandedly. "I sent a shipment of them myself a week ago. It should be arriving tomorrow morning. I'm afraid, my friend, that your caravan will arrive to a saturated market—not to mention the fact that your melons will be slightly overripe."

Ahan cursed, the plate going limp in his hand, shellfish

tumbling unnoticed to the grass below. "How in the name of Domi did you manage that?"

"Oh, didn't you know?" Roial asked. "I was half partner in young Lukel's venture. I got all the unripened fruits from his shipment last week—they should be ready by the time they hit Svorden."

Ahan shook his head, laughing in a low voice. "You got me again, Roial. But just you watch—one of these days I'm finally going to get the better of you, and you'll be so surprised that you won't be able to look at yourself for a week!"

"I look forward to it," Roial said as they left the serving tables behind.

Sarene chuckled, the sound of Seaden scolding her husband rising behind. "You really are as good a businessman as they say, aren't you?"

Roial spread his hands in humility. Then he said, "Yes. Every bit as good."

Sarene laughed.

"However," Roial continued, "that young cousin of yours puts me to shame. I have no idea how he kept that sourmelon shipment a secret—my Duladen agents are supposed to inform me of such things. I only got in on the deal because Lukel came to me for capital."

"Then it's a good thing he didn't go to Ahan instead."

"A good thing indeed," Roial agreed. "I would never hear the end of it if he had. Ahan's been trying to best me for two decades now—one of these days he's going to realize I only *act* brilliant to keep him off-balance, and then life isn't going to be half as entertaining."

They continued to walk, speaking with guests and enjoying Roial's excellent gardens. The early-blooming flower beds were cleverly lit with torchlight, lanterns, and even candles. Most impressive were the crosswood trees, whose branches—leafed with pink and white blossoms—were lit from behind by lanterns running up the trunks. Sarene was enjoying herself so much that she almost lost track of time. Only Ashe's sudden appearance reminded her of the night's true purpose.

"My lady!" Ashe exclaimed. "The king is leaving the party!"

"Are you certain?" she asked, her attention snapping away from the crosswood flowers.

"Yes, my lady," Ashe said. "He left furtively, claiming he needed to use the privy, but he called his carriage instead."

"Excuse me, Your Grace," Sarene curtly told Roial. "I must be going."

"Sarene?" Roial asked with surprise as Sarene walked back toward the house. Then, more urgently, he called again. "Sarene! You can't go."

"I apologize, Your Grace, but this is important!"

He tried to follow her, but her legs were longer. In addition, the duke had a party to attend. He couldn't just disappear in the middle of it.

Sarene rounded the side of Roial's house in time to see the king climbing into his carriage. She cursed—why hadn't she thought to arrange transportation of her own? She looked around frantically, searching for a vehicle to requisition. She picked a likely candidate as the king's carriage pulled away, hooves clopping against the cobblestones.

"My lady!" Ashe warned. "The king is not in that carriage."

Sarene froze. "What?"

"He slipped out the other side and disappeared into the shadows on the far side of the driveway. The carriage is a ruse."

Sarene didn't bother to question the Seon—his senses were much more acute than those of a human. "Let's go," she said, heading in the proper direction. "I'm not dressed for sneaking; you'll have to keep watch on him and tell me where he goes."

"Yes, my lady," Ashe said, dimming his light to a nearly imperceptible level and flying after the king. Sarene followed at a slower pace.

They continued in that manner, Ashe staying close to the king and Sarene following at a less conspicuous distance. They covered the ground surrounding Roial's mansion quickly, then moved into the city of Kae. Iadon moved strictly through alleys, and Sarene realized for the first time that she might be putting herself in danger. Women didn't travel alone after dark—even in Kae, which was one of the safest cities in Opelon. She considered turning back a half-dozen times, once nearly dashing away in a panic as a drunk man moved in the darkness next to her. However, she kept going. She was only going to get one chance to find out what Iadon was up to, and her curiosity was stronger than her fear . . . for the moment at least.

Ashe, sensing the danger, advised that she let him follow the king alone, but she pressed on with determination. The Seon, accustomed to Sarene's ways, gave no further argument. He flitted back and forth between her and the king, doing his best to keep watch over Sarene while at the same time following Iadon.

Eventually, the Seon slowed, returning to Sarene with an apprehensive bob. "He just entered the sewers, my lady."

"The sewers?" Sarene asked incredulously.

"Yes, my lady. And he is not alone—he met two cloaked men just after he left the party, and was joined by a half-dozen more at the mouth of the sewers."

"And you didn't follow them in?" she asked with disappointment. "We'll never be able to tail them."

"That is unfortunate, my lady."

Sarene ground her teeth in frustration. "They'll leave tracks in the muck," she decided, stalking forward. "You should be able to follow them."

Ashe hesitated. "My lady, I must insist that you return to the duke's party."

"Not a chance, Ashe."

"I have the solemn duty of your protection, my lady," Ashe said. "I can't allow you to go climbing through refuse in the middle of the night—I was wrong to let you go this far. It is my responsibility to stop this before it goes any further."

"And how will you do that?" Sarene asked impatiently.

"I could call your father."

"Father lives in Teod, Ashe," Sarene pointed out. "What is he going to do?"

"I could go get Lord Eondel or one of the others."

"And leave me to get lost in the sewers on my own?"

"You would never do something that foolish, my lady," Ashe declared. Then he paused, hovering uncertainly in the air, his Aon so dim it was translucent. "All-right," he finally admitted. "You are indeed that foolish."

Sarene smiled. "Come on—the fresher those tracks are, the easier it will be for you to follow them."

The Seon sullenly led the way down the street, which soon ended in a dirty, fungus-lined arch. Sarene strode forward with determination, paying no heed to the damage the sludge would do to her dress.

The moonlight lasted only as far as the first turnoff. Sarene stood for a moment in the suffocating, dank blackness, realizing that even she would never have been foolish enough to enter the directionless maze without guidance. Fortunately, her bluff had convinced Ashe—though she wasn't sure whether or not to be offended by the level of arrogant idiocy of which he thought her capable.

Ashe increased his light slightly. The sewer was a hollow tube, a remnant of the days when Elantris's magic provided running water for every house in Kae. Now the sewers were used as a receptacle for trash and excrement. They were flushed out by a periodic diversion of the Aredel—something which obviously hadn't been done in a while, for the wet muck at the bottom of the corridor came up to her ankles. She didn't want to consider what that sludge must be composed of, but the pungent stink was an overpowering clue.

All of the tunnels looked the same to Sarene. One thing reassured her: the Seon sense of direction. It was impossible to get lost when accompanied by Ashe. The creatures always knew where they were, and could point the exact direction to any place they had ever been.

Ashe led the way, floating close to the muck's surface. "My lady, may I be allowed to know just how you knew the king would sneak away from Roial's party?"

"Surely you can figure it out, Ashe," she chided.

"Let me assure you, my lady, I have tried."

"Well, what day of the week is it?"

"MaeDal?" the Seon replied, leading her around a corner.

"Right. And what happens every week on MaeDal?"

Ashe didn't answer immediately. "Your father plays ShinDa with Lord Eoden?" he asked, his voice laced with uncharacteristic frustration. The night's activities—especially her belligerence—were wearing away even Ashe's formidable patience.

"No," Sarene said. "Every week on MaeDal at eleven o'clock I hear scrapings in the passage that runs through my wall—the one that leads to the king's rooms."

The Seon made a slight "ah" of understanding.

"I heard noises in the passage some other nights as well," Sarene explained. "But MaeDal was the only consistent day."

"So you had Roial throw a party tonight, expecting that the king would keep to his schedule," the Seon said.

"Right," Sarene said, trying not to slip in the muck. "And I had to make it a late party so that people would stay at least until midnight—the eclipse provided a convenient excuse. The king had to come to the party; his pride wouldn't let him stay away. However, his weekly appointment must be important, for he risked leaving early to attend it."

"My lady, I don't like this," Ashe said. "What good could the king be doing in the sewers at midnight?"

"That is exactly what I intend to find out," Sarene said, brushing away a spiderweb. One thought drove her through muck and darkness—a possibility she was barely willing to acknowledge. Perhaps Prince Raoden lived. Maybe Iadon hadn't confined him to the dungeons, but in the sewers. Sarene might not be a widow after all.

A noise came from ahead. "Turn down your light, Ashe," she said. "I think I hear voices."

He did so, becoming nearly invisible. There was an intersection just ahead, and torchlight flickered from the rightmost tunnel. Sarene approached the corner slowly, intending to peek around it. Unfortunately, she hadn't noticed that the floor declined slightly just before the intersection, and her feet slipped. She waved desperate arms, barely stabilizing herself as she slid a few feet down the incline and came to a halt at the bottom.

The motion placed her directly in the middle of the intersection. Sarene looked up slowly.

King Iadon stared back, looking as stunned as she felt.

"Merciful Domi," Sarene whispered. The king stood facing her behind an altar, a red-streaked knife raised in his hand. He was completely naked except for the blood smearing his chest. The remains of an eviscerated young woman lay tied to the altar, her torso sliced open from neck to crotch.

The knife dropped from Iadon's hand, hitting the muck below with a muffled plop. Only then did Sarene notice the dozen black-robed forms standing behind him, Duladen runes sewn into their clothing. Each one carried a long dagger. Several approached her with quick steps.

Sarene wavered between her body's urge to retch and her mind's insistence that she scream.

The scream came out on top.

She stumbled backward, slipping and splashing down into the slime. The figures rushed for her, their cowled eyes intent. Sarene kicked and struggled in the slime, still screaming as she tried to regain her feet. She almost missed the sounds of footsteps from her right.

Then Eondel was there.

The aged general's sword flashed in the dim light, cleanly slicing off an arm that was reaching for Sarene's ankle. Other figures moved through the corridor as well, men in the livery of Eondel's legion. There was also a man in a red robe—Dilaf, the Derethi priest. He didn't join the fighting, but stood to the side with a fascinated look on his face.

Dumbfounded, Sarene tried to stand again, but only ended up slipping in the sewage once more. A hand grabbed her arm, helping her up. Roial's wrinkled face smiled in relief as he pulled Sarene to her feet.

"Maybe next time you'll tell me what you are planning, Princess," he suggested.

"*YOU* told him," Sarene realized, shooting Ashe an accusatory look.

"Of course I told him, my lady," the Seon responded, pulsing slightly to punctuate the remark. She sat in Roial's study with Ashe and Lukel. Sarene wore a robe that the duke had borrowed from one of his maids. It was too short, of course, but it was better than a sewage-covered velvet dress.

"When?" Sarene demanded, leaning back in Roial's deep plush couch and wrapping herself in a blanket. The duke had ordered a bath drawn for her, and her hair was still wet, chilled in the night air.

"He called Opa as soon as you left my drive," Roial explained, walking into the room, carrying three steaming cups. He handed one to her and another to Lukel before taking a seat.

"That soon?" Sarene asked with surprise.

"I knew you would never turn back, no matter what I said," Ashe said.

"You know me too well," she muttered, taking a sip of her drink. It was Fjordell garha—which was good; she couldn't afford to fall asleep just yet.

"I will admit to that failing without argument, my lady," Ashe said.

"Then why did you try and stop me before leading me into the sewer?" she asked.

"I was stalling, my lady," Ashe explained. "The duke insisted on coming himself, and his group moved slowly."

"I might be slow, but I was not going to miss whatever you had planned, Sarene," Roial said. "They say age brings wisdom, but it only gave me a torturous case of curiosity."

"Eondel's soldiers?" Sarene asked.

"Were already at the party," Lukel said. He had insisted on knowing what had happened as soon as he saw Sarene sneaking into Roial's house, covered in slime. "I saw some of them mingling with the guests."

"I invited Eondel's officers," Roial explained. "Or, at least, the half-dozen of them that were in town."

"All right," Sarene said. "So after I ran off, Ashe called your Seon and told you I was pursuing the king."

"'The foolish girl is going off to get herself killed' were his exact words, I believe," Roial said with a chuckle.

"Ashe!"

"I apologize, my lady," the Seon said, pulsing in embarrassment. "I was rather out of sorts."

"Anyway," Sarene continued, "Ashe called Roial and he gathered Eondel and his men from the party. You all followed me to the sewers, where you had your Seon guide you."

"Until Eondel heard you screaming," Roial finished. "You are a very lucky lady to have that man's loyalty, Sarene."

"I know," Sarene said. "That's the second time this week his sword has proved useful. Next time I see Iadon, remind me to kick him for convincing the nobility that military training is beneath them."

Roial chuckled. "You might have to stand in line to do that kicking, Princess. I doubt the city's priests—Derethi or Korathi—will let the king get away with taking part in the Jeskeri Mysteries."

"And sacrificing that poor woman," Ashe said quietly.

The tone of the conversation grew subdued as they remembered just what they were discussing. Sarene shuddered at the image of the blood-covered altar and its occupant. *Ashe's right,* she thought somberly. *This is no time for joking.*

"That's what it was, then?" Lukel asked.

Sarene nodded. "The Mysteries sometimes involve sacrifices. Iadon must have wanted something very badly."

"Our Derethi friend claimed to have some knowledge on the subject," Roial said. "He seemed to think the king was petitioning the Jesker spirits to destroy someone for him."

"Me?" Sarene asked, growing cold despite her blanket.

Roial nodded. "Arteth Dilaf said the instructions were written on the altar in that woman's blood."

Sarene shivered. "Well, at least now we know what happened to the maids and cooks who disappeared from the palace."

Roial nodded. "I'd guess he's been involved with the Mysteries for a long time—perhaps even since the Reod. He was obviously the leader of that particular band."

"The others?" Sarene asked.

"Minor nobles," Roial said. "Iadon wouldn't have involved anyone who could challenge him."

"Wait a moment," Sarene said, her brows furled. "Where did that Derethi priest come from, anyway?"

Roial looked down at his cup uncomfortably. "That's my fault. He saw me gathering Eondel's men—I was kind of in a hurry—and followed us. We didn't have time to deal with him."

Sarene sipped at her drink petulantly. The night's events definitely hadn't turned out as she had planned.

Suddenly Ahan waddled through the door. "Rag Domi, Sarene!" he declared. "First you oppose the king, then you rescue him, and now you dethrone him. Would you please make up your mind?"

Sarene pulled her knees up against her chest and dropped her head between them with a groan. "There's no chance of keeping it under cover, then?"

"No," Roial said. "The Derethi priest saw to that—he's already announced it to half of the city."

"Telrii will almost certainly seize power now," Ahan said with a shake of his head.

"Where is Eondel?" Sarene asked, her voice muffled by the blankets.

"Locking the king in the jailhouse," Ahan said.

"And Shuden?"

"Still seeing that the women got home safely, I assume," Lukel said.

"All right," Sarene said, raising her head and brushing her hair out of her eyes. "We'll have to proceed without them. Gentlemen, I'm afraid I just destroyed our brief respite of peace. We have some heavy planning to do—and most of it is going to be in the way of damage control."

CHAPTER 33

SOMETHING changed. Hrathen blinked, washing away the last remnants of his waking dream. He wasn't sure how much time had passed—it was dark now, hauntingly black save for a few lonely torches burning high above on Elantris's wall. There wasn't even any moonlight.

He fell into the stupor more and more often lately, his mind fuzzing as he knelt in the same penitent stance. Three days was a long time to spend in prayer.

He was thirsty. Hungry as well. He had expected that; he had fasted before. However, this time seemed different. His hunger seemed more urgent, as if his body were trying to warn him of something. Elantris had much do with his discomfort, he knew. There was a desperation about the town, a sense of anxiety in every vile, cracking stone.

Suddenly, light appeared in the sky. Hrathen looked up with awe, blinking tired eyes. The moon slowly appeared from darkness. First a scythe-shaped sliver, it grew even as Hrathen watched. He hadn't realized that there would be a lunar eclipse this night—he had stopped paying attention to such things since he left Duladel. That nation's now extinct pagan religion had ascribed special importance to the heaven's movements, and the Mysteries often practiced their rituals on such nights.

Squatting in the courtyard of Elantris, Hrathen finally understood what had prodded the Jeskers to regard nature with religious wonder. There was something beautiful about the pale-faced goddess of the heavens, a mysticism to her eclipse. It was as if she really were disappearing for a time—traveling to another place, as opposed to just falling into the planet's shadow, as Svordish scientists now claimed. Hrathen could almost feel her magic.

Almost. He could understand how, perhaps, a primitive culture could worship the moon—but he could not take part in that worship. Yet he wondered—was this the awe he should feel for his God? Was his own belief flawed because he did not regard Jaddeth with the same mixture of curious fear and wonder with which the people of Jesker had regarded the moon?

He would never have such emotions; he was not capable of irrational veneration. He understood. Even if he envied men who could gush praises to a god without understanding his teachings, Hrathen could not separate fact and religion. Jaddeth bestowed attributes on men as He saw fit, and Hrathen had been given a logical intellect. He would never be content with simpleminded devotion.

It was not what Hrathen had been hoping for, but it was an answer, and he found comfort and strength within it. He was not a zealot; he would never be a man of extreme passion. In the end, he followed Derethi because it made sense. That would have to be enough.

Hrathen licked his drying lips. He didn't know how long it would be until he left Elantris; his exile could last days yet. He hadn't wanted to show signs of physical dependence, but he knew that he would need some nourishment. Reaching over, he retrieved his sacrificial basket. Caked with slime, the offerings were growing stale and moldy. Hrathen ate them anyway, resolve breaking as he finally made the decision to eat. He devoured it all—flaccid vegetables, moldy bread, meat, even some of the corn, the hard grains softened slightly by their extended bath in Elantris slime. At the end he downed the entire flask of wine with one prolonged gulp.

He tossed the basket aside. At least now he wouldn't have to worry about scavengers coming to steal his offerings, though he hadn't seen any more of them since the earlier attack. He was thankful to Jaddeth for the respite. He was becoming so weak and dehydrated that he might not have been able to fend off another assault.

The moon was almost completely visible now. Hrathen stared up with renewed resolve. He might lack passion, but he had an ample serving of determination. Licking his now wetted lips, Hrathen restarted his prayer. He would continue as he always had, doing his best to serve in Lord Jaddeth's empire.

There was nothing else God could expect of him.

CHAPTER 34

RAODEN was wrong about Shaor's men. A few of them came to him that night to cook their food, the light of consciousness shining weakly in their eyes. The rest—the majority of Shaor's followers—did not.

They came to him for another reason.

He watched several of them pull a large stone block on one of Mareshe's sleds. Their minds were gone—their capacity for rational thought atrophied somehow by their extended submersion in bestial madness. While several had recovered—if only partially—the rest seemed beyond help. They never made the connection between fires and cooking; they had simply stood howling over the grain, outraged and confused by their inability to devour it.

No, these men had not fallen into his trap. But, they had come anyway—for Raoden had dethroned their god.

He had entered Shaor's territory and had escaped unscathed. He had power over food; he could make it inedible for one but succulent for another. His soldiers had repeatedly defeated Shaor's band. To their simple, degenerate minds there was only one thing to do when faced by a god more powerful than their own: convert.

They came to him the morning after his attempt at restoring their intelligence. He had been walking the perimeter of New Elantris's short defensive wall, and seen them slinking down one of the city's main thoroughfares. He had raised the call, thinking they had finally decided to mount a coordinated attack.

But Shaor's men had not come to fight. They had come to

give him a gift: the head of their former god. Or, at least, her hair. The lead madman had tossed the golden wig at Raoden's feet, its follicles stained with dark, stagnant Elantrian blood.

Despite searching, his people never found Shaor's body.

Then, the fleece of their fallen goddess lying in the slime before them, the wildmen had bowed their faces to the ground in supplication. They now did exactly as Raoden said in all things. In turn, he had rewarded them with morsels of food, just as one would a favored pet.

It disturbed him, using men like beasts. He made other efforts to restore their rational minds, but even after just two days he knew that it was a futile hope. These men had surrendered their intellect—and, regardless of whether psychology or the Dor was to blame, it would never return.

They were remarkably well behaved—docile, even. The pain didn't seem to affect them, and they performed any duty, no matter how menial or laborious. If Raoden told them to push on a building until it fell over, he would return days later to find them still standing against the same wall, their palms pressed against the belligerent stone. Yet, despite their apparent obedience, Raoden didn't trust them. They had murdered Saolin; they had even killed their former master. They were calm only because their god currently demanded it.

"Kayana," Galladon declared, joining him.

"There's not much left, is there?" Karata agreed.

The Kayana was Galladon's name for them. It meant the "Insane."

"Poor souls," Raoden whispered.

Galladon nodded. "You sent for us, sule?"

"Yes, I did. Come with me."

THE increased manpower of the Kayana had given Mareshe and his workers the means to reconstruct some stone furniture, thereby conserving their already dwindling wood resources. Raoden's new table inside the chapel was the same one that he had used to make Taan remember his stonecarving days. A large crack—patched with mortar—ran down the middle, but other than that it was remarkably intact, the carvings worn but distinct.

The table held several books. The recent restoration of New Elantris required Raoden's leadership, making it difficult for him to sneak away to the hidden library, so he had brought out several volumes. The people were accustomed to seeing him with books, and hadn't thought to question him—even though these tomes still had leather covers on them.

He studied AonDor with increasing urgency. The pain had grown. Sometimes, it struck with such ferocity that Raoden collapsed, struggling against the agony. It was still manageable, if only barely, but it was growing worse. It had been a month and a half since he entered Elantris, and he doubted he would see another month come and go.

"I don't see why you insist on sharing every AonDor detail with us, sule," Galladon said, sighing as Raoden approached an open tome. "I barely understand half of what you tell us."

"Galladon, you *must* force yourself to remember these things," Raoden said. "No matter what you claim, I know you have the intellect for it."

"Perhaps," Galladon admitted, "but that doesn't mean I enjoy it. AonDor is your hobby, not mine."

"Listen, my friend," Raoden said, "I know AonDor holds the secret to our curse. In time, with study, we can find the clues we need. But," he continued, holding up a finger, "if something should happen to me, then there has to be someone to continue my work."

Galladon snorted. "You're about as close to becoming a Hoed as I am to being a Fjordell."

I hide it well. "That doesn't matter," Raoden said. "It is foolish not to have a backup. I'll write these things down, but I want you two to hear what I have to say."

Galladon sighed. "All right, sule, what have you discovered? Another modifier to increase the range of an Aon?"

Raoden smiled. "No, this is far more interesting. I know why Elantris is covered with slime."

Karata and Galladon perked up. "Really?" Karata asked, looking down at the open book. "Does it explain that here?"

"No, it's a combination of several things," Raoden said.

"The key element, however, is right here." He pointed to an illustration.

"Aon Ashe?" Galladon asked.

"Correct," Raoden said. "You know that Elantrian skin was so silvery that some people claimed it glowed."

"It did," Galladon said. "Not brightly, but when my father walked into a dark room, you could see his outline."

"Well, the Dor was behind it," Raoden explained. "Every Elantrian's body is connected constantly to the Dor. The same link existed between Elantris itself and the Dor, though the scholars don't know why. The Dor infused the entire city, making stone and wood shine as if some quiet flame were burning within."

"It must have been difficult to sleep," Karata noted.

"You could cover it up," Raoden said. "But the effect of the lighted city was so spectacular that many Elantrians just accepted it as natural, learning to sleep even with the glow."

"Fascinating," Galladon said indifferently. "So, what does this have to do with slime?"

"There are fungi and molds that live on light, Galladon," Raoden explained. "The Dor's illumination was different from regular light, however, and it attracted a different kind of fungus. Apparently, a thin translucent film grew on most things. The Elantrians didn't bother to clean it off—it was practically imperceptible, and it actually enhanced the radiance. The mold was tough, and it didn't make much mess. Until it died."

"The light faded . . ." Karata said.

"And the fungi rotted," Raoden said with a nod. "Since the mold once covered the entire city, now the slime does as well."

"So, what's the point?" Galladon asked with a yawn.

"This is another string in the web," Raoden explained, "another clue as to what happened when the Reod struck. We have to work backward, my friend. We are only now starting to learn symptoms of an event that happened ten years ago. Maybe after we understand everything the Reod did, we can begin to guess what might have caused it."

"The slime explanation makes sense, my prince," Karata

said. "I've always known that there was something unnatural about that grime. I've stood outside in the rain, watching waves of water pound against a stone wall without cleaning it a speck."

"The slime is oily," Raoden said, "and repels water. Have you heard Kahar talk about how difficult it is to scrub away?"

Karata nodded, leafing through the tome. "These books contain much information."

"They do," Raoden said. "Though the scholars who wrote them could be frustratingly obscure. It takes a great deal of studying to find answers to specific questions."

"Such as?" Karata asked.

Raoden frowned. "Well, for one thing, I haven't found a single book that mentions how to make Seons."

"None at all?" Karata asked with surprise.

Raoden shook his head. "I always assumed that Seons were created by AonDor, but if so, the books don't explain how. A lot of them talk about the Passing of famous Seons from one person to another, but that's about it."

"Passing?" Karata asked with a frown.

"Giving the Seon to another person," Raoden said. "If you have one, you can give it to someone else—or you can tell it who it's supposed to go and serve if you should die."

"So, a regular person could have a Seon?" she asked. "I thought it was only noblemen."

Raoden shook his head. "It's all up to the previous owner."

"Though a nobleman's not likely to Pass his Seon to some random peasant," Galladon said. "Seons, like wealth, tend to say in the family. Kolo?"

Karata frowned. "So . . . what happens if the owner dies, and hasn't told the Seon who to move on to?"

Raoden paused, then shrugged, looking to Galladon.

"Don't look at me, sule," Galladon said. "I never had a Seon."

"I don't know," Raoden admitted. "I guess it would just choose its next master on its own."

"And if it didn't want to?" Karata asked.

"I don't think it would have a choice," Raoden said.

"There's . . . something about Seons and their masters. They're bonded, somehow. Seons go mad when their masters are taken by the Shaod, for instance. I think they were created to serve—it's part of their magic."

Karata nodded.

"My lord Spirit!" called an approaching voice.

Raoden raised an eyebrow, closing the tome.

"My lord," Dashe said as he rushed through the door. The tall Elantrian looked more confused than worried.

"What is it, Dashe?" Raoden asked.

"It's the gyorn, my lord," Dashe said with an excited look. "He's been healed."

CHAPTER 35

A month and a half and you've already dethroned the king. Never let it be said that you don't work quickly, 'Ene." Her father's words were jovial, though his glowing face betrayed concern. He knew, as she did, that chaos in the wake of an uprooted government could be dangerous for both peasant and noble.

"Well, it isn't as if I *intended* it," Sarene protested. "Merciful Domi, I tried to save the fool. He shouldn't have gotten mixed up in the Mysteries."

Her father chuckled. "I should never have sent you over there. You were bad enough when we let you visit our enemies."

"You didn't 'send' me here, Father," Sarene said. "This was my idea."

"I'm glad to know that my opinion counts for so much in my daughter's eyes," Eventeo said.

Sarene felt herself soften. "I'm sorry, Father," she said with a sigh. "I've been on edge ever since . . . you don't know how *horrible* it was."

"Oh, I do—unfortunately. How in Domi's name could a monstrosity like the Mysteries come from a religion as innocent as Jesker?"

"The same way Shu-Dereth and Shu-Korath could both come from the teachings of one little Jindoeese man," Sarene replied with a shake of her head.

Eventeo sighed. "So, Iadon is dead?"

"You've heard?" Sarene asked with surprise.

"I sent a few new spies into Arelon recently, 'Ene," her father said. "I'm not going to leave my daughter alone in a country on the edge of destruction without at least keeping an eye on her."

"Who?" Sarene asked curiously.

"You don't need to know," her father said.

"They must have a Seon," Sarene mused. "Otherwise you wouldn't know about Iadon—he only hanged himself last night."

"I'm not going to tell you, 'Ene," Eventeo said with an amused tone. "If you knew who it was, you would inevitably decide to appropriate him for your own purposes."

"Fine," Sarene said. "But when this is all over, you'd better tell me who it was."

"You don't know him."

"Fine," Sarene repeated, feigning indifference.

Her father laughed. "So, tell me about Iadon. How in Domi's name did he get a rope?"

"Lord Eondel must have arranged it," Sarene guessed, resting her elbows on her desk. "The count thinks like a warrior, and this was a very efficient solution. We don't have to force an abdication, and suicide restored some dignity to the monarchy."

"Bloodthirsty this afternoon, are we 'Ene?"

Sarene shivered. "You didn't see it, Father. The king didn't just murder that girl, he . . . enjoyed doing it."

"Ah," Eventeo said. "My sources say Duke Telrii will probably take the throne."

"Not if we can help it," Sarene said. "Telrii is even worse

than Iadon. Even if he weren't a Derethi sympathizer, he'd make a terrible king."

"'Ene, a civil war will help no one."

"It won't come to that, Father," Sarene promised. "You don't understand how unmilitaristically minded these people are. They lived for centuries under Elantrian protection—they think the presence of a few overweight guards on the city wall is enough to dissuade invaders. Their only real troops belong to Lord Eondel's legion, which he's ordered to gather at Kae. We might just be able to get Roial crowned before anyone's the wiser."

"You've united behind him, then?"

"He's the only one rich enough to challenge Telrii," Sarene explained. "I didn't have enough time to stamp out Iadon's foolish monetary-title system. That is what the people are accustomed to, and so we're going to have to use it, for now."

A knock at the door was followed by a maid with a lunch tray. Sarene had returned to live in the palace after spending only one night in Roial's manor, despite her allies' concerns. The palace was a symbol, and she hoped it would lend her authority. The maid put the tray on the table and departed.

"Was that lunch?" Her father seemed to have a sixth sense regarding food.

"Yes," Sarene said, cutting herself a piece of cornbread.

"Is it good?"

Sarene smiled. "You shouldn't ask, Father. You'll only upset yourself."

Eventeo sighed. "I know. Your mother has a new fascination—Hraggish weed soup."

"Is it good?" Sarene asked. Her mother was the daughter of a Teoish diplomat, and had spent most of her growing years in Jindo. As a result, she had picked up some very odd dietary preferences—ones she forced upon the entire palace and its staff.

"It's horrible."

"Pity," Sarene said. "Now, where did I put that butter?"

Her father groaned.

"Father," Sarene chided. "You know you need to lose weight." While the king was nowhere as large—in either muscle or fat—as his brother Kiin, he was more portly than he was stocky.

"I don't see why," Eventeo said. "Did you know that in Duladel they consider fat people attractive? They don't care about Jindoeese notions of health, and they're perfectly happy. Besides, where has it been proven that butter makes you fat?"

"You know what the Jindos say, Father," Sarene said. "If it burns, it isn't healthy."

Eventeo sighed. "I haven't had a cup of wine in ten years."

"I know, Father. I used to live with you, remember?"

"Yes, but she didn't make you stay away from alcohol."

"I'm not overweight," Sarene pointed out. "Alcohol burns."

"So does Hraggish weed soup," Eventeo replied, his voice turning slightly impish. "At least, it does if you dry it out. I tried."

Sarene laughed. "I doubt Mother responded very well to that little experiment."

"She just gave me one of her looks—you know how she is."

"Yes," Sarene said, recalling her mother's features. Sarene had spent far too much time on diplomatic missions in the last few years to suffer from homesickness now, but it would be nice to be back in Teod—especially considering the seemingly endless series of surprises and disasters that had filled the last few weeks.

"Well, 'Ene, I have to go hold court," her father finally said. "I'm glad you occasionally take the time to call your poor old father—especially to let him know when you've overthrown an entire nation. Oh, one more thing. As soon as we found out about Iadon's suicide, Seinalan commandeered one of my fastest ships and set sail for Arelon. He should be arriving within a few days."

"Seinalan?" Sarene asked with surprise. "What part does the patriarch have in all this?"

"I don't know—he wouldn't tell me. But, I really have to go, 'Ene. I love you."

"I love you too, Father."

"I'VE never met the patriarch," Roial confessed from his seat in Kiin's dining room. "Is he much like Father Omin?"

"No," Sarene said firmly. "Seinalan is a self-serving egotist with enough pride to make a Derethi gyorn look humble."

"Princess!" Eondel said with indignation. "You're talking about the father of our Church!"

"That doesn't mean I have to like him," Sarene said.

Eondel's face whitened as he reached reflexively for the Aon Omi pendant around his neck.

Sarene scowled. "You don't have to ward off evil, Eondel. I'm not going to reject Domi just because He put a fool in charge of His Church; fools need to have a chance to serve too."

Eondel's eyes turned down toward his hand; then he lowered it with an embarrassed look. Roial, however, was laughing quietly to himself.

"What?" Sarene demanded.

"It's just that I was considering something, Sarene," the old man said with a smile. "I don't think I've ever met anyone, male or female, that's quite as opinionated as you are."

"Then you've lived a sheltered life, my duke," Sarene informed. "And where is Lukel, anyway?"

Kiin's table wasn't as comfortable as Roial's study, but for some reason they all felt most at home in Kiin's dining room. While most people added personal touches to their study or reception room, Kiin's love was his food, and the dining room the place where he shared his talent. The room's decorations—mementos from Kiin's travels including everything from dried vegetables to a large, ornamental axe—were comfortingly familiar. There was never any discussion about it; they all just naturally came to this room when they met.

They had to wait a few more moments before Lukel finally decided to return. Eventually, they heard the door open and close, then her cousin's amiable face popped in the door. Ahan and Kiin were with him.

"Well?" Sarene asked.

"Telrii definitely intends to take the throne," Lukel said.

"Not with my legion backing Roial, he won't," Eondel said.

"Unfortunately, my dear general," Ahan said, settling his bulk into a chair, "your legion isn't here. You have barely a dozen men at your disposal."

"It's more than Telrii has," Sarene pointed out.

"Not anymore, it isn't," Ahan said. "The Elantris City Guard left their posts to set up camp outside Telrii's mansion."

Eondel snorted. "The Guard is hardly more than a club for second sons who want to pretend they're important."

"True," Ahan said. "But there *are* over six hundred people in that club. At fifty-to-one odds, even *I* would fight against your legion. I'm afraid the balance of power has shifted in Telrii's favor."

"This is bad," Roial agreed. "Telrii's superior wealth was a great problem before, but now . . ."

"There's got to be a way," Lukel said.

"I don't see one," Roial confessed.

The men frowned, deep in thought. However, they had all been pondering this very problem for two days. Even if they'd had the military edge, the other aristocrats would be hesitant to support Roial, who was the less wealthy man.

As Sarene studied each lord in turn, her eyes fell on Shuden. He seemed hesitant rather than worried.

"What?" she asked quietly.

"I think I may have a way," he said tentatively.

"Speak on, màn," Ahan said.

"Well, Sarene is still very wealthy," Shuden explained. "Raoden left her at least five hundred thousand deos."

"We discussed this, Shuden," Lukel said. "She has a lot of money, but still less than Roial."

"True," Shuden agreed. "But *together* they would have far more than Telrii."

The room grew quiet.

"Your marriage contract *is* technically void, my lady," Ashe said from behind. "It dissolved as soon as Iadon killed himself, thereby removing his line from the throne. The moment someone else becomes king—be it Telrii or

Roial—the treaty will end, and you will cease to be an Arelish princess."

Shuden nodded. "If you unify your fortune with that of Lord Roial, it would not only give you the money to stand against Telrii, it would also legitimize the duke's claim. Don't assume that lineage doesn't matter in Arelon. The nobles would much rather give their loyalty to one of Iadon's relatives."

Roial found her with eyes like those of a benevolent grandfather. "I must admit that young Shuden has a point. The marriage would be strictly political, Sarene."

Sarene took a breath. Things happened so quickly. "I understand, my lord. We will do what must be done."

And so, for the second time in only two months, Sarene was engaged to be married.

"THAT wasn't very romantic, I'm afraid," Roial apologized. The meeting was over, and Roial had discreetly offered to escort Sarene back to the palace. The others, including Ashe, had realized that the two needed to talk alone.

"It's all right, my lord," Sarene said with a slight smile. "That is how political marriages are supposed to be—dry, contrived, but extremely useful."

"You're very pragmatic."

"I have to be, my lord."

Roial frowned. "Must we return to the 'my lords,' Sarene? I thought we were beyond that."

"I'm sorry, Roial," Sarene said. "It's just hard to separate my personal self from my political self."

Roial nodded. "I meant what I said, Sarene. This will be strictly a union of convenience—do not fear yourself obligated in any other way."

Sarene rode quietly for a moment, listening to the horse's hooves clop in front of them. "There will need to be heirs."

Roial laughed quietly. "No, Sarene. Thank you, but no. Even if such were physically possible, I couldn't go through with it. I am an old man, and can't possibly survive more than a few years. This time, your wedding contract won't forbid you from remarrying after I die. When I'm gone, you can finally choose a man of your own preference—by then we will have replaced Iadon's silly system with something more stable, and your children with the third husband will inherit the throne."

Third husband. Roial spoke as if he were already dead, herself a widow twice over. "Well," she said, "if things *do* happen as you suggest, then at least I wouldn't have trouble attracting a husband. The throne would be a tempting prize, even if I were attached to it."

Roial's face hardened. "This is something I've been meaning to discuss with you, Sarene."

"What?"

"You're far too harsh on yourself. I've heard the way you speak—you assume that nobody wants you."

"They don't," Sarene said flatly. "Trust me."

Roial shook his head. "You're an excellent judge of character, Sarene—except your own. Often, our own opinions of ourselves are the most unrealistic. You may see yourself as an old maid, child, but you *are* young, and you *are* beautiful. Just because you've had misfortune in your past doesn't mean you have to give up on your future."

He looked into her eyes. For all his mischievous shows, this was a man of sage understanding. "You *will* find someone to love you, Sarene," Roial promised. "You are a prize—a prize even greater than that throne you'll be attached to."

Sarene blushed, looking down. Still . . . his words were encouraging. Perhaps she did have a hope. She would probably be in her mid-thirties, but she would have at least one more chance to find the right man.

"Anyway," Roial said. "Our wedding will have to come soon if we are going to beat Telrii."

"What do you suggest?"

"The day of Iadon's funeral," Roial said. "Technically, Iadon's reign doesn't end until his burial."

Four days. It would be a short engagement indeed.

"I just worry at the necessity of putting you through all of this," Roial said. "It can't be easy to consider marrying such a dusty old man."

Sarene laid her hand on that of the duke, smiling at the sweetness in his tone. "All things considered, my lord, I think I'm rather fortunate. There are very few men in this world I would actually consider it an honor to be forced to marry."

Roial smiled a wrinkly smile, his eyes twinkling. "It's a shame Ahan's already married, isn't it?"

Sarene removed her hand and swatted him on the shoulder. "I've had enough emotional shocks for one week, Roial—I'll kindly thank you not to make me sick to my stomach as well."

The duke laughed at length. When his merriment died down, however, another sound replaced it—yelling. Sarene tensed, but the yells weren't ones of anger or pain. They seemed joyful and excited. Confused, she looked out the carriage window and saw a crowd of people surging through a cross street.

"What in the name of Domi is that?" Roial asked.

Their carriage drew closer, allowing Sarene to make out a tall form at the center of the crowd.

Sarene grew numb. "But . . . but that's impossible!"

"What?" Roial asked, squinting.

"It's Hrathen," Sarene said with wide eyes, "He's left Elantris!" Then she realized something else. The gyorn's face was unspotted. Flesh-colored.

"Merciful Domi—he's been healed!"

CHAPTER 36

WHEN dawn signaled the fifth day of Hrathen's exile, he knew that he had made a mistake. He would die in Elantris. Five days was too long to go without drink, and he knew there was no water to be had in the city of the damned.

He didn't regret his actions—he had behaved in the most logical way. It had been desperate logic, but rational nonetheless. Had he continued in Kae, he would have grown more impotent with each turning day. No, it was much better to die of dehydration.

He grew increasingly delirious as the fifth day passed. At times, he saw Dilaf laughing over him; at others the Teoish princess did the same. Once he even thought he saw Jaddeth himself, His face burning red with the heat of Godly disappointment as he looked down on Hrathen. The delusions soon changed, however. He no longer saw faces, no longer felt humiliated and scorned. In their place, he was confronted with something much more horrid.

Memories of Dakhor.

Once again, the dark, hollow cubicles of the monastery surrounded him. Screams echoed through the black stone hallways, cries of bestial agony mixing with solemn chanting. Chanting that had a strange power to it. The boy Hrathen knelt obediently, waiting, crouched in a cubical no larger than a closet, sweat streaming past terrified eyes, knowing that eventually they would come for him.

Rathbore Monastery trained assassins, Fjeldor Monastery trained spies. Dakhor . . . Dakhor Monastery trained demons.

HIS delirium broke sometime in the early afternoon, releasing him for a time—like a cat allowing its prey to run free one last time before striking a deadly blow. Hrathen roused his weakened body from the hard stones, his matted clothing sticking to the slimy surface. He didn't remember pulling into a fetal position. With a sigh, Hrathen rubbed a hand over his dirty, grime-stained scalp—a senseless but reflexive attempt to wipe away the dirt. His fingers scraped against something rough and bristly. Stubble.

Hrathen sat upright, shock providing momentary strength. He reached with trembling fingers, searching out the small flask that had contained his sacrificial wine. He wiped the glass as best he could with a dirty sleeve, then peered at his spectral reflection. It was distorted and unclear, but it was enough. The spots were gone. His skin, though covered with dirt, was as fresh and unblemished as it had been five days before.

Forton's potion had finally worn off.

He had begun to think that it never would, that Forton had forgotten to make the effects temporary. It was amazing enough that the Hroven man could create a potion that made one's body mimic the afflictions of an Elantrian. But Hrathen had misjudged the apothecary: he had done as asked, even if the effects had lasted a bit longer than expected.

Of course, if Hrathen didn't get himself out of Elantris quickly, he might still die. Hrathen stood, gathering his remaining strength and bolstering it with excited adrenaline. "Behold!" he screamed toward the guardhouse above. "Witness the power and glory of Lord Jaddeth! I have been healed!"

There was no response. Perhaps it was too far for his voice to carry. Then, looking along the walls, he noticed something. There were no Guards. No patrols or watches marched their rounds, no telltale tips of spears marked their presence. They had been there the day before . . . or, had it been the day before that? The last three days had become something of a blur in his mind—one extended set of prayers, hallucinations, and the occasional exhausted nap.

Where had the guards gone? They considered it their solemn duty to watch Elantris, as if anything threatening could ever come from the rotting city. The Elantris City Guard performed a useless function, but that function gave them notoriety. The Guards would never give up their posts.

Except they had. Hrathen began to scream again, feeling the strength leak from his body. If the Guard wasn't there to open the gates, then he was doomed. Irony tickled at his mind—the only Elantrian to ever be healed would die because of a collection of incompetent, negligent guards.

The gate suddenly cracked open. Another hallucination? But then a head poked through the gap—the avaricious captain that Hrathen had been nurturing.

"My lord . . . ?" the guard asked hesitantly. Then, looking Hrathen up and down with wide eyes, he inhaled sharply. "Gracious Domi! It's true—you've been healed!"

"Lord Jaddeth has heard my pleas, Captain," Hrathen announced with what strength he could manage. "The taint of Elantris has been removed from my body."

The captain's head disappeared for a moment. Then, slowly, the gate opened all the way, revealing a group of wary guards.

"Come, my lord."

Hrathen rose to his feet—he hadn't even noticed sinking to his knees—and walked on shaky legs to the gate. He turned, resting his hand on the wood—one side filthy and grime-stained, the other side bright and clean—and looked back at Elantris. A few huddled shapes watched him from the top of a building.

"Enjoy your damnation, my friends," Hrathen whispered, then motioned for the guards to shut the gate.

"I really shouldn't be doing this, you know," the captain said. "Once a man is thrown into Elantris . . ."

"Jaddeth rewards those who obey Him, Captain," Hrathen said. "Often at the hands of His servants."

The captain's eyes brightened, and Hrathen was suddenly very grateful he had begun bribing the man. "Where are the rest of your men, Captain?"

"Protecting the new king," the captain said proudly.

"New king?" Hrathen asked.

"You've missed a lot, my lord. Lord Telrii rules in Arelon now—or, at least, he will as soon as Iadon's funeral is over."

Weakened as he was, Hrathen could only stand in shock. *Iadon dead? Telrii seizing control?* How could five days bring about such drastic events?

"Come," Hrathen said firmly. "You can explain it to me on the way to the chapel."

THE crowds gathered around him as he walked; the captain owned no carriage, and Hrathen didn't want to bother waiting for one. For the moment, the exhilaration of a plan fulfilled was enough to keep him moving.

The crowds helped as well. As news spread, the people—servants, merchants, and nobles alike—came to stare at the recovered Elantrian. All parted before him, regarding him with looks that ranged from stunned to worshipful, some reaching out to touch his Elantrian robe in awe.

The trip was crowded, but uneventful—except for one moment when he looked down a side street and recognized the Teoish princess's head poking out of a carriage window. In that moment, Hrathen felt a sense of fulfillment that rivaled the day he had become a full gyorn. His healing wasn't just unexpected, it was unfathomable. There was no way Sarene could have planned for it. For once, Hrathen had total and complete advantage.

When he reached the chapel, Hrathen turned to the mass of people with raised hands. His clothing was still stained, but he held himself as if to make the grime a badge of pride. The dirt signaled his suffering, proving that he had traveled to the very pit of damnation and returned with his soul intact.

"People of Arelon!" he yelled. "Know ye this day who is Master! Let your hearts and souls be guided by the religion which can offer evidence of divine support. Lord Jaddeth is the only God in Sycla. If you need proof of this, look at my hands that are clean from rot, my face that is pure and unblemished, and my scalp rough with stubble. Lord Jaddeth tested me, and as I relied on Him, He blessed me. I have been healed!"

He lowered his hands and the crowd roared their approval. Many had probably doubted after Hrathen's apparent fall, but they would return with renewed dedication. The converts he made now would be stronger than any that had come before.

Hrathen entered the chapel, and the people remained outside. Hrathen walked with increasing fatigue, the energy of the moment finally giving way to five days' worth of strain. He flopped to his knees before the altar, bowing his head in sincere prayer.

It didn't bother him that the miracle was an effect of Forton's potion—Hrathen had found that most supposed miracles were either natural or the result of human intervention. Jaddeth was behind them, as He was behind all things, using natural phenomena to increase the faith of man.

Hrathen raised praises to God for giving him the capacity to think of the plan, the means to execute it, and the climate to make it succeed. The captain's arrival had certainly been a result of divine will. That the man would leave Telrii's camp just when Hrathen needed him, and that he would hear Hrathen yelling through the thick wood, was simply too much to be a coincidence. Jaddeth might not have "cursed" Hrathen with the Shaod, but He had certainly been behind the plan's success.

Drained, Hrathen finished his prayer and lurched to his feet. As he did so, he heard a chapel door open behind him. When he turned, Dilaf stood behind him. Hrathen sighed. This was a confrontation he had hoped to avoid until he'd had some rest.

Dilaf, however, fell to his knees before Hrathen. "My hroden," he whispered.

Hrathen blinked in surprise. "Yes, Arteth?"

"I doubted you, my hroden," Dilaf confessed. "I thought Lord Jaddeth had cursed you for incompetence. Now I see that your faith is much stronger than I realized. I know why you were chosen to hold the position of gyorn."

"Your apology is accepted, Arteth," Hrathen said, trying to keep the fatigue from his voice. "All men question in times of trial—the days following my exile must have been difficult for you and the other priests."

"We should have had more faith."

"Learn from these events then, Arteth, and next time do not allow yourself to doubt. You may go."

Dilaf moved to leave. As the man rose, Hrathen studied his eyes. There was respect there, but not as much penitence as the arteth was trying to show. He looked more confused than anything; he was amazed and unsettled, but he was not pleased. The battle was not over yet.

Too tired to worry about Dilaf for the moment, Hrathen stumbled back to his quarters and pulled open the door. His possessions were piled in one corner of the room, as if waiting to be hauled away for disposal. Suddenly apprehensive, Hrathen rushed to the pile. He found the Seon trunk beneath a pile of clothing; its lock was broken. Hrathen opened the lid with anxious fingers and pulled out the steel box inside. The front of the box was covered with scrapes, scratches, and dents.

Hurriedly, Hrathen opened the box. Several of the levers were bent, and the dial stuck, so he was extremely relieved when he heard the lock click open. He lifted the lid with anxious hands. The Seon floated inside, unperturbed. The three remaining vials of potion lay next to it; two had cracked, leaking their contents into the bottom of the box.

"Did anyone open this box since I last spoke through you?" Hrathen asked.

"No, my lord," the Seon replied in her melancholy voice.

"Good," Hrathen said, snapping the lid closed. After that, he drank a careful amount of wine from a flask he got from the pile, then collapsed on the bed and fell asleep.

IT was dark when he awakened. His body was still tired, but he forced himself to rise. A vital piece of his plans could not wait. He summoned a particular priest, who arrived a short time later. The priest, Dothgen, was a tall man with a powerful Fjordell build and muscles that even managed to bulge through his red Derethi robes.

"Yes, my lord?" Dothgen asked.

"You were trained in Rathbore Monastery, were you not, Arteth?" Hrathen asked.

"I was, my lord," the man responded in a deep voice.

"Good," Hrathen said, holding up the last vial of potion. "I have need of your special skills."

"Who is it for, my lord?" the priest asked. Like every graduate of Rathbore, Dothgen was a trained assassin. He had received far more specialized training than Hrathen had at Ghajan Monastery, the place Hrathen had gone after Dakhor proved too much for him. Only a gyorn or a ragnat, however, could make use of Rathbore-trained priests without Wyrn's permission.

Hrathen smiled.

CHAPTER 37

IT struck while Raoden was studying. He didn't hear himself gasp in agonized shock, nor did he feel himself tumble from his seat in a spastic seizure. All he felt was the pain—a sharp torment that dropped upon him suddenly and vengefully. It was like a million tiny insects, each one latching on to his body—inside and out—to eat him alive. Soon he felt as if he had no body—the pain *was* his body. It was the only sense, the only input, and his screams were the only product.

Then he felt *it*. It stood like an enormous slick surface, without crack or pocket, at the back of his mind. It pressed demandingly, pounding the pain into every nerve in his body, like a workman driving a spike into the ground. It was vast. It made men, mountains, and worlds seem paltry. It was not evil, or even sentient. It didn't rage or churn. It was immobile, frozen by its own intense *pressure*. It wanted to move—to go anywhere, to find any release from the strain. But there was no outlet.

Raoden's vision cleared slowly as the force retreated. He lay on the cold marble floor of the chapel, staring up at the bottom of his table. Two hazy faces hovered above him.

"Sule?" an urgent voice asked, as if from far away. "Doloken! Raoden, can you hear me?"

His view sharpened. Karata's usually stern features were concerned, while Galladon was livid.

"I'm all right," Raoden croaked, shamed. They would realize how weak he was, that he couldn't stand the pain of even a month-long stay in Elantris.

The two helped him sit. He remained on the floor for a moment before indicating that he wanted to move to the chair. His entire body was sore, as if he had tried to lift a dozen different weights at the same time. He groaned as he slid into the uncomfortable stone seat.

"Sule, what happened?" Galladon asked, retreating hesitantly to his own chair.

"It was the pain," Raoden said, holding his head in his hands and resting his elbows on the table. "It was too much for me for a moment. I'm all right now; it retreated."

Galladon frowned. "What are you talking about, sule?"

"The pain," Raoden said with exasperation. "The pain of my cuts and bruises, the bane of life here in Elantris."

"Sule, the pain doesn't come in waves," Galladon said. "It just remains the same."

"It comes in waves for me," Raoden said tiredly.

Galladon shook his head. "That can't be. Kolo? When you fall to the pain, you snap and your mind is gone. That's the way it always is. Besides, there's no way you could have accumulated enough cuts and bruises to go Hoed yet."

"You've said that before, Galladon, but this is how it works for me. It comes all of a sudden, as if trying to destroy me, then moves away. Maybe I'm just worse at dealing with it than everyone else."

"My prince," Karata said hesitantly, "you were glowing."

Raoden looked up at her with shock. "What?"

"It's true, sule," Galladon said. "After you collapsed you began glowing. Like an Aon. Almost as if . . ."

Raoden's mouth fell open slightly in amazement. ". . . as if the Dor were trying to come through *me*." The force had been searching for an opening, a way out. It had tried to use him like an Aon. "Why me?"

"Some people are closer to the Dor than others, sule," Galladon said. "In Elantris, some people could create Aons much more powerful than others, and some seemed more . . . intimate with the power."

"Besides, my prince," Karata said, "are you not the one who knows the Aons best? We see you practicing them every day."

Raoden nodded slowly, almost forgetting about his agony. "During the Reod, they say the most powerful Elantrians were the first to fall. They didn't fight when the mobs burned them."

"As if they were overwhelmed by something. Kolo?" Galladon asked.

Sudden and ironic relief soothed Raoden's mind. As much as the pain hurt, his insecurity had worried him more. Still, he was not free. "The attacks are getting worse. If they continue, they will take me, eventually. If that happens . . ."

Galladon nodded solemnly. "You will join the Hoed."

"The Dor will destroy me," Raoden said, "ripping my soul apart in a futile attempt to break free. It isn't alive—it's just a force, and the fact that I am not a viable passage won't stop it from trying. When it does take me, remember your vow."

Galladon and Karata nodded. They would take him to the pool in the mountains. Knowing they would take care of him if he did fall was enough to keep him going—and enough to make him wish, just a little, that the day of his failure was not far away.

"That doesn't have to happen though, sule," Galladon said. "I mean, that gyorn was healed. Maybe something's happening; maybe something has changed."

Raoden paused. "If he really was healed."

"What do you mean?" Karata asked.

"There was a lot of fuss pulling him from the city," Raoden said. "If I were Wyrn, I wouldn't want a Derethi Elantrian hanging around to bring shame on my religion. I'd send an envoy to pull him out, telling everyone he'd been healed, then hide him back in Fjordell."

"We never did get a good look at the man after he was 'healed,'" Karata acknowledged.

Galladon looked a little crestfallen at the line of conversation. He, like others in Elantris, had received a measure of hope from Hrathen's healing. Raoden hadn't said anything outright to discourage the people's optimism, but inside he was more reserved. Since the gyorn's departure, nobody else had been healed.

It was a hopeful sign, but somehow Raoden doubted it would mean much of a change for the Elantrian people. They needed to work and improve their own lives, not wait for some external miracle.

He turned back to his studies.

CHAPTER 38

SARENE watched the gyorn with displeased eyes. Hrathen no longer gave his sermons at the Derethi chapel; there were too many people. Instead he organized meetings on the edge of the city, where he could stand on Kae's five-foot border wall, his followers sitting at his feet to listen. The gyorn preached with more vibrancy and enthusiasm than he had before. For now, he was a saint. He had suffered the Shaod, and had proven himself superior to its curse.

He was, Sarene had to admit, an impressive opponent. Outfitted in his red armor, he stood like a bloodied metal statue above the crowd.

"It must have been some kind of trick," she noted.

"Of course it was, Cousin," Lukel said, standing beside her. "If we thought otherwise, we might as well join Shu-Dereth. Personally, I look horrible in red."

"Your face is too pink," Sarene said offhandedly.

"If it was a trick, Sarene," Shuden said, "then I am at a

loss to explain it." The three of them stood at the periphery of the morning meeting. They had come to see for themselves the amazing numbers Hrathen's meetings drew, even on the very day of the king's funeral.

"It could have been makeup," Sarene said.

"That survived the ritual washing?" Shuden said.

"Maybe the priests were in on it," Lukel said.

"Have you ever tried to bribe a Korathi priest, Lukel?" Shuden asked pointedly.

Lukel looked around uncomfortably. "I'd rather not answer that question, thank you."

"You sound almost as if you believe his miracle, Shuden," Sarene said.

"I do not discount it," Shuden said. "Why wouldn't God bless one of his devout? Religious exclusivism is a Korathi and Derethi addition to Shu-Keseg."

Sarene sighed, nodding for her friends to follow as she pushed her way through the outlying crowds and walked toward their waiting carriage. Trick or not, Hrathen had an uncomfortably strong hold on the people. If he managed to place a sympathizer on the throne, it would all be over. Arelon would become a Derethi nation, and only Teod would remain—though probably not for long.

Her companions were undoubtedly thinking along similar lines; both Lukel and Shuden's faces bore disturbed, contemplative looks. They entered the coach in silent thought, but finally Lukel turned to her, his hawkish features troubled.

"What do you mean, my face is too pink?" he asked with a hurt tone.

THE ship's mast bore the royal crest of Teod—a gold Aon Teo on a blue background. Long and thin, there was no faster vessel on the water than a Teoish strightboat.

Sarene felt it her duty to give the patriarch a better reception than she herself had received upon arriving at those same docks. She didn't like the man, but that was no excuse for incivility, and so she had brought Shuden, Lukel, Eondel, and several of the count's soldiers as an honor guard.

The thin ship came into dock smoothly, sailors throwing out a gangplank as soon as the vessel was secured. A blue-robed form strode past the sailors and down the gangplank with a firm step. Over a dozen attendants and lesser priests followed; the patriarch liked to be well cared for. As Seinalan approached, Sarene masked her face with controlled courtesy.

The patriarch was a tall man with delicate features. His golden hair was long, like that of a woman, and it blended with the enormous gold cape that fluttered behind him. The blue robe was embroidered with so much gold thread it was difficult at times to see the material underneath. He smiled with the benevolently tolerant face of one who wanted you to know he was patient with your inferiority.

"Your Highness!" Seinalan said as he approached. "It has been too long since my old eyes beheld your sweet features."

Sarene did her best to smile, curtsying before the patriarch and his "old" eyes. Seinalan was no more than forty, though he tried to make himself seem more aged and wise than he really was.

"Your Holiness," she said. "All of Arelon is blessed by your presence."

He nodded, as if to say that he understood just how fortunate they all were. He turned toward Shuden and the others. "Who are your companions?"

"My cousin Lukel and Baron Shuden and Count Eondel of Arelon, Your Holiness." Each man bowed as she made the introductions.

"Only barons and counts?" Seinalan asked with disappointment.

"Duke Roial sends his greetings, Your Grace," Sarene said. "He is busy preparing for King Iadon's burial."

"Ah," Seinalan said, his luxurious hair—untouched by gray—waving in the sea wind. Sarene had wished many times to have locks half as fine as those of the patriarch. "I assume I am not too late to attend the funeral?"

"No, Your Holiness," Sarene said. "It will occur this afternoon."

"Good," Seinalan said. "Come, you may show me to my lodgings now."

"THAT was . . . disappointing," Lukel confessed as soon as they climbed back in their carriage. The patriarch had been given his own vehicle, courtesy of Roial, and the gift had cooled his dissatisfaction at the duke's absence.

"He's not exactly what you expect, is he?" Sarene said.

"That isn't what Lukel meant, Sarene," Shuden said.

Sarene glanced at Lukel. "What *do* you mean?"

"I was just hoping for something more entertaining," Lukel said, twin flops of hair bouncing against his cheeks as he shrugged.

"He has been looking forward to this ever since he heard you describe the patriarch, Your Highness," Eondel explained with a dissatisfied look. "He assumed you two would . . . argue more."

Sarene sighed, giving Lukel a withering look. "Just because I don't like the man doesn't mean I'm going to make a scene, Cousin. Remember, I was one of my father's chief diplomats."

Lukel nodded with resignation.

"I will admit, Sarene," Shuden said, "your analysis of the patriarch's personality seems accurate. I am left wondering how such a man could be chosen for such an important position."

"By mistake," Sarene said curtly. "Seinalan gained the seat about fifteen years ago, when he was barely your age. It was just after Wulfden became Wyrn, and the leaders of Shu-Korath felt threatened by his vigor. For some reason, they got it into their minds that they needed to elect a patriarch who was just as young as Wulfden—if not younger. Seinalan was the result."

Shuden raised an eyebrow.

"I agree completely," Sarene said. "But, I have to give them a bit of credit. Wulfden is said to be one of the most handsome men to ever take the Fjordell throne, and the Korathi leaders wanted someone who would be equally impressive."

Lukel snorted. "Handsome and pretty are two completely different things, Cousin. Half the women who see that man will love him, the other half will just be jealous."

Throughout the conversation, Lord Eondel grew progressively more pale. Finally, he found voice for his indignation. "Remember, my lords and lady, this is Domi's holy chosen vessel."

"And he couldn't have picked a vessel more lovely," Lukel quipped—earning him an elbow in the ribs from Sarene.

"We will try to make our comments more respectful, Eondel," she apologized. "The patriarch's looks are unimportant anyway—I'm more interested in why he came."

"Isn't a king's funeral enough of a reason?" Shuden asked.

"Perhaps," Sarene said, unconvinced, as the carriage pulled to a halt outside the Korathi chapel. "Come on, let's see His Holiness settled as soon as possible—the funeral is in less than two hours, and after that it appears that I'm getting married."

WITH no obvious heir, and with Eshen completely unhinged by her husband's disgrace and subsequent death, Duke Roial took the burden of the funeral arrangements upon himself.

"Pagan murderer or not, Iadon was once my friend," the duke had explained. "He brought stability to this country in a time of need. For that much, he at least deserves a decent burial."

Omin had requested that they not use the Korathi chapel for the services, so Roial decided to use the king's throne room instead. The choice made Sarene a little uncomfortable—the throne room was the same place they would hold the wedding. However, Roial thought it symbolic that the same room would serve both the passing of the old king and the ascension of the new.

The decorations were tasteful and subdued. Roial, characteristically frugal, had planned arrangements and colors that would work for both a funeral and a wedding. The room's pillars were wrapped with white ribbons, and there were various arrangements of flowers—mostly white roses or aberteens.

Sarene entered the room, looking to the side with a smile. Near the front, next to one of the pillars, was the place where she had first set up her easel. It seemed like so long ago, though barely more than a month had passed. Forgotten with shame were the days when she had been considered an empty-headed girl—the nobility now regarded her with something akin to awe. Here was the woman who had manipulated the king, then made a fool of him, and finally toppled him from his throne. They would never love her as they had loved Raoden, but she would accept their admiration as an inferior substitute.

To the side, Sarene saw Duke Telrii. The bald, over-dressed man actually looked displeased, rather than simply uncaring. Roial had announced his wedding to Sarene only a few hours earlier, giving the pompous Telrii little time to consider a response. Sarene met Telrii's eyes, and sensed . . . frustration in the man's bearing. She had expected something from him—some kind of attempt to block their marriage—but he had made no move. What held him back?

Roial's arrival called the group to order, and the crowd fell silent. Roial walked to the front of the room, where the king's casket lay sealed, and began to speak.

It was a short offering. Roial spoke of how Iadon had forged a country from the ashes of Elantris, and how he had given them all their titles. He warned them against making the same mistake as the king, counseling them not to forget Domi in their riches and comfort. He closed by advocating that they refrain from speaking ill of the deceased, remembering that Domi would see to Iadon's soul, and such was none of their concern.

With that, he motioned for several of Eondel's solders to pick up the casket. However, another form stepped forward before they could go more than a few steps.

"I have something to add," Seinalan announced.

Roial paused in surprise. Seinalan smiled, showing perfect teeth to the room. He had already changed clothing, and was wearing a robe similar to the first, except it had a wide golden band running up his back and down his chest instead of the embroidery.

"Of course, Your Holiness," Roial said.

"What is this about?" Shuden whispered.

Sarene simply shook her head as Seinalan walked up to stand behind the casket. He regarded the crowd with a self-important smile, melodramatically whipping a scroll from the sleeve of his robe.

"Ten years ago, just after his ascension, King Iadon came to me and made this statement," Seinalan said. "You can see his seal at the bottom, as well as my own. He ordered that I present this to Arelon at his funeral, or fifteen years from the date of its creation, whichever arrived first."

Roial moved across the side of the room until he was standing next to Sarene and Shuden. His eyes showed curiosity, and concern. At the front of the room, Seinalan broke the seal on the scroll and unrolled it.

"'My lords and ladies of Arelon,'" Seinalan read, holding the paper before him as if it were a shining relic. "'Let the will of your first king, Iadon of Kae, be known. I swear solemnly before Domi, my ancestors, and whatever other gods may be watching that this proclamation is lawful. If it be that I am dead or for some other reason unable to continue as your king, then let it be understood that I made this decree of sound mind, and it is binding according to the laws of our nation.

"'I order that all titles of noble rank are to be frozen as they stand, to be handed down from generation to generation, father to son, as is commonly done in other nations. Let wealth no longer be the measure of a man's nobility—those who have held to their rank this long have proven themselves worthy. The attached document is a codified list of inheritance laws patterned after those in Teod. Let this document become the law of our country.'"

Seinalan lowered the paper to a stunned room. There was no sound, except for a quiet exhale from beside Sarene. Finally, people began to speak in hushed, excited tones.

"So that's what he was planning all along," Roial said softly. "He knew how unstable his system was. He *intended* it that way. He let them go at each other's throats just to see who would be strong enough, or treacherous enough, to survive."

"A good plan, if an unconscionable one," Shuden said. "Perhaps we underestimated Iadon's craftiness."

Seinalan still stood at the front of the room, eyeing the nobles with knowing looks.

"Why him?" Shuden asked.

"Because he's absolute," Sarene said. "Not even Hrathen would dare question the word of the patriarch—not yet, at least. If Seinalan says that order was made ten years ago, then everyone in Arelon is bound to agree with him."

Shuden nodded. "Does this change our plans?"

"Not at all," Roial said, shooting a look toward Telrii, whose expression had turned even darker than before. "It strengthens our claim—my union with Iadon's house will be even more creditable."

"Telrii still bothers me," Sarene said as the patriarch added a few platitudes about the wisdom of adopting the inheritance system. "His claim is definitely weakened by this—but will he accept it?"

"He'll have to," Roial said with a smile. "None of the nobility would dare follow him now. Iadon's proclamation grants the thing they have all been wanting—stable titles. The nobility aren't going to risk crowning a man who has no valid blood claim to the throne. The legality of Iadon's declaration doesn't matter; everyone is going to act as if it were Church doctrine."

Eondel's soldiers were finally allowed to come forward and pick up the casket. Faced with no precedent regarding the proper burial of an Arelish king, Roial had turned to the culture most similar to his own: Teod. The Teos favored large ceremonies, often burying their greatest kings with an entire shipload of riches, if not the ship itself. While such was obviously unfit for Iadon, Roial had adapted other ideas. A Teoish funeral procession was a long, drawn-out exercise, often requiring the attendants to walk an hour or more to reach the prepared site. Roial had included this tradition, with a slight modification.

A line of carriages waited outside the palace. To Sarene, using vehicles seemed disrespectful, but Shuden had made a good point.

"Roial is planning to make a bid for the crown this very afternoon," the Jindo had explained. "He can't afford to offend the plush lords and ladies of Arelon by requiring a forced march all the way out of the city."

Besides, Sarene had added to herself, *why worry about disrespect? This is, after all, only Iadon.*

With the carriages, it took only about fifteen minutes to reach the burial site. At first it looked like a large hole that had been excavated, but careful inspection would have shown it to be a natural depression in the earth that had been further deepened. Once again, Roial's frugality had been behind the choice.

With little ceremony, Roial ordered the coffin lowered into the hole. A large group of workers began to build the mound over it.

Sarene was surprised how many nobles stayed to watch. The weather had turned cold lately, bringing a chill wind from the mountains. A drizzle hung in the air, clouds obscuring the sun. She had expected most of the nobility to trickle away after the first few shovels of dirt were thrown.

But they stayed, watching the work with silent eyes. Sarene, dressed for once in black, pulled her shawl close to ward off the cold. There was something in the eyes of those nobles. Iadon had been the first king of Arelon, his rule—short though it had been—the beginning of a tradition. People would recall Iadon's name for centuries, and children would be taught how he had risen to power in a land whose gods were dead.

Was it any wonder he had turned to the Mysteries? With all he had seen—the glory of pre-Reod Elantris, then the death of an era thought eternal—was it any wonder he sought to control the chaos that seemed to reign in the land of the gods? Sarene though she understood Iadon a little bit better, standing in the chill dampness, watching the dirt slowly envelop his coffin.

Only when the last shovel of dirt was thrown, the last part of the mound patted down, did the Arelish nobility finally turn to leave. Their going was a quiet procession, and Sarene barely noticed. She stood for a while longer, looking at the king's barrow in the rare afternoon fog. Iadon was gone; it was time for new leadership in Arelon.

A hand fell lightly on her shoulder, and she turned to look into Roial's comforting eyes. "We should get ready, Sarene."

Sarene nodded and allowed herself to be led away.

SARENE knelt before the altar in the familiar, low-ceilinged Korathi chapel. She was alone; it was customary for a bride to have one last private communion with Domi before taking her marriage vows.

She was draped head to foot in white. She wore the dress that she had brought for her first wedding—a chaste, high-necked gown that her father had chosen. She wore white silken gloves that reached all the way to her shoulders, and her face was swathed in a thick veil—which, by tradition, wouldn't be lifted until she entered the hallway where her fiancé waited.

She wasn't certain what to pray about. Sarene considered herself religious, though she was nowhere near as devout as Eondel. Still, her fight for Teod was really a fight for the Korathi religion. She believed in Domi and regarded Him with reverence. She was faithful to the tenets the priests taught her—even if she was, perhaps, a little too headstrong.

Now it appeared that Domi had finally answered her prayers. He had delivered her a husband, though he was not at all what she had expected. *Perhaps,* she thought to herself, *I should have been a little more specific.*

There was no bitterness in the thought, however. She had known most of her life that she was meant for a marriage of policy, not of love. Roial really was one of the most decent men she had ever met—even if he was old enough to be her father, or even her grandfather. Still, she had heard of state marriages far more unbalanced; several Jindoeese kings were known to have taken brides as young as twelve years old.

So, her prayer was one of thanks. She recognized a blessing when she saw one: With Roial as her husband, she would be queen of Arelon. And, if Domi did decide to take Roial from her in a few years, she knew the duke's promise was true. She would have another opportunity.

Please, she added as a close to her simple prayer, *just let us be happy.*

Her lady attendants waited outside, most of them daughters of nobility. Kaise was there, looking very solemn in her little white dress, as was Torena. They held Sarene's long, cloaklike train as she walked the short distance to her carriage, then again as she alighted and entered the palace.

The throne-room doors were open, and Roial stood in a white suit near the front of the room. It was his intention to sit on the throne as soon as the ceremony was finished. If the duke did not make his claim in a forceful, unquestionable manner, then Telrii might still try to seize control.

The diminutive Father Omin stood beside the throne, clutching the large tome of the *Do-Korath*. There was a dreamy look on his face; the little priest obviously enjoyed weddings. Seinalan stood beside him, petulant that Sarene hadn't asked him to officiate. She didn't really care. Living in Teod, she had always assumed that the patriarch would wed her. Now that she had an opportunity to use a priest she actually liked, she wasn't going to give in.

She stepped into the room, and all eyes turned toward her. There were as many people at the wedding as there had been at the funeral—if not more. Iadon's funeral had been an important political event, but Roial's marriage was even more vital. The nobility would see it as paramount that they begin Roial's reign with the proper level of sycophantic flattery.

Even the gyorn Hrathen was there. It was odd, Sarene thought, that his face appeared so calm. Her wedding to Roial was going to be a major obstacle to his conversion plans. For the moment, however, Sarene put the Fjordell priest out of her mind. She had been waiting for this day for a long time, and even if it wasn't what she had once hoped for, she would make the best of it.

It was finally happening. After all the waiting, after two near misses, she was actually going to get married. With that thought, both terrifying and vindicating, she raised her veil.

The screaming started immediately.

Confused, mortified, and shocked, Sarene reached to pull off her veil, thinking perhaps that there was something wrong with it. When it came off, her hair went with it.

Sarene stared down at the long tresses with stupefaction. Her hands began to shake. She looked up. Roial was stunned, Seinalan outraged, and even Omin clutched his Korathi pendant with shock.

Sarene turned frantically, her eyes finding one of the broad mirrors on either side of the throne room. The face that stared back was not her own. It was a repulsive thing covered with black spots, defects that stood out even more markedly against her white dress. Only a few fugitive strands of hair still clung to her diseased scalp.

Inexplicable and mysterious, the Shaod had come upon her.

CHAPTER 39

HRATHEN watched several Korathi priests lead the stunned princess from the quiet room. "Such are the judgments of Holy Jaddeth," he announced.

The duke, Roial, sat on the edge of the throne dais, head held between his hands. The young Jindo baron looked as if he wanted to follow the priests and demand Sarene's release, and the martial Count Eondel was weeping openly. Hrathen was surprised to realize that he took no joy from their sorrow. Princess Sarene's fall was necessary, but her friends were of no concern—or, at least, they shouldn't be. Why was he bothered that no one had shed tears at his own fall before the Shaod?

Hrathen had begun to think that the poison would take effect too late, that the surprise marriage between Sarene and Roial would go forward unchallenged. Of course, Sarene's fall would probably have been just as disastrous after the marriage—unless Roial had intended to take the throne this very evening. It was an uncomfortable possibility. One, fortunately, Hrathen would never have the opportunity to see fulfilled.

Roial wouldn't crown himself now. Not only did he lack the legal right, but his fortune was still less than that of Telrii. Hrathen had checked the wedding contract—this time a death was *not* the same as a marriage.

Hrathen pushed his way through the stunned crowd toward the exit. He had to work quickly: Sarene's potion would wear off in five days. Duke Telrii met Hrathen's eyes as he passed, nodding with a respectful smile. The man had received Hrathen's message, and had not acted against the wedding. Now his faith would be rewarded.

The conquest of Arelon was almost complete.

CHAPTER 40

"THERE should be a way to get up there," Raoden said, shading his eyes as he looked at the Elantris city wall. During the last few hours the sun had emerged, burning away the morning mists. It hadn't, however, brought much warmth with it.

Galladon frowned. "I don't see how, sule. Those walls are rather high."

"You forget, my friend," Raoden said, "the walls weren't made to keep people in, or even really to keep enemies out. The old Elantrians built stairs and viewing platforms on the outside of the wall—there should be others in here."

Galladon grunted. Ever since the Guards had mysteriously disappeared from the walls, Raoden had wanted to find a way up. The walls belonged to Elantris, not the out-side world. From them, perhaps they could find out what was happening in Kae.

The Guard's inattentiveness bothered him. The disappear-ance was fortunate, in a way; it lessened the possibility that someone would notice New Elantris. However, Raoden could only think of a couple of reasons why the soldiers would leave their post on the walls, and the most likely one was also the most worrisome. Could the East finally have in-vaded?

Raoden knew that an invasion was all too possible. Wyrn was too opportunistic to let a gem like post-Reod Arelon go unmolested forever. Fjorden would attack eventually. And, if Arelon fell before Wyrn's holy war, then Elantris would be destroyed. The Derethi priests would see to that.

Raoden didn't voice his fears to the other Elantrians, but he did act on them. If he could place men on the walls, then he would have prior warning of an army's approach. Perhaps with advance notice, Raoden would have time to hide his people. One of the three empty, ruined towns outside of Elantris was probably their best hope. He would lead them there, if he had the chance.

Assuming he was in any condition to help. The Dor had come against him twice in the last four days. Fortunately, while the pain was growing stronger, so was his resolve. Now, at least, he understood.

"There," Galladon said, pointing to an outcropping.

Raoden nodded. There was a chance the stone column held a stairwell. "Let's go."

They were far from New Elantris, which was positioned in the center of the city to hide it from prying wall-top eyes. Here, in old Elantris, the slime still covered all. Raoden smiled: The dirt and grime was becoming repulsive to him again. For a while he had almost forgotten how disgusting it was.

They didn't get very far. Soon after Galladon pointed out the stairwell, a messenger from New Elantris appeared from a side street behind them. The man approached on quick feet, waving toward Raoden.

"My lord Spirit," the man said.

"Yes, Tenrao?" Raoden asked, turning.

"A newcomer has been thrown into the city, my lord."

Raoden nodded. He preferred to greet each newcomer personally. "Shall we go?" he asked Galladon.

"The walls will wait," the Dula agreed.

THE newcomer turned out to be a she. The woman sat with her back to the gate, her knees pulled up against her chest, her head buried in her sacrificial robes.

"She's a feisty one, my lord," said Dashe, who had been serving as watcher when the newcomer arrived. "She screamed at the gate for a full ten minutes after they tossed her in. Then she threw her offering basket against the wall and sank down like she is now."

Raoden nodded. Most newcomers were too stunned to do much besides wander. This one had strength.

Raoden gestured for the others to remain behind; he didn't want to make her nervous by bringing a crowd. He strolled forward until he was directly in front of her, then squatted down to regard her at eye level.

"Hello, there," he said affably. "I'm willing to guess you've had an awful day."

The woman looked up. When he saw her face, Raoden nearly lost his balance in surprise. Her skin was splotched and her hair was missing, but she had the same thin face and round, mischievous eyes. Princess Sarene. His wife.

"You don't know the half of it, Spirit," she said, a small, ironic smile coming to her lips.

"I'll bet I understand more than you think I do," Raoden said. "I'm here to make things a little less dreary."

"What?" Sarene asked, her voice suddenly turning bitter. "Are you going to steal the offering the priests gave me?"

"Well, I will if you really want me to," Raoden said. "Though I don't think we need it. Someone was kind enough to deliver us several large batches of food a few weeks back."

Sarene regarded him with hostile eyes. She hadn't forgotten his betrayal.

"Come with me," he urged, holding out his hand.

"I don't trust you anymore, Spirit."

"Did you ever?"

Sarene paused, then shook her head. "I wanted to, but I knew that I shouldn't."

"Then you never really gave me a chance, did you?" He stretched his hand out a little closer. "Come with me."

She regarded him for a moment, studying his eyes. Eventually she reached out her fine, thin-fingered hand and placed it in his own for the first time, allowing him to pull her to her feet.

CHAPTER 41

THE sudden change was nothing less than stupefying. It was as if Sarene had stepped from darkness into sunlight, burst from brackish water into warm air. The dirt and grime of Elantris stopped in a crisp line, beyond which the cobblestones were pure and white. Anywhere else the street's simple cleanliness would have been noticeable, but not remarkable. Here, with the rot of Elantris behind her, it seemed as if Sarene had stumbled into Domi's Paradise.

She stopped before the stone gate, staring at the city-within-a-city, her eyes wide and disbelieving. People talked and worked within, each bearing the cursed skin of an Elantrian, but each wearing a pleasant smile as well. None wore the rags she had assumed were the only available clothing in Elantris; their outfits were simple skirts or trousers and a shirt. The cloth was strikingly colorful. With amazement Sarene realized that these were the colors *she* had chosen. What she had seen as offensive, however, the people wore with joy—the bright yellows, greens, and reds highlighting their cheerfulness.

These were not the people she had seen just a few weeks before, pathetic and begging for food. They looked as if they belonged to some pastoral village of lore—people who expressed a good-natured joviality Sarene had thought unrealistic in the real world. Yet, they lived in the one place everyone knew was even more horrible than the real world.

"What . . . ?"

Spirit smiled broadly, still holding her hand as he pulled her through the gateway into the village. "Welcome to New Elantris, Sarene. Everything you assumed is no longer valid."

"I can see that."

A squat Elantrian woman approached, her dress a mixture of vibrant greens and yellows. She eyed Sarene critically. "I doubt we've got anything in her size, Lord Spirit."

Spirit laughed, taking in Sarene's height. "Do your best, Maare," he said, walking toward a low-ceilinged building at the side of the gate. The door was open, and Sarene could see rows of clothing hanging on pegs inside. Embarrassed, she was suddenly aware of her own clothing. She had already stained the white garment with slime and muck.

"Come, dearie," Maare said, leading her to a second building. "Let's see what we can do."

The motherly woman eventually found a dress that fit Sarene reasonably well—or, at least, a blue skirt that showed her legs only up to midcalf, along with a bright red blouse. There were even undergarments, though they too were constructed of bright materials. Sarene didn't complain—anything was better than her filth-soiled robe.

After pulling on the clothing, Sarene regarded herself in the room's full-length mirror. Half of her skin was still flesh-toned, but that only made the dark splotches more striking. She assumed that her flesh tones would dim with time, becoming gray like those of the other Elantrians.

"Wait," she asked hesitantly, "where did the mirror come from?"

"It isn't a mirror, dearie," Maare informed as she sifted

through socks and shoes. "It's a flat piece of stone—part of a table, I think—with thin sheets of steel wrapped around it."

Looking closely, Sarene could see the folds where sheets of steel overlapped one another. All things considered, it made a remarkable mirror. The stone must have been extremely smooth.

"But where—" Sarene stopped. She knew exactly where they had gotten sheets of steel that thin. Sarene herself had sent them, again thinking to get the better of Spirit, who had demanded several sheets of metal as part of his bribe.

Maare disappeared for a moment, then returned with socks and shoes for Sarene. Both were different colors from either her shirt or her skirt. "Here we are," the woman said. "I had to go over and pilfer these from the men."

Sarene felt herself blush as she accepted the items.

"Don't mind, dearie," Maare said with a laugh. "It makes sense you'd have big feet—Domi knows you need more on the bottom to support all that height! Oh, and here's the last thing."

The woman held up a long scarflike piece of orange cloth. "For your head," Maare said, pointing at the similar cloth wrapped around her own head. "It helps us forget about the hair."

Sarene nodded thankfully, accepting the scarf and tying it around her scalp. Spirit waited for her outside, wearing a pair of red trousers and a yellow shirt. He smiled as she approached.

"I feel like an insane rainbow," Sarene confessed, looking down at the menagerie of colors.

Spirit laughed, holding out his hand and leading her deeper into the city. Unconsciously, she found herself judging his height. *He's tall enough for me,* she thought almost offhandedly, *if only barely.* Then, realizing what she was doing, she rolled her eyes. The entire world was toppling around her, and all she could do was size up the man walking next to her.

". . . get used to the idea that we all look like secabirds in the spring," he was saying. "The colors don't bother you all that much once you wear them for a while. Actually, after the dull monotones of old Elantris, I find them quite refreshing."

As they walked, Spirit explained New Elantris to her. It wasn't very large, perhaps fifty buildings in all, but its compact nature made it feel more unified. Though there couldn't have been many people in the town—five or six hundred at most—there always seemed to be motion around her. Men worked on walls or roofs, women sewed or cleaned—even children ran in the streets. It had never occurred to her that the Shaod would take children as well as adults.

Everyone greeted Spirit as he passed, calling out with welcoming smiles. There was true acceptance in their voices, displaying a level of loving respect Sarene had rarely seen given to a leader; even her father, who was generally well liked, had his dissenters. Of course, it was easier with such a small population, but she was still impressed.

At one point they walked by a man of indecipherable age—it was hard to put years with faces in Elantris—sitting on a stone block. He was short with a large belly, and he didn't greet them. His inattention, however, was not a sign of incivility—he was just focused on the small object in his hand. Several children stood around the man, watching his bent-over work with eager eyes. As Sarene and Spirit passed, the man held the object out to one of the children; it was a beautifully carved stone horse. The girl clapped ecstatically, accepting the piece with exuberant fingers. The children ran off as the sculptor reached down to select another rock from the ground. He began to scrape at the stone with a short tool; as Sarene peered closely at his fingers, she realized what it was.

"One of my nails!" she said. "He's using one of the bent nails I sent you."

"Hmm?" Spirit asked. "Oh, yes. I have to tell you, Sarene, we had quite a time figuring out what to do with that particular box. It would have taken far too much fuel to melt them all down, even assuming we had the tools for smelting. Those nails were one of your more clever adaptations."

Sarene flushed. These people were fighting to survive in a city deprived of resources, and she had been so petty as to send them bent nails. "I'm sorry. I was afraid you would make weapons out of the steel."

"You were right to be wary," Spirit said. "I did, after all, betray you in the end."

"I'm sure you had a good reason," she said quickly.

"I did," he said with a nod. "But that didn't matter much at the time, did it? You were right about me. I was—am—a tyrant. I kept food back from a part of the population, I broke our agreement, and I caused the deaths of some fine men."

Sarene shook her head, her voice growing firm. "You are *not* a tyrant. This community proves that—the people love you, and there cannot be tyranny where there is love."

He half smiled, his eyes unconvinced. Then, however, he regarded her with an unreadable expression. "Well, I suppose the time during your Trial wasn't a complete loss. I gained something very important during those weeks."

"The supplies?" Sarene asked.

"That too."

Sarene paused, holding his eyes. Then she looked back at the sculptor. "Who is he?"

"His name is Taan," Spirit said. "Though you might know of him by the name Aanden."

"The gang leader?" Sarene asked with surprise.

Spirit nodded. "Taan was one of the most accomplished sculptors in Arelon before the Shaod took him. After coming to Elantris, he lost track of himself for a while. He came around eventually."

They left the sculptor to his work. Spirit showing her through the last few sections of the city. They passed a large building that he referred to as "the Hall of the Fallen," and the sorrow in his voice kept her from asking about it, though she did see several mindless Shaod Seons floating around above its roof.

Sarene felt a sudden stab of grief. *Ashe must be like that now,* she thought, remembering the mad Seons she had occasionally seen floating around Elantris. Despite what she'd seen, she'd continued to hope through the night that Ashe would find her. The Korathi priests had locked her in some sort of holding cell to wait—apparently, new Elantrians were only thrown into the city once a day—and she'd stood by the window, wishing he would arrive.

She'd waited in vain. With the confusion at the wedding,

she couldn't even remember the last time she'd seen him.
Not wanting to enter the chapel, he'd gone ahead to wait for
her in the throne room. When she'd arrived, had she seen
him floating inside the room? Had she heard his voice, calling out amid the other shocked members of the wedding
party? Or, was she simply letting hope cloud her memories?

Sarene shook her head, sighing as she let Spirit lead her
away from the Hall of the Fallen. She kept looking over her
shoulder, glancing upward, expecting Ashe to be there. He
always had been before.

At least he isn't dead, she thought, forcing aside her grief.
*He's probably in the city somewhere. I can find him ...
maybe help him, somehow.*

They continued to walk, and Sarene intentionally let herself be distracted by the scenery—she couldn't bear to think
of Ashe anymore. Soon, Spirit led her past several open areas that—looking closely—Sarene realized must be fields.
Tiny sprouts were appearing in careful rows piled in the dirt,
and several men walked among them, searching for weeds.
There was a distinct smell in the air.

Sarene paused. "Fish?"

"Fertilizer," Spirit said with a chuckle. "That's one time
we managed to get the better of you. We asked for trike
knowing full well you would find the nearest barrel of rotten
fish to include in the shipment."

"It seems like you got the better of me more times than
not," Sarene said, remembering with shame the time she had
spent gloating over her sly interpretations of the demands. It
seemed no matter how twisted her attempt, the New Elantrians had found uses for all of her useless gifts.

"We don't have much choice, Princess. Everything from
pre-Reod Elantris is rotten or befouled; even the stones are
starting to crumble. No matter how defective you may have
thought those supplies, they were still far more useful than
anything left in the city."

"I was wrong," Sarene said morosely.

"Don't start that again," Spirit said. "If you begin feeling
sorry for yourself, I'll lock you in a room with Galladon for
an hour so that you can learn what *true* pessimism is."

"Galladon?"

"He was the large fellow you met briefly back at the gates," Spirit explained.

"The Dula?" Sarene asked with surprise, recalling the large, broad-faced Elantrian with the thick Duladen accent.

"That's him."

"A pessimistic Dula?" she repeated. "I've never heard of such a thing."

Spirit laughed again, leading her into a large, stately building. Sarene gasped in wonder at its beauty. It was lined with delicate, spiraled arches, and the floor was crafted of pale white marble. The wall reliefs were even more intricate than those on the Korathi temple in Teoras.

"It's a chapel," she said, running her fingers over the intricate marble patterns.

"Yes, it is. How did you know that?"

"These scenes are straight out of the *Do-Korath*," she said, looking up with chiding eyes. "Someone didn't pay much attention in chapel school."

Spirit coughed to himself. "Well . . ."

"Don't even try and convince me you didn't go," Sarene said, turning back to the carvings. "You're obviously a nobleman. You would have gone to church to keep up appearances, even if you weren't devout."

"My lady is very astute. I am, of course, Domi's humble servant—but I'll admit that my mind sometimes wandered during the sermons."

"So, who were you?" Sarene asked conversationally, finally asking the question that had bothered her ever since she first met Spirit weeks before.

He paused. "The second son of the Lord of Ien Plantation. A very minor holding in the south of Arelon."

It could be the truth. She hadn't bothered memorizing the names of minor lords; it had been difficult enough to keep track of the dukes, counts, and barons. It could also be a lie. Spirit appeared to be at least a passable statesman, and he would know how to tell a convincing falsehood. Whatever he was, he had certainly learned some excellent leadership skills—attributes she had found, for the most part, lacking in the Arelish aristocracy.

"How long—" she began, turning away from the wall. Then she froze, her breath catching in her throat.

Spirit was glowing.

A spectral light grew from somewhere within; she could see the lines of his bones silhouetted before some awesome power that burned within his chest. His mouth opened in a voiceless scream; then he collapsed, quivering as the light flared.

Sarene rushed to his side, then paused, unsure what to do. Gritting her teeth, she grabbed him, lifting his head up to keep the spasms from pounding it repeatedly against the cold marble floor. And she felt something.

It brought bumps to her arms and sent a frigid shiver through her body. Something large, something impossibly immense, pressed against her. The air itself seemed to warp away from Spirit's body. She could no longer see his bones; there was too much light. It was as if he were dissolving into pure whiteness; she would have thought him gone if she hadn't felt his weight in her arms. His struggles jerked to a stop, and he fell limp.

Then he screamed.

A single note, cold and uniform, flew from his mouth in a defiant yell. The light vanished almost immediately, and Sarene was left with her heart pounding a rhythm in her breast, her arms bathed in anxious sweat, her breathing coming deeply and rapidly.

Spirit's eyes fluttered open a few moments later. As comprehension slowly returned, he smiled wanly and rested his head back against her arm. "When I opened my eyes, I thought that time I had died for certain."

"What happened?" she asked anxiously. "Should I go for help?"

"No, this is becoming a common occurrence."

"Common?" Sarene asked slowly. "For . . . all of us?"

Spirit laughed weakly. "No, just me. I'm the one the Dor is intent on destroying."

"The Dor?" she asked. "What does Jesker have to do with this?"

He smiled. "So, the fair princess is a religious scholar as well?"

"The fair princess knows a lot of things," Sarene said dismissively. "I want to know why a 'humble servant of Domi' thinks the Jesker overspirit is trying to destroy him."

Spirit moved to sit, and she helped. "It has to do with AonDor," he explained with a tired voice.

"AonDor? That's a heathen legend." There wasn't much conviction to her words—not after what she had just seen.

Spirit raised an eyebrow. "So, it's all right for us to be cursed with bodies that won't die, but it's not possible for our ancient magic to work? Didn't I see you with a Seon?"

"That's different. . . ." Sarene trailed off weakly, her mind turning back to Ashe.

Spirit, however, immediately drew her attention again. He raised his hand and began drawing. Lines appeared in the air, following his finger's movement.

Korathi teaching of the last ten years had done its best to downplay Elantris's magic, despite the Seons. Seons were familiar, almost like benevolent spirits sent by Domi for protection and comfort. Sarene had been taught, and had believed, that Elantris's magics had mostly been a sham.

Now, however, she was faced with a possibility. Perhaps the stories were true.

"Teach me," she whispered. "I want to know."

IT wasn't until later, after night had fallen, that Sarene finally allowed herself to cry. Spirit had spent the better part of the day explaining all he knew of AonDor. Apparently, he had done some extensive research on the subject. Sarene had listened with enjoyment, because of both the company and the distraction he provided. Before they had known it, dusk was falling outside the chapel windows, and Spirit had found her lodgings.

Now she lay curled up, shivering in the cold. The room's two other women slept soundly, neither one bothering with a blanket despite the frigid air. The other Elantrians didn't seem to notice temperature variation as much as Sarene did. Spirit claimed that their bodies were in a kind of stasis, that they had stopped working as they waited for the Dor to finish transforming them. Still, it seemed unpleasantly cold to Sarene.

The dismal atmosphere didn't do much for her mood. As she bunched up against the hard stone wall, she remembered the looks. Those awful looks. Most other Elantrians had been taken at night, and they would have been discovered quietly. Sarene, however, had been exhibited before the entire aristocracy. And at her own wedding, no less.

It was a mortifying embarrassment. Her only consolation was that she would probably never see any of them again. It was a small comfort, for by the same reasoning she would probably never see her father, mother, or brother again. Kiin and his family were lost to her. So, where homesickness had never hit her before, now it attacked with a lifetime's worth of repression.

Coupled with it was the knowledge of her failure. Spirit had asked her for news from the outside, but the topic had proven too painful for her. She knew that Telrii was probably already king, and that meant Hrathen would easily convert the rest of Arelon.

Her tears came silently. She cried for the wedding, for Arelon, for Ashe's madness, and for the shame dear Roial must have felt. Thoughts of her father were worst of all. The idea of never again feeling the love of his gentle banter—never again sensing his overwhelming, unconditional approval—brought to her heart an overpowering sense of dread.

"My lady?" whispered a deep, hesitant voice. "Is that you?"

Shocked, she looked up through her tears. Was she hearing things? She had to be. She couldn't have heard . . .

"Lady Sarene?"

It was Ashe's voice.

Then she saw him, hovering just inside the window, his Aon so dim it was nearly invisible. "Ashe?" she asked with hesitant wonder.

"Oh, blessed Domi!" the Aon exclaimed, approaching quickly.

"Ashe!" she said, wiping her eyes with a quivering hand, numbed by shock. "You never use the Lord's name!"

"If He has brought me to you, then He has His first Seon convert," Ashe said, pulsing excitedly.

She could barely keep herself from reaching out and trying to hug the ball of light. "Ashe, you're talking! You shouldn't be able to speak, you should be . . ."

"Mad," Ashe said. "Yes, my lady, I know. Yet, I feel no different from before."

"A miracle," Sarene said.

"A wonder, if nothing else," the Seon said. "Perhaps I *should* look into converting to Shu-Korath."

Sarene laughed. "Seinalan would never hear of it. Of course, his disapproval has never stopped us before, has it?"

"Not once, my lady."

Sarene rested back against the wall, content to simply enjoy the familiarity of his voice.

"You have no idea how relieved I am to find you, my lady. I have been searching for two days. I had begun to fear that something awful had happened to you."

"It did, Ashe," Sarene said, though she smiled when she said the words.

"I mean something more horrible, my lady," the Seon said. "I have seen the kind of atrocities this place can breed."

"It has changed, Ashe," Sarene said. "I don't quite understand how he did it, but Spirit brought order to Elantris."

"Whatever he did, if it kept you safe, I bless him for it."

Suddenly, something occurred to her. If Ashe lived . . . Sarene had a link to the outside world. She wasn't completely separated from Kiin and the others.

"Do you know how everyone is doing?" she asked.

"No, my lady. After the wedding dismissed, I spent an hour demanding that the patriarch let you free. I don't think he was disappointed by your fall. After that, I realized that I had lost you. I went to Elantris's gates, but I was apparently too late to see you get thrown into the city. However, when I asked the guards where you had gone, they refused to tell me anything. They said it was taboo to speak of those who had become Elantrians, and when I told them that I was your Seon, they grew very uncomfortable and stopped speaking to me. I had to venture into the city without information, and I've been searching for you ever since."

Sarene smiled, picturing the solemn Seon—essentially, a

pagan creation—arguing with the head of the Korathi religion. "You didn't arrive too late to see me get thrown into the city, Ashe. You arrived too *early*. Apparently, they only throw people in before a certain time of day, and the marriage happened quite late. I spent the night in the chapel, and they brought me to Elantris this afternoon."

"Ah," the Seon said, bobbing with comprehension.

"In the future you can probably find me here, in the clean section of the city."

"This is an interesting place," Ashe said. "I had never been here before—it is well masked from the outside. Why is this area different from the others?"

"You'll see," she said. "Come back tomorrow."

"Come back, my lady?" Ashe asked indignantly. "I don't intend to leave you."

"Just briefly, my friend," Sarene said. "I need news from Kae, and you need to let the others know I am all right."

"Yes, my lady."

Sarene paused for a moment. Spirit had gone through great efforts to make sure no one on the outside knew of New Elantris; she couldn't betray his secret so offhandedly, even if she did trust the people Ashe would tell. "Tell them you found me, but don't tell them any of what you see in here."

"Yes, my lady," Ashe said, his voice confused. "Just a moment, my lady. Your father wishes to speak with you." The Seon began to pulse, then his light melted, dripping and reforming into Eventeo's large oval head.

"'Ene?" Eventeo asked with frantic concern.

"I'm here, Father."

"Oh, thank Domi!" he said. "Sarene, are you unharmed?"

"I'm fine, Father," she assured him, strength returning. She suddenly knew that she could do anything and go anywhere as long as she had the promise of Eventeo's voice.

"Curse that Seinalan! He didn't even try to let you free. If I weren't so devout, I'd behead him without a second thought."

"We must be fair, Father," Sarene said. "If a peasant's daughter can be cast into Elantris, then a king's daughter shouldn't be exempt."

"If my reports are true, then no one should be thrown into that pit."

"It's not as bad as you think, Father," Sarene said. "I can't explain, but things are more hopeful than anticipated."

"Hopeful or not, I'm getting you out of there."

"Father, no!" Sarene said. "If you bring soldiers to Arelon you'll not only leave Teod undefended, but you'll alienate our only ally!"

"It won't be our ally for long, if my spy's predictions are accurate," Eventeo said. "Duke Telrii is waiting a few days to consolidate power, but everyone knows he'll soon take the throne—and he is on very friendly terms with that Gyorn Hrathen. You tried, 'Ene, but Arelon is lost. I'm going to come get you—I won't really need all that many men—and then I'm going to fall back and prepare for an invasion. No matter how many men Wyrn raises, he'll never get them past our armada. Teod has the finest ships on the sea."

"Father, you might have given up on Arelon, but I can't."

"Sarene," Eventeo said warningly, "do not start that again. You are no more Arelish than I—"

"I mean it, Father," Sarene said firmly. "I will not leave Arelon."

"Idos Domi, Sarene, this is lunacy! I am your father and your king. I am going to bring you back, whether you want to come or not."

Sarene calmed herself; force would never work with Eventeo. "Father," she said, letting love and respect sound in her voice, "you taught me to be bold. You made me into something stronger than the ordinary. At times I cursed you, but mostly I blessed your encouragement. You gave me the liberty to become myself. Would you deny that now by taking away my right to choose?"

Her father's white head hung silently in the dark room.

"Your lessons won't be complete until you let go, Father," Sarene said quietly. "If you truly believe the ideals that you gave me, then you will allow me to make this decision."

Finally he spoke. "You love them that much, 'Ene?"

"They have become my people, Father."

"It has been less than two months."

"Love is independent of time, Father. I need to stay with

Arelon. If it is to fall, I must fall with it—but I don't think it will. There has to be a way to stop Telrii."

"But you're trapped in that city, Sarene," her father said. "What can you do from there?"

"Ashe can act as messenger. I can no longer lead them, but I might be able to help. Even if I cannot, I still must stay."

"I see," her father finally said, sighing deeply. "Your life is yours, Sarene. I have always believed that—even if I forget it once in a while."

"You love me, Father. We protect what we love."

"And I do," Eventeo said. "Never forget that, my daughter."

Sarene smiled. "I never have."

"Ashe," Eventeo ordered, calling the Seon's consciousness into the conversation.

"Yes, my king," Ashe's voice said, its deep tone deferential and reverent.

"You will watch and protect her. If she is injured, you will call me."

"As I ever have, and ever will, my king," Ashe responded.

"Sarene, I'm still going to set the armada in a defensive pattern. Let your friends know that any ship approaching Teoish waters will be sunk without question. The entire world has turned against us, and I cannot risk the safety of my people."

"I'll warn them, Father," Sarene promised.

"Goodnight then, 'Ene, and may Domi bless you."

CHAPTER 42

HRATHEN was back in control. Like a hero from the old Svordish epics, he had descended to the underworld—physically, mentally, and spiritually—and returned a stronger man. Dilaf's hold was broken. Only now could Hrathen see that the chains Dilaf had used to bind him had been forged from Hrathen's own envy and insecurity. He had felt threatened by Dilaf's passion, for he had felt his own faith inferior. Now, however, his resolve was firm—as it had been when he first arrived in Arelon. He *would* be the savior of this people.

Dilaf backed down unhappily. The arteth grudgingly promised to hold no meetings or sermons without Hrathen's overt permission. And, in exchange for being officially named head arteth of the chapel, Dilaf also consented to relieve his numerous odivs from their vows, instead swearing them to the less binding position of krondet. The biggest change, however, wasn't in the arteth's actions, but in Hrathen's confidence. As long as Hrathen knew that his faith was as strong as Dilaf's, then the arteth would not be able to manipulate him.

Dilaf would not, however, relent in his pursuit of Elantris's destruction. "They are unholy!" the arteth insisted as they walked toward the chapel. This night's sermon had been extremely successful; Hrathen could now claim over three-fourths of the local Arelish nobility as Derethi members or sympathizers. Telrii would crown himself within the week, and as soon as his rule stabilized a bit, he would announce his conversion to Shu-Dereth. Arelon was Hrathen's, and he still had a month left before Wyrn's deadline.

"The Elantrians have served their purpose, Arteth," Hrathen explained to Dilaf as they walked. It was cold this night, though not cold enough for one's breath to mist.

"Why do you forbid me to preach against them, my lord?" Dilaf's voice was bitter—now that Hrathen forbade him to speak about Elantris, the arteth's speeches seemed almost emasculated.

"Preaching against Elantris no longer has a point," Hrathen said, matching Dilaf's anger with logic. "Do not forget that our hate had a purpose. Now that I have proven Jaddeth's supreme power over Elantris, we have effectively shown that our God is true, while Domi is false. The people understand that subconsciously."

"But the Elantrians are still unholy."

"They are vile, they are blasphemous, and they are definitely unholy. But right now they are also unimportant. We need to focus on the Derethi religion itself, showing the people how to link themselves to Jaddeth by swearing fealty to yourself or one of the other arteths. They sense our power, and it is our duty to show them how to partake of it."

"And Elantris goes free?" Dilaf demanded.

"No, most certainly not," Hrathen said. "There will be time enough to deal with it after this nation—and its monarch—is firmly in Jaddeth's grasp."

Hrathen smiled to himself, turning away from the scowling Dilaf.

It's over, he realized. *I actually did it—I converted the people without a bloody revolution.* He wasn't finished yet, however. Arelon was his, but one nation still remained.

Hrathen had plans for Teod.

CHAPTER 43

THE door had been barred shut from the inside, but the wooden portal was part of the original Elantris—subject to the same rot that infested the rest of the city. Galladon said the mess had fallen off its hinges practically at a touch. A dark stairwell lay hidden inside, ten years of dust coating its steps. Only a single set of footprints marked the powder—footprints that could have been made only by feet as large as Galladon's.

"And it goes all the way to the top?" Raoden asked, stepping over the sodden wreck of a door.

"Kolo," Galladon said. "And it's encased in stone the entire way, with only an occasional slit for light. One wrong step will send you tumbling down a series of stone steps as long—and as painful—as one of my hama's stories."

Raoden nodded and began climbing, the Dula following behind. Before the Reod, the stair must have been lit by Elantrian magic—but now the darkness was broken only by occasional thin spears of light from the scattered slits. The stairs circled up against the outer wall of the structure, and the lower curves were dimly visible when one peered down the center. There had been a railing once, but it had long since decayed.

They had to stop often to rest, their Elantrian bodies unable to bear the strain of vigorous exercise. Eventually, however, they reached the top. The wooden door here was newer; the Guard had probably replaced it after the original rotted away. There was no handle—it wasn't really a door, but a barricade.

"This is as far as I got, sule," Galladon said. "Climbed all the way to the top of the Doloken stairs, only to find out I needed an axe to go on."

"That's why we brought this," Raoden said, pulling out the very axe Taan had almost used to topple a building down on Raoden. The two set to work, taking turns hacking at the wood.

Even with the tool, cutting through the door was a difficult task. Raoden tired after just a few swings, and each one barely seemed to nick the wood. Eventually, however, they got one board loose and—spurred by the victory—they finally managed to break open a hole large enough to squeeze through.

The view was worth the effort. Raoden had been atop the walls of Elantris dozens of times, but never had the sight of Kae looked so sweet. The city was quiet; it appeared as if his fears of invasion had been premature. Smiling, Raoden enjoyed the sense of accomplishment. He felt as if he had climbed a mountain, not a simple stairwell. The walls of Elantris were once again back in the hands of those who had created them.

"We did it," Raoden said, resting against the parapet.

"Took us long enough," Galladon noted, stepping up beside him.

"Only a few hours," Raoden said lightly, the agony of the work forgotten in the bliss of victory.

"I didn't mean cutting through the door. I've been trying to get you to come up here for three days."

"I've been busy."

Galladon snorted, mumbling something under his breath.

"What was that?"

"I said, 'A two-headed ferrin would never leave its nest.'"

Raoden smiled; he knew the Jindoeese proverb. Ferrins were talkative birds, and could often be heard screaming at one another across the Jindoeese marshes. The saying was used in reference to a person who had found a new hobby. Or a new romance.

"Oh, come now," Raoden said, eyeing Galladon. "I'm not that bad."

"Sule, the only time in the last three days I've seen you two apart is when one of you had to go to the privy. She'd be here now if I hadn't snatched you when no one was looking."

"Well," Raoden said defensively, "she *is* my wife."

"And do you ever intend to inform her of that fact?"

"Maybe," Raoden said lightly. "I wouldn't want her to feel any obligation."

"No, of course not."

"Galladon, my friend," Raoden said, completely unruffled by the Dula's comments, "your people would be mortified to hear how unromantic you are." Duladen was a notorious hotbed of melodramatic romances and forbidden love.

Galladon snorted his response, showing what he thought of the average Dula's romantic inclinations. He turned, scanning the city of Kae. "So, sule, we're up here. What do we do now?"

"I don't know," Raoden confessed. "You're the one who forced me to come."

"Yes, but it was *your* idea to search for a stairwell in the first place."

Raoden nodded, remembering back to their short conversation three days ago. *Has it really been that long?* he wondered. He'd barely noticed. Perhaps he had been spending a little too much time with Sarene. However, he didn't feel a bit guilty.

"There," Galladon said, squinting and pointing at the city.

"What?" Raoden said, following the Dula's gesture.

"I see a flag," Galladon said. "Our missing Guards."

Raoden could barely pick out a hint of red in the distance—a banner. "Are you sure?"

"Positive," Galladon said.

Raoden squinted, recognizing the building over which the banner flew. "That's Duke Telrii's mansion. What could the Elantris City Guard possibly have to do with him?"

"Perhaps he's under arrest," Galladon said.

"No," Raoden said. "The Guard isn't a policing force."

"Why would they leave the walls, then?" Galladon asked.

Raoden shook his head. "I'm not sure. Something, however, is very wrong."

———

RAODEN and Galladon retreated back down the stairwell, deep in thought.

There was one way to find out what was going on with the Guard. Sarene was the only Elantrian to be thrown into the city since the disappearance of the Guard. Only she could explain the current political climate of the city.

Sarene, however, still resisted talking about the outside. Something about the last few days before her exile had been extremely painful. Sensing her hurt, Raoden had avoided prying; he didn't want to risk alienating her. The truth was, he really did enjoy his time with Sarene. Her wry wit made him smile, her intelligence intrigued him, and her personality encouraged him. After ten years of dealing with women whose only apparent thought was how good they looked in their dress—a state of forced obtuseness led by his own weak-willed stepmother—Raoden was ready for a woman who wouldn't cower at the first sign of conflict. A woman such as he remembered his mother being, before she died.

However, that same unyielding personality was the very thing that had kept him from learning about the outside. No amount of subtle persuasion—or even direct manipulation—could pry a single unwilling fact out of Sarene's mouth. He couldn't afford to be delicate any longer, however. The Guard's strange actions were troubling—any shift in power could be extremely dangerous to Elantris.

They reached the bottom of the stairwell and moved on toward the center of the city. The walk was a relatively long one, but it passed quickly as Raoden considered what they had seen. Despite the fall of Elantris, Arelon had spent the last ten years in relative peace—at least, on a national level. With an ally to the south, Teod's armada patrolling the northern ocean, and the mountains to their east, even a weakened Arelon had faced little external danger. Internally, Iadon had kept a strong grip on military might, encouraging the nobility toward political squabbling as opposed to militaristic posings.

Raoden knew that peace couldn't last long, even if his father refused to see that fact. Raoden's decision to marry Sarene had been influenced greatly by the chance to enter a formal treaty with Teod—giving Arelon at least partial access to the Teoish armada. Arelenes weren't accustomed to battle; they had been bred for pacifism by centuries of Elantrian protection. The current Wyrn would have to be a fool not to strike soon. All he needed was an opening.

Internal strife would provide that opening. If the Guard had decided to betray the king, civil conflict would throw Arelon into chaos once again, and the Fjordells were infamous for capitalizing on such events. Raoden had to find out what was happening beyond those walls.

Eventually, he and Galladon reached their destination. Not New Elantris, but the squat, unassuming building that was the passage to the holy place. Galladon hadn't said a word when he'd found out that Raoden had taken Sarene to the library; the Dula had actually looked as if he'd expected such a development.

A few moments later, Raoden and Galladon strode into the underground library. Only a few of the wall lamps burned—an effort to save fuel—but Raoden could easily make out Sarene's form sitting in one of the cubicles at the back, leaning over a book just where he had left her.

As they approached, her face became more distinct, and Raoden wasn't able to keep himself from remarking again at her beauty. The dark-splotched skin of an Elantrian was prosaic to him now; he didn't really notice it anymore. Actually, Sarene's body seemed to be adapting remarkably well to the Shaod. Further signs of degeneration were usually visible after just a few days—wrinkles and creases appearing in the skin, the body's remaining flesh color dulling to a pallid white. Sarene showed none of this—her skin was as smooth and vibrant as the day she had entered Elantris.

She claimed that her injuries didn't continue hurting the way they should—though Raoden was certain that that was just because she had never lived outside of New Elantris. Many of the more recent newcomers never experienced the worst of Elantrian pain, the work and positive atmosphere keeping them from focusing on their injuries. The hunger hadn't come upon her either—but, again, she had the fortune of coming at a time when everyone had the opportunity to eat at least once a day. Their supplies wouldn't last more than a month, but there was no reason to stockpile. Starvation was not deadly to Elantrians, just uncomfortable.

Most beautiful were her eyes—the way she studied everything with keen interest. Sarene didn't just look, she examined. When she spoke, there was thought behind her words. That intelligence was what Raoden found most attractive about his Teoish princess.

She looked up as they approached, an excited smile on her face. "Spirit! You are *never* going to guess what I found."

"You're right," Raoden confessed with a smile—unsure how to approach the topic of information about the outside. "Therefore, you might as well just tell me."

Sarene held up the book, showing him the spine, which read *Seor's Encyclopedia of Political Myths*. Though Raoden had shown Sarene the library in an effort to sate her interest in AonDor, she'd postponed that study as soon as she had realized that there was an entire shelf of books on political theory. Part of the reason for her shift in interest probably had to do with her annoyance at AonDor. She couldn't draw Aons in the air; she couldn't even get the lines to start appearing behind her fingers. Raoden had been perplexed at first, but Galladon had explained that such a thing wasn't uncommon. Even before the Reod, it had taken some Elantrians years to learn AonDor; if one began even the first line with an improper slant, nothing would appear. Raoden's own immediate success was nothing short of extraordinary.

Sarene, however, didn't see it that way. She was the type who grew annoyed when it took her longer to learn than someone else. She claimed she was drawing the Aons perfectly—and, in truth, Raoden couldn't see any flaws in her form. The characters just refused to appear—and no amount of princessly indignation could convince them to behave.

So Sarene had turned her interest to political works—though Raoden guessed she would have ended up there anyway. She was interested in AonDor, but she was fascinated by politics. Whenever Raoden came to the library to practice Aons or study, Sarene picked out a volume by some ancient historian or diplomatic genius and began to read in the corner.

". . . it's amazing. I have never read anything that so soundly debunks Fjorden's rhetoric and manipulation."

Raoden shook his head, realizing he had simply been staring at her, enjoying her features rather than paying attention to her words. She was saying something about the book—about how it exposed Fjordell political lies.

"Every government lies occasionally, Sarene," he said as she paused.

"True," she said, flipping through the book. "But not with such magnitude—for the last three hundred years, ever since Fjorden adopted the Derethi religion, the Wyrns have been blatantly altering their country's own histories and literature to make it seem as if the empire has *always* been a manifestation of divine purpose. Look at this." She held up the book again, this time showing him a page of verse.

"What is that?"

"*Wyrn the King*—the entire three-thousand-line poem."

"I've read it," Raoden said. *Wyrn* was said to be the oldest recorded piece of literature—older, even, than the *Do-Kando,* the holy book that Shu-Keseg, and eventually Shu-Dereth and Shu-Korath, had come from.

"You may have read *a* version of *Wyrn the King,*" Sarene said, shaking her head. "But not this one. Modern versions of the poem make references to Jaddeth in an almost Derethi way. The version in this book shows that the priests rewrote the literature from the original to make it sound as if Wyrn were Derethi—even though he lived long before Shu-Dereth was founded. Back then Jaddeth—or, at least, the god of the same name that Shu-Dereth adopted—was a relatively unimportant god who cared for the rocks under the earth.

"Now that Fjorden is religious, they can't have it sounding like their greatest historical king was a pagan, so the priests went through and rewrote all of the poems. I don't know where this man Seor got an original version of *Wyrn,* but if it got out, it would provide a major source of embarrassment to Fjorden." Her eyes sparkled mischievously.

Raoden sighed, walking over and crouching down next to Sarene's desk, putting her face at eye level. Any other time, he would have liked nothing more than to sit and listen to her talk. Unfortunately, he had more pressing things on his mind.

"All right," she said, her eyes thinning as she put down the book. "What is it? Am I really that boring?"

"Not at all," Raoden said. "This is just the wrong time. You see . . . Galladon and I just climbed to the top of the city wall."

Her face grew perplexed. "And?"

"We found the Elantris City Guard surrounding Duke Telrii's mansion," Raoden said. "We were kind of hoping you could tell us why. I know you're hesitant to talk about the outside, but I'm worried. I need to know what is happening."

Sarene sat with one arm leaning on the desktop, hand raised and tapping her cheek with her index finger as she often did when she was thinking. "All right," she finally said with a sigh. "I guess I haven't been fair. I didn't want to concern you with outside events."

"Some of the other Elantrians may seem uninterested, Sarene," Raoden said, "but that's just because they know we can't change what is going on in Kae. I'd prefer to know about things on the outside, however—even if you are a bit hesitant to talk about them."

Sarene nodded. "It's all right—I can talk about it now. I guess the important part began when I dethroned King Iadon—which, of course, is why he hanged himself."

Raoden sat down with a thump, his eyes wide.

CHAPTER 44

EVEN as she spoke, Sarene worried about what Spirit had said. Without her, the others had no legitimate claim on the throne. Even Roial was stumped; they could only watch helplessly as Telrii solidified control over the nobility.

She expected to receive news of Telrii's coronation by the end of the day.

It took her a few moments to realize the look of stunned shock her comment had caused Spirit. He had fallen back into one of the room's chairs, his eyes wide. She chastened herself for lack of tact; this was, after all, Spirit's king she was talking about. So much had happened in court the last few weeks that she had grown desensitized.

"I'm sorry," Sarene said. "That was a little blunt, wasn't it?"

"Iadon is dead?" Spirit asked in a quiet voice.

Sarene nodded. "It turns out he was involved with the Jeskeri Mysteries. When that got out, he hanged himself rather than face the shame." She didn't expand on her role in the events; there was no need to complicate them further.

"Jeskeri?" Spirit repeated, then his face turned dark and he gritted his teeth. "I always thought of him as a fool, but . . . How far did his . . . involvement go?"

"He was sacrificing his cooks and maids," Sarene said, feeling sick. There was a reason she had avoided explaining these things.

Spirit apparently noticed her pallor. "I'm sorry."

"It's all right," Sarene said. However, she knew no matter what else happened, no matter where she went in her life, the shadowed vision of Iadon's sacrifice would always lurk in her mind.

"Telrii is king then?" Spirit asked.

"Soon," Sarene said. "He might have been crowned already."

Spirit shook his head. "What about Duke Roial? He's both richer and more respected. He should have taken the throne."

"He's not richer anymore," Sarene said. "Fjorden has supplemented Telrii's income. He's a Derethi sympathizer, which, I'm afraid, has increased his social standing."

Spirit's brow furled. "Being a Derethi sympathizer makes one popular? I've missed a lot, haven't I?"

"How long have you been in here?"

"A year," Spirit answered offhandedly. That matched what some of the other New Elantrians had told her. No one knew for certain how long Spirit had been in the city, but they all guessed at least a year. He had seized control of the rival gangs in recent weeks, but that wasn't the sort of thing a person accomplished without a great deal of planning and work.

"I guess that answers how Telrii got the Guard to back him," Spirit mumbled. "They've always been far too eager to support whoever seemed most popular at the moment."

Sarene nodded. "They relocated to the duke's mansion shortly before I was thrown in here."

"All right," Spirit said. "You're going to have to start at the beginning—I need as much information as you can give me."

So, she explained. She began with the fall of the Duladen Republic and Fjorden's increasing threat. She told him of her engagement to Prince Raoden, and of the Derethi incursions into Arelon. As she spoke, she realized that Spirit understood the political climate of Arelon more soundly than she would have thought possible. He quickly grasped the implications of Iadon's posthumous declaration. He knew a lot about Fjorden, though he didn't have a working knowledge of how dangerous its priests could be; he was more worried about Wyrn-controlled soldiers.

Most impressive was his understanding of the various lords and nobles of Arelon. Sarene didn't need to explain their personalities and temperaments; Spirit already knew them. In fact, he seemed to understand them better than Sarene herself. When she questioned him on the matter, he simply explained that in Arelon it was vital to know of each noble with a rank of baron or higher. Many times a lesser nobleman's only means of advancement was to make deals and take contracts with the more powerful aristocrats, for they controlled the markets.

Only one thing beyond the king's death shocked him.

"You were going to *marry* Roial?" he asked incredulously.

Sarene smiled. "I can't believe it either—the plan developed rather quickly."

"Roial?" Spirit asked again. "The old rascal! He must have thoroughly enjoyed suggesting *that* idea."

"I found the duke to be an unquestionable gentleman," Sarene said.

Spirit eyed her with a look that said "And I thought you were a better judge of character."

"Besides," she continued, "he didn't suggest it. Shuden did."

"Shuden?" Spirit said. Then, after a moment's thought, he nodded. "Yes, that does sound like a connection he would make, though I can't see him even mentioning the word 'marriage.' The very concept of matrimony frightens him."

"Not anymore," Sarene said. "He and Ahan's daughter are growing very close."

"Shuden and Torena?" Spirit asked, even more dumbfounded. Then, he regarded Sarene with narrowed eyes. "Wait a moment—how were you going to marry Roial? I thought you were already married."

"To a dead man," Sarene huffed.

"But your wedding contract said you could never marry again."

"How did you know that?" Sarene asked with narrowed eyes.

"You explained it just a few minutes ago."

"I did not."

"Sure you did—didn't she, Galladon?"

The large Dula, who was flipping through Sarene's political book, didn't even look up. "Don't look at me, sule. I'm not getting involved."

"Anyway," Spirit said, turning away from his friend. "How is it that you were going to marry Roial?"

"Why not?" Sarene asked. "I never knew this Raoden. Everyone says he was a fine prince, but what do I owe him? My contract with Arelon dissolved when Iadon died; the only reason I made the treaty in the first place was to provide a link between Arelon and my homeland. Why would I honor a contract with a dead man when I could form a more promising one with the future king of Arelon?"

"So you only agreed to marry the prince for politics." His tone sounded hurt for some reason, as if her relationship with the crown prince of Arelon reflected directly on its aristocracy.

"Of course," Sarene said. "I am a political creature, Spirit. I did what was best for Teod—and for the same reason I was going to marry Roial."

He nodded, still looking a bit melancholy.

"So, I was in the throne room, ready to marry the duke," Sarene continued, ignoring Spirit's pique. What right did he have to question her motives? "And that was exactly when the Shaod took me."

"Right then?" Spirit asked. "It happened at your wedding?"

Sarene nodded, suddenly feeling very insecure. It seemed that every time she was about to find acceptance, something disastrous alienated her once again.

Galladon snorted. "Well, now we know why she didn't want to talk about it. Kolo?"

Spirit's hand found her shoulder. "I'm sorry."

"It's over now," Sarene said with a shake of her head. "We need to worry about Telrii's coronation. With Fjorden supporting him . . ."

"We can worry about Telrii, but I doubt there's anything we can do. If only there were a way to contact the outside!"

Suddenly ashamed, Sarene's eyes darted up to where Ashe hid in the room's shadows, his Aon nearly invisible. "There might be a way," she admitted.

Spirit looked up as Sarene waved to Ashe. Ashe started to glow, the Aon's light expanding into a luminescent ball around him. As the Seon floated down to hover above her desk, Sarene shot Spirit an embarrassed look.

"A Seon?" he said appreciatively.

"You're not angry at me for hiding him?" Sarene asked.

Spirit chuckled. "In all honesty, Sarene, I expected you to hold some things back from me. You seem like the type of person who needs secrets, if only for the sake of having them."

Sarene blushed slightly at the astute comment. "Ashe, go check with Kiin and the others. I want to know the moment Telrii declares himself king."

"Yes, my lady," Ashe said, hovering away.

Spirit fell silent. He hadn't commented on Ashe's inexplicable lack of Shaod madness—but, of course, Spirit couldn't know that Ashe had been Sarene's own Seon.

They waited in silence, and Sarene didn't interrupt Spirit's thoughts. She had given him an overwhelming mass of information, and she could see his mind picking through it behind his eyes.

He was hiding things from her as well. Not that she mistrusted him. Whatever his secrets were, he probably felt he had a good reason for keeping them. She had been involved with politics far too long to take the holding of secrets as a personal offense.

That didn't, of course, mean she wasn't going to find out what she could. So far, Ashe hadn't been able to discover anything about a second son of Ien Plantation's ruler, but he was very restricted in his movements. She had allowed him to reveal himself only to Kiin and the others; she didn't know why he had survived where other Seons did not, but she didn't want to lose any potential edge his existence might give her.

Apparently realizing they weren't going to go anywhere soon, the Dula Galladon shuffled over to one of the chairs and seated himself. Then he closed his eyes and appeared to fall asleep. He might be unstereotypically pessimistic, but he was still a Dula. It was said that his people were so relaxed that they could fall asleep in any position at any time.

Sarene eyed the large man. Galladon didn't seem to like her. But, then, he was so determinedly grouchy that she couldn't tell. He seemed a well of knowledge at times, but in other areas he was completely ignorant—and totally unconcerned by that fact. He seemed to take everything in stride, but he complained about it at the same time.

By the time Ashe came back, Sarene had returned her attention to the book on political cover-ups. The Seon had to make a throat-clearing sound before she even realized he was there. Spirit looked up as well, though the Dula continued snoring until his friend elbowed him in the stomach. Then all three sets of eyes turned to Ashe.

"Well?" Sarene asked.

"It is done, my lady," Ashe informed them. "Telrii is king."

CHAPTER 45

HRATHEN stood in the moonlight atop the Elantris City wall, curiously studying the hole. One of the stairwell barricades was broken and scarred, the boards pulled free. The hole was strikingly similar to one that might have been made by rodents—Elantrian rodents, seeking to escape from their nest. This was one of the sections of the wall kept clean by the Guard, and some slime tracks from the stairwell gave ample proof that those below had been up the wall several times.

Hrathen strolled away from the stairwell. He was probably the only one who knew about the hole; Elantris was now watched by only two or three Guards, and they rarely—if ever—patrolled the wall walk. For now, he wouldn't tell the Guards about the hole. It didn't matter to him if the Elantrians snuck out of their city. They wouldn't be able to go anywhere; their appearance was too distinctive. Besides, he didn't want to bother the people with worries about Elantris; he wanted them to remain focused on their new king, and the allegiances he would soon declare.

He walked, Elantris to his right, Kae to his left. A small concentration of lights shone in the evening's darkness—the royal palace, now Telrii's home. The Arelish nobility, eager to show devotion to their new king, were in near unanimous attendance at his coronation party—each man vying to prove his loyalty. The pompous former duke was obviously enjoying the attention.

Hrathen continued to stroll in the calm night, feet clinking against the stones. Telrii's coronation had occurred with expected flair. The former duke, now king, was an easy man to understand, and men who could be understood could be manipulated. Let him enjoy his diversion for the moment. On the morrow, the time would come for payment of debts.

Telrii would undoubtedly demand more money from Hrathen before he joined Shu-Dereth. Telrii would think himself clever, and would assume that the crown gave him even greater leverage with Fjorden. Hrathen, of course, would feign indignation at the cash demands, all the while understanding what Telrii never could. Power was not in wealth, but in control—money was worthless before a man who refused to be bought. The king would never understand that the wyrnings he demanded wouldn't give him power, but would instead put him beneath the power of another. As he glutted himself on coins, Arelon would slip away from him.

Hrathen shook his head, feeling mildly guilty. He used Telrii because the king made himself such a wonderful tool. However, there would be no conversion in Telrii's heart—no true acceptance of Jaddeth or His empire. Telrii's promises would be as empty as the power of his throne. And yet, Hrathen would use him. It was logical, and as Hrathen had come to understand, the strength of his faith was in its logic. Telrii might not believe, but his children—raised Derethi—would. One man's meaningless conversion would provide for the salvation of a kingdom.

As he walked, Hrathen found his eyes consistently drawn toward the darkened streets of Elantris. He tried to focus his thoughts on Telrii and the impending conquest of Arelon, but another matter tickled at his mind.

Grudgingly, Hrathen admitted to himself that he had wanted to walk the wall of Elantris this night for more than one reason. He was worried about the princess. The emotion bothered him, of course, but he didn't deny that he felt it. Sarene had been a wonderful opponent, and he knew how dangerous Elantris could be. He had realized this when he gave the poisoning order, determining the risk to be worth the gain. After waiting three days, however, his resolve was beginning to waver. He needed her to live for more reason than one.

So, Hrathen watched the streets, foolishly hoping that he might see her below and console his conscience that she was unharmed. Of course, he hadn't seen anything of the sort; in fact, there didn't seem to be any Elantrians about this evening. Hrathen didn't know if they had just moved to other parts of the city, or if the place had grown so violent that they had destroyed themselves. For the princess's sake, he hoped the second was not true.

"You are the gyorn, Hrathen," a sudden voice said.

Hrathen spun, eyes searching for the man who had approached him unseen and unheard. A Seon hovered behind him, glowing vibrantly in the darkness. Hrathen squinted, reading the Aon at its center. Dio.

"I am he," Hrathen said cautiously.

"I come on behalf of my master, King Eventeo of Teod," the Seon said with a melodious voice. "He wishes to speak with you."

Hrathen smiled. He had been wondering how long it would take Eventeo to contact him. "I am anxious to hear what His Majesty has to say."

The Seon pulsed as its light pulled inward, outlining the face of a man with an oval face and a full chin.

"Your Majesty," Hrathen said with a slight nod. "How may I serve you?"

"No need for useless civility, Gyorn," Eventeo said flatly. "You know what I want."

"Your daughter."

The king's head nodded. "I know that somehow you have power over this sickness. What would it take for you to heal Sarene?"

"I have no power of myself," Hrathen said humbly. "It was Lord Jaddeth who performed the healing."

The king paused. "Then, what would it take for your Jaddeth to heal my daughter?"

"The Lord might be persuaded if you gave Him some form of encouragement," Hrathen said. "The faithless receive no miracles, Your Majesty."

King Eventeo slowly bowed his head—he had obviously known what Hrathen would demand. He must love his daughter very much.

"It will be as you say, priest," Eventeo promised. "If my daughter returns safely from that city, I will convert to Shu-Dereth. I knew it was coming anyway."

Hrathen smiled broadly. "I will see if I can . . . encourage Lord Jaddeth to return the princess, Your Majesty."

Eventeo nodded. His face was that of a man defeated. The Seon ended the contact and floated away without a word.

Hrathen smiled, the final piece of his plan falling into place. Eventeo had made a wise decision. This way, at least, he got to demand something in return for his conversion—even if it was something he would have received anyway.

Hrathen looked down at Elantris, more anxious than ever that Sarene return to him unharmed. It was beginning to appear that within the next few months he would be able to hand Wyrn not one heathen nation, but two.

CHAPTER 46

THERE had been times when Raoden had wished his father dead. Raoden had seen the people's suffering, and knew his father was to blame. Iadon had proven himself deceitful in his success and merciless in his determination to crush others. He had delighted in watching his nobles squabble while his kingdom collapsed. Arelon would be better off without King Iadon.

Yet, when news of his father's demise actually came, Raoden found his emotions traitorously melancholy. His heart wanted to forget the Iadon of the last five years, instead remembering the Iadon of Raoden's childhood. His father had been the most successful merchant in all of Arelon—respected by his countrymen and loved by his son. He had seemed a man of honor and of strength. Part of Raoden would always be that child who saw his father as the greatest of heroes.

Two things helped him forget the pain of loss—Sarene and the Aons. When he wasn't with one, he was with the other. New Elantris all but ran itself now; the people found their own projects to keep them busy, and there were rarely arguments that required his attention. So, he came to the library often, drawing Aons while Sarene studied.

"There is surprisingly little information here about modern Fjorden," Sarene said, poking through a tome so large she had nearly needed Raoden's help to carry it.

"Maybe you just haven't found the right book yet," Raoden said as he traced Aon Ehe. She sat at her customary desk, a pile of books next to her chair, and he stood with his back to the wall, practicing a new batch of Aon modifiers.

"Perhaps," Sarene said, unconvinced. "Everything in here seems to be about the Old Empire; only that book on historical reconstruction even mentions the Fjorden of the last hundred years. I assumed that the Elantrians would have studied other religions with care—if only to know what they were up against."

"As I understand it, the Elantrians didn't really mind competition," Raoden said. As he spoke his finger slipped slightly, breaking its line. The Aon held for a moment in the air, then faded away, his mistake invalidating the entire construction. He sighed before continuing his explanation. "The Elantrians figured they were so obviously superior to anything else that they didn't need to worry about other religions. Most of them didn't even care if they were worshipped or not."

Sarene considered his comment, then looked back at her book, pushing aside the empty plate that had held this afternoon's rations. Raoden didn't tell her that he increased her portion of food—just as he did for every newcomer during their first week. He had learned from experience that gradual reductions in food intake helped a mind adjust to the hunger.

He started his drawing again, and a few moments later the library door opened. "Is he still up there?" Raoden asked as Galladon entered.

"Kolo," the Dula replied. "Still screaming at his god."

"You mean 'praying.'"

Galladon shrugged, wandering over to take a seat next to Sarene. "You'd think a god would be able to hear him no matter how softly he spoke."

Sarene looked up from her book. "Are you talking about the gyorn?"

Raoden nodded. "He's been standing on the wall above the gate since early this morning. Apparently, he's been petitioning his god to heal us."

Sarene started. "*Heal* us?"

"Something like that," Raoden said. "We can't hear him very well."

"Healing Elantris? That's a switch." Her eyes were suspicious.

Raoden shrugged, continuing his drawing. Galladon selected a book on farming and began searching through it. Over the last few days he had been trying to devise a method of irrigation that would work under their particular circumstances.

A few minutes later, when Raoden had nearly completed the Aon and its modifiers, he realized that Sarene had put down her book and was watching him with interested eyes. The scrutiny made him slip again, and the Aon faded away before he even realized what he had done. She was still regarding him as he raised his hand to begin Aon Ehe again.

"What?" he finally asked. His fingers instinctively drew the first three strokes—the line across the top, line down the side, and dot in the middle that were the beginning of every Aon.

"You've been drawing that same one for the last hour now," she noted.

"I want to get it right."

"But you have—at least a dozen times in a row."

Raoden shrugged. "It helps me think."

"About what?" she asked curiously, apparently bored of the Old Empire for the time being.

"Lately, about AonDor itself. I understand most of the theory now, but I still don't seem any closer to discovering what has blocked the Dor. I feel that the Aons have changed, that the old patterns are slightly wrong, but I can't even begin to guess why that would be."

"Maybe something's wrong with the land," Sarene said offhandedly, leaning back in her chair so the front two legs rose off the ground.

"What do you mean?"

"Well," Sarene said speculatively, "you say that the Aons and the land are linked—though even I could have told you that."

"Oh?" Raoden asked, smiling as he drew. "Did your training as a princess include some secret lessons in Elantrian magic?"

"No," Sarene said with a dramatic toss of her head. "But it did include training in the Aons. To begin every Aon, you draw a picture of Arelon. I learned that as a little girl."

Raoden froze, his hand pausing in midline. "Say that again."

"Hum?" Sarene asked. "Oh, it's just a silly trick my teacher used to make me pay attention. See? Every Aon starts the same way—with a line at the top to represent the coast, a line down the side that looks like the Atad Mountains, and a dot in the middle to be Lake Alonoe."

Galladon stood, wandering over to look at Raoden's still glowing Aon. "She's right, sule. It *does* kind of look like Arelon. Didn't your books say anything about that?"

"No," Raoden said with amazement. "Well, they claimed there was a connection between the Aons and Arelon, but they never mentioned that the characters actually *represented* the land. Perhaps the concept was just too elementary."

Galladon picked up his book, folding something out of its back—a map of Arelon. "Keep drawing, sule. Otherwise that Aon's going to vanish away."

Raoden complied, forcing his finger back into motion. Galladon held up the map and Sarene moved to stand at the Dula's side. They looked through the thin paper at the glowing Aon.

"Doloken!" Galladon swore. "Sule, the proportions are exactly the same. They even slant the same way."

Raoden finished the Aon with one last stroke. He joined

the other two, regarding the map, then looked over at
Sarene. "But, what's wrong, then? The mountains are still
there, as is the coast, and the lake."

Sarene shrugged. "Don't look at me. You're the expert—I
can't even get the first line right."

Raoden turned back to the Aon. A few seconds later it
flashed briefly and disappeared, its potential blocked for
some inexplicable reason. If Sarene's hypothesis was right,
then the Aons were even more closely linked to Arelon than
he had assumed. Whatever had stopped AonDor must have
affected the land as well.

He turned, intending to praise Sarene for the clue. However, his words choked in his mouth. Something was wrong.
The dark splotches on the princess's skin were the wrong
color: they were a mixture of blues and purple, like bruises.
They seemed to fade before his eyes.

"Merciful Domi!" he exclaimed. "Galladon, look at her!"

The Dula turned with alarm, then his face changed from
worried to awed.

"What?" the princess demanded, shooting them nervous
looks.

"What did you do, sule?" Galladon asked.

"Nothing!" Raoden insisted, looking at the place where
his Aon had been. "Something else must be healing her."

Then he made the connection. Sarene had never been able
to draw Aons. She had complained of being cold, and she
still insisted that her wounds didn't hurt. Raoden reached out
and felt Sarene's face. Her flesh was warm—too warm, even
for a new Elantrian whose body hadn't completely cooled
yet. He pushed the scarf off her head with trembling fingers,
and felt the nearly invisible blond stubble on her scalp.

"Idos Domi," he whispered. Then he grabbed her hand,
pulling her out of the library.

"SPIRIT, I don't understand," she protested as they entered
the courtyard before Elantris's gate.

"You were never an Elantrian, Sarene," he said. "It was a
trick—the same one that gyorn used to appear as if he were

an Elantrian. Somehow Hrathen can make it seem that you've been taken by the Shaod when you haven't."

"But—" she objected.

"Think, Sarene!" Raoden said, spinning her around to look him in the eyes. The gyorn preached on the wall above them, his loud voice garbled by the distance. "Your wedding to Roial would have put an opponent of Shu-Dereth on the throne. Hrathen had to stop that wedding—and he did it in the most embarrassing way he could contrive. You don't belong here."

He pulled on her arm again, attempting to lead her toward the gates. She resisted, pulling against him with equal strength. "I'm not going."

Raoden turned with surprise. "But you have to go—this is *Elantris,* Sarene. No one *wants* to be here."

"I don't care," she insisted, voice defiantly firm. "I'm going to stay."

"Arelon needs you."

"Arelon will be better off without me. If I hadn't interfered, Iadon would still be alive, and Telrii wouldn't have the throne."

Raoden fell still. He wanted her to stay—he longed for her to stay. But he would do whatever it took to get her out of Elantris. The city was death.

The gates were opening; the gyorn had recognized his prey.

Sarene regarded Raoden with wide eyes, her hand reaching up toward him. The splotches had nearly completely vanished now. She was beautiful.

"You think we can afford to feed you, Princess?" Raoden said, forcing harshness into his voice. "You assume we will waste food on a woman who is not one of us?"

"That won't work, Spirit," Sarene shot back. "I can see the truth in your eyes."

"Then believe this truth," Raoden said. "Even with severe rationing, New Elantris only has enough food for a few more weeks. We raise crops, but it will be months before we can harvest them. During that time we will starve. All of us—the men the women and the children. We will starve unless someone on the outside can get us more supplies."

She hesitated, then she was in his arms, pulling close against his chest. "Curse you," she hissed. "Domi curse you."

"Arelon does need you, Sarene," he whispered back. "If what you say is right, and a Fjordell sympathizer is on the throne, there may not be much time left for Elantris. You know what the Derethi priests would do to us if they had their way. Things have gone very wrong in Arelon, Sarene, and you are the only one I trust to fix them."

She looked into his eyes. "I will return."

Men in yellow and brown churned around them, pulling the two apart. They shoved Raoden aside, and he fell back against the slick cobblestones as the figures pulled Sarene away. Raoden was left lying on his back, feeling the slime squish beneath him, looking up at a man in bloodred armor. The gyorn stood quietly for a moment, then turned and followed Sarene out of the city. The gates slammed shut behind him.

CHAPTER 47

THE gates slammed shut. This time they didn't lock Sarene in Elantris, but out of it. Emotions snapped at her soul like a pack of angry wolves, each one demanding her attention. Five days before, she had thought her life ruined. She had wished, prayed, and begged for Domi to heal her. Now she found herself craving to return to her damnation, as long as Spirit was there.

Domi, however, had made the decision for her. Spirit was right: She could no more live in Elantris than he could exist outside of the city. The worlds, and the demands of their flesh, were far too different.

A hand fell on her shoulder. Shaking off her numbness, Sarene turned. There weren't many men she had to crane her neck to look up at. Hrathen.

"Jaddeth has preserved you, Princess," he said in a lightly accented voice.

Sarene shook his arm away. "I don't know how you did this, priest, but I know one thing with absolute certainty. I owe your god nothing."

"Your father thinks differently, Princess," Hrathen said, his face hard.

"For a man whose religion claims to spread truth, priest, your lies are strikingly vulgar."

Hrathen smiled thinly. "Lies? Why don't you go and speak with him? In a way, it could be said that *you* gave us Teod. Convert the king, and often you convert the kingdom as well."

"Impossible!" Sarene said, growing uncertain. Gyorns were usually far too wily to tell direct falsehoods.

"You fought with wisdom and cleverness, Princess," Hrathen said, taking a slow step forward and extending his gauntleted hand. "But true wisdom knows when further fighting is pointless. I have Teod, and Arelon will soon be mine as well. Do not be like the stonelark, ever trying to dig a pit in the sand's wet beaches and ever having your work destroyed by the tide. Embrace Shu-Dereth, and let your efforts become more than vanity."

"I will die first!"

"You already have," the gyorn pointed out. "And *I* brought you back." He took another step forward, and Sarene shied back, pulling her hands up against her chest.

Steel whipped in the sunlight, and suddenly the point of Eondel's sword was at Hrathen's neck. Sarene felt herself enfolded in enormous, powerful arms, a scratchy voice crying out in joy beside her.

"Blessed be Domi's name!" Kiin praised, lifting her off the ground with his hug.

"Blessed be *Jaddeth's* name," Hrathen said, sword tip still pressed against his flesh. "Domi left this one to rot."

"Say no more, priest," Eondel said, angling his sword threateningly.

Hrathen snorted. Then, moving more quickly than Sarene's eyes could track, the gyorn bent backward and pulled his head out of the sword's range. He kicked at the same time, smashing his foot into Eondel's hand and knocking the weapon free.

Hrathen spun, crimson cape billowing, bloodred hand plucking the sword from the air. Steel reflected sunlight as Hrathen spun the weapon. He snapped its tip against the cobblestones, holding it as a king would his scepter. Then, he let it drop, the hilt falling back into Eondel's stunned hand. The priest stepped forward, passing the confused general.

"Time moves like a mountain, Sarene," Hrathen whispered, so close that his breastplate nearly brushed against Kiin's protective arms. "It comes so slowly that most don't even notice its passing. It will, however, crush those who don't move before it."

With that he spun, his cape fluttering against both Eondel and Kiin as he marched away.

Kiin watched Hrathen go, hatred in his eyes. Finally, he turned to Eondel. "Come, General. Let's take Sarene home to rest."

"There is no time for rest, Uncle," Sarene said. "I need you to gather our allies. We must meet as soon as possible."

Kiin raised an eyebrow. "There will be time enough for that later, 'Ene. You're in no condition—"

"I've had a fine vacation, Uncle," she declared, "but there is work to be done. Perhaps when it is finished, I'll be able to escape back to Elantris. For now, we need to worry about stopping Telrii from giving our country to Wyrn. Send messengers to Roial and Ahan. I want to meet with them as soon as possible."

Her uncle's face looked utterly dumbfounded.

"Well, she *seems* all right," Eondel noted, smiling.

THE cooks in her father's household had learned one thing: When Sarene wanted to eat, she could eat.

"You'd better move faster, Cousin," Lukel said as she finished her fourth plate. "You looked like you almost had time to taste that one."

Sarene ignored him, motioning for Kiin to bring in the next delicacy. She had been told that if one starved oneself long enough, the stomach would shrink, thereby reducing the amount of food one could eat. The man who had invented that theory would have thrown up his hands in despair if he could have seen Sarene feasting.

She sat at the table across from Lukel and Roial. The elderly duke had just arrived, and when he had seen Sarene, she thought for a moment he was going to collapse from the shock. Instead, he had breathed a prayer to Domi, seating himself speechlessly in the chair across from her.

"I can honestly say that I have never seen a woman eat this much," Duke Roial noted appreciatively. There was still a hint of disbelieving wonder in his eyes as he looked at her.

"She's a Teoish giantess," Lukel said. "I don't think it's fair to make comparisons between Sarene and regular women."

"If I weren't so busy eating, I'd respond to that," Sarene said, waving her fork at them. She hadn't realized exactly how hungry she was until she'd entered Kiin's kitchen, where the lingering scents of past banquets hung in the air like a delectable fog. She was only now appreciating how useful it was to have a world-traveled chef as an uncle.

Kiin entered with a pan of semi-boiling meat and vegetables in a red sauce. "It's Jindoeese RaiDomo Mai. The name means 'meat with fiery skin.' You're fortunate I had the proper ingredients, the Jindo RaiDel pepper had a poor crop last season, and . . ." He trailed off as Sarene began heaping meat onto her plate. "You don't care, do you?" he asked with a sigh. "I could have boiled it in dishwater, and it would be the same to you."

"I understand, Uncle," Sarene said. "You suffer for your art."

Kiin sat down, looking at the empty dishes scattered across the table. "Well, you certainly inherited the family appetite."

"She's a big girl," Lukel said. "It takes a lot of fuel to keep that body going."

Sarene shot him a look between bites.

"Is she slowing down at all?" Kiin asked. "I'm running out of supplies."

"Actually," Sarene said, "I think this should about do it. You don't understand what it was like in there, gentlemen. I did actually enjoy myself, but there wasn't a lot of food to be had."

"I'm surprised there was any at all," Lukel said. "Elantrians like to eat."

"But they don't actually need to," Kiin said, "so they can afford to stockpile."

Sarene kept eating, not looking up at her uncle and cousin. Her mind, however, paused. How did they know so much about Elantrians?

"Whatever the conditions, Princess," Roial said, "we thank Domi for your safe return."

"It isn't as miraculous as it seems, Roial," Sarene said. "Did anyone count how many days Hrathen was in Elantris?"

"Four or five," Lukel said after a moment's thought.

"I'd be willing to bet it was five days—exactly the same amount of time it took me to get thrown in and then be 'healed.'"

Roial nodded. "The gyorn had something to do with this. Have you spoken with your father yet?"

Sarene felt her stomach turn. "No. I'm . . . going to do that soon."

There was a knock at the door, and a few moments later Eondel entered, Shuden in tow. The young Jindo had been out riding with Torena.

As he entered, the baron's face broke into an uncharacteristically wide smile. "We should have known you'd be back, Sarene. If anyone could be sent to hell and return untouched, it would be you."

"Not exactly untouched," Sarene said, raising her hand to feel her bald scalp. "Did you find anything?"

"Here, my lady," Eondel said, holding out a short blond wig. "It was the best I could find—most of the others felt so thick I would have sworn they were made of horse hair."

Sarene looked over the wig with a critical eye—it would

barely come down to her shoulders. But, it was better than baldness. In her estimation, her hair was the greatest loss incurred by her exile. It was going to take years to grow it to a decent length again.

"Too bad no one gathered up my own hair," she said, tucking the wig away until she could find time to put it on properly.

"We didn't exactly anticipate your return, Cousin," Lukel said, picking at the last few pieces of meat in the pan. "It was probably still attached to your veil when we burned it."

"Burned it?"

"Arelish custom, 'Ene," Kiin explained. "When someone is thrown into Elantris, we burn their possessions."

"Everything?" Sarene asked weakly.

"I'm afraid so," Kiin said with embarrassment.

Sarene closed her eyes, exhaling. "Never mind," she said, regarding them. "Where's Ahan?"

"At Telrii's palace," Roial said.

Sarene frowned. "What's he doing there?"

Kiin shrugged. "We figured we should send someone, at least, to make an overture to the new king. We're going to have to work with him, so we might as well see what kind of cooperation we can expect."

Sarene eyed her companions. Despite their obvious joy at seeing her, she sensed something in their expressions. Defeat. They had worked so hard to keep Telrii off the throne, and they had failed. Inside, Sarene barely acknowledged that she felt many of the same emotions. She felt sick. She couldn't decide what she wanted; everything was so confused. Fortunately, her sense of duty provided guidance. Spirit was correct: Arelon was in serious danger. She didn't want to even contemplate the things Hrathen had said about her father—she only knew that no matter what else happened, she had to protect Arelon. For Elantris's sake.

"You speak as if there weren't anything we could do about Telrii's claim of the throne," Sarene said to the quiet room.

"What could we do?" Lukel said. "Telrii's been crowned, and the nobility supports him."

"So does Wyrn," Sarene reminded. "Sending Ahan is a good idea, but I doubt you'll find any leniency in Telrii's reign—for us, or for the rest of Arelon. My lords, Raoden should have been king, and I am his wife. I feel responsible for his people. They suffered under Iadon. If Telrii turns this kingdom over to Wyrn, then Arelon will become nothing more than another Fjordell province."

"What are you implying, Sarene?" Shuden asked.

"That we take action against Telrii—any action we can."

The table fell silent. Finally, Roial spoke. "This is different from what we were doing before, Sarene. We opposed Iadon, but we did not plan to remove him. If we take direct action against Telrii, then we will be traitors to the Crown."

"Traitors to the Crown, but not the people," Sarene said. "In Teod, we respect the king because he protects us. It is a bargain—a formal agreement. Iadon did nothing to protect Arelon. He built no army to keep Fjorden away, he devised no legal system to ensure that his subjects were treated fairly, and he did nothing to care for the spiritual welfare of his nation. My instincts warn me that Telrii will be even worse."

Roial sighed. "I don't know, Sarene. Iadon overthrew the Elantrians to seize his power, and now you suggest that we do the same thing. How much of this can a country stand before it breaks apart?"

"How much of Hrathen's string pulling do you think it can stand?" Sarene asked pointedly.

The gathered lords looked at each other. "Let us sleep on it, Sarene," Shuden requested. "You speak of difficult matters—ones that should not be entered into without careful meditation."

"Agreed," Sarene said. She was looking forward to the night's rest herself. For the first time in almost a week, she was going to actually be warm as she slept.

The lords nodded, rising to go their separate ways. Roial hung back for a moment. "It looks as if there is no reason to continue our betrothal, is there, Sarene?"

"I don't think so, my lord. If we take the throne now, it will be through force, not manipulation of politics."

The elderly man nodded wistfully. "Ah, it was far too good to be true anyway, my dear. Goodnight, then."

"Goodnight," Sarene said, smiling fondly as the aged duke left. Three engagements and no weddings. She was amassing a poor track record indeed. With a sigh, she watched Roial close the door, then turned to Kiin, who was fastidiously clearing away the remains of her meal.

"Uncle," she said. "Telrii has moved into the palace and my things have been burned. I find myself suddenly without lodgings. Might I accept your offer of two months ago and move in here?"

Kiin chuckled. "My wife will be seriously annoyed if you don't, 'Ene. She spent the last hour preparing a room for you."

SARENE sat on her new bed, wearing one of her aunt's nightgowns. Her legs were pulled tightly against her chest, and her bowed head was sorrowful.

Ashe fuzzed for a moment, her father's face disappearing as the Seon returned to his normal shape. He was silent for a long moment before saying, "I am sorry, my lady."

Sarene nodded, her bald head rubbing against her knees. Hrathen had not been lying—he hadn't even been exaggerating. Her father had converted to Shu-Dereth.

The ceremony hadn't been performed yet; there were no Derethi priests in Teod. However, it was apparent that as soon as Hrathen finished with Arelon, he intended to travel to her homeland and personally collect her father's formal oath. The oath would place Eventeo at the bottom of the Derethi hierarchy, forcing him to submit to the whims of even a simple priest.

No amount of raving or explaining had changed her father's resolve. Eventeo was an honest man. He had sworn to Hrathen that if Sarene returned safely, he would convert. It didn't matter that the gyorn's trickery was behind both her curse and restoration; the king would honor his promise.

Where Eventeo led, Teod would follow. It would take time, of course; the people of Teod were not sheep. However, as the arteths flooded her homeland, the people would give ear where they would have given only fists before—all because they knew that their king was Derethi. Teod had been changed forever.

And he had done it for her. Of course, he claimed that he

also knew it was best for the country. No matter how good Teod's navy was, sheer numbers insured that a determined Fjordell campaign would eventually punch through the armada. Eventeo claimed he would not fight a hopeless war.

Yet, this was the same man who had instructed Sarene that principle was always worth fighting to protect. Eventeo had sworn that truth was immutable, and that no battle—even a hopeless one—was in vain when defending what was right. But, apparently, his love was stronger than truth. She was flattered, but the emotion made her sick. Teod would fall because of her, becoming just another Fjordell state, its king little more than Wyrn's servant.

Eventeo had implied that she should lead Arelon to do as he had done, though she could tell from his voice that he was proud when she refused. She would protect Arelon, and Elantris. She would struggle for the survival of her religion, because Arelon—poor sickly Arelon—was now Shu-Korath's final sanctuary. Where Arelon had once been a nation populated by gods, now it would serve as the final haven for Domi Himself.

CHAPTER 48

HRATHEN sat in the palace waiting room with growing dissatisfaction. Around him, the signs of a changing government were already evident. It seemed remarkable that one man could own so many tapestries, rugs, and brocades. The palace sitting room was so draped with cloth plushness that Hrathen had been forced to shove a virtual mountain of pillows out of the way before finding a stone ledge upon which to seat himself.

He sat near the stone hearth, jaw clenched as he regarded the assembled nobility. As could be expected, Telrii had quite suddenly become a very busy man. Every nobleman, landholder, and ambitious merchant in the city wanted to pay his "respects" to the new king. Dozens waited in the sitting room, many without firm appointments. They hid their impatience poorly, but not a one was brave enough to voice annoyance at the treatment.

Their inconvenience was unimportant. The intolerable factor was Hrathen's inclusion in the group. The rabble of supposed nobility was a pandering, indolent lot. Hrathen, however, was backed by the power of Wyrn's kingdom and Jaddeth's empire—the very power that had given Telrii the wealth he needed to claim the throne.

And yet Hrathen was forced to wait. It was maddening, it was discourteous, and it was unbelievable. Yet Hrathen had no choice but to endure it. Backed by Wyrn's power though he was, he had no troops, no might to force Telrii's hand. He could not denounce the man openly—despite his frustration, Hrathen's political instinct was too keen to let him do something like that. He had worked hard to get a potential sympathizer on the throne; only a fool would let his own pride ruin such an opportunity. Hrathen would wait, tolerating disrespect for a short time, to achieve the eventual prize.

An attendant entered the room, draped in fine silks—the exaggerated livery of Telrii's personal heralds. The room's occupants perked up, several men standing and straightening their clothing.

"Gyorn Hrathen," the attendant announced.

The noblemen wilted, and Hrathen stood and brushed past them with a dismissive step. It was about time.

Telrii waited beyond. Hrathen paused just inside the door, regarding the chamber with displeasure. The room had once been Iadon's study, and at that time it had been marked by a businessman's efficiency. Everything had been well placed and orderly; the furniture had been comfortable without being lavish.

Telrii had changed that. Attendants stood at the sides of the room, and beside them sat carts heaped with exotic foods, purchased from the merchants of the Arelene Market.

Telrii reclined in a massive pile of cushions and silks, a pleasant smile on his purple-birthmarked face. Rugs coated the floor, and tapestries overlapped one another on the walls.

The men I am forced to work with . . . Hrathen thought with an inward sigh. Iadon, at least, had been businesslike.

"Ah, Hrathen," Telrii said with a smile. "Welcome."

"Your Majesty," Hrathen said, masking his disgust. "I was hoping we could speak in private."

Telrii sighed. "Very well," he said with a wave of his hand, dismissing the attendants. They left, pulling the outer doors closed.

"Now," Telrii said, "why have you come? Are you interested in the tariffs on your merchants setting up for the Arelene Market?"

Hrathen frowned. "I have more important matters to consider, Your Majesty. As do you. I have come to collect on the promises of our allegiance."

"Promises, Hrathen?" Telrii asked idly. "I made no promises."

And so the game began. "You are to join the Derethi religion," Hrathen said. "That was the deal."

"I made no such deal, Hrathen," Telrii said. "You offered me funds; I accepted them. You have my gratitude for the support, as I said that you would."

"I will not squabble with you, merchant," Hrathen said, wondering how much money Telrii would demand to "remember" their agreement. "I am no sycophant to be baited. If you do not do as Jaddeth expects, then I will find someone else. Do not forget what happened to your predecessor."

Telrii snorted. "Don't take credit for something you had no hand in, priest. Iadon's fall was, as I recall, caused by the Teoish princess. You were in Elantris at the time. Now, if Fjorden wishes a Derethi on the throne of Arelon, that can probably be arranged. There will be, however, a price."

Finally, Hrathen thought. He clenched his jaw, feigning anger, and waited a moment. Then he sighed. "Very well. How much—"

"However," Telrii interrupted, "it is not a price you can pay."

Hrathen froze. "Excuse me?"

"Yes," Telrii said. "My price must be paid by someone with a little more . . . authority than yourself. You see, I've learned that Derethi priests cannot appoint men to their own position in the Church hierarchy."

Hrathen felt a chill grow within him as he connected the pieces of Telrii's statements. "You can't possibly be serious," he whispered.

"I know more than you assume, Hrathen," Telrii said. "You think me a fool, ignorant of the ways of the East? Kings bow to gyorns. What power will I hold if I let you make me into nothing more than a Derethi slave? No, that will not do for me. I don't plan to bow anytime one of your priests comes to visit. I will convert to your religion, but I will do so only with the promise of an ecclesiastic rank to match my civil one. Not just King Telrii, but *Gyorn* Telrii."

Hrathen shook his head in wonder. How easily this man claimed that he was not "ignorant" of the ways of the East, yet even Fjordell children knew enough doctrine to laugh at such a ridiculous suggestion. "My lord Telrii," he said with amusement. "You have no idea—"

"I said, Hrathen," Telrii interrupted, "that there is nothing you can do for me. I have sought to deal with a higher power."

Hrathen's apprehension returned. "What are you saying?"

"Wyrn," Telrii said with a wide smile. "I sent him a messenger several days ago, informing him of my demand. You are no longer necessary, Hrathen. You may withdraw."

Hrathen stood, stunned. The man had sent a letter to Wyrn himself . . . Telrii had made *demands* of the Regent of All Creation? "You are a foolish, foolish man," Hrathen whispered, finally realizing the severity of his problems. When Wyrn received that message . . .

"Go!" Telrii repeated pointing toward the door.

Slightly dazed, Hrathen did as commanded.

CHAPTER 49

A T first Raoden stayed away from the library, because it reminded him of her. Then, he found himself drawn back to it—because it reminded him of her.

Instead of thinking about his loss, Raoden focused on the connection Sarene had made. He studied Aon after Aon, noticing other features of the landscape in their forms. Aon Eno, the character for water, included a wiggling line that matched the meanderings of the Aredel River. The character for wood—Aon Dii—included several circles that represented the southern forests.

The Aons were maps of the land, each one a slightly different rendering of the same general picture. Each one had the three basic lines—the coast line, the mountain line, and the dot for Lake Alonoe. Many often had a line at the bottom to represent the Kalomo River, which separated Arelon from Duladel.

Some of the features completely baffled him, however. Why did Aon Mea, the character for thoughtfulness have an X that crossed somewhere in the middle of the Eon County? Why was Aon Rii specked with two dozen seemingly random dots? The answers might have been held in one of the library's tomes, but so far he had found nothing in the way of explanation.

The Dor attacked him at least twice a day now. Each battle seemed like it would be his last, and each time he seemed a little weaker when the fight was through—as if his energy were a finite well, dribbling a little lower with each confrontation. The question was not whether he would fall or not, but whether he would find the secret before he did.

RAODEN pounded the map with frustration. Five days had passed since Sarene's departure, and he still couldn't find the answer. He was beginning to feel that he would continue for eternity, agonizingly close to the secret of AonDor yet forever unable to find it.

The large map, now hung from the wall near his desk, fluttered as he pushed it flat, studying its lines. Its edges were worn with age, and the ink was beginning to fade. The map had lived through Elantris's glory and collapse; how he wished it could speak, whisper to him the mysteries it knew.

He shook his head, sitting down in Sarene's chair, his foot knocking over one of her book stacks. With a sigh, he leaned back in the chair and began to draw—seeking solace in the Aons.

He had recently moved on to a new, more advanced Aon-Dor technique. The texts explained that Aons were more powerful when drawn with attention not only to line length and slant, but line width as well. While they would still work if the lines were all the same width, variance in the proper locations added extra control and strength.

So, Raoden practiced as they instructed, using his fifthfinger to draw small lines and his thumb to construct larger ones. He could also use tools—such as a stick or a quill—to draw the lines. Fingers were the convention, but form mattered far more than the utensils used. After all, the Elantrians had used AonDor to carve permanent symbols into rock and stone—and had even constructed them from wire, pieces of wood, and a host of other materials. Apparently, it was difficult to create AonDor characters from physical materials, but the Aons still had their same effect, regard-less of whether they were drawn in the air or smelted from steel.

His practice was futile. It didn't matter how efficient his Aons were; none of them worked. He used his fingernails to draw some lines so delicate that they were nearly invisible; he drew others with three fingers side by side—exactly as instructed in his texts. And it was pointless. All his memorization, all of his work. Why had he even bothered?

Feet snapped in the hallway. Mareshe's newest technological advance was shoes with thick leather soles, studded with nails. Raoden watched through his translucent Aon as the door opened and Galladon entered.

"Her Seon just stopped by again, sule," the Dula said.

"Is he still here?"

Galladon shook his head. "He left almost immediately—he wanted me to tell you that she's finally convinced the lords to rebel against King Telrii."

Sarene had been sending her Seon to give them daily reports of her activities—a service that was a mixed blessing. Raoden knew he should listen to what was happening on the outside, but he longed for the stress-free relative ignorance of before. Then, he had only needed to worry about Elantris; now he had to fret over the entire kingdom—a fact he had to stomach along with the painful knowledge that there was nothing he could do to help.

"Did Ashe say when the next supply dump would come?"

"Tonight."

"Good," Raoden said. "Did he say if she would come herself?"

"Same stipulations as before, sule," Galladon said with a shake of his head.

Raoden nodded, keeping the melancholy out of his face. He didn't know what means Sarene was using to deliver the supplies, but for some reason Raoden and the others weren't allowed to retrieve the boxes until after their deliverers had gone.

"Stop moping, sule," Galladon said with a grunt. "It doesn't suit you—it takes a fine sense of pessimism to brood with any sort of respectability."

Raoden couldn't help smiling. "I'm sorry. It just seems that no matter how hard I push against our problems, they just push back equally."

"Still no progress with AonDor?"

"No," Raoden said. "I checked older maps with new ones, looking for changes in the coast or the mountain range, but nothing seems to have changed. I've tried drawing the basic lines with slightly different slants, but that's fruitless. The lines won't appear unless I put them at exactly the right slant—the same slant as always. Even the lake is in the same place, unchanged. I can't see what is different."

"Maybe none of the basic lines have changed, sule," Galladon said. "Perhaps something needs to be added."

"I considered that—but what? I know of no new rivers or lakes, and there certainly aren't any new mountains in Arelon." Raoden finished his Aon—Aon Ehe—with a dissatisfied stroke of his thumb. He looked at the Aon's center, the core that represented Arelon and its features. Nothing had changed.

Except. *When the Reod occurred, the land cracked.* "The Chasm!" Raoden exclaimed.

"The Chasm?" Galladon said skeptically. "That was caused by the Reod, Sule, not the other way around."

"But what if it wasn't?" Raoden said with excitement. "What if the earthquake came just *before* the Reod? It caused the crack to the south, and suddenly all of the Aons were invalid—they all needed an extra line to function. All of AonDor, and therefore Elantris, would have fallen immediately."

Raoden focused on the Aon hanging just before him. With a hesitant hand, he swiped his finger across the glowing character in an approximation of where the Chasm stood. Nothing happened—no line appeared. The Aon flashed and disappeared.

"I guess that is that, sule," Galladon said.

"No," Raoden said, starting the Aon again. His fingers whipped and spun. He moved with a speed even he hadn't realized he'd achieved, re-creating the Aon in a matter of seconds. He paused at the end, hand hovering at the bottom, below the three basic lines. He could almost feel . . .

He stabbed the Aon and slashed his finger through the air. And a small line streaked across the Aon behind it.

Then it hit him. The Dor attacked with a roaring surge of power, and this time it hit no wall. It exploded through Raoden like a river. He gasped, basking in its power for just a moment. It burst free like a beast that had been kept trapped in a small space for far too long. It almost seemed . . . joyful.

Then it was gone, and he stumbled, dropping to his knees.

"Sule?" Galladon asked with concern.

Raoden shook his head, unable to explain. His toe still burned, he was still an Elantrian, but the Dor had been freed. He had . . . fixed something. The Dor would come against him no more.

Then he heard a sound—like that of a burning fire. His Aon, the one he had drawn before him, was glowing brightly. Raoden yelped, gesturing for Galladon to duck as the Aon bent around itself, its lines distorting and twirling in the air until they formed a disk. A thin prick of red light appeared in the disk's center, then expanded, the burning sounds rising to a clamor. The Aon became a twisting vortex of fire; Raoden could feel the heat as he stumbled back.

It burst, spitting out a horizontal column of flame through the air just above Galladon's head. The column crashed into a bookshelf, immolating the structure in a massive explosion. Books and flaming pages were tossed into the air, slamming into walls and other bookcases.

The column of fire disappeared, the heat suddenly gone, and Raoden's skin felt clammy in contrast. A few burning scraps of paper fluttered to the ground. All that was left of the bookcase was a smoldering pile of charcoal.

"What was that?" Galladon demanded.

"I think I just destroyed the biology section," Raoden replied with wonder.

"NEXT time, sule, I recommend that you *not* test your theories with Aon Ehe. Kolo?" Galladon set down a pile of mostly burned books. They had spent the last hour cleaning up the library, making certain they doused any smoldering flame.

"Agreed," Raoden said, too happy to be defensive. "That just happened to be the one I was practicing—it wouldn't have been so dramatic if I hadn't put so many modifiers on it."

Galladon looked back over the library. A dark scar still marked the place of the incinerated bookcase, and several piles of half-charred tomes lay scattered around the room.

"Shall we try another?" Raoden asked.

Galladon snorted. "As long as no fire is involved."

Raoden nodded, raising his hand to begin Aon Ashe. He finished the character's double box shape and added the Chasm line. He stepped back, waiting anxiously.

The Aon began to glow. The light started at the tip of the coast line, then burned through the entire Aon like flames sweeping across a pool of oil. The lines turned red at first, then, like metal in a forge, turned a bright white. The color stabilized, bathing the area in soft luminescence.

"It works, sule," Galladon whispered. "By Doloken—you actually did it!"

Raoden nodded with excitement. He approached the Aon hesitantly, putting his hand up against it. There was no heat—just as the books had explained. One thing was wrong, however.

"It's not as bright as it should be," he said.

"How can you be sure?" Galladon asked. "This is the first one you've seen work."

Raoden shook his head. "I've read enough to know. An Aon Ashe this big should be powerful enough to light the entire library—it's barely as bright as a lantern."

He reached up, tapping the Aon in the center. The glow faded immediately, the Aon's lines vanishing one at a time, as if some invisible finger were undrawing them. Then he drew another Aon Ashe, this time including all the power-increasing modifiers he knew. When this Aon finally stabilized, it appeared slightly brighter than the first one, but nowhere near as powerful as it should have been.

"Something is still wrong," Raoden said. "That Aon should be too bright for us to look at."

"You think the Chasm line is wrong?" Galladon asked.

"No, it was obviously a large part of the problem. AonDor works now, but it's handicapped in power. There must be something else—another line, perhaps, that we need to add."

Galladon glanced down at his arms. Even against the dark-brown Dula skin, it was easy to make out his sickly Elantrian splotches. "Try a healing Aon, sule."

Raoden nodded, tracing Aon Ien in the air. He added a modification stipulating Galladon's body as the target, as well as all three power-increasing marks. He finished with the small Chasm line. The Aon flashed briefly then disappeared.

"Do you feel anything?" Raoden asked.

The Dula shook his head. Then, raising his arm, he inspected the cut on his elbow—an injury caused just the other day when he slipped in one of the fields. It was unchanged.

"The pain is still there, sule," Galladon said with disappointment. "And my heart does not beat."

"That Aon didn't behave properly," Raoden said. "It disappeared like before, when we didn't know about the Chasm line. The Dor couldn't find a target for its power."

"Then what good is it, sule?" Galladon's voice was bitter with frustration. "We'll still rot in this city."

Raoden laid a comforting hand on the Dula's shoulder. "It isn't useless, Galladon. We have the power of the Elantrians—some of it might not work, but that might just be because we haven't experimented enough. Think about it! This is the power that gave Elantris its beauty, the power that fed all of Arelon. Don't give up hope when we're so close."

Galladon looked at him, then smiled ruefully. "No one can give up when you're around, sule. You utterly refuse to let a man despair."

AS they tried more Aons, it became more apparent that something was still blocking the Dor. They made a stack of papers float, but not an entire book. They turned one of the walls blue, then changed it back, and Raoden managed to convert a small pile of charcoal into a few grains of corn. The results were encouraging, but many Aons failed completely.

Any Aon, for instance, that targeted either of them flashed away ineffectually. Their clothing was a valid target, but their flesh was not; Raoden broke off the tip of his thumbnail and tried to make that float, and was completely unsuccessful. The only theory Raoden could offer was the one he had expressed earlier.

"Our bodies are frozen in the middle of being changed, Galladon," he explained, watching a sheet of paper hover in front of him, then burst into flames. Linked Aons appeared to work. "The Shaod hasn't finished with us—whatever's keeping the Aons from reaching their full potential is also stopping us from becoming true Elantrians. Until our transformation is finished, it appears that no Aons can affect us."

"I still don't understand that first explosion, sule," Galladon said, practicing Aon Ashe in front of himself. The Dula knew only a few Aons, and his thick-fingered hands had trouble drawing them precisely. Even as he spoke, he made a slight error, and the character faded away. He frowned, then continued his question. "It seemed so powerful. Why hasn't anything else worked that well?"

"I'm not sure," Raoden said. A few moments earlier he had hesitantly redrawn Aon Ehe with the same modifications, creating the complex rune that was supposed to form another column of flame. Instead, the Aon had barely sputtered out enough fire to warm a cup of tea. He suspected that the first explosion had something do with the Dor's surge through him . . . an expression of its long-awaited freedom.

"Perhaps there was some sort of buildup in the Dor," Raoden said. "Like a pocket of gas trapped in the top of a cave. The first Aon I drew drained that reserve."

Galladon shrugged. There was just so much they didn't understand. Raoden sat for a moment, eyes falling on one of his tomes, a thought occurring.

He rushed over to his stack of AonDor books, selecting a large volume that contained nothing but page after page of Aon diagrams. Galladon, whom he had left behind midsentence, followed with a grumpy expression, peeking over Raoden's shoulder at the page Raoden chose.

The Aon was extensive and complex. Raoden had to take several steps to the side as he drew it, the modifications and stipulations going far beyond the central Aon. His arm ached by the time he had finished, and the construction hung in the air like a wall of glowing lines. Then, it began to gleam, and the sheet of inscriptions twisted, turning and wrapping around Raoden. Galladon yelped in surprise at the suddenly bright light.

In a few seconds, the light vanished. Raoden could tell from the startled look on Galladon's face that he had been successful.

"Sule . . . you've done it! You've healed yourself!"

"I'm afraid not," Raoden said with a shake of his head. "It's only an illusion. Look." He held up his hands, which were still gray and spotted with black. His face, however, was different. He walked over, regarding his reflection in a polished plaque on the end of a bookshelf.

The garbled image showed an unfamiliar face—it was free from spots, true, but it didn't look anything like his real face had before the Shaod had taken him.

"An illusion?" Galladon asked.

Raoden nodded. "It's based on Aon Shao, but there are so many things mixed in that the base Aon is almost irrelevant."

"But it shouldn't work on you," Galladon said. "I thought we decided the Aons couldn't target Elantrians."

"It doesn't," Raoden said, turning. "It targets my shirt. The illusion is like an article of clothing—it only covers up my skin; it doesn't change anything."

"Then what good is it?"

Raoden smiled. "It is going to get us out of Elantris, my friend."

CHAPTER 50

"WHAT took you so long?"

"I couldn't find Spirit, my lady," Ashe explained, floating into her carriage window. "So I had to deliver the message to Master Galladon. After that, I went to check on King Telrii."

Sarene tapped her cheek with annoyance. "How is he doing, then?"

"Galladon or the king, my lady?"

"The king."

"His Majesty is quite busy lounging in his palace while half of Arelon's nobility waits outside," the Seon said with a disapproving tone. "I believe his largest current complaint is that there aren't enough young women left on the palace staff."

"We've exchanged one idiot for another," Sarene said with a shake of her head. "How did that man ever acquire enough wealth to become a duke?"

"He didn't, my lady," Ashe explained. "His brother did most of the work. Telrii inherited upon the man's death."

Sarene sighed, leaning back as the carriage hit a bump. "Is Hrathen there?"

"Often, my lady," Ashe said. "Apparently, he visits the king on a daily basis."

"What are they waiting for?" Sarene asked with frustration. "Why doesn't Telrii just convert?"

"No one is certain, my lady."

Sarene frowned. The continued game left her baffled. It was well known that Telrii had attended Derethi meetings, and there was no reason for him to maintain an illusion of Korathi conservatism. "No new news on that proclamation the gyorn has supposedly drafted?" she asked with trepidation.

"No, my lady," came the blessed reply. Rumors claimed that Hrathen had drawn up a bill that would force all of Arelon to convert to Shu-Dereth or face incarceration. Though the merchants put on a face of normalcy, holding the spring Arelene Market, the entire city was on edge with a sense of tense anxiety.

Sarene could easily imagine the future. Soon Wyrn would send a fleet of priests into Arelon, followed closely by his warrior monks. Telrii, at first a sympathizer, then a convert, would eventually become less than a pawn. In just a few years Arelon wouldn't be just a country of Derethi believers, but a virtual extension of Fjorden itself.

Once Hrathen's bill passed, the priest would waste no time in arresting Sarene and the others. They would be locked away or, more likely, executed. After that, there would be no one to oppose Fjorden. The entire civilized world would belong to Wyrn, a final fulfillment of the Old Empire's dream.

And yet, despite all of this, her allies debated and talked. None of them believed that Telrii would actually sign a document forcing conversion; such atrocities didn't happen in their world. Arelon was a peaceful kingdom; even the so-called riots of a decade past hadn't been that destructive—unless one was an Elantrian. Her friends wanted to move carefully. Their caution was understandable, laudable even, but their timing was terrible. It was a good thing she had an opportunity to practice fencing this day. She needed to release a little aggression.

As if in response to her thoughts, the carriage pulled to a halt in front of Roial's manor. In the wake of Telrii's move into the palace, the women had relocated their fencing practice to the old duke's gardens. The weather of late had been warm and breezy, as if spring had decided to stay this time, and Duke Roial had welcomed them.

Sarene had been surprised when the women insisted that they continue the fencing practice. However, the ladies had shown strength in their resolve. This one meeting would continue, every second day, as it had for over a month now. Apparently, Sarene wasn't the only one who needed an opportunity to work out her frustration with a sword.

She climbed out of the carriage, dressed in her usual white jumpsuit and wearing her new wig. As she rounded the building, she could make out the sounds of syres clashing in the background. With shade and a wooden floor, Roial's garden pavilion was a perfect place for practice. Most of the women had already arrived, and they greeted Sarene with smiles and curtsies. None of them had quite gotten over her sudden return from Elantris; now they regarded her with even more respect, and fear, than they had before. Sarene nodded back with polite affection. She liked these women, even if she could never be one of them.

Seeing them, however, reminded her of the strange loss she still felt at having left Elantris behind. It wasn't just Spirit; Elantris was the one place where she could remember feeling unconditional acceptance. She had not been a princess, she had been something far better—a member of a community where every individual was vital. She had felt warmth from those motley-skinned Elantrians, a willingness to accept her into their lives and give her part of themselves.

There, in the center of the most cursed city in the world, Spirit had constructed a society that exemplified Korathi teachings. The church taught of the blessings of unity; it was ironic that the only people who practiced such ideals were those who had been damned.

Sarene shook her head, snapping her sword forward in a practice thrust, beginning her warm-ups. She had spent her adult life in an unending quest to find acceptance and love. When, at long last, she had finally found both, she had left them behind.

She wasn't sure how long she practiced—she fell into her forms easily once the warm-ups were finished. Her thoughts rotated around Elantris, Domi, her feelings, and the indecipherable ironies of life. She was sweating heavily by the time she realized the other women had stopped sparring.

Sarene looked up with surprise. Everyone was huddled at one side of the pavilion, chattering among themselves and looking at something Sarene couldn't see. Curious, she edged her way to the side until her superior height gave her a good look at the object of their attention. A man.

He was dressed in fine blue and green silks, a feathered hat on his head. He had the creamy brown skin of a Duladen aristocrat—not as dark as Shuden's, but not as light as Sarene's. His features were round and happy, and he had a foppish, unconcerned air. Duladen indeed. The dark-skinned servant at his side was massive and bulky, like most Dulas of lower birth. She had never seen either man before.

"What is going on here?" Sarene demanded.

"His name is Kaloo, my lady," Ashe explained, floating over to her. "He arrived a few moments ago. Apparently, he's one of the few Duladen Republicans that escaped the massacre last year. He has been hiding in southern Arelon until just recently, when he heard that King Iadon was looking for a man to take Baron Edan's holdings."

Sarene frowned; something about the man bothered her. The women suddenly burst into laughter at one of his comments, giggling as if the Dula were an old and favored member of the court. By the time the laughter died down, the Dula had noticed Sarene.

"Ah," Kaloo said, bowing ornately. "This must be the Princess Sarene. They say you are the most fair woman in all of Opelon."

"You should not believe all of the things that people say, my lord," Sarene replied slowly.

"No," he agreed, looking up into her eyes. "Only the ones that are true."

Despite herself, Sarene started to blush. She did *not* like men who could do that to her. "I'm afraid you have caught us off guard, my lord," Sarene said through narrowed eyes. "We have been exercising quite vigorously, and are in no position to receive you like proper ladies."

"I apologize for my abrupt arrival, Your Highness," Kaloo said. Despite the polite words, he appeared unconcerned that he had interrupted an obviously private gathering. "Upon arriving in this glorious city, I first paid my respects to the palace—but was told that I would have to wait for at least a week to see the king himself. I put my name on the lists, then had my coachman drive me around your lovely city. I had heard of the illustrious Duke Roial, and decided to pay him a visit. How surprised I was to find all these lovelies in his gardens!"

Sarene snorted, but her rebuttal was interrupted by the arrival of Duke Roial. Apparently, the old man had finally realized that his property had been invaded by a roving Dula. As the duke approached, Kaloo gave another one of his silly bows, sweeping his large, floppy hat out in front of him. Then he launched into praises of the duke, telling Roial how honored he was to meet such a venerable man.

"I don't like him," Sarene declared quietly to Ashe.

"Of course not, my lady," Ashe said. "You never have gotten along very well with Duladen aristocrats."

"It's more than that," Sarene insisted. "Something about him seems false. He doesn't have an accent."

"Most Republic citizens spoke Aonic quite fluently, especially if they lived near the border. I have met several Dulas in my time without hint of an accent."

Sarene just frowned. As she watched the man perform, she realized what it was. Kaloo was *too* stereotypical. He represented everything a Duladen aristocrat was said to be—foolishly haughty, overdressed and overmannered, and completely indifferent when it came to just about everything. This Kaloo was like a cliché that shouldn't exist, a living representation of the idealized Duladen noble.

Kaloo finished his introductions and moved on to a dramatic retelling of his arrival story. Roial took it all in with a smile; the duke had done lots of business with Dulas, and apparently knew that the best way to deal with them was to smile and nod occasionally.

One of the women handed Kaloo a cup. He smiled his thanks and downed the wine in a single gulp, never breaking his narrative as he immediately brought his hand back into the conversation. Dulas didn't just talk with their mouths, they used their entire bodies as part of the storytelling experience. Silks and feathers fluttered as Kaloo described his surprise at finding King Iadon dead and a new king on the throne.

"Perhaps my lord would care to join us," Sarene said, interrupting Kaloo—which was often the only way to enter a conversation with a Dula.

Kaloo blinked in surprise. "Join you?" he asked hesitantly, his flow of words stopping for a brief moment. Sarene could sense a break in character as he reoriented himself. She was becoming increasingly certain that this man was not who he claimed. Fortunately, her mind had just alighted on a method to test him.

"Of course, my lord," Sarene said. "Duladen citizens are said to be the finest fencers in all of the land—better, even, than Jaadorians. I am certain the ladies here would be much intrigued to see a true master at work."

"I am very thankful at the offer, Your Gracious Highness," Kaloo began, "but I am hardly dressed—"

"We will make it a quick bout, my lord," Sarene said, picking up her bag and sliding out her two finest syres—the ones with sharpened points rather than simple balls. She whipped one through the air expertly as she smiled at the Dula.

"All right," the Dula said, tossing aside his hat. "Let us have a bout, then."

Sarene stopped, trying to judge whether he was bluffing. She hadn't intended to actually fight him; otherwise she wouldn't have chosen the dangerous blades. She considered for a moment, and then, with a casual shrug, tossed him one of the weapons. If he was bluffing, then she intended to call him in a very embarrassing—and potentially painful—way.

Kaloo pulled off his bright turquoise jacket, revealing the ruffled green shirt underneath; then, surprisingly, he fell into a fencing stance, his hand raised behind him, the tip of his syre raised offensively.

"All right," Sarene said, then attacked.

Kaloo jumped backward at the onslaught, twirling around the stunned Duke Roial as he parried Sarene's blows. There were several startled cries from the women as Sarene pushed through them, snapping her blade at the offending Dula. Soon she emerged into the sunlight, jumping off the wooden dais and landing barefoot in the soft grass.

As shocked as they were at the impropriety of the battle, the women made certain not to miss a single blow. Sarene could see them following as she and Kaloo moved out into the flat courtyard at the center of Roial's gardens.

The Dula was surprisingly good, but he was no master. He spent too much time parrying her attacks, obviously unable to do much but defend. If he truly was a member of the Duladen aristocracy, then he was one of their poorer fencers. Sarene had met a few citizens who were worse than she, but on average three out of four could defeat her.

Kaloo abandoned his air of apathy, concentrating solely on keeping Sarene's syre from slicing him apart. They moved all the way across the courtyard, Kaloo retreating a few steps with each new exchange. He seemed surprised when he stepped onto brick instead of grass, arriving at the fountain centerpiece of Roial's gardens.

Sarene advanced more vigorously as Kaloo stumbled up onto the brick deck. She forced him back until his thigh struck the edge of the fountain itself. There was nowhere else for him to go—or so she thought. She watched with surprise as the Dula leapt into the water. With a kick of his leg, he sent a splash in her direction, then leapt out of the fountain to her right.

Sarene's syre pierced the water as Kaloo passed through the air beside her. She felt the tip of her blade strike something soft, and the nobleman let out a quiet, almost unnoticeable, yelp of pain. Sarene spun, raising her blade to strike again, but Kaloo was on his knee, his syre stuck point-first into the soft earth. He held up a bright yellow flower to Sarene.

"Ah, my lady," he said in a dramatic voice. "You have found my secret—never have I been able to face a beautiful woman in combat. My heart melts, my knees shake, and my sword refuses to strike." He bowed his head, proffering the flower. The collected women behind him sighed dreamily.

Sarene lowered her sword uncertainly. Where had he gotten the flower? With a sigh, she accepted the gift. They both knew that his excuse was nothing more than a sneaky method of escaping embarrassment—but Sarene had to respect his cleverness. He had not only managed to avoid looking like a fool, but had impressed the women with his courtly sense of romance at the same time.

Sarene studied the man closely, searching for a wound. She'd been certain her blade had scratched him on the face as he jumped out of the fountain, but there was no sign of a hit. Uncertain, she looked down at the tip of her syre. There was no blood on it. She must have missed after all.

The women clapped at the show, and they began to urge the dandy back toward the pavilion. As he left, Kaloo looked back at her and smiled—not the silly, foppish smile he had used before, but a more knowing, sly smile. A smile she found strikingly familiar for some reason. He performed another one of his ridiculous bows, then allowed himself to be led away.

CHAPTER 51

THE market's tents were a bright burst of color in the center of the city. Hrathen walked among them, noting the unsold wares and empty streets with dissatisfaction. Many of the merchants were from the East, and they had spent a great deal of money shipping their cargoes to Arelon for the spring market. If they failed to sell their goods, the losses would be a financial blow from which they might never recover.

Most of the merchants, displaying dark Fjordell colorings, bowed their heads respectfully at his passing. Hrathen had been away so long—first in Duladel, then in Arelon—that he had almost forgotten what it was like to be treated with proper deference. Even as they bowed their heads, Hrathen could see something in these merchants' eyes. An edginess. They had planned for this market for months, their wares and passage purchased long before King Iadon's death. Even with the upheaval, they had no choice but to try and sell what they could.

Hrathen's cloak billowed behind him as he toured the market, his armor clinking comfortably with each step. He displayed a confidence he didn't feel, trying to give the merchants some measure of security. Things were not well, not at all. His hurried call via Seon to Wyrn had come too late; Telrii's message had already arrived. Fortunately, Wyrn had displayed only slight anger at Telrii's presumptuousness.

Time was short. Wyrn had indicated that he had little patience for fools, and he would never—of course—name a foreigner to the title of gyorn. Yet Hrathen's subsequent meetings with Telrii had not gone well. Though he seemed to be a bit more reasonable than he had been the day he'd tossed Hrathen out, the king still resisted all suggestions of monetary compensation. His lethargy to convert gave mixed signs to the rest of Arelon.

The empty market was a manifestation of the Arelish nobility's confused state. Suddenly, they weren't certain if it were better to be a Derethi sympathizer or not—so they simply hid. Balls and parties slowed, and men hesitated to visit the markets, instead waiting to see what their monarch would do. Everything hung on Telrii's decision.

It will come, Hrathen, he told himself. *You still have a month left. You have time to persuade, cajole, and threaten. Telrii will come to understand the foolishness of his request, and he will convert.*

Yet, despite self-assurances, Hrathen felt as if he were at a precipice. He played a dangerous game of balance. The Arelish nobility weren't really his, not yet. Most of them were still more concerned about appearances than substance. If he delivered Arelon to Wyrn, he would deliver a batch of halfhearted converts at best. He hoped it would be enough.

Hrathen paused as he saw a flutter of movement near a tent at his side. The tent was a large blue structure with extravagant embroidery and large winglike pavilions to the sides. The breeze brought hints of spice and smoke: an incense merchant.

Hrathen frowned. He was certain he had seen the distinctive bloodred of a Derethi robe as someone ducked inside the tent. The arteths were supposed to be in solitary meditation at the moment, not idly shopping. Determined to discover which priest had disobeyed his command, Hrathen strode across the path and entered the tent.

It was dark inside, the thick canvas walls blocking out sunlight. A lantern burned at one side of the tent, but the large structure was so piled with boxes, barrels, and bins that Hrathen could see only shadows. He stood for a moment, eyes adjusting. There didn't seem to be anyone inside the tent, not even a merchant.

He stepped forward, moving through waves of scents both pungent and enticing. Sweetsands, soaps, and oils all perfumed the air, and the mixture of their many odors left the mind confused. Near the back of the tent, he found the solitary lantern sitting beside a box of ashes, the remnants of burned incense. Hrathen pulled off his gauntlet, then reached to rub the soft powder between his fingers.

"The ashes are like the wreckage of your power, are they not, Hrathen?" a voice asked.

Hrathen spun, startled by the sound. A shadowed figure stood in the tent behind him, a familiar form in Derethi robes.

"What are you doing here?" Hrathen asked, turning from Dilaf and brushing off his hand, then replacing his gauntlet.

Dilaf didn't respond. He stood in the darkness, his unseen face unnerving in its stare.

"Dilaf?" Hrathen repeated, turning. "I asked you a question."

"You have failed here, Hrathen," Dilaf whispered. "The fool Telrii is playing with you. You, a gyorn of Shu-Dereth. Men do not make demands of the Fjordell Empire, Hrathen. They should not."

Hrathen felt his face redden. "What know you of such things?" he snapped. "Leave me be, Arteth."

Dilaf didn't move. "You were close, I admit, but your foolishness cost you the victory."

"Bah!" Hrathen said, brushing past the small man in the darkness, walking toward the exit. "My battle is far from over—I still have time left."

"Do you?" Dilaf asked. Out of the corner of his eye, Hrathen saw Dilaf approach the ashes, running his fingers through them. "It has all slipped away, hasn't it, Hrathen? My victory is so sweet in the face of your failure."

Hrathen paused, then laughed, looking back at Dilaf. "Victory? What victory have you achieved? What . . . ?"

Dilaf smiled. In the wan light of the lantern, his face pocketed with shadow, he smiled. The expression, filled with the passion, the ambition, and the zeal that Hrathen had noted on that first day so long ago, was so disturbing that Hrathen's question died on his lips. In the flickering light, the arteth seemed not a man at all, but a Svrakiss, sent to torment Hrathen.

Dilaf dropped his handful of ashes, then walked past Hrathen, throwing open the tent flap and striding out into the light.

"Dilaf?" Hrathen asked in a voice far too soft for the arteth to hear. "What victory?"

CHAPTER 52

"OW!" Raoden complained as Galladon stuck the needle into his cheek.

"Stop whining," the Dula ordered, pulling the thread tight.

"Karata's much better at this," Raoden said. He sat before a mirror in their rooms at Roial's mansion, his head cocked to the side, watching Galladon sew the sword wound.

"Well, wait until we get back to Elantris, then," the Dula said grumpily, punctuating the remark by sticking Raoden again.

"No," Raoden said with a sigh, "I've waited too long already—I can feel this one ripping a little bit each time I smile. Why couldn't she have hit me on the arm?"

"Because we're Elantrians, sule," Galladon explained. "If a bad thing can happen to us, it will. You're lucky to escape with only this. In fact, you're lucky you were even able to fight at all with that body of yours."

"It wasn't easy," Raoden said, keeping his head still as the Dula worked. "That's why I had to end it so quickly."

"Well, you fight better than I expected."

"I had Eondel teach me," Raoden said. "Back when I was trying to find ways to prove that my father's laws were foolish. Eondel chose fencing because he thought it would be most useful to me, as a politician. I never figured I'd end up using it to keep my wife from slicing me to pieces."

Galladon snorted in amusement as he stabbed Raoden again, and Raoden gritted his teeth against the pain. The doors were all bolted tightly and the drapes closed, for Raoden had needed to drop his illusionary mask to let Galladon sew. The duke had been kind enough to board them—Roial seemed to be the only one of Raoden's former friends who was intrigued, rather than annoyed, by his Kaloo personality.

"All right, sule," Galladon said, tugging the final stitch.

Raoden nodded, looking at himself in the mirror. He had almost begun to think that the handsome Duladen face belonged to him. That was dangerous. He had to remember that he was still an Elantrian, with all the weaknesses and pains of his kind, despite the unconcerned personality he had adopted.

Galladon still wore his mask. The Aon illusions were good as long as Raoden left them alone. Whether they were drawn in air or in mud, Aons could be destroyed only by another Elantrian. The books claimed that an Aon inscribed in dust would continue to function even if the pattern was scuffed or erased.

The illusions were attached to their underclothes, allowing them to change outfits each day without needing to redraw the Aon. Galladon's illusion was that of a nondescript, broad-faced Dula, an image Raoden had found at the back of his book. Raoden's face had been much harder to choose.

"How's my personality?" Raoden asked, pulling out the AonDor book to begin re-creating his illusion. "Am I convincing?"

Galladon shrugged, taking a seat on Raoden's bed. "*I* wouldn't have believed you were a Dula, but they seem to. I don't think you could have made a better choice, anyway. Kolo?"

Raoden nodded as he drew. The Arelish nobility were too well known, and Sarene would have immediately seen through any attempt at pretending to be from Teod. Assuming he wanted to speak Aonic, that left only Duladen. It had been obvious from his failed attempts to imitate Galladon's accent that he could never make a convincing member of the

Duladen underclass; even his pronunciation of a simple word such as "kolo" had sent Galladon into gales of laughter. Fortunately, there were a good number of lesser-known Duladen citizens—men who had been mayors of small towns or members of unimportant councils—who spoke flawless Aonic. Raoden had met many such individuals, and mimicking their personality required only a sense of flamboyance and a nonchalant attitude.

Getting the clothing had been a little difficult—requiring Raoden, in another illusion, to go purchase it from the Arelene Market. Since his official arrival, however, he'd been able to get some better-tailored outfits. He thought he played a fairly good Dula, though not everyone was convinced.

"I think Sarene's suspicious," Raoden said, finishing the Aon and watching it spin around him and mold to his face.

"She's a bit more skeptical than most."

"True," Raoden said. He intended to tell her who he was as soon as possible, but she had resisted any attempts by "Kaloo" to get her alone; she'd even refused the letter he'd sent, returning it unopened.

Fortunately, things were going better with the rest of the nobility. Since Raoden had left Elantris two days before, entrusting New Elantris to Karata's care, he had managed to wiggle his way into Arelish high society with an ease that surprised even him. The nobles were too busy worrying about Telrii's rule to question Kaloo's background. In fact, they had latched on to him with startling vigor. Apparently, the sense of free-willed silliness he brought to gatherings gave the nobles a chance to laugh and forget the chaos of the last few weeks. So he soon became a necessary guest at any function.

Of course, the true test was going to be getting himself into Roial and Sarene's secret meetings. If he was ever going to do any good for Arelon, he needed to be admitted into that special group. They were the ones who were working to determine the fate of the country. Galladon was skeptical about Raoden's chances—of course, Galladon was skeptical about everything. Raoden smiled to himself; he was the one who had actually started the meetings. It seemed ironic that he should now be forced to work to regain admittance.

Kaloo's face once again masking his own, Raoden pulled on his green gloves—articles that held the illusion that made his arms seem non-Elantrian—then spun and twirled for Galladon. "And the magnificent Kaloo returns."

"Please, sule, not in private. I come close enough to strangling you in public."

Raoden chuckled. "Ah, what a life. Loved by all women, envied by every man."

Galladon snorted. "Loved by all of the women but one, you mean."

"Well, she *did* invite me to spar with her any time I wanted," Raoden said, smiling as he walked over to pull open the drapes.

"Even if it was just to get another chance to impale you," Galladon said. "You should be glad she hit you on the face, where the illusion covered the wound. If she'd stabbed through your clothing, it would have been very difficult to explain why your cut didn't bleed. Kolo?"

Raoden slid open the balcony door, walking out to look over Roial's gardens. He sighed as Galladon joined him. "Tell me this. Why is it that every time I meet her, Sarene is determined to hate me?"

"Must be love," Galladon said.

Raoden laughed wryly. "Well, at least this time it's Kaloo she hates, rather than the real me. I suppose I can forgive her for that—I've almost gotten to the point where I hate him too."

A knock came at the door, drawing their attention. Galladon looked at him and he nodded. Their costumes and faces were complete. Galladon, playing the part of a servant, walked over and unlocked the door. Roial stood outside.

"My lord," Raoden said, approaching with outreached arms and a broad smile. "I trust your day has been as fine as my own!"

"It has, Citizen Kaloo," Roial said. "May I come in?"

"Certainly, certainly," Raoden said. "It is, after all, your house. We are so unspeakably indebted to your kindness that I know I shall never manage to repay you."

"Nonsense, citizen," Roial said. "Though, speaking of payments, you will be pleased to know that I made a good trade on those lamp mounts you gave me. I deposited your credit in an account at my bank—it should be enough to see that you live comfortably for several years at least."

"Excellent!" Raoden proclaimed. "We shall immediately seek another place to reside."

"No, no," the old duke said, holding up his hands. "Stay here as long as you wish. I get so few visitors in my old age that even this small house often seems too large."

"Then we shall stay as long as you suffer us!" Raoden declared with characteristically Duladen lack of decorum. It was said that the moment you invited a Dula to stay, you would never get rid of him—or his family.

"Tell me, citizen," Roial said, strolling to the balcony. "Where did you find a dozen lamp mounts made of solid gold?"

"Family heirlooms," Raoden said. "I pried them off our mansion walls even as the people burned it down."

"It must have been horrible," Roial said, leaning against the balcony rail.

"Worse than horrible," Raoden said with somberness. Then he smiled. "But those times are over now, my lord. I have a new country and new friends! You shall become my family now."

Roial nodded absently, then shot wary eyes back at Galladon.

"I see something occupies your mind, Lord Roial," Raoden said. "Fear not to speak it—good Dendo has been with me since I was born; he is worthy of any man's trust."

Roial nodded, turning back to look out over his estate. "I do not mention the harsh times in your homeland indiscriminately, citizen. You said they are over now, but I fear for us the terror is just beginning."

"Ah, you speak of the problems with the throne," Raoden said with a click of his tongue.

"Yes, citizen," Roial said. "Telrii is not a strong leader. I fear Arelon will soon fall to Duladel's fate. We have Fjordell wolves nipping at us, smelling blood, but our nobility pretends to see nothing more than favored hounds."

"Oh troubled times," Raoden said. "Where can I go to find simple peace?"

"Sometimes we must make our own peace, citizen."

"What do you mean?" Raoden asked, trying to keep the excitement out of his voice.

"Citizen, I hope I do not injure you when I point out that the others see you as rather frivolous."

Raoden laughed. "I hope they see me that way, my lord. I should hate to think I've been playing the fool for nothing."

Roial smiled. "I sense a wit in you that is not completely masked by your foppishness, citizen. Tell me, how did you manage to escape from Duladen?"

"I am afraid that is one secret which must remain untold, my lord," Raoden said. "There are those who would suffer dearly if their part in my escape became known."

Roial nodded. "I understand. The important part is that you survived when your countrymen did not. Do you know how many refugees came up through the border when the Republic fell?"

"I am afraid not, my lord," Raoden replied. "I was a little busy at the time."

"None," Roial said. "Not a single one that I know of—yourself excluded. I hear that the republicans were too shocked to even think of escaping."

"My people are slow to act, my lord," Raoden said with upraised hands. "In this case, our lax manner proved our downfall. The revolution rolled over us while we were still discussing what to have for dinner."

"But you escaped."

"I escaped," Raoden agreed.

"You have already been through what we might have to suffer, and that makes your advice valuable—no matter what the others may think."

"There is a way to escape Duladel's fate, my lord," Raoden said cautiously. "Though it could be dangerous. It would involve a . . . change in leadership."

Roial's eyes narrowed knowingly, and he nodded. Something passed between them—an understanding of the duke's offer and Raoden's willingness.

"You speak of dangerous things," Roial warned.

"I have been through a lot, my lord. I would not be averse

to a little more danger if it provided me a means of living the rest of my life in peace."

"I cannot guarantee that will happen," Roial said.

"And I cannot guarantee that this balcony won't suddenly collapse, sending us to our doom. All we can do is count on luck, and our wits, to protect us."

Roial nodded. "You know the house of the merchant Kiin?"

"Yes."

"Meet me there tonight at sunset."

Raoden nodded, and the duke excused himself. As the door shut, Raoden winked at Galladon. "And you thought I couldn't do it."

"I'll never doubt you again," Galladon said dryly.

"The secret was Roial, my friend," Raoden said, pulling the balcony door shut as he walked back into the room. "He sees through most façades—but, unlike Sarene, his primary question is not 'Why is this man trying to fool me?' but 'How can I make use of what I know?' I gave him hints, and he responded."

Galladon nodded. "Well, you're in. Now what will you do?"

"Find a way to put Roial on the throne instead of Telrii," Raoden said, picking up a cloth and a jar of brown makeup. He smeared some of the makeup on the cloth, then tucked the cloth in his pocket.

Galladon raised an eyebrow. "And what is that?" he asked, nodding to the cloth.

"Something I hope I won't have to use."

CHAPTER 53

"WHAT is *he* doing here?" Sarene demanded, standing at the doorway to Kiin's kitchen. The idiot Kaloo sat inside, dressed in a montage of garish reds and oranges. He spoke animatedly with Kiin and Roial, and apparently hadn't noticed her arrival.

Lukel closed the door behind her, then glanced toward the Dula with apparent distaste. Her cousin was known as one of the wittiest, most colorful men in Kae. Kaloo's reputation, however, had quickly eclipsed even Lukel's, leaving the young merchant a bitter second.

"Roial invited him for some reason," Lukel muttered.

"Has Roial gone mad?" Sarene asked, perhaps more loudly than she should have. "What if that cursed Dula is a spy?"

"A spy for whom?" Kaloo asked merrily. "I don't think your pompous king has the political acumen to hire spies— and let me assure you, no matter how much I exasperate you, Princess, I bother Fjordells even more. That gyorn would rather stab himself in the chest than pay me for information."

Sarene flushed with embarrassment, an action that only sent Kaloo into another peal of laughter.

"I think, Sarene, you will find Citizen Kaloo's opinions helpful," Roial said. "This man sees things differently from Arelenes, and he also has a fresh opinion of events in Kae. I seem to remember that you yourself used a similar argument when you first joined us. Do not discount Kaloo's value because he happens to be a little more eccentric than you find comfortable."

Sarene frowned, but allowed herself to be rebuked. The

duke's observations held weight; it would be helpful to have a new perspective. For some reason Roial seemed to trust Kaloo. She could sense a mutual respect between them. Grudgingly, she admitted that perhaps the duke had seen something in Kaloo that she hadn't. The Dula had, after all, been staying with Roial for several days.

Ahan was late, as usual. Shuden and Eondel spoke quietly at one end of the table, their subdued conversation a stark contrast to Kaloo's vibrant narrative. Kiin had provided appetizers—crackers with some sort of creamy white glaze atop them. Despite her insistences that he not prepare dinner, Kiin had obviously been unable to let this many people congregate without giving them something to eat. Sarene smiled; she doubted that other treasonous conspiracies enjoyed gourmet snacks.

A few moments later, Ahan waddled in, not bothering to knock. He plopped himself down in his customary seat and proceeded to attack the crackers.

"We're all here, then," Sarene said, speaking sharply to interrupt Kaloo. All heads turned toward her as she stood. "I trust you all have given our predicament much thought. Does anyone want to start?"

"I will," Ahan said. "Maybe Telrii can be persuaded not to convert to Shu-Dereth."

Sarene sighed. "I thought we discussed this, Ahan. Telrii isn't debating whether or not to convert; he's waiting to see how much money he can get out of Wyrn."

"If only we had more troops," Roial said with a shake of his head. "With a proper army, we could intimidate Telrii. Sarene, what chance is there of getting aid from Teod?"

"Not much," Sarene said, sitting. "Remember, my father swore himself to Shu-Dereth. Besides, Teod has a wonderful navy, but few ground troops. Our country has a small population—we survive by sinking our enemies before they land."

"I hear there are resistance fighters in Duladel," Shuden suggested. "They harass caravans occasionally."

All eyes turned toward Kaloo, who raised his hands palms forward. "Trust me, my friends, you do not want their help. The men of which you speak are mostly former republicans, like myself. They can duel one another with fine proficiency, but a syre isn't much good against a trained solider, especially if he has five friends beside him. The resistance only survives because the Fjordells are too lazy to chase it out of the swamps."

Shuden frowned. "I thought they were hiding in the caves of the Duladen Steppes."

"There are several pockets of them," Kaloo said smoothly, though Sarene detected a hint of uncertainty in his eyes. *Who are you?* she thought as the conversation moved forward.

"I think we should bring the people into it," Lukel said. "Telrii has indicated that he intends to maintain the plantation system. If we encourage the common people to our cause, they should be willing to rise against him."

"It could work," Eondel said. "Lady Sarene's plan to sharecrop my peasants has given them a taste of freedom, and they've grown far more self-confident over the last few months. But, it would take a great deal of time—you don't train men to fight overnight."

"Agreed," Roial said. "Telrii will be Derethi long before we finish, and Hrathen's proclamation will be law."

"I could pretend to be Derethi for a while," Lukel said. "If only while I'm planning the king's demise."

Sarene shook her head. "If we give Shu-Dereth that kind of foothold in Arelon, we'll never be free of it."

"It's only a religion, Sarene," Ahan said. "I think we should focus on real problems."

"You don't think Shu-Dereth is a 'real problem,' Ahan?" Sarene asked. "Why don't you try and explain that to Jindo and Duladel?"

"She's right," Roial said. "Fjorden embraced Shu-Dereth as a vehicle for domination. If those priests convert Arelon, then Wyrn will rule here no matter who we put on the throne."

"Then raising an army of peasants is out?" Shuden asked, bringing the conversation back on topic.

"Too time-consuming," Roial said.

"Besides," Kaloo noted, "I don't think you want to throw this country into war. I've seen what a bloody revolution can do to a nation—it breaks the people's spirit to fight one another. The men in the Elantris City Guard might be fools, but they are still your countrymen. Their blood would be on your hands."

Sarene looked up at the comment, made without a hint of Kaloo's normal flamboyance. Something about him made her increasingly suspicious.

"Then what?" Lukel said with exasperation. "We can't fight Telrii and we can't wait for him to convert. What do we do?"

"We could kill him," Eondel said quietly.

"Well?" Sarene asked. She hadn't expected that suggestion to come out quite so early in the meeting.

"It has merits," Kiin agreed, showing a cold dispassion that Sarene had never seen in him before. "Assassinating Telrii would solve a lot of problems."

The room fell quiet. Sarene felt a bitter taste in her mouth as she studied the men. They knew what she knew. She had determined long before the meeting began that this was the only way.

"Ah, one man's death to save a nation," Kaloo whispered.

"It seems the only alternative," Kiin said with a shake of his head.

"Perhaps," the Dula said. "Though I wonder if we aren't underestimating the people of Arelon."

"We already discussed this," Lukel said. "We don't have enough time to rally the peasants."

"Not just the peasants, young Lukel," Kaloo said, "but the nobility. Have you not sensed their hesitance to back Telrii? Have you not seen the discomfort in their eyes? A king with no support is no king at all."

"And the Guard?" Kiin asked pointedly.

"I wonder if we couldn't turn them," Kaloo said. "Certainly they could be persuaded to see that what they have done is not right."

"You" had become "we." Sarene's brow furled; she almost had it. There was something familiar about his words. . . .

"It's an interesting suggestion," Roial said.

"The Guard and the nobility support Telrii because they

don't see another alternative," Kaloo explained. "Lord Roial was shamed by the failed wedding, and Lady Sarene was thrown into Elantris. Now, however, the embarrassment has been removed. Perhaps if we can show the Guard the ultimate result of their decision—occupation by Fjorden and a virtual enslavement of our people—they will realize that they supported the wrong man. Give men an honest choice, and I believe they will choose wisely."

That was it. Sarene knew that faith somewhere—that pure belief in the basic goodness of all men. And, when she suddenly realized where she had seen it before, she couldn't stop herself from jumping up and yelping in surprise.

RAODEN cringed, immediately recognizing his mistake. He had let go of Kaloo too quickly, allowing too much of his true self to show. The others hadn't noticed the change, but Sarene—dear suspicious Sarene—hadn't been so lax. He looked into her shocked, wide eyes, and knew that she knew. Somehow, despite their short time together, she had recognized him when his best friends could not.

Uh-oh, he thought to himself.

"SARENE?" Roial asked. "Princess, are you all right?"

Sarene looked around sheepishly, standing in front of her chair. She quickly forgot her embarrassment, however, as her eyes fell on the furtive Kaloo.

"No, my lord, I don't think so," she said. "I think we need a break."

"We haven't really been going that long . . ." Lukel said.

Sarene silenced him with a look, and no one else braved her wrath.

"A break it is," Roial said slowly.

"Good," Kiin said, rising from his seat. "I have some Hraggish meatwraps cooling out back. I'll go get them."

Sarene was so flustered that she barely even considered chastising her uncle for preparing a meal when she had expressly told him not to. She shot Kaloo a telling look, then stalked away from the table, apparently on her way to the privy. She waited in Kiin's study for a moment before the hapless impostor finally strolled around the corner.

Sarene grabbed his shirt and all but threw him against the wall as she pressed her face up against his.

"*Spirit?*" she demanded. "What in the name of Gracious Domi are you doing here?"

Spirit looked to the side apprehensively. "Not so loudly, Sarene! How do you think those men would react if they discovered they'd been sitting with an Elantrian?"

"But . . . how?" she asked, her anger turning to excitement as she realized it really was him. She reached up to wiggle his nose, which was far too long to be his real one. She was surprised when her fingers passed through the tip as if it weren't there.

"You were right about the Aons, Sarene," Spirit said quickly. "They're maps of Arelon—all I had to do was add one line, and the entire system started working again."

"One line?"

"The Chasm," Spirit explained. "*It* caused the Reod. It was enough of a change in the landscape that its presence needs to be reflected in the Aons."

"It works!" Sarene said. Then she released his shirt and gave him a bitter punch to the side. "You've been lying to me!"

"Ow!" Spirit complained. "Please, no punching—my body doesn't heal, remember?"

Sarene gasped. "That didn't . . . ?"

"Change when we fixed AonDor?" Spirit asked. "No. I'm still an Elantrian under this illusion. There's something else wrong with AonDor."

Sarene resisted the urge to punch him again. "Why did you lie to me?"

Spirit smiled. "Oh, and you're going to try and tell me it wasn't more fun this way?"

"Well . . ."

He laughed. "Only you would consider that a valid excuse, my princess. Actually, I never got the chance to tell you. Every time I tried to approach you these last few days, you ducked away—and you ignored the letter I sent you. I couldn't just jump in front of you and drop my illusion. I actually came to Kiin's last night in the hopes I would see you in the window."

"You did?" Sarene asked with a smile.

"Ask Galladon," Raoden said. "He's back at Roial's right now eating all of the duke's Jaadorian candy. Did you know he had a weakness for sweets?"

"The duke or Galladon?"

"Both. Look, they're going to wonder what's taking us so long."

"Let them," Sarene said. "All the other women have been mooning over Kaloo so much, it's about time I fell into line."

Spirit began to chuckle, then he caught the dangerous look in her eyes and let it taper off. "It really was the only way, Sarene. I didn't have much choice—I had to act the part."

"I think you acted it a little too well," she said. Then she smiled, unable to remain angry.

He obviously caught the softening in her eyes, for he untensed. "You have to admit, it was fun at times. I had no idea you were *that* good of a fencer."

Sarene smiled slyly. "My talents are plentiful, Spirit. And apparently so are yours—I had no idea *you* were that good of an actor. I hated you!"

"It's nice to feel appreciated," Spirit said, letting his arms wrap around her.

Suddenly she was aware of his close proximity. His body was room temperature, and the unnatural coolness was unnerving. However, rather than pulling away, she let her head rest on his shoulder. "So, why did you come? You should be back in New Elantris, preparing your people. Why risk coming out into Kae?"

"To find you," he said.

She smiled. That was the right answer.

"And," he continued, "to keep you all from slaughtering each other. This country certainly is a mess, isn't it?"

Sarene sighed. "And it's partially my fault."

Spirit reached up to put his hands on her neck, rotating her head so she could see into his eyes. His face was different, but those eyes were the same. Deep and blue. How had she ever mistaken him for anyone else?

"You are *not* allowed to berate yourself, Sarene," he said. "I get enough of that from Galladon. You've done a wonderful job here—better than I could have even imagined. I assumed that these men would stop meeting after I left."

Sarene paused, shaking herself from the trance of being lost in those eyes. "What was that you just said? After you left . . . ?"

Voices called from the other room, and Spirit winked at her, his eyes twinkling. "We need to go back in. But . . . let's just say I have something else I need to tell you, once the meeting is through and we can speak more privately."

She nodded in a half daze. Spirit was in Kae, and AonDor worked. She walked back into the dining room and sat down at the table, and Spirit entered the room a few moments later. One chair was still empty, however.

"Where's Ahan?" Sarene asked.

Kiin frowned. "He left," he declared in a bitter tone.

Lukel laughed, shooting Sarene a smile. "The count claims that something he ate didn't agree with him. He . . . stepped out."

"It's impossible," Kiin grumbled. "There was nothing in those crackers that could have upset his stomach."

"I'm sure it wasn't the crackers, Uncle," Sarene said with a smile. "It must be something he ate before he came."

Lukel laughed in agreement. "Domi knows, that man eats so much it's a wonder he doesn't end up sick every night by pure laws of probability."

"Well, we should continue without him," Roial said. "There's no telling how long he will be indisposed."

"Agreed," Sarene said, preparing to begin again.

Roial, however, beat her to it. He stood slowly, his old body looking surprisingly weak. The duke sighed, shaking his head. "If you will all forgive me, I have something to say."

The nobles nodded, sensing the duke's solemnity.

"I will not lie to you; I never once debated whether or not action should be taken against Telrii. He and I have spent the last ten years as mercantile enemies. He is a flagrant, wasteful man—he will make a worse king, even, than Iadon. His willingness to even consider Hrathen's silly proclamation was the final proof I needed.

"No, my reason for demanding more time before we met was not to wonder if we should depose Telrii. The reason I asked for more time was to wait for some . . . associates of mine to arrive."

"Associates?" Sarene said.

"Assassins," Roial said. "Men I have hired out of Fjorden. Not all the people of that country are perfectly loyal to their god—some are sworn to gold instead."

"Where are they?" Sarene asked.

"Staying in an inn not far away," Roial said.

"But," Sarene said with confusion, "just last week you warned us against letting bloodshed advance our revolt."

Roial bowed his head. "The guilt was speaking, dear Sarene, for I had already sent for these men. However, I have changed my mind. This young man from Dula—"

Roial was interrupted by the sound of feet clomping in the entry hallway: Ahan had returned. *Odd,* Sarene thought to herself as she turned, *I didn't hear the front door close.*

When she turned, it was not Ahan she found standing in the doorway. Instead, she was confronted by a group of armed soldiers with a well-dressed man at their front. King Telrii.

Sarene jumped up, but her yell of surprise was lost among other similar exclamations. Telrii stepped to the side, allowing a dozen men in Elantris City Guard uniforms to fill the room. They were followed by the portly Count Ahan.

"Ahan!" Roial said. "What have you done?"

"I finally got you, old man," the count said gleefully, his jowls shaking. "I told you I would. Joke about how my caravans to Svorden are doing *now,* you cursed old idiot. We'll see how yours do while you spend the next few years in prison."

Roial shook a mournful, white-haired head. "You fool . . . Didn't you realize when this stopped being a game? We aren't playing with fruits and silks anymore."

"Protest if you will," Ahan said with a triumphant shake of his finger. "But you have to admit, I got you! I've been waiting to do this for months—I could never get Iadon to believe me. Can you believe that he actually thought you incapable of betraying him? He claimed your old friendship went too deep."

Roial sighed, regarding Telrii, who was smiling broadly, obviously enjoying the exchange. "Oh, Ahan," Roial said. "You have always been so fond of acting without thought."

Sarene was stunned. She couldn't move, or even speak. Traitors were supposed to be men with dark eyes and sour dispositions. She couldn't connect that image with Ahan. He was arrogant and impetuous, but she *liked* him. How could someone she liked do something so horrible?

Telrii snapped his fingers, and a soldier stepped forward and rammed his sword directly into Duke Roial's belly. Roial gasped, then crumpled with a moan.

"Thus are the judgments of your king," Telrii said.

Ahan yelled, eyes widening in his fat face. "No! You said prison!" He rushed past Telrii, blubbering as he knelt beside Roial.

"Did I?" Telrii asked. Then he pointed at two of his soldiers. "You two, gather some men and find those assassins, then . . ." He tapped his chin thoughtfully. ". . . throw them off the walls of Elantris."

The two men saluted, then marched from the room.

"The rest of you," Telrii said, "kill these traitors. Start with the dear princess. Let it be known that this is the punishment for all those who try to usurp the throne."

"No!" Shuden and Eondel yelled in unison.

The soldiers started to move, and Sarene found herself behind a protective wall formed by Shuden, Eondel, and Lukel. Only Eondel was armed, however, and they were faced by ten men.

"Interesting you should mention usurpers, Duke Telrii," a voice said from across the table. "I was under the impression that the throne belonged to Iadon's family."

Sarene followed the sound. Her eyes found Spirit—or, at least, someone wearing Spirit's clothing. He had pale Aonic skin, sandy brown hair, and keen blue eyes. Spirit's eyes. But his face didn't show any signs of Elantris's taint. He tossed a rag on the table, and she could see the brown stains on one side—as if he wanted them to believe he had simply wiped away his makeup to reveal a completely different face underneath.

Telrii gasped, stumbling back against the wall. "Prince

Raoden!" he choked. "No! You died. They told me you were dead!"

Raoden. Sarene felt numb. She stared at the man Spirit, wondering who he was, and if she had ever really known him.

Spirit looked at the soldiers. "Would you dare slay the true king of Arelon?" he demanded.

The Guard members stepped back, faces confused and frightened.

"Men, protect me!" Telrii yelped, turning and scrambling from the room. The soldiers watched their leader flee, then unceremoniously joined him, leaving the conspirators alone.

Spirit—Raoden—hopped over the table, brushing past Lukel. He shoved the still blubbering Ahan out of his way and knelt next to Kiin—the only one who had thought to try treating Roial's wound. Sarene watched dumbly from behind, her senses paralyzed. It was obvious that Kiin's care would be nowhere near enough to save the duke. The sword had passed completely through the man's body, delivering a painful wound that was certainly mortal.

"Raoden!" Duke Roial gasped. "You have returned to us!"

"Be still, Roial," Raoden said, stabbing the air with his finger. Light burst from its tip as he began to draw.

"I should have known it was you," the duke rambled. "All of that silly talk about trusting the people. Can you believe I actually started to agree with you? I should have sent those assassins to do their work the moment they arrived."

"You are too good a man for that, Roial," Spirit said, his voice taut with emotion.

Roial's eyes focused, perceiving for the first time the Aon that Spirit was drawing above him. He breathed out in awe. "Have you returned the beautiful city as well?"

Spirit didn't respond, instead concentrating on his Aon. He drew differently from the way he had before, his fingers moving more dexterously and quickly. He finished the Aon with a small line near the bottom. It began to glow warmly, bathing Roial in its light. As Sarene watched, the edges of Roial's wound seemed to pull together slightly. A scratch on Roial's face disappeared, and several of the liver spots on his scalp faded.

Then the light fell away, the wound still belching blood with each futile pump of the duke's dying heart.

Spirit cursed. "It's too weak," he said, desperately beginning another Aon. "And I haven't studied the healing modifiers! I don't know how to target just one part of the body."

Roial reached up with a quivering arm and grabbed Spirit's hand. The partially completed Aon faded away as the duke's movement caused Spirit to make a mistake. Spirit did not start again, bowing his head as if weeping.

"Do not cry, my boy," Roial said. "Your return is blessed. You cannot save this tired old body, but you can save the kingdom. I will die in peace, knowing you are here to protect it."

Spirit cupped the old man's face in his hands. "You did a wonderful job with me, Roial," he whispered, and Sarene felt intensely that she was intruding. "Without you to watch over me, I would have turned out like my father."

"No, boy," Roial said. "You were more like your mother from the start. Domi bless you."

Sarene turned away then as the duke's death turned gruesome, his body spasming and blood coming to his lips. When she turned back, blinking the tears from her eyes, Raoden was still kneeling over the old man's corpse. Finally he took a deep breath and stood, turning to regard the rest of them with sad—but firm—eyes. Beside her, Sarene felt Shuden, Eondel, and Lukel fall to their knees, bowing their heads reverently.

"My king," Eondel said, speaking for all of them.

"My . . . husband," Sarene realized with shock.

CHAPTER 54

"HE did *what*?" Hrathen asked with amazement.

The priest, startled by Hrathen's sudden reaction, stuttered as he repeated the message. Hrathen cut the man off halfway through.

The Duke of Ial Plantation, dead? By Telrii's command? What kind of random move was this? Hrathen could tell from the messenger's face that there was more, so he motioned for the man to continue. Soon Hrathen realized that the execution hadn't been random at all—that in fact it had been completely logical. Hrathen couldn't believe Telrii's fortune. Roial was said to be a crafty man; catching the duke in the act of treason had been amazingly propitious.

What the messenger related next, however, was even more shocking. The rumors said that Prince Raoden had returned from the grave.

Hrathen sat, dumbfounded, behind his desk. A tapestry fluttered on the wall as the messenger closed the door on his way out.

Control, he thought. *You can deal with this.* The rumor of Raoden's return was false, of course, but Hrathen had to admit that it was a masterful stroke. He knew of the prince's saintly reputation; the people regarded Raoden with a level of idolizing adoration that was given only to dead men. If Sarene had somehow found a look-alike, she could call him husband and continue her bid for the throne even now that Roial was dead.

She certainly works quickly, Hrathen thought with a respectful smile.

Telrii's slaughter of Roial still bothered Hrathen. Murdering the duke without trial or incarceration would make the other nobles even more apprehensive. Hrathen rose. Perhaps it wasn't too late to convince Telrii to at least draft a warrant of execution. It would ease the aristocratic minds if they were able to read such a document.

TELRII refused to see him. Hrathen stood in the waiting room again, staring down two of Telrii's guards, arms folded in front of him. The two men looked at the ground sheepishly. Apparently, something had unsettled Telrii so much that he wasn't taking any visitors at all.

Hrathen didn't intend to let himself be ignored. Though he could not force his way into the room, he could make himself such a nuisance that Telrii eventually agreed to meet with him. So he had spent the last hour demanding a meeting every five minutes.

In fact, the time was approaching for another request. "Soldier," he commanded. "Ask the king if he will see me."

The soldier sighed—just as he had the last half-dozen times Hrathen had made the demand. However, the soldier opened the door and obeyed, going in to search out his commander. A few moments later, the man returned.

Hrathen's query froze in his throat. *It wasn't the same man.*

The "guard" whipped out his sword and attacked the second guard. Sounds of metal against metal exploded from the king's audience chamber, and men began to scream—some in rage, others in agony.

Hrathen cursed—a battle on the one night he had left his armor behind. Gritting his teeth, he spun past the fighting guards and entered the room.

The tapestries were in flames, and men struggled desperately in the close confines. Several guards lay dead at the far doorway. Some wore the brown and yellow of the Elantris Guard. The others were in silver and blue—the colors of Count Eondel's legion.

Hrathen dodged a few attacks, ducking blades or smashing them out of men's hands. He had to find the king. Telrii was too important to—

Time froze as Hrathen saw the king through the melee, burning strips of cloth dripping from the brocades above. Telrii's eyes were wild with fear as he dashed toward the open door at the back of the room. Eondel's sword found Telrii's neck before the king had taken more than a few steps.

Telrii's headless corpse fell at Count Eondel's feet. The count regarded it with grim eyes, then collapsed himself, holding a wound in his side.

Hrathen stood quietly in the melee, chaos forgotten for the moment, regarding the two corpses. *So much for avoiding a bloody change in power,* he thought with resignation.

Part Three

THE
SPIRIT
OF
ELANTRIS

CHAPTER 55

IT seemed unnatural to look at Elantris from the outside.
Raoden belonged in the city. It was as if he stood outside
of his own body, looking at it from another person's perspective. He should no more be separated from Elantris than
his spirit should be separated from his body.

He stood with Sarene atop Kiin's fortresslike house in the
noonday sun. The merchant, showing both foresight and
healthy paranoia following the massacre ten years before,
had built his mansion more like a castle than a house. It was
a compact square, with straight stone walls and narrow windows, and it even stood atop a hill. The roof had a pattern of
stones running along its lip, much like the battlements atop a
city wall. It was against one such stone that Raoden leaned
now, Sarene pressed close to his side, her arms around his
waist as they regarded the city.

Soon after Roial's death the night before, Kiin had barred
his doors and informed them that he had enough supplies
stockpiled to last years. Though Raoden doubted the doors
would survive long against a determined attack, he welcomed
the feelings of safety Kiin inspired. There was no telling how
Telrii would react to Raoden's appearance. Chances were,
however, that he would give up all pretense and seek Fjordell
aid. The Elantris Guard might have been hesitant to attack
Raoden, but Fjordell troops would have no such inhibitions.

"I should have figured it out," Sarene mumbled at Raoden's side.

"Hum?" Raoden asked, raising his eyebrows. She was
wearing one of Daora's dresses—which was, of course, too

short for her, though Raoden rather liked the amount of leg it showed. She wore her short blond wig, which was cut in a style that made her look younger than she was, a schoolgirl instead of a mature woman. Well, Raoden revised, a six-foot-tall schoolgirl.

Sarene raised her head, looking into his eyes. "I can't believe I didn't put it together. I was even suspicious about your—meaning Raoden's—disappearance. I assumed the king had killed you off, or at least exiled you."

"He certainly would have liked to," Raoden said. "He tried to send me away on numerous occasions, but I usually wiggled out of it somehow."

"It was so *obvious*!" Sarene said, resting her head on his shoulder with a petulant thud. "The cover-up, the embarrassment . . . it makes perfect sense."

"It's easy to see the answers once the puzzle is solved, Sarene," Raoden said. "I'm not surprised that no one connected my disappearance with Elantris—that isn't the sort of thing an Arelene would assume. People don't talk about Elantris, and they certainly don't want to associate it with those they love. They would *prefer* to believe that I'd died than know that I'd been taken by the Shaod."

"But I'm not an Arelene," Sarene said. "I don't have the same biases."

"You lived with them," Raoden said. "You couldn't help being affected by their disposition. Besides, you haven't lived around Elantris—you didn't know how the Shaod worked."

Sarene huffed to herself. "And you let me go along in ignorance. My own husband."

"I gave you a clue," he protested.

"Yes, about five minutes before you revealed yourself."

Raoden chuckled, pulling her close. No matter what else happened, he was glad he had made the decision to leave Elantris. This short time with Sarene was worth it.

After a few moments, he realized something. "I'm not, you know."

"Not what?"

"Your husband. At least, the relationship is disputable. The betrothal contract said our marriage would be binding if either of us died before the wedding. I didn't die—I went to Elantris. Though they're essentially the same thing, the contract's words were very specific."

Sarene looked up with concern.

He laughed quietly. "I'm not trying to get out of it, Sarene," he said. "I'm just saying we should make it formal, just so everyone's mind is put at ease."

Sarene thought for a moment, then she nodded sharply. "Definitely. I've been engaged twice during the last two months, and I never got a wedding. A girl deserves a good wedding."

"A queen's wedding," Raoden agreed.

Sarene sighed as she looked back at Kae. The city seemed cold and lifeless, almost unpopulated. The political uncertainty was destroying the economy of Arelon as surely as Iadon's rule had destroyed its spirit. Where there should have been busy commerce, only a few hearty pedestrians slipped furtively through the streets. The only exception was the great city square, which held the tents of the Arelene Market. While some of the merchants had decided to cut their losses—moving on to Teod to sell what they could—a surprising number had stayed. What could have persuaded so many to remain to try and push wares upon a people that just weren't buying?

The only other place that showed any sign of activity was the palace. Elantris City Guard members had been poring over the area like worried insects all morning. Sarene had sent her Seon to investigate, but he had yet to return.

"He was such a good man," Sarene said softly.

"Roial?" Raoden asked. "Yes, he was. The duke was the role model I needed when my father proved unworthy."

Sarene chuckled softly. "When Kiin first introduced Roial to me, he said he wasn't sure if the duke helped us because he loved Arelon, or because he was just bored."

"Many people took Roial's craftiness as a sign of deceitfulness," Raoden said. "They were wrong; Roial was clever, and he enjoyed intrigue, but he was a patriot. He taught me to believe in Arelon, even after its many stumbles."

"He was like a wily old grandfather," Sarene said. "And he almost became my husband."

"I still can't believe that," Raoden said. "I loved Roial . . . but to imagine him married? To you?"

Sarene laughed. "I don't think we believed it either. Of course, that doesn't mean we wouldn't have gone through with it."

Raoden sighed, rubbing her shoulder. "If only I had known what capable hands I was leaving Arelon in. It would have saved me a great deal of worry."

"And New Elantris?" Sarene asked. "Is Karata watching it?"

"New Elantris watches itself without much trouble," Raoden said. "But, I did send Galladon back this morning with instructions to begin teaching the people AonDor. If we fail here, I don't want to leave Elantris unable to protect itself."

"There probably isn't much time left."

"Time enough to make sure they learn an Aon or two," Raoden said. "They deserve to know the secret to their power."

Sarene smiled. "I always knew you would find the answer. Domi doesn't let your kind of dedication go wasted."

Raoden smiled. The night before, she had made him draw several dozen Aons to prove that they actually worked. Of course, they hadn't been enough to save Roial.

A rock of guilt burned in Raoden's chest. If he had known the proper modifiers, he might have been able to save Roial. A gut wound took a long time to kill a man; Raoden could have healed each organ separately, then sealed the skin. Instead, he had been able only to draw a general Aon that affected Roial's entire body. The Aon's power, already weak, had been diluted so much by the broad target that it did no good.

Raoden had stayed up late memorizing modifiers. Aon-Dor healing was a complex, difficult art, but he was determined to make certain no one else died because of his inability. It would take months of memorizing, but he would learn the modifier for every organ, muscle, and bone.

Sarene turned back to her contemplation of the city. She retained a strong grip on Raoden's waist—Sarene did *not* like heights, especially if she didn't have something to hold on to. Looking over at the top of her head, Raoden suddenly remembered something from the night's studies.

Reaching out, he pulled off her wig. It resisted as the glue held, then fell away, revealing the stubble underneath. Sarene turned with questioning, annoyed eyes, but Raoden was already drawing.

It wasn't a complex Aon; it required him only to stipulate a target, how the target was to be affected, and a length of time. When he finished, her hair began to grow. It went lethargically, sliding out of her head like a breath slowly exhaled. In a few minutes, however, it was finished—her long golden hair once again reaching to the middle of her back.

Sarene ran disbelieving fingers through the hair. Then she looked up at Raoden with teary eyes. "Thank you," she whispered, pulling him close. "You have no idea what that means."

After a moment, she pulled back, staring at him with intent, silvery gray eyes. "Show yourself to me."

"My face?" Raoden asked.

Sarene nodded.

"You've seen it before," he said hesitantly.

"I know, but I'm getting too used to this one. I want to see the real you."

The determination in her eyes stopped him from arguing further. With a sigh, he reached up, tapping the collar of his undershirt with his index finger. To him, nothing changed, but he could feel Sarene stiffen as the illusion fell away. He felt suddenly ashamed, and hurriedly began to draw the Aon again, but she stopped him.

"It isn't as horrid as you think, Raoden," she said, running her fingers across his face. "They say your bodies are like corpses, but that isn't true. Your skin may be discolored and a little wrinkled, but there is still flesh underneath."

Her finger found the cut on his cheek, and she gasped slightly. "I did this, didn't I?"

Raoden nodded. "As I said—I had no idea how good of a fencer you are."

Sarene ran her finger down the wound. "It confused me terribly when I couldn't find the wound. Why does the illusion show your expressions, but not a cut?"

"It's complicated," Raoden said. "You have to link each muscle in the face with its companion in the illusion. I could never have figured it out myself—the equations are all in one of my books."

"But you altered the illusion so quickly last night, changing from Kaloo to Raoden."

He smiled. "That's because I had *two* illusions on, one connected to my undershirt and the other to my coat. As soon as I dissolved the one on the top, the one underneath showed. I'm just glad it looks enough like me that the others recognized it. There weren't, of course, any equations describing how to create my own face—I had to figure that out on my own."

"You did a good job."

"I extrapolated from my Elantrian face, telling the illusion to use it as a base." He smiled. "You're a lucky woman, having a man who can change faces at any time. You'll never get bored."

Sarene snorted. "I like this one just fine. This is the face that loved me when it thought I was an Elantrian, all rank and title abandoned."

"You think you can get used to this?" Raoden asked.

"Raoden, I was going to marry Roial last week. He was a dear old man, but he was so incredibly homely that rocks looked handsome when he stood next to them."

Raoden laughed. Despite everything—Telrii, Hrathen, and poor Roial's demise—his heart was jubilant.

"What *are* they doing?" Sarene said, looking back at the palace.

Raoden turned to follow her view—an action that bumped Sarene forward slightly. She reacted by locking a deathlike grip on Raoden's shoulder, her fingers biting into his flesh. "Don't do that!"

"Oops," he said, putting an arm around her shoulder. "I forgot about your fear of heights."

"I am *not* afraid of heights," Sarene said, still holding on to his arm. "I just get dizzy."

"Of course," Raoden said, squinting at the palace. He could barely make out a group of soldiers doing something in the grounds before the building. They were laying out blankets or sheets of some sort.

"It's too far," Sarene said. "Where is Ashe?"

Raoden reached up and sketched Aon Nae—a large circular character—in the air before them. When he was finished, the air inside Aon Nae's circle rippled like water, then cleared to show a magnified view of the city. Placing his palm in the center of the circle, Raoden maneuvered the Aon until it was pointing at the palace. The view unblurred itself, and they were able to see the soldiers with such detail that they could read their rank insignias.

"That's useful," Sarene noted as Raoden raised the Aon slightly. The soldiers were indeed laying out sheets—sheets with what appeared to be bodies on them. Raoden grew cold as he moved the disk along the line of corpses. The last two corpses in the row were familiar.

Sarene gasped in horror as Eondel's and Telrii's dead faces came into focus.

CHAPTER 56

"HE attacked late last night, my lady," Ashe explained. The remaining members of their group—Kiin, Lukel, and Shuden—were gathered atop the house, watching as Raoden focused his Aon spyglass on the funeral pyres being built in the palace courtyard.

Baron Shuden sat morosely on the stone roof, shaking his head in disbelief. Sarene held the young Jindo's hand in an attempt to provide comfort, painfully aware of how difficult the last few days must have been for him. His future father-in-law had turned out to be a traitor, Torena had reportedly disappeared, and now his best friend was dead.

"He was a brave man," Kiin said, standing beside Raoden.

"That was never in question," Raoden said. "His actions were foolish nonetheless."

"He did it for honor, Raoden," Sarene said, looking up from the despondent Shuden. "Telrii murdered a great man last night—Eondel acted to avenge the duke."

Raoden shook his head. "Revenge is always a foolish motivation, Sarene. Now we have lost not only Roial, but Eondel as well. The people are left with their second dead king in the space of a few weeks."

Sarene let the matter drop. Raoden spoke as a ruler, not as a friend. He couldn't afford to give Eondel leeway, even in death, because of the situation the count had created.

The soldiers did not wait on ceremony to immolate the fallen men. They simply lit the pyre, then saluted en masse as the bodies burned away. Whatever else could be said about the Guard, they performed this one duty with solemnity and honor.

"There," Raoden said, pointing his Aon at a detachment of about fifty soldiers who left the pyre and galloped toward Kiin's house. All wore the brown capes that marked them as officers in the Elantris City Guard.

"This could be bad," Kiin said.

"Or it could be good," Raoden said.

Kiin shook his head. "We should collapse the entryway. Let them try to break down my door with a ton of stone behind it."

"No," Raoden said. "Trapping us inside won't do any good. I want to meet with them."

"There are other ways out of the building," Kiin said.

"Still, wait for my command to collapse your entryway, Kiin," Raoden said. "That is an order."

Kiin ground his teeth for a moment, then nodded. "All right, Raoden, but not because you order it—but because I trust you. My son may call you king, but I accept the rule of no man."

Sarene regarded her uncle with a look of shocked surprise. She had never seen him speak in such a manner; he was usually so jovial, like a happy circus bear. Now his face was flat and grim, covered with whiskers he had allowed to start growing the moment Iadon was found dead. Gone was the brusque but compliant chef, and in his place was a man who seemed more like a grizzled admiral from her father's navy.

"Thank you, Kiin," Raoden said.

Her uncle nodded. The horsemen approached quickly, fanning out to surround Kiin's hilltop fortress. Noticing Raoden on the roof, one of the soldiers urged his horse a few steps closer.

"We have heard rumors that Lord Raoden, crown prince of Arelon, still lives," the man announced. "If there is truth to this, let him come forward. Our country has need of a king."

Kiin untensed visibly, and Raoden let out a quiet sigh. The Guard officers stood in a row, still mounted, and even from the short distance, Raoden could see their faces. They were harried, confused, yet hopeful.

"We have to move quickly, before that gyorn can respond," Raoden said to his friends. "Send messengers to the nobility—I plan to hold my coronation within the hour."

RAODEN strode into the palace throne room. Beside the throne dais stood Sarene and the young-looking patriarch of the Korathi religion. Raoden had only just met the man, but Sarene's description of him had been accurate. Long golden hair, a smile that claimed to know things it didn't, and a self-important air were his most striking features. However, Raoden needed him. The statement made by choosing the patriarch of Shu-Korath to crown him was an important precedent.

Sarene smiled encouragingly as Raoden approached. It amazed him how much she had to give, considering what she had been through recently. He joined her on the dais, then turned to regard the nobility of Arelon.

He recognized most of the faces. Many of them had supported him before his exile. Now most were simply confused. His appearance had been sudden, as had Telrii's death. Rumors were widespread that Raoden had been behind the assassination, but most of the people didn't seem to care. Their eyes were dull from the shock, and they were beginning to show the wearied signs of extended stress.

It will change now, Raoden promised them silently. *No more questioning. No more uncertainty. We will put forth a united front, with Teod, and face Fjorden.*

"My lords and ladies," Raoden said. "People of Arelon. Our poor kingdom has suffered too much over the last ten years. Let us set it at right once again. With this crown, I promise—"

He froze. He felt . . . a power. At first, he thought the Dor was attacking. However, he realized this was something else—something he had never experienced before. Something external.

Someone else was manipulating the Dor.

He searched through the crowd, masking his surprise. His eyes fell on a small red-robed form almost invisible among the noblemen. The power was coming from him.

A Derethi priest? Raoden thought incredulously. The man was smiling, and his hair was blond beneath his hood. *What?*

The mood of the congregation changed. Several people fainted immediately, but most simply stared. Dumbfounded. Shocked. Yet somehow unsurprised. They had been beaten down so much, they had expected something horrible to happen. Without checking, Raoden knew that his illusion had fallen.

The patriarch gasped, dropping the crown as he stumbled away. Raoden looked back to the crowd, his stomach sick. He had been so close. . . .

A voice came at his side. "Look at him, nobles of Arelon!" Sarene declared. "Look at the man who would have been your king. Look at his dark skin and his Elantrian face! Then, tell me. Does it really matter?"

The crowd was quiet.

"Ten years you were ruled by a tyrant because you rejected Elantris," Sarene said. "You were the privileged, the wealthy, but in a way you were the most oppressed, for you could never be secure. Were your titles worth your freedom?

"This is the man who loved you when all others sought to steal your pride. I ask you this: Can being an Elantrian make him any worse a king than Iadon or Telrii?"

She knelt before him. "I, for one, accept his rule."

Raoden watched the crowd tensely. Then, one at a time, they began to kneel. It began with Shuden and Lukel, who stood near the front of the crowd, but it soon spread to the others. Like a wave, the forms knelt—some in a stupor, others with resignation. Some, however, dared to be happy.

Sarene reached down and snatched up the fallen crown. It was a simple thing—no more than a hastily constructed gold band—but it represented so much. With Seinalan stunned, the princess of Teod took his duty upon herself and, reaching up, placed the crown on Raoden's head.

"Behold, your king!" she exclaimed.

Some of the people actually started cheering.

ONE man was not cheering, but hissing. Dilaf looked as if he wanted to claw his way through the crowd and rip Raoden apart with his bare hands. The people, whose cheers increased from a few scattered yells to a general exclamation of approval, kept him back. The priest looked around him with loathing, then forced his way through the crowd and escaped through the doors, out into a darkening city.

Sarene ignored the priest, instead looking over at Raoden. "Congratulations, Your Majesty," she said, kissing him lightly.

"I can't believe they accepted me," Raoden said with wonder.

"Ten years ago they rejected the Elantrians," Sarene said, "and found that a man could be a monster no matter what he looked like. They're finally ready to accept a ruler not because he's a god or because he has money, but because they know he will lead them well."

Raoden smiled. "Of course, it helps when that ruler has a wife who can deliver a moving speech at precisely the right moment."

"True."

Raoden turned, looking out over the crowd toward the fleeing Dilaf. "Who was that?"

"Just one of Hrathen's priests," Sarene said dismissively.

"I imagine he isn't having a very good day—Dilaf is known for his hatred of Elantrians."

Raoden didn't seem to think her dismissal was justified. "Something's wrong, Sarene. Why did my illusion drop?"

"You didn't do that?"

Raoden shook his head. "I . . . I think that priest did it."

"What?"

"I sensed the Dor the moment before my Aon fell, and it was coming from that priest." He paused for a moment, grinding his teeth. "Can I borrow Ashe?"

"Of course," Sarene said, waving the Seon closer.

"Ashe, would you deliver a message for me?" Raoden asked.

"Of course, my lord," the Seon said with a bob.

"Find Galladon in New Elantris and tell him what just happened," Raoden said. "Then warn him to be ready for something."

"For what, my lord?"

"I don't know," Raoden said. "Just tell him to be prepared—and tell him that I'm worried."

CHAPTER 57

HRATHEN watched as "Raoden" strode into the throne room. No one challenged the impostor's claim—this man, Raoden or not, would soon be king. Sarene's move was a brilliant stroke. Telrii assassinated, a pretender on the throne . . . Hrathen's plans were in serious danger.

Hrathen eyed this pretender, feeling an odd surge of hatred as he saw the way that Sarene looked at the man. Hrathen could see the love in her eyes. Could that foolish adoration really be serious? Where had this man come from so suddenly? And how had he managed to capture Sarene, who was normally so discerning?

Regardless, she had apparently given her heart to him. Logically, Hrathen knew his jealousy was foolish. Hrathen's own relationship with the girl had been one of antagonism, not of affection. Why should he be jealous of another man? No, Hrathen needed to be levelheaded. Only one month remained until the armies of united Derethi would wash over Arelon, slaughtering the people—Sarene included. Hrathen had to work quickly if he was going to find a way to convert the kingdom with so little time remaining.

Hrathen pulled back as Raoden began the coronation. Many a king ordered his enemies' incarceration as a first royal decree, and Hrathen didn't want his presence to give the impostor a reminder.

He was, however, close enough to the front to witness the transformation. Hrathen was confused by the sight; the Shaod was supposed to come suddenly, but not *that* suddenly. The oddity forced him to reconsider his assumptions. What if Raoden hadn't died? What if he had been hiding in Elantris all along? Hrathen had found a way to feign being an Elantrian. What if this man had done the same?

Hrathen was shocked by the transformation, but he was even more shocked when the people of Arelon did nothing about it. Sarene gave her speech, and people just stood dully. They did not stop her from crowning the Elantrian king.

Hrathen felt sick. He turned, and by happenstance he saw Dilaf slipping away from the crowd. Hrathen trailed behind—for once, he shared Dilaf's disgust. He was amazed that the people of Arelon could act so illogically.

At that moment, Hrathen realized his mistake. Dilaf had been right: If Hrathen had focused more on Elantris, the people would have been too disgusted to grant Raoden kingship. Hrathen had neglected to instill in his followers a true sense of Jaddeth's holy will. He had used popularity to convert, rather than doctrine. The result was a fickle congregation, capable of returning to their old ways as quickly as they had left.

It is this cursed deadline! Hrathen thought to himself as he strode down Kae's quickly darkening evening streets. Three months was not enough time to build a stable following.

Ahead of him, Dilaf turned down a side street. Hrathen paused. That wasn't the way to the chapel—it was the way to the center of the city. Curiosity overcoming brooding, Hrathen turned to follow the arteth, staying far enough behind to diffuse the clicking of his armored feet on the cobblestones. He needn't have worried; the arteth strode through the blackening night with single-minded purpose, not bothering to look back.

Dusk had almost passed, and darkness cloaked the market square. Hrathen lost track of Dilaf in the waning light and stopped, looking around at the quiet tents.

Suddenly, lights appeared around him.

A hundred torches winked into existence from within dozens of different tents. Hrathen frowned, and then his eyes opened wide as men began to pour from the tents, torchlight glistening off bare backs.

Hrathen stumbled back in horror. He knew those twisted figures. Arms like knotted tree branches. Skin pulled tight over strange ridges and unspoken symbols.

Though the night was quiet, memories howled in Hrathen's ears. The tents and merchants had been a ruse. That was why so many Fjordells had come to the Arelene Market despite the political chaos, and that was why they had stayed when others left. They weren't merchants at all, but warriors. The invasion of Arelon was to begin a month early.

Wyrn had sent the monks of Dakhor.

CHAPTER 58

RAODEN awoke to strange sounds. He lay disoriented for a moment in Roial's mansion. The wedding wasn't slated to happen until the following afternoon, and so Raoden had chosen to sleep in Kaloo's rooms back in Roial's mansion instead of staying at Kiin's house, where Sarene had already taken the guest bedroom.

The sounds came again—sounds of fighting.

Raoden leaped from his bed and threw open the balcony doors, staring out over the gardens and into Kae. Smoke billowed in the night sky, fires blazing throughout the city. Screams were audible, rising from the darkness like the cries of the damned, and metal clanged against metal from someplace nearby.

Hurriedly throwing on a jacket, Raoden rushed through the mansion. Turning a corner, he stumbled across a squad of Guardsmen battling for their lives against a group of . . . demons.

They were bare-chested, and their eyes seemed to burn. They looked like men, but their flesh was ridged and disfigured, as if a carved piece of metal had somehow been inserted beneath the skin. One of Raoden's soldiers scored a hit, but the weapon left barely a mark—scratching where it should have sliced. A dozen soldiers lay dying on the floor, but the five demons looked unharmed. The remaining soldiers fought with terror, their weapons ineffective, their members dying one by one.

Raoden stumbled backward in horror. The lead demon

jumped at a soldier, dodging the man's thrust with inhuman speed, then impaling him on a wicked-looking sword.

Raoden froze. He recognized this demon. Though its body was twisted like the rest, its face was familiar. It was Dilaf, the Fjordell priest.

Dilaf smiled, eyeing Raoden. Raoden scrambled for one of the fallen soldiers' weapons, but he was too slow. Dilaf darted across the room, moving like the wind, and brought his fist up into Raoden's stomach. Raoden gasped in pain and dropped to the floor.

"Bring him," the creature ordered.

"MAKE certain you deliver these tonight," Sarene said, pulling the lid closed on the final box of supplies.

The beggar nodded, casting an apprehensive glance toward the wall of Elantris, which stood only a few feet away.

"You needn't be so afraid, Hoid," Sarene said. "You have a new king now. Things are going to change in Arelon."

Hoid shrugged. Despite Telrii's death, the beggar refused to meet with Sarene during the day. Hoid's people had spent ten years fearing Iadon and his farms; they weren't used to acting without the enveloping presence of night, no matter how legal their intentions. Sarene would have used someone else to make the delivery, but Hoid and his men already knew how and where to deposit the boxes. Besides, she would rather the populace of Arelon not discover what was in this particular shipment.

"These boxes are more heavy than the ones before, my lady," Hoid noted astutely. There was a reason he had managed to survive a decade on the streets of Kae without being caught.

"What the boxes contain is none of your business," Sarene replied, handing him a pouch of coins.

Hoid nodded, his face hidden in the darkness of his hood. Sarene had never seen his face, but she assumed from his voice that he was an older man.

She shivered in the night, eager to get back to Kiin's house. The wedding was set for the next day, and Sarene had a hard time containing her excitement. Despite all the trials, difficulties, and setbacks, there was finally an honorable king on the throne of Arelon. And, after years of waiting, Sarene had finally found someone her heart was as willing to marry as her mind.

"Goodnight then, my lady," Hoid said, following the train of beggars who slowly climbed the stairs of Elantris's wall.

Sarene nodded to Ashe. "Go tell them that a shipment is coming, Ashe."

"Yes, my lady," Ashe said with a bob, and hovered away to follow Hoid's beggars.

Pulling her shawl close, Sarene climbed into her carriage and ordered the coachman home. Hopefully, Galladon and Karata would understand why she had sent crates full of swords and bows. Raoden's apprehensive warning earlier in the day had disturbed Sarene immensely. She kept worrying about New Elantris and its bright, accepting people, and so she had finally decided to do something.

Sarene sighed as the carriage rolled down the quiet street. The weapons probably wouldn't help much; the people of New Elantris were not soldiers. But it had been something she could do.

The carriage pulled to a sudden stop. Sarene frowned, opening her mouth to call out a question to the coachman. Then she paused. Now that the rumbling of the coach had ceased, she could hear something. Something that sounded faintly like . . . screams. She smelled the smoke a second later. Sarene pulled back the carriage curtain, poking her head out the window. She found a scene as if from hell itself.

The carriage stood at an intersection. Three streets were calm, but the one directly before her blazed red. Fires billowed from homes, and corpses slumped on the cobblestones. Men and women ran screaming through the streets; others simply stood in dazed shock. Among them stalked shirtless warriors, their skin glistening with sweat in the firelight.

It was a slaughter. The strange warriors killed with dispassion, cutting down man, woman, and child alike with casual swipes of their swords. Sarene watched for a stunned moment before screaming at the coachman to turn them around. The man shook himself from his stupor, whipping at the horses to turn.

Sarene's yell died in her throat as one of the shirtless

warriors noticed the carriage. The soldier dashed toward them as the carriage began to turn. Sarene yelled a warning to the coachman too late. The strange warrior leapt, sailing an incredible distance to land on the carriage horse's back. The soldier crouched lithely upon the beast's flesh, and for the first time Sarene could see the inhuman twisting of his body, the chilling fire in his eyes.

Another short hop took the soldier to the top of the carriage. The vehicle rocked slightly, and the coachman screamed.

Sarene threw open her door and stumbled out. She scrambled across the cobblestones, shoes thrown from her feet in haste. Just up the street, away from the fires, lay Kiin's house. If she could only—

The coachman's body slammed into a building beside her, then slumped to the ground. Sarene screamed, lurching back, nearly tripping. To the side, the demonic creature was a dark silhouette in the firelight as he dropped from the carriage top, prowling slowly along the street toward her. Though his motions seemed casual, he moved with a lithe alertness. Sarene could see the unnatural shadows and pockets beneath his skin, as if his skeleton had been twisted and carved.

Pushing down another scream, Sarene scrambled away, running up the hill toward her uncle's house. Not fast enough. Catching her would barely be a game for this monster; she could hear his footsteps behind. Approaching. Faster and faster. She could see the lights up ahead, but—

Something grabbed her ankle. Sarene jerked as the creature yanked with incredible strength, twisting her leg and spinning her so she smashed to the ground on her side. Sarene rolled onto her back, gasping at the pain.

The twisted figure loomed above her. She could hear it whispering in a foreign tongue. Fjordell.

Something dark and massive slammed into the monster, throwing it backward. Two figures struggled in the darkness. The creature howled, but the newcomer bellowed louder. Dazed, Sarene pushed herself up, watching the shadowed forms. An approaching light soon unmasked them. The shirtless warrior was expected. The other was not.

"Kiin?" Sarene asked.

Her uncle held an enormous axe, large as a man's chest. He smashed it into the creature's back as it wiggled across the stones, reaching for its sword. The creature cursed in pain, though the axe didn't penetrate far. Kiin wrenched the weapon free, then raised it in a mighty swing and brought it down directly into the demon's face.

The creature grunted, but did not stop moving. Neither did Kiin. He swung again and again, hacking at the monster's head with repeated swings, howling Teoish battle cries in his scratchy voice. Bones crunched, and finally the creature stopped moving.

Something touched her arm, and Sarene yelped. Lukel, kneeling beside her, raised his lantern. "Come on!" he urged, grabbing her hand and pulling her to her feet.

They dashed the short distance to Kiin's mansion, her uncle lumbering behind. They pushed through the doors, then stumbled into the kitchen, where a frightened group waited for their return. Daora rushed to her husband as Lukel slammed the door.

"Lukel, collapse the entryway," Kiin ordered.

Lukel complied, throwing the lever Sarene had always mistaken for a torchholder. A second later there was a mighty crash from the entryway, and dust poured through the kitchen door.

Sarene plopped into a chair, staring at the quiet room. Shuden was there, and he had managed to find Torena, who sniffled quietly in his arms. Daorn, Kaise, and Adien huddled in a corner with Lukel's wife. Raoden was not there.

"What . . . what *are* those things?" Sarene asked, looking up at Lukel.

Her cousin shook his head. "I don't know. The attack started just a short time ago, and we were worried that something had happened to you. We were outside waiting—it's a good thing Father spotted your coach down at the bottom of the hill."

Sarene nodded, still a bit numb.

Kiin stood with his wife in one arm, looking down at the bloodied axe in his other hand. "I swore I would never take up this cursed weapon again," he whispered.

Daora patted her husband's shoulder. Despite her shock, Sarene realized that she recognized the axe. It used to hang on the kitchen wall, with other mementoes of Kiin's travels. Yet he had held the weapon with obvious skill. The axe wasn't a simple ornament as she had assumed. Looking closely, she could see nicks and scratches on its blade. Etched into the steel was a heraldic Aon—Aon Reo. The character meant "punishment."

"Why would a merchant need to know how to use one of those?" Sarene asked, almost to herself.

Kiin shook his head. "A merchant wouldn't."

Sarene knew of only one person who had used Aon Reo, though he was more a myth than a man. "They called him Dreok," she whispered. "The pirate Crushthroat."

"That was always a mistake," Kiin said in his raspy voice. "The true name was Dreok *Crushed*throat."

"He tried to steal the throne of Teod from my father," Sarene said, looking up into Kiin's eyes.

"No," Kiin said, turning away. "Dreok wanted what belonged to him. He tried to take back the throne that his younger brother, Eventeo, stole—stole right from under Dreok's nose while he foolishly wasted his life on pleasure trips."

DILAF strode into the chapel, his face bright with satisfaction. One of his monks dropped an unconscious Raoden next to the far wall.

"This, my dear Hrathen," Dilaf said, "is how you deal with heretics."

Appalled, Hrathen turned away from the window. "You are massacring the entire town, Dilaf! What is the point? Where is the glory for Jaddeth in this?"

"Do not question me!" Dilaf screamed, his eyes blazing. His raging zeal had finally been released.

Hrathen turned away. Of all the titles in the hierarchy of the Derethi Church, only two outranked gyorn: Wyrn, and gragdet—leader of a monastery. The gragdets were usually discounted, for they generally had little to do with the world outside their monasteries. Apparently that had changed.

Hrathen ran his eyes over Dilaf's bare chest, seeing the twisted patterns that had always been hiding beneath the arteth's robes. Hrathen's stomach turned at the lines and curves that ran like varicose veins beneath the man's skin. It was bone, Hrathen knew—hard, unyielding bone. Dilaf wasn't just a monk, and he wasn't just a gragdet; he was monk and gragdet of the most infamous monastery in Fjorden. Dakhor. The Order of Bone.

The prayers and incantations used to create Dakhor monks were secret; even the gyorns didn't know them. A few months after a boy was initiated into the Dakhor order, his bones started to grow and twist, adopting strange patterns like those visible beneath Dilaf's skin. Somehow, each of those patterns gave its bearer abilities, such as heightened speed and strength.

Horrible images washed through Hrathen's mind. Images of priests chanting over him; memories of an awesome pain rising within, the pain of his bones reshaping. It had been too much—the darkness, the screams, the torment. Hrathen had left after just a few months to join a different monastery.

He had not left behind the nightmares or memories, however. One did not easily forget Dakhor.

"So you were a Fjordell all this time?" Hrathen whispered.

"You never suspected, did you?" Dilaf asked with a smile. "You should have realized. It is far easier to imitate an Arelene speaking Fjordell than it is for an actual man of Arelon to learn the Holy Language so perfectly."

Hrathen bowed his head. His duty was clear; Dilaf was his superior. He didn't know how long Dilaf had been in Arelon—the Dakhor lived unusually long lives—but it was obvious that Dilaf had been planning Kae's destruction for a very long time.

"Oh, Hrathen," Dilaf said with a laugh. "You never did understand your place, did you? Wyrn didn't send you to convert Arelon."

Hrathen looked up with surprise. He had a letter from Wyrn that said otherwise.

"Yes, I know of your orders, Gyorn," Dilaf said. "Reread that letter sometime. Wyrn didn't send you to Arelon to convert, he sent you to inform the people of their impending destruction. You were a distraction, something for people like Eventeo to focus their attention on while I prepared for the city's invasion. You did your job perfectly."

"Distraction . . . ?" Hrathen asked. "But the people . . ."

"Were never to be saved, Hrathen," Dilaf said. "Wyrn always intended to destroy Arelon. He needs such a victory to insure his grip on the other countries—despite your efforts, our control of Duladel is tenuous. The world needs to know what happens to those who blaspheme against Jaddeth."

"These people don't blaspheme," Hrathen said, feeling his anger rise. "They don't even know Jaddeth! How can we expect them to be righteous if we don't give them a chance to convert!"

Dilaf's hand shot out, slapping Hrathen across the face. Hrathen stumbled back, cheek flaring with pain from the blow—delivered by an unnaturally strong hand, hardened by extra bones.

"You forget to whom you speak, Gyorn," Dilaf snapped. "This people is unholy. Only Arelenes and Teos can become Elantrians. If we destroy them, then we end the heresy of Elantris forever!"

Hrathen ignored his throbbing cheek. With growing numbness, he finally realized how deeply Dilaf's hatred went. "You will slaughter them all? You would murder an entire nation of people?"

"It is the only way to be certain," Dilaf said, smiling.

CHAPTER 59

RAODEN awoke to new pains. The sharpest was at the back of his head, but there were others—scratches, bruises, and cuts across his entire body.

For a moment it was almost too much. Each wound stung sharply, never deadening, never weakening. Fortunately, he had spent weeks dealing with the Dor's all-powerful attacks. Compared to those crushing monuments of agony, the regular pains of his body—no matter how severe—seemed weaker. Ironically, the very force that had nearly destroyed him now allowed him to keep insanity at bay.

Though dazed, he could feel himself being picked up and thrown onto something hard—a saddle. He lost track of time as the horse cantered, and he was forced to struggle against the darkness of insensibility. There were voices around him, but they spoke in Fjordell, which he didn't understand.

The horse stopped. Raoden opened his eyes with a groan as hands pulled him off the beast and set him on the ground.

"Wake up, Elantrian," said a voice speaking Aonic.

Raoden raised his head, blinking confused eyes. It was still night, and he could smell the thick scent of smoke. They were at the base of a hill—Kiin's hill. The blockish house stood only a few yards away, but he could barely make it out. His vision swam, everything blurry.

Merciful Domi, he thought, *let Sarene be safe.*

"I know you can hear me, Princess," Dilaf yelled. "Look who I have here. Let us make a deal."

"No!" Raoden tried to say, but it came out as a croak. The blow to his head had done something to his brain. He could barely keep himself upright, let alone speak. The worst part was, he knew it would never improve.

He could not heal—now that the dizziness had come upon him, it would never leave.

"YOU realize that there is no dealing with him," Kiin said quietly. They watched Dilaf and the staggering Raoden through one of Kiin's slitlike windows.

Sarene nodded quietly, feeling chill. Raoden wasn't doing well; he wobbled as he stood, looking disoriented in the firelight. "Merciful Domi. What have they done to him?"

"Don't look, 'Ene," Kiin said, turning away from the window. His enormous axe—the axe of Dreok the Pirate—stood ready in the corner.

"I can't look away," Sarene whispered. "I have to at least speak to him—to say goodbye."

Kiin sighed, then nodded. "All right. Let's go to the roof. At the first sign of bows, however, we're locking ourselves back in."

Sarene nodded solemnly, and the two climbed the steps up onto the roof. She approached the roof's ledge, looking down at Dilaf and Raoden. If she could convince the priest to take her in exchange for Raoden, she would do it. However, she suspected that Dilaf would demand the entire household, and Sarene could never agree to such a thing. Daora and the children huddled in the basement under Lukel's care. Sarene would not betray them, no matter whom Dilaf held hostage.

She opened her mouth to speak, knowing that her words would probably be the last Raoden ever heard.

"GO!" Dilaf ordered.

Hrathen stood by, a dismayed observer, as Sarene fell into Dilaf's trap. The Dakhor monks sprang forward, jumping from hiding places along the base of the building. They leaped to the walls, their feet seeming to stick as they found tiny footholds between bricks and arrow slits. Several monks, already in place hanging from the back of the rooftop, swung up and cut off Sarene's escape.

Hrathen could hear startled yells as Sarene and her companion realized their predicament. It was too late. A few moments later, a Dakhor jumped down from the rooftop, a struggling princess in his arms.

"Hrathen, get me your Seon," Dilaf ordered.

Hrathen complied, opening the metal box and letting the ball of light float free. Hrathen hadn't bothered asking how the monk knew about the Seon. The Dakhor were Wyrn's favored warriors; their leader would be privy to many of his secrets.

"Seon, I wish to speak with King Eventeo," Dilaf said.

The Seon complied. Soon its light molded into the head of an overweight man with a proud face.

"I do not know you," Eventeo said. "Who calls for me in the middle of the night?"

"I am the man who has your daughter, King," Dilaf said, prodding Sarene in the side. The princess yelped despite herself.

Eventeo's head turned, as if searching out the source of the sound, though he would only be able to see Dilaf's face. "Who are you?"

"I am Dilaf. Gragdet of the Dakhor Monastery."

"Merciful Domi . . ." Eventeo whispered.

Dilaf's eyes thinned, and he smiled evilly. "I thought you had converted, Eventeo. No matter. Wake your soldiers and gather them on their ships. I will arrive in Teod one hour from now, and if they are not ready to present a formal surrender, I will kill the girl."

"Father no!" Sarene yelled. "He can't be trusted!"

"Sarene?" Eventeo asked anxiously.

"One hour, Eventeo," Dilaf said. Then he swiped his hand in the air dismissively. The king's confused face melted back into the smooth spherical shape of a Seon.

"You will kill the Teos as well," Hrathen said in Fjordell.

"No," Dilaf said. "Others will perform those executions. I will just kill their king, then burn Teod's ships with the sailors still on them. Once the armada is gone, Wyrn can land his armies on Teod's shore and use the country as a battleground to prove his might."

"It is unnecessary you know," Hrathen said, feeling sick. "I had him—Eventeo was mine."

"He might have converted, Hrathen," Dilaf said, "but you are simpleminded if you think he would have allowed our troops to land on his soil."

"You are a monster," Hrathen whispered. "You will slaughter two kingdoms to feed your paranoia. What happened to make you hate Elantris so much?"

"*Enough!*" Dilaf shouted. "Do not think I won't hesitate to kill you, Gyorn. The Dakhor are outside the law!" The monk stared at Hrathen with menacing eyes, then slowly calmed, breathing deeply as he noticed his captives again.

The still disoriented Raoden was stumbling toward his wife, who was being held by a quiet Dakhor. The prince reached out to her, his arm wavering.

"Oh," Dilaf said, unsheathing his sword. "I forgot about you." He smiled wickedly as he rammed the blade through Raoden's stomach.

THE pain washed over Raoden like a sudden wave of light. He hadn't even seen the thrust coming.

He felt it, however. Groaning, he stumbled to his knees. The agony was unimaginable, even for one whose pain had been building steadily for two months. He held his stomach with trembling hands. He could feel the Dor. It felt . . . close.

It was too much. The woman he loved was in danger, and he could do nothing. The pain, the Dor, his failure . . . The soul that was Raoden crumpled beneath their combined weight, giving a final sigh of resignation.

After that there was no longer pain, for there was no longer self. There was nothing.

SARENE screamed as Raoden fell to the ground. She could see the suffering in his face, and she felt the sword as if it had been run through her own stomach. She shuddered,

weeping as Raoden struggled for a moment, his legs working. Then he just . . . stopped.

"Failed . . ." Raoden whispered, his lips forming a Hoed
mantra. "Failed my love. Failed. . . ."

"Bring her," Dilaf said. The words, spoken in Fjordell,
barely registered in Sarene's mind.

"And the others?" a monk asked.

"Gather them with the rest of the people in this accursed
town and take them into Elantris," Dilaf said. "You will find
the Elantrians near the center of the city, in a place that
seems more clean."

"We found them, my gragdet," the monk said. "Our men
have already attacked."

"Ah, good," Dilaf said with a hiss of pleasure. "Make certain you gather their bodies—Elantrians do not die as easily
as normal men, and we do not want to let any of them escape."

"Yes, my gragdet."

"When you have them all in one place, bodies, Elantrians,
and future Elantrians, say the purification rites. Then burn
them all."

"Yes, my gragdet," the warrior said, bowing his head.

"Come, Hrathen," Dilaf said. "You will accompany me to
Teod."

Sarene fell into a disbelieving stupor as they pulled her
away, watching Raoden until his slumped form was no
longer visible in the night.

CHAPTER 60

GALLADON hid in the shadows, careful not to move until the gyorn and his strange, bare-chested companions were gone. Then, motioning to Karata, he crept up to Raoden's body. "Sule?"

Raoden did not move.

"Doloken, Sule!" Galladon said, choked with emotion. "Don't do this to me!"

A noise came from Raoden's mouth, and Galladon leaned in eagerly, listening.

"Failed . . ." Raoden whispered. "Failed my love . . ." The mantra of the fallen; Raoden had joined the Hoed.

Galladon sank down on the hard cobblestones, his body shaking as he wept tearlessly. The last hour had been a horror. Galladon and Karata had been at the library, planning how to lead the people away from Elantris. They had heard the screams even at that distance, but by the time they had arrived at New Elantris, no one but Hoed remained. As far as he knew, he and Karata were the last two conscious Elantrians.

Karata placed a hand on his shoulder. "Galladon, we should go. This place is not safe."

"No," Galladon said, climbing to his feet. "I have a promise to keep." He looked up at the mountain slope just outside of Kae, a slope that held a special pool of water. Then, reaching down, he tied his jacket around Raoden to cover the wound, and hefted his friend up onto his shoulder.

"Raoden made me vow to give him peace," Galladon said. "After I see to him, I intend to do the same for myself. We are the last, Karata; there is no more room for us in this world."

The woman nodded, moving to take part of Raoden's burden on herself. Together, the two of them began the hike that would end in oblivion.

LUKEL didn't struggle; there was little use in it. His father, however, was a different story. It took three Fjordells to bind Kiin and throw him on a horse—and even then, the large man managed to get off the odd kick at a passing head. Eventually, one of the soldiers thought to smash him on the back of the skull with a rock, and Kiin fell still.

Lukel held his mother and wife close as the warriors herded them toward Elantris. There was a long line of people—nobles gathered from the corners of Kae, their clothing and faces ragged. Soldiers kept a watchful eye on the captives—as if any of them had the courage or will left to try escaping. Most of the people didn't even look up as they were pushed through the streets.

Kaise and Daorn clung to Lukel, wide-eyed and frightened. Lukel pitied them the most, for their youth. Adien walked along behind him, apparently unconcerned. He slowly counted the steps as he moved. "Three hundred fifty-seven, three hundred fifty-eight, three hundred fifty-nine . . ."

Lukel knew that they were marching to their own execution. He saw the bodies that lined the streets, and he understood that these men were not intent on domination. They were here to commit a massacre, and no massacre would be complete with victims left alive.

He considered fighting back, grabbing a sword in some hopeless feat of heroism. But in the end, he simply plodded along with the others. He knew that he was going to die, and he knew there was nothing he could do to stop it. He was no warrior. The best he could hope for was a quick end.

HRATHEN stood next to Dilaf, remaining perfectly still as instructed. They stood in a circle—fifty Dakhor, Sarene, and Hrathen, with one solitary monk in the center. The Dakhor raised their hands, and the men on either side of Hrathen placed a hand on his shoulder. His heart began to pound as the monks began to glow, the bone inscriptions beneath their skin shining. There was a jarring sensation, and Kae vanished around them.

They reappeared in an unfamiliar city. The houses lining the nearby street were tall and connected, rather than separated and squat like those of Kae. They had arrived in Teod.

The group still stood in a circle, but Hrathen did not fail to notice that the man in the center was now missing. Hrathen shuddered, images from his youth returning. The monk in the center had been fuel, his flesh and soul burned away—a sacrifice in return for the instantaneous transportation to Teod.

Dilaf stepped forward, leading his men up the street. As far as Hrathen could tell, Dilaf had brought the bulk of his monks with him, leaving Arelon in the care of regular Fjordell soldiers and a few Dakhor overseers. Arelon and Elantris had been defeated; the next battle was Teod. Hrathen could tell from Dilaf's eyes that the monk would not be satisfied until every person of Aonic descent was dead.

Dilaf chose a building with a flat roof and motioned for his men to climb. It was easy for them, their enhanced strength and agility helping them leap and scramble up surfaces no normal man could possibly scale. Hrathen felt himself lifted and thrown over a monk's shoulder, and the ground fell away as he was carted up the side of the wall— carried without difficulty despite his plate armor. The Dakhor were unnatural monstrosities, but one couldn't help being awed at their power.

The monk dropped Hrathen unceremoniously on the roof, his armor clanking against the stone. As Hrathen pulled himself to his feet, his eyes found those of the princess. Sarene's face was a tempest of hatred. She blamed him, of course. She didn't realize that, in a way, Hrathen was as much a prisoner as she.

Dilaf stood at the edge of the roof, scanning the city. A fleet of ships was pulling into Teod's enormous bay.

"We are early," Dilaf said, squatting down. "We will wait."

GALLADON could almost imagine that the city was peaceful. He stood on a mountainside boulder, watching the morning's light creep across Kae—as if an invisible hand were pulling back a dark shade. He could almost convince himself that the rising smoke was coming from chimneys, not the ashen wrecks of buildings. He could nearly believe that the specks lining the streets were not bodies, but bushes or boxes, the crimson blood on the streets a trick of the early sunlight.

Galladon turned away from the city. Kae might be peaceful, but it was the peace of death, not of serenity. Dreaming otherwise did little good. Perhaps if he had been less inclined to delusion, he wouldn't have let Raoden pull him out of Elantris's gutters. He wouldn't have allowed one man's simplistic optimism to cloud his mind; he wouldn't have begun to believe that life in Elantris could be anything but pain. He wouldn't have dared to hope.

Unfortunately, he had listened. Like a rulo, he had allowed himself to give in to Raoden's dreams. Once, he'd thought that he could no longer feel hope; he'd chased it far away, wary of its fickle tricks. He should have left it there. Without hope, he wouldn't have to worry about disappointment.

"Doloken, sule," Galladon mumbled, looking down at the mindless Raoden, "you certainly made a mess of me."

The worst of it was, he still hoped. The light that Raoden had kindled still flickered inside Galladon's chest, no matter how hard he tried to stomp it out. The images of New Elantris's destruction were still crisp in his memory. Mareshe, an enormous, ragged hole torn in his chest. The quiet craftsman Taan, his face crushed beneath a large stone, but his fingers still twitching. The old Kahar—who had cleaned all of New Elantris practically by himself—missing an arm and both legs.

Galladon had stood amid the carnage, screaming at Raoden for abandoning them, for leaving them behind. Their prince had betrayed them for Sarene.

And still, he hoped.

It was like a small rodent, cowering in the corner of his soul, frightened by the anger, the rage, and the despair. Yet every time he tried to grab hold of it, the hope slipped to another part of his heart. It was what had spurred him to leave the dead behind, to crawl from Elantris in search of Raoden, believing for some irrational reason that the prince could still fix everything.

You are the fool, Galladon. Not Raoden, Galladon told himself bitterly. *He couldn't help being what he was. You, however, know better.*

Yet, he hoped. A part of Galladon still believed that Raoden would somehow make things better. This was the curse his friend had set upon him, the wicked seed of optimism that refused to be uprooted. Galladon still had hope, and he probably would until the moment he gave himself up to the pool.

Silently, Galladon nodded to Karata, and they picked Raoden up, ready to trek the last short distance to the pond. In few minutes he would be rid of both hope and despair.

ELANTRIS was dark, even though dawn was breaking. The tall walls made a shadow, keeping the sunlight out, expanding the night for a few moments. It was here, at one side of the broad entry plaza, that the soldiers deposited Lukel and the other nobles. Another group of Fjordells was building an enormous pile of wood, hauling scraps of buildings and furniture into the city.

Surprisingly, there were very few of the strange demon warriors; only three directed the work. The rest of the men were regular soldiers, their armor covered with red surcoats marking them as Derethi monks. The worked quickly, keeping their eyes off of their prisoners, apparently trying not to think too hard about what the wood would be used for.

Lukel tried not to think about that either.

Jalla pulled close to him, her body trembling with fright. Lukel had tried to convince her to plead for freedom because of her Svordish blood, but she would not go. She was so quiet and unassertive that some mistook her for weak, but if they could have seen her as she was, voluntarily staying with her husband though it meant certain death, they would have realized their mistake. Of all the deals, trades, and recognitions Lukel had won, the prize of Jalla's heart was by far the most valuable.

His family pulled close to him, Daora and the children having no place to turn now that Kiin was unconscious. Only Adien stood apart, staring at the pile of lumber. He kept mumbling some number to himself.

Lukel searched through the crowd of nobles, trying to smile and give encouragement, though he himself felt little confidence. Elantris would be their grave. As he looked, Lukel noticed a figure standing near the back of the group, hidden by bodies. He was moving slowly, his hands waving in front of himself.

Shuden? Lukel thought. The Jindo's eyes were closed, his hands moving fluidly in some sort of pattern. Lukel watched his friend with confusion, wondering if the Jindo's mind had snapped; then he remembered the strange dance that Shuden had done that first day in Sarene's fencing class. ChayShan.

Shuden moved his hands slowly, giving only a bare hint of the fury that was to come. Lukel watched with growing determination, somehow understanding. Shuden was no warrior. He practiced his dance for exercise, not for combat. However, he was not going to let the ones he loved be murdered without some sort of fight. He would rather die struggling than sit and wait, hoping that fate would send them a miracle.

Lukel took a breath, feeling ashamed. He searched around him, his eyes finding a table leg that one of the soldiers had dropped nearby. When the time came, Shuden would not fight alone.

RAODEN floated, senseless and unaware. Time meant nothing to him—he *was* time. It was his essence. Occasionally he would bob toward the surface of what he had once called consciousness, but as he approached he would feel pain, and back away. The agony was like a lake's surface: if he broke through it, the pain would return and envelop him.

Those times he got close to the surface of pain, however, he thought he saw images. Visions that might have been real, but were probably just reflections of his memory. He saw Galladon's face, concerned and angry at the same time. He saw Karata, her eyes heavy with despair. He saw a mountain landscape, covered with scrub and rocks.

It was all immaterial to him.

"I often wish that they'd just let her die."

Hrathen looked up. Dilaf's voice was introspective, as if he were talking to himself. However, the priest's eyes were focused on Hrathen.

"What?" Hrathen asked hesitantly.

"If only they had let her die . . ." Dilaf trailed off. He sat at the edge of the rooftop, watching the ships gather below, his face reminiscent. His emotions had always been unstable. No man could keep Dilaf's level of ardor burning for long without doing emotional damage to his mind. A few more years, and Dilaf would probably be completely insane.

"I was already fifty years old back then, Hrathen," Dilaf said. "Did you know that? I have lived nearly seventy years, though my body doesn't look older than twenty. She thought I was the most handsome man she'd ever seen, even though my body had been twisted and destroyed to fit the mold of an Arelene."

Hrathen remained quiet. He had heard of such things, that the incantations of Dakhor could actually change the way a person looked. The process had undoubtedly been very painful.

"When she fell sick, I took her to Elantris," Dilaf mumbled, his legs pulled tightly against his chest. "I knew it was pagan, I knew it was blasphemous, but even forty years as a Dakhor wasn't enough to keep me away . . . not when I thought Elantris could save her. Elantris can heal, they said, while Dakhor cannot. And I took her."

The monk was no longer looking at Hrathen. His eyes were unfocused. "They changed her," he whispered. "They said the spell went wrong, but I know the truth. They knew me, and they hated me. Why, then, did they have to put their curse on Seala? Her skin turned black, her hair fell out, and she began to die. She screamed at night, yelling that the pain was eating her from the inside. Eventually she threw herself off the city wall."

Dilaf's voice turned reverently mournful. "I found her at the bottom, still alive. Still alive, despite the fall. And I burned her. She never stopped screaming. She screams still. I can hear her. She will scream until Elantris is gone."

THEY reached the ledge, behind which lay the pool, and Galladon laid Raoden down. The prince slumped idly against the stone, his head hanging slightly over the side of the cliff, his unfocused eyes staring out over the city of Kae. Galladon leaned back against the rock face, next to the door of the tunnel that led down to Elantris. Karata slumped next to him in exhaustion. They would wait a brief moment, then find oblivion.

ONCE the wood was gathered, the soldiers began a new pile—this one of bodies. The soldiers went searching through the city, seeking the corpses of Elantrians who had been slain. Lukel realized something as he watched the pile grow. They weren't all dead. In fact, most of them weren't.

Most of them had wounds so grievous that it sickened Lukel to look at them, yet their arms and legs twitched, their lips moving. *Elantrians,* Lukel thought with amazement, *the dead whose minds continue to live.*

The pile of bodies grew higher. There were hundreds of them, all of the Elantrians that had been collecting in the city for ten years. None of them resisted; they simply allowed themselves to be heaped, their eyes uncaring, until the pile of bodies was larger than the pile of wood.

"Twenty-seven steps to the bodies," Adien whispered suddenly, walking away from the crowd of nobles. Lukel reached for his brother, but it was too late.

A soldier yelled for Adien to get back with the others. Adien didn't respond. Angry, the soldier slashed at Adien with a sword, leaving a large gash in his chest. Adien stumbled, but kept walking. No blood came from the wound. The soldier's eyes opened wide, and he jumped back, making a ward against evil. Adien approached the pile of Elantrians and joined its ranks, flopping down among them and then lying still.

Adien's secret of five years had finally been revealed. He had joined his people.

"I remember you, Hrathen." Dilaf was smiling now, his grin wicked and demonic. "I remember you as a boy, when you came to us. It was just before I left for Arelon. You were frightened then, as you are frightened now. You ran from us, and I watched you go with satisfaction. You were never meant to be Dakhor—you are far too weak."

Hrathen felt chilled. "You were there?"

"I was gragdet by then, Hrathen," Dilaf said. "Do you remember me?"

Then, looking into the man's eyes, Hrathen had a flash of remembrance. He remembered evil eyes in the body of a tall, unmerciful man. He remembered chants. He remembered fires. He remembered screams—his screams—and a face hanging above him. They were the same eyes.

"You!" Hrathen said with a gasp.

"You remember."

"I remember," Hrathen said with a dull chill. "You were the one that convinced me to leave. In my third month, you demanded that one of your monks use his magic and send you to Wyrn's palace. The monk complied, giving up his life to transport you a distance that you could have walked in fifteen minutes."

"Absolute obedience is required, Hrathen," Dilaf whispered. "Occasional tests and examples bring loyalty from the rest." Then, pausing, he looked out over the bay. The armada was docked, waiting as per Dilaf's order. Hrathen scanned the horizon, and he could see several dark specks—the tips of masts. Wyrn's army was coming.

"Come," Dilaf ordered, rising to his feet. "We have been successful; the Teoish armada has docked. They will not be able to stop our fleet from landing. I have only one duty remaining—the death of King Eventeo."

A vision sprang into Raoden's passive mind. He tried to ignore it. Yet, for some reason, it refused to leave. He saw it through the shimmering surface of his pain— a simple picture.

It was Aon Rao. A large square with four circles around it, lines connecting them to the center. It was a widely used Aon—especially among the Korathi—for its meaning. Spirit. Soul.

Floating in the white eternity, Raoden's mind tried to discard the image of Aon Rao. It was something from a previous existence, unimportant and forgotten. He didn't need it any longer. Yet, even as he strove to remove the image, another sprung up in its place.

Elantris. Four walls forming a square. The four outer cities surrounding it, their borders circles. A straight road leading from each city to Elantris.

Merciful Domi!

THE soldiers opened several barrels of oil, and Lukel watched with revulsion as they began pouring them over the heap of bodies. Three shirtless warriors stood at the side, singing some sort of chant in a foreign language that sounded too harsh and unfamiliar to be Fjordell. *We will be next,* Lukel realized.

"Don't look," Lukel ordered his family, turning away as the soldiers prepared Elantris for immolation.

KING Eventeo stood in the distance, a small honor guard surrounding him. He bowed his head as Dilaf approached. The monk smiled, preparing his knife. Eventeo thought he was presenting his country for surrender—he didn't realize that he was offering it up for a sacrifice.

Hrathen walked beside Dilaf, thinking about necessity

and duty. Men would die, true, but their loss would not be meaningless. The entire Fjordell Empire would grow stronger for the victory over Teod. The hearts of men would increase in faith. It was the same thing Hrathen himself had done in Arelon. He had tried to convert the people for political reasons, using politics and popularity. He had bribed Telrii to convert, giving no heed to saving the man's soul. It was the same thing. What was a nation of unbelievers when compared with all of Shu-Dereth?

Yet, even as he rationalized, his stomach grew sick.

I was sent to save these people, not to slaughter them!

Dilaf held Princess Sarene by the neck, her mouth gagged. Eventeo looked up and smiled reassuringly as they approached. He could not see the knife in Dilaf's hand.

"I have waited for this," Dilaf whispered softly. At first, Hrathen thought the priest referred to the destruction of Teod. But Dilaf wasn't looking at the king. He was looking at Sarene, the blade of his knife pressed into her back.

"You, Princess, are a disease," Dilaf whispered in Sarene's ear, his voice barely audible to Hrathen. "Before you came to Kae, even the Arelenes hated Elantris. You are the reason they forgot that loathing. You associated with the unholy ones, and you even descended to their level. You are worse than they are—you are one who is not cursed, but seeks to be cursed. I considered killing your father first and making you watch, but now I realize it will be much worse the other way around. Think of old Eventeo watching you die, Princess. Ponder that image as I send you to Jaddeth's eternal pits of torment."

She was crying, the tears staining her gag.

RAODEN struggled toward consciousness. The pain hit him like an enormous block of stone, halting his progress, his mind recoiling in agony. He threw himself against it, and the torment washed over him. He slowly forced his way through the resistant surface, coming to a laborious awareness of the world outside himself.

He wanted to scream, to scream over and over again. The

pain was incredible. However, with the pain, he felt something else. His body. He was moving, being dragged along the ground. Images washed into his mind as sight returned. He was being pulled toward something round and blue.

The pool.

NO! he thought desperately. *Not yet! I know the answer!*

RAODEN screamed suddenly, twitching. Galladon was so surprised that he dropped the body.

Raoden stumbled forward, trying to get his footing, and fell directly into the pool.

CHAPTER 61

DILAF reached around the princess to press his dagger against her neck. Eventeo's eyes opened wide with horror.

Hrathen watched the dagger begin to slice Sarene's skin. He thought of Fjorden. He thought of the work he had done, the people he had saved. He thought of a young boy, eager to prove his faith by entering the priesthood. Unity.

"*No!*" Spinning, Hrathen drove his fist into Dilaf's face.

Dilaf stumbled for a moment, lowering his weapon in surprise. Then the monk looked up with rage and plunged the dagger at Hrathen's breast.

The knife slid off Hrathen's armor, scraping ineffectually along the painted steel. Dilaf regarded the breastplate with stunned eyes. "But, that armor is just for show. . . ."

"You should know by now, Dilaf," Hrathen said, bringing his armored forearm up and smashing it into the monk's face. Though the unnatural bone had resisted Hrathen's fist, it crunched with a satisfying sound beneath steel. "*Nothing* I do is just for show."

Dilaf fell, and Hrathen pulled the monk's sword free from its scabbard. "Launch your ships, Eventeo!" he yelled. "Fjorden's armies come not to dominate, but to massacre. Move now if you want to save your people!"

"Rag Domi!" Eventeo cursed, yelling for his generals. Then he paused. "My daughter—"

"I will help the girl!" Hrathen snapped. "Save your kingdom, you fool!"

Though Dakhor bodies were unnaturally quick, their minds recovered from shock no more quickly than those of regular men. Their surprise bought Hrathen a few vital seconds. He brought his sword up, shoving Sarene toward an alleyway and backing up to block the entrance.

THE water held Raoden in a cool embrace. It was a thing alive; he could hear it calling in his mind. *Come,* it said, *I give you release.* It was a comforting parent. It wanted to take away his pain and sorrows, just as his mother had once done.

Come, it pled. *You can finally give up.*

No, Raoden thought. *Not yet.*

THE Fjordells finished dousing the Elantrians with oil, then prepared their torches. During the entire process, Shuden moved his arms in restrained circular patterns, not increasing their speed as he had the time at the fencing class. Lukel began to wonder if Shuden wasn't planning an assault at all, but simply preparing himself for the inevitable.

Then Shuden burst into motion. The young baron snapped forward, spinning like a dancer as he brought his fist around, driving it into the chest of a chanting warrior monk. There was an audible crack, and Shuden spun again, slapping the monk across the face. The demon's head spun completely around, his eyes bulging as his reinforced neck snapped.

And Shuden did it all with his eyes closed. Lukel couldn't

be certain, but he thought he saw something else—a slight glow following Shuden's movements in the dawn shadows.

Yelling a battle cry—more to motivate himself than frighten his foes—Lukel grabbed the table leg and swung it at a soldier. The wood bounced off the man's helmet, but the blow was powerful enough to daze him, so Lukel followed it with a solid blow to the face. The soldier dropped and Lukel grabbed his weapon.

Now he had a sword. He only wished he knew how to use it.

THE Dakhor were faster, stronger, and tougher, but Hrathen was more determined. For the first time in years, his heart and his mind agreed. He felt power—the same strength he had felt that first day when he had arrived in Arelon, confident in his ability to save its people.

He held them off, though just barely. Hrathen might not have been a Dakhor monk, but he was a master swordsman. What he lacked in comparative strength and speed he could compensate for in skill. He swung, thrusting his sword at a Dakhor chest, slamming it directly in between two bone ridges. The blade slid past enlarged ribs, piercing the heart. The Dakhor gasped, dropping as Hrathen whipped his sword free. The monk's companions, however, forced Hrathen to retreat defensively into the alleyway.

He felt Sarene stumbling behind him, pulling off her gag. "There are too many!" she said. "You can't fight them all."

She was right. Fortunately, a wave moved through the crowd of warriors, and Hrathen heard the sounds of battle coming from the other side. Eventeo's honor guard had joined the affray.

"Come on," Sarene said, tugging his shoulder. Hrathen risked a glance behind him. The princess was pointing at a slightly ajar door in the building next to them. Hrathen nodded, battering away another attack, then turned to run.

RAODEN burst from the water, gasping reflexively for breath. Galladon and Karata jumped back in surprise. Raoden felt the cool blue liquid streaming from his face. It wasn't water, but something else. Something thicker. He paid it little heed as he crawled from the pool.

"Sule!" Galladon whispered in surprise.

Raoden shook his head, unable to respond. They had expected him to dissolve—they didn't understand that the pool couldn't take him unless he wanted it to.

"Come," he finally rasped, stumbling to his feet.

DESPITE Lukel's energetic assault and Shuden's powerful attack, the other townspeople simply stood and watched in dumb stupefaction. Lukel found himself desperately fighting three soldiers; the only reason he stayed alive was because he did more dodging and running than actual attacking. When aid finally did come, it was given by an odd source: the women.

Several of Sarene's fencers snatched up pieces of wood or fallen swords and fell in behind Lukel, thrusting with more control and ability than he could even feign to know. The brunt of their onslaught was pushed forward by surprise, and for a moment Lukel thought they might actually break free.

Then Shuden fell, crying out as a sword bit into his arm. As soon as the Jindo's concentration broke, so did his war dance, and a simple club to the head knocked him from the battle. The old queen, Eshen, fell next, a sword rammed through her chest. Her horrible scream, and the sight of the blood streaming down her dress, unnerved the other women. They broke, dropping their weapons. Lukel took a long gash on the thigh as one of his foes realized he had no clue how to use his weapon.

Lukel yelled in pain and fell to the cobblestones, holding his leg. The soldier didn't even bother to finish him off.

RAODEN dashed down the side of the mountain at a horrifying pace. The prince leapt and scrambled, as if he hadn't been practically comatose just a few minutes earlier. One slip at this pace, one wrong step, and he wouldn't stop rolling until he hit the foot of the mountain.

"Doloken!" Galladon said, trying his best to keep up. At this rate they would reach Kae in a matter of minutes.

SARENE hid beside her unlikely rescuer, holding perfectly still in the darkness.

Hrathen looked up through the floorboards. He had been the one to spot the cellar door, pulling it open and shoving her through. Underneath they had found a terrified family huddled in the blackness. They had all waited quietly, tense, as the Dakhor moved through the house then left out the front door.

Eventually, Hrathen nodded. "Let's go," he said, reaching over to lift the trapdoor.

"Stay down here," Sarene told the family. "Don't come up until you absolutely have to."

The gyorn's armor clinked as he climbed the steps, then peeked cautiously into the room. He motioned for Sarene to follow, then moved into the small kitchen at the back of the house. He began pulling off his armor, dropping its pieces to the floor. Though he gave no explanation, Sarene understood the action. The bloodred gyorn's armor was far too distinctive to be worth its protective value.

As he worked, Sarene was surprised at the apparent weight of the metal. "You've been walking around all these months in real armor? Wasn't that difficult?"

"The burden of my calling," Hrathen said, pulling off his final greave. Its bloodred paint was now scratched and dented. "A calling I no longer deserve." He dropped it with a clank.

He looked at the greave, then shook his head, pulling off his bulky cotton underclothing, meant to cushion the armor. He stood bare-chested, wearing only a pair of thin, knee-length trousers and a long, sleevelike band of cloth around his right arm.

Why the covered arm? Sarene wondered. *Some piece of Derethi priest's garb?* Other questions were more pressing, however.

"Why did you do it, Hrathen?" she asked. "Why turn against your people?"

Hrathen paused. Then he looked away. "Dilaf's actions are evil."

"But your faith . . ."

"My faith is in Jaddeth, a God who wants the devotion of men. A massacre does not serve Him."

"Wyrn seems to think differently."

Hrathen did not respond, instead selecting a cloak from a nearby chest. He handed it to her, then took another for himself. "Let us go."

RAODEN'S feet were so covered with bumps, lacerations, and scrapes that he no longer related to them as pieces of flesh. They were simply lumps of pain burning at the end of his legs.

But still he ran on. He knew that if he stopped, the pain would claim him once again. He wasn't truly free—his mind was on loan, returned from the void to perform a single task. When he was finished, the white nothingness would suck him down into its oblivion again.

He stumbled toward the city of Kae, feeling as much as seeing his way.

LUKEL lay dazed as Jalla pulled him back toward the mass of terrified townspeople. His leg throbbed, and he could feel his body weakening as blood spilled from the long gash. His wife bound it as best she could, but Lukel knew that the action was pointless. Even if she did manage to stop the bleeding, the soldiers were only going to kill them in a few moments anyway.

He watched in despair as one of the bare-chested warriors tossed a torch onto the pile of Elantrians. The oil-soaked bodies burst into flames.

The demon-man nodded to several soldiers, who pulled out their weapons and grimly advanced on the huddled townspeople.

"WHAT is he doing?" Karata demanded as they reached the bottom of the slope. Raoden was still ahead of them, running in an unsteady gait toward Kae's short border wall.

"I don't know," Galladon said. Ahead, Raoden grabbed a long stick from the ground, then he started to run, dragging the length of wood behind him.

What are you up to, sule? Galladon wondered. Yet he could feel stubborn hope rising again. "Whatever it is, Karata, it is important. We must see that he finishes." He ran after Raoden, following the prince along his path.

After a few minutes, Karata pointed ahead of them. "There!" A squad of six Fjordell guards, probably searching the city for stragglers, walked along the inside of Kae's border wall. The lead soldier noticed Raoden and raised a hand.

"Come on," Galladon said, dashing after Raoden with sudden strength. "No matter what else happens, Karata, don't let them stop him!"

RAODEN barely heard the men approaching, and he only briefly recognized Galladon and Karata running up behind him, desperately throwing themselves at the soldiers. His friends were unarmed; a voice in the back of his head warned that they would not be able to win him much time.

Raoden continued to run, the stick held in rigid fingers. He wasn't sure how he knew he was in the right place, but he did. He *felt* it.

Only a little farther. Only a little farther.

A hand grabbed him; a voice yelled at him in Fjordell. Raoden tripped, falling to the ground—but he kept the stick steady, not letting it slip even an inch. A moment later there was a grunt, and the hand released him.

Only a little farther!

Men battled around him, Galladon and Karata keeping the soldiers' attention. Raoden let out a primal sob of frustration, crawling like a child as he dug his line in the ground. Boots slammed into the earth next to Raoden's hand, coming within inches of crushing his fingers. Still he kept moving.

He looked up as he neared the end. A soldier finished the swing that separated Karata's beleaguered head from her body. Galladon fell with a pair of swords in his stomach. A soldier pointed at Raoden.

Raoden gritted his teeth, and finished his line in the dirt.

Galladon's large bulk crashed to the ground. Karata's head knocked against the short stone wall. The soldier took a step.

Light exploded from the ground.

It burst from the dirt like a silver river, spraying into the air along the line Raoden had drawn. The light enveloped him—but it was more than just light. It was essential purity. Power refined. The Dor. It washed over him, covering him like a warm liquid.

And for the first time in two months, the pain went away.

THE light continued along Raoden's line, which connected to Kae's short border wall. It followed the wall, spurting from the ground, continuing in a circle until it completely surrounded Kae. It didn't stop. The power shot up the short road between Kae and Elantris, spreading to coat the great city's wall as well. From Elantris it moved to the other three outer cities, their rubble all but forgotten in the ten years since the Reod. Soon all five cities were outlined with light—five resplendent pillars of energy.

The city complex was an enormous Aon—a focus for Elantrian power. All it had needed was the Chasm line to make it begin working again.

One square, four circles. Aon Rao. The Spirit of Elantris.

RAODEN stood in the torrent of light, his clothing fluttering in its unique power. He felt his strength return, his pains evaporate like unimportant memories, and his wounds heal. He didn't need to look to know that soft white hair had grown from his scalp, that his skin had discarded its sickly taint in favor of a delicate silver sheen.

Then he experienced the most joyful event of all. Like a thundering drum, his heart began to beat in his chest. The Shaod, the Transformation, had finally completed its work.

With a sigh of regret, Raoden stepped from the light, emerging into the world as a metamorphosed creature. Galladon, stunned, rose from the ground a few feet away, his skin a dark metallic silver.

The terrified soldiers stumbled away. Several made wards against evil, calling upon their god.

"You have one hour," Raoden said, raising a glowing finger toward the docks. "Go."

LUKEL clutched his wife, watching the fire consume its living fuel. He whispered his love to her as the soldiers advanced to do their grisly work. Father Omin whispered behind Lukel, offering a quiet prayer to Domi for their souls, and for those of their executioners.

Then, like a lantern suddenly set aflame, Elantris erupted with light. The entire city shook, its walls seeming to stretch, distorted by some awesome power. The people inside were trapped in a vortex of energy, sudden winds ripping through the town.

All fell still. They stood as if at the eye of an enormous white storm, power raging in a wall of luster that surrounded the city. Townspeople cried out in fear, and soldiers cursed, looking up at the shining walls with confusion. Lukel wasn't watching the walls. His mouth opened slightly in amazement as he stared at the pyre of corpses—and the shadows moving within it.

Slowly, their bodies glistening with a light both more luminous and more powerful than the flames around them, the Elantrians began to step from the blaze, unharmed by its heat.

The townspeople sat stunned. Only the two demon priests seemed capable of motion. One of them screamed in denial, dashing at the emerging Elantrians with his sword upraised.

A flash of power shot across the courtyard and struck the monk in the chest, immolating the creature in a puff of energy. The sword dropped to the cobblestones with a clang, followed by a scattering of smoking bones and burnt flesh.

Lukel turned bewildered eyes toward the source of the attack. Raoden stood in the still open gate of Elantris, his hand upraised. The king glowed like a specter returned from the grave, his skin silver, his hair a brilliant white, his face effulgent with triumph.

The remaining demon priest screamed at Raoden in

Fjorden, cursing him as a Svrakiss. Raoden raised a hand, quietly sketching in the air, his fingers leaving gleaming white trails—trails that shone with the same raging power that surrounded Elantris's wall.

Raoden stopped, his hand poised next to the gleaming character—Aon Daa, the Aon for power. The king looked through the glowing symbol, his eyes raised in a challenge to the lone Derethi warrior.

The monk cursed again, then slowly lowered his weapon.

"Take your men, monk," Raoden said. "Board those ships and go. Anything Derethi, man or vessel, that remains in my country after the next hour's chime will suffer the force of my rage. I dare you to leave me with a suitable target."

The soldiers were already running, dashing past Raoden into the city. Their leader slunk behind them. Before Raoden's glory, the monk's horrible body seemed more pitiful than it did terrifying.

Raoden watched them go, then he turned toward Lukel and the others. "People of Arelon. Elantris is restored!"

Lukel blinked dizzily. Briefly, he wondered if the entire experience had been a vision concocted by his overtaxed mind. When the shouts of joy began to ring in his ears, however, he knew that it was all real. They had been saved.

"How totally unexpected," he declared, then proceeded to faint from blood loss.

DILAF tenderly prodded at his shattered nose, resisting the urge to bellow in pain. His men, the Dakhor, waited beside him. They had easily slain the king's guards, but in the combat they had somehow lost not only Eventeo and the princess, but the traitor Hrathen as well.

"Find them!" Dilaf demanded, rising to his feet. Passion. Anger. The voice of his dead wife called in his ears, begging for revenge. She would have it. Eventeo would never launch his ships in time. Besides, fifty Dakhor already roamed his capital. The monks themselves were like an army, each one as powerful as a hundred normal men.

They would take Teod yet.

CHAPTER 62

SARENE and Hrathen shambled down the city street, their nondescript cloaks pulled close. Hrathen kept his hood up to hide his dark hair. The people of Teod had gathered in the streets, wondering why their king had brought the armada into the bay. Many wandered in the direction of the docks, and with these Sarene and Hrathen mingled, stooped and subservient, trying their best to look commonplace.

"When we arrive, we will seek passage on one of the merchant ships," Hrathen said quietly. "They will bolt from Teod as soon as the armada launches. There are several places in Hrovell that don't see a Derethi priest for months at a time. We can hide there."

"You talk as if Teod will fall," Sarene whispered back. "You may go, priest, but I will not leave my homeland."

"If you value its safety, you will," Hrathen snapped. "I know Dilaf—he is a man obsessed. If you stay in Teod, so will he. If you leave, perhaps he will follow."

Sarene ground her teeth. The gyorn's words had apparent sense in them, but it was possible he was concocting things to get her to accompany him. Of course, there was no reason for him to do such a thing. What cared he for Sarene? She had been his fervent enemy.

They moved slowly, unwilling to set themselves apart from the crowd by increasing their speed. "You didn't really answer my question before, priest," Sarene whispered. "You have turned against your religion. Why?"

Hrathen walked in silence for a moment. "I . . . I don't know, woman. I have followed Shu-Dereth since I was a child—the structure and formality of it have always called to me. I joined the priesthood. I . . . thought I had faith. It turned out, however, that the thing I grew to believe was not Shu-Dereth after all. I don't know what it is."

"Shu-Korath?"

Hrathen shook his head. "That is too simple. Belief is not simply Korathi or Derethi, one or the other. I still believe Dereth's teachings. My problem is with Wyrn, not God."

HORRIFIED at his show of weakness before the girl, Hrathen quickly steeled his heart against further questions. Yes, he had betrayed Shu-Dereth. Yes, he was a traitor. But, for some reason, he felt calm now that he had made the decision. He had caused blood and death in Duladel. He would not let that happen again.

He had convinced himself that the Republic's fall was a necessary tragedy. Now he had dispelled that illusion. His work in Duladel had been no more ethical than what Dilaf had attempted here in Teod. Ironically, by opening himself to truth, Hrathen had also exposed himself to the guilt of his past atrocities.

One thing, however, kept him from despair—the knowledge that whatever else happened to him, no matter what he had done, he could say that he now followed the truth in his heart. He could die and face Jaddeth with courage and pride.

The thought crossed his mind right before he felt the stab of pain in his chest. He reached over in surprise, grunting as he brought his hand up. His fingers were stained with blood. He felt his feet weaken, and he slumped against a building, ignoring Sarene's startled cry. Confused, he looked out into the crowd, and his eyes fell on the face of his murderer. He knew the man. His name was Fjon—the priest Hrathen had sent home from Kae the very day he had arrived. That had been two months ago. How had Fjon found him? How . . . ? It was impossible.

Fjon smiled, then disappeared into the throng of people.

As the darkness closed in, Hrathen discarded all questions. Instead his view and consciousness was filled with Sarene's worried face. The woman who had destroyed him. Because of her, he had finally rejected the lies he had believed all of his life.

She would never know that he had come to love her.

Goodbye, my princess, he thought. *Jaddeth, be merciful to my soul. I only did the best I could.*

SARENE watched the light fading from Hrathen's eyes.

"No!" she cried, pressing her hand against his wound in a futile attempt to stop the blood. "Hrathen, don't you dare leave me alone here!"

He didn't respond. She had fought with him over the fate of two countries, but had never really known who he was. She never would.

A startled scream shocked Sarene back into the tangible world. People gathered around her, upset by the sight of a dying man in the street. Stunned, Sarene realized she had become the center of attention. She lifted her hand, pulled away as if to hide, but it was too late. Several bare-chested forms appeared from an alley to investigate the disturbance. One of them had blood on his face, the sign of a broken nose.

FJON slipped away from the crowd, exulting at the ease of his first kill. They had told him that it would be simple: He needed only to knife a single man, and then he would be admitted into the monastery of Rathbore, where he would be trained as an assassin.

You were right, Hrathen, he thought. *They did give me a new way to serve Jaddeth's empire—an important one.*

How ironic that the man he had been ordered to kill had turned out to be Hrathen himself. How had Wyrn known that Fjon would find Hrathen here, on the streets of Teod of all places? Fjon would probably never know; Lord Jaddeth moved in ways beyond the understanding of men. But Fjon had performed his duty. His period of penance was over.

With a merry step, Fjon went back to his inn and ordered breakfast.

"LEAVE me," Lukel said with a pained tone. "I'm nearly dead—see to the others."

"Stop whining," Raoden said, drawing Aon Ien in the air above the wounded Lukel. He crossed it with the Chasm line, and the wound in the merchant's leg resealed instantly. Not only did Raoden know the proper modifiers this time, but his Aons had the power of Elantris behind them. With the resurrection of the city, AonDor had regained its legendary strength.

Lukel looked down, experimentally bending his leg and feeling where the cut had been. Then he frowned. "You know, you could have left a scar. I had to go through an awful lot to get that wound—you should have seen how courageous I was. My grandchildren are going to be disappointed that I don't have any scars to show them."

"They'll live," Raoden said, rising and walking away.

"What's wrong with you?" Lukel said from behind. "I thought we *won*."

We won, Raoden thought, *but I failed.* They had searched the city—there was no sign of Sarene, Dilaf, or Hrathen. Raoden had captured a straggling Derethi soldier and demanded to know where they were, but the man had pled ignorance, and Raoden had released him with disgust.

He brooded, watching the people celebrate. Despite the deaths, despite the near-complete destruction of Kae, they were happy. Fjorden had been cast out and Elantris had returned. The days of the gods had come again. Unfortunately, Raoden couldn't enjoy the sweetness of his victory. Not without Sarene.

Galladon approached slowly, ambling away from the group of Elantrians. The mass of sliver-skinned people were, for the most part, disoriented. Many of them had been Hoed for years, and knew nothing of current events.

"They're going to be—" the Dula began.

"My lord Raoden!" a voice suddenly interrupted—a voice Raoden recognized.

"Ashe?" he asked anxiously, seeking out the Seon.

"Your Majesty!" Ashe said, zipping across the courtyard.

"A Seon just spoke with me. The princess! She is in Teod, my lord. My kingdom is under attack as well!"

"Teod?" Raoden asked, dumbfounded. "How in Domi's name did she get *there*?"

SARENE backed away, wishing desperately for a weapon. The townspeople noticed Dilaf and his warriors and, seeing the Fjordells' odd twisted bodies and malevolent eyes, scattered in fright. Sarene's reflexes urged her to join them, but such a move would only put her directly in Dilaf's hands. The small monk's warriors quickly fanned out to cut off Sarene's escape.

Dilaf approached—his face stained with drying blood, his bare torso sweating in Teod's cold air, the intricate patterns beneath the skin on his arms and chest bulging, his lips curved in a wicked smile. At that moment, Sarene knew that this man was the most horrifying thing she would ever see.

RAODEN climbed to the top of Elantris's wall, taking the steps two at a time, his restored Elantrian muscles moving more quickly and tirelessly than even those of his pre-Shaod self.

"Sule!" Galladon called with concern, rushing up behind him.

Raoden didn't respond. He topped the wall, pushing his way through the crowds of people who stood looking over the remains of Kae. They parted as they realized who he was, some kneeling and mumbling "Your Majesty." Their voices were awed. In him they saw a return to their former lives. Hopeful, luxurious lives filled with ample food and time. Lives nearly forgotten over a decade of tyranny.

Raoden gave them no heed, continuing until he stood on the northern wall, which overlooked the broad blue Sea of Fjorden. On the other side of those waters lay Teod. And Sarene.

"Seon," Raoden ordered, "show me the exact direction Teod's capital is from this point."

Ashe hovered for a moment, then moved to a spot in front of Raoden, marking a point on the horizon. "If you wanted to sail to Teod, my lord, you would go in this direction."

Raoden nodded, trusting the Seon's innate sense of direction. He began to draw. He constructed Aon Tia with frantic hands, his fingers tracing patterns he had learned by rote, never thinking they would do any good. Now, with Elantris somehow feeding the Aons' strength, lines no longer simply appeared in the air when he drew—they exploded. Light streamed from the Aon, as if his fingers were ripping tiny holes through a mighty dam, allowing only some of the water to squirt through.

"Sule!" Galladon said, finally catching up to him. "Sule, what is going on?" Then, apparently recognizing the Aon, he cursed. "Doloken, Raoden, you don't know what you're doing!"

"I am going to Teod," Raoden said, continuing to draw.

"But sule," Galladon protested. "You yourself told me how dangerous Aon Tia can be. What was it you said? If you don't know the exact distance you need to travel, you could be killed. You can't go into this blind. Kolo?"

"It's the only way, Galladon," Raoden said. "I have to at least try."

Galladon shook his head, laying a hand on Raoden's shoulder. "Sule, a meaningless attempt won't prove anything but your stupidity. Do you even know how far it is to Teod?"

Raoden's hand fell slowly to his side. He was no geographer; he knew Teod was about four days' sail, but he had no practical knowledge of how many miles or feet that was. He had to work a frame of reference into Aon Tia, give it some sort of measurement, so that it knew how far to send him.

Galladon nodded, clapping Raoden on the shoulder. "Prepare a ship!" the Dula ordered to a group of soldiers—the last remnants of the Elantris City Guard.

It will be too late! Raoden thought with sorrow. *What good is power, what good is Elantris, if I can't use it to protect the one I love?*

"One million, three hundred twenty-seven thousand, forty-two," said a voice from behind Raoden.

Raoden turned with surprise. Adien stood a short distance away, his skin shining with a silvery Elantrian glow. His eyes betrayed none of the mental retardation that had cursed him since birth; instead they stared lucidly ahead.

"Adien," Raoden said with surprise. "You're . . ."

The young man, looking strikingly like Lukel now that he was healed, stepped forward. "I . . . I feel like my entire life has been a dream, Raoden. I remember everything that happened. But, I couldn't interact—I couldn't say anything. That's changed now, but one thing remains the same. My mind . . . I've always been able to figure numbers. . . ."

"Footsteps," Raoden whispered.

"One million, three hundred twenty-seven thousand, forty-two," Adien repeated. "That is how many steps it is to Teod. Measure my stride, and use that as your unit."

"Hurry, my lord!" Ashe exclaimed with fear. "She's in danger. Mai—he's watching the princess now. He says she's surrounded. Oh, Domi! Hurry!"

"Where, Seon!" Raoden snapped, kneeling down and measuring Adien's stride with a strip of cloth.

"Near the docks, my lord," Ashe said. "She's standing on the main road leading to the docks!"

"Adien!" Raoden said, drawing a line in his Aon that duplicated the length of the boy's stride.

"One million, three hundred twenty-six thousand, eight hundred and five," Adien said. "That will take you to the docks." He looked up, frowning. "I . . . I'm not sure how I know that. I went there as a child once, but . . ."

It'll have to be enough, Raoden thought. He reached up and wrote a modifier beside his Aon, telling it to transport him one million, three hundred twenty-six thousand, eight hundred and five lengths of the line.

"Sule, this is insane!" Galladon said.

Raoden looked at his friend, nodded in agreement, then with a broad stroke drew the Chasm line across his Aon.

"You are in charge of Arelon until I return, my friend," Raoden said as Aon Tia began to shake, spewing light before him. He reached up and grabbed the center of the trembling Aon, and his fingers latched on to it, as if it were solid.

Idos Domi, he prayed, *if you have ever heard my prayers before, direct my path now.* Then, hoping Ashe had the angle correct, he felt the Aon's power rush through and envelop his body. A moment later the world disappeared.

SARENE pressed her back against the hard brick wall. Dilaf approached with gleeful eyes. He crept forward, his line of monks closing on Sarene.

It was over. There was nowhere for her to run.

Suddenly, a spray of light crashed into one of the monks, throwing the creature into the air. Stupefied, Sarene watched the monk's body as it arced before her, then fell to the ground with a thud. The other monks paused, stunned.

A figure dashed between the surprised line of monks, scrambling toward Sarene. His skin was silvery, his hair a blazing white, his face . . .

"Raoden?" she asked with shock.

Dilaf growled, and Sarene yelped as the priest dove at Raoden, moving supernaturally quickly. Yet somehow Raoden reacted just as quickly, spinning and backing away before Dilaf's attack. The king's hand whipped out, scrawling a quick Aon in the air.

A burst of light shot from the Aon, the air warping and twisting around it. The bolt took Dilaf in the chest and exploded, throwing the monk backward. Dilaf crashed into the side of a building and collapsed to the ground. Then, however, the priest groaned, stumbling back to his feet.

Raoden cursed. He dashed the short distance and grabbed Sarene. "Hold on," he ordered, his free hand tracing another Aon. The designs Raoden crafted around Aon Tia were complex, but his hand moved dexterously. He finished it just as Dilaf's men reached them.

Sarene's body lurched, much as it had when Dilaf had brought them to Teod. Light surrounded her, shaking and pulsing. A brief second later the world returned. Sarene stumbled in confusion, falling against the familiar Teoish cobblestones.

She looked up with surprise. About fifty feet down the street she could see the bare chests of Dilaf's monks standing in a confused circle. One of them raised a hand, pointing at Raoden and Sarene.

"Idos Domi!" Raoden cursed. "I forgot what the books said! The Aons grow weaker the farther one goes from Elantris."

"You can't get us home?" Sarene asked, climbing to her feet.

"Not by Aon, I can't," Raoden said. Then, taking her hand, he started running.

Her mind was so full of questions the entire world seemed a confused jumble. What had happened to Raoden? How had he recovered from the wound Dilaf gave him? She choked the questions back. It was enough that he had come.

FRANTIC, Raoden searched for a means of escape. Perhaps alone he could have outrun Dilaf's men, but never with Sarene in tow. Their street emptied onto the docks, where Teod's large warships were ponderously moving from the bay to engage a fleet bearing Fjorden's flag. A man in royal green robes stood at the far side of the docks, conversing with a couple of adjuncts. King Eventeo—Sarene's father. The king didn't see them, instead turning to walk in a rushed step down a side alley.

"Father!" Sarene yelled out, but the distance was too far.

Raoden could hear footsteps approaching. He spun, thrusting Sarene behind him, and raised his arms to begin an Aon Daa with each hand. The Aons were weaker in Teod, but they weren't ineffectual.

Dilaf held up a hand, slowing his men. Raoden froze, unwilling to commit himself to a final battle unless he had to. What was Dilaf waiting for?

Bare-chested monks poured from alleys and streets. Dilaf smiled, waiting as his warriors gathered. Within a few minutes his group had grown from twelve to fifty, and Raoden's odds had plummeted from bad to hopeless.

"Not much of a rescue," Sarene muttered, stepping forward to stand next to Raoden, staring down the group of monstrosities with a contemptuous air.

Her defiant irony brought a smile to Raoden's lips. "Next time, I'll remember to bring an army with me."

DILAF'S monks charged. Raoden completed his duplicate Aons—sending out a pair of powerful energy blasts—then quickly began drawing again. Yet, holding to his waist with tense hands, Sarene could see that Raoden wouldn't finish before the supernaturally quick warriors arrived.

The docks shook with a powerful force. Wood cracked and stone shattered, and an explosion of wind blasted across her. She had to cling to Raoden's somehow more stable body to keep from being thrown to the ground. When she finally dared open her eyes, they were surrounded by hundreds of silver-skinned forms.

"Aon Daa!" Galladon ordered with a booming voice.

Two hundred hands raised in the air, scribbling Aons. About half of them made mistakes, their Aons evaporating. Enough finished, however, to send a wave of destruction toward Dilaf's men that was so powerful it tore completely through the first few monks.

Bodies collapsed and others were thrown backward. The remaining monks paused in shock, staring at the Elantrians.

Then the Dakhor scattered in an offensive charge, turning from Raoden and Sarene to attack this new foe.

DILAF was the only one of his men who thought to duck. The rest, confidently arrogant in their strength, simply allowed the powerful blasts to hit them.

Fools! Dilaf thought as he rolled away. Every Dakhor was blessed with special skills and powers. They all had increased strength and nearly indestructible bones, but only Dilaf bore the power that made him resistant to attacks by the Dor—a power that had required the deaths of fifty men to create. He felt, rather than saw, as his men were torn apart by the Elantrians' attack.

The remaining monks were horribly outnumbered. They attacked bravely, trying to kill as many of the vile Elantrians as they could. They had been trained well. They would die fighting. Dilaf yearned to join them.

But he did not. Some thought him mad, but he was not a fool. The screams in his head demanded revenge, and there was still a way left. One way to get vengeance on the Teoish princess and her Elantrians. One way to fulfill Wyrn's commands. One way to turn the tide of this battle.

Dilaf scrambled away, stumbling slightly as a bolt of energy sprayed against his back. His bone wardings held, and he was left unharmed by the attack.

When he had entered the docks a few moments before, he had seen King Eventeo disappear down a side alley. He now dashed toward that same alley.

His prey would follow.

"RAODEN!" Sarene said, pointing at the fleeing Dilaf.

"Let him go," Raoden said. "He can do no more damage."

"But that's the way my father went!" Sarene said, tugging him toward the alley.

She's right, Raoden thought with a curse. He took off behind Dilaf. Sarene waved him on, and he left her behind, letting his newly reconditioned Elantrian legs carry him to the alleyway at an extraordinary speed. The other Elantrians didn't see him go, but continued to fight the monks.

Raoden entered the alleyway, barely puffing. Dilaf tackled him a second later. The monk's powerful body appeared out of a shadowed corner, slamming Raoden into the alley wall.

Raoden cried out, feeling his ribs crack. Dilaf backed away, unsheathing his sword with a smile. The priest lunged forward, and Raoden barely rolled away in time to avoid being impaled. As it was, Dilaf's attack sliced through the flesh of Raoden's left forearm, spilling silvery-white Elantrian blood.

Raoden gasped as pain washed through his arm. This pain, however, was weak and dull compared to his former agonies. He forgot it quickly, rolling again as Dilaf's blade sought his heart. If his heart stopped again, Raoden would die. Elantrians were strong and quick-healing, but they were not immortal.

As he dodged, Raoden searched through his memory of Aons. Thinking quickly, he rolled to his feet, rapidly scribbling Aon Edo before him. It was a simple character, requiring only six strokes, and he finished it before Dilaf could make a third attack. The Aon flashed briefly, and then a thin wall of light appeared between himself and Dilaf.

Dilaf tested the wall hesitantly with the tip of his sword, and the wall resisted. The more one pressed against it, the more it drew from the Dor, pressing back with equal strength. Dilaf could not reach him.

Casually, Dilaf reached up and tapped the wall with his bare hand. His palm flashed briefly, and the wall shattered, shards of light scattering through the air.

Raoden cursed his stupidity—this was the man who had destroyed his illusionary face just a day before. Somehow, Dilaf had the power to negate Aons. Raoden jumped back, but the sword snapped forward more quickly. The tip did not strike Raoden's chest, but struck his hand instead.

Raoden cried out as the sword pierced his right palm. He brought his other hand up to cup it around the injured one, but the wound on his forearm blazed with renewed vigor. Both hands were incapacitated; he could no longer draw Aons. Dilaf's next attack was a casual kick, and Raoden's already wounded ribs cracked further. He cried out and dropped to his knees.

Dilaf laughed, tapping Raoden on the side of the face with the tip of his sword. "The Skaze are right, then. Elantrians are not indestructible."

Raoden didn't answer.

"I will still win, Elantrian," Dilaf said, his voice passionate and frenzied. "After Wyrn's fleets defeat the Teoish armada, I will gather my troops and march on Elantris."

"No one defeats the Teoish armada, priest," a feminine voice interjected, a blade flashing out to strike at Dilaf's head.

The priest yelped, barely bringing his own sword up in time to block Sarene's attack. She had found a sword somewhere, and she whipped it in a pattern that moved too quickly for Raoden to track. He smiled at Dilaf's surprise, remembering how easily the princess had defeated his own skills. Her weapon was thicker than a syre, but she still handled it with remarkable proficiency.

Dilaf, however, was no ordinary man. The bone patterns beneath his skin started glowing as he blocked Sarene's attack, and his body began to move even more quickly. Soon Sarene stopped advancing, and almost immediately she was forced to begin retreating. The battle ended as Dilaf's sword pierced her shoulder. Sarene's weapon clanged to the cobblestones, and she stumbled, slumping down next to Raoden.

"I'm sorry," she whispered.

Raoden shook his head. No one could be expected to win a sword fight against one such as Dilaf.

"And my revenge begins," Dilaf whispered reverently, bringing up his sword. "You may stop yelling, my love."

Raoden grabbed Sarene protectively with a bleeding hand. Then he paused. There was something moving behind Dilaf—a form in the shadows of the alleyway.

Frowning, Dilaf turned to follow Raoden's gaze. A figure stumbled from the darkness, holding his side in pain. The figure was a tall, broad-chested man with dark hair and determined eyes. Though the man no longer wore his armor, Raoden recognized him. The gyorn, Hrathen.

Strangely, Dilaf didn't seem happy to see his companion. The Dakhor monk spun, raising his sword, eyes flashing with anger. He leapt, screaming something in Fjordell, and swung his sword at the obviously weakened gyorn.

Hrathen stopped, then whipped his arm out from beneath his cloak. Dilaf's sword hit the flesh of Hrathen's forearm.

And stopped.

Sarene gasped beside Raoden. "He's one of them!" she whispered.

It was true. Dilaf's weapon scraped along Hrathen's arm, pushing back the sleeve there and revealing the skin beneath. The arm was not that of a normal man; it showed twisting patterns beneath the skin, the outcroppings of bone that were the sign of a Dakhor monk.

Dilaf, obviously, was surprised by the revelation as well.

The monk stood stunned as Hrathen's hand whipped out and grabbed Dilaf by the neck.

Dilaf began to curse, squirming in Hrathen's grasp. The gyorn, however, began to stand up straighter, his grip tightening. Beneath his cloak, Hrathen was bare-chested, and Raoden could see that his skin there bore no Dakhor markings, though it was wet with blood from a wound at his side. Only the bones in his arm had the strange twisted patterns. Why the partial transformation?

Hrathen stood tall, ignoring Dilaf, though the monk began to swing at Hrathen's enhanced arm with his short sword. The blows bounced off, so Dilaf swung at Hrathen's side instead. The sword bit deeply into Hrathen's flesh, but the gyorn didn't even grunt. Instead, he tightened his grip on Dilaf's neck, and the little monk gasped, dropping his sword in pain.

Hrathen's arm began to glow.

The strange, twisting lines beneath Hrathen's skin took on an eerie radiance as the gyorn lifted Dilaf off the ground. Dilaf squirmed and twisted, his breath coming in gasps. He struggled to escape, prying at Hrathen's fingers, but the gyorn's grip was firm.

Hrathen held Dilaf aloft, as if toward the heavens. He stared upward, toward the sky, eyes strangely unfocused, Dilaf proffered like some sort of holy offering. The gyorn stood there for a long moment, immobile, arm glowing, Dilaf becoming more and more frantic.

There was a snap. Dilaf stopped struggling. Hrathen lowered the body with a slow motion, then tossed it aside, the glow in his arm fading. He looked toward Raoden and Sarene, stood quietly for a moment, then toppled forward lifelessly.

WHEN Galladon arrived a few moments later, Raoden was trying unsuccessfully to heal Sarene's shoulder with his wounded hands. The large Dula took in the scene, then nodded for a couple of Elantrians to check on Dilaf and Hrathen's corpses. Then Galladon settled down, letting Raoden tell him how to draw Aon Ien. A few moments later, Raoden's hands and ribs had been restored, and he moved to help Sarene.

She sat quietly. Despite her wound, she had already checked on Hrathen. He was dead. In fact, either one of the wounds in his sides should have killed him long before he managed to break Dilaf's neck. Something about his Dakhor markings had kept him alive. Raoden shook his head, drawing a healing Aon for Sarene's shoulder. He still didn't have an explanation as to why the gyorn had saved them, but he quietly blessed the man's intervention.

"The armada?" Sarene asked anxiously as Raoden drew.

"Looks to me like it's doing fine," Galladon said with a shrug. "Your father is searching for you—he came to the docks soon after we arrived."

Raoden drew the Chasm line, and the wound in Sarene's arm disappeared.

"I have to admit, sule, you are lucky as Doloken," Galladon said. "Jumping here blind was just about the most idiotic thing I've ever seen a man do."

Raoden shrugged, pulling Sarene tight. "It was worth it. Besides, you followed, didn't you?"

Galladon snorted. "We had Ashe call ahead to make sure you arrived safely. We're not kayana, unlike our king."

"All right," Sarene declared firmly. "Somebody is going to start explaining things to me *right now*."

CHAPTER 63

SARENE straightened Raoden's jacket, then stood back, tapping her cheek as she studied him. She would have preferred a white suit rather than a gold one, but for some reason white seemed pale and lifeless when placed next to his silvery skin.

"Well?" Raoden asked, holding his arms out to the sides.

"You'll have to do," she decided airily.

He laughed, approaching and kissing her with a smile. "Shouldn't you be alone in the chapel, praying and preparing? What ever happened to tradition?"

"I tried that once already," Sarene said, turning to make sure he hadn't mussed up her makeup. "This time I intend to keep a close eye on you. For some reason, my potential husbands have a way of disappearing."

"That might say something about you, Leky Stick," Raoden teased. He had laughed long when her father explained the nickname to him, and since then he had been careful to use it at every possible occasion.

She swatted at him absently, straightening her veil.

"My lord, my lady," said a stoic voice. Raoden's Seon, Ien, floated in through the doorway. "It is time."

Sarene grabbed Raoden's arm in a firm grip. "Walk," she ordered, nodding toward the doorway. This time, she wasn't letting go until someone married them.

RAODEN tried to pay attention to the ceremony, but Korathi wedding services were lengthy and often dry. Father Omin, well aware of the precedent set by an Elantrian asking a Korathi priest to officiate at his wedding, had prepared an extensive speech for the occasion. As usual, the short man's eyes took on a semiglazed look as he rambled, as if he had forgotten that there was anyone else present.

So Raoden let his mind wander too. He couldn't stop thinking of a conversation he had held with Galladon earlier in the day, a conversation initiated because of a piece of bone. The bone, retrieved from the body of a dead Fjordell monk, was deformed and twisted—yet it was more beautiful than disgusting. It was like a carved piece of ivory, or a bundle of engraved wooden rods all twisted together. Most disturbingly, Raoden swore he could make out slightly familiar symbols in the carving. Symbols he recognized from his schooling—ancient Fjordell characters.

The Derethi monks had devised their own version of Aon-Dor.

The worry pressed on his mind with such vigor that it drew his attention even in the middle of his own wedding. Over the centuries, only one thing had kept Fjorden from conquering the West: Elantris. If Wyrn had learned to access the Dor . . . Raoden kept remembering Dilaf and his strange ability to resist, and even destroy, Aons. If a few more of the monks had possessed that power, then the battle could easily have gone another way.

Ien's familiar bubble-like ball of light floated approvingly at Raoden's side. The Seon's restoration almost made up for the dear friends Raoden had lost during the final battle to restore Elantris. Karata and the others would be missed. Ien claimed to remember nothing of his time of madness, but something seemed a little . . . different about the Seon. He was more quiet than normal, even more thoughtful. As soon as he had some free time, Raoden planned to interrogate the other Elantrians in the hopes of discovering more about the Seons. It disturbed him that throughout his studies, readings, and learning, he had never discovered exactly how Seons were created—if, indeed, they were even creations of AonDor.

That wasn't the only thing that bothered him, however. There was also the question of Shuden's strange ChayShan dance. Onlookers, including Lukel, claimed that the Jindo had managed to defeat one of Dilaf's monks alone—with his eyes closed. Some even said they had seen the young baron glowing as he fought. Raoden was beginning to suspect there was more than one way to access the Dor—far more. And one of those methods was in the hands of the most brutal, domineering tyrant in Opelon: Wyrn Wulfden the Fourth, Regent of All Creation.

Apparently, Sarene noticed Raoden's inattention, for she elbowed him in the side when Omin's speech began to wind down. Ever the stateswoman, she was poised, in control, and alert. Not to mention beautiful.

They performed the ceremony, exchanging Korathi pendants that bore Aon Omi and pledging their lives and deaths to one another. The pendant he gave to Sarene had been delicately carved from pure jade by Taan himself, then overlaid with bands of gold to match her hair. Sarene's own gift was less extravagant, but equally fitting. Somewhere she had found a heavy black stone that polished up as if it were metal, and its reflective darkness complimented Raoden's silvery skin.

With that, Omin proclaimed to all of Arelon that its king was married. The cheering began, and Sarene leaned over to kiss him.

"Was it everything you hoped for?" Raoden asked. "You said you have been anticipating this moment for your entire life."

"It was wonderful," Sarene replied. "However, there is one thing I have looked forward to even more than my wedding."

Raoden raised an eyebrow.

She smiled mischievously. "The wedding night."

Raoden laughed his reply, wondering what he had gotten himself, and Arelon, into by bringing Sarene to Arelon.

EPILOGUE

THE day was warm and bright, a complete contrast to the day of Iadon's burial. Sarene stood outside Kae, regarding the former king's barrow. Everything Iadon had fought for had been overturned; Elantris had been revitalized and serfdom proclaimed illegal. Of course, his son did sit on the throne of Arelon, even if that throne was inside of Elantris now.

Only a week had passed since the wedding, but so much had happened. Raoden had ended up allowing the nobility to keep their titles, though he had first tried to abolish the entire system. The people wouldn't have it. It seemed unnatural for there not to be counts, barons, or other lords. So, Raoden had instead twisted the system to his own ends. He made each lord a servant of Elantris, charging them with the responsibility of caring for the people in remote parts of the country. The nobility became less aristocrats and more food distributors—which, in a way, was what they should have been in the first place.

Sarene watched him now, speaking with Shuden and Lukel, his skin glowing even in the sunlight. The priests who said the fall of Elantris had revealed its occupants' true selves had not known Raoden. This was the true him, the glowing beacon, the powerful source of pride and hope. No matter how metallically bright his skin became, it could never match the radiance of his soul.

Beside Raoden stood the quiet Galladon, his skin glowing as well, though in a different way. It was darker, like polished iron, a remnant of his Duladen heritage. The large man's head was still bald. Sarene had been surprised at that fact, for all the other Elantrians had grown heads of white hair. When asked about the oddity, Galladon had simply shrugged in his characteristic manner, mumbling, "Seems right to me. I've been bald since I hit my third decade. Kolo?"

Just behind Raoden and Lukel, she could make out the silver-skinned form of Adien, Daora's second son. According to Lukel, the Shaod had taken Adien five years before, but the family had determined to cover up his transformation with makeup rather than throw him into Elantris.

Adien's true nature was no more baffling than that of his father. Kiin hadn't been willing to explain much, but Sarene saw the confirmation in her uncle's eyes. Just over ten years ago, he had led his fleets against Sarene's father in an attempt to steal the throne—a throne that Sarene was beginning to believe might legally have belonged to Kiin. If it was true that Kiin was the older brother, then he should have inherited, not Eventeo. Her father still wouldn't speak on the subject, but she intended to get her answers eventually.

As she pondered, she noticed a carriage pulling up to the grave site. The door opened and Torena climbed out, leading her overweight father, Count Ahan. Ahan hadn't been the same since Roial's death; he spoke in a dazed, sickly voice, and he had lost an alarming amount of weight. The others hadn't forgiven him for his part in the duke's execution, but their scorn could never match the self-loathing he must feel.

Raoden caught her eye, nodding slightly. It was time. Sarene strode past Iadon's grave and four just like it—the resting places of Roial, Eondel, Karata, and a man named Saolin. This last barrow held no body, but Raoden had insisted that it be raised with the others.

This area was to become a memorial, a way of remembering those who had fought for Arelon—as well as the man who had tried to crush it. Every lesson had two sides. It was as important for them to remember Iadon's sickening greed as it was to remember Roial's sacrifice.

She slowly approached one final grave. The earth was raised high like the others, forming a barrow that would someday be covered with grass and foliage. For now, however, it was barren, the freshly piled earth still soft. Sarene hadn't needed to lobby hard for its creation. They all now knew the debt they owed to the man buried within. Hrathen of Fjorden, high priest and holy gyorn of Shu-Dereth. They had left his funeral until the last.

Sarene turned to address the crowd, Raoden at their front. "I will not speak long," she said, "for though I had more contact with the man Hrathen than most of you, I did not know him. I always assumed that I could come to understand a man through being his enemy, and I thought that I understood Hrathen—his sense of duty, his powerful will, and his determination to save us from ourselves.

"I did not see his internal conflict. I could not know the man whose heart drove him, eventually, to reject all that he had once believed in the name of what he knew was right. I never knew the Hrathen who placed the lives of others ahead of his own ambition. These things were hidden, but in the end they are what proved most important to him.

"When you remember this man, think not of an enemy. Think of a man who longed to protect Arelon and its people. Think of the man he became, the hero who saved your king. My husband and I would have been killed by the monster of Dakhor, had Hrathen not arrived to protect us.

"Most important, remember Hrathen as the one who gave that vital warning that saved Teod's fleets. If the armada had fallen, then be assured that Teod wouldn't have been the only country to suffer. Wyrn's armies would have fallen on Arelon, Elantris or no Elantris, and you all would be fighting for survival at this moment—if, that is, you were even still alive."

Sarene paused, letting her eyes linger on the grave. At its head stood a carefully arranged stack of bloodred armor. Hrathen's cloak hung on the end of a sword, its point driven into the soft earth. The crimson cape flapped in the wind.

"No," Sarene said. "When you speak of this man, let it be known that he died in our defense. Let it be said that after all else, Hrathen, gyorn of Shu-Dereth, was not our enemy. He was our savior."

GLOSSARY

The following is a dictionary of some of the common Aons used in the text. It is by no means comprehensive. The words included in parenthesis are examples of names or terms that incorporate that particular Aon.

AAN
Truth, Fact
(Aandan, Taan)

ALA
Beauty, Handsomeness
(Meala, Seinalan)

AHA
Breath, Air
(Ahan, Dahad, Kahar)

AON
First, Language
(AonDor, Aonic)

ARE
Unity, Cohesion
(Arelon, Aredel,
Maare, Waren)

DAO
Stability, Security
(Daora, Daorn)

ASHE
Light, Illumination
(Seon Ashe, Dashe)

DEO
Gold, Metal
(Deos, Deo Plantation)

ATA
Grace, Smoothness
(Karata, Atad Mountains,
Atara)

EDA
Superior, Lofty
(Edan)

DAA
Power, Energy

EDO
Protection, Safety

EHE
Fire, Warmth

ENE
Wit, Cleverness
(Sarene)

ELA
Focus, Center
(Elantris, Elao)

ESHE
Gift, Endowment
(Eshen, Mareshe)

EON
Willpower, Endurance
(Eondel, Eonic)

IAD
Trust, Reliable
(Iadon)

ENA
Kindness
(Torena)

IAL
Helpfulness, Aid
(Roial)

IEN
Wisdom
(Seon Ien, Adien)

KAE
The Direction East
(The City of Kae)

IRE
Time, Age
(Diren)

KII
Justice
(Kiin)

IDO
Mercy, Forgiveness
("Idos Domi")

NAE
Sight, Clarity

KAI
Calmness, Solemnity
(Kaise)

OMI
Love
(Domi, Omin)

OPA
Flower
(Seon Opa,
Opais, Opelon)

TEO
Royal, Majestic
(Eventeo, Teod,
Teois, Teoras, Teorn)

RAO
Sprit, Essence
(Raoden, Tenrao)

MAI
Honor

REO
Punishment, Retribution
(Dreok Crushthroat, Reod)

MEA
Thoughtfulness, Caringness
(Meala)

RII
Wealth, Affluence
(Telrii, Sorii)

SAO
Intelligence, Learning
(Saolin)

SEA
Chastity, Faithfulness
(Seaden, Seala)

SHEO
Death

SEO
Loyalty, Service
(Seon, Seor)

TIA
Travel, Transportation

SHAO
Transform, Change
(Shaod, Shaor)

Here is a preview of

MISTBORN

BY BRANDON SANDERSON

Available now

Sometimes I worry that I'm not the hero everyone thinks I am.

The philosophers assure me that this is the time, that the signs have been met. But I still wonder if they have the wrong man. So many people depend on me. They say I will hold the future of the entire world on my arms.

What would they think if they knew that their champion—the Hero of Ages, their savior—doubted himself? Perhaps they wouldn't be shocked at all. In a way, this is what worries me most. Maybe, in their hearts, they wonder—just as I do.

When they see me, do they see a liar?

Ash fell from the sky.

Lord Tresting frowned, glancing up at the ruddy midday sky as his servants scuttled forward, opening a parasol over Tresting and his distinguished guest. Ashfalls weren't that uncommon in the Final Empire, but Tresting had hoped to avoid getting soot stains on his fine new suit coat and red vest, which had just arrived via canal boat from Luthadel itself. Fortunately, there wasn't much wind; the parasol would likely be effective.

Tresting stood with his guest on a small hilltop patio that overlooked the fields. Hundreds of people in brown smocks worked in the falling ash, caring for the crops. There was a sluggishness to their efforts—but, of course, that was the way of the skaa. The peasants were an indolent, unproductive lot. They didn't complain, of course; they knew better than that. Instead, they simply worked with bowed heads, moving about their work with quiet apathy. The passing whip of a taskmaster would force them into dedicated motion for a few moments, but as soon as the taskmaster passed, they would return to their languor.

Tresting turned to the man standing beside him on the hill. "One would think," Tresting noted, "that a thousand years of working in fields would have bred them to be a little more effective at it."

The obligator turned, raising an eyebrow—the motion done as if to highlight his most distinctive feature, the intricate tattoos that laced the skin around his eyes. The tattoos were enormous, reaching all the way across his brow and up the sides of his nose. This was a full prelan—a very important obligator indeed. Tresting had his own, personal obligators back at the manor, but they were only minor functionaries, with barely a few marks around their eyes. This man had arrived from Luthadel with the same canal boat that had brought Tresting's new suit.

"You should see city skaa, Tresting," the obligator said, turning back to watch the skaa workers. "These are actually quite diligent, compared to those inside Luthadel. You have more . . . direct control over your skaa here. How many would you say you lose a month?"

"Oh, a half dozen or so," Tresting said. "Some to beatings, some to exhaustion."

"Runaways?"

"Never!" Tresting said. "When I first inherited this land from my title, I had a few runaways—but I executed their families. The rest quickly lost heart. I've never understood men who have trouble with their skaa—I find the creatures easy to control, if you show a properly firm hand."

The obligator nodded, standing quietly in his gray robes. He seemed pleased—which was a good thing. The skaa weren't actually Tresting's property. Like all skaa, they belonged to the Lord Ruler; Tresting only leased the workers from his god, much in the same way he paid for the services of His obligators.

The obligator looked down, checking his pocket watch, then glanced up at the sun. Despite the ashfall, the sun was bright this day, shining a brilliant crimson red behind the smoky blackness of the upper sky. Tresting removed a handkerchief and wiped his brow, thankful for the parasol's shade against the midday heat.

"Very well, Tresting," the obligator said. "I will carry your proposal to Lord Venture, as requested. He will have a favorable report from me on your operations here."

Tresting held in a sigh of relief. An obligator was required to witness any contract or business deal between noblemen. True, even a lowly obligator like the ones Tresting employed could serve as such a witness—but it meant so much more to impress Straff Venture's own obligator.

The obligator turned toward him. "I will leave back down the canal this afternoon."

"So soon?" Tresting asked. "Wouldn't you care to stay for supper?"

"No," the obligator replied. "Though there is another matter I wish to discuss with you. I came not only at the behest of Lord Venture, but to . . . look in on some matters for the Canton of Inquisition. Rumors say that you like to dally with your skaa women."

Tresting felt a chill.

The obligator smiled; he likely meant it to be disarming, but Tresting only found it eerie. "Don't worry yourself, Tresting," the obligator said. "If there had been any *real* worries about your actions, a Steel Inquisitor would have been sent here in my place."

Tresting nodded slowly. Inquisitor. He'd never seen one of the inhuman creatures, but he had heard . . . stories.

"I have been satisfied regarding your actions with the skaa women," the obligator said, looking back over the fields. "What I've seen and heard here indicates that you always clean up your messes. A man such as yourself—efficient, productive—could go far in Luthadel. A few more years of work, some inspired mercantile deals, and who knows?"

The obligator turned away, and Tresting found himself smiling. It wasn't a promise, or even an endorsement—for the most part, obligators were more bureaucrats and witnesses than they were priests—but to hear such praise from one of the Lord Ruler's own servants . . . Tresting knew that some nobility considered the obligators to be unsettling—some men even considered them a bother—but at that moment, Testing could have kissed his distinguished guest.

Tresting turned back toward the skaa, who worked quietly beneath the bloody sun and the lazy flakes of ash. Tresting had always been a country nobleman, living on his plantation, dreaming of perhaps moving into Luthadel itself. He had heard of the balls and the parties, the glamour and the intrigue, and it excited him no end.

I'll have to celebrate tonight, he thought. There was that young girl in the fourteenth hovel that he'd been watching for some time . . .

He smiled again. A few more years of work, the obligator had said. But could Tresting perhaps speed that up, if he worked a little harder? His skaa population had been growing lately. Perhaps if he pushed them a bit more, he could bring in an extra harvest this summer, fulfill his contract with Lord Venture in extra measure.

Tresting nodded as he watched the crowd of lazy skaa, some working with their hoes, others on hands and knees, pushing the ash away from the fledgling crops. They didn't complain. They didn't hope. They barely dared think. That was the way it should be, for they were skaa. They were—

Tresting froze as one of the skaa looked up. The man met Tresting's eyes, a spark—no, a fire—of defiance showing in his expression. Tresting had never seen anything like it, not in the face of a skaa. Tresting stepped backward reflexively, a chill running through him as the strange, straight-backed skaa held his eyes.

And smiled.

Tresting looked away. "Kurdon!" he snapped.

The burly taskmaster rushed up the incline. "Yes, my lord?"

Tresting turned, pointing at . . .

He frowned. Where had that skaa been standing? Working with their heads bowed, bodies stained by soot and sweat, they were so hard to tell apart. Tresting paused, searching. He thought he knew the place . . . an empty spot, where nobody now stood.

But, no. That couldn't be it. The man couldn't have disappeared from the group so quickly. Where would he have gone? He must be in there, somewhere, working with his head now properly bowed. Still, his moment of apparent defiance was inexcusable.

"My lord?" Kurdon asked again.

The obligator stood at the side, watching curiously. It would not be wise to let the man know that one of the skaa had acted so brazenly.

"Work the skaa in that southern section a little harder," Tresting ordered, pointing. "I see them being sluggish, even for skaa. Beat a few of them."

Kurdon shrugged, but nodded. It wasn't much of a reason for a beating—but, then, he didn't need much of a reason to give the workers a beating.

They were, after all, only skaa.

KELSIER had heard stories.

He had heard whispers of times when once, long ago, the sun had not been red. Times when the sky hadn't been clogged by smoke and ash, when plants hadn't struggled to grow and when skaa hadn't been slaves. Times before the Lord Ruler. Those days, however, were nearly forgotten. Even the legends were growing vague.

Kelsier watched the sun, his eyes following the giant red disk as it crept toward the western horizon. He stood quietly for a long moment, alone in the empty fields. The day's work was done; the skaa had been herded back to their hovels. Soon the mists would come.

Eventually, Kelsier sighed, then turned to pick his way across the furrows and pathways, weaving between large heaps of ash. He avoided stepping on the plants—though he wasn't sure why he bothered. The crops hardly seemed worth the effort. Wan, with wilted brown leaves, the plants seemed as depressed as the people who tended them.

The skaa hovels loomed in the waning light. Already, Kelsier could see the mists beginning to form, clouding the air and giving the moundlike buildings a surreal, intangible look. The hovels stood unguarded; there was no need for watchers, for no skaa would venture outside once night arrived. Their fear of the mists was far too strong.

I'll have to cure them of that someday, Kelsier thought as he approached one of the larger buildings. *But, all things in their own time.* He pulled open the door and slipped inside.

Conversation stopped immediately. Kelsier closed the door, then turned with a smile to confront the room of about thirty skaa. A firepit burned weakly at the center, and the large cauldron beside it was filled with vegetable-dappled water—the beginnings of an evening meal. The soup would be bland, of course. Still, the smell was enticing.

"Good evening, everyone," Kelsier said with a smile, resting his pack beside his feet and leaning against the door. "How was your day?"

His words broke the silence, and the women returned to their dinner preparations. A group of men sitting at a crude table, however, continued to regard Kelsier with dissatisfied expressions.

"Our day was filled with work, traveler," said Tepper, one of the skaa elders. "Something you managed to avoid."

"Fieldwork hasn't ever really suited me," Kelsier said. "It's far too hard on my delicate skin." He smiled, holding up hands and arms that were lined with layers and layers of thin scars. They covered his skin, running lengthwise, as if some beast had repeatedly raked its claws up and down his arms.

Tepper snorted. He was young to be an elder, probably barely into his forties; at most, he might be five years Kelsier's senior. However, the scrawny man held himself with the air of one who liked to be in charge.

"This is no time for levity," Tepper said sternly. "When we harbor a traveler, we expect him to behave himself and avoid suspicion. When you ducked away from the fields this morning, you could have earned a whipping for the men around you."

"True," Kelsier said. "But those men could also have been whipped for standing in the wrong place, for pausing too long, or for coughing when a taskmaster walked by. I once saw a man beaten because his master claimed that he had 'blinked inappropriately.' "

Tepper sat with narrow eyes and a stiff posture, his arm resting on the table. His expression was unyielding.

Kelsier sighed, rolling his eyes. "Fine. If you want me to go, I'll be off then." He slung his pack up on his shoulder and nonchalantly pulled open the door.

Thick mist immediately began to pour through the portal, drifting lazily across Kelsier's body, pooling on the floor and creeping across the dirt like a hesitant animal. Several people gasped in horror, though most of them were too stunned to make a sound. Kelsier stood for a moment, staring out into the dark mists, their shifting currents lit feebly by the cooking pit's coals.

"Close the door." Tepper's words were a plea, not a command.

Kelsier did as requested, pushing the door closed and stemming the flood of white mist. "The mist is not what you think. You fear it far too much."

"Men who venture into the mist lose their souls," a woman whispered. Her words raised a question. Had Kelsier walked in the mists? What, then, had happened to his soul?

If you only knew, Kelsier thought. "Well, I guess this means I'm staying." He waved for a boy to bring him a stool. "It's a good thing, too—it would have been a shame for me to leave before I shared my news."

More than one person perked up at the comment. This was the real reason they tolerated him—the reason even the timid peasants would harbor a man such as Kelsier, a skaa who defied the Lord Ruler's will by traveling from plantation to plantation. A renegade he might be—a danger to the entire community—but he brought news from the outside world.

"I come from the north," Kelsier said. "From lands where the Lord Ruler's touch is less noticeable." He spoke in a clear voice, and people leaned unconsciously toward him as they worked. On the next day, Kelsier's words would be repeated to the several hundred people who lived in other hovels. The skaa might be subservient, but they were incurable gossips.

"Local lords rule in the west," Kelsier said, "and they are far from the iron grip of the Lord Ruler and his obligators. Some of these distant noblemen are finding that happy skaa make better workers than mistreated skaa. One man, Lord Renoux, has even ordered his taskmasters to stop unauthorized beatings. There are whispers that he's considering paying wages to his plantation skaa, like city craftsmen might earn."

"Nonsense," Tepper said.

"My apologies," Kelsier said. "I didn't realize that Goodman Tepper had been to Lord Renoux's estates recently. When you dined with him last, did he tell you something that he did not tell me?"

Tepper blushed: skaa did not travel, and they certainly didn't dine with lords. "You think me a fool, traveler," Tepper said, "but I know what you're doing. You're the one they call the Survivor; those scars on your arms give you away. You're a troublemaker—you travel the plantations, stirring up discontent. You eat our food, telling your grand stories and your lies, then you disappear and leave people like me to deal with the false hopes you give our children."

Kelsier raised an eyebrow. "Now, now, Goodman Tepper," he said. "Your worries are completely unfounded. Why, I have no intention of eating your food. I brought my own." With that, Kelsier reached over and tossed his pack onto the earth before Tepper's table. The loose bag slumped to the side, dumping an array of foods to the ground. Fine breads, fruits, and even a few thick, cured sausages bounced free.

A summerfruit rolled across the packed earthen floor and bumped lightly against Tepper's foot. The middle-aged skaa regarded the fruit with stunned eyes. "That's nobleman's food!"

Kelsier snorted. "Barely. You know, for a man of renowned prestige and rank, your Lord Tresting has remarkably poor taste. His pantry is an embarrassment to his noble station."

Tepper paled even further. "That's where you went this afternoon," he whispered. "You went to the manor. You . . . *stole from the master!*"

"Indeed," Kelsier said. "And, might I add that while your lord's taste in foods is deplorable, his eye for soldiers is far more impressive. Sneaking into his manor during the day was quite a challenge."

Tepper was still staring at the bag of food. "If the taskmasters find this here . . ."

"Well, I suggest you make it disappear then," Kelsier said. "I'd be willing to bet that it tastes a fare bit better than watered-down farlet soup."

Two dozen sets of hungry eyes studied the food. If Tepper intended further arguments, he didn't make them quickly enough, for his silent pause was taken as agreement. Within a few minutes, the bag's contents had been inspected and distributed, and the pot of soup sat bubbling and ignored as the skaa feasted on a meal far more exotic.

Kelsier settled back, leaning against the hovel's wooden wall and watching the people devour their food. He had spoken correctly: the pantry's offerings had been depressingly mundane. However, this was a people who had been fed on nothing but soup and gruel since they were children. To them, breads and fruits were rare delicacies—usually eaten only as aging discards brought down by the house servants.

"Your storytelling was cut short, young man," an elderly skaa noted, hobbling over to sit on a stool beside Kelsier.

"Oh, I suspect there will be time for more later," Kelsier said. "Once all evidence of my thievery has been properly devoured. Don't you want any of it?"

"No need," the old man said. "The last time I tried lords'

food, I had stomach pains for three days. New tastes are like new ideas, young man—the older you get, the more difficult they are for you to stomach."

Kelsier paused. The old man was hardly an imposing sight. His leathered skin and bald scalp made him look more frail than they did wise. Yet he had to be stronger than he looked; few plantation skaa lived to such ages. Many lords didn't allow the elderly to remain home from daily work, and the frequent beatings that made up a skaa's life took a terrible toll on the elderly.

"What was your name again?" Kelsier asked.

"Mennis."

Kelsier glanced back at Tepper. "So, Goodman Mennis, tell me something. Why do you let him lead?"

Mennis shrugged. "When you get to be my age, you have to be very careful where you waste your energy. Some battles just aren't worth fighting." There was an implication in Mennis's eyes; he was referring to things greater than his own struggle with Tepper.

"You're satisfied with this, then?" Kelsier asked, nodding toward the hovel and its half-starved, overworked occupants. "You're content with a life full of beatings and endless drudgery?"

"At least it's a life," Mennis said. "I know what wages malcontent and rebellion bring. The eye of the Lord Ruler, and the ire of the Steel Ministry, can be far more terrible than a few whippings. Men like you preach change, but I wonder. Is this a battle we can really fight?"

"You're fighting it already, Goodman Mennis. You're just losing horribly." Kelsier shrugged. "But, what do I know? I'm just a traveling miscreant, here to eat your food and impress your youths."

Mennis shook his head. "You jest, but Tepper might have been right. I fear your visit will bring us grief."

Kelsier smiled. "That's why I didn't contradict him—at least, not on the troublemaker point." He paused, then smiled more deeply. "In fact, I'd say calling me a troublemaker is probably the only accurate thing Tepper has said since I got here."

"How do you do that?" Mennis asked, frowning.

"What?"

"Smile so much."

"Oh, I'm just a happy person."

Mennis glanced down at Kelsier's hands. "You know, I've only seen scars like those on one other person—and he was dead. His body was returned to Lord Tresting as proof that his punishment had been carried out." Mennis looked up at Kelsier. "He'd been caught speaking of rebellion. Tresting sent him to the Pits of Hathsin, where he was worked until he died. The lad lasted less than a month."

Kelsier glanced down at his hands and forearms. They still burned sometimes, though he was certain the pain was only in his mind. He looked up at Mennis and smiled. "You ask why I smile, Goodman Mennis? Well, the Lord Ruler thinks he has claimed laughter and joy for himself. I'm disinclined to let him do so. This is one battle that doesn't take very much effort to fight."

Mennis stared at Kelsier, and for a moment Kelsier thought the old man might smile in return. However, Mennis eventually just shook his head. "I don't know. I just don't—"

The scream cut him off. It came from outside, perhaps to the north, though the mists distorted sounds. The people in the hovel fell silent, listening to the faint, high-pitched yells. Despite the distance and the mist, Kelsier could hear the pain contained in those screams.

Kelsier burned tin.

It was simple for him now, after years of practice. The tin sat with other Allomantic metals within his stomach, swallowed earlier, waiting for him to draw upon them. He reached inside with his mind and touched the tin, tapping powers he still barely understood. The tin flared to life within him, burning his stomach like the sensation of a hot drink swallowed to quickly.

Allomantic power surged through his body, enhancing his senses. The room around him became crisp, the dull firepit flaring to near-blinding brightness. He could feel the grain in the wood of the stool beneath him. He could still taste the remnants of the loaf of bread he'd snacked on earlier. Most importantly, he could hear the screams with supernatural ears. Two separate people were yelling. One was an older woman, the other a younger woman—perhaps a child. The younger screams were getting farther and farther away.

"Poor Jess," a nearby woman said, her voice booming in Kelsier's enhanced ears. "That child of hers was a curse. It's better for skaa not to have pretty daughters."

Tepper nodded. "Lord Tresting was sure to send for the girl sooner or later. We all knew it. Jess knew it."

"Still a shame, though," another man said.

The screams continued in the distance. Burning tin, Kelsier was able to judge the direction accurately. Her voice was moving toward the lord's manor. The sounds set something off within him, and he felt his face flush with anger.

Kelsier turned. "Does Lord Tresting ever return the girls after he's finished with them?"

Old Mennis shook his head. "Lord Tresting is a law-abiding nobleman—he has the girls killed after a few weeks. He doesn't want to catch the eye of the Inquisitors."

That was the Lord Ruler's command. He couldn't afford to have half-breed children running around—children who might possess powers that skaa weren't even supposed to know existed. . . .

The screams waned, but Kelsier's anger only built. The yells reminded him of other screams. A woman's screams from the past. He stood abruptly, stool toppling to the ground behind him.

"Careful, lad," Mennis said apprehensively. "Remember what I said about wasting energy. You'll never raise that rebellion of yours if you get yourself killed tonight."

Kelsier glanced toward the old man. Then, through the screams and the pain, he forced himself to smile. "I'm not here to lead a rebellion among you, Goodman Mennis. I just want to stir up a little trouble."

"What good could that do?"

Kelsier's smile deepened. "New days are coming. Survive a little longer, and you just might see great happenings in the Final Empire. I bid you all thanks for your hospitality."

With that, he pulled open the door and strode out into the mist.

MENNIS lay awake in the early hours of morning. It seemed that the older he became, the more difficult it was for him to sleep. This was particularly true when he was troubled about something, such as the traveler's failure to return to the hovel.

Mennis hoped that Kelsier had come to his senses and decided to move on. However, that prospect seemed unlikely; Mennis had seen the fire in Kelsier's eyes. It seemed such a shame that a man who had survived the Pits would instead find death here, on a random plantation, trying to protect a girl everyone else had given up for dead.

How would Lord Tresting react? He was said to be particularly harsh with anyone who interrupted his nighttime enjoyments. If Kelsier had managed to disturb the master's pleasures, Tresting might easily decide to punish the rest of his skaa by association.

Eventually, the other skaa began to awake. Mennis lay on the hard earth—bones aching, back complaining, muscles exhausted—trying to decide if it was worth rising. Each day, he nearly gave up. Each day, it was a little harder. One day, he would just stay in the hovel, waiting until the taskmasters came to kill those who were too sick or too elderly to work.

But not today. He could see too much fear in the eyes of the skaa. They knew that Kelsier's nighttime activities would bring trouble. They needed Mennis; they looked to him. He needed to get up.

And so, he did. Once he started moving, the pains of age decreased slightly, and he was able to shuffle out of the hovel toward the fields, leaning on a younger man for support.

It was then that he caught a scent in the air. "What's that?" he asked. "Do you smell smoke?"

Shum—the lad upon whom Mennis leaned—paused. The last remnants of the night's mist had burned away, and the red sun was rising behind the sky's usual haze of blackish clouds.

"I always smell smoke, lately," Shum said. "The Ash-mounts are violent this year."

"No," Mennis said, feeling increasingly apprehensive. "This is different." He turned to the north, toward where a group of skaa were gathering. He let go of Shum, shuffling toward the group, feet kicking up dust and ash as he moved.

At the center of the group of people, he found Jess. Her daughter, the one they all assumed had been taken by Lord Tresting, stood beside her. The young girl's eyes were red from lack of sleep, but she appeared unharmed.

"She came back not long after they took her," the woman was explaining. "She came and pounded on the door, crying in the mist. Flen was sure it was just a mist-wraith impersonating her, but I had to let her in! I don't care what he says, I'm not giving her up. I brought her out in the sunlight, and she didn't disappear. That proves she's not a mistwraith!"

Mennis stumbled back from the growing crowd. Did none of them see it? No taskmasters came to break up the group. No soldiers came to make the morning population counts. Something was very wrong. Mennis continued to the north, moving frantically toward the manor house.

By the time he arrived, others had noticed the twisting line of smoke that was just barely visible in the morning light. Mennis wasn't the first to arrive at the edge of the short hill-top plateau, but the group made way for him when he did.

The manor house was gone. Only a blackened, smoldering scar remained.

"By the Lord Ruler!" Mennis whispered. "What happened here?"

"He killed them all."

Mennis turned. The speaker was Jess's girl. She stood looking down at the fallen house, a satisfied expression on her youthful face.

"They were dead when he brought me out," she said. "All of them—the soldiers, the taskmasters, the lords . . . dead. Even Lord Tresting and his obligators. The master had left me, going to investigate when the noises began. On the way out, I saw him lying in his own blood, stab wounds in his chest. The man who saved me threw a torch in the building as we left."

"This man," Mennis said. "He had scars on his hands and arms, reaching past the elbows?"

The girl nodded silently.

"What kind of demon was that man?" one of the skaa muttered uncomfortably.

"Mistwraith," another whispered, apparently forgetting that Kelsier had gone out during the day.

But he did go out into the mist, Mennis thought. *And how did he accomplish a feat like this . . . ? Lord Tresting kept over two dozen soldiers! Did Kelsier have a hidden band of rebels, perhaps?*

Kelsier's words from the night before sounded in his ears. *New days are coming . . .*

"But, what of us?" Tepper asked, terrified. "What will happen when the Lord Ruler hears this? He'll think that we did it! He'll send us to the Pits, or maybe just send his koloss to slaughter us outright! Why would that troublemaker do something like this? Doesn't he understand the damage he's done?"

"He understands," Mennis said. "He warned us, Tepper. He came to stir up trouble."

"But, why?"

"Because he knew we'd never rebel on our own, so he gave us no choice."

Tepper paled.

Lord Ruler, Mennis thought. *I can't do this. I can barely get up in the mornings—I can't save this people.*

But what other choice was there?

Mennis turned. "Gather the people, Tepper. We must flee before word of this disaster reaches the Lord Ruler."

"Where will we go?"

"The caves to the east," Mennis said. "Travelers say there are rebel skaa hiding in them. Perhaps they'll take us in."

Tepper paled further. "But . . . we'd have to travel for days. Spend nights *in the mist.*"

"We can do that," Mennis said, "or we can stay here and die."

Tepper stood frozen for a moment, and Mennis thought the shock of it all might have overwhelmed him. Eventually, however, the younger man scurried off to gather the others, as commanded.

Mennis sighed, looking up toward the trailing line of smoke, cursing the man Kelsier quietly in his mind.

New days indeed.

TOR BOOKS *by*

THE STORMLIGHT ARCHIVE®

The Way of Kings, Words of Radiance, Oathbringer

With more than ten years spent in research, world-building, and writing, The Stormlight Archive is a true epic in the making, a multi-volume masterpiece in the grand tradition of The Wheel of Time®.

THE MISTBORN® SAGA

Mistborn, The Well of Ascension, The Hero of Ages

This modern fantasy classic dares to ask a simple question: What if the hero of prophecy fails, and the Dark Lord takes over? What follows is a story full of surprises and political intrigue, driven by a memorable heist crew.

The Alloy of Law, Shadows of Self, The Bands of Mourning

Three hundred years after the events of the Mistborn trilogy, the world is on the verge of modernity, but one scion returning from the Roughs discovers that the civilized world isn't as civilized as he'd thought.